HEATHER GRAHAM

MARIE FORCE

DANGEROUS NIGHTS

ISBN-13: 978-0-7783-3131-5

Recycling programs for this product may not exist in your area.

Dangerous Nights

Copyright © 2017 by Harlequin Books S.A.

The publisher acknowledges the copyright holders of the individual works as follows:

Night of the Blackbird
Copyright © 2001 by Heather Graham

Fatal Affair
Copyright © 2010 by Marie Force

For questions and comments about the quality of this book, please contact us at CustomerService@Harlequin.com.

www.Harlequin.com

Printed in U.S.A.

Praise for Heather Graham

"Graham stands at the top of the romantic suspense category."
—Publishers Weekly

"Intricate, fast-paced, and intense, this riveting thriller blends romance and suspense in perfect combination and keeps readers guessing and the tension taut until the very end."
—Library Journal on *Flawless*

"Graham is a master at world building and her latest is a thrilling, dark, and deadly tale of romantic suspense."
—Booklist, starred review, on *Haunted Destiny*

"Graham is the queen of romantic suspense."
—RT Book Reviews

Praise for Marie Force

"Fans of *Scandal* and *House of Cards* will love the Fatal Series."
—New York Times bestselling author Cindy Gerard

"Force's skill is also evident in the way that she develops the characters, from the murdered and mutilated senator to the detective and chief of staff who are trying to solve the case. The heroine, Sam, is especially complex and her secrets add depth to this mystery… This novel is *The O.C.* does D.C., and you just can't get enough."
—RT Book Reviews on *Fatal Affair* (4½ stars)

"Force pushes the boundaries by deftly using political issues like immigration to create an intricate mystery."
—RT Book Reviews on *Fatal Consequences* (4 stars)

CONTENTS

NIGHT OF THE BLACKBIRD

Heather Graham

Prologue

Belfast, Northern Ireland
Summer, 1977

"All right, my son, my fine lad!" his mum said, bursting into his square little room without even knocking. "Your da has made it home, and we are going to the movies!"

The mother was flushed and eager. Her work-worn face was transformed into beauty, for her smile was a young girl's smile, and brightness touched her eyes. He held his breath, barely able to believe. He wanted to go to the movies so badly. It was the new American film, making its debut downtown. At nine, he spent much of his time in the streets; few promises his parents made came to pass. Not their faults, just the way of the world, and there were many things that were the way of the world, or the way of his particular world, and that was just that, and he understood it. His father had his work, his mother had hers, and they had their time at the pub, as well, with their meetings and such. He was a tough kid, strong for his nine years, street smart and, sadly—as even he was aware—already wary and weary. But this...

It was a science fiction movie. Full of futuristic

knights, space vehicles, great battles. The fight for right and, in the end—or so he figured—the victory of right over evil.

He threw down the comic book he was reading and stared at her with disbelief, then jumped up, throwing his arms around her. "The movies! Really? Wow!"

"Comb your hair now, boy. Get ready. I'll get your baby sister."

And soon they were walking down the street.

The street was something of a slum. Old brick walls were covered with graffiti. The houses were old, as well, small, drafty, and still required peat fires in winter. But it was a good neighborhood in which to live. There were plenty of dark, secret places in the crevices in the walls; there were gates to be jumped, places to hide.

Here and there, they passed a neighbor. Men tipped their hats. Women greeted them with cordial voices. The boy was so pleased, walking along with his folks. He held his sister's hand. She was just five, younger than he, with eyes still so bright and alive. She didn't know yet that the smiles that greeted them were usually grim smiles, that the people were as gray and strained as the sky that ever seemed dark, as the old buildings that always seemed somber and shadowed. She looked up at him, and her smile was real, beautiful, and though they fought at times, though he was a tough kid, a nine-year-old boy, and she just a little girl, he loved her fiercely. Her pleasure and awe in their outing touched him deeply.

"We're really going to see the movie?"

"We're really going to see the movie!" he assured her.

Their father turned around, grinning. "Aye, girl, and we're buying popcorn, as well!"

She laughed, and the sound of her laughter made them all smile; it even seemed to touch the ancient grimed walls and make them lighter.

They reached the movie theater. Some there were their friends, some were their enemies. They all wanted to see the movie, so some of the smiles were a bit grimmer, and now and then his parents exchanged stiff nods with others.

As he'd promised, their father bought popcorn. And sodas. Even candy.

He'd seldom felt closer to his parents. More like a boy. For a few hours he left his own dark reality for a far-off time and place. He laughed, he cheered, he gave his sister the last little kernel of popcorn. He explained what she didn't understand. He lifted her onto his lap. He watched his mother hesitate, then let her head fall on his father's shoulder. His father let his hand fall upon her knee.

They were halfway home when the gunmen suddenly appeared.

They had come from one of those dark and secretive places in the wall that the boy had learned so well himself.

The masked man in the front suddenly called his father by name.

"I am he, and proud of it, I am!" his father replied with strength and defiance, pushing his wife behind him. "But me family is with me—"

"Aye, ye'd hide behind skirts!" the second man said contemptuously.

The popping of gunfire, so suddenly and so close, was deafening.

The boy reached for his sister even as he watched his father fall. It had happened so fast, yet it was almost like slow motion in the movies. He could see the terrible end; he couldn't stop it.

The gunmen had come for his father. But a stray bullet hit his sister, as well. Somewhere in his mind, he knew that the gunmen hadn't intended it, nor could they afford to regret it. She was simply a casualty of this strange war.

He heard his mother shout his father's name. She didn't know as yet that her baby was gone, as well.

The lad held his sister, seeing the blood stain her dress. Her eyes were open. She didn't even feel pain; she didn't realize what was happening. She smiled, her bright eyes touching his as she whispered his name.

"I want to go home now," she said. Then she closed her eyes, and he knew she was dead.

He just held her, in the darkness of the street and the darkness of his life, and he listened to his mother's screams and, soon, the wailing of the police cars and the ambulances in the shadows of the night.

They had the services for his father and sister on a Saturday afternoon. They had waked them in the house in the old way, and family and friends had come and sat vigil by the coffins. They had drunk whiskey and ale, and his father had been hailed and put upon a pedestal, the loss of his baby sister made into a cause. There was so much press from around the world that many whispered that the sacrifice of the poor wee dear might well have been God's way in their great cause.

They hadn't seen her smile. They didn't know that she'd been just a child with hopes and dreams and a wealth of life within her smile and the brightness of her eyes.

At last it was time for the final service, the time

when they would be buried—though nothing here, he knew, was ever really buried.

Father Gillian read the prayers, and a number of men gave impassioned speeches. His mother wailed, tore at her hair, beat her breast. Women helped her, held her, grieved with her. They cried and mourned and wailed, as well, sounding like a pack of banshees, howling to the heavens.

He stood alone. His tears had been shed.

The prayers and the services over, the pipers came forward, and the old Irish pipes wheezed and wailed.

They played "Danny Boy."

Soon after, he stepped forward with some of the other men, and they lifted the coffins. Thankfully, he was a tall lad, and he carried his sister's coffin with cousins much older than he. She had been such a little thing, it was amazing that the coffin could be so heavy. Almost as if they carried a girl who had lived a life.

They were laid into the ground. Earth and flowers were cast upon them. It was over.

The other mourners began to move away, Father Gillian with an arm around his mother. A great aunt came up to him. "Come, lad, your mother needs you."

He looked up for a moment, his eyes misting with tears. "She does not need me now," he said, and it was true—he had tried to be a comfort to her, but she had her hatred, and her passion, and she had a newfound cause.

He didn't mean to hurt anyone, so he added, "I need to be here now, please. Me mum has help now. Later, when she's alone, she'll need me."

"You're a good lad, keen and sharp, that you are," his aunt said, and she left him.

Alone, he stood by the graves. Silent tears streamed down his cheeks.

And he made a vow. A passionate vow, to his dead father, his poor wee sister. To his God—and to himself.

He would die, he swore, before he ever failed in that vow.

Darkness fell around his city.

And around his heart.

1

New York City, New York
The Present

"What do you mean, you're not coming home for Saint Patrick's Day?"

Moira Kelly flinched.

Her mother's voice, usually soft, pleasant and well-modulated, was so shrill that Moira was certain her assistant had heard Katy Kelly in the next room—despite the fact that they were talking by phone, and that her mother was in Boston, several hundred miles away.

"Mum, it's not like I'm missing Christmas—"

"No, it's worse."

"Mum, I'm a working woman, not a little kid."

"Right. You're a first-generation American, forgetting all about tradition."

Moira inhaled deeply. "Mother, that's the point. We are living in America. Yes, I was born here. As disheartening and horrible as it may be, Saint Patrick's Day is not a national holiday."

"There you go. Mocking me."

Moira inhaled deeply again, counted, sighed. "I'm not mocking you."

"You work for yourself. You can work around any holiday you want."

"I don't actually just work for myself. I have a partner. We have a whole production company. A schedule. Deadlines. And my partner has a wife—"

"That Jewish girl he married."

Moira hesitated again.

"No, Mum. Andy Garson, the New York reporter, the one who sometimes cohosts that mid-morning show, just married a Jewish girl. Josh's wife is Italian." She smiled slightly, staring at the receiver. "And very Catholic. You'd like her. And their little eight-month-old twins. A few of the reasons we both really want to keep this company going!"

Her mother only heard what she wanted to hear. "If his wife is Catholic, she should understand."

"I don't think the Italians consider Saint Patrick's Day a national holiday, either," Moira said.

"He's a Catholic saint!" her mother said.

"Mother—"

"Moira, please. I'm not asking for myself." This time, her mother hesitated. "Your father just had to have another procedure…"

Her heart skipped a beat. "What do you mean?" she asked sharply.

"They may have to do another surgery."

"You didn't call me!"

"I'm calling you now."

"But not about Dad!"

"He wouldn't let me call and tell you—he hasn't been feeling all that well and he didn't want to disturb you before the holiday. You've always come home before. We figured we'd tell you when you got here. He has to have a test on Monday—outpatient, and not life-threatening—and then…well, then they'll decide just what to do. But, darling, you know…he really would like you home, though he won't admit it. And Granny Jon is…well, she seems to be failing a bit."

Granny Jon was ninety-something years in age and, at best, maybe a good eighty-five pounds in weight. She was still the fiercest little creature Moira had ever met.

She would live forever, Moira was convinced.

But Moira was concerned about her father. He'd had open-heart surgery a few years earlier, a valve replacement, and since then, she'd worried about him. He never complained, always had a smile and was therefore, in her mind, dangerous—simply because he was too prone to being half-dead before he would agree to see a doctor. She knew that her mother worked very hard to keep him on a proper heart-healthy regime, but that couldn't solve everything.

And as to Saint Patrick's Day…

"Patrick is coming," her mother informed her.

Naturally, she thought.

Her brother, who had property in western Massachusetts, wouldn't dare miss his own saint's day. Few men would have such courage.

Still, it was easy for Patrick. He was in Boston often anyway.

In fact, she realized with a small touch of guilt, she had counted on her brother and her sister, Colleen, to make it all right that she wasn't there for the great family holiday that much of the country saw as an excuse to drink green beer or send out cute little leprechaun cards, though it meant far more to them.

"You want to see Patrick, don't you?"

"Of course, but I'm mostly worried about Dad."

"If your father and I were both to drop dead tomorrow—"

"My brother, sister and I would still see each other,

Mum. Honestly, you're not going to drop dead tomorrow, but don't worry, we love each other, we'd see each other."

It was an old argument. Her mother said the same thing to her, she said the same thing back. Her mother said the same thing to her brother—who said the same thing back.

Her sister just sighed and rolled her eyes each time. But Moira did love her family.

"Mum, I'll be home." She wasn't that far away, and it wasn't that she didn't get home frequently. This time, this Saint Patrick's Day, she hadn't thought much about it—just because she did get home so often. She had just been home for the Christmas holidays. Going home now hadn't seemed crucial, in part because of the filming schedule.

But it was crucial now.

"Did you hear me, Mum? I *will* be home for Saint Patrick's Day."

"Bless you, baby. I do need you."

"I'll call you back as soon as I get things straightened out. You make Dad behave, okay?"

"I will."

She started to set the receiver down, but then she heard her mother's voice. "Oh, sweetheart, I forgot to tell you—"

"Yes?" She brought the receiver back to her ear.

"You'll never guess who's coming."

"The great leprechaun?" She couldn't quite help herself.

"No!"

"Auntie Lizbeth?" She wasn't really an aunt, just an old neighbor from back home. She came to the States every few years. Moira liked her, though she seldom understood her—she simply smiled at the old woman a lot. She was even older than Granny Jon, had the thickest brogue known to man—and her wolfhound had chewed up her false teeth, since she hated them and was always leaving them on the table. To Moira, she had been almost totally incomprehensible even when she'd had her teeth, and now, well, it was almost impossible for Moira to make sense of her words. Still, Granny Jon and her folks seemed to do just fine understanding the old woman.

"No, silly. Not Auntie Lizbeth."

"I give up, Mum. Who?"

"Dan. Daniel O'Hara. Isn't that wonderful? You two were always such good friends. I know you wouldn't have wanted to miss him."

"Uh…no," she said, and her voice cracked only slightly.

"Goodbye, darling."

"Bye, Mum."

Danny was coming.

She didn't realize that she was still holding the receiver with a death grip until her hand began to hurt and the low buzzing sound from the phone began to sink in. Then a recorded operator's voice. If you'd like to make a call…

She hung up, stared at the phone, then shook her head in disgust. How long since she had seen Danny? Two years, maybe three? He'd been the love of her life—the love of her *young* life, she corrected herself. But he'd come and gone like the wind. She'd refused to see him the last time he had called to say he was in the States. He was about as dependable as good weather in a Boston winter. And still…

Her heart quivered with a little pang. It would be good to see Danny.

Now that she was really over him.

And she was seeing someone, so she really would be immune to his, "Ah, Moira, just a quick beer." Or, "Moira Kelly, you'd not take a stroll with me?" Or even, "You'd not like to make time stand still, hop in bed with me, girl, because you know, you do, that we were magic?"

No more, Daniel.

She had a hectic life; she would be busy, especially since she was about to ask everyone to reschedule everything for her.

She loved her business. She was still in awe of the fact that she and Josh had made a go of it, that they were a production company and that their show was a modest success. Ireland, the old country, remained a passion for her parents. America was hers. She'd been born here and she'd grown up here, and the diversity of her country was what she loved best. Since she'd first gone to college, she'd kept very busy. Forgetting what could never be. Or trying to.

Maybe, though, in the corner of her mind, she had always dreamed that Danny would come back. To stay.

With annoyance, she realized that the very thought made her wistful.

Okay, she cared for Danny, she always would. In a far, far corner of her mind! As far as a distant galaxy. She was a realist. She'd seen people through the years—not too seriously, because of her work. And she was seeing someone now, someone bright, compelling and with shared interests, someone who'd entered her life at the right time, in the right way…

So Danny was coming to Boston. Good for him. He would like…

For a moment, her mind went blank.

Michael! She was dating a man named Michael McLean. Of Irish descent, as well, but of normal Irish descent. They had a really great relationship. Michael loved a good movie and didn't whine about a bad one. He was an avid sports fan but liked a day at a museum just as well and was up for a Broadway show—or Off Broadway, for that matter.

He was nearly perfect. He worked hard for her company, too. He was always on the go, seeing people, checking on logistics and permits. In fact, he was off somewhere right now. She wasn't even sure where. Well, of course, she knew…she just couldn't think of it right now. Talking to her mother had that effect on her.

It didn't matter where he was. Michael always had his cell phone on him, and he always returned messages, whether they were personal or business related. It was part of his being so wonderful.

And still, just thinking about Danny…

Impatiently, she picked up a pencil and tapped it on her desk. She had other things to think about. Like business. She reached for the phone again and buzzed her partner, Josh.

It would be good to see Danny again.

She was startled by the wave of heat that seemed to wash through her with the thought. Like a longing to hop into bed this very second. She could close her eyes and see him. See him naked.

Stop it! she chastised herself.

"What's up?"

"What?"

"You called me," Josh said. "What's up?"

"Can we go somewhere for lunch?"

Mentally, she put clothes on Danny.

Then she sternly forced him to the far corner of her mind.

She realized that Josh had hesitated, and as if she were in front of him, she could see his shaggy brows tightening into a frown. Danny retreated to memory. Her partner was very real, always a part of her life, steady, and just a downright, decent good guy. Josh Whalen was tall and lean, almost skinny. Good-looking. They had met in film school at NYU, almost had an affair, realized instead that they could remain friends for a lifetime but never lovers, and became partners instead.

Danny had been in her life then, coming and going. Josh would have been only an attempt to convince herself that she wouldn't have to wait forever for a man to love, but she'd realized that before she'd done anything they would both regret.

Once again, she firmly pushed Danny back where he belonged.

Josh was better than any man she had ever dated. They shared a vision—and a work ethic. They'd both slaved in numerous restaurants to raise the capital they had needed to get their small production company going; he had also worked in construction and dug ditches. They had both been willing to give a hundred percent.

"You don't want me just to come to your office?" Josh asked.

"No. I want to take you to a nice restaurant, buy you a few glasses of good wine…"

His groan interrupted her. "You want to change the schedule."

"I—"

"Make it a sports bar, and buy me a beer."

"Where?"

He named his favorite little hole-in-the-wall, just a few blocks from their offices in the Village. He had an interview with a potential new cameraman, she was supposed to have coffee with a potential guest, but they decided to meet right after their appointments.

As it happened, their potential guest missed her connection and called in to find out if Moira would be available in the afternoon. Relieved, Moira cheerfully agreed.

She went out walking. And walked and walked until it was nearly time to meet Josh.

Moira reached Sam's Sports Spectacular—a true hole-in-the-wall but a great neighborhood place—before her partner. She seldom drank anything at all during the day and was cautious even at night, but this afternoon, she ordered a draft. She was nursing it at the farthest table from the bar when Josh came in. He was a handsome, appealing guy in a tall, lanky, artistic way. He looked like a director or, she mused with a flash of humor, a refugee from some grunge band. His eyes were dark and beautiful, his hair reddish brown and very curly, and despite his wife's objection, he wore a full beard and mustache.

"Where's my beer?" he asked, sliding into a chair by the table.

"I wasn't sure what you wanted."

He stared at her as if she had lost her mind. "How many years have you known me?"

"Almost ten. Since we were eighteen. But—"

"What do I always drink?"

"Miller Lite. But—"

"There you have it."

"I'm a bit off today."

"You *are* a bit off." He raised his hand, and their waiter saw him. He gave his order, and the young man nodded in acknowledgment and started for the bar.

"Why are you off today?" Josh asked, leaning forward.

"My mother called."

He grimaced. "My mother calls almost every day. That's no excuse."

"You don't know my mother."

"I do." He grinned and feigned a slight accent. "She's a lovely lady, she is."

"Um. My dad's ill."

"Oh." Josh was quickly serious. "I'm sorry."

"I—" She hesitated. That wasn't really it. "I think he's going to be okay, although it appears he may need another surgery."

"So you want to go home for Saint Patrick's Day."

"I know we were supposed to be shooting at the theme parks in central Florida, and I know how hard you worked to straighten out all the paperwork and rights and—"

"Things have been postponed before."

"I truly appreciate your attitude," she told him softly, swallowing her draft, her eyes lowered.

"I never believed we'd be going to Florida in March." She looked at him and flushed. "You think I have no spine?"

"I think your mother could take on the Terminator."

She flashed him a grateful smile. "I do have another idea. We can do a real ethnic Irish show and arrange with the Leisure Channel to do a live feed. It really might be a great idea. I think the viewers would love it."

Josh mused over the idea. He lifted his hands. "You could be right. 'Fun, food, and fantasy—live from the home of the hostess herself.'"

"How do you feel about Boston in March?"

"Wretched, but then, it's not much worse than New York." He smiled at her suddenly. "Actually, I thought something like this might come up. I've had Michael checking into the permit situation in Boston as well as Orlando."

"You're kidding! He didn't say a word."

"He knows how to keep a confidence. I didn't want you to suspect I was second-guessing you."

"Great."

"Hey, kid, it's a show we should have done before this."

She grinned, suddenly feeling a tremendous sense of relief. "But you and Gina were looking forward to doing the whole Disney thing."

"We'll still do it. We'll just reschedule. And the kids won't mind—they didn't really understand what was going on anyway."

She smiled. He had a point. At eight months, the twins undoubtedly didn't care one way or the other whether they got to see Mickey Mouse or not.

"Do you want something to eat?" he asked her. "Or are you just going to drink your lunch?" He indicated her beer glass. It was empty, and she didn't even remember drinking the whole thing.

"I *am* Irish," she muttered.

He laughed, leaning forward again. "Hey! No ill will intended. I just wondered if you wanted food or not."

"Yes, yes, I guess I should eat."

"They make a nice salad here."

"Great. I think I'll have a hamburger."

"Ah, we're being a wild renegade today, eh?" He teased, motioning to their waiter.

"What? Are you trying to be just a wee bit condescending, so I don't have to be eternally grateful for making you change the entire schedule for the season?"

He laughed. "Maybe. Maybe it's just amusing to see you so afraid of going home."

"I am not afraid of going home! I go home all the time. Here comes the waiter. Just order me a hamburger—and another beer."

Josh did so diligently, but there was still a sparkle in his eyes.

"So what are you so afraid of?" he asked softly, once the waiter had taken their order and departed.

"I'm not afraid. I go home all the time."

"But this time you seem uneasy. Is it the fact that you think we should film at your home as an excuse to go there? The whole thing does fit nicely. There are a lot of Irish in the United States. And on Saint Patrick's Day—"

"Everyone is Irish. Yes, I know," she murmured. Her second beer arrived. She flashed the waiter a smile. He grinned and left. She took a sip of the brew immediately, then sat back, running her fingertip along the edge of the glass.

"So? It's perfect," Josh said.

"Perfect—and what a cast of characters we have."

"Your mother is charming. So is your father."

"Mmm. They are. Just…"

"Just what?"

"Well, they are…eccentric."

"Your parents? No."

"Stop teasing. You know Granny Jon. She had me convinced for years that I had to be really good or the banshees would get me on the way to the outhouse. I think that Colleen, Patrick and I were all out of high school before we suddenly realized the great flaw in her terror tactics—we didn't have an outhouse."

"Your grandmother is adorable."

"Like a hedgehog," Moira agreed. "Then there's my father, who has yet to accept the fact that in the U.S., the Fighting Irish are a football team."

"Not true! I've watched college football games with him. Though he does root for Notre Dame, I'll give you that."

"My mother will give speeches on how the traditional dish is bacon and cabbage, not corned beef, and somewhere along the line, if you're not careful, Dad will get going on English imperialism against the rights of the Gaelic-speaking people of the world, and then he'll get going on the wonders of America. He'll forget that as a country we massacred hundreds of thousands of Indians and he'll start to list famous Americans of Irish descent, from the founding fathers to the Civil War—both sides, of course."

"Maybe he'll avoid talking about Irishmen who rode with Custer."

"Josh, I'm serious. You know my dad. Please, God, make sure no one brings up the question of Irish nationalism or the IRA."

"Okay, we'll keep him off politics."

She barely heard him as she rested an elbow on the table, leaning over, preoccupied. "Patrick will bring my little nieces and nephew, so Mum, Dad and Granny Jon will all be running around pretending there are stray leprechauns in the house. They'll have beer kegs everywhere, and everything will be green."

"It sounds great."

"We'll have all kinds of company—"

"The more the merrier."

She straightened and looked him in the eye. "Danny is coming," she told him.

"Oh, I see," he said softly.

He awoke very late and very slowly, and in luxurious comfort. The mattress he lay on was soft, the sheets cool and clean. The woman beside him still smelled sweetly of perfume, and of the scent of their lovemaking. She was young, but not too young. Her skin was tanned and sleek. Her hair was dark, and a wealth of it graced the hotel pillow. She'd had her price, but what the hell, so did he. They'd had fun together.

Coffee had brewed in a pot he'd set to go on a timer last night. Brewed and probably burned. He'd never imagined he would sleep so late.

He leaned against his pillow and the headboard.

America was good.

He had always enjoyed it.

There was so much here. Such an abundance. And such foolish people, who didn't begin to understand what they had. Aye, they had their problems; he wasn't at all blind to the world, nor did he lack compassion. But problems were different here. Spoiled rich kids, racial tensions, Republicans, Democrats...and, he had to say, though with all compassion, if they didn't have enough problems, they just made more for themselves. But it didn't change the fact that life was good.

The phone rang. He reached to the bedside table; picked it up.

"Hello?"

"Have you the order ready, sir?"

"I do. Shall I deliver, or do you want to come here?"

"It's probably better if you come here. We may have more business to discuss."

"That will be fine. When?"

He was given a time; then the phone clicked. He hung up.

The woman at his side stirred and moaned. She turned toward him, her eyes flickering open. She smiled. "Morning."

"Morning." He leaned over and kissed her. She was still a cute little thing. Dark-haired, dark-eyed, tanned.

She reached for him beneath the sheets, her hand curling around his sex.

He arched a brow at her.

She laughed. "Freebie. I don't usually stay until morning—"

"I don't usually keep a who—a woman—till morning," he amended kindly.

Her fingers were talented, and he found himself quickly aroused. He noted, though, the light that was beginning to show around the edges of the curtains.

"What's the matter?" she asked him.

He smiled, crushed out his cigarette. "Nothing," he told her, drawing her head toward his, kissing her lips, then drawing her downward to continue a more liquid approach to her sensual assault on his body. He glanced at his watch. Plenty of time.

She was very good, and it had been a long time since he'd had such an opportunity to dally. He let her have her way, then returned the favor, and when he made love to her—if one could, even politely, call the act "making love" when it was with a woman who was a stranger and a whore at that—he did so with energy and pleasure, a courteous partner despite the fact that he swiftly climaxed. Even as he rolled to her side, he checked his watch again.

"Late," he muttered, then kissed her lips and headed for the shower. "Coffee's on. Cigarettes are by the bed."

He showered quickly, with an economy of motion learned over the years. He emerged well scrubbed, hair washed. He grabbed a towel from the rack and studiously worked at drying his hair while he opened the bathroom door and exited, head covered, body naked.

"Did you get your cof—" he began politely, but then paused, muscles tightening. "What are you doing?" he asked sharply.

She was on her knees, his pants in her hands.

"I—" she began, dropping his pants, looking at him.

She stumbled to her feet. Had she been about to rob him?

He wondered what she had seen. He noted quickly that she had been through more than his pants. Drawers weren't quite closed; the dust ruffle around the bed was still up at the foot of it. What had she discovered that had caused the look of fear she wore?

Or was it merely what she was seeing in his eyes?

She stood, clad in her bra slip and stockings. He watched the workings of her mind. She was wishing she'd got dressed and got the hell out while he had showered.

But she hadn't.

Her eyes, glued to his, registered her fear. He didn't look away; he saw the room with his peripheral vision. She'd done a good job in the time she'd had. Thorough. She was just a working girl—and, it appeared, a thief.

Or was she?

"I was just looking around, just curious," she said, moistening her lips.

Whatever else she was, she was a damn poor liar.

"Ah, love," he said softly. "Hadn't you ever heard? Curiosity killed the cat."

"Ah, your good friend Daniel O'Hara," Josh teased. "Think of it. If it hadn't been for old Danny boy, you and I might be married now."

"And divorced—we'd have killed each other in a week," Moira reminded him.

"Maybe, maybe not. Let's see, you were intellectually in love with me, but you lusted after your old flame. I was the good, decent man who meant to do all the honorable things, but he was an unobtainable, intriguing and dashing young lover, and though never present, he took your heart as well as your—well, you know."

"Josh, we would never have gotten married."

"Probably not," he agreed, a bit too cheerfully.

"Well, I don't appreciate the dramatics. He's an old family friend—"

"And the fact that he's built like a linebacker and looks like an Adonis has nothing to do with it?"

"You're being incredibly...shallow. As if I don't judge men by other standards. Besides, you're a very good-looking man yourself."

"Thanks. I'll take that. But I'm not sure I compare with your exotic foreign lover. And no, it's not just his looks that affect you. It's the accent, the voice, the tradition, the fact that he's an old family friend." He put on a Hollywood Irish accent. "Aye, me lass, your lover has a definite presence."

"He's not my lover!"

"How quickly you protest."

"I haven't even seen him in years."

"I can tell you when you saw him last. Summer, almost three years ago. And you wound up lying to your family, saying you were coming back to New York, but you stayed at the Copley with him in Boston. You thought he'd stay here, because you wanted him to. He wasn't ready, you got mad. And when he called again the following Christmas, you refused to see him."

"I never told you all that!"

"Well, I may not have made it as husband material, but I *am* your best friend. And there's something about him you can't quite shake."

"You're wrong."

"Am I?"

"Trust me, I *have* shaken him." She looked at her watch. "How time flies when you're being tortured by your supposed best friend. I have to meet Mrs. Grisholm. She missed her connection this morning.

She's the lady from that little mystery theater group in Maine where the audience joins in and they do the show together. They even cook and eat dinner together. You know. I told you all about her, and it sounds like a—"

"What's Michael going to say about the return of your old flame? Did you ever tell *him* about Daniel O'Hara?" Josh interrupted, amused.

"Dan is my past, Michael is none of your business."

Josh started laughing. Her cheeks flamed.

"Saint Patrick's Day could be lots of fun. Your sleeping arrangements may be none of my business, but we hired Michael as location manager before you two became involved, so I assume he'll be joining us in Boston."

"Yes, of course he'll be joining us in Boston."

Josh was still grinning.

"Oh, will you wipe that smirk off your face?"

"I'm sorry. As your one-time would-be lover, I find it amusing that you've spent half your adult life in celibacy and now you're going to have both of the great loves of your life home for the holiday."

"Josh…" she said warningly.

"Maybe that's not so bad. Mum and Dad can protect you."

She stood up. "I would thank you for being such a great business partner—"

"If I wasn't being such a prick." He was still laughing.

"I could tell your wife you're being a horse's ass."

"She knows all about my ancient crush on you. I think she'll find the situation just as much fun as I do."

"You're impossible, and I'm leaving."

"You're leaving because you're late, and you love me anyway," he called after her, since she was already heading for the door.

"I don't love you," she called, turning around. "Make sure you get the check, and leave a decent tip."

"You adore me!" he called after her.

At the door, she looked back. He was still wearing the same shit-eating grin. He arched a brow to her and started humming "Danny Boy."

2

It had been a damned long day. Michael McLean took his work to heart, and he accomplished what he set out to do, whether it took diplomacy and tact or a dead-set determination and a few strong-arm techniques.

When the phone rang, Michael jumped. He'd been lying there, half asleep, and though his work meant that he got calls at all hours, he hadn't been expecting the abrasive ring. He'd been traveling large expanses of the country—they had to be prepared for every contingency—and he was tired. For a moment the ringing was simply jarring, and he let it go on. Then he forced himself up, dragging his legs over the side of the bed, running his fingers through his hair. He started for his bedside phone, then realized that it was his cellular ringing. He rose, running his fingers through his hair, found his pants and dug out the phone.

He glanced at the caller ID. Moira.

"Hey, babe, what's up? You're all right, aren't you? It's late."

"I know, I'm sorry. I should have called earlier."

"You can call me any time, day or night. You know that."

"Thanks," she said, her voice soft.

There were lots of women in the world. He'd known

his share. But the tenor of her voice slipped into him. There were others, yes. But none quite like her. He pictured her. Moira was a beauty, with her true deep red hair and blue-green eyes. Tall, elegant, with a natural sophistication and the ability to dirty her hands and nails, laugh at any obstacle and get involved with the most absurd situations. When he'd answered the ad for an associate producer and locations manager for KW Productions, he'd known her from seeing her on the air, having studied what tapes he could find before applying for the job. She was good on tape. She was even better in person. He hadn't been ready for the excitement she could create or the emotion she could invoke. He wished she were there right now. Amazing what the sound of her voice could do to a man.

"I should have called you—*could* have called you—hours ago," she went on, then halted suddenly. "You haven't heard from Josh already, have you?"

"No."

He heard her sigh. "Yeah, he would make me do this one myself. And it's so late because I've been trying to get up the nerve to call you."

He was about to assure her that she never needed nerve to call him when she rushed on.

"I know how much work you've already done—"

"You are the boss, you know."

"Not really. Josh and I have always made decisions together, and since you've been with us, well, you've just been the perfect addition to the show... Oh, Lord, Michael, I'm so sorry to be doing this, but...we're making a sudden switch in plans."

He'd been expecting this; still, he felt every muscle in his body tense. He knew what she was about to say.

"I know that you and Josh have made an incredible effort on the Orlando angle, that acquiring permits to tape has been a bitch…but we're switching locations for Saint Patrick's Day. I'm so sorry. I know—"

"Family pressure, eh?" he asked quietly.

"My father has to go in for tests next week. Nothing serious, Mum assures me, but I'm willing to bet he's still working the pub himself until all hours of the night. Anyway, she made it sound as if I were punching the Easter Bunny or something, and I… I caved in."

"Don't worry," he told her. "I've already looked into the Boston situation."

"What?"

"Josh and I both kind of expected this," he said.

She was silent.

"Moira, it's all right. Hey, I'm going to love meeting your family. I'll get to feel important, right? The man in your life, someone who means everything in the world to you, right?"

"You're incredible, you know that?"

"Well, of course, you'd have nothing less, right?" he said.

"You know what?"

"What?"

"You sound so good."

Her voice was almost like silk.

"I was just thinking the same about you."

"They're crazy, you know."

"Who?"

"My folks."

"Moira, you've hit the right guy here. My family is Irish, too. Okay, we don't own a pub and no one runs around whistling 'Danny Boy' all day, but I can deal with the leprechaun and banshee stories. Don't be so worried."

She was still silent. Then she said, "Mine do."

"What?"

"They run around whistling 'Danny Boy' all the time."

He laughed. "I've got nothing against the song. Hey, Josh and I had a wager going, you know."

"Who bet that I wouldn't cave in to family pressure?"

"Neither of us. The wager was on the date you'd finally do it."

"I can't wait to see you," she said. Once again, he pictured her. Not the woman on television. The one who should be here with him now. Softly scented, sleek and smooth, hair down and wild, naked as the day she was born. Maybe that was part of her allure. She could be so elegant and almost aloof in public, and so incredibly sensual and volatile in private.

"I don't think there are any planes at this time of night," he said regretfully. "Can't even hop a train. I could rent a car...if you're really needy."

"You're good. Very good."

"No, what I am is—"

"Never mind," she said, laughing again. "You know you can't rent a car in Florida and be here that quickly. And I have to—*have* to—tie up a few things here tomorrow and then head up right after. That will give us a week before the actual big day. Time so I can see my folks and so we can give the Leisure Channel a really good show."

"I can be there, if you want." He wondered if he should tell her that he wasn't in Florida. Maybe he'd better leave that one for Josh.

He was silent for a moment. Yes, there were other women in the world, he knew that well. The fingers of his free hand tensed and eased, tensed and eased. But none like her.

"Aye, me love, at ye olde pub!" he said, giving her his best Irish accent. "If you insist that we wait that long."

"You'd really drive all night…?"

"I would."

"I'd rather have you alive in the future than dead in such an effort," Moira said firmly. "Boston, night after next, Kelly's Pub, you'll meet the folks. I'll see you there?"

"All right," he told her. Then, though he had expected it, he found himself dreading the fact that they would all be in Boston together. He, Moira, her family, her past—and the future. "I love you," he added, and he was surprised by the almost desperate ardor in his voice.

"I love you, too," she said, and he believed her.

A few moments later, they rang off.

Though it was late and he was still exhausted, Michael found himself rising and getting dressed. He glanced at the clock. Not that late; just after midnight.

He dressed and left the hotel room.

His destination was within easy walking distance. Boston was a good city in that respect. Narrow, winding streets in the old section and even in the newer areas. There was little distance here between the colonial and the modern. He liked Boston. Great seafood. A sense of history.

He walked quickly and came to the street he had checked out earlier that day. There, in the middle of the block, beneath a soft yellow streetlight, was the sign.

Kelly's Pub.

He stood there, staring at it.

And damning the days to come.

The doors were still open, though it looked quiet within. Weeknight. He thought about sauntering in, quietly ordering a draft, sitting in a corner, taking a look.

No.

At twelve-thirty, he turned and walked away.

Twelve forty-five.

From the shadows cast by the long buildings, another man watched Michael McLean leave the premises. He hadn't really seen his face, had never known the man previously, but even so, he was fully aware of who he was.

Dan O'Hara watched the man thoughtfully until he had disappeared. He had avoided the streetlight on the opposite side of the block and therefore had hardly been even a dark silhouette in the night.

He leaned against the old building. With the street clear, he lit a cigarette, slowly allowing the smoke to filter out of his lungs. Bad habit. He needed to quit, he thought idly. So that was Michael. He didn't have enough basis for any rational judgments, but by virtue of instinct, he disliked the guy. But then, Moira could be seeing a Nobel Peace Prize-winning certified saint and he would still dislike the guy.

He had to force himself to hold back any conclusions on Michael McLean. He couldn't even blame the guy for wanting a good look at the pub.

Kelly's. Dan loved the place himself.

How long had he been gone this time? Too long. Of course, last time he had come back, things had been different. No Moira.

How many times had he pushed her away? Doing the right thing, of course. At first she'd been too young. Then, even when they'd become lovers, he'd just known that he was wrong for her. Yet he hadn't realized that he still lived with the belief that she was his, that she would still be there. He truly wanted her to be happy, but he wasn't a man without an ego. Somewhere inside, he had believed that happiness for her would mean waiting for him.

Okay, so he was an ass.

An ass…yet he had done the right thing. She was a strong character, with a sense of the world, of right and wrong and everything that being an American meant. He hadn't been able to help it; he was Irish. An Irishman who loved America, but who felt…

Obligated.

Was he always going to feel obligated?

Hell, was he going to survive?

He thought angrily of how much he didn't like what was going on, and there seemed to be no help in the knowledge that it wasn't his fault. He'd never put any of this into motion, but there wasn't a damn thing he could do.

Moira was coming home. He'd talked to Katy Kelly on the phone today, and she'd been in heaven, knowing that she would have her whole family home and in one place for the special holiday. She was also a little nervous. "She's been seeing a man, one her da and I have yet to meet," Katy had informed him, trying to keep her disapproval out of her voice.

"He's probably a great guy," Dan had told her. "She's grown up a smart woman, Katy, you know that. You should be proud."

"He's in television, too. Working for her and Josh." Katy had sighed. "Now Josh…there's a good man."

"A fine man." Danny could say so easily. He liked Moira's partner. And the fellow was married, was truly a friend and had never had an intimate relationship with Moira.

"Well, this new fellow is Irish."

"Oh? And what's his name?"

"Michael. Michael McLean."

"Well, there you go. What more can you ask for?"

Katy sighed again. "Well, I suppose…for you two to have married, Danny."

"Ah, Katy. We were going different ways. Besides, I wasn't meant for marriage."

"I think you were."

She had gone on to insist that it wouldn't matter that Moira and her crew would be there—the back room of the pub was his, as it always was when he came to Boston. And yes, Moira knew that he was coming.

A strange sense of nostalgia stole over him. This place really was home to him, certainly as much as any other. His early years seemed a very long time ago. Living with his uncle, he had traveled a great deal. Brendan O'Toole, his mother's brother, who had married a cousin of Katy Kelly, had been a scholar and broker for antique manuscripts. He had given Dan his first love of literature. Of the written word and the power within it. He'd been a storyteller, another talent he had passed on to Dan. His house in Dublin had been home, but they'd been on the go constantly. Dan had seen many foreign countries, and he had spent a great deal of time in America. He did love the States.

And after any length of time away, he missed this old place.

It was time for him to be there. He could go on in. But he had said he was arriving in the morning. He would wait. No reason to tell the folks that he had been in Boston a bit before checking in with them.

Aye, he would wait.

As he stood there against the building, he saw another man striding down the street. He wore a huge overcoat and a low-brimmed hat. Nothing odd in that. Boston could be frigid this time of year.

But this man approached the pub oddly; then, as Dan had done himself, he paused, staring at the windows.

He stood there for a long time. Dan dropped his cigarette to the ground and remained still, watching the watcher.

The man was peering through the windows, trying to see who was in the pub.

Apparently he didn't see the person—or people—he was seeking, because after a long moment, he turned away and started down the street again, back in the direction from which he had come.

Nothing odd in that. A guy out to find friends at a pub, taking a look for them, realizing they weren't there, deciding to leave.

Nothing odd in that.

Except that the man in the huge coat and low-brimmed hat was Patrick Kelly, son of the owners of Kelly's Pub.

Dan lit another cigarette, feeling a new tension, as if rocks were forming in his gut.

He waited a while longer, then hiked up the collar of his coat and started off down the street, as well.

Moira seldom paused to window-shop; she was usually running somewhere, and besides, she had been in New York a long time. She still loved the beautiful displays that were put out for holidays, and she appreciated the fact that she could buy almost anything in the world in the city where she lived and worked. She loved clothes, but she also loved a day when she could take the time to try on outfits, go through a zillion pair of shoes, driving salesmen crazy.

But that morning, walking toward the new French restaurant in the Village where she was to meet the lady from Maine to discuss their taping schedule, she found herself stopping to stare at an incredible Saint Patrick's showcase. The stores usually had out all their Easter wares along with their Saint Patrick's Day items. This particular window had been done with real love. There were shamrocks everywhere, arranged artfully. A field of lovely porcelain fairies had been hung to fly above a rainbow with the traditional pot of gold at the end. Finely carved leprechauns with charming faces were set around the rainbow, as if they were busy at daily tasks. The leprechaun in the middle sat on a pedestal, facing a fairy on another pedestal. The fairy was exquisite, poised on one toe, with wings painted the colors of the rainbow. Pausing without realizing it, she stared at the fairy, charmed. She realized that it was a music box.

She glanced quickly at her watch and decided she had time to take a closer look. She went into the store, not surprised to discover that the shop owner was the cashier, that she still carried a bit of an Irish accent and that she was delighted with Moira's interest in the item.

"My mother would absolutely love that piece," Moira told her, and asked the price.

It was high, but the woman quickly explained. "The piece is one of a kind. The fairies and leprechauns, you see. The porcelain fairies are limited, but the carved pieces are hand-crafted by two brothers in Dublin. Each is individual, and signed. I believe they'll be very popular in the future, but it's not the fact that they may be highly collectible one day that makes them so dear. It's the time taken for the work that goes into each one."

"I hate to ask you to take it out of the window."

"Oh, no, dear, I love the darling little things. Please, it's my pleasure, even if you don't buy. You seem to truly appreciate the art of it."

Moira assured her that she did, indeed. And when the woman took the piece from the window and put it before her, she found that it was even more beautiful than she had thought. The carving of the face was exquisite. The fairy created a feeling that was totally ethereal. She was simply magical. *All that is good and enchanting about the Irish people,* Moira thought.

"I'll take her," Moira said.

"Don't you wish to hear her play?" the woman asked, twisting the key at the bottom of the small pedestal.

"Sure, thank you. What song does she play?"

The woman laughed softly. She allowed her accent to deepen as she jokingly said, "Why, besure and begorrah, dear. She plays 'Danny Boy.' You know, 'Londonderry Air.'"

The little fairy began to spin, to fly on her pedestal. The music tinkled out, charming, beautiful, sweet, the haunting melody familiar and yet light, different.

"Danny Boy." Of course. What else? There were so many beautiful old Irish tunes, but naturally this box would play "Danny Boy."

"Is something wrong?" the woman asked.

"No, she's lovely, thank you so much. I'll definitely buy her for my mum."

"I'll wrap her very carefully for you."

"Thanks so much."

As Moira waited, she realized that she would be spending the next week listening to "Danny Boy." Might as well get used to it now.

"Are you sure there's nothing wrong, dear?"

"Not at all. In fact, I'd like both of those little stuffed leprechauns, please. They'll make cute little gifts for my nieces. Then I need something for a boy."

"I have a small, hand-held video game just in. Banshees against fairies, with the leprechauns being the chance factor, some of them good, some of them bad."

"Sounds perfect," Moira said. "Thank you so much."

Tomorrow she was going home. And suddenly, here in this shop, anticipation mingled with her dread.

Kelly's Pub was already in full nightly swing when Dan O'Hara emerged from the back room of the tavern, the guest quarters, where he had been staying. The pub band, Blackbird, was already playing a mixture of old and new Irish music with a bit of American pop thrown in here and there. He knew all the members from way back.

It was the first time he had come into the pub during opening hours, and he was ready for the greeting he knew he would receive.

"And there he is!" Eamon Kelly called from behind the bar. "The best and brightest of you lot of reprobates, Mr. Daniel O'Hara."

"Hey, Danny, how are you?" asked old Seamus.

"Danny boy, you're back in town!" Liam McConnahy said.

The lineup at the bar was made up of Eamon's longtime friends, some old country, some born and bred in the USA. He recognized Sal Costanza, an old school chum who had grown up in the Italian sector along the North Shore. Eamon Kelly had created his own little Gaelic empire here, but he was a good-hearted, friendly fellow, with a keen interest in everyone around him and—usually—a nose for a decent character in any man. But now Dan didn't like what was happening here. He would have done anything in his power to keep Kelly's Pub and the Kellys themselves out of what was happening. But things had been set in motion; he had no choice. Whatever was going down had been given the code name Blackbird, and that could only refer to Kelly's Pub.

Hell, a Kelly could be involved.

"Back in town," Dan said easily, embracing both old Seamus and Liam, then shaking hands with the others as each man spoke a quick greeting.

"So," Seamus said, his thick, snow-white brows rising over cloudy blue eyes, "have you been hanging around back in the old country or gallivantin' around the States?"

"A bit of both," Dan said.

"You've been in Ireland recently?" Liam asked. He had the same cap of white hair as Seamus, except that his was thinning now.

"That I have," Dan said.

"The Republic—or the North?" Seamus asked, a slight frown denoting his worry.

"A bit of both," Dan said. "Eamon, how about a round for my old friends at the bar? It's good to see them again. Sal, how's it going in the pasta business in Little Italy? I've been hankering for a taste of your mum's lasagna. No one makes it as good as she does."

Sal answered, and Dan kept smiling, nodding in reply to the thanks he received for the round of drinks. But as he engaged in the banter at the bar, he looked around the room. Though the band was in action at one end, the scene remained fairly quiet. An attractive young couple, with either his or her parents, were having dinner at a center table. A group just off from work—probably from the IBM offices or the bank around the corner—huddled around a couple of tables near the band, winding down from their nine-to-five workday. Patrick Kelly was in. Eamon's son, tall, with a head full of dark hair touched by a reddish sheen. He was a good-looking fellow, on stage now with the band, playing along with the violinist. He saw Daniel and gave him a wave and a grin, beckoning to him. Daniel nodded and smiled in return, motioning that he would join them all soon. Patrick nudged Jeff Dolan, lead guitarist and group leader, and Jeff, too, nodded Dan's way.

Still scanning the room, Dan saw a lone man in a business suit seated at a far corner table, a darkened table. A stranger. Dan had the feeling the man was surveying the occupants of the pub, just as he was doing himself.

"What are you drinking yourself?" Eamon asked him.

"What's he drinking?" Seamus said indignantly. "Give him a whiskey and a Guinness!"

"Now, Seamus, I'm in the grand old USA," Dan protested. "A Bud Lite on draft, if you will, Eamon. It may prove to be a long night—back with a party of Boston's black sheep!"

"How's the place look, Danny?" Liam asked. "You miss it when you're away?"

"Why, the pub looks just fine, and old friends look even better," Dan replied. He lifted the stein Eamon had brought him. "Slainte! To old times, old friends."

"And to the old country!" Eamon declared.

"Aye, to the old country," Dan said softly.

The sky was overcast when Moira's shuttle from New York to Boston made its initial descent for landing. Even so, she stared out the window for a bird's-eye view of the city where she had grown up, and which she still loved so much. Coming home. She was excited; she loved her family dearly. They were all entirely crazy, of course. She was convinced of that. But she loved them and was happy at the prospect of seeing them.

But then…then there was this whole Danny thing.

The plane landed. She was slow to take off her seat belt and slow to deplane. No one was picking her up; she had made the last-minute decision to take an earlier shuttle than the rest of the cast and crew, who would be taking the last flight. When the people in the seats behind her had filed out, she grabbed her overnight bag and walked out, thanking the flight attendant and the pilots, who were waiting for her exit to leave themselves.

Outside Logan, she hailed a taxi. Once seated, she realized that the driver, a young man of twenty-something with a lean face and amber eyes, was staring at her by way of the rearview mirror.

"You're Moira Kelly!" he said, flushing as she caught his eye.

"Yes."

"In my cab! Fancy that. You just travel on a regular plane and get in a regular taxi?"

"Seems to be the best way to get around," she told him, smiling.

"You mean you don't have a private jet and a limo waiting?" the man demanded.

She laughed. "I don't have a private jet at all, though sometimes we do hire private cars."

"And no one recognizes you—and hounds you?"

"I'm afraid that all of America doesn't tune in to the Leisure Channel. And even those who do don't necessarily watch our show."

"Well, they should."

"Thank you. Very much."

"What are you doing in Boston?"

"I'm from here."

"Wow. Right. And you're Irish, right? Are you home to see family, or are you going to film stuff here?"

"Both."

"Wow. Well, great. Hey, it's a privilege. If you need more transportation while you're here, call me. I've got the cleanest cab in the city. I grew up here, too.

I know the place backward and forward. No charge, even. Honest."

"I'd never take advantage that way of anyone making a living," Moira said. "But give me your card, and I promise when we need transportation we'll call you." In fact, he did seem to be a good driver. Boston's traffic was as crazy as ever. There was always construction; the freeway was as often as not a stop-and-go place. Once they were out of the tunnel and off the highway, the streets were narrow and one-way. And then there were the traffic circles… The old character and ultrathin roadways were part of the charm of the city—and the bane of it, as well.

The young man kept his right hand solidly on the steering wheel and slipped her a card with his left hand.

"Hey, I'm Irish, too."

"Your name is Tom Gambetti."

He grinned at her in the rearview mirror. "My mum is Irish, Dad is Italian. Hey, this is Boston. There are lots of us living on pasta and potatoes! Both your folks are Irish?"

"Oh, Lord, yes!" Moira laughed.

"Right off the old potato boat, eh?"

"Something like that," she said, then leaned forward, pointing. "There it is—Kelly's Pub."

The street was narrow. Though both corners held large new office buildings, the rest of the block still had a lot of old character. The building that housed the pub was two stories, with a basement and an attic. It dated from Colonial days, as did many of its nudged-in neighbors. An old iron tethering pole remained in front, from the days when the country's forefathers had come to knock back a pint or two. Kelly's Pub was lettered on an attractive board above the door, and there were soft friendly lights issuing from lamps on either side.

When the weather was warm, tables spilled onto the narrow enclosed patio in front. There were two windows in the front, as well; they were closed now, in deference to the winter, but within the pub, the lace-edged curtains were drawn back so that passersby could see the welcoming coziness to be found inside. "Want your suitcase right in the pub?" Tom asked.

"No, thanks, just on the sidewalk. I'm going upstairs first."

"I'll be happy to take it up for you," he suggested.

She shook her head. "No, thanks. I appreciate it, but—"

"But a homecoming is best alone," he said.

She paid him as he set her bag down. "Thanks. And I will call you if we need transportation."

"You may not have to call me. It looks like a great pub."

"It is," she murmured, listening to the laughter and music coming from within. "It's everything a pub is supposed to be. *Céad mile fáilte.*"

"What does that mean?"

She looked at him, smiling wryly. "A hundred thousand welcomes."

"Nice. Well, good luck. I'll be seeing you."

"Thanks."

He got in his car and drove away, it seemed regretfully. Nice kid, she thought. Then she hefted her suitcase and started up the outside stairs that led to the family living quarters above the thriving business.

Her mother was a model of domesticity. The porch beside the front door of the home area was set with white wicker café tables, and the canvas overhang was clean as a whistle, even in the dying days of winter. Moira set her case down by the door and knocked, her fingers colder than she had realized inside her gloves. Knocking was easier than trying to find her key.

The door opened. Her mother was there, taking one look at her face and giving her the kind of smile that would have made a trek halfway around the world worthwhile. "Moira Kathleen!" And then, though Katy Kelly was thin as a reed and two inches shorter than Moira's five feet eight, she enveloped her daughter in a fierce hug with the strength of a grizzly.

"Moira Kathleen, you're home!" Katy said, stepping back at last, hands on her hips as she surveyed her daughter.

"Mum, of course I'm home. You knew I was coming."

"Seems so long, Moira," Katy said, shaking her head. "And you look like a million."

Moira laughed. "Thanks, Mum. Good genes," she said affectionately. Her mother was a beautiful woman. Katy didn't dye the tendrils of silver threading through her auburn hair. God was granting her age, in her words. A head full of silver wasn't going to matter. Katy was trim from moving a thousand miles an hour every day of her life. Her eyes were the green of her old County Cork, and her face had a classical beauty.

"Ah, sweetie, I miss you so!" Katy said, kissing her. "It's been so long."

"Mum, we're just heading into Saint Patrick's Day. I spent Christmas here. And we all did First Night in the city together, remember?"

"Aye, and maybe it's not so long, but your brother, Patrick, you know, manages to get back at least once a month, he does."

"Ah, yes, my brother. Saint Patrick," Moira murmured.

"Now would you be mocking the likes of your

brother?" The question came from behind Katy. Moira looked past her mother to see her grandmother standing there, Granny Jon. On a good day, Granny Jon might be considered an even five feet. At ninety-something—no one, including Granny Jon, was quite sure what year she'd been born—she was still as straight as a ramrod and spry as a young girl. Her keen sense of humor sparkled in hazel eyes as she playfully accosted Moira.

"And there—the heart of Eire herself!" Moira laughed, stepping forward to hug her grandmother. As she hugged Granny Jon, she felt the old woman shake a little. Spry and straight she might be, but her grandmother was still a tiny mass of delicate bones, and Moira adored her. She'd given Moira leprechauns and legends, wonderful tales about the banshees being tricked or bribed to go away, and then, when she'd been older, true tales of the fight for freedom for the Irish through long years of mayhem throughout history. She was keen and wise and had seen the battlefield of her city torn to shreds, yet had somehow maintained a love for all the humanity around her, a glorious sense of humor, and a sound judgment regarding both politics and people.

"Why, Moira, you haven't aged a day," Granny Jon teased. "Katy, have a heart now. The girl is out there doing us proud. And she is living in New York, while Patrick has stayed in the state of Massachusetts."

"Um. As if western Mass weren't nearly as far away as New York City," Katy said.

"But it hasn't the traffic," Granny Jon said.

"Then there's my evil younger sister," Moira teased, rolling her eyes.

Katy inclined her head with a wry smile for the two of them. "Well, then, Colleen has gone as far as the west of the entire country now, hasn't she? And she'd never even consider not being here for Saint Patrick's Day."

Moira sighed. "Mum, I'm here, and I'm even bringing in the non-Irish for you to convert," Moira told her.

"Ah, now, 'tis enough," Katy said. "We'll give you a quick cup of tea. Granny Jon was just brewing—"

"And it will be strong enough to pick itself up and walk itself right across the table, eh?" Moira said, teasing her grandmother and putting on her accent.

"We'll have none of that," Granny Jon said. "And I do make a good pot of tea, a real pot of tea, nothing wishy-washy about it. And what have we here?"

The main entry to the living quarters was a foyer, with the kitchen—a very large room with added warmth in winter from the oven—and a hallway leading to the bedrooms, library and office straight ahead. Moira hadn't heard a thing, but when she looked beyond Granny Jon, she saw three little heads bobbing into sight.

Patrick and his wife, Siobhan, had nearly repeated her parents' pattern of procreation; their son Brian was nine and daughters Molly and Shannon were six and four respectively.

"Hey, guys!" Moira called delightedly, hunching down on the balls of her feet and putting her arms out for the kids. They came running to her with whoops and hollers, kissing her, hugging her.

"Auntie Mo," Brian said. As a baby, he'd never quite gotten her name right. She'd been Auntie Mo to the kids ever since. "Is it true we're going to be on the telly?"

"On the *telly?* Oh, dear, you've been hanging around the Irish too long, me lad!" she teased. "Yes, of course, if you wish, you'll be on the telly."

"Cool!" Molly told her.

"Cool!" Shannon repeated, wide-eyed.

"Oh, yes, all the kids at the preschool will be talking!" Moira said, ruffling her nieces' hair. Brian was almost a Mini-Me of her brother, with his hazel eyes and deep auburn hair. The girls had acquired their mother's soft true-blond hair and huge blue eyes. Leave it to Patrick. They were wonderful children, well-behaved without being timid, full of personality and love. Chalk that all up to Siobhan, Moira thought. Her sister-in-law was a doll. Patrick…well, as Granny Jon had once said, he could fall into a mire of cow dung and come up smelling like roses. She adored her brother, of course. She just wished he didn't manage to go his own way all the time and still wind up appearing to be the perfect child on every occasion. He should have been a politician. Maybe he would be one day. He'd gotten his law degree and now practiced in a tiny town in western Massachusetts, where he also owned land, kept horses and a few farm animals and still maintained a home that always seemed as beautifully kept as something out of *Architectural Digest.* Business frequently brought him to Boston, where, naturally, he always stopped in to see his parents.

Her brother had married well, she decided. She knew Siobhan, née O'Malley, had taken a chance with Patrick after his wild days in high school, but apparently the chance had paid off. They both seemed happy and still, after ten years of marriage, deeply in love.

"Cool, cool, cool, Auntie Mo!" Shannon repeated.

"Cool. I like that. Good American slang term," Moira said seriously.

Her mother let out a tsking sound. "Now, Moira, if you can't hold on to a few traditions…"

"Mum! I adore tradition," she said.

"And you, you little leprechauns!" Katy chastised the

children. "It's nearly nine. You're supposed to be asleep now. You've gotten to see Auntie Mo, now back in bed."

"Ah, Nana K!" Brian protested.

"I'll not have your mother telling me I can't handle her poppets in my old age," Katy said. "'Tis back in bed with you. Off now."

"Wait! I'll take full responsibility! One more hug each," Moira said. The girls giggled; Brian was more serious. She kissed their cheeks, hugged them tightly one more time.

"Auntie Mo has to go down and see your father—and Granda," Katy said. "Besides, she'll be here for the week, like the lot o' you. And she's promised to get you on the telly, so you'll be needing your sleep."

Brian nodded seriously.

"We don't want bags under your eyes," Moira teased, then winked. Brian's lips twitched in a smile, and he gave his grandmother a rueful glance. "And," she added, "I have presents for all three of you. So if you go back to bed right now, you'll get them first thing when I see you in the morning," she promised.

"Presents?" Molly said happily.

"One apiece!" Moira said, laughing. "Now, like Granny Katy has told you, back off to bed! And sound asleep. Or the Auntie Mo fairy—just like Santa and the tooth fairy—will know that you've been awake, and no present beside the teacup in the morning!"

Her mother gazed at her and rolled her eyes. Moira grimaced, then laughed.

"Night, Auntie Mo," Brian said. "Come on, girls." He led them toward the bedrooms.

Molly tugged on his hand and stopped him. "Granny Jon," she said seriously. "There aren't really any banshees around tonight, are there?"

"Not a one," Granny Jon said.

"No monsters at all!" Brian said firmly.

"Not in this house! I'll see to it. I'm as mean as any old banshee," Granny Jon said, her eyes alight.

The kids called good-night again and went traipsing off down the hall. Moira rose and stared at her grandmother sternly. "Now, have you been telling tales again?"

"Not on your life! They spent the day watching 'Darby O'Gill and the Little People.' I'm entirely innocent," her grandmother protested with a laugh. "And you, young lady, you'd best get downstairs to the pub. Your father will be heartbroken if he hears you've been here all this time and haven't been to give him a hug."

"Patrick, Siobhan and Colleen are down there?" Moira asked.

"Siobhan's off to see her folks, but your brother and sister are both downstairs," Katy said. "Get along with you."

"Wait, wait, let her have a sip of her tea before they ply her with alcohol," Granny Jon protested, bringing a cup to Moira. Moira thanked her with a quick smile. No one made tea like Granny Jon. Not cold, not scalding. A touch of sugar. Never like syrup, and never bitter.

"It's delicious, Granny Jon," Moira said.

"Then swallow it down and be gone with you," her mother said.

She gulped the tea—grateful that it wasn't scalding.

"I'll put your bag in your room—give me your coat, Moira Kathleen," Katy said. "Take the inside stairs down. You know your father will be behind the bar."

"I'll be rescuing the teacup," Granny Jon said dryly.

Moira slid obediently out of her coat and handed it to her mother. "I'll take my bag, Mum. It's heavy."

"Away with you, I can handle a mite of luggage."

"All right, all right, I'm going. 'So happy you're here, now get out,'" she teased her mother.

"'Tis just your father, girl," Katy protested.

"How is he?" she asked anxiously.

Her mother's smile was the best answer she could have received. "His tests came out well, but he was told that he must come in without fail for a checkup every six months."

"He's working too hard," Moira murmured.

"Well, now, that was my thought, but the doctors say that work is good for a man, and sitting around and getting no exercise is not. So he got all the permission he needed to keep right on running his pub, though the Lord knows, he has able help."

"I'm going down right now to see him."

Her mother nodded, pleased.

Moira gave both her mother and grandmother another kiss, then started through the foyer to the left; there was a little sitting room there, and a spiral staircase that led down to a door at the foot of the stairs that opened to the office and storage space behind the polished oak expanse of the bar, where she would find the rest of her family—and all the mixed emotions that coming home entailed.

3

As soon as she opened the door, Moira could hear the chatter in the bar and the sounds of the band. She groaned inwardly. Blackbird was doing a speeded-up number from the Brendan Behan play *The Hostage*.

"Great," she muttered aloud. "They're all toasting the Republic already."

She slipped in, walked through the office and the swinging doors, and saw her father's back. Eamon Kelly was a tall, broad-shouldered man with graying hair that had once been close to a true, luxurious black. Though he was pouring a draft, she sneaked up behind him, winding her arms around his waist. "Hey, Dad," she said softly.

"Moira Kathleen!" he cried, spilling a bit of draft as he set the glass down, spun around and picked her up by the waist. He lifted her high, and she kissed his cheek, quickly protesting his hold, worried about his heart.

"Dad, put me down!" She laughed.

He shook his head, beautiful blue eyes on her. "Now when the day comes that I cannot lift my girl, that will be a sad day indeed!"

"Put me down," she said again, still laughing, "because I feel as if everyone in the pub is looking at me!"

"And why not? Me daughter has come home!"

"You've got another daughter in her—"

"And I've already made quite a spectacle of Colleen, I have. Now it's your turn!"

She managed to regain her footing, then hugged him fiercely again.

"You know the boys at the bar, eh, daughter? Seamus and Liam, Sal Costanza, the Italian here, Sandy O'Connor down there, his wife, Sue—"

"Hello!" Moira called to them all.

"Well, now, I'd be taking a hug and a kiss," Seamus told her.

"And you'd not leave me out!" Liam protested.

"One more for Dad, then I'll come around the bar," she said, holding her father closely to her once again. "Are you supposed to be working this hard?" she asked him softly.

"Ah, now, pouring a draft isn't hard work," he told her. Then he pulled back and frowned. "And you, did you fly in alone?"

She smiled. "Dad, I live and work in New York City. I travel all over the country."

"But there's usually someone with you."

Puzzled, Moira shook her head. "I took a cab to the airport, got on a plane, then took a cab here."

"Boston's not the safest city in the world these days," Liam said. Moira noted that he and Seamus had a newspaper spread out between them at the bar.

"I don't think it's ever been crime free," Moira said lightly. "No major metropolis goes without crime. That's why you raised intelligent, streetwise children, Dad."

"He's thinking about the girl," Liam told her.

Moira frowned. "What girl?"

"A prostitute found in the river," Seamus said.

"Dead," Liam added sadly.

"Strangled," Seamus finished with sorrowful drama.

She looked at her father, finding the situation sad, as well, but wondering why this news should suddenly make him worried about her. "Dad, I promise you, I haven't taken up the world's oldest profession as a sideline."

He shrugged. "Now, Moira—"

"He's afraid there might be a serial killer in the city," Liam said, shaking his head. "Apparently the woman plied her trade around the hotel and attracted men of means. Therefore, you see, any lovely lass might be a target. But we're not here to get you down, Moira, girl. There are fine things happening as well. Let's look to the good news! We're getting one of the most important politicians in Northern Ireland for our very own Saint Patrick's Day parade. Mr. Jacob Brolin is coming here, right to Boston, can you imagine?"

"Oh?" Moira murmured, afraid to say more. Josh, who hailed from the deep South, had told her about a round table he had attended where men still sat together, engaging in deep and sometimes passionate discussions regarding the American Civil War. Josh was an American history buff. At Kelly's, too, often they relived battles—and the fighting that had eventually led to the Irish Free State and the Republic of Ireland. They drank to the Easter Rebellion solemnly, bemoaning the fate of the freedom fighters executed after the surrender. They argued the strategies of the leaders, they spoke for and against the hero Michael Collins and ripped apart Eamon De Valera, the American-born first president of the Irish Republic. Of course, it always came back to the same thing: if only, from the very beginning, the island had been recognized as one nation—an Irish nation—they would never have had The Troubles that followed. She personally felt rather sorry for

Michael Collins. He'd risked his life time and again, devoted himself wholeheartedly to the cause, managed the first true liberation of any of his people, and, in the end, been killed by a faction of his own people for not managing to take the entire island at once.

"Aye, a fine man, this Jacob Brolin," her father said, brightening. "Why, the flyers are out at the front entry, daughter. We're privileged, we are. You ought to know this already."

She tried to keep quiet, but she couldn't. She shook her head. "Dad, you'll all have to excuse me if I think that violence against anyone is horrible and if I don't know every move made in a foreign country regarding the hoped-for union of an island nation. You all can dream of a united Ireland, but I'm sorry if I think that bombing innocent people is beyond despicable. I have friends who are English who have no desire to hurt anyone Irish—"

"Why, Moira Kathleen Kelly! I have good Englishmen in here all the time," her father said indignantly. "Englishmen, Scotsmen, Australians, Cornishmen, Welsh and a good helping of our close friends the Canadians, not to mention Mexicans, French, Spanish—"

"And excuse me, but have you forgotten your truly closest friends in Boston? The Italians, naturally. To the Italians! Salute!" Sal said, smiling, meeting Moira's gaze and winking in his attempt to defuse the argument.

"God, yes, the Italians! Salute!" Moira said.

"To the Italians!"

The men at the bar were always happy to toast to anyone and everyone.

It did nothing, however, to change the gist of the conversation.

"Moira, you would admire this man Jacob Brolin,"

Seamus said earnestly. "He's a pacifist, working for the rights of every last man in Northern Ireland. He's arranged social events where all attend; he's worked hard for the downtrodden and poor and he's loved by Orangemen and Catholics alike. There's seldom been so fine and fair a man to reach a position of power."

Moira let out a long breath, feeling a bit foolish. All she'd wanted was to get everyone off the subject. Instead, she'd nearly created a passionate argument herself.

"Well, then, I'm thrilled that this man is coming to our country, to our city—"

"You'll want him on your program," Seamus said.

"Aye, and then maybe we'll all get to meet him," Liam agreed.

"Well, we'll see," Moira murmured. "We planned on asking Mum to make a traditional Irish meal, tell leprechaun stories, things like that."

"Aye, but you'll want the parade on your show," her father insisted.

"Moira?"

She had seldom been so relieved to hear her name called. She spun around, delighted to see her younger sister, Colleen, coming to her, threading her way through the crowd.

They'd fought like cats and dogs as children, but now Colleen was incredibly dear to her. Her sister was beautiful, Moira's height, with red hair a far softer shade than Moira's deep auburn. She had Granny Jon's hazel eyes and a face of sheer light and beauty. She had been living in Los Angeles for the last two years, to their parents' great dismay. But she had been hired as the lead model for a burgeoning new cosmetics line, and though they were disconsolate that she spent so much time so far away, they were also as proud as it was possible to be. Her face was appearing in magazines across the country.

Colleen hugged her. "When did you get in?"

"Thirty minutes ago. You?"

"Earlier this afternoon. Have you seen Patrick yet?"

"No, but he's down here, right?"

"With the band. Along with Danny."

Moira jerked her head around. She'd heard the band playing since she'd come in, but Jeff Dolan had been doing the singing—she'd heard Jeff play and sing at least a third of her life, and she knew the sound of his voice like the back of her hand. Now she saw that her brother was indeed up with the group, playing bass guitar.

And Danny was there, as well, sitting in for the drummer this time. As if he had known the exact moment she would look his way, he suddenly stared across the room, meeting her eyes.

He smiled slowly. Just a slight curl of his lips. He didn't miss a beat on the drums. *Ah, yes, Moira, love, I'm here.* Was that part of his appeal? The slow grin that could slip into a soul, amber eyes that seemed always to be a bit mocking, and a bit rueful, as well? She tried to stare at him analytically. He was a tall man, which seemed oddly apparent even as he sat behind the drums. His hair, a sandy shade that still carried a hint of red, was perpetually unruly, an annoyance to him when it fell low on his brow, but somehow rakish and sensual to the female gender.

His shoulders, she assured herself, were not as broad as Michael's. Michael was quintessentially tall, dark and handsome. And more. He was decent. Kind, entertaining, courteous and concerned with the well-being of those around him. When she'd first met Michael, right after the Christmas holidays, she'd thought he was definitely appealing, sexy. Then she'd thought he was intelligent, bright and witty. Then she'd started becoming emotionally involved with him. But with Danny...

He had just been there. A whirlwind in her life, coming and going, visiting her folks with his uncle when he'd been young, coming on his own once he'd turned eighteen. He was Patrick's age, three years older than she was, and he'd been someone she'd adored when she'd been ten and he'd been thirteen, the first time he had arrived. He'd come back when she was fourteen, fifteen, sixteen and then eighteen, and it had been that year when she'd realized there was nothing in the world that she wanted as badly as she wanted Dan O'Hara. Maybe he'd resisted at first. He'd just graduated from college with a degree in journalism. He had a passion to write, to change the world, and she was still wet behind the ears, not to mention the fact that she was also the child of his good American friends. So she'd set out to have what she wanted. She was enthralled, in awe, and being with him changed none of that. Neither did it change Danny. He'd told her that he was bad for her, that she was young, that she needed to see the world, know the world. And still, year after year, she had waited, going to school, loving the learning, looking, always looking, hoping for someone who could make her forget Danny was in the world somewhere. Danny, with his passion and, always, a level of energy about him that was electric. She knew that he cared for her; perhaps in his way he loved her. Just not as much as he loved the rest of the world—or at least his precious Ireland. As she'd gotten older, she'd begun to understand him in a way. She was an American, and she loved being an American. And she had her own dreams and aspirations. They weren't meant to be together, but that had never stopped her from wanting him.

But now she had found someone. Michael. She inhaled deeply, forced a casual smile. *So you're here, Danny. Good for you, nice to see you. Now, if you'll excuse me, I have a great life that I'm living....*

She meant to turn away, but Danny's smile deepened as the number ended, and in the midst of the applause, she saw him lean over to whisper to Jeff Dolan and her brother.

"Oh, no," Colleen breathed. "They've seen us together."

"So what?" Moira whispered.

"I said I wouldn't sing until you showed up."

"Colleen!" Moira protested.

"Hey, folks, we've got a special performance for you this evening," Jeff announced over the mike. "The prodigal daughters have returned for Saint Patrick's Day. We're going to get them both up here for a special number in honor of all the Irish in America—and remember, on Saint Patrick's Day, all Americans are a wee bit Irish!"

"Daughters, go on now," Eamon said proudly.

"Come on up, Kelly girls," Jeff said, encouraging them determinedly. "Ladies and gentlemen, a real treat. The Kelly girls. No one can do a rendition of 'Danny Boy' with quite such melodious Irish beauty."

"What do we do?" Colleen whispered. "I can't believe they're doing this to us. I haven't even heard the song in ages."

"Um. Not since the last time we were here," Moira said dryly. "I guess we go up there. We can't hurt Dad."

Danny had instigated this. She knew it. She walked toward Jeff, trying to ignore Danny with casual negligence as she took the mike. "Irish-American melodious beauty," she said, smiling at Jeff and apologizing to the patrons in the pub. "No guarantees, but we'll do our best."

The first strains of the violin brought a sigh from the crowd. Moira reflected briefly that, with this particular audience, she and Colleen could have sung like two crows and sentiment alone would have evoked wild applause. But she did love the song, and she and Colleen had done it together since the Saint Pat's program at church when they had been in grammar school. Her sister's voice harmonized perfectly with hers. They might not have produced the most melodious Irish beauty ever, but they did the song proud. She loved the music. There was a magic to it, to being home, to singing with Colleen…and even in knowing that Daniel O'Hara was playing a soft beat on the drums behind her.

Naturally the crowd went wild when they ended the tune. Of course, here, it was singing to a group of proud relatives. Moira smiled along with Colleen, thanking those who called out compliments. She felt an arm around her, and before she could completely stiffen, she realized it was her brother.

"Patrick, hey." She hugged him.

"What about me?" Jeff protested.

Jeff Dolan looked like a latter-day hippie. She gave him a hug and a kiss. Jeff had put himself through the wringer. On drugs, off drugs, politically wild— protesting everything from toxic waste to government spending. He'd survived. Cleaned up. He was still an activist, but one with temperance and vision. At least, she hoped so. She gave him a warm hug, along with the three other regulars, Sean, Peter and the odd man out, Ira, an Israeli.

"Did you notice me back here?" Danny asked her. "Or am I supposed to line up?"

"Danny," she murmured, trying to sound as if missing him was an oversight. She kissed his cheek perfunctorily. "How could anyone ever forget you?"

He grinned, catching her after the kiss, hugging her tightly and planting a kiss firmly on her lips. She escaped his touch as quickly as possible. It was far too easy to underestimate Danny. The quick strength with which he held her belied the lean appearance his height afforded him. Energy always seemed to radiate from Danny. In a flash of time, she felt as if her flesh burned.

"Good to see you, Danny," she murmured.

"Something light, fellows," Jeff instructed the band members.

"'Rosie O'Grady,'" Ira suggested.

Stepping from the stage, Moira looked across the room to the bar—and froze. Josh and Michael were in the pub, standing behind the taps near her father.

They had arrived far earlier than she had anticipated.

Josh had a camera running. Michael was still applauding, meeting her eyes, a sparkle in his. She wasn't sure why, but she felt as if she had been caught off guard. She was irritated with Josh, filming her unaware, and yet warmed by Michael's presence and his never faltering support. She also wondered if Danny, pounding out a new beat, was aware that Josh had arrived with another man. She was sure that he had noticed; Danny always seemed to be aware of what was happening around him. And certainly, since Danny had apparently been there a while, he had spoken with her parents and knew there was a man in her life.

She wasn't given to effusive public demonstrations, but she smiled at Michael and hurried across the room, leaning past a bar stool to give him a welcoming, open-mouthed kiss. Very emotional, she thought. And perfectly natural, despite the sound of her father clearing his throat. She hadn't seen Michael in a while. He'd been traveling, making connections, when she'd made the decision to come here for Saint Patrick's Day.

"Beautiful, babe," he said softly.

"Thanks."

"Very nice," Josh agreed.

She gritted her teeth, wondering why she was so irritated with Josh for taping the performance and wondering just how much of it he had captured on camera. Why was she angry? This was the centerpiece of their planned coverage: an Irish pub in America. She was a performer; she was on a show almost every day of her life, vulnerable to criticism and ridicule. Part of the game. But this...

This was her personal life. Danny had kissed her on stage.

An old friend, that was all.

And she herself had opened this can of worms.

She lowered her head, counting for a minute.

Her smile was still forced when she looked at Josh. "Josh, you know my dad. And, Dad, I guess Josh has introduced you to Michael... I didn't know they'd be arriving so early."

"I did all the introductions," Josh said.

"Great. When did you arrive?" she asked him.

He arched a brow, knowing her well, and noting the tone of her voice when no one else did. "In time to tape the whole thing," Josh told her.

"You know your partner," Eamon said, making an attempt to speak lightly. She grimaced inwardly, aware that her father was a bit put out that she had greeted a man he had just met with such public affection.

"It was terrific," Josh said, determined to show her that he was amused by her restrained annoyance. "A real demonstration of the diversity of Americana. You'll like it—trust me."

"How did you two manage to get here so early?" she queried.

Michael slipped an arm around her, grinning. He had a terrific smile. Dimples. A square face that still offered a fine bone structure and a strong chin. He was tall, well-built, as gorgeous as usual in a handsome business suit. She loved the aftershave he used. Everything about him was perfect—perfect for her. She knew her own mind and who she should be with.

As long as Michael was there. As long as he stood beside her.

"Josh gave me a call at the hotel and said you'd left already, so he managed to get us on an earlier flight, as well," Michael said. "I met him at the airport, then we came straight here."

"Wonderful," she murmured

"I can tell you're thrilled," Josh teased.

"I like to know when I'm on camera," she said.

"Well, there, then, that's the beauty of it, eh?" Liam chimed in. Her father's cronies never seemed to think that there might be a conversation in which they weren't included. "You're doing a real live Saint Paddy's Day show, me darling, and what's better than a picture of you and your sister singing 'Danny Boy' at home? It was lovely, girl, lovely."

"Thank you, Liam."

"Your nose isn't a-shinin' or anything, Moira Kathleen," Seamus added.

"Thanks, guys, thanks so much," she said softly, and her words were genuine. The men were all sincerity, her true supporters. "Dad, I think I'll take Michael up to meet Mum—"

"Aye, daughter, don't be a' leaving me now! The place is getting busy. Come back here and give your old man a hand."

"Colleen—"

"Now, do you see your sister? She's escaped somehow."

"I'll take Michael up to meet your mother and Granny Jon," Josh volunteered cheerfully.

She tried to skewer him with her eyes.

Michael looked at her with a rueful smile and a shrug, his countenance assuring her that he totally understood her situation. "I'll be fine with Josh."

"Be prepared for strong tea," she warned him, walking around the bar to join her father.

He caught her hands and whispered softly, "Save those kisses for later. Maybe at the hotel—after pub hours? Totally discreetly, of course," he teased, his eyes rolling. "I don't want your father hating me before he gets to know me."

"Just make sure he knows your family is Irish. He'll love you," she whispered.

"Come on, Michael," Josh said. "I'll show you the back way."

As Josh brushed by Moira, she caught his arm and hissed at him. "Just you wait! See if I ever baby-sit again."

"Turning coward on me now, are you, Moira Kathleen?" he teased. "Sorry, kid, face this den of lions yourself. Or is it only one lion that frightens you?"

With that, he was gone, leading Michael behind the office and storeroom to show him the stairs.

"Bastard," she muttered.

"You don't mean me, do you, Moira Kathleen?"

She spun around. She should have known that Dan O'Hara had joined her behind the bar. He wore his distinctive brand of aftershave. She should have felt him there, next to her, helping himself to a beer from the tap.

"Does it fit?" she inquired sweetly.

He didn't respond, just drank deeply and looked her up and down. "Maybe it does," he said at last, with a casual shrug. "You're looking quite the sophisticated lady. Lovely, as usual."

"Thank you so much."

"Work is good?"

"Wonderful. And you? Stirring up strife and rebellion, as usual?"

"Ah, now, my weapon, if I have one, is the pen, you know. Or the computer, these days."

"Whatever."

"You never understood me, love."

"I think I understood enough."

He leaned against the bar next to her. Too close. "You need to spend time with me, Moira."

"Can't, this trip. Sorry, I'm in love."

"Ah, yes, with perfect Michael."

"He's quite wonderful, really."

"As good as me?"

She was surprised to find herself moving closer to him, eyes slightly narrowed. "Better. So damned good, in fact, that it was only my father's presence that kept me from full-fledged sex on the bar."

To her annoyance, he started to laugh.

"I'm so glad I always amuse you."

He shook his head, sobering. "Sorry. It's just that… well, if he were that good, you wouldn't have felt the need to tell me."

She straightened, staring at him with all the cool dignity with which she could cloak herself. "No, no, it's different this time. Sure there were those years when I just hopped from man to man, affair to affair, my heart bleeding for you, but things change. Now I'm in love."

"Sure you are. And like hell you hopped from man

to man. You want a dossier on a man before you go to dinner with him."

She turned, clearing away empty glasses. "Things change, your ego doesn't. Did you really think you were the only man who ever made me happy and fulfilled?"

She was surprised at the seriousness with which he spoke. "I didn't think I could ever make you happy, and that's why I never stayed," he said. His tone changed instantly, so that she thought she might have imagined the strange passion in his first comment. "Now, as to the fulfilled part…come see me. I understand the love of your life travels all the time, as well. On your business, of course, but still… I'll be just down here, right in ye olde guest quarters, for the next few days. Come see me when you admit to yourself that it's exactly what you want to do."

He tipped an imaginary hat to her and started around the bar.

"That will be a freezing day in hell, Danny boy," she called softly after him.

She couldn't see his face as he left her, but she thought she saw his shoulders shaking slightly.

He was laughing.

He stopped suddenly and came back to her, leaning against the bar. "A freezing day in hell before you admit it—or before you do it?" he asked.

She didn't respond fast enough.

"I feel a chill coming on," he said softly, and once again turned to thread his way through the crowd and head for the stage.

This time, he didn't turn back.

She was tempted to throw a glass.

Is it only one lion that frightens you?

Josh's words came back to haunt her. She wasn't

frightened, she was furious. And she was furious because...

Because she was afraid of lions. Or at least...

One lion.

Yet, turning to look at that lion, she realized he wasn't looking at her. Danny was playing the drums again, apparently enjoying his time with the band. His interest seemed to be totally on the task at hand.

Yet when he looked up, she got the sense that he was watching the room. Not casually. It was as if he was looking for something, or someone, in particular.

Moira looked around. The room had gotten busy. Couples, nine-to-fivers easing down after work, the old crowd at the bar, a few loners at tables. One man alone, in a casual suit, sitting at a table in the far corner. Business traveler, probably.

Everyone seemed as ordinary as ever.

So just who was Danny looking for?

Josh's word flitted through her mind again.

Lions.

That was it. Danny was watching the room like a lion. Lying in the sun. Tail twitching. Calculating. Watching...

As if he could spring into action at any moment. She couldn't help but wonder, just what prey was Danny watching?

Strangely, she felt a sense of fear. As if something near and dear to her was somehow being threatened.

She turned to a man at the bar who had asked her for something, determined then to shake her feelings. It was Danny doing this to her, damn him.

Just Danny.

4

Surprisingly, it turned into a very nice night.

Michael and Josh returned to the bar after having tea with her mother and grandmother. Josh was happy; he had spoken to his wife, who was coming up with the babies the next day. Michael had looked in on her nieces and nephew as they slept and insisted on telling her just how adorable they were, as if she didn't know that already. That always sat well with her. Love me, love my dog, she realized. She didn't have a dog, but the same thought applied. She might be a bit wary of her family, but she did take tremendous pride in them, and she couldn't help but be pleased that Michael seemed to be fitting in so well.

He really was wonderful. He got behind the bar for a while. He chatted with her dad's friends as if he had known them all his life. He had a conversation with Patrick regarding a group of Americans that was forming to support Irish orphans and provide scholarships for those, Protestant and Catholic, who were of college age and had lost their parents through natural causes or violent events.

He was amazing.

She smiled at him across the bar at one point, hoping that he could sense what she was thinking.

At last it came time for Kelly's Pub to close. The band stopped, and the last of the customers, the old-timers, departed. She was wiping down the bar when she felt Danny behind her. This time she knew he was there before he spoke. "You've not introduced me to the new love of your life, Moira," he murmured.

"Oh, really? Imagine that—and when I've seen so much of you, too."

"I've been playing hard, all for the good of the cause," he said softly.

"Don't even use the word 'cause' near me, Daniel O'Hara," she said, voice lowered.

"Moira, it's just an innocent word," he said, amused.

Michael was walking toward her, a bulwark against this thorn in her side.

"Here he comes. So you get to meet him," she said softly. "There you are, Michael," she said in a normal tone, dropping her bar rag and walking toward Michael to slip an arm around him. He hugged her back. She gave him an adoring gaze, then pretended to realize that, oh, yes, Danny, an old friend, was standing there. "Dan O'Hara, Michael McLean. Michael's working with us as an associate producer and locations manager," Moira said.

Michael, smiling, stretched out his right hand to shake Danny's. His left arm remained around Moira's shoulder. "I hope I'm a lot more than that," he said ruefully. "Dan O'Hara, it's nice to meet you. I understand you're an old family friend."

"Oh, much more than that," Danny said lightly. "A pleasure to meet you, too, Michael McLean. If I can be of any assistance while you're in the city, please don't hesitate."

"An Irishman who knows Boston so well?" Michael said.

"My home away from home," Danny said.

"He's a citizen of the world," Moira's father announced, joining them and throwing an arm around Danny. "We're about to close up the place, Moira Kathleen. And if you've such a busy workload tomorrow, perhaps your friends should get on to their hotel rooms."

"Moira, are you coming back with us for a while? Check out what we've done with the scheduling?" Michael asked. His voice was all innocence; after all, her father was standing there.

Moira was determined, under Danny's watchful eye, to say yes and to say it with enthusiasm. But before she could open her mouth, her father was speaking.

"Ah, daughter, not tonight. Please, don't be going out on the streets tonight."

"Dad, I'm not going far. Just over to the Copley."

"It's late."

"Dad..."

"They've just found that poor girl's body."

"Dad, I'm as disturbed as you are about the murder, but I'm not going out soliciting—"

"Moira Kathleen! It's the hour. And what makes you think the innocent are less likely than the sinners to be harmed?"

"She may not have been a sinner. She might have just been trying to get by," Moira told her father, then wondered why she was arguing the point.

"Moira, perhaps your dad is right. It's very late, and it's your first night home," Michael said. His eyes spoke his regret, but it made her happy that once again he was trying to make everything work with her family. That kind of attitude meant that they were in it for the long haul.

"All right, it is late," Moira said. "I'll see you in the

morning," she told Michael. She stood on tiptoe to give him a kiss good-night. He smelled good, she thought. The texture of his jacket was nice against her hands. *I really do care about this man,* she thought. *He's handsome, sexy and so much more. Solid, decent, confident, exciting.*

"Girl, he's leaving for the night, not the millennium," her father said with a soft sigh.

She laughed, letting go of Michael. She gave Josh a kiss on the cheek. "You two be careful going back to the hotel."

"We'll be fine," Josh assured her.

They both bade her father and Danny good-night, and she walked them to the door of the pub, catching Michael's scarf to stop him after the men had donned their coats and kissing him one last time.

"Well, it's about all done," her father said when the door had closed. "You go to bed, Moira Kathleen, and Dan and I will finish up here."

"No, Dad, I'm home tonight. You go up to bed and get some rest. I think you're supposed to be resting far more than you are."

"If a man stops working, he stops moving, and it's all over after that," Eamon said, shaking his head.

"Dad, I'm here, safe and sound in the house, and it won't hurt you to go to bed this one night," she insisted. She made a mental note to have a long talk with her mother. Kelly's was open every day of the week. Eamon employed good people, but he had a tendency to make his business a very personal affair, and she was sure he let his work put too much strain on him.

"Well, then, fine. Tonight you and Danny can pick up the slack for the old man," he told her, winking.

He pulled her to him, giving her a strong, fierce hug

once again and kissing the top of her head. "Love you, girl, that I do," he said, a husky timbre to his voice.

"You, too, Dad. Now get up to bed. You've got a full house tonight."

"Aye, but I've a sainted mother, who puts up with everything and manages a house like the best of construction foremen. Aye, she's a rough taskmaster, that one," he said. "Good night, Moira, and, Danny, see that she gets up to bed soon herself."

"That I will, Eamon," Danny assured him.

As her father headed for the inner stairway, Moira walked to the bar. There were only a few glasses still sitting out and the beautiful old bar to be wiped down. The place had been a tavern in colonial days, and the bar was several hundred years old. She had always loved it and loved the sense of history she felt when wiping it down.

Danny checked the door to the street, making sure it was locked, then walked to where she was cleaning. He leaned against the bar, his eyes sparkling as he looked at her.

"I believe you're supposed to be working with me," she told him, not looking up from her task.

He shrugged. "You shouldn't be dating him, you know."

Moira didn't stop wiping the polished wood of the bar. She forced Danny to move an elbow.

"You're listening to me, love, and we both know it," he said, leaning against the wood once again. "You shouldn't be dating him."

"Oh?" she said, staring at him, surprised to find that the amusement had left his eyes. "And why not? Because you've decided to grace us with a visit?"

"No, not because of me at all."

"Why, then?"

"He has beady eyes."

"Beady eyes?"

"Dangerous eyes."

"Dangerous eyes? Well, how lovely. How wonderfully exciting—and sexy. I hadn't realized just how much Michael has to offer."

"You should have married Josh. Now there's a good fellow, and safe."

Moira took up scrubbing the perfectly clean bar once again. "Now that will be great for Josh's ego—you calling him safe."

"What? A man doesn't want to be dependable and safe?"

Moira sighed deeply. "I don't know, Danny, you'd have to answer that one. Have you ever been dependable—or safe?"

"As dependable as a rock."

"A rock that skips all over the place."

He shrugged. "I love the United States. I was born in Ireland. That creates a divided heart, you know."

"I read somewhere the other day that there are far more Irish in America than there are in Ireland."

"Are you asking me to move here permanently?" he queried.

"I'm merely informing you that since you seemed beguiled into coming to the States time and time again, you might want to consider immigration."

"If I did, would you put a cease and desist on the fellow with the beady eyes?"

"No. And please, get going, grab those glasses and get them washed. I want to go up to bed."

"Ah, now, was that an invitation? In your father's house? Moira Kelly!"

"That was definitely not an invitation. What are you

doing here now, anyway? Shouldn't you be at home celebrating Saint Patrick's Day?"

"I'm visiting old friends," he said.

"Don't you have any friends in Ireland who need to be visited?"

"All over the island. I wanted to be here."

"Why? Will you be preaching to the Americans again? Do you have a new book out? All about the imperialism of the English and how the entire world should just stop whatever else it's doing and force the unification of Ireland?"

He arched a brow. "That's a rather biased way of seeing the situation—and me."

"Oh, I agree, but isn't it *your* way of seeing it?"

"No, not at all. I think you've mixed up a bit of personal resentment with logical judgment. I was never a fire starter. I never claimed to have all the answers, and I don't begin to claim to have them now. You're American, right? You do insist that everyone knows that all the time."

"I *am* an American. I was born here."

"Okay, so you're first generation. The 'English' in Northern Ireland have been there a much longer time. Centuries, for some families. The difficulties are easy to see. For so many centuries, the Irish people were reduced to second-class citizens in their own country. The English, the Protestants, had the power and the money, and vicious hatreds have been inbred into the people. But what to do now…well, that's a very difficult question. In my mind, there has to be a reconciliation between the people there themselves, and only then can you ever have a united Ireland."

She stopped and stared at him. "You think that one morning all the people in Northern Ireland are going to wake up and say, 'Hey, this whole thing has been ridiculous, let's just get on with each other'?"

"Things have been much better in the last ten years or so," he told her.

"Danny, I watched you speak once, after your first book was published, and your talk was about ancient history and all the wars the Irish have fought."

"I was young then, but you never heard me suggest that there was an easy solution, or that anyone should take up arms against anyone else. Yes, I was a student of Irish history, from the Tuath de Danaan to the Easter Rebellion and beyond, and in the middle of trying to decipher how such a mess between people came about, I discovered I loved both writing and speaking. I hope I'm not quite the total ham I was as a very young man, but I still love to lecture. Especially to Irish Americans. But never about taking up arms. You should know that about me."

"Danny, you know what? I don't know you, or anything about you, anymore. I probably *never* knew you. But I *am* an American. And I deplore violence no matter what."

"You haven't been listening to me. What do you think I'm about? Carrying an Uzi in the street?"

"I just told you, I don't know. And I don't care. I'm American to the bone, and we have enough of our own problems in this country. I'm going to bed. Good night. Finish up the glasses, since you told my father you were going to help."

She headed for the winding stairs to the house.

"Moira."

"What?" She stopped. At first she didn't turn around, but held still, her shoulders stiff. At last she turned to face him. "What?" she repeated.

"You do know me. Deep inside, you do know me."

"Great. Good night."

"I'm still your friend. Whether you know it or not. And here's a friendly warning. Watch out for men with beady eyes."

"Michael has beautiful eyes."

"Beautiful? If you say so. Rather hard for me to tell. So okay, beautiful, if you insist, but still beady."

She sighed with impatience. "Good night, Danny."

"Good night, Moira."

As she started up the stairs, she could hear the clink of glasses. She hurried to her home above the pub and quickly locked the door at the top of the stairs.

The house was very quiet. Down the hallway, all the bedroom doors were closed. Her parents had taken Patrick's old room and given him and Siobhan the master bedroom, with the little nursery off it for the kids, Brian happily taking possession of the air mattress. She had offered to sleep with Colleen, so the children could have her room and her parents could stay in theirs, or to take a room at the Copley with the rest of her crew, but her parents had wanted no part of that. They were too happy just to have their family together. Their children, their grandchildren and Siobhan, whom they loved like a daughter.

She hadn't seen her sister-in-law yet, she thought. Unusual. Siobhan had gone to visit her folks, but it was odd that she hadn't taken the children or come into the pub when she returned.

Moira passed the master bedroom as she headed for her room. She had nearly reached her door when she was startled to hear the sound of voices. Muffled, low, angry voices. One masculine, one feminine. Obviously her brother and sister-in-law.

"Oh, Christ, Siobhan, get off it!"

Then Siobhan's voice, so low that Moira couldn't catch the words.

"I'm not involved in anything."

Siobhan again, still too soft to hear.

"No, it's not going to lead to anything else. It's a cause for children, for God's sake!"

Siobhan must have spoken, though Moira didn't even hear her voice.

"Baby, baby, please, believe me, believe in me…"

His voice trailed off. A few seconds later, she heard her parents' old bed squeak.

Standing alone in the hallway, she flushed so hotly that she felt her face flame. Great. First she'd been standing there eavesdropping on her brother and sister-in-law, and now she was listening to them have sex.

"At least someone is getting some."

She jumped and almost screamed at the sound of her sister's soft whisper.

"Colleen," she managed to say.

Colleen covered a giggle, dragging her down the hall.

"I didn't even hear your door open," Moira said.

"I wasn't in my room. I was on the phone."

"The phone?"

"It's only eleven in California."

"Business at eleven?" Moira asked.

Colleen waved a hand in the air.

"A guy. A new guy, nothing deep or heavy or anything like that. I mean, I wouldn't crawl all over him in Dad's own pub in front of Dad the way you did with your Michael tonight."

"Do you crawl all over him when Dad isn't around?"

Colleen laughed. "What have you become suddenly? The moral conscience of the family?" she said teasingly.

"I didn't mean to be eavesdropping. I just... I heard voices on the way to my room."

"Voices, yeah, right."

"Seriously, Colleen, they were arguing. And I really didn't mean to listen."

"But since you did, you're about to ask me if I know if anything is wrong between them."

"Well?"

"Not that I know about. But I just came in today, too. Speaking of which, should we make tea? No, no, way too late, and you're here working, right? We'll have to talk tomorrow. I'm dying to hear. He's good-looking— your Michael, that is. Tall, broad-shouldered. Big feet. And you know what they say about men with big feet."

"That's an old wives' tale."

"I'm sorry to hear that."

"Damn it, Colleen, what about asking me how the show is going, what's coming up next—"

"I watch television, and the show is doing just fine. And if I had anything good to tell you, I'd give you all the juicy details."

"More so than I'd need to know," Moira agreed.

"I was wondering, with Danny here and all..."

"Danny has nothing to do with anything."

"Oh, you liar."

"He's an old friend."

"Come on, big sister, your nose will grow," Colleen warned her. "The heat waves used to bounce off you two. And tonight...it was like one of those static electricity things. Wow, come to think of it, I don't envy you. Tall, dark and handsome on the one side, wild wicked past with the bad boy of Eire on the other."

"Colleen, be quiet, will you? Mum and Dad never knew—"

"They're Catholic, Moira, not stupid. And not even

a deaf, dumb and blind female would be immune to Mr. Daniel O'Hara. I think he's as tall, or maybe taller, than your new love. Hmm. Taut muscles, great buns. Wow, choices, choices, kid."

"Danny is ancient history, Colleen."

"Sure he is," Colleen said skeptically.

"You just said that Michael—"

"Yeah, he's pretty damn perfect. Great voice. But then again, Danny's got that wee touch of an accent…"

Moira groaned. "This coming home thing isn't easy. I expect to be tortured by my parents, but you're worse than they are."

"I'm your sister, the only one you've got, and you're supposed to thank Mum and Dad daily for giving you a sister," Colleen informed her.

"I get that speech, too. But enough about me. What about this guy in California? What's his name? Is he tall? Big feet? You can check out that anatomy equation for yourself."

"His name is Chad Storm, and yes, he's tall."

"Chad Storm?" Moira rolled her eyes. "Is he an actor? Couldn't he have made up a better name?"

"He's a graphic arts designer, and he didn't make up the name, it's the one he was born with," Colleen said indignantly.

"Shush! We're going to wake up the house."

"All right, all right, we don't want our cherubic little rug rats waking up. Patrick and Siobhan will kill us. I mean…well, they'd really kill us! I'm going to bed, and I'll let you get your beauty rest. But tomorrow I want details. Down and dirty, graphic and—"

"Go to bed, Colleen."

"You're going to confess all, you know."

"Good night, Colleen."

"Yeah, yeah, good night." They exchanged a warm,

brief hug and started down the long corridor to their doors, opposite one another at the end of the hallway.

As they passed the master bedroom, they could still hear the bed creaking. They looked at one another, burst into laughter and quickly slipped into their own rooms.

Daniel thoughtfully dried the last of the glasses and glanced at the nineteenth-century clock at the rear of the bar.

Nearly two. He'd taken his time picking up the place, feeling distracted and wounded. Tense night. Naturally. Here he was, closing in on Saint Patrick's Day.

He'd scoured a number of the pubs in the city, learning what he could, watching, always watching.

Just as he was probably being watched himself.

He would keep watching, too. He'd seen the man who had sat by himself at the rear table before. The man wasn't all that good at what he did. A man came into a pub and interacted if he wanted to go unnoticed. Still, Daniel was convinced that the man he was looking for was going to be someone he had never seen before. Someone who shouldn't know him, either.

Unless, of course, it turned out to be Patrick.

"You're slowing down, boy," he told himself, setting the last glass on the wooden ledge behind the bar. Maybe he hadn't taken so long. The pub had stayed open late that night.

Kelly's didn't always keep the doors open until one, though sometimes, on a Saturday night, the pub was known to be open until two. It all depended on the clientele. On what was happening. The kitchen closed at ten, but if a hungry soul wandered in after that hour, someone could usually be found to scrounge up some food. Kelly's never changed. From the time Daniel had been little more than a kid, he'd been coming here.

Eamon was a good man. A hard worker and a lover of mankind. No harm should ever come to Eamon or anyone in his family.

The phone began to ring. Danny picked it up. "Kelly's," he said automatically. Then his fingers tensed around the receiver.

"Kelly's," he repeated. He hesitated, then added, "Where Blackbird plays."

"Blackbird?" a deep-throated, husky voice inquired. Male or female?

"Yes, Blackbird," he said firmly.

"I—" the caller began, then, "Wrong number," the voice uttered harshly. And that was it.

The line went dead. Not the wrong number, he wanted to shout.

Then he heard a slight clicking sound.

The phone had been answered by someone upstairs, as well. Had the caller paused because two people had answered? He hit star sixty-nine on the phone. The number came up as unavailable.

With a sudden fury, he hurled the rag he'd been using across the bar. He shook his head and, gritting his teeth, opted for a shot of whiskey before bed. He swallowed it in a gulp. Damn, but it burned.

He walked through the office and storeroom to the stairs leading to the home above. At the top, he checked the door. Locked.

In the bar, he suddenly bolted out the front and ran to the side, taking the stairs two at the time. The outside door to the residence was also firmly locked, although anyone with a real intent to get in and a talent for breaking and entering could jimmy the bolts.

He went down the stairs, into the pub, to his allotted room.

He took a hot shower, then slid beneath the sheets

and comforter. He flicked on the telly. CNN. The world was in bad shape. Violence flaring in the Middle East. In Eastern Europe, a terrible train wreck, the fault of an antiquated switching system. The weather taking a gruesome toll in South America.

Then the news reporter, who had just given a grim tale regarding flooding in Venezuela, put a smile on her face and began talking about Saint Patrick's Day. She showed a cheery scene in Dublin, crowds in New York, then a brief interview with the Belfast politician, hailed worldwide, who was en route to Boston to help celebrate with the Boston Irish.

The news continued. Dan stared at the picture on the screen but didn't hear much more.

It was a very long time before he slept.

5

The house seemed quiet when Moira left her bedroom the following morning. She saw that Colleen was just ahead of her, walking down the hall to the kitchen.

She followed her sister. "Good morning," she murmured, as they entered the kitchen together. Her mother had evidently been up already; coffee had been brewed in the automatic coffeemaker, and a pot of tea sat on the big kitchen table, as well. Her brother was up, sitting at the table, sipping coffee, reading the newspaper.

"Top o' the morning to you," Colleen returned, eyes rolling as she turned them on Patrick. "And you, brother, dear. You're looking well-rested for a man who spent half the night playing—"

"With the band," Moira interrupted in horror, amazed that Colleen would make any reference to the fact that they'd been outside his door the previous night. She slid into her old chair at the table and cast Colleen a warning glare.

"Playing with the band," Colleen repeated. "That's exactly what I was saying," she continued, glaring at Moira, eyes wide with innocence and mock indignation.

Moira felt like hell. She hadn't fallen asleep until three or four. And then, perhaps out of force of habit, she'd found herself wide awake and unable to pound her pillow into any semblance of comfort when she'd realized she didn't have to be awake so early this morning. She did have things to do, of course. Michael and Josh had done their work well. Permits to tape the parade and the goings-on in various areas of the city had been procured. But she needed a plan of action, and she needed to pretend that she had been on it from the moment she had hung up after talking to her mother and making the decision to come to Boston.

Patrick looked at them both, slightly puzzled. "I feel just fine, thanks. Colleen, you look all right, but Moira…hmm. Trust me, you don't look as bad as you sound. Wouldn't do, would it? Can't have bags beneath your eyes that stretch to your chin when you're on camera, now, can you?"

"Great. How come Colleen looks all right but I merely look better than you think I feel?" Moira asked him.

Patrick grinned. "You've had this shell-shocked look since you arrived," he told Moira.

"Has she?" Pouring coffee, Colleen turned to study Moira.

"If you're going to turn that cup-filling ritual into a daylong event, perhaps you could let me go first," Moira said.

"Give her the coffee—she needs it," Patrick said.

Moira glared at her brother. "How come you're saying that?"

"I heard you tossing around all night."

"Me!" Moira protested. She stared at Colleen, and suddenly she couldn't help it; she burst into laughter, and Colleen followed suit.

"What's the inside joke?" Patrick asked, eyes narrowing as he looked from one of them to the other.

"Well, we were trying to be discreet..." Colleen began.

"But honest to God, surely, that old bed frame hasn't created such a noise since...well, probably since Colleen was conceived," Moira said.

Patrick's heritage was instantly visible as his cheeks flamed a brilliant shade of red.

"You two are full of it," Patrick managed to sputter. "How rude. I mean, this is our parents' house..."

"Hey, we're not chastising you," Colleen said, retrieving the coffeepot from Moira.

"No, we're simply happy—"

"For you both, of course," Colleen interrupted.

"That after all your years of marriage," Moira continued.

"And at your ripe old age," Colleen added.

"You can still get it up, that's all," Moira finished.

Patrick set his cup down, shaking his head, eyes lowered. Then he stared at them both across the table. "Well, all that from the woman who nearly attacked a stranger in the bar last night."

"Michael's not a stranger," Moira protested.

"Hey, we've never met him before."

"I know him very well."

"Apparently so. What, you met him after the Christmas holidays? That doesn't exactly make you eligible for a diamond anniversary band."

"Cute," she told Patrick.

"Well, she probably only did it because of Danny," Colleen said, yawning.

Moira glared at her sister. "Hey, whose side are you on here?"

Colleen instantly looked sheepish. "Sorry."

"You're not supposed to be taking sides against me to begin with," Patrick protested.

"Ah, now, are the girls beating up on you again, Patrick?" their mother asked, sweeping into the kitchen from the hallway. "Shame on you, the both of you. Now, don't I spend half my life reminding you that—"

"That we're all the greatest gifts you ever gave to any one of us," the three of them said in unison, creating an outbreak of laughter around the table.

Katy shook her head. "One day you'll know the truth of it. When the world is against you, when friends have failed you, you always have your family."

"Oh, Mum," Moira said, rising and walking to her brother to give his shoulders a hug—and his arm a pinch. "I adore my big brother. Honestly."

"And me, too, of course," Colleen said.

"And you, Patrick?" Katy demanded of him firmly.

"And me?" Patrick asked, grinning at Moira. "Why, my sisters are the light of my life. Though there is that other person. My wife. Oh, and my kids, bless the little demons. My life is just one big radiant ray of light."

"Enough of that," Katy said with a grin. "Moira, move back a bit. Patrick, scooch in your chair. The children are awake—they'll be out for breakfast any minute now. Let me get the eggs going. Girls, would you give me a hand?"

"Girls?" Colleen asked.

"Aye?" Katy asked, puzzled.

Moira slipped an arm around her mother. "Mum, what she's saying is that you're being sexist. Patrick can help out just as well."

"After all, you're cooking for his children."

"Well, now, Patrick can't help out," Katy said.

"And why is that?" Colleen asked.

"Because he's the most useless human being in a kitchen I've ever seen. Granny Jon says that he's the only person she's ever met who's incapable of boiling a pot of water."

"He only pretends he can't cook," Moira said.

"To get out of the work," Colleen explained.

"Now, the lot of you!" Katy said indignantly.

"Just kidding, Mum," Moira said. "I'll get the bacon."

"The bottom batch, please. The lean stuff at the top from McDonnell's is for the bacon and cabbage we're having tonight."

"Bacon and cabbage," Moira murmured.

"And colcannon," Katy said. "And some broccoli and spinach, because they're good for your father's heart. Moira Kathleen, I need the oatmeal, as well. Your dad has taken to getting it down plain every morning, for his cholesterol."

Moira brought out the requested items from the refrigerator, then got the oatmeal from the cabinet. She looked at her mother. "That's it. We'll cook. For the show, we'll let you take over, and we'll videotape your preparation of the Saint Patrick's Day meal."

"We're not having bacon and cabbage for Saint Patrick's Day, we'll be having a roast," Katy said.

"Mum," Moira groaned. "I don't care what we're really having on Saint Patrick's Day. Bacon and cabbage is a traditional Irish meal. It will be a terrific segment for the show."

"Oh, now, daughter, I'm not good on camera," Katy protested.

"Can we put Patrick in an apron?" Colleen asked hopefully.

"Not on your life," Patrick protested.

"Oh, yeah, great. Let him be traditionally Irish by drinking beer and playing with the band," Colleen teased.

"You know, it's just one of those things," Patrick said. "I can wear a suit well, which is good for an attorney. I look pretty good in hats. Aprons… I just don't seem to have the right build."

"We won't film you in an apron," Moira said. "Since you can't cook, you can do the dishes when we're done."

"I've got an appointment this morning," Patrick protested.

"I bet he just thought it up," Colleen said.

"Do you really have an appointment?" Katy asked him.

Before he could answer, there was a tap on the inner door. Moira felt an inexplicable wave of tension instantly tighten her muscles.

Her mother and sister had turned toward the sound. Only Patrick was looking at her.

"So, it is Danny," he said softly.

"Don't be ridiculous," she murmured. "Should I get it?" she asked her mother.

"No, it's just Danny, at this hour," Katy said. "Come in, Dan!" she called.

"I locked it last night when I came up," Moira said.

"Danny has a key, of course," her mother replied impatiently.

She heard the key twisting in the lock even as her mother spoke.

She wondered why it bothered her so much that he had a key. To her home. No, not *her* home, her *parents'* home.

And he had always been welcome here.

He walked in, freshly showered and scrubbed, as evidenced by the dampness that remained in his combed hair and gleamed on newly shaven cheeks. He was wearing jeans and a gold knit sweater beneath a casual leather jacket. She had to admit that he looked good. A bit of age had given his natural ease a slightly weathered and dignified look. He wasn't as handsome a man as Michael, she thought, almost analytically, and only partially defensively. Michael had classic good looks. Pitch dark hair, striking blue eyes and a clean-cut face. Daniel was craggier. His chin a bit squarer, cheeks leaner, features more jagged. He had good eyes, though. A strange shade of hazel that made them amber at times, almost gold at others. He saw her studying him but only smiled, addressing her mother.

"I could smell Katy Kelly's coffee way down in my room," he told her, slipping his arms around her waist affectionately and kissing her cheek.

"There's a coffeepot behind the bar," Moira said rather sharply. Patrick looked at her. She widened her eyes. "How else would we make Irish coffee?"

"I think we're all aware that there's a coffeepot behind the bar," her brother said.

"I was merely suggesting—" she began.

"Ah, but my coffee would never be as good as Katy's," Danny interrupted.

"And you'd not be wanting to have it alone," Katy said firmly. "You've been up here every morning, and now the girls are here, as well. Naturally you want to spend time together." Katy said the last casually, but sincerely.

"Of course we want to spend time with him. He's like another older brother. A nice one," Colleen teased.

Patrick groaned audibly.

"Just like a brother," Moira said sweetly.

Danny had poured coffee and taken a seat next to Patrick. "Sibling torture this morning, eh?"

"Tell me, would you wear an apron so that your sister could humiliate you on national television?" Patrick asked.

"It's just a cable show," Moira murmured.

"A highly rated cable show," Patrick said. "Well?"

For a moment, as Danny stared at her, Moira thought that his face had hardened strangely with anger. "I don't have a sister," he said.

"But you're just like a nicer older brother," Patrick reminded him.

"Oh, right. Well, what does the apron look like?" Danny asked, and the casual conviviality was back in his voice.

"I'm sure Mum has one with a leprechaun on it somewhere," Colleen said.

"No one has to wear an apron!" Moira protested.

"Right. We'll cook neatly," Danny said.

"I didn't say anyone but Mum needed to be in the show," Moira reminded them.

"That's right. The long-suffering siblings get to wash dishes offstage," Patrick said.

"Hey," Colleen protested, "I've got the kind of face they say can launch a thousand ships."

"Naturally you're invited to cook with us on camera," Moira told her sister.

"Thanks. I'll have to check with my agent."

"Colleen Mary!" Katy said indignantly.

"Just kidding, Mum."

"That *is* a face that could launch a thousand ships—*sis,*" Danny told Colleen. "Congratulations. I'm seeing it more and more every day now."

"Really, Danny?" Colleen asked, her voice a little anxious. For a moment Moira reflected that her sister was really just a nice kid. She was doing exceptionally well, yet she was still amazed that people really thought her looks worthy of attention. She had managed to develop enough confidence to go forward and retain enough humility to remain grounded.

"Really. And I've heard from Patrick and your folks that there's a budding romance in the west?"

"Just budding," Katy said firmly. "So my daughter tells me."

"Absolutely just budding," Colleen said, laughing. "Mum, I'd never get serious without bringing the poor guy home first and making sure he had the stamina for a real relationship."

Patrick looked at his sister without the twitch of a smile. "Um, stamina?"

"He's a nice guy?" Danny asked. "Nothing else would do for my, uh, baby sister."

"The nicest. Hey, you come to California now and then. Maybe you'll be out there soon. I'd love for you to meet him."

"Dan can size him up for you just like that," Patrick told her.

"Colleen has a good head on her shoulders. I'm sure he's a fine fellow," Danny said. "Now, as to Moira…"

"Moira and her Michael," Katy said.

"He's great, Mum, and you know it," Moira said.

"He does seem decent," Patrick acknowledged.

"He's a hunk," Colleen said decisively.

"Beady eyes," Danny said, shaking his head.

"Oh, God, that again," Moira said irritably.

"Well, I think his eyes are fine," Katy said thoughtfully, taking the comment entirely literally.

"Look again—they're beady," Danny said, staring at Moira.

"Fine, I'll take another really good look at the man, Danny," Katy said, setting strips of bacon into a huge frying pan with incredible precision, getting more bacon into the pan than Moira would have thought possible. "But really, he's courteous, and very handsome. And he does adore Moira."

"Yes, I guess he does," Danny said grudgingly.

"A vote of approval at last?" Moira inquired.

"I'm withholding final judgment."

"And he's been so effusive with his comments regarding you," Moira said.

"Really?" Danny asked.

"Actually, no. He hasn't mentioned you at all."

"Well, I'm just an old family friend. Not a real member of the family who he needs to impress."

"But you'll definitely be on top of the guest list for the wedding," Moira said over the rim of her coffee cup.

Her mother gasped. "Moira Kathleen!"

"No, no, no, Mum," she said quickly, with a sigh. She had to watch this sparring with Danny in front of her parents. "We're not planning anything—yet."

"I truly wish you every happiness," Danny said. His eyes were steady on hers; his voice was sincere.

For some reason, that made her more irritated.

Maybe she didn't want him to be happy for her. Yup, that was it. Completely. She wanted him to be sorry he'd blown everything himself.

"Thanks." She forced herself to speak casually. "Excuse me for a minute, please. I've got to make a phone call and get going on the day. Mum, would you really mind if I taped the preparation of tonight's meal? If it will really make you uncomfortable…"

"No, no, it's all right. I mean, I just don't want to appear…foolish. You'll be with me all the time, right?"

"Of course. And we'll have Colleen and Siobhan and even the kids, if they'd like. It will be fun. Honestly, Mum."

"Maybe."

"No maybe about it," Colleen assured her.

Katy nodded again. Moira started to her room to

make a call, just as the kids came scampering out of the master bedroom.

"Auntie Mo!" Brian said.

"Morning, handsome," she told her nephew.

Molly was right behind him. "Auntie Mo, Auntie Mo! Presents!" she said, hurling herself into Moira's arms.

"Molly," Shannon said as she came up behind her sister, very mature at six, "we don't ask for presents."

"It's all right," Moira assured them both quickly. "You can ask your aunt but not other people," she reminded Molly. "But I'm your aunt, and I've promised you a present, so it's okay. I've got to make a call, and then I'll bring the presents out."

"Thanks, Auntie Mo," Brian said.

"Where's your mum? I haven't seen her yet."

"On her way out," Shannon said. "She told me she didn't sleep much last night, and that when you get older, it's harder to wash away the wrinkles."

Moira laughed. "Tell your mum that she doesn't have anything that so much as resembles a wrinkle." She smiled suddenly and couldn't help adding, "Tell her I'm sorry she didn't sleep well."

She slipped past Brian and the girls and went into her room, where she dialed the Copley and asked for Michael. No answer. She asked for Josh's room, and he quickly picked up, telling her they'd just talked to the four-man crew Michael had hired and that they would all be ready to go in about half an hour.

"So what are we doing? I mean, we've flown by the seat of the pants before, but…"

"We're going to tape right here today. Traditional Irish cooking. Come on over whenever you're all ready. Oh! I couldn't reach Michael."

"I talked to him earlier. I'll give his cell a buzz and tell him to be at your place."

Moira hung up, then gathered the presents before starting down the hall to the kitchen. When she got there, she saw that her sister-in-law had preceded her and was talking to her mother at the sink. She turned as Moira came in, smiled broadly and hurried over to her.

Siobhan was a beautiful woman, with long blond hair and deep blue eyes. She looked wonderful, but she also looked tired, really tired. Her slender features were leaner than ever. She was pale, and there was a hint of mauve beneath her eyes, despite her practiced application of makeup.

"Moira, hey!"

"Siobhan, you look terrific," she said, hugging her sister-in-law tightly and wondering if she sounded as if she was lying.

"Thanks, but I feel like hell this morning," Siobhan said with a laugh. "So we're doing a typical, natural, completely unaffected and spontaneous cooking section for your program, hmm?"

"Completely spontaneous," Moira agreed with a laugh. "Even though you'll have to open the door five times so we can get all the right angles on tape, trust me, you'll be completely spontaneous."

"I was joking. You want me in it, too?"

"Sure, it will be fun. We'll whip up some scones first, so the kids can sit in the dining room and eat them, and then the four of us will do all the stuff in the kitchen. A family thing."

"A family thing? What about the guys?"

"We'll film them lounging around on the couch, drinking beer, scratching and watching a football game."

Siobhan laughed. Eamon Kelly, hearing the conversation, instantly protested. "Daughter, how can you say such a thing?"

"Eamon, don't complain," Danny said lazily from the kitchen table, where he was playing a game of war with Molly, who was slapping her little hand on the cards on the table with a happy giggle. "Sitting on the couch, drinking beer, watching a game—scratching an itch now and then—sounds like a fine way to spend the day," he said.

"Dad, everyone knows that you work like a horse," Moira said, ignoring Danny. "You sit on the couch and take it easy."

"I'll be down seeing to the pub, girl, you know that," Eamon told her.

"I'll open for you, Eamon," Danny said. "That way you can watch your daughter at work."

"I really do have an appointment at one," Patrick said regretfully.

"Patrick, I thought this was a family vacation," Siobhan protested.

"Honey, it's an hour's meeting with an important client," Patrick said.

"Auntie Mo!" Molly suddenly wailed. "Presents!"

"Molly!" Siobhan was the one to chastise her that time.

"Hey, I promised her a present ten minutes ago. That's an eternity when you're only four," Moira said. "Molly, catch!"

She tossed one of the wrapped plush leprechauns to Molly, who missed. Danny retrieved the gift from the floor for her, while Moira turned to pass out the gifts for Brian and Shannon. When she was done, she walked over with the music box and set it next to her mother.

Katy looked at her with a question in her eyes.

"It screamed your name," Moira explained.

"Moira, it's neither Christmas nor my birthday—"

"Mum, chill," Colleen said lightly. "Just open the gift, let us ooh and aah, and say thank-you to Moira."

Katy grinned sheepishly, then opened the present almost as quickly as the children. Molly squealed happily over her stuffed toy, and Patrick let out an affirming, "Oh, wow, cool."

But Moira was busy watching her mother as she unwrapped the delicate little fairy and her eyes widened with delight.

"Moira, she's breathtaking."

"She's a music box."

"What does she play?"

Moira picked up the figure to wind it.

"'Danny Boy,'" Danny said softly before the music began.

Moira turned to stare at him as the rest of the room watched the little fairy dance. He was watching her strangely, she thought. The light in the room reflected off his eyes, making them appear golden and yet oddly shielded.

"How did you know?" she asked him.

"Lucky guess," he said with a shrug. "Hey—bacon's starting to snap."

"Mary, Jesus, and Joseph," Katy gasped, seeing her pan smoking.

"I've got it, Mum. Go put her on the mantel or wherever you'd like her," Moira said, quickly flipping the breakfast bacon.

"I'll grab the eggs," Colleen said.

"Danny, Patrick, you get the juice," Moira suggested.

"Juice?" Molly said.

"Hey, where's Granny Jon?" Patrick asked.

"I'll see if she's up," Danny volunteered, leaving the kitchen.

Katy left the room with her little treasure but was back quickly. With an efficiency that only appeared to be confusion, breakfast arrived on the table. Danny came in escorting Granny Jon, who was apologizing for oversleeping.

"Everything is under control, Mum," Katy assured her.

"Tea?" Granny Jon asked.

"Strong enough to walk itself across the table," Moira said in unison with not only her brother and sister, but her parents, as well.

Everyone laughed at that except for Granny Jon, who gave them all an indignant sniff as they grouped around the kitchen table. It was big, but there were eleven of them, and they were tightly packed. For a few minutes the conversation centered entirely around such comments as, "Can you pass the salt, please?" and, "Who has the juice?" and, "Oh, no, Molly, that glass is way too full."

As Moira was rescuing the glass from her niece, the doorbell rang. "I'll get it," she said, jumping up. "Must be my crew."

She poured some of the juice from Molly's plastic cup into her glass, set it down, then headed for the door. When she opened it, she saw that Michael had arrived. There was a nip in the air, and she shivered as she felt the chill. Michael didn't seem to notice it. He looked like an ad for Armani, in a long wool coat and black scarf.

"Morning," he said. His voice was nicely husky.

"Good morning. Come in, it's freezing out there."

"The cold is okay, but last night was awfully lonely," he told her.

"I'm sorry," she murmured. "My dad, you know..."

"I've got it perfectly," he said softly. "It's still just

a shade, well, you know, lonely." He was looking over her shoulder. She saw that Danny had followed her to the door.

"Michael, good to see you. You must be a man accustomed to the cold, standing around on the porch like that. What's your pleasure, coffee or tea?"

"Coffee," Michael said, moving in as Moira shut the door. He slipped out of his coat, allowing Moira to hang it on the eighteenth-century hall tree, and removed his gloves, meeting Danny's eyes. "Coffee, please. I think I've had six cups this morning, and it still doesn't seem like enough."

"Right you are. One coffee coming up."

Danny turned to get Michael coffee, his attitude as courteous and casually friendly as could be.

"Don't trust him," Moira whispered to Michael.

"Oh?"

She shook her head, leading him into the kitchen.

"Morning, Michael. Bacon and eggs—or oatmeal?" Eamon asked, rising to shake Michael's hand in greeting.

"Nothing, thanks, I grabbed a bite early."

"Michael, you haven't met my sister-in-law, Siobhan, yet," Moira said, introducing the two.

"Hello, Siobhan. A pleasure."

"Very nice to meet you," Siobhan replied, studying him with an open smile.

"Was that bacon and eggs you decided on?" Katy asked.

"I think he said he ate, Mum," Moira said.

"They're only happy, and they'll only love you, if you eat, you know," Danny warned Michael.

"Then bacon and eggs it is," Michael said.

"Now, Dan O'Hara, that's not at all true," Katy protested. "Though surely everything here will be better than at your hotel."

"Oh, I'm positive of that," Michael said. "But, Katy, all this food… And you're just going to clean up and start cooking again so we can film?"

"I'm cooking again because we're planning on having dinner," Katy said. "And I've lots of help."

"Except for me," Patrick said. "Appointment," he explained. "And I want to go by and check on the boat." Besides his wife and children, his one real love in life was his boat. He kept it berthed at the docks in Boston because he loved going out on the open sea, except that it was something he seldom did in winter when the seas were too rough. It was a nice toy, forty-five feet, sleek as a devil, with sleeping facilities for eight people.

Patrick glanced at his watch. "In fact, I've got to get moving. Moira, I'll try to be back in plenty of time to do my part, sitting on the couch, scratching, drinking beer—and doing the dishes, as well. Sweetheart…" He paused by Siobhan's chair to give her cheek a kiss.

She didn't offer him anything more.

"Okay, munchkins," he said to the kids, delivering only slightly distracted kisses to the three of them. "Behave now, okay?"

"The kids are always fine," Eamon said. Moira was curious at his tone. She wondered if her father wasn't a little bit disturbed by her brother's exit.

"Bye, then," Patrick said, taking his coat from the hall tree. Maybe he felt all eyes on him. He turned at the door. "Honest, I'll drink a lot of beer and do a lot of scratching," he said. Moira offered her brother a slightly pained smile. His eyes fell on his wife.

But Siobhan wasn't watching him. Her eyes were purposely lowered as she buttered toast for Molly.

Patrick departed, and Danny cleared his throat.

"Well, now, can't let Patrick be the only bad child. I'm off for some cigarettes. Nasty habit, I know. I'll keep it outside. Katy, do you need anything while I'm out? Something traditionally Irish you might be missing for your meal?"

"Now, Danny, you know that between the pub and the house, we don't often run out of what we need," Katy said.

"Actually, I think we're a bit low on butter," Colleen murmured. "The real thing, no margarine."

"Colleen, we can't be making a guest go to the store," Katy said.

"Sure we can," Colleen said quickly. "He's not a guest, he's a big brother, remember?"

"Katy, how much butter?" Danny asked, starting for the stairs that led out through the pub.

"Better make it two pounds. We've a full house," Katy said.

"Right," Danny said. "I'll be back soon. I don't want to miss the fun."

"You told my father you'd open up the pub," Moira reminded him.

"And so I did. I guess I, like Patrick, will have to do my share of scratching and guzzling a bit later."

With that he left, but something about his departure seemed odd to Moira.

Only Michael was still eating. Siobhan rose, picking up plates from the table. "I'll wash," she said.

"Fine, I'll dry," Colleen added.

"Then I'll get the rest," Moira said, quickly busying herself with plates and condiments.

"Now, let Michael finish his meal before you go stealing his plate," Eamon told her.

"Right, Dad." As she took her grandmother's plate, she saw that Granny Jon was looking curiously at the floor. But she looked at Moira quickly, as if her attention had never been anywhere else. "The kids drop something?" Moira asked, ducking.

But the kids hadn't dropped anything.

Granny Jon had been staring at the brand-new pack of cigarettes that lay on the floor beneath the chair where Danny had been sitting.

Patrick hurried down the street, tightening his wool scarf around his neck and hiking up his collar. Having spent the majority of his life in Massachusetts, he was accustomed to weather that could be brutal far into the spring. Stopping at a traffic light, he stomped his feet and spoke aloud to himself. "No wonder the fucking Pilgrims all died," he muttered. He looked up. At least, for the moment, there was no snow. Just a blue sky with puffs of white clouds, fast-moving.

The light changed. He suddenly looked back, struck by an eerie feeling of being followed.

No one on the streets except a kid on a scooter. *Wait till the ice forms toward night, kid, you'll be sorry,* he thought. It was a Saturday morning, still fairly early. Bostonians took some time to get going on Saturdays. Still, it seemed as odd to him that the street was empty as if it had been full.

Why had he thought someone was following him? Nerves? Guilty conscience? Maybe it was just the weather.

He moved quickly, then glanced back again. No one there.

Still, that feeling. Unnerving. As if he heard silent footfalls echoing in his mind.

Someone's breath, whispering at the back of his neck.

Right. And maybe he was being followed by leprechauns, little people in green, trailing along behind him.

And maybe he'd just been home too long, listened to too many stories as his parents and grandmother entertained the kids.

Tales about fairies, mischievous leprechauns...

And then, of course, there were banshees, black shadow creatures tracking a man, wailing in the night, foretelling his death.

He looked back once again and hesitated, eyes scanning the street.

There were no fairies, no leprechauns or banshees. Both the good and the evil in the world came from men.

He started forward with determination. He had made up his mind, set his course.

He was going to do what he thought was right.

6

Moira was delighted to see that her mother was a natural in front of the camera. After a few minutes of being a little bit nervous about the camera, the lights and the overhead mike, held on a pole above her head by a total stranger, she was just fine. Katy Kelly loved to cook. She warmed to her subject, instructing her daughters and talking about being a little girl in Dublin, how times had changed drastically in a way, and then again, not at all. Somehow, in the midst of cooking, instructing Colleen to keep an eye on the cabbage, Moira to watch the meat and Siobhan to make sure that the mixture of chopped cabbage and onions was properly sauteed for the colcannon, she also got going on the temperament of the Irish people. Too many people thought of Ireland as a divided island, she said, but what they forgot was that over the years everyone had become Irish. Northern Ireland might technically be part of Great Britain, but Eire was a great place whose spirit entered the souls of those who loved her. The Vikings had come and invaded and created terrible havoc, but then many had settled and stayed. The English had begun coming to conquer in the eleven hundreds, but from those ancient invaders had come some of the most well-known Irish surnames of today. Being Irish was more than being born on the island, more than heritage. It was a spirit of warmth, of storytelling, of a special magic, and it was in so many Americans today.

Moira, meeting Josh's eyes at one point, signaled her pleasure with her mother's natural dialogue, as well as her amazement. Josh gave her a thumbs-up and a big smile. It was going to be a good show. Her family was charming. It was all going to work.

Eamon Kelly was beaming with pride at his wife. Watching them both, Moira realized that she was lucky in many ways. So many of her friends had parents who were divorced, had never known what it was like to grow up in a household with both a mother and a father. And her parents weren't together just for the children or any other practical reason. After all these years of marriage, they still loved one another.

Michael and Josh were getting along wonderfully with her family, and the crew was great, too. She watched some of the tape as they reran it, and it was excellent. Katy was pleased, blushing at the congratulations bestowed on her by both her family and the crew. She was like an old pro when Josh asked that she repeat steps over and over again so the cameraman could focus with more detail on exactly how to prepare the meal.

The kids had been taped sitting at the table, but then, not long ago, they had disappeared. While Josh was busy talking about how to edit the segment, Moira wandered into the family room. Granny Jon, who was scheduled to have her moment in the sun discussing, naturally, the elements of a really good cup of tea, was busy with needlework as she waited. She told Moira that the kids were in the pub; they had grown restless, and Danny had returned to entertain them.

"I didn't see him come back," Moira murmured.

"He was careful not to disturb the work, but he told

your father he'd open the pub, and so he did, taking the kids down to help set up," Granny Jon said.

"I'll walk down and see how things are going," Moira said.

When she got downstairs, she realized how late it had gotten. The lunch crowd had come and gone. Danny was behind the bar, while Chrissie Dingle, Larry Donovan and a new young waitress, Marty, whom Moira had never met before, worked the floor. Joey Sullivan and Harry Darcy were cooking in the kitchen. Brian, Shannon and Molly were at a table in the corner. When Moira approached them, she discovered that Danny had brought them Irish coloring books. Molly's leprechauns were bright purple instead of green. Moira rather liked them.

"I don't really color like this often, you know," Brian told his aunt gravely. "Uncle Dan asked me to keep an eye on the girls, so I'm watching them."

"And a fine job you're doing," Moira said, and winced. There she went, sounding like her mother or Granny Jon again.

"We had ice cream for lunch," Shannon told her.

"Brrr," Moira said. "Great coloring. You're being little angels. Patrick doesn't deserve you."

Brian frowned at her seeming criticism of his beloved father.

Moira quickly hugged him. "Your daddy is my brother, you know. I love him with all my heart, but you know how you tease the girls sometimes? I like to tease Patrick that way."

Brian smiled, happy again.

"I'll be back," Moira promised.

She walked to the bar, ready to bite the bullet and thank Danny for helping her dad out while they'd been filming. But when she reached the bar, Chrissie was at

the taps. Thirty and attractive, Chrissie was also efficient, with a no-nonsense manner.

"Where's Danny?"

"He just walked over to see to the kids," Chrissie
said.

When Moira turned around, she saw that not only
had Danny gone to sit at the table with the kids, but Michael had come down, as well. They were both there,
each with a pint of beer.

"We're going to include your dad in this thing, too,
Moira," Michael told her, rising. "He's going to tell us
about the Irish beers he has on tap and the Irish whis-
kies he carries."

"Great idea," she said. "We'll stay entirely away
from the political."

"What are you so afraid of, Moira?" Danny inquired,
watching her.

There was something about his voice. She should
have walked away quickly.

"I'm not afraid of anything, Danny."

"Then why are you so determined to be 'politically
correct'?"

"Because I do a friendly little travel show, that's
why," she said angrily.

"And we're making sure all the Irish look good,"
Michael added lightly.

"All the Irish. Well, you know, that's just great,"
Danny said, his tone equally light. "Let's just pretend
that everything is always perfect. That the Irish haven't
been trod upon since the time Henry the Second came
to power and forced the Irish chieftains to submit to
him. And that Henry the Eighth didn't come to power,
want a divorce, create his own church, fight the Irish
of the established church who couldn't see changing
their religion because he wanted a new wife, beat them

to a pulp and confiscate the lands of all those who opposed him. And let's just forget about William of Orange and the Battle of the Boyne and the subjugation of the people who had supported the rightful king."

"Dan, those things happened hundreds of years ago," Michael reminded him.

"And the Easter Rebellion, where the leaders of the hoped-for Irish Republic were shot dead, executed *after* they had surrendered." Dan was speaking as if he hadn't even heard Michael's words.

Moira was about to speak when Michael answered Danny sharply. "And let's not forget those leaders who willfully and cold-bloodedly assassinated English public servants in Ireland. And let's not forget the bombs that went off and killed dozens of innocent people, including children."

Moira realized that though Molly and Shannon were still coloring, ignoring the tones taken on by the adults at their sides, Brian was staring at them.

"Is there still a war in Ireland?" he asked.

"No," Moira said.

"Yes," Michael answered angrily, staring at Danny. "Some people insist on fighting one."

Danny shrugged suddenly, a slow smile curving his lips. Moira realized that he had intentionally provoked Michael. Trying to break the tension, she said, "I think we should go shopping, maybe take the kids down to Quincy Market. Have pasta for lunch in Little Italy. Or find a Chinese restaurant."

"The kids just ate," Danny told her placidly.

"They're kids. They'll be hungry again," Moira said sharply.

Danny shrugged.

Michael sighed, rising. "I've got to get back to Josh. We're going to bring your father down now, while there's a lull after the lunch crowd." He curled his fingers around Moira's. "Later? We'll do something later?"

"Absolutely," she told him.

He rose and walked by her, close, slipping an arm around her, kissing her cheek. "Sorry," he whispered softly.

"Not your fault," she told him, purposely letting Danny hear her. Michael frowned, then squeezed her hand and walked by.

"What the hell is the matter with you?" Moira asked Danny angrily as she dragged him away to where the children couldn't overhear.

His eyes narrowed on her speculatively and seemed to gleam with a golden, predatory light. He shrugged. "Just trying to suss out the lay of the land."

"Why? Leave him alone."

"He's Irish, isn't he? That's what your mother told me."

Moira waved a hand impatiently. "Emigration has been going on for hundreds of years. Some people get to the States and become Americans. He's Irish—he's just not *Irish*, the way some people insist on being."

"Moira, I'm sorry, but I *am* Irish."

"Fine. But this is America."

"So it is."

"Auntie Mo," Brian called suddenly, "are you going to marry Michael?"

"No," Danny assured him.

"Yes, I think I just might," Moira said.

"Your auntie Mo is willing to go to great lengths to aggravate me," Danny said.

"To aggravate you?" Moira said incredulously. "Gee, he's smart, good-looking, charming and willing to tolerate a lot of abuse for my sake. What on earth could be wrong with my marrying such a man?"

To her surprise, Danny replied softly, "I don't know. That's the problem. I just don't know." She realized that he wasn't looking at her. The television set over the bar was on. He rose, and said, distracted, "Excuse me." Standing before the television, he slid his hand into his pocket and watched the set. Curiously, Moira walked over and joined him.

"Turn it up, please, will you, Chrissie?" he asked the woman behind the bar, who obliged him with a quick smile.

There was a tall, broad-shouldered, white-haired man standing on the steps of New York's Plaza Hotel, answering questions put to him by news crews on his way into the hotel.

"Mr. Brolin, how does it feel to be in America?" a tall, dark-haired reporter asked.

"Great," the man replied. "It always feels wonderful to be in America." He had a deep, rich speaking voice and a light brogue, enough of an accent to mark him as Irish. He was clearly comfortable with the mikes thrust in front of his face.

"Have you come here for diplomatic reasons, sir?" a woman queried, getting her question in next.

"Well, now, as part of the U.K., Northern Ireland has a fine relationship with America. As part of the Irish people, we in Northern Ireland want you Americans to come see us when you're visiting the Republic in the south. Some of the greatest places of legend, for Northerner and Republican alike, are in the north. Armagh, Tara, landscapes so beautiful they take your breath away. They belong to all of us, and to the Irish in America, as well."

"Mr. Brolin, do you have a campaign to see the island of Ireland reunited again?"

"My first campaign is to see people united again," Brolin said.

"Can such a thing ever happen?"

"We're into the twenty-first century now. I believe we see more clearly, that we can get to the root of our problems. Not to say that decades of bitterness can be wiped away overnight. But in the past ten years, we've made some giant leaps. We are working together in the North. Come now, you all know that we want your American tourist dollars. That's a goal that can get all the people working together right there."

He started to turn away. For a split second, it was possible to see the exhaustion on the man's face.

"Mr. Brolin, Mr. Brolin, one more question, please," a tiny woman, who had just maneuvered her mike near the politician, called. Brolin hesitated, and she went on. "We've thousands of good Irish Americans right here in New York. What made you choose Boston for your appearance on Saint Patrick's Day?"

Brolin smiled slowly, eyes alight. "New York is as fine a city as a man can find, with many a good Irish American, indeed. I didn't choose Boston, though it, too, is a fine American city. They invited me. Invite me to New York next year. I'll be delighted to come."

With that, he waved a hand in the air and started up the steps of the hotel. Moira noted the police in attendance, protecting him.

"He's charming," she murmured. "So even and moderate. I wonder why on earth he has such a large police escort?"

Danny looked at her strangely. "Because some people don't want to be moderate," he told her. "Ah, look, here comes your father. I guess you're back on. Time to give Eamon a chance to promote the brews of Eire— and Boston, of course." He turned away, walking to the street door at the front of the pub. He lifted his coat from a hook and left without so much as a glance back.

She could hear her father, Michael, Josh and some of the others coming down to the pub but, curious, she followed Danny, sliding past one of the tables by the window and looking out. He'd been in such a hurry to leave, but he hadn't gone anywhere. He was just standing in front of the pub, lighting a cigarette. He turned, almost as if he knew she was there, and she shrank from the window. Danny looked at the Kelly's Pub sign for several long moments. Then he crushed out his cigarette and started down the street.

"Moody bastard," Moira murmured to herself, then turned to the others.

They went to work. Lights and sound levels were set. Eamon stood at his taps, while Moira settled onto a bar stool in front of him. Eamon gave a great recitation, explaining the differences between lagers and ales and stouts. Customers began to filter in, making it all work perfectly. Chrissie, shy at first, got into the act. Seamus and Liam arrived and talked about the heart of the pub, how it was a place like home, a haven where you came to be with friends. "A beer…a beer you buy anywhere," Liam told the camera. "But a place where a man belongs, with friends to argue and agree, where the bartender always knows what you're drinking, now that's not so easy to come by."

Moira was stunned to find herself having fun as she began to move around the room to speak with customers. She put the kids on camera again, coloring at their table. Jeff Dolan had come in to set up early for the night, and she caught him teasing the kids while they laughed and crawled all over him. Jeff was the one to tell the video camera, "A pub is far more than a bar. A pub offers family fare, meals for the kids, good warm

food, as well as ale. Well, now, I grant you, until recent times there existed many a pub in Ireland where
the men had their place, and the women, well, they had
their place, as well, but not on the same side with the
men. I'd be willing to bet such a place or two still exists
in the old country. But nowadays, I know I can come
here alone—when I'm not working, of course—and I
know I can come with kids, relatives, more. There's a
dartboard in the back, and I was teaching my nephew
just last week how to play. We always have the games
on—I'm a big Patriots fan myself. The point is, you can
get a good beer, but also a whole lot more. The true
Irish pub is the heart of the neighborhood. Kelly's has
a lot of heart, even here in America, and that's a fact."

Josh, who'd been following Moira with the camera,
switched off the tape. Moira smiled with delight and
kissed Jeff on the cheek. "That was wonderful."

He blushed. "I'm glad. Thank God you didn't warn
me. I'd have been awful."

"I'm glad we didn't warn you either," Josh told him.
"This is going to be one of the best pieces we've done.
Moira, I'm going over to talk with Michael and the
sound guy. I want to make sure we're good with what
we've got." She nodded, and Josh walked away.

Jeff seemed really pleased. "Seems to me you've got
enough tape for a ten-hour show," he told her.

She shook her head. "We'll be editing everything
we've got, taking out pauses, the amazing long spaces
you get once you look over the video. Cutting and slic-
ing shots…you'll see."

"You mean you're still going to be taping in here?"
he queried.

"Sure, why not? Hey, I didn't know Josh was going
to come in last night and tape while Colleen and I were
onstage, but it might be good stuff. I haven't looked it

over yet. That's how you get a lot that's really good for a show like this. Spontaneous pieces, you know."

"I don't think it's such a good idea," Jeff said.

"Why not?"

He hesitated, gazing toward the equipment he'd been setting up.

"What happens," he asked her, "when you get someone on tape who doesn't want to be seen on camera?"

"Jeff, we do what the big guys like Disney do. We put up signs warning people that there are cameras going."

"And you think everyone reads signs?"

"We ask for releases from anyone we feature," she told him, then frowned. "Jeff, I'm not sure what you're so worried about. So far, I've come across an incredible group of hams. They all want to be on camera."

"Yes, but..."

She shook her head, smiling. "Jeff, you're not into any... I mean, there are no drugs being passed around in my dad's place, right?"

"Moira, I've been clean as a whistle for over five years. Ask your dad—I barely have a beer or two now and then."

"I wasn't accusing you, Jeff..."

"I'm just a little worried about you, Moira, all right? Be careful what you get on camera. I don't think your own brother is going to want everything going on in here videotaped."

"My brother!" Despite her surprised tone, she'd had her own uneasy suspicions regarding her brother's activities since overhearing his conversation with Siobhan.

"Yeah, yeah, you know, he's an attorney. Has to be careful."

"Jeff, this is a friendly little travel show!"

"Right. I know. Just watch what you're filming. For me, okay? This place is important to me. I admit to being a wild child. Well, hell, you were there, you know. I was on drugs, off drugs. I went through a spell of being a tough guy on the streets and I tried to raise money to send arms overseas. I spent a night or two in jail. Your dad kept faith in me when my own folks were ready to call it quits. You be careful. Just be careful."

He didn't wait for an answer, just ran his fingers through his unruly dark hair and turned to the band equipment.

She wanted to quiz him further, but she couldn't because Michael came up behind her, slipping his arms around her waist. His aftershave smelled good. The texture of his cheek against hers as he leaned down was pleasant and alluring. She felt warmed and was glad for the moment.

"Want to slip away somewhere?" he asked huskily.

"I do."

"I mean, really away. We don't want to find out that Josh has decided to film Saint Patrick's Day mating rituals or anything like that."

She laughed aloud, turning to face him. "He wouldn't dare."

"Let's sneak away to the hotel."

"Let's."

Moira started across the pub to tell her father she was leaving. It wasn't busy at the moment. Chrissie was tending to the three women at the bar, and Eamon was poring over a newspaper.

Moira was surprised to feel a little bit like a guilty kid as she approached her dad. She wasn't sure what she was going to say. She was well over twenty-one, of course, but she knew she was going to make up a story about needing something or going to scout locales or some such thing. What woman, no matter how old, would ever want to admit to her father that she was getting a little bit desperate to get away from her family for just a few minutes of…quality time with the new man in her life?

"Dad…" she began.

"They haven't found a thing," Eamon said, looking up.

"Pardon?"

"On that poor girl, murdered the other day. The police have been questioning half the city, and they haven't found out anything. She was at a bar the night she died, a high-priced place. I guess she was what they call an escort these days, a high-priced girl herself. Everyone remembers her sitting at the bar by herself. No one remembers who she left with. They haven't been able to connect her murder with any others in the city."

"Dad, unfortunately, it often takes months, even years, for the police to crack down on a killer," Moira said. "And sometimes, as you know, people get away with murder."

"I don't like it," Eamon said.

"Of course not, Dad, it's tragic."

Michael was behind Moira. "Eamon, I can tell you're afraid for your daughters, and I'm making no judgments, but it's true that a call girl takes her chances. Your daughters would never be in such a position."

"It just bothers me, in the bones," her father said.

"I'll be safe in the city. I'm always with Michael or Josh, Dad," Moira said. There was her opening. "And as to that—"

Just then Colleen came in from the office behind the bar and straight up behind her father. "Hey, it's time for dinner," Colleen said.

"Dinner?" Moira repeated blankly.

"Dinner. Remember that stuff we cooked all day for your program? Well, Mum has it in her head that we're all going to gather around and eat it. You know. Dinner."

"Now?" Moira said.

"Six o'clock seems like a pretty good time for dinner to me," someone said from behind Moira.

She turned. Danny was back. Golden eyes on her speculatively. He seemed to know she'd been about to leave. With Michael. And he obviously found her situation amusing.

Colleen leaned over the bar to whisper to her, "Don't you dare walk out on dinner after all the effort Mum went to get it right for your show!"

"She'd kill me, huh?"

"*I'd* kill you," Colleen assured her.

She was going to have to explain to Michael. No, she wasn't. She felt his hands at her waist. "Dinner sounds great," he said softly.

She turned into his arms, meeting his eyes. "You're really too good," she told him.

He shook his head. "You're worth any wait, Moira."

She touched his cheek. Then, aware that she was still being watched by Danny, she took Michael's hand and said softly, "Let's go on up."

Upstairs, the delicious scent of her mother's Irish bacon and cabbage dinner filled the air. The kids were already in their chairs, and Siobhan was helping them butter their Irish soda bread. It was a wonderful scene; Moira immediately thought she should be filming again.

"No cameras when we sit down to dinner," her mother announced firmly, as if she had read her mind.

"No cameras," she quickly agreed.

No cameras.

She suddenly remembered how worried Jeff had been about her continuing to tape in the pub.

Why?

What was he afraid she would catch on camera?

America was an amazing place. From his hotel room high above New York City, Jacob Brolin looked at the hive of activity below him. His windows overlooked both the street below and the park, and he could see people moving. They were faceless figures from his distance, some obviously taking in the sights, others walking as if they were in a rush to return home from whatever they'd been doing. Tourists stopped and haggled with the carriage drivers on the street. He'd been gratified earlier to see that the horses all seemed to be in fine shape. No scrawny, ill-fed nags pulled the people along the streets and through the park. Many of the horses wore blankets in the chill of mid-March, and some were festooned with flowers. One, almost directly below him, seemed to be wearing a hat. Many of the drivers were Irish; they had watched and cheered when he had checked into the hotel. Aye, he was glad to see how well-kept the horses were. It was strange, he thought, or maybe not so strange. Many a man like himself had witnessed terrible violence against human beings yet found himself torn by the plight of an animal. But the horses were kept in fine shape, and that was good.

"Mr. Brolin?"

He turned from the window. Peter O'Malley, one of his aides, had tapped on the door connecting the parlor with the bedroom. O'Malley was one big son of a bitch. Six-four if he was an inch. Close to three hundred pounds of hard muscle. He wore a suit, and wore it well. Brolin thought few people would realize that a

wee bit of the man's bulk was the bulletproof vest he
wore beneath his jacket.

"Peter?"

"The call has come."

"Thank you. I'll take it in here."

He picked up the phone and identified himself. The
caller spoke in Gaelic. He listened gravely, then spoke
with soft determination.

"I'll not cancel. I'll be there tomorrow afternoon."

After a brief exchange, he hung up the phone and
walked to the window. This time, however, he closed
his eyes.

1973. He had taken a different road. It had seemed
the only choice. He'd been running with Jenna Mc-
Cleary, and things had gone badly awry. The battle had
taken to the street. Bullets had been flying as they ran.

"We have to split," Jenna had said.

He'd nodded. Split, disappear right into the midst of
it. Where to hide but in plain sight? So he had agreed.

He'd gone into the first pub and ordered an ale. He
wasn't sure what path Jenna had taken; all he knew was
that, later that night, she'd been picked up.

He'd heard about it. About the way she'd been questioned. How the official in charge had sent her back
with soldiers who had just lost a chum. Shot down in
the street when they'd been running. Maybe Jenna had
pulled the trigger that particular round. Maybe he had.
Jenna had paid. She had been young, beautiful and
taught vengeance since she'd been a wee babe.

She hadn't been beautiful when they'd finished with
her. There had been a plan, of course; they'd never simply deserted their own. But by the time they stopped
the convoy transporting her from holding cell to prison,
something had been dead within her already. When the
bomb had exploded in front of the car and they'd gone

to release her, she hadn't run. She had just stood there, knowing that the bullets would fly again.

He had watched her fall. Watched the motion as the bullet had struck, watched her jerk, spin and hit the earth. And he had seen her face clearly for a moment. Seen the hopelessness, seen the death in her eyes before they had glazed over. He had stood in the street, and it was surely a miracle that he hadn't been struck. And in those moments, he had suddenly known that they had all killed her. They had all of them, every one of them, killed her as surely as if they had shot her down themselves.

There was a tap on the door again. O'Malley had returned.

"Mr. Brolin?"

"We'll be on the one o'clock shuttle, right after the television appearance, just as planned, Peter."

"Sir, perhaps, with what we know, and with what we don't know—"

"Just as planned, Peter."

O'Malley inclined his head and left, quietly closing the door.

Brolin looked at the street.

Aye, it was good to see that the horses were in such fine shape.

7

Dinner was pleasant. Moira sat beside Michael, and Danny was down the table between Brian and Molly. After the conversation they'd had in front of the kids that afternoon, Moira was a little worried about what Danny might be saying to them. She made a point of rising throughout the meal for more drinks or anything else that might be needed, just to walk by Danny's end of the table and see what he was saying. She needn't have worried. He was doing nothing more than telling them about Saint Patrick. As always, Danny was a good storyteller.

"Patrick's life, you know, is shrouded in mystery," Danny explained. "He was the son of a man named Calpurnius, who was most probably a wealthy Roman living in Britain. Now the Romans had gone just about everywhere, you know, but they didn't do much more than skirt the edges of Ireland. The island was very wild at the time, and the people were fierce, and they lived in tribes. They were good-looking, of course, even back then, but they believed very much in magic, and in the wind and the sky and the power of the earth. They were fine seamen, too. So Patrick was a boy growing up in Britain—Wales, many people believe. And he was out late at night when he shouldn't have been—which is a

lesson to the three of you to stay close to your parents
and family when you're out. Patrick wound up being
captured by pagan Irish sea raiders and taken across
the Irish Sea to be sold as a slave. To a nasty fellow,
so they say. Patrick became a shepherd, and he tended
his sheep well, but he knew he must escape. It was
very dangerous for him, because slaves attempting to
escape could be executed at the will of their masters.
But Patrick was a brave fellow, and he meant to go. In
time, he convinced rivals of his master to help him escape across the sea again, and he came back home. His
parents were very happy to see him, of course, but Patrick believed that God had come to him and told him
that he must go back and help the Irish people. Patrick
knew he had a special calling. His father wanted him
to go to be a businessman—"

"Like Daddy," Shannon said.

"Like Daddy. Being a businessman is certainly a
fine enough thing to do in life," Danny assured her.
"But Patrick knew that he couldn't do what his parents
wanted. So he convinced them at last that he must go
on to become a man of the Church. Years later, he returned to Ireland to preach a message of peace to the
pagans, who were still practicing their strange beliefs.
He might have been caught by the mean master he had
escaped and put to death, but he came back anyway.
Some say God helped him by letting the pagans see
certain miracles. Others say that Patrick's wit and mind
were miraculous in themselves, and that his power was
in his words and his way with people."

"Either way, gifts from God," Granny Jon added.

Danny smiled across the table at her. "True enough.
So here's our good Patrick among these people. He
walked all over Ireland, North and South, because they
were just one back then, with many kings ruling dif-

ferent areas and sometimes an Ard-Ri, or High King, sitting at Tara. When Patrick came, so legend has it, there was a High King at Tara, and he was a powerful man with deep belief in his pagan priest. The pagan priest wanted to trick Patrick into a fire, where Patrick would burn to death and leave the pagan priest as the most powerful one. But the Ard-Ri wanted the truth, and he forced both his own priest and Patrick to walk through the flames. Patrick proved that his faith in God was the greatest magic in the world, for he passed easily through fire, and the pagan priest who wanted to hurt Patrick was the one who perished in the flames. Ah, but that didn't end the trials Patrick had to go through. He had trouble with other churchmen, jealous of his success in Ireland. But in the end, Patrick plugged away, sure of his love of Ireland and the Irish people, and sure of his faith in God, and he passed through all his trials, changed Ireland forever, and guess what?"

"What?" Brian demanded.

"He went on to live to a ripe old age, still in his beloved Ireland, and so we celebrate a special day for him every year, even here in America."

"Saint Patrick's Day is a public holiday in Ireland, Moira, you know," Katy said.

She smiled. "Yes, Mum. In Ireland."

"Did he really pass through fire?" Brian asked Danny very seriously.

"Well, now, I wasn't there. Is that truth, or legend?" Danny said. "It's all a matter of belief."

"Did Saint Patrick bring the leprechauns to Ireland?" Molly asked.

"No, you see, the wee people were always there, living in the magic of the mind," Danny told her, and winked.

Moira left a bottle of soda in front of the group at the end of the table and moved back to her seat.

Michael leaned close to speak softly to her. "He's quite a fine storyteller."

"Oh, yes, he has lots of stories."

"You're not so fond of your old family friend?" Michael asked curiously.

She hesitated. She'd never mentioned Danny to Michael before this had all come up. No reason to. They hadn't torn apart their pasts. She hadn't given him a questionnaire about his previous relationships or talked about her own. Now she felt guilty.

And still totally disinclined to tell the truth.

"He can be very charming, and very irritating," she said simply. She looked at Danny. "Like a brother," she said, loudly enough for Danny to hear.

A slight smile curved his lips. He went on to tell Molly about a special girl leprechaun called Taloola. Moira had heard a lot of Irish fairy tales in her day, but she had never heard that one. She decided Danny must have been making up the story as he went along, creating it especially for the kids.

That was fine. Just as long as he didn't launch into a speech about the oppression faced by their people over the years.

Moira looked across the table to discover that her grandmother was watching her with a grave expression. She arched a brow. "Pass the colcannon, please, Moira, will you?" Granny Jon said.

Moira obediently passed the food over, wondering why her grandmother had been watching her so strangely.

After dinner, she, Colleen and Siobhan made her mother go sit in the den with Granny Jon. They served them tea there, making a big deal of putting them into the most comfortable chairs, pulling up footrests and making them do nothing but rest. Granny Jon seemed bemused, her mother restless. Once the tea was served, the younger women forced the older women to stay put and went in to clean up the dining room and kitchen. It seemed strangely empty with just the three of them.

"Where are the kids?" Moira asked. "They don't have the poor little things back down in the pub again, do they?"

"Patrick is putting them to bed."

"Good," Moira said to her sister-in-law.

"Yeah, well, usually he's a good father."

Rinsing a dish, then setting in into the dishwasher, Moira wondered whether to say something further or to keep her mouth shut.

"Has he been really busy lately?" she asked.

"Yeah," Siobhan said, handing Moira a plate. She looked as if she was about to say something, hesitated, then shrugged. "I really don't know what this new deal is. He met these people involved with a charitable association in Northern Ireland. They raise American money for Irish kids who've been orphaned, to help them pay for an education."

"It sounds like a decent cause," Colleen said.

"Yes, it does, doesn't it?" Siobhan said.

"I'm lost, then," Moira murmured. "What's the problem?"

Siobhan shook her head. "He's been in Boston an awful lot lately. Times when he hasn't even stopped by to see your folks."

"Well," Moira murmured, surprised to realize she was coming to her brother's defense, "if he's just coming in for some quick business, he may not stop to see them because he thinks he'd never get back home if he did."

"Yeah, sure," Siobhan said.

Siobhan's words might have meant that she agreed with Moira or that she didn't believe a word Moira had said. All that was clear was that she didn't want to talk about it anymore. And all that Moira knew was that something about her brother's behavior was troubling.

"Hey," Colleen said, breaking in on the awkward moment, "I've got to tell you, Siobhan, every time I see them, I'm prouder than ever of being an aunt to those little munchkins of yours."

"Beyond a doubt," Moira agreed wholeheartedly. "They're adorable and well behaved, even though they're still so young."

"Thanks," Siobhan said, smiling. "They are kind of worth everything, aren't they? You're going to make a terrific parent yourself one day, you know. Whoops, sorry, both of you are going to make terrific parents. I was merely addressing Moira because she's older," Siobhan explained to Colleen.

"Thank you for pointing that out," Moira said.

"Well, you are closing in on the big three-oh," Siobhan said.

"That's right, Moira, no matter how old I get, you'll be older."

"You're both so kind," Moira said.

Siobhan laughed. "So is this Michael thing serious?"

"He's definitely great to look at," Colleen said.

"Looks aren't everything," Siobhan reminded her.

"But when you're not speaking to one another, at least the scenery's nice," Colleen said.

"He's not the temperamental type, is he?" Siobhan asked.

"Not at all," Moira said.

"He's practically perfect in every way," Colleen remarked.

"I'd say he's doing exceptionally well," Siobhan noted. "I mean, this isn't an easy household to crash, and he's holding his own quite nicely."

"Yes, he is."

"So *is* it serious?" Siobhan persisted.

"Could be."

"You would have great-looking children," Colleen murmured.

"Just because you're now the face on a zillion magazine covers, you shouldn't obsess about looks," Moira chastised.

"Okay, what a dog you're dating."

Moira sighed, Siobhan laughed, and the cleanup went on, the next line of inquiry focused on Colleen's love life. Moira kept from questioning Siobhan further, because her sister-in-law obviously didn't want to answer questions, but when they finished and Siobhan excused herself to see to the kids, Moira still felt uneasy.

After Siobhan walked down the hall and left them, Colleen asked Moira, "You don't think Patrick could be cheating on her, do you?"

"I can't imagine it," Moira said. "If he is, he's a fool."

"Think we ought to tell him so?"

"I… I think we need to stay out of it, unless one of them decides to talk to us," Moira said.

"I guess you're right, except that…"

"You don't think that…" Moira began.

"What?"

"Patrick wouldn't be involved in…anything illegal, would he?"

"He's an attorney! What are you talking about?"

"I know. Never mind. I don't know what I'm talking about myself."

"I'm going to head down to the pub and see if Dad needs any help," Colleen said. She set the dish towel she'd been using on the counter. "He loves it when we're down there, you know."

"I know. I'll just check on Mum and Granny Jon, then be right down," Moira said.

They went their separate ways. When Moira slipped into the den, she found that her mother had gone to bed and Granny Jon was watching the news. She smiled at Moira, nodding toward the sofa next to the big upholstered chair where she was sitting.

"All cleaned up, eh?"

"Yep, all done. I came to see if I can get you anything else."

"You know, Moira, thank the good Lord, I'm still mobile."

"I thank Him all the time," Moira said earnestly. "You're very precious to us."

Granny Jon nodded, smiling. "Thank you. It's truly good to have you children home. It's good to be able to take care of yourself, but it's also very nice to have loved ones who want to do things for you."

"We're lucky, too."

"Oh?"

Moira waved a hand in the air. "I have so many friends whose parents are divorced and don't really have a home to go back to. Every time they have an important occasion in their lives, they have to figure out how to manage the logistics. I know I'm lucky."

Granny Jon nodded gravely. "Good. Half the time in life, people don't appreciate what they have." She paused. "Don't be too hard on them for remembering the old country, though, Moira."

"I… I don't mean to be."

Granny Jon was silent for a minute, then she said, "I am very old, you know."

"Age is relative," Moira said.

"Yes, but there is a lot I remember, you see. I was a child in Dublin at the time of the Easter Rebellion, you know. I saw the streets in flames. I had friends—little children—who were killed in the crossfire."

"I'm so sorry," Moira said. "You've never talked about it."

Granny Jon shrugged. "Dublin is a wonderful city now. And the Irish are a wonderful people. I'm just saying this because...well, sometimes when people are born into violence, scars remain. Sometimes the old-timers can't help talking about what was—and about what they hope for in the future."

"Granny Jon, I just can't believe that bombs and bullets—"

"Bombs and bullets are wrong. The murder of innocents is wrong. I'll never say otherwise. I just want you to understand how people feel at times."

"I do understand. Honestly, Granny Jon, I know the history of Ireland. It was impossible to grow up with you and Mum and Dad and not know it."

"Your father wanted to come here, you know. To America. Not that he didn't realize that every country had its injustices to fight. But we had family in the North."

"I understand."

"I'm not sure if you really do. In the last few years, there have been giant steps taken toward real peace, the ceasefire in 1997, the Good Friday Agreement in 1998. President Clinton spent time in Northern Ireland, working things out. But you know as well as I do that there remain those who wish to die and don't mind sacrificing the lives of others for their beliefs. You've just got to remember, Moira, that we are Irish and proud of it, and that you're Irish, too."

Moira stood, then kneeled down by her grandmother, putting her arms around her. "I'm so sorry if I led you to believe that I was ever anything but completely proud of all of you," she said softly.

Granny Jon pulled away, smiling at her, smoothing her hair. "I don't say there aren't problems in Ireland. But you know, though it may well be the greatest country in the world, there are problems in America, as well."

"I always knew you were wonderful," Moira told her, "but I don't think I ever knew before just how incredibly savvy you were."

Granny Jon grinned. "Sometimes…well, there are times when I'm afraid, too. But get on down to the pub now, girl. Go sing 'Danny Boy' for your dad."

"We sang it last night."

"Sing it again—it makes him happy."

"You don't need anything…"

"If I did, I'd ask."

Moira smiled and started out of the room.

"Moira?"

She paused in the doorway. "Yes?"

"Remember, the country we're from is beautiful. The Irish in years past kept the art of books alive. In the Dark Ages, Irish monks worked endlessly to keep the written word going. Some of the finest craftsmen in the world were Irish. There's a spirit there, as well, in the wind, the sea, the crags and cairns. Legends and stories, art and drama. Remember it all, Moira."

"I do, Granny, I do. Honestly."

Granny Jon nodded. "Go on with you, then. Go have fun being with your family. The taping you did today was lovely."

"Thanks. Hey, would you let me tape you telling the kids a story tomorrow?"

"If you're sure you want an old woman on your show."

"I want an incredibly bright and wonderful woman on my show."

Granny Jon smiled her pleasure. "Go on now."

"You sure? You're not watching the television or reading or anything. I hate to leave you alone."

"I'm thinking, girl. Reflecting. At my age, it's an interesting occupation."

Moira nodded and left her, ready to head down to the pub.

Dan saw the man in the navy sweater at the corner table the minute he came down and stepped behind the bar with Michael McLean.

McLean was evidently wary of him, but the guy was doing everything he could to fit in. He was obviously very much in love with Moira and willing to prove it. Not that he was behaving like a sycophant in any way. He was steady, determined and willing, unafraid to speak his mind and capable of doing so with diplomacy. Actually, Dan reflected, under other circumstances, he might have liked the guy.

They'd come together behind the bar to allow Eamon Kelly time to sit with his old cronies for a while, and solve the future of the free world. Working the bar was easy enough—most orders were for drafts. The pub was busy, but there was still time to watch the floor and talk to the regulars. The band was playing, and the television was on with the sound turned down. It seemed a typical enough night. Something going on everywhere.

The guy in the corner was alone. At a two-seater table, he nursed a single beer. He'd been at it for a while. A nondescript fellow, brown hair cut short, Ivy League look. He might have been an accountant, a banker, a lawyer or a businessman of any variety. White-collar type, though, beyond a doubt.

"They're at it again," Michael said, then added a quick, "sorry."

Dan arched a brow at him.

Michael McLean shrugged. "I forgot how important it is to all of you—every event in the history of Ireland."

Dan nodded, tuning in to the old men's conversation. It was a familiar one.

"Well, I ask you again," Seamus said. "Are you an American?"

"Don't be daft, man," Eamon Kelly replied, shaking his head. "Yes, I'm an American. I applied for my citizenship the day I'd been in the country long enough. I'd had a son by then, and Moira was on her way. Katy and I had talked about it long and hard. We'd decided that we were bringing the children up in Boston, and that was that."

"But you're still an Irishman."

Eamon groaned. "I was born an Irishman."

"So what if America went to war with Ireland?" Seamus demanded.

"America will never go to war with Ireland."

"But what if it did?"

"Seamus, I'm telling you again, you're daft, man."

"You're missing the point."

"I'm not missing the point. You're saying that an Irishman is always an Irishman, above and beyond anything else. The American Irish and the Northern Irish both."

"But you do think the island should be united."

"*You* think the island should be united."

"Aye, but I don't know how it's to come about."

"That's why a man like Jacob Brolin is so important. He knows The Troubles backward and forward. He knows that the religious divide is an economic divide, that laws in the past have created half the problems, that the healing has to come from the people. And if you can unite the people, you can eventually unite Ireland."

"What about those who like their financial ties with England?"

"Why are we arguing about this, Seamus? We both feel the same way," Eamon said, irritated. The two men looked as if they were about to exchange blows. Dan knew that they often looked this way.

Seamus shook his head, looking sorrowful. "There's trouble brewing."

"In my pub?" Eamon said scornfully.

Seamus suddenly lowered his voice. "Do you remember that soldier in seventy-one?"

"I'm a Dubliner, Seamus."

"But you remember, because you knew him. Family ties, Eamon, and they run deep. The poor kid was a twenty-year-old British soldier. The IRA kidnapped him after a street brawl in Belfast. He lived in Paddy McNally's house for two weeks, and everyone who met the fellow liked the chap. But the British refused to free a few of the IRA men who had been picked up, so they took that poor kid out and shot him dead, despite the fact that they had all but adopted the lad."

"And the world condemned the IRA faction that did the deed as terrorists," Eamon said angrily. "Seamus, what are you going on about? I'm telling you, I can't solve the problem and I know it. I'm an American, running a pub in Boston. Praying for peace everywhere, like the whole damned rest of the world. The governments of North and South both know that the time of war and revolution is over, that in the small world we live in now, negotiation is the way to go. Jesus, Seamus, how you're going on. We've both seen it. Kids taught to throw rocks from the time they're walking, rocks that turn into bullets when they're old enough to tote a gun. We've learned to fight with words—"

"Oh, aye. And every time there's an agreement signed, there's sure to be a bomb going off somewhere."

"Excuse me, Seamus, but I was over in Belfast not more than a year and a half ago, and I'm telling you, the Northern Irish want tourist dollars the same as the rest of the world. They're on the road to change."

"*Most* of the Northern Irish," Seamus muttered.

"Seamus, just what are you trying to say to me?"

Seamus suddenly looked straight at Dan. "I'm saying that the North still has terrorists."

"And what would you have me do?"

Seamus shook his head suddenly, looking into his beer. "Whispering," he muttered. "Gaelic. I've been hearing it, here in the pub. There's something going on—I've yet to put my finger on it, but I've heard… Gaelic."

"I can still speak the old language myself, Seamus, so what in the Lord's name does that have to do with anything?"

Seamus looked up and caught Dan watching him.

He lifted his beer. "It's a fine old language."

Colleen was at the service end of the bar with a tray, ready to place an order. "Hey, one of you guys want to make a blackbird?"

"I thought Blackbird was the band?" Michael said, setting a Guinness in front of a balding man near the end of the bar.

"The blackbird is an old house specialty," Seamus told him. "Coffee, two parts Irish cream and one part Irish whiskey. A dollop of whipped cream on top. Haven't had an order for one in a long time."

"I know the drink," Dan said. "I'll get it."

"Who asked for it?"

"Some guy over there," Colleen said, pointing vaguely to the back of the room.

"I'll make it and take it to him," Dan said.

"Just make it for me, I'll take it to him," Colleen said, rolling her eyes slightly. "We don't want Dad thinking he's got to get behind the bar again himself, not when he and Seamus are having such a good time."

Dan made the drink. Though the bar became more crowded and people were standing behind the stools calling out orders, he watched as Colleen delivered it.

As he had suspected, it went to the man in the navy sweater at the table in the corner.

The pub was a zoo. Well, it was Saturday night preceding the week when Saint Patrick's Day would fall. As she entered the bar area, Moira was glad that she had come down. Her father was a good businessman; he had planned for the crowd. But it was very busy.

She was surprised to see Michael behind the bar with Danny. He looked a little frazzled, but he was gamely pouring beer and mixing drinks. She slipped up behind him.

"You all right?"

"Fine, I think. Working hard at it, anyway." He dropped his voice, whispering, "Trying to earn points, you know. Think I can make it into the family circle?"

She laughed, delighted that he was trying so hard. "You have the right background. Good last name. I think you'll make it just fine. You're doing an exceptional job. But I had thought you might want to slip away tonight."

"Moira, if you'd suggested that earlier, we might have had a chance."

He was watching her with a rueful grin, and she knew he was right. She could never leave when the place was roaring along full tilt, as it was now, and every hand was needed. She slipped her arms around him. "You're incredible."

"Don't press so tightly. I'm suffering the agony of the damned as it is."

"I can slip out later, you know." She sighed. "Much later, of course."

"Now that's an enticing possibility."

"You know I mean it, Michael. You're really wonderful."

"In more ways than one, if you recall."

"Vaguely," she teased. "I'd love to have my memory refreshed."

"We'll see," Michael said, his lips curved in a smile. "Will you really sneak out of Dad's house?"

"Hey!" Chrissie called. "Is anybody back there actually working?"

"Sorry, Chrissie," Moira said quickly. She strode to the service area.

"I need a Gibson, extra onions, two Guinness drafts, a Murphy's, two white wines and a burgundy."

"Got it," Moira said.

"Know what? You're better at this than I am, but I *can* write down orders," Michael said. He cast a glance along the bar. "I'll leave you with good old Danny boy there and work the floor with the others."

She nodded. It was true; she could make the drinks a lot faster than he could.

Moira took over the service area and was surprised when she heard Danny whispering in her ear a few minutes later.

"He's racking up some points tonight, eh?"

She turned halfway around while still keeping her attention on the drinks she was pouring.

"What are you talking about?"

"Tall, dark and handsome. Old beady eyes. He's worming his way in."

"He's helping out. And even if he *is* doing it all to make my father like him, I appreciate the effort."

"Beady eyes, Moira."

"Danny, I hear someone calling you."

"Am I too close? Is that it? Is the memory of what's really good shooting through your bloodstream? Is your pulse pounding? Let me answer for you. You're feeling the heat. You're watching my hands on the taps and remembering just how good they felt on your flesh."

"Oh, yeah, heat, Danny. I'm under a friggin' blowtorch." She leaned closer to him. "Know what I'm really thinking?"

"That I'm to die for?"

"I'm thinking you're delusional," she told him.

He grinned. "Maybe, love. Maybe I'm the one with the memories, recalling just how good it feels to have my hands on you. We were good together, eh?"

"That was then, this is now," she said simply. "Chrissie!" she shouted over the heads of the customers packing the bar. "Was that martini up or on the rocks?"

"Rocks!" Chrissie called.

"I do love you, Moira Kelly," Danny said softly.

His whisper seemed to touch the back of her neck. Like the stroke of a finger. Suddenly she was filled with memories. She found herself staring at his hands on the taps. A hot flush rushed over her, and she found herself thinking she was a terrible person. But it was true. He *was* good in bed.

So was Michael. She had been in love with Danny once. Maybe half her lifetime. She'd waited for years for something else. Something real. Michael. She wasn't a fool. She was mature enough to have learned that what felt good wasn't always right.

And still…

Danny's eyes. The curl of his lips, his humor. The way he could laugh with her or at himself. The way he could slip an arm around her, hold her, give warmth and a sense of understanding at just the right moment. And then suddenly turn sensual, purely sexual in a way that left her gasping…

"Seamus needs another draft," she said, to distract herself from her dangerous thoughts.

"Seamus has had too many."

"Patrick is back. I see him over there. He'll walk old Seamus home—he's just a few blocks away. Give him another draft. He's having fun with Dad."

"I think *you* should have a beer."

"Maybe I will."

"Maybe I can get you to have enough of them."

"Enough of them for what? For you to get me back in bed? Are you bored to tears or something this trip, Danny? Have I become a challenge because Michael is here? Because I really care for someone else after all these years?"

"Because I really love you."

"Danny, you don't know the meaning of the word."

"I've always known it, Moira."

"Moira, do we have Fosters?" Colleen called.

"Only on tap."

"That's fine. I need one Fosters, two Buds and a Coors in the bottle with lemon instead of lime."

"Danny, get me the Coors," she said. He was too close. She had always liked his aftershave. The scent was subtle, and…

And it filled her with memories.

Maybe she *would* have that beer. No, maybe she would have a straight shot of whiskey and slap herself in the face.

As she made the drinks for Chrissie, Moira heard the phone ringing. "I'll get it," she told Danny as he set the Coors on the serving tray.

"I've got it," he told her.

She heard him answer the phone with the single word *Kelly's.*

"Moira, I need two more Buds!" Colleen called. "In the bottle."

As Moira walked to the cooler, she heard Danny talking. His voice had dropped very low.

She tried to make out the words but couldn't hear him.

Then she realized that she *was* hearing him; she simply wasn't understanding him. He was speaking in Gaelic.

His voice was very low, but tense.

He caught her watching him and grinned, shrugging. But it wasn't Danny's usual grin. A moment later, he hung up.

"Who was that?" she asked.

"Oh, just some old-timer. Wanted to know if it was a real Irish pub. I thought I'd convince him that it was."

She didn't speak Gaelic. Oh, she knew a few words here and there, but she had never really learned the language. She had taken both French and Spanish in school. Far more useful in the United States.

She decided to lie. "You know, I've been taking some Gaelic, Danny," she told him.

She wondered why he hadn't decided to be an actor. She was certain that he tensed, but he wasn't going to allow her to see whatever it was that really bothered him. Or else he was calling her bluff.

"It's about time, Moira Kelly," he said. "It's calming down in here. I'm going to leave the bar to you," he told her, walking toward the exit.

But he paused and came back and took her suddenly by the shoulders, no hint of amusement in his eyes as they met hers.

"If that's the truth, Moira, don't go letting anyone know, do you hear me?"

"Danny—"

"Listen to me for once in your life, Moira. Don't let anyone know that you understand a single word."

"Danny, what—"

"I mean it, Moira."

His fingers were hurting her, they bit into her shoulders so deeply. There was something so serious about his face that she felt a strange whisper of fear seep into her.

"Danny—"

"Please, Moira, for the love of God."

She suddenly realized she had really never known this man.

She found herself nodding. "All right. Damn it, Danny, stop it, you're hurting me."

"Sorry." His hold eased. "Moira, you've got to be careful."

"Of what?"

"People who are too passionate."

"And what the hell does that mean? You, Michael, old Seamus there?"

"Anyone and everyone. Do you understand me?"

"No, I don't."

"Moira, leave it alone. Just leave it alone."

She suddenly realized that Michael was watching her from the floor. She wanted to get Danny away from her.

"Leave 'it' alone? What 'it'? Leave *me* alone." She tried to back away.

"Moira—"

"I don't really speak or understand Gaelic, Danny.

I know nothing more than good morning, good night, please, thank you and Erin go bragh."

"Then don't pretend you do."

He turned and left the bar area. She stared at him as he went out on the floor. Chrissie asked her for something, and she responded mechanically.

Michael came up to the service area. "Are you all right?" he asked.

"Of course."

"That looked like a very intense moment."

"Disagreement over drink recipes," she lied.

"You look…frazzled."

"It's a really busy night."

"I know. I'm worn out, too."

"I'll make this all up to you."

"I'll hold you to that."

"What's your room number?"

He smiled and gave it to her, then added, "Oh, I need three draft beers."

"What kind?"

"Buds. And I need another one of those bird things."

"A blackbird?"

"Yeah, that's it."

She laughed and made the drinks. She watched him as he delivered the beers, then took the blackbird to the man at the corner table who had been sitting alone for several hours, listening to the band, nursing his drink.

Michael wasn't as bad at this as he seemed to think he was. He had talked with the threesome who'd ordered the beers, and he paused long enough to exchange words with the fellow in the navy sweater. Someone called her name at the bar, and she gave her attention to the taps.

When she looked up, she saw Danny walking across the room. She realized that he was approaching the man in the corner. The man in the navy sweater, the one who had ordered the blackbird.

A few moments later, Danny got his coat from the hook by the bar and left the pub.

Not five minutes went by before the man in the navy sweater did the same.

She wondered if the man was known to anyone in the pub. She decided to ask her brother if he knew the fellow.

But looking around, she realized that she didn't see Patrick anywhere.

Nor, for that matter, did Michael seem to be anywhere on the floor, either. In fact, in a few minutes' time, it seemed that the bar had half emptied; people who had been there throughout the evening had all seemed to vanish into thin air.

"Damn them all," she murmured to herself. She couldn't even see her father anywhere.

A feeling of deep unease settled over her. It was Danny again, damn it. His ridiculous temper after she had lied to him about the Gaelic.

Tomorrow, she decided, she would have it out with him.

"Moira, one more Guinness for me old bones," Seamus said to her. He was sitting alone. She finally saw her father, who had gone to speak with Jeff by the bandstand.

She poured the drink and brought it to Seamus, then set it down with a disapproving frown. "That's the last, now, Seamus."

He nodded. "As you wish, Moira." She started to walk away. "Moira Kelly," he called, stopping her. She turned back.

"Moira, be a good girl, eh? See how quiet it's become? Ominous," Seamus muttered. "Watch the streets of Boston these days."

"Seamus, what are you on about?"

"That girl was found dead."

She sighed, then walked to him, leaned across the bar and kissed the top of his head. "I promise not to go out soliciting, Seamus. I especially promise not to solicit using the Gaelic language. How's that?"

"Stay close to home," he told her seriously.

"Seamus…"

"There are always troubles," he said softly.

They'd all gone daft, she thought.

She poured herself the shot of whiskey she'd been debating about ever since her conversation with Danny and downed it in one neat swallow.

It was so hot—it indeed burned like a blowtorch.

Coming home was never easy, she decided.

"Watch out for strangers," Seamus said. "Don't go talking to any."

"Seamus, this is a public establishment. We serve strangers all the time."

"And friends, even," Seamus said sorrowfully. "Sometimes friends…can be stranger than…strangers."

"Seamus, you are definitely cut off."

"I am not drunk, Moira Kelly," he said defensively.

"Then you're talking like a madman."

Seamus leaned forward, very close. "There are whispers, Moira."

"About what, Seamus?"

He sat back, shaking his head and looking around uneasily. As if he had said too much. "You take care, girl," he said again. Then he stood up, leaving his drink half finished. "Night, lass."

"Seamus, wait, I'll get someone to walk you home."

"Walk me home? Moira, I'm sober, I swear it, and

I've been walking meself home from this pub more years than you've been alive."

"Seamus, you're not drunk, but you *have* had a few. I wouldn't let you drive tonight, and I'm not so sure you should be walking."

He lifted a hand in farewell.

"Seamus!"

But Seamus was already across the room on his way toward the door. She couldn't help but be worried about him. "Chrissie!" she called. "Can you take the bar, please?"

She didn't wait for an answer but slipped out and hurried after old Seamus. He had made it to the door already. Moira didn't have a coat handy, but she followed him anyway.

Once outside, she was amazed to see that he had already disappeared. The streets were deserted and cold. Very cold. The chill bit into her.

The night was dark, clouds covering the moon. Beyond the spill of lights from the pub, the street was cast in shadows.

"Seamus?" she called anxiously.

She started down the street, knowing the path Seamus would take to reach his home. Down the block, she turned to the left, stepping into the shadows.

The cold wrapped around her.

As she walked, she cursed herself for the idiocy of leaving without a coat. Then she cursed herself for running out in the darkness at this hour of the night. The sidewalks were slick with a thin sheen of ice. And yet...

It was more than just the dark, icy grip of the Boston winter night that held her, she realized. The chill was inside and out. She had walked these neighborhood streets for most of her life, and the family knew their neighbors. She knew the cold, and she even knew the shadows. She had never felt this kind of unease before, never felt as if the chill were inside her, something that would never go away.

She turned the corner to the left. Ahead, the eaves of an old building cast a spill of total Stygian blackness over the sidewalk. Moira moved against the building, instinctively afraid, seeking the protection of darkness.

She was almost upon the two figures before she realized they were there. And she couldn't help but hear the exchange of low murmurs. Whispers, the words just barely audible in the stillness of the night.

"So it's definite. Let the blackbird fly."

"Which piece?"

"You'll receive it."

There was a sudden silence; it seemed to stretch forever, but it was probably no more than the beat of a second. She had stopped walking without realizing it.

Blackbird...

It was as if a giant blackbird had suddenly erupted from the shadow, wings sweeping over the street, brushing her. It was as if the wind picked her up, spinning her around. She found herself moving, catapulted forward. Her feet found no grip on the ice. She went sliding, desperately trying to catch her balance, terrified of the dark presence that suddenly menaced her from behind, darkness rising with a stealthy force. Something struck her hard. She found herself falling to the ground, the shadows rising all around her, the stars glimmering in a sky that had been nothing but cloud and darkness before.

8

When she tried to get up, Moira slid again. She was staring at the sky when a face appeared in the cloud-covered night.

"Moira Kelly! What on earth are you doing out here like this?"

Danny. He reached down, catching her hands. He didn't pull her straight up but hunkered at her side first, studying her eyes. "Whoa, now. Did you hurt yourself?"

"I don't think so."

"You're all right? Nasty spill on the ice? Where's your coat, girl? It's freezing out here."

"I'm well aware that it's freezing, thank you."

"What are you doing out here?"

"It's freezing, Danny. Stop asking questions and help me up."

"Good shoes for the ice," he observed. "You're sure you're not really hurt? So what was it? Lovers' quarrel? Were you racing after that beady-eyed Michael?"

"No," she said indignantly. "Michael and I don't quarrel, and I don't think anything is really hurt. I was—"

She broke off suddenly as he helped her up. *Pushed.* She'd been about to say that she'd been pushed. Instinct kept her from speaking the truth. There was no one out here except Danny. The man who'd been warning her not to let people think that she spoke or understood Gaelic.

Had he pushed her from the shadows, then turned around to help her?

"You were what?" he asked her, eyeing her closely.

"Nothing, I was… I was concerned about Seamus. He'd been drinking quite a bit. I came out after him, and I fell."

As she spoke, Danny took his coat off, draping it around her. The warmth felt awfully good. She also realized, as she began to thaw a bit, that she was sore from head to toe. "What are *you* doing out here?" she asked him.

"Saying good-night to a few old chums."

"Where is my brother? Were you with him?"

"Haven't seen Patrick in a bit," he told her. He arched a brow. "Are we all supposed to report in to you these days?"

"I couldn't find anyone to walk Seamus home, that's all," she lied. She wondered why she didn't tell Danny the truth. That she'd come outside, overheard two men talking about a flying blackbird and been pushed to the ground.

The reason was obvious. She was alone on the street with Danny. As much as she hated to think it, he might have been the one who had pushed her.

"Let's get in," she said. "It's freezing out here."

He nodded, taking her arm as they turned toward the pub.

"Did you see someone out here?" he asked.

"No."

"Why are you lying to me?"

"I'm not." She wasn't. She hadn't actually seen anyone. Just shadows. Figures in the dark.

She was looking straight ahead, but she could tell that he was watching her suspiciously.

"Fine, then."

A statement that he didn't believe her. She was suddenly very anxious to get into the pub.

Danny obliged, moving quickly. She nearly went sliding again. He caught her instantly, keeping her from going down. As they neared the door, she increased her speed.

She felt herself slide on the ice the moment she hit it. This time, not even Danny's hold could keep her from falling. He tried so hard, though, that even as she flailed in what seemed like slow motion, he lost his footing, as well. He managed to get beneath her as they went down. She wound up sprawled on top of him, staring into his amber eyes. For a moment they just lay there, winded, staring at one another. Then Danny smoothed a stray hair from her forehead.

"Hey, this isn't bad," he told her.

She immediately struggled to rise, slipped, then slammed hard against him once again. The breath was knocked out of him, but he laughed.

"Quit laughing!"

"Hey, I'm the injured party here. Throw your flesh and bones down to be chivalrous, and what do you get? A knee in the groin."

"I did not jab my knee into your groin."

"Not on purpose. I don't think."

She let out a sound of total aggravation, rolling off him. Danny was already up, offering her a hand. She took it. Looking at the door to the pub, she saw that Colleen was standing there, laughing, as well. "If you children are through playing in the snow, it's much warmer inside."

Danny's coat was lying on the ice. She bent to retrieve it, but he had already picked up the garment. "Inside, yes. I guess that would be good. Although, I was rather enjoying myself," he said with a grin.

Moira went through the door. Danny entered behind her, his arm around Colleen. "And what were you doing, venturing out in the ice and snow?"

"It's not snowing."

"Figure of speech."

"I was wondering how the entire pub suddenly seemed to disappear," Colleen said lightly. "Even the band has quit for the night, and Jeff took off somewhere. Oh, Moira?"

"Yes?"

"Michael was in a moment ago, looking for you. He said to tell you he was heading back to the hotel."

"Thanks."

She'd practically promised to slip out to join him at the hotel, and she knew she should keep that promise. Except that she was tired and sore, and afraid that she would give away the fact that people at her father's pub were all behaving very strangely. Especially her brother.

And Danny.

Moira saw that Chrissie was behind the bar, picking up glasses, breaking down. Moira took a tray from the bar and went on the floor, where she started clearing tables. Behind her, Colleen and Danny did the same.

"Moira Kathleen!" her father suddenly exclaimed.

She nearly dropped her tray full of glasses. "What?"

"What happened to you?"

"Nothing. Why?"

"You're bleeding, girl!"

She looked down to discover that her stockings had torn and a thin trickle of blood was seeping from her knee down her shinbone.

"Just a meeting with the sidewalk, Dad. I tripped outside," she said. "Danny helped me up."

"You need to take care of that right away."

"I'll go upstairs," Moira said.

"There's a first-aid kit right in the office," Eamon said.

"I can just go up—"

"Not on your life," Danny said. "You might need stitches. We'll have to take a look at that."

He was by her side in a moment, golden mischief in his eyes.

"Danny, I skinned my knee."

"Ah, but you're *the* Moira Kelly. Can't have scraped knees showing on camera. Let's take care of it right away."

He ushered her around the bar toward the back.

"First-aid kit is in the—" Eamon began.

"Top drawer," Danny finished.

A minute later, Moira found herself seated at the desk, with Danny on his knees before her, digging in the drawer.

"What are you doing?" she asked him.

"Taking every lecherous opportunity I can to get closer."

She started to rise, but he already had her shoe off. She gave up.

"Let's get those stockings off, as well," he said.

"They aren't stockings. They're panty hose."

"All the better."

"Danny…"

"You've got to be careful, Moira. You can't go running out of the pub after people."

There was no lightness to his tone. Nor was there a teasing look in his eyes. He was suddenly dead serious.

"Okay, Danny, I won't go running out of the pub after people anymore," she said. She lowered her head, speaking softly. "If you had been around, I could have asked you to go after Seamus."

"That's right. But Seamus is a grown man."

"Seamus was acting very strange tonight."

"Oh? What did he say?"

"I don't remember," she lied. "He was just speaking…strangely."

"Was he afraid?"

"Should he have been?"

"I'm just trying to figure out why you went running after him. Moira, take off the panty hose. I'll close my eyes. Promise. Not that…"

"Danny, I'll just go up and take care of my own injuries."

"You're that afraid of me touching your leg?"

"I'm not at all afraid of you touching my leg. So apparently what I'm supposed to do now is prove it by slipping out of my panty hose?"

"Well, yeah," he said, offering a rueful grin.

She was suddenly tempted to reach out and touch his hair. Always a bit unruly and unkempt, it fit him. Like the half smile he so frequently wore.

"You're trying to ruin my life," she told him.

"Never."

"I have a great job and a wonderful relationship."

"He has beady eyes."

"He's a bona fide decent man."

"I disagree. Besides, is that what you want to settle for? Decent?"

"You told me I should have married Josh."

"I didn't mean it."

She rose suddenly and stepped behind the desk to shimmy out of her panty hose. Then she sat in the chair. His fingers were gentle as he studied the gash on her knee. "And you didn't even feel this?"

"I felt like an icicle from head to toe, how was I going to feel anything else? And what is that you're about to put on me? Don't you dare—"

"Peroxide. It won't hurt."

It didn't. The peroxide bubbled and nothing more. He wiped at the wound with a square of cotton. She watched his hands and his lowered head. Great hands. Danny always had great hands. Long fingers, clipped nails.

Strong hands. He had always been able to open the most stubborn jar known to man.

"And what's that?" she demanded cautiously.

"Neosporin. It won't hurt you, and since when do you act like such a big baby?"

"Since I'm so tired and aggravated. What were you doing outside?"

"I told you, I was saying goodbye to some friends. My turn—what were you really doing out there?"

"Running after Seamus. Danny, damn it, what's going on around here?"

"Nothing, most certainly nothing." He placed a Band-Aid on her knee. "Not if I have any say in it," he murmured.

She caught his chin, lifting his eyes to hers. "What are you going on about?"

"Nothing, Moira. All I'm saying is that I'd die before I'd let anything happen to anyone in your family."

"Why should anything happen to anyone in my family?"

He let out an aggravated sigh. "I was just speaking hypothetically, Moira, all right?"

She stood abruptly. He wasn't going to say anything more to her. "I'm going up to bed. Thanks for the first aid."

"Hey!"

She started and looked toward the doorway to the bar. Patrick was standing there, staring at her and Danny, who remained on the floor as she stood.

"It's getting to her head, eh, the television thing? She's got you on your knees before her," Patrick observed.

"He was giving me first aid," Moira said.

"I've heard she likes her men on their knees," Danny quipped in return.

"Careful there, I'm her older brother, remember?"

"And where have you been?" she demanded.

Patrick arched a brow. "The guy from that charity thing was here tonight. I was just walking down the street with him, pointing out how close his hotel was to the pub. Why? You know, I have a wife now, to give me a third degree. What's the matter?"

"I wanted somebody to walk Seamus home."

"He lives a few blocks away."

"He'd had a few too many," she said.

"I was gone, you were gone—even her precious Michael was nowhere to be found," Danny said. "And then, poor lass, trying to be an escort herself, she went sliding right across the ice."

"Where was precious Michael?" Patrick asked.

"Precious Michael—" she began, then sighed with aggravation. "Michael doesn't work here."

"Neither do I."

"It's our pub."

"Right. I'll try not to let you down next time. Good thing you didn't skin your ass, huh, Moira?" Patrick said.

"Cute, big brother, real cute."

"That could have been interesting," Danny murmured.

"Go to hell, both of you," she said sweetly.

She turned and went upstairs.

She could feel Danny watching her as she went.

It was late night. Very late.

Or early morning, depending on one's point of view.

At that time of night—or morning—he went by a different name. He had identification to match many names.

The art of subterfuge, of course, was always to hide in plain sight. The eyes didn't always believe what they saw because the mind went by what it was told. Glasses could change a man, a change of hairstyle or color, facial hair, no facial hair. For the most part, people went along their day-by-day routines noting very little.

He had always felt sorry for the kids he knew as faces on milk cartons. Few people, pouring a drop into their coffee or drowning their cereal, ever looked twice at those little faces. And that was how they were in life, too.

It worked well for him.

He should have been keeping a low profile. They were in the waiting period now. Nothing to do but wait and see how events progressed.

Wait...

Days were easy enough. Nights were hard.

Restlessly, he walked the streets. He picked a different bar for a nightcap. A place in a not-so-great section of town where the hours went by unnoticed and the drinks were watered but cheap. He'd really had no plans other than a drink, but there was something about the girl at the end of the bar. She had long hair, thick, with a reddish tinge.

Dye.

No matter. The bar was dark and dingy.

Her skirt was very short; her stockings had a snag. Her boots, displayed nicely by legs wound around her bar stool, were stilettos. *Sweet love, you should just wear a sign around your neck that says prostitute,* he thought with some amusement. But there was a forlorn quality about her face. From a distance, she was even pretty. A little girl lost, gone the wrong way. And now here she was in this life, no way out…

She looked up and noticed him watching her. He offered a smile. "Hi."

She smiled back, perking up, surveying the cut of his clothing. He had dressed down for tonight. Still, for this place, he was well attired.

"Can I buy you a drink?" he asked.

Her smile broadened, and she slid off her stool, hurrying to take the one next to his. "Lovely," she said. He frowned, noting an accent in the one word. "I'm Cary. How do you do, and thank you very much. And you are…?"

"Richard. Richard Jordan," he lied.

"English?" she said with a frown, trying to place his accent. "I should really know, I suppose."

"Australian," he said. "But I've been around."

"It's a glorious accent, really."

"And yours."

She made a face. "I can't seem to leave County Cork behind."

"And do you want to?"

"Oh, yes. Things back home are so fucked up."

"It's a beautiful place."

"Not if you had me mum and da," she told him. "Him going off all the time, fighting a silly war, cheatin' on her. Her taken' in boarders. That's what she called her men. When I told her that no matter what I did, I'd call a spade a spade, she hit me and threw me out of the house. I don't give a damn about the old country, except that…" She paused, looking at him ruefully. "Sorry, this isn't what you expected. I'm a little tired. There are masses of Americans in town who think they're Irish. So many assholes!"

"Ah, I see," he murmured.

"Cold?" she asked him.

"Eh?"

"You have gloves on—inside."

"Um. It's a bit chilly."

"I can warm you up, you know," she told him. Then shrugged. "I told you, I call a spade a spade myself. I was about all in. Too many assholes. But you're…different. I mean, I'm not offering a freebie or anything, I am a working girl. But with you… I'd throw in a few extras at no charge."

There was that look about her. Innocence turned to dime trash. Optimism ground down by weariness. She had attracted him, angered him and aroused him. She was trash. Gutter trash.

But he was restless. In a mood to roll in the dirt.

"Fine. Get your coat while I pay for the drinks."

On Sunday morning, the first and foremost event in the Kelly household was church. Moira, on the phone with Michael, told him he certainly wasn't obliged to go.

"I wouldn't miss it," he assured her. "I'm very carefully working my way into your father's heart, you know."

"Well, I admit, an appearance at Mass always sits well with him."

"What happened to you last night?" he asked her. "Did the Sunday thing kick in after midnight?"

"What happened to me? Where did you go? You left without saying goodbye."

She heard a soft sigh. "I'm embarrassed to tell you."

"Tell me anyway."

"I forgot to collect a check. The people walked out. My indignation kicked in, and I went out after them."

"People walked out on a check? At my dad's place?"

"I must be a very bad waiter."

"No, you're a wonderful waiter, I'm sure. Most of the people who come in are regulars, but it is a public establishment. You simply lucked out and got the bad eggs."

"Ah, there you go. Loyal to the core. No wonder I love you."

"I love you, too."

"Anyway, I never found the people, so I slipped back in and paid the check myself so I wouldn't have to tell anyone. Then I looked for you, to say goodbye, but you weren't around, so I went back to the hotel. I waited up, though."

"I'm sorry. Things happened, and I…"

"This family bit isn't easy, is it?"

"Michael, truly…"

"Hey, I understand. Saint Patrick's Day will come. And go. I'll meet you at the church."

"You can come here—"

"You've got enough people there to keep track of. I'll go with Josh and his wife and the twins. We'll meet you there."

There was definitely confusion, getting out of the Kelly household. In a thousand years, Moira knew, she would never be the kind of mother Katy Kelly managed to be. Despite the confusion, breakfast had to be served early enough to make sure all food would be consumed an hour before communion. Siobhan got the girls into the tub, sending Patrick to pound on Moira's bathroom door, telling her that he had to take a shower, too.

"Hey, I just got in here!" she shouted at her brother.

"Just wash all body parts once—soaking is only necessary for laundry."

"Oh, yeah? Like you know anything about laundry."

"Moira, how dirty can you be?"

"Go shout at Colleen to get out of her bathroom."

"I think she fell asleep in there. And aren't you supposed to be helping Mum or something?"

"You can help Mum, too, you chauvinist."

"I'm not a chauvinist. I give credit where credit is due. You're a wiz with toast, Moira Kelly, that you are."

"Go use Mum's and Dad's bathroom."

"Brian is in there. He's a big lad now, you know. He doesn't hop into the tub with the girls."

"Then next time you can drag your butt out of bed faster than your kids, Patrick."

"You could have been done by now, little sister, if you weren't so intent on fighting with me."

"Quit tormenting me. Go downstairs and kick Danny out of the guest bathroom."

"How rude. You want me to torment a guest?"

"Danny's no guest."

"Besides, he's a guy, and he probably took a normal shower."

Her brother disappeared, much to her delight. When she emerged, she discovered that Siobhan had finished with her shower and the kids' bath; the girls were outfitted beautifully in velvet dresses. They were at the table, helping their grandmother by smothering toast with enough butter for a dozen batches of cookies. "Whoa there, let me give you a hand," Moira suggested, sitting with the girls.

"Thanks," Siobhan said softly. She was in the process of flipping bacon. When her sister-in-law turned, Moira saw that she seemed even paler than she had the day before. Circles rimmed her beautiful eyes.

"Just a bit, that's all we need," Moira told Shannon.

"I have it right, Auntie Mo," Shannon said gravely. "It's Molly. She likes to eat butter just plain, you know."

"Well, Molly, today we're going to have a little toast with our butter," Moira said. Her niece giggled and looked at her adoringly. She patted the little head of angel soft hair. "Today we're going to be really good, okay? I have a special treat in store for you later. Your mum looks a little tired, so be really, really good for me, okay?"

Molly nodded gravely. "Toast with the butter."

"Right." Moira walked to Siobhan at the stove. "Are you all right?"

"Of course," Siobhan said, too quickly.

"You need a break. You and Patrick need to get out without the kids."

"Patrick is always out without the kids. Our kids, at any rate," she murmured. She quickly flashed a glance Moira's way. "You know, he's busy."

"So are you."

"A different busy, I guess. He's the breadwinner and all that. I'm not being disloyal. I love your brother."

"So do I, but that doesn't mean he might not need a good kick in the butt. I needed him last night, and he was nowhere to be found."

"Oh, really?" Siobhan murmured, staring at the bacon she flipped. "What was wrong?"

"I thought Seamus needed someone to walk him home. Naturally I couldn't find any of the guys."

"Men!" Colleen announced, sweeping into the kitchen and making the announcement as if she'd been in on the entire conversation. "That's the way it goes." She looked around to see if her mother was anywhere in the vicinity. "They're like leeches when they want something, especially sex. Need them, and only the good Lord knows where they've gotten to."

"Now, darlin', that's not true a'tall," Danny said, making an appearance from the den. He had apparently been upstairs for some time, Moira thought, and wondered why that made her uneasy. "I'm here, right here. And I can cook. Siobhan Kelly, you take a seat. I'll finish this up."

"Where's Mum?" Moira asked as Danny ushered Siobhan into a chair.

"Finally taking a shower," Danny said. "Colleen, me fine beauty, take a seat."

"Thanks, I'll sit and watch you, too—closely," Moira said.

"Ach, there she goes, the star in motion. Moira, take care of the bacon there while I whip up the eggs."

She had a fork in her hands before she knew it, and Danny got busy with the eggs. Colleen didn't sit; she started bringing out juice, coffee and tea.

Moira flipped the bacon onto a plate covered with paper towels to absorb the grease, watching Danny. He could cook, and he was efficient. He looked damned good in the jacket and trousers he had donned for church, and he was freshly shaven, his scent far too appealing.

"Where's lover boy?" he asked.

"Meeting us at church."

"Ah, he's a good Catholic boy, is he? Or is he just making more Brownie points with your father?"

"Naturally he's a good Catholic boy," she said

sweetly. "And of course you know, if we're married, being the daughter I am, we'll be married in the family church in Boston, so it's good that he gets to attend a mass there now."

"If," Danny said.

"What?"

"You didn't say when, you said if. There must be some doubt in your mind."

"Not a lick," she told him sweetly.

"Oh, thank the Lord. It's all under control," Katy said, sweeping in from the hallway. "Danny, you are a doll."

"Danny? Siobhan was doing it all," Moira said.

"No, actually, Danny was in here before. He just had to make a phone call," Siobhan said.

"A phone call? In the middle of making bacon? How important it must have been," Moira muttered.

"All my phone calls are important," Danny informed her. "Eggs are on, and the oatmeal for Eamon is just about right. Katy Kelly, you have a seat. I'll serve."

Eamon came out from the long hallway, wishing everyone a good morning. Molly ran over to him with a piece of toast. "Granda! I made it just for you."

"Oh, Molly dear, Granda can't have that toast. He'll be in the hospital with a coronary for sure," Katy protested.

"Katy, I'll not really eat it," Eamon assured his wife. "Molly Kelly, you bring me that toast. It will be extra special delicious."

Patrick arrived from downstairs, Granny Jon walked in, and the family sat. Eamon said grace, but before the amen he paused and looked around the table. "Thank you, Lord, for letting me have me family all here. Thank you for this squabbling tribe of ruffians who still do their old dad proud by coming home for Saint

Patrick's Day, and thank you, too, for old friends who are like kin, and giving us Danny here for this happy occasion, as well."

"Amen to that, and let's eat," Patrick said.

"Patrick, your father was praying," Katy moaned.

"Aye, and bless the Irish, and let's eat!" Patrick said.

"I wasn't quite finished," Eamon said sternly. "I was about to bless the Lord for gracing me with a daughter-in-law like Siobhan, beautiful inside and out, a lady who has given me three of the greatest gifts a man could ever hope for, Brian, Shannon and Molly, who helps to make the world's most incredible toast."

"Here, here," Moira said, staring at her brother. "To Siobhan—and the kids, of course."

Molly giggled. Granny Jon glanced at the old silver watch pendant she always wore. "To Siobhan. And Patrick's right—let's eat. We'll be closing in on communion if we're not careful."

"The very last toast," Danny announced, lifting his coffee cup. "To Eamon Kelly, his lovely wife Kathleen, and to the bacon and toast."

"Ah, there we go. Now, let's wolf this down and get going," Patrick said.

"Busy day?" Siobhan asked him sweetly.

He looked at his wife. "Church," he replied, just as sweetly.

"Mass waits for no man," Danny murmured.

Michael, Josh and his family were already at the church. Since it was her family's church, Moira greeted Michael instantly and affectionately but discreetly, despite the fact that she had sat in the back of the family car between Siobhan and Danny on the way to Mass and had been dying to throw herself at Michael the moment she stepped into the cathedral. She was able to be more openly enthusiastic with Gina, Josh's wife, hugging her friend and admiring the twins, who seemed to grow by leaps and bounds every week. She instantly picked up one of the twins to hold during the service. The babies were angelic little boys who already looked like Josh. She held Gregory, the older of the two, who lay in her arms sweetly sleeping.

She sat during the sermon, giving more attention to the warm bundle in her arms than to the priest, until she heard him talking about Saint Patrick's Day and announcing the arrival of Jacob Brolin in the city of Boston and asking his congregation to pray for Brolin and the message of peace he brought not only to Northern Ireland, but to all men in Ireland, all men of Irish descent and all men throughout the world. His sermon was stirring, one that reminded his congregation that more than the arms procured for violence in other places came from American financing, that American businesses and tourists helped bring prosperity and the hope of peace. It was a good sermon, earning a round of applause at the end, despite the final words being, "Let us pray."

The applause woke Gregory, who immediately began to cry. Moira tried to soothe him, only to find the infant being plucked from her arms by Danny, who lifted the boy high in his arms, whispered a few words and immediately—to Moira's annoyance—elicited a coo of soft baby laughter. "I'll take him back," she whispered.

"You'll only get him crying again."

"I will not."

"You're edgy, and he knows it."

"I'm not edgy."

"You reek of hostility. You're even angry that I can manage an infant."

"I am not."

"You're arguing, Moira, during the most holy passages of the Eucharist."

"Damn it, keep the baby."

"Moira Kathleen Kelly! We're in church."

"Darn it, then. Keep the baby. What are you doing next to me, anyway?"

"I slipped past Colleen when I saw that you were in distress."

"I'm not in distress."

"There's your good Michael, on his knees next to you, love. Don't you just feel the urge to kneel down beside him? He's praying. What do you think he's praying for? Peace among the Irish, or for you to make good on a promise and show up in his hotel room in the middle of the night? Or even…for something more sinister?"

"Danny…"

"I know what I'm praying for."

"Peace in the world?"

"Oh, that, too, of course."

"I'm going to hit you in a minute, even if we are in church."

"Your whispers are growing awfully loud."

"*My* whispers?"

"You're supposed to be on your knees, Moira. Bonding with your love. I truly wish I could hear your Michael's prayers."

"You should be on your knees."

"I'm holding a baby, in case you haven't noticed."

Moira ignored him, kneeling beside Michael, taking his hand. He squeezed hers in return. When Moira rose for the Lord's Prayer, she managed to take the baby from Danny, and, after kissing or shaking hands with her family and everyone nearby, she changed her position to Danny's other side.

Outside the church, the Kelly children dutifully

greeted all their parents' old friends, and Moira introduced Michael around.

Danny had enough friends of his own.

Standing with Michael, waiting for her folks to finish the after-Mass coffee, Moira felt the warmth of their close-knit little community within the large city. She closed her eyes for a minute. She loved New York, but she also loved Boston. She even loved the Irish eccentricities of her family and friends. Everyone was so enthused about the arrival of Jacob Brolin. They spoke about him as if they were speaking about the Second Coming.

"He's from Belfast, isn't he?" Michael said.

"What?"

"Your old friend. Danny. He's from Belfast."

"He was born there, yes. I don't know that much about when he was really young. He was brought up by an uncle who traveled a great deal. He was here a lot, and he also spent some time growing up in Dublin, I think."

"I've heard he was a wild man in his youth. IRA?"

"Was Danny actually in the IRA? I don't think so," Moira said, noticing that the man in question was approaching them.

"Well, Michael, how did you survive family day at church?" Danny asked cheerfully.

"It's rather charming," Michael said.

"Yup. Everyone praying for Jacob Brolin."

"He must be quite a man. Moira, you should call him, ask about an interview for the show."

"You're the locations manager, right?" Danny said. "You haven't tried to reach him yourself?"

Michael shrugged, ignoring the suggestion of rebuke in the question.

"I'm not Moira Kelly. I think that kind of request

would be better coming from her. I just handle places, she handles people. Having him on tape. That would be a coup for the show. Right, Moira?"

She was listening to Michael but noting that Seamus was in a group not far from them. "Excuse me, will you? There's Seamus. I have a bone to pick with him."

"We'll say hi, as well," Danny said, following her as she started in Seamus's direction.

The group around Seamus was saying goodbye. Seamus didn't seem to notice. He was too busy staring at the three of them as they approached.

"Seamus, there you are," Moira said. "Why did you run out on me like that last night?"

Seamus wasn't looking at her. He was watching the two men.

"Seamus?"

He suddenly snapped his attention to her. "Ah, Moira, I merely took myself on home."

"You were behaving so strangely."

"I'm Irish, eh? We all talk fairy tales. I'll be seeing you later, Moira Kelly, at the pub. Drinking me ale and nothing more. Ta, now."

He turned and left.

"What on earth is up with him?" Moira murmured, more to herself than to Danny or Michael.

"He's Irish, like he says. You can't go worrying about every one of your father's friends. The old coot is eccentric. Let it go, Moira," Michael said.

She felt Danny's hand on her arm and heard his soft whisper. "For once, lover boy is right. Let it go, Moira. Let it go."

9

"Beady eyes, eh?" Moira whispered to Danny.

He seemed impossible to shake.

They had decided to take their filming to the streets of Boston that afternoon. Moira still wanted a segment on her grandmother telling the old tales, but after a meeting with Jeff and Michael, they had decided that they also needed more general scenes in the Boston area, so she'd decided to combine the two. Michael had already arranged a permit for Quincy Market and the Faneuil Hall area, so they had brought the cast and crew to the historic area where shops designed to meet contemporary tastes now abounded.

Her mother, always concerned that things work out, had arranged for friends to bring their children. Moira had her grandmother seated on a bench, surrounded by a flock of children.

It was an old adage, but true—it was never easy filming animals and children. She hadn't asked for any animals, but the children were all going crazy over every pooch being walked through the area by a pup-loving Bostonian.

Michael was doing the best anyone could expect on critter control, herding children to where they were supposed to be, assuring dog owners that they could be in a crowd shot as long as they were willing to sign releases. As the last-minute camera angles were set up, Michael took control of the children, assuring them that since there were a few monsters in Irish lore, they would be entertained. After getting the last child seated, he left, placing a gentle hand on Molly's head as he went. Moira hadn't been about to keep her nieces and nephew out of this group, and she'd been glad of it, because Patrick and Siobhan had come to watch the taping, and their offspring, together.

"Okay, so he's good with kids and canines," Danny admitted, drawing her line of thought away from her family. "Just remember, Hansel and Gretel thought the witch in the woods was a kind old lady until they were nearly stuffed in the oven."

"Wise, Danny, wise. I'll remember that."

"Your grandmother is holding her own," he pointed out.

It was true. Granny Jon had her crowd spellbound. "The banshee, you see, is a death ghost. She howls and cries in the night when she comes for the souls of those about to depart this world. In America you have hundreds of monsters—so many from the cinema, right? Well, when I was a little girl in Ireland, we had the banshees. We knew the terrible wail they could make and knew when to be afraid. And the older folk used to warn us to behave, because if we didn't, do you know what could happen?"

The kids were all watching her expectantly.

"What?" whispered one young boy, perhaps eight or nine years old.

"The banshees would get you on your way in or out of the outhouse."

"What's an outhouse?" a little girl asked.

"Ah, well, there I go, showing just how old an old

woman I am," Granny Jon said. "Way back when I was
a girl in Dublin, we didn't have a bathroom right in our
house. No charming little place with tile and scented
soaps and the like. Our loos—" She paused and looked
at the kids and laughed. "Sorry, our toilets were in a
little house behind the main house. And sometimes, at
night, when it was very, very dark, and maybe a storm
was coming, and you slipped outside at night, you could
hear the wind howling in the trees. The branches would
sway and cast huge shadows, and in those shadows,
you could see the sad, dark form of the banshee as she
swept down into the night."

"Did she ever get you?" a little boy asked anxiously.

"Well, now, no, of course not, or I'd not be here to
tell the tale."

The kids burst into laughter.

"Please tell me they had the tape running for that,"
Moira murmured.

"You've got it," Danny said, pointing to the cameraman.

"There's another tale involving children," Granny
Jon went on. "There was a great king, and his name was
Lir. He had four children, and he loved them dearly. He
lost his lovely wife and later remarried. But his love for
his children remained the greatest love in his life. His
new wife had magical powers, and she was very jealous of the children. She took them to the lake and cast
a spell upon them, turning them into swans for nine
hundred years. She wasn't really a terrible witch, and
she felt guilty immediately, so she gave the swans the
gift of song. They could sing like nightingales. The
swans became honored all over Ireland. That was in
the ancient days, and during those nine hundred years,
a man named Saint Patrick brought Christianity to Ireland. The nine hundred years ended, and the children

turned into people again, but their years of being swans had weakened them, and they were frail. They were baptized, however, before they passed on, and became children of God. Their father was bereft and ordered that, in their honor, no swan should be killed in Ireland, and to this day there is a law protecting swans in all Ireland."

"Their father was still alive?" a towheaded girl asked, amazed. "He was even older than my daddy!"

"Oh, yes, he was very, very old," Granny Jon said, and winked. "That's why we have stories, though, myths and legends and tales. And in most legends, a little bit is true, a little bit is exaggerated, and some of the story is a downright lie. But Irish stories are like all others, tales we tell to explain what goes on in life, or perhaps stories that are just for fun."

"Like leprechauns?" a boy asked.

"Oh, no," Granny Jon said. "Leprechauns are real. Well, so legend has it."

The taping went wonderfully. Stray children wandered over to join the crowd. Patrick and Siobhan watched delightedly, arm and arm, as they observed their own brood piping up with pieces of information they already knew, becoming stars to the kids around them.

When filming was finished, the Boston crew broke quickly, making arrangements with Michael and Josh for the following day. Granny Jon was tired, eager to go home. Danny immediately volunteered to take her and suggested the kids might want to go, too, telling Patrick and Siobhan not to worry, if Mum was worn out, he would do the baby-sitting. Siobhan gratefully accepted the offer.

Josh suggested that they have supper somewhere in the area.

"Little Italy has some of the best food in the world," Patrick said.

"Not as good as Kelly's Pub, surely," Michael said.

"Sal's family has a place down here, and it's excellent," Moira said. "And Italian will be a wonderful change."

"I won't tell Mum you said that," Patrick told her.

"Mum loves Italian food," Moira said. "But we won't stay late, anyway. This may be Sunday, but that never stopped an Irishman from going to a pub. And we're getting closer and closer to Saint Patrick's Day. I don't want to leave Dad in the lurch."

"Colleen is home," Patrick reminded her.

"Yes, but he may need more help."

"That's true," Patrick said. "We should stick around and help, as much as possible."

"Yes," Siobhan murmured. "You have so many friends and associates coming in these days, after all."

There was an underlying bitterness to her tone, Moira thought, but she was the only one who seemed to hear it.

"We won't be long," Josh said. "But Italian food sounds great right now."

"Josh, you sure as hell don't have to work at the pub," Patrick said. "Why are you worried about time?"

"I can't leave Gina at the hotel all night with the kids alone."

"Call her and tell her to come down," Moira suggested.

"No, she'll have eaten and she'll be getting the twins to sleep. I'll grab something with you, then head on back. It shouldn't take too much time."

"No, it's early for the real dinner crowd. We can walk over. Little Italy is right across the road," Siobhan said.

As they walked, Patrick commented that they never quit with the roadwork in Boston. Siobhan pointed out that they were in the very heart of a city that was trying to accommodate a growing population, so the work was necessary.

"It's a crazy city," Patrick said.

"I love Boston," Moira protested. "It has something for everyone—the old, with buildings dating from the birth of the nation, and the new."

"It has the ethnic—the Irish and the Italians," Siobhan added.

"And everyone else now. A growing Asian population, Hispanic, European, everyone," Moira protested.

"Let's not forget Boston baked beans," Patrick said dryly.

"And if the kids were here, they'd tell you that Boston baked beans make the snobby people fart, and then they can't be so snobby anymore," Siobhan said.

"There you go, a city with everything, culture—and wicked good farting," Patrick said.

He slipped an arm around his wife. As they walked, Moira found that she and Michael were at the rear of the crowd, almost alone. They passed a restaurant where an outside sign advertised Live Maine Lobster, 2 for 19.95.

"Does that mean we'd have to eat them while they were still alive?" Michael queried lightly.

"A grim thought, those claws snapping at you as you munched down," she responded.

"This is nice," Michael said.

"What?"

"Me, you. A distance from the rest of your world. The absence of your old buddy boy, Dan O'Hara."

"Michael, he's a longtime family friend. There's not much I can do about that."

"I'm delighted that he skipped dinner."

"So am I."

His arm around her shoulder, he squeezed her tightly to him. "You know, he was right about one thing."

"What's that?"

"I should have contacted Jacob Brolin's people."

"I'm sure he's being bombarded by the networks and the major cable stations."

"But you have an edge. You're a beautiful woman, and you're Irish."

"I'm an American—and thanks for the compliment."

"First generation, and the compliment is due. I think you definitely have an edge. Maybe…maybe I was afraid to say much more at the time. I feel this macho power struggle thing with your Mr. O'Hara, and I didn't want to admit that I might fall short in any way. But in all honesty, I think you might want to try to make contact yourself. You are an Irish American, a woman, and your father does run one of the most prestigious Irish pubs in the city."

"Hmm."

"What?"

"I don't know. I never thought of the pub as being prestigious. Warm, fun, a great place. My dad is an excellent host. He creates a really great atmosphere. But we're not like a gourmet restaurant or anything."

"I'm willing to bet that if old Jacob Brolin has heard anything about Boston, he'll have heard about Kelly's Pub."

"There are tons of pubs here."

"But your father's is down-home authentic."

"All right, I'll call Brolin. Or call his people—that may be as close as I can get."

"Good for you. I'm convinced you're the best man— sorry, woman—for breaking the ice."

"Maybe you're right." She pointed to a shop along

their way. "You can buy the best cannoli in the world in that store. Sal's aunt owns it. The older generation sits outside, arguing in Italian and playing checkers—when the weather is decent, of course. The Old—"

"—North Church is right down there," Michael finished for her. "Hey, I'm your locations manager. I scout things out."

She laughed, hugging him.

"C'mon, quick kiss. Your brother isn't looking."

"My brother knows all about you."

"You talk about that with your brother?"

"Well, no, but I'm sure he knows the extent of our relationship."

They paused in the street, where he pressed the lightest kiss against her lips. She felt the bulk of his shoulders in arms, the strength in his height as he cradled her to him. She buried her face against his chest. Yes, she was in love with him.

"You know," he murmured.

"What?"

"Watch out for him."

"Who?"

"Your friend. Danny."

She drew back. "Watch out for him. Why?"

He shook his head. "Last night, when I was trying to hunt down the group that stiffed me on the bill, he was outside. In the shadows. Looking very suspicious. The guy *is* from Belfast. He could be a loose cannon. I don't know—maybe I'm just jealous of his position in the bosom of your family. But…for me, be careful. Something about him makes me uneasy. I know he's a good friend and all, and this is just a feeling, but keep your distance a little, huh? Just to humor me?"

He was staring at her, deep blue eyes incredibly serious.

"Hey, are you two coming?" Patrick called.

Moira realized that they were standing in front of Paul Revere's house. The sun was completely gone; the last of the tourists were leaving.

The restaurant was right around the corner.

"Sure," Moira called.

Michael thought that she was agreeing with him, as well, and he smiled. Taking her hand, he hurried toward Patrick, who was waiting impatiently at the corner as if, after all these years, Moira just might forget where Sal's family's restaurant was situated.

"Kids, Granny Jon, I've got one quick stop to make, if you'll allow me. I want to pick up some of those cannoli Katy likes so much," Dan told his passengers. He was driving Eamon Kelly's minivan. The kids were wearing their seat belts; they were well-trained. Even little Molly immediately buckled up the minute she got into a car.

Granny Jon, next to him, nodded. "Pick up a few of those Italian cookies, too, please, Danny. The ones with vanilla, not anise."

"Got ya. Kids?"

"Chocolate!" Shannon said. And with a sigh way older than her years, she added, "You can just buy a stick of butter for Molly."

"Butter cookies," Brian said.

"Chocolate-covered butter cookies." Molly giggled. "Candy."

"No candy. It's an Italian bakery, silly girl," Dan teased.

The first parking space he could squeeze into was about a block from the restaurant. Perfect. He left the car running, the heat on.

"No driving," he warned Brian.

Brian grinned.

"I'll hurry," Dan said.

"We're just fine here. I'll keep the kids amused," Granny Jon said.

Dan nodded, closed the driver's door and started down the street at a brisk walk. He knew the exact shop he wanted and slipped in quickly. He smiled at the dark-haired girl behind the counter. Elena. He'd bought pastries here before.

"A box of cannoli, some sugar cookies…biscotti with vanilla, not anise, and…have you got anything with chocolate?"

"Frosted butter cookies?" Elena suggested.

"Perfect. I'll be making a phone call."

The phone was right inside the doorway. He dropped coins into the slot and dialed the number he needed. A soft female voice answered with a simple hello.

"Liz, it's Dan."

"Where are you?"

"Public phone. Have you got anything for me?"

"Well, I've checked out your man."

"And?"

"Born in Ohio, actually, Irish-American parents. Good schools, good jobs. Film major, degree from UCLA. He's worked as a production assistant, cameraman, sound tech—anything and everything behind the camera. Never acted. He won some film school prizes for production and direction. Left California, worked in Florida, Vancouver and, last year, made the move to New York."

Idly staring out the window, Dan tensed. Patrick and Siobhan Kelly were ambling past the shop. Josh was walking alone, catching up with the two of them. Dan stepped back against the support beam that would allow him to look out but keep passersby from noticing him.

"So he came to New York—and took his first job with Moira Kelly's show?"

"That's what I've got here. And you know I know how to trace people."

"You're sure? There's nothing on him at all? No political activities, no protests against cruelty to animals, nothing? No protests against American military action?"

"Dan, the guy doesn't have his own Web page. I haven't managed to get any warm, fuzzy photos of him with his old teddy bear. But from everything I can find, the guy is clean. I can tell you he has no arrest record, no known political affiliations—his voter's registration even has him as an independent. He's never even been late paying a parking ticket, as far as I can make out."

"He seems suspicious to me anyway. And there's word on the street about something going down."

"Well, if there's anything dirty about him, it's well-hidden, that much I can tell you."

Frustrated, Dan kept looking out the window. The object of his inquiry was walking by, an arm tightly wrapped around Moira's shoulder. *Slime bucket.* Moira was smiling at him, laughing. Oh, yeah, the guy was picture-perfect. Dan narrowed his eyes. Tall, in damned good shape, probably lifted weights, kickboxed and had a black belt in karate.

All the better to be…

Fucking picture-perfect.

And, on paper at least, he was as pure as the driven snow.

"Keep looking," Dan said. The pair had stopped outside the Revere house. They didn't seem to notice the tourists streaming by them.

Together, they were definitely picture-perfect. Moira, absolutely stunning, red-tinged hair streaming down her back as she lifted her classically beautiful face to his ever so tender kiss. McLean, tall, seeming to tower over her in masculine protection, though Moira was tall herself.

"Dan, you there?"

"Keep looking," Dan insisted.

"For what?" Liz asked.

"I don't know. But something isn't right."

"You're obsessed, Dan O'Hara."

"It's my job to be wary."

"It's your job to do a hell of a lot more than that," Liz reminded him.

"Has he ever been to Ireland?"

"Yes—his first semester of college."

"Hmm. There. There's something."

"Oh, yeah, there's something. Something done by countless college kids with money. He toured Ireland, England, Scotland and the Continent. Spent most of his time in Florence and Rome. Dan, I've checked him out with a fine-tooth comb."

"Keep looking," Dan insisted. There they went, down the street, Moira still in his arms.

"Dan—"

"Keep looking."

"Just in case you're interested," Liz said dryly, "Patrick Kelly has gotten pretty deeply involved with a group called Americans for Children."

"It's a legitimate charity, right?"

"It's new, but it appears so. Still, some of the founders are old IRA guys, émigrés to the States. May be Patrick Kelly has his eye on your movements."

"Right."

"Then there's Jeff Dolan."

"Dolan has a rap sheet that would put the toughest

inner-city kid to shame," Dan said impatiently. "But he's burned out."

"He could still be keeping his eyes on you. He could be the one."

"Lizzie, like I said, I'm wary. By nature. *I'm* watching him, and I'm sure he's keeping tabs on me, as well. Have you talked to The Man?"

"Of course. I'm in constant communication."

"And we're still on? For sure?"

"Yes."

"Damn."

"What's the matter? You're supposed to be good."

"Oh, Lizzie," he teased back. "You don't know just how good. It's what's at stake that chills my blood."

"Keep your eyes open. He can't be swayed. And he'll contact you in his own way, in his own time."

"Yeah. And you keep checking on Michael McLean."

"Don't you go letting your heart—or your dick—get in your way," Liz said bluntly.

"You know me, Lizzie," he said lightly. "I never let anything get in my way. Never."

He hung up the phone. Elena had finished his order. He paid her, hurried out of the shop and down to the car.

Dinner was going beautifully—and then Danny arrived.

"Hey, where are my kids?" Siobhan asked, seeing him come in the door. He was not to be missed. The restaurant was small and intimate, as were many of the restaurants in Boston, especially in Little Italy, and he was a big man.

Danny strode over, shedding his wool coat as he did so and hanging it on the rack. Moira hadn't thought to worry that she was at the edge of the semicircular booth, Michael beside her, Siobhan beside him, Patrick next and Josh in the chair drawn up to the free edge of the table.

Bad choice, she realized, as Danny slid in beside her. "The kids? Oh, I dropped them in traffic, naturally."

"Seriously…" Siobhan began.

Patrick let out an impatient snort. "Seriously, he dropped them in traffic."

"Seriously," Danny said, smiling at Siobhan, "your mother was delighted to have some time alone with them. What's good, huh? Everything, right? Hey, I see that Sal is working his own restaurant for a change."

"We're having the house special," Patrick said. "A pasta sampler with ziti, lasagna, spaghetti, and an antipasto."

"I'm not sure what it all is, but it's great," Siobhan added, looking at the large platter filled with Italian delicacies in the middle of the table.

Sal had reached the table, taking Danny's hand, shaking it. "Hey, it's my Italian amico," he said. "Benvenuto."

"Grazie, Salvatore," Danny said. "Hey, this looks wonderful. What is everything?"

"I don't want to tell you, not in front of Siobhan."

"Ah, now, Siobhan managed to eat haggis when Katy made it for that Scottish convention a few years back," Danny said, smiling at Siobhan. He made a face. "Sheep's stomach or bladder or some such filled with entrails. Thank the Lord the Scots came up with it or we Irish would be to blame again."

"Well, there's nothing more evil than octopus on that tray," Sal said, "so I guess the Italians are off the hook for the moment, too."

"I don't know, Sal. You all fool around with squid ink an awful lot," Danny said warily.

"It makes good pasta," Sal said. "Excuse me, I'll add another order of the special special for the table."

Sal left, and Danny helped himself to wine from the bottle already at the table. "So, what did I miss?"

"Earth-shattering events," Moira said sharply.

"A lovely time," Siobhan said. "We've been getting to know Michael. He does great imitations. You know, Michael, you should be in front of the camera. You're not just gorgeous, you're talented."

"Are you now?" Danny said, looking past Moira to Michael.

"He can do your accent to perfection," Siobhan said, and Moira wanted to kick her for the innocent remark. Michael had been great, surprising even her with his mastery of a Boston accent, a Bronx intonation, a deep South drawl and, a moment ago, Danny's light brogue.

"I was a film major," Michael said with a shrug. "I never wanted to be in front of the camera, but…thanks," he told Siobhan. "We had to take speech and dialect classes to get through school."

"I'd love to hear you do me," Danny told Michael.

"Can't do it when I'm put on the spot," Michael said.

"Just do a quick Granny Jon, then," Siobhan urged.

Moira moved closer to Michael, distancing herself from Danny. Michael sighed. "Now I'll mess it all up," he said. "All right. 'I'd like me tea strong enough to pick itself up and walk itself right across the table,'" he mimicked, his brogue heavy, but missing here and there, as it had not been before. "See why I can't be in front of the camera?" he asked Siobhan. "I fold under pressure."

"No, no," Danny said. "That was excellent. Why, I would have believed you were from the Old Country meself."

Michael smiled along with the others, but Moira didn't think he was particularly amused.

"Look, here comes dinner," Patrick said, breaking the tension.

Sal assisted the waiter, serving them all quickly. "Delicious," Danny said, digging in. "And safe—no black pasta on the plate, Siobhan."

"Black pasta?"

"Flavored with squid ink," Sal told her, winking. "It's safe, entirely safe. Unless you've gone vegetarian?"

"No, I'm afraid I still chow down on cows."

"Cows have those big brown eyes," Patrick teased her. "So much better to eat them than some creepy-looking squid."

Siobhan smiled at him and looked at Sal. "Whatever it is, it's wonderful. My husband hasn't left the table once to say a quick hello to a business associate. I think I may just turn in the Irish flag and become Italian, Sal."

Sal took her hand. "Cara mia, you may become Italian anytime."

"Sal, let go of my wife and behave, before your own very Italian wife comes out of the kitchen and hits you with a frying pan."

Sal grinned. "Okay, maybe I'll become a Mormon. How about you, Danny?"

"I'm afraid for some of us, Sal, there's just no way out of being Irish," Danny said. "But thank the Lord, even in Ireland, we have lots of Italian restaurants." He looked at Michael, smiling. "Good imitation there, Mikey. Damn good. You're better than you think."

"Oh, I know what I'm good at," Michael told him.

"And you're damn good at whatever it is, right?" Danny asked.

"Damn good," Michael repeated evenly.

"So am I," Danny told him. "So am I."

Moira felt strangely as if she were the buffer between two boxers spoiling for a confrontation.

And oddly, she didn't feel as if she was the prize in the competition.

Josh turned the conversation to his pleasure at the way the filming had gone that day, approving when Moira told him that she was going to try to get an interview with Jacob Brolin. "Danny actually pushed it a bit, and Michael told me later how right he was," Moira said, hoping to create an atmosphere of peace.

"Well, we can try," Josh said. "And we're fine with the crew. I've booked them through the eighteenth. That way we can cover anything we might want to have for a postshow. We do that sometimes, follow-ups on places or events we've covered," he told the others, then glanced at his watch. "I've got to go. My hopes for a few in-room dirty movies and a night of wild passion dwindle with each passing moment. The twins are a handful. These days it's a late night for Gina when she makes nine o'clock."

"But the twins are worth it, right?" Moira said.

"Yes. And I'm going to remind you of that when you finally decide to procreate. Only I'm going to wish triplets on you. Night, all."

Josh departed. Sal came by, offering coffee. Danny declined, saying he thought he should get back to the bar.

"You said Katy was fine with the kids," Siobhan reminded him.

"But I'm worried about Eamon with the pub. Chrissie called in sick tonight—seems she ate a bad taco for lunch or something," Danny said.

"Then I should get back, too," Moira said.

"Stay, spend your time with Michael and Siobhan and Patrick. A double date with your brother and his wife, eh?" Danny said. "I've still got your father's car, and you all are in Patrick's." He shook his pocket to jingle the keys and left them.

"We should be there," Moira said to Patrick.

"We'll only be a few minutes longer. I would love to have my coffee in peace before we return to the Irish zoo," Patrick said.

"A cappuccino would be heavenly," Siobhan agreed.

"Espresso for me," Michael told Moira, smiling.

She nodded. "Espresso, sure."

The first person she noticed when she walked into the pub that night was the stranger. The man who had been there before, ordering the blackbird.

She wanted to walk straight to him, but the bar was three deep, so she hurried around to help her father, dropping her purse in one of the empty wells.

"Ah, Moira, how was your dinner?" her father called cheerfully.

"Good, Dad. I should have been back here sooner, though."

"Thank you, daughter, but we do survive when you and your brother and sister are off living your own lives—as you should be," he added quickly.

She took the time to give him a quick kiss on the cheek before she started taking orders and filling glasses. She saw that Seamus was at the bar with Liam. As soon as she had a moment to breathe, she walked toward Seamus's stool. "Are you all right?" she asked him.

"Couldn't be better, Moira Kathleen," he assured her. "Now, don't you go staring at me beer mug. I've had one real beer and one of those nonalcoholic things."

"Good for you, Seamus."

"I'll just spend the evening keeping track of meself,

Moira. One and one. Slowly, of course. Don't want you worrying about me. Danny said you took a nasty spill chasing after me."

"I'm fine. Danny shouldn't have said anything."

"Well, he's a good lad. Worried about us both."

She forced a smile for Seamus, then noted that her father was doing just fine at the bar. When Colleen came up with an order for a blackbird, Moira told her sister she would make the drink and deliver it herself. "It's the guy in the corner, right?"

"Yeah, how did you know?"

"Same guy who ordered one the other night."

Moira didn't bother with a tray, since she only had the one drink. She made her way through the tables until she reached the man. Tonight he was in a dark brown sweater. He appeared to be of medium build, perhaps thirty or thirty-five, with brown eyes and neatly trimmed dark hair.

"Hello, welcome to Kelly's. You've been here a few nights now."

"Great band," he told her. He didn't smile, just watched her gravely.

"We hadn't had an order for a blackbird in a while."

"Heard about it from a friend," he said casually. "You're Moira Kelly?"

"Yes."

"I've seen your show." He didn't mention whether he had liked it or not. She was surprised when he said, "Can you sit a minute?"

Moira looked around. Danny was behind the bar with her father, and Colleen was out on the floor. The crowd had thinned out enough that Patrick and Michael had taken seats at the end of the bar and were talking to each other.

"I suppose," she murmured, taking a seat opposite him in the booth against the wall.

"Interesting place you have here," the man said.

He smiled, but there was something insincere in it, Moira thought.

"Lots of people," he went on.

"It's a pub," Moira said flatly.

"Very Irish."

"It's an Irish pub."

"Have you ever had any trouble here?"

"Trouble?" Moira said. "Um, let me see. Once a man got ornery when my father said he'd had too much and refused to serve him. We called the cops, and he was escorted out."

"Hasn't your band man, Jeff Dolan, been arrested a few times?"

"He was a wild kid. He's straightened out."

"Don't always count on people being what they seem."

"Excuse me, what's your name?"

"Kyle. Kyle Browne," the man said, smiling and offering his hand across the table. Moira shook it briefly.

"You know, Americans finance half the trouble that goes on around the world."

"In Northern Ireland, you mean."

Kyle Browne shrugged. "Your father is a very political man."

"He is not!"

"Then there's your brother."

"He's an attorney, and he doesn't even live in Boston."

"You don't know all your clientele."

"Are you insinuating," she asked, keeping a check on her anger, "that my father's place is some kind of harbor for the IRA and their sympathizers?"

"I'm not insinuating anything. What about your family friend? The writer. Just how well do you know him? Think he's up to something?"

"Are you a cop?" Moira asked bluntly.

"Let's just say I'm a friend, keeping an eye on things."

"Fine. You keep an eye on things. Let me tell you about my father. He's one of the nicest men you'll ever meet. He came to America because my family was mixed. Good Irish Catholics with a few Orangemen thrown in. You know—marriage, in-laws, things like that. My dad didn't like the kind of conflict that could arouse back home. He never believed in any man killing another over his belief in God. Of course, in this day and age, the religious thing has really become political and economic. Sure, a united Ireland would be great. But my father doesn't believe that thousands of people born in Ireland, whose families have been in Ireland for hundreds of years, should all be lined up and shot. My dad holds nothing against the English for something a brutal king did hundreds of years ago, and he understands how the Protestants in Northern Ireland are afraid of what will happen if they're not part of the United Kingdom. He's an American citizen, a Catholic and a man of the Republic, but he's a moderate who hopes that time and negotiation and good and honest men will bring peace. Does that answer your questions about the pub?"

She stood angrily and started to walk away, then returned to the table, still angry. "See the couple at the end of the bar? They're English, and they moved into the neighborhood about two years ago. They love to come here, and they're more than welcome. Danny, my good friend, was born in Belfast. As was Peter Lacey, the tall skinny guy talking to my dad right now.

He's a Protestant. Well, he was. He married a stunning young Jewish woman and converted. He's welcome here, too. Sal who just came in, well, Sal is half Italian. We love his food, he loves our beer. And you, God knows where you're from or what religion you practice, or if you practice any at all. Hell, my father even lets atheists drink in here. He puts up decorations for Kwanzaa, for God's sake. So you're welcome in here just like everyone else. You can come in and drink any time you want, or eat—we serve good food. You can sit there and watch and listen all you like. But take it from me, if you're looking for a conspiracy going on here, you're crazy."

She started away again. He caught her hand, smiling.

"Hey, sorry," he said softly.

"Yeah. Great."

"No, I mean it, I'm really sorry to have upset you. You're a beautiful woman, and it's a fine place. I'd hate to see bad things happen here."

"They won't."

"How about the old codger at the bar?"

"Seamus?" she said incredulously. "He's harmless. Completely. Don't you want to accuse my sister of something, as well? Or my mother, perhaps?"

"I'm not making accusations. I'm watching."

"Fine. It's a public establishment, as I've said."

"The drink is terrific."

"Good. It's on the house."

She freed her hand and walked away, and was startled to realize that she was rattled. She walked behind the bar. The Englishman, Roald Miller, lifted his glass. "Finally, a good bartender. Hey, Moira, how come you had to go off and become successful? We really miss you around here."

"Thanks, Roald. What was in that glass you're lifting to me?"

"Sarah and I are having Fosters."

She set the beers down and was startled to hear Danny behind her a moment later. "You really gave that fellow a piece of your mind."

She flushed. "You heard me?"

"Most of it. I was trying to appear far away and busy."

"The nerve! Insinuating that my father—"

Danny interrupted her with a sigh. "He doesn't have to be insinuating anything about your father. There are lots of people in this pub."

She spun on him and whispered softly, "What is going on, Danny?"

He shook his head. "I don't know. I wish I did. But now that you've given that bloke the what for, I suggest you stay away from him."

"I think he's a cop."

"Maybe. Maybe not. But don't go dating him, eh?"

"You know that—"

"You're in love. Right. With old beady eyes. You should stay away from him, too."

"If I were to listen to the guy in the corner, I'd definitely be staying away from you."

"But you have to go on instinct, don't you, Moira? And you know I'd never hurt you."

"If you only knew. You've hurt me time and time again."

"I'm sorry for that. It was never my intention. Honest to God, I'm trying to make up for it now."

"And I'm sorry, but you're too late."

"Am I? Am I really, Moira?"

She looked down the bar, where Michael was still

talking to Patrick. The two had gotten into a conversation with Liam and Seamus.

Michael looked up as if he had sensed her needing him. He smiled and lifted his glass. I'm doing my best to be part of it all, he seemed to be saying.

She smiled in return and looked at Danny.

"Yes, you're really too late," she said softly, and turned away.

As she did so, she caught the eye of the man in the corner. Kyle Browne. He was frowning, as if…

Warning her.

About what, or…

Who?

10

Moira wasn't sure why, but she was still worried about Seamus, despite the fact that he had been drinking more moderately that night. Her brother was next to her behind the bar when the place finally wound down for the night. Liam had long gone, as had most everyone else, but Seamus was still there.

"Patrick?"

"Yeah?"

"Do me a favor."

"What?"

"Walk Seamus home."

"Why? He only lives a couple of blocks from here."

"Please? Just humor me."

"Oh, sure, let me just run out into the bitter cold in the middle of the night to humor you."

"I'll ask someone else."

"No, Moira, damn, I'll do it. I was teasing you. Remember what teasing is? But why are you worried about the old coot?"

"I don't know." She walked past her brother to the end of the bar, facing Seamus. "Patrick is going to walk you home tonight."

"Now, Moira, I switched between the real stuff and the unleaded all night."

"And how many did you have in all?"

"Just a few."

"About ten, I believe." Colleen piped up from the floor. She was gathering bottles and glasses from the tables.

"Ten? It's amazing you have kidneys left, Seamus," Moira said.

"Irish kidneys. The best to be had," Seamus said.

"I'm proud of you for switching. Next time, just not quite so many altogether. I wouldn't have served you so many."

"Ah, but that's the trick, lass. You get the real stuff from a different bartender each time."

"Shame on you, Seamus," she said firmly.

"Now, I don't drive, Moira."

"You'd be cut off after the first one if you did."

"All right, girl. I'm going home."

"With Patrick."

"Sorry, Patrick," Seamus said sheepishly.

"No bother," Patrick said cheerfully, grimacing over his head at Moira. "Come on, then."

Kyle Browne had departed at about one. It was nearly two now.

Saint Patrick's Day made for a long week.

"Get Dad to go on up," Patrick told Moira in a soft whisper as he followed Seamus.

"Right," she said, but Colleen was already chastising their father, urging him up the steps.

"I guess I should get out, too, let the family close up," Michael said quietly to Moira. She looked at him, saw the gentle concern in his eyes.

"One of these nights I *will* get over there."

"I'll be waiting."

"My dad is gone. Kiss me goodbye?" she said, walking him to the door.

He curled his arms around her, then lifted her chin with his thumb and forefinger. He kissed her lips lightly, but she clung to him, demanding more. She turned it into a long, wet, openmouthed kiss, the kind that would have stirred her had she any energy left in her body whatsoever.

Michael withdrew when her sister cleared her throat and asked, "Shall we all leave the room?"

Michael's eyes were on her, intense, curious. "Was that a kiss?" he whispered. "Or a performance?"

She felt a shiver snake through her. "A kiss," she said firmly. "And maybe a performance. I'm just establishing a few things. Is…that all right?"

"Oh, yeah."

He touched her lips briefly with his. "It's after two. We'll all be as tired as you look in the morning."

"Thanks," she murmured.

He grinned. "Good night. I'm out of here."

Cold wind swept in as he departed. She closed and locked the door and turned. Colleen and Danny were staring at her.

Danny applauded, clapping his hands slowly.

"You could have gone with him. I can clean up with Danny," Colleen said.

"I— Great. You two clean up. I'm going to get some sleep."

She started around the bar and through to the office, then remembered her purse in the well. She came back in, but couldn't find it where she had thrown it.

"Hey, Colleen, did you move my purse?"

"Nope. Haven't seen it."

"Did you leave it at the restaurant?" Danny asked.

"No, I'm certain. I came in, the place was wild, I walked behind the bar and threw my purse in the well."

"Maybe Dad picked it up. Or Patrick," Colleen suggested.

"Maybe," Moira said, frowning and haphazardly moving bottles around to see if she had stuck it somewhere else. "Damn, I can't find it."

"It's got to be there somewhere," Danny said. "I didn't see any customers hop the bar to make off with it."

"Moira, calm down. That's Dad's best aged whiskey you're pushing around there. What's in your purse that—"

"Just my identification, my credentials, everything!" Moira said.

"I was about to ask what was in it that you needed before the morning," Colleen said. "I'm sure someone merely moved it."

Moira sighed. "Yeah, I guess you're right."

Danny caught her by the shoulders. "Hey, go up to bed. You really do look worn out. Go up and get some sleep."

"You're right."

"And don't be going back out at night."

She looked at him warily.

"Really. Please," he said softly.

"I wasn't going back out tonight."

"Good."

"That's not going to keep me from sleeping with him, Danny."

"I don't think I need to be in on this conversation," Colleen said, humming, trying to make a racket as she picked up the tables.

"Maybe you're not really so sure you want to," Danny said, his hand on her arm. "Maybe that's why you gave that Academy Award-winning performance at the door."

"And maybe I'm just really, really tired."

"There is no such thing as really, really, tired, not if you're really, really certain and if you've been with your family this much time."

"How do you know where I've been all this time?" she demanded.

"Trust me. I know."

"Great. You're spying on me? Watching me?"

"Circumstances, Moira, nothing more."

Colleen started singing "The Irish Washwoman." Loudly.

"Look, just for now, don't be on the streets at night alone, okay? A sensible woman wouldn't go wandering out alone in the wee hours of the morning anyway. Right?"

"I carry Mace."

"In the purse you can't find. And Mace is no defense against a gun."

"Why would someone use a gun against me?"

He sighed with impatience. "Moira, Boston is a big city. Remember the dead prostitute? And God knows how many murders there are here a year. That's the way of the world. Please, don't go out alone late at night."

"I'm not going anywhere, Danny, except to bed."

He released her at last. Tawny eyes met hers. She wished she didn't like his face so much. An interesting face. She wished fervently that Danny had been called to Timbuktu to give a speech that particular Saint Patrick's Day.

"Night. Night, Colleen," she called, and turned her back, going upstairs.

"Hey, Patrick?" Seamus said sheepishly as they walked down the street.

"Yeah, Seamus?"

"You don't have to do this. I don't know what got your sister going, but you know I'm a man who can hold me ale."

"Seamus, it never hurts to have company on the walk home. Besides," he said with a shrug and a smile, "it gives me another chance to slip away."

"To slip away to do what, at this hour of the night?" Seamus asked.

"Well, I really have had business here. I haven't been around as much as I should have been these past few days. I'd like to head downtown. And stare at my boat."

"In the middle of the night?"

"Sounds weird, huh?"

"Sounds like an excuse for something else," Seamus told him.

"Oh, yeah?" Patrick said, stopping and staring at Seamus.

"But then," Seamus said quickly, "that's what you *were* doing. Something else. Everyone knows a man can stay in a pub till all hours, not even drinking, just talking. Talking. There's the crux," he suddenly muttered. "I shouldn't have talked so much. Or maybe I should have talked some more."

"What are you going on about, Seamus?"

"Nothing, nothing." Seamus looked sideways at his escort. Patrick Kelly was a tall man, lean, but solid. He had a fine face. All of Eamon Kelly's children had fine faces, probably thanks to Katy Kelly. Hard to tell, though; he and Eamon had aged and wrinkled and grizzled together, but Eamon Kelly had been a fine-looking man in his prime.

"Are you all right?" Patrick asked.

"Oh, I'm fine. I'm a big fellow. Did you know I used to box?"

"I'm sure you were a hard hitter."

"Aye, that I was. And only a wee bit of me ale has gone to me belly."

"You're still a heartthrob, Seamus, I'm sure."

"I'm tired and worried, that's what I am," Seamus muttered.

"Worried? About what?"

Seamus shook his head, wondering if he should pour his heart out or muzzle his lips. "Those orphans you've been looking into, Patrick. What's the deal with that? You need money? I can donate a bit. I'm not a charity case, you know. In the old days, we needed sponsors and jobs to get into the United States. Me uncle sponsored me, and I worked hard in the fishing business for over twenty years. I made some good investments, too."

"Seamus, I've just gotten involved, but as soon as I know a little more myself, you'll be the first man I hit up, how's that?"

Seamus thought Patrick was looking at him a bit strangely. "Sure, sure," he said quickly. "Well, now, there's me house, just along the street. Old man Kowalski lives on the first floor. Polish fellow. Nice enough. Has his kids in all the time, always lots of people around. You don't have to see me in, Patrick."

There was sweat on his upper lip, Seamus realized.

"You don't want help walking up the stairs?" Patrick asked doubtfully.

"No, no. The day I can't make it up one flight of stairs…well, I'll move to a ground floor somewhere, that's what I'll do."

He slipped his key into the lock, opened the door and waved to Patrick, who waved back, then turned to go.

Seamus went up the steps two at a time. "There," he told himself. "I'm spry as a young rooster still, when need be."

At the top of the stairs, he realized that he hadn't

locked the lower door. He'd been so eager to rid himself of his escort and find the safety of solitude. Now he worried and started down the stairs.

As he did, the downstairs door opened. He heard the creaking. He squinted, looking out. The streetlights outside made his visitor no more than a dark image, a silhouette. A man in a hat and a coat. That was all he knew.

"Seamus, Seamus, Seamus. Shame on you, Seamus," a voice said. Deep, rich, throaty, menacing, with the soft cadence of the Old Country.

He knew instinctively that, indeed, he knew too much. Had said too much.

He turned, his heart thundering. His door was not so far away. And he *was* spry, spry as a young rooster.

He missed the first step he tried to take. He wavered briefly, then fell.

He hit his head. Hard. Every bone in his old body ached.

"Sorry, me old man. Sorry," that Irish-inflected voice said. Seamus was vaguely aware of footfalls landing lightly on the stairs, coming toward him. "Indeed, sorry, old man. But I can't take the chance of you giving me away. Nothing, you see, must stand in my way."

Seamus wanted to scream. He'd lied. Old Kowalski was deaf as a stone, and he'd never had a wife, much less children. Seamus wanted to scream anyway.

He couldn't. He felt the powerful grip that seized him. Then he was falling. Flying first, then falling, falling, falling.

When he landed that time, there was an instant of agony.

The sound of something snapping.

Then no pain. No pain at all.

* * *

On her way through the house to her bedroom, Moira noticed a small box sitting at the edge of the kitchen table. Inspecting it, she saw that it was a videotape. Frowning to see the title in the dim light, she saw that it had been recorded by someone off TV. Her brother's handwriting on the cover announced his title for whatever he had taped: The Results of the Troubles in Ireland. She started to put the tape down, then hesitated. They had shared things all their lives, and Patrick had left the tape out where anyone could see it. She took it to her room.

Was she prying? Too bad. She wanted to know what Patrick was up to.

She slid the tape into the VCR in her room and watched for a minute, but the tape seemed to be little more than a travelogue. Yawning, she went into the bathroom, listening as she washed her face and brushed her teeth. She heard music with a voice-over talking about traditional Irish music and dance.

Nothing too evil so far.

Letting it run, she hopped quickly in and out of the shower. Wrapped in a towel, she walked from the bathroom to the bedroom, where she slipped into a T-shirt with a yawning, frazzled cat on the front, saying, "Got coffee?" The Irish music and dance were finished; the narrator had gone on to talk about The Troubles, the thirty years of violence that had gripped Northern Ireland at the end of the twentieth century. Then-President Clinton was on the screen saying, "I don't think reversal is an option." She rewound the tape. The narrator spoke about Clinton's visit, his meetings with Irish Prime Minister Bertie Ahern, Gerry Adams and Martin McGuinness of the Sinn Fein. It went on to discuss his journey to Dundalk, a town just south of the Northern

Ireland border long known as a recruiting station for the Real IRA, a left-wing faction, that had claimed responsibility for the 1998 car bombing that killed twenty-nine people in the town of Omagh and threatened the fragile Good Friday Agreement, providing for a joint Catholic-Protestant government and approved in April of 1998. Clinton's face appeared on the screen again as he pointed out how past violence had destroyed the lives not just of those killed, but of those left behind. The important issue of tourism and American business dollars was brought up. Another speaker appeared on the screen, pleading for reason and the value of every human life to both the Unionists, mainly Protestants who worked for continued unification with Great Britain, and the Nationalists, mainly Catholics longing for a united Ireland. The tape went on with shots of Clinton visiting David Trimble, Protestant first minister in the new Northern Ireland government, and Seamus Mallon, the senior Catholic in the government. The tape moved on to interviews with children, orphaned or left with one struggling surviving parent due to the violence. They all talked about the future, about turning Ireland around, making her as prosperous and welcoming as her age-old adage promising hospitality. One attractive teenager, raised by nuns after the deaths of her parents, walked the photographer around the county of Armagh and Tara, the beautiful site made royal by the ancient kings. Northern Ireland, often shunned by tourists because of The Troubles, offered wonderful archeological locations, striking Norman fortifications, haunted castles, magical vistas and more. The girl was charming and sincere, ending her speech with a longing for the kind of education that would allow her generation to offer the world an Ireland at peace. She ended with the words, "There are more Irish in the United States now than there are in Ireland. This is still your home. Please help us, and the land that remains in your heart."

The soundtrack ended, and a loud buzzing filled the room. Moira quickly hopped up and hit the reverse button, rewinding the tape. As she did so, she thought she heard a strange thumping sound. She stopped the tape, listening. She heard nothing, but remained certain that she had heard a noise coming from the pub below.

"Danny," she murmured aloud. It had to be Danny. But what was he up to?

She exited her room, closing the door quietly behind her. She didn't bother with slippers or a robe, just tiptoed along the hall, listening. She thought she heard movement downstairs again. Was he going for a beer? It was nearly half past three in the morning.

Maybe her brother had returned, and he and Danny were talking.

Whatever was going on, she wanted the truth.

She opened the door at the top of the spiral stairway, closing it behind her very quietly. She waited there a moment, listening. Voices. Droning voices. People talking? Or a television or radio left on?

Silently and slowly, she moved down the winding stairway, inwardly damning the fact that a night-light was on in the office, while the bar beyond lay in darkness. Still, she moved downward, step by step, trying to discern just what she was hearing and from where the sound was coming. She came to the ground floor and held very still. She couldn't make out the words being said. It had to be a radio or television. After a minute, she stepped forward carefully, realizing only then that the floor was very cold, the wooden boards covering concrete, and her feet were freezing. Goose bumps were breaking out on her arms, as well.

She left the office area, creeping behind the bar. The

noise, she thought, was coming from the rear of the bar. Probably from Danny's room. The bar was empty. At least Danny and her brother weren't sitting around conspiring together.

She started very carefully through the tables in the darkened room toward the guest room door. She wasn't going to knock or anything like that. She just wanted to assure herself that she was hearing the droning of a television.

Halfway to the rear of the pub, she realized that she was feeling a cold draft. She paused, looking around. It was so dark, both inside and outside, that she couldn't make out the door. She should have been able to; there were streetlights just outside. But they didn't seem to be bright enough that night. Finally her eyes grew accustomed to the darkness, and she could see the door. It appeared to be closed, but it might be ajar. It had to be ajar. Cold air was coming in. A deep, bone-chilling cold. How the heck could the door be open? Patrick would never be so careless as to forget to lock up when he came in.

Hugging her arms around herself, she started weaving her way through the tables and around the bar. When she reached the end of the bar, still staring at the front door, she suddenly felt an entirely new sensation, as if a ghost were whispering at the nape of her neck, warning her to stop, to turn back. She did so, coming to a dead halt and turning.

The door to Danny's room seemed to be ajar, a faint ray of light spilling from it. That door had not been open before. She was certain. She would have noticed the light. It suddenly seemed imperative that she reach the front door, make sure it was closed and locked.

She turned back. The darkness seemed to thicken before her, as if a cloud had converged on the room.

Groping blindly, she slid her feet forward. There was something in her path. She tripped, stumbling. She reached out, trying to find something to break her fall. Cloth…a body? Something…someone…blocking the light.

But there was nothing for her to grip. She flailed helplessly, then went down, her feet entangled in something. She crashed to the floor, hands ahead of her to break her fall.

She hit the ground face forward, her forehead connecting with the green linoleum behind the bar. Pain suddenly shot through her head. Odd, it seemed to come from the back of her skull rather than the front. Sharp… then fading. The room became blacker than ever.

She closed her eyes.

"Moira, now what the hell are you up to?"

She blinked, then realized that she must have passed out, if only for a few minutes. There was a light on behind the bar, and she was being held in a man's arms. Danny's. She was still on the floor, but he had lifted her up and was studying her face.

"Danny," she breathed. She stared at him, not sure whether to fling herself against him or find the strength to leap away in terror.

"Who else were you expecting down here?"

"Were you out?" she asked.

His eyes narrowed. "For a bit. Why? What are you doing down here? Judging by the way you're dressed, I don't imagine you trekked down the stairs to seduce me."

"Danny, damn it, did you just conk me on the head?"

"Are you daft?"

"Who was in your room?"

"No one I know about." He seemed tense. "Why?"

"There were sounds. Voices."

"From my room?"

"Yes."

"The television?"

She hesitated, staring into his eyes. In the murky light, they seemed a pure gold. His features were in shadow, which seemed to emphasize the lean planes and rugged angles of his bone structure. She had been so frightened. Here, in her family business. In a room where she had spent half her life, in a place where she had never been afraid before.

She'd heard voices, seen shadows, touched...something. She'd sensed the danger, felt it at her nape, known it in her bones...

And it might well have been him.

But the fear was ebbing from her, just as the darkness had ebbed from the area around the bar.

"Moira, what's up? You said you heard voices."

She sighed, sitting up, rubbing the back of her head. There didn't seem to be a bump there.

"It might have been a television," she admitted. "I thought the front door was open...then it seemed your door was open. It was cold, and I thought Patrick had come back and forgotten to lock up properly..." Her voice trailed off.

"You weren't on your way out to lover boy's hotel room, eh?" he teased.

"Shoeless and in a T-shirt?" she retorted.

"Ah. You save the bare feet and T-shirts for me. How sweet."

She frowned. "I really hit my head. I think I blacked out."

He leaned toward her. "You hit your forehead. Poor baby. Hang on."

He rose, walking behind the bar, finding a clean

towel and filling it with ice. As he came back to her, she tried to rise. "No, no, you might be dizzy, don't try to stand. Hey, were you drinking tonight?"

"No!" she said indignantly. "Two glasses of wine at dinner. Danny, I could have sworn there was someone in front of me when I fell. Were—were you there all along?"

"No, I wasn't, and the front door was locked when I came in." He hunkered down by her, pressing the ice to her temple. She shivered.

"That floor is probably cold. Grab the ice."

She did so automatically. She was cold, and the ice, though it felt good against her head, sent rivers of frost racing through her.

She realized he had given her the command so he could scoop her up. "Danny," she murmured, still holding the ice but slipping her free arm around his neck so she wouldn't fall.

"You're like an ice cube yourself," he said huskily. He strode with her in his arms toward the back, making his way through the tables much more fluidly than she had. Of course, he had light to guide him.

He juggled her weight so he could open the door to his room, which was also closed, though not locked.

"Hey!" she protested.

"I'm not going to attack you or anything. Just warm you up," he assured her.

He paused in the doorway with her in his arms. He smelled good. The underlying scent of the aftershave she had always known and loved so much.

She realized that he was studying his room—his guest suite, as her father called it. Not really a suite. Her father had always imagined that in the old days, the room might have been a secret little harbor where the American Founding Fathers had met to ponder the question of separation from the mother country. Sam Adams might have written some of his stirring rhetoric here. Now it held a queen-size bed, two dressers, a mahogany entertainment center and a modern bath.

The doors to the entertainment center were open. The television was on. CNN. Headlines on the hour.

"Nothing seems out of place," he murmured.

"I guess I heard the television," she replied.

He remained still, looking around. He didn't seem to notice her weight. She had forgotten that although Danny appeared slim, he was built like rock. A lean machine, pure, supple muscle. He turned, still not seeming to notice that he was carrying her.

"Danny, you can put me down."

"Yeah. Let's get you under a blanket."

Still holding her with seemingly little effort in one arm, he stripped the throw and comforter from the bed, then placed her against the pillows and immediately covered her up.

"Danny—"

"Are you any warmer?"

"A little. I've got to go upstairs. I must have been imagining things."

"Let me take a look around out there. Keep that ice on your forehead."

He left her in the bed. She stared at the television. The volume was low, but she could hear every word clearly. She wondered why the sound had been so strange and garbled before. Because she had been listening through a closed door?

Danny seemed to be gone awhile. She turned from the television to see that he had returned and was standing in the doorway to the bedroom with something in his hands. Her black knit purse.

"My purse." She rose from the pillows. "Where was it?"

"By the end of the bar. It's what you must have tripped over."

She frowned as he brought it to her. "Danny, I know damn well I didn't set it there. And if it was there, why didn't you and Colleen see it when you were cleaning up?"

He shrugged. "Maybe it was wedged beneath the bar."

He slipped out of his coat, hanging it on the hook by the door, then pulled his sweater over his head and took a seat by her on the bed. "Check it out," he told her. "See if anything seems to be missing."

"You think someone stole my purse and put it back?" she queried.

He shook his head, eyes on the purse, his slow, rueful smile slipping into place. "I think someone moved it from the well, meant to give it to you, walked around with it, set it down by the bar and forgot it. But since it seems to have mysteriously moved of its own volition, perhaps you should check it out. Besides, I want to see if you've got a bump on your forehead." He reached out, taking the ice-laden towel from her hand and her head, studying her seriously.

"No bump. Not even a bruise."

"Good," she murmured.

"Headache?"

"Not really."

"Want an aspirin?"

"For my imagined injury?"

"I never suggested you had an imagined injury." He rose, disappearing into the bathroom, returning with two aspirin and a paper cup of water.

She took the pills from him. "I really don't feel bad," she murmured. "I should. I'm sure I blacked out."

He wasn't listening to her. He was watching the television. The reporter was explaining the route the parade would follow on Saint Patrick's Day.

Then suddenly he was looking at her. He reached out, smoothing a tangle from her hair.

He was close. Warm. His fingertips were like magic. "You know, you're really beautiful."

"You're not supposed to be attacking me," she murmured.

"I'm not attacking you. I'm trying to smooth out your hair."

"How romantic."

"I'm not supposed to be romantic, since I'm not allowed to attack you, remember? Of course, the devastating negligee is a real turn-on. Are you sure you didn't come down here with the express thought of attacking *me?*"

"Attacking *you?*"

"Seducing me?"

"Danny…"

"You know, the lovely heroine in distress, fallen on the floor. The strong, silent hero sweeping her up and all that?"

"When the hell were you ever the silent type?"

"You have a point there."

His fingers were still moving through her hair. And somewhere along the way he'd stretched out beside her. When she closed her eyes, she breathed him. She seemed overwhelmed by a sea of physical memory. Sight, touch, the sound of his voice, the huskiness, the slight touch of a brogue. She could even remember the taste of his lips on hers, his flesh beneath the pressure of her whisper-soft kisses, and more. How long had it been? How in God's name could she feel so natural, lying here with him, wanting to reach out and touch and taste and breathe and more again?

"You know, even dressed that way, you're absolutely beautiful," he said softly.

"That's a stock line."

"I mean it."

"You're prejudiced. Being an old family friend and all."

"Longtime friend, not old. You're not going to marry him."

"Michael?"

"You have to ask?"

"Maybe I am."

He shook his head. "You're here with me. You never risked the night to run out and be with him."

"Honestly, Danny, if I don't marry him, I'm a fool. He's doing everything in his power to get close to my family. He knows what's important to me. And he cares. He isn't trying to save the world, or destroy it, whichever you're after. I've never been sure. He's an American." Danny's fingers were still moving through her hair. He seemed to have settled more comfortably beside her, radiating a startling heat. "Grounded," she continued, wishing it didn't seem quite so hard to keep her focus on what she was saying. He was smiling at her, apparently listening. His face was close. His scent and warmth seemed to seep into her, sweep through her. Irish magic. "Good-looking," she managed. "Damned good-looking. Dependable. Reliable."

He curled a tendril of her hair in his fingers, amused. "Dependable. Reliable. What words to describe a passionate relationship."

"You should listen to a few of my friends who have been divorced. They'd go for dependable over exciting any day."

He shook his head. "Some of your friends probably

do need reliable and dependable. But *you* need reliable, dependable—and exciting."

"Michael is—" she began.

His lips touched hers, very gentle. Then he moved his face a fraction of an inch away. "Touch of friendship, not an attack," he swore, his whisper brushing her cheek. "Michael is…?"

"Um…exciting and dependable…"

This time his lips touched hers with a greater force. His kiss parted her lips, brought a wealth of wet, sweeping heat. She was wrapped in his arms, tangled in her T-shirt and the comforter, and the kiss went on and on, wet, ragged, his plunging tongue seeming to reach inside to her womb, caressing every erotic zone in her body. She didn't protest. The amazing thing was that she didn't protest. Every ethic, every tenet of right and wrong, seemed to slip away. Her fingertips moved against his face, threaded into his hair. His lips broke from hers. "That's an actual kiss," he murmured.

"What? Um…no more so than what I shared with…"

"Michael," he supplied.

Somehow he was over her. She felt the T-shirt tangled around her waist.

"Michael," she agreed.

"No, no. With Michael, it was a performance. With me, it was a kiss. Allow me. I'll show you the difference again."

"You're not supposed to be attacking me," she reminded him.

"This isn't an attack," he whispered. "You're free to go, you know."

"With you draped over me?"

"Well, I don't actually want to make it easy for you to leave."

She could have pushed him away, but it was easier

to convince herself that he was blocking her exit. She lay perfectly still, staring into his eyes. When he kissed her again, she brought her hands between them but still made no move to push him away. As they rolled to the side, mouths still fused together, she found her fingers curling around the buttons of his shirt. She touched his bare flesh. So familiar. The mat of tawny hair that teased her fingertips, the taut muscle beneath. A second later he was halfway up, struggling out of his shirt. Then his hands were on her and her shirt was on the floor. When he wrapped her in his arms again, she was instantly aware of the length of him. Wired muscle, tension, heat. She loved his chest, the feel of her lips against his throat and collarbone, the cradling way he cupped the back of her head. He used one foot against the other to shove off his boots, and she felt his foot move along her calf. The stroke of his hand was on her thighs, fingering the delicate panties she wore. His mouth closed over her breast, and he worked his body down the length of her. He knew how to do things with his tongue that defied silk and mesh. If there had ever been a time to protest, this was it. She spoke his name, but it was nothing more than a whisper. Her hips were moving, arching to his erotic, liquid manipulation. Lava seemed to burn deep inside her, then erupt and flow like a cascade. She nearly screamed aloud at the force of her climax, bit her lip, shuddered in his hold and allowed the volatile climax to sweep through her.

She was barely aware of his movement, his jeans joining the rest of their clothes on the floor, the force of his body between her thighs when he settled over her and into her. Her fingers laced together against his back; her legs locked around his hips. She had forgotten this; she had never forgotten this. Danny made love like he lived, passionately, vehemently, with electric force.

He filled her with his physical presence, aroused her anew where she had been shaken and sated, pulsing slowly, giving, taking away, then finding a beat that raced like thunder, building a need within her that was a sweet agony until she bit lightly against his shoulder, feeling her climax seize hold of her again, euphoric pleasure like a blanket of honey streaming through her system. Danny eased to her side, flesh bathed in a fine sheen of perspiration. He had a way of holding a woman after sex that kept the warmth glowing. Fingers in her hair, smoothing dampened strands. Sated, catching her breath, she felt the wave of thoughts bombarding her mind, thoughts that the previous moments had not allowed. She was an evil human being. If there had been any chance of this happening, she should have been honest with Michael. But there *shouldn't* have been a chance of this happening. She was an adult, she was mature, she was…not as much in love as she had tried to convince herself she was. But what she had done was still wrong. Really wrong.

"I have to go," she murmured.

"That's all you have to say?"

"I have to go *now.*"

He drew his arms away. Shadows hid his amber eyes.

"What did you expect?" she whispered.

"Oh, I don't know. Something like, 'What was I thinking, even pretending to be so totally in love with another man, when here's Danny, and together we're just so damned good.'"

"Obviously you're good," she murmured with a trace of bitterness. "I'm here."

"Well, you know me. I don't just want to be good. I want to be the best there is."

She didn't tell him that he'd certainly managed that.

"And I should have spent my life waiting for those moments when you chose to be in the country?"

"You're right," he said. "I'm being unfair."

She had said she needed to go, yet she was still lying beside him, loath to leave. Her knuckles brushed over his abdomen.

"Now you're being an evil woman," he informed. "That's truly unfair if you're intending on leaving."

His abdomen gave new meaning to the term "six-pack."

"You're in incredible shape," she told him. "Curious, for a writer and lecturer."

"The better to seduce you during those moments when I'm in the same country."

"You're being flippant. I'm talking about real life."

"You shouldn't marry Michael."

"Apparently," she murmured, "Michael shouldn't marry me."

"You're on a misdirected guilt trip."

"Oh, right. He's in a hotel room where I keep saying I'll appear, but I shouldn't feel guilty for being in your bed instead."

"He's not right for you."

"Because he happens to be here when you are?"

He shook his head, staring at her intently. "Because he has beady eyes."

"Oh, God, Danny, stop with that." She almost managed to rise at that point, but their legs were still tangled together. "Danny, I really should leave," she said softly.

He shook his head stubbornly. "For what? So you can race upstairs, feed on your guilt and decide to make it up to the guy by running over there and throwing yourself into his arms? Either confessing—or not confessing—and trying to make it up with another performance?"

"No!" she protested angrily. "I would never do anything like that. It isn't me, and you know it."

"That's right. You're far too Catholic. You'd need a long hot shower, cleanse away the sin and all that."

"Damn it, Danny, if we'd had any time at all together in the last several weeks—"

"Aha," he murmured.

"Aha, what?"

"That's not love," he told her. "I mean, to come to me just because you haven't had time with him... I'm sorry, but you're not in love with him."

"There's love and then there's sex," she said primly.

"Yeah, and it's a hell of a lot nicer when they go together."

"Oh, yeah? Well, in all those years, it never actually occurred to me that you'd come back one day and declare that you actually loved me. To total distraction, above all else, et cetera, et cetera," she murmured dryly.

"I never said that love should rule your every moment, or that it should make you behave insanely, or take precedence over everything else, like responsibilities, living, et cetera, et cetera."

"I never know what you're actually saying, Danny. Or what you mean. Maybe that's half our problem."

"There you go. You're admitting we have a problem, which means we're an us."

"Danny, *you* are the problem."

"I'm going to be a lot more of a problem if you keep tickling my ribs that way."

She clenched her fingers into a fist.

"I didn't really mean you should stop."

"Danny, I shouldn't be here. I shouldn't have been here. I certainly shouldn't stay."

"But the sin has occurred already," he said, shifting

his weight so that he pinned her to the mattress. "And, you know, I really do love you."

"Danny, I believe that you care about me."

He groaned softly, lowering his head. His hair brushed against her breasts. She wondered how such a simple thing could feel so terribly erotic. "The sin has already been committed," he repeated softly.

"I think it's worse when you sin twice. Especially when you should have known better the first time."

"That's the point. You did know better the first time. And since you've already sinned, at least in your own mind, you should go with it. All the way. Everything in life should be done with passion, commitment, all the way." His eyes rose to hers for a moment, glowing amber.

"Danny," she murmured, "if I stay now, for a while, you can't go thinking that..."

"That?"

"It means..."

"Don't worry, I won't go thinking anything. It's simply easier, more convenient, to go for the guy in the house rather than the one outside it. Nothing personal. You need sex, just sex, hey, I'm happy to oblige." He spoke sarcastically, but with an underlying note of bitterness that somehow dulled the anger she had felt at his words.

"No, Danny, I..."

She felt the pressure of his lips against her throat, her collarbone.

"That was rude. Uncalled for. I should...hit you," she whispered.

"Never opt for violence," he murmured against her breast. "And you can't hit me, I mean, that would mean that one of us was taking this...personally."

His hand sculpted the length of her body. Fingers

caressed her flesh. Zeroed in. Moved with practice and subtle precision. He was her every breath, close, hot. Breathing Danny was too easy, too natural, as familiar and electric as life…

"Damn you, Danny," she murmured.

"My name…how personal and intimate," he said. "It's only courteous to respond in kind."

His caress traveled the length of her.

Very personally, very intimately.

"Danny…" It came out like a long moan when she said his name again.

"I've always believed in actions rather than words."

11

Hours later, before the crack of dawn, Moira rose to leave.

She rescued her T-shirt from the pile of clothing by the bed. Danny had been sleeping. Or so she had thought, until she turned to see that he was wide awake, watching her. If he'd been sleeping, he'd awakened at her first slight movement.

She thought he meant to protest her leaving again, though surely he knew it was nearly morning and the household would be stirring soon.

He rose on one elbow, watching her. "Tell me again. Exactly why did you come down here last night?" he asked.

"What?"

"What were you doing down here last night? You asked me if I'd been out, said you thought there might have been someone in my room. And you thought that someone was in the bar area—you suggested I might have knocked you on the head. Why were you down here in the first place? Dressed the way you were, you weren't on your way out to the hotel to meet Michael."

"I heard a noise."

"A noise? You heard this noise in your room?"

"Yes."

"And you thought it came from down here?"

"Yes."

"What kind of a noise?"

"I don't know. A thumping noise. As if…as if someone were moving things around or dropped something. I don't know. I just heard a noise."

"You're certain?"

"I don't seem to be certain about anything these days," she told him.

He rolled out of the bed, strolling to her naked, taking her by the shoulders. "All the way, Moira, remember, all the way. Go with your instincts. Passion, commitment. Get rid of old beady eyes, today."

"Don't you dare say a word to him or try to make up my mind for me about right and wrong and my future."

"I don't need to make up your mind for you. I know you. You did that last night. As for old beady eyes, my love, I intend to let you wrestle with your demons all by yourself."

"Maybe my mind isn't made up. Maybe you're not as good as you think." She lifted her chin, meeting his eyes.

"Moira, whatever you're thinking, be careful. When you hear noises in the night, you shouldn't go prowling around."

"This is my family home and my family's business," she reminded him. "I grew up here, learning to clear tables from the time I was a little girl. Why should I have to be afraid to walk around my dad's place, even in the middle of the night?"

He watched her, weighing the question for a minute.

"Because there's evil in the world, that's why. When you're a child, your parents teach you to watch out for strangers. Think of Son of Sam, the Boston Strangler, the Zodiac Killer, Jack the Ripper."

"Right. But none of them has keys to my dad's pub."

"Yes, but your brother is here these days, I'm here, your associates are here. Doors may be left open."

"Danny, why don't you just tell me the truth?"

"About what?"

"About whatever is going on."

"I'm not privy to anything that might be going on."

She watched him for another moment. Her eyes slid down the length of him, far more analytically than in the previous hours. Danny was really toned. He could have stepped right out of the pages of a brochure on martial arts. Again she wondered how a lecturer and writer stayed in such excellent shape.

"All right, Danny," she murmured. She turned, starting for the door.

"Moira."

"What?"

"You know, *you* are keeping things from *me*."

"Oh?"

"Like what really happened out on the ice the night before last."

"I slid."

"Trust is a two-way street, Moira."

"So it is."

"And?"

"I don't see any cars coming toward me, Danny. No one to meet halfway."

She turned again. He caught her arm. "Moira, listen to me. If you hear something, anything strange at all, it's important that you let me know."

"I'll keep that in mind." She looked at his hand where he held her arm. The slightest unease swept over her. "I have to go upstairs, Danny."

He let her go. She walked out, closed the door to his room quietly behind her, then made her way through the bar and up the winding stairs. When she slipped into the house, she carefully locked the door. In her room, she took the videotape from her machine and put it on the table where she had found it. It was still very early. She showered and dressed, then sat in her room, staring at the phone and hesitating. She went to the living room and found Sunday's newspaper. There was an article about Jacob Brolin, talking about his expected arrival in the city and mentioning the hotel where he would be staying.

She walked to the kitchen, where her mother, in a terry bathrobe, had just risen to start breakfast. "Mum," she said, walking behind her and slipping her arms around her waist.

"Moira, darlin', 'tis so early."

"Yep."

"What's on your agenda for today?"

"Well, I'll definitely be helping Dad in the pub tonight."

Katy turned around and cupped Moira's face between her hands. "You children are not responsible for the pub."

"But it's fun, and I like helping Dad. And we're getting a great show, really."

"Then I'm glad. Since I did rather manipulate you into coming home."

"Dad seems to be in great health," she commented with a smile.

Katy shrugged. "He did have to have a battery of tests." She sighed. "I was worried because he works so much. But the doctor told me that work was good for him, just like an ale or a stout a day would do him no harm. Too many men retire and sit around becoming couch potatoes, and that's what kills them, the doctor said."

"You know who works too hard, don't you?"

"Who?" Katy asked.

"You."

"Oh, no, Moira, dear."

"Cooking, cooking, cooking."

"When it's just your dad and me, there's oatmeal in the morning. And I don't fix his breakfast because he's a tyrant, I fix his breakfast because I love to, and I like being a wife and mum. I'm happy as a lark that my girls have gone off and done well, but for me, well, I like my lot in life just fine."

"I know you do, Mum. But today…" Moira paused, feeling a bit guilty. Her mother was vindicating her desire to be a housewife, confessing to manipulation, and she was manipulating things herself.

"Mum, I still say there's no job in the world harder than yours. The coffee is going, and that's the thing we all need first. Now, I want you out of your bathrobe. I'm taking you out to breakfast this morning."

"Moira! The children are here, your sister, brother—"

"I don't mean any insult, but Granny Jon can cook, and Danny will come up, and Siobhan and Colleen are here—not to mention the fact that it would be good for Patrick to try cooking for a change. I've an urge to get away with just my mother, to have you all to myself."

"But, Moira—"

"Please."

"I'll just tell your father."

"We can leave a note."

"Moira, I have to change out of me robe anyway."

"You've got a point. But hurry, please."

Katy did as she was asked, flushing like a schoolgirl. Moira wasn't sure whether to feel guilt or pleasure that her scheme seemed to have made her mother so happy.

* * *

Jacob Brolin was staying close to the New England Aquarium, just outside Little Italy. Moira told a little white lie, assuring Katy that she'd heard of the hotel's restaurant and that they were known to prepare very special eggs Benedict, which she'd been harboring a craving for the last few days.

"You know, Moira Kathleen," Katy said as they sat, "I can cook eggs Benedict. You only needed to say you wanted some."

"Oh, I know, Mum. Like I said, I wanted to get you out."

Moira looked around the dining room, wondering if Brolin and his party would come down to breakfast. This was really a wild shot. He would probably order room service.

She realized suddenly that her mother had put down her menu and was studying her, sliding her reading glasses down her nose and watching her suspiciously.

"Moira Kathleen."

"What, Mum?"

"There are no eggs Benedict on this menu."

"You're kidding!"

"You're not a good enough actress for your mother, girl."

"No, Mum, I thought that—"

"Don't add insult to injury, daughter. What are we doing here?"

She leaned forward. "All right, Mum. I thought that we might run into Jacob Brolin here."

Katy put down her menu. "Why didn't you just try calling him?"

"I'm not with one of the networks, or even a major cable channel, Mum," Moira said. "And... I kind of wanted to do this on my own, too."

Katy nodded. "All right. Why didn't you just ask me to help you scope out the situation?"

"I really haven't had any time with you alone, Mum," Moira said earnestly, giving her entire attention to her mother.

Their waiter arrived, wishing them both a good morning and asking if they needed more time.

"Not at all," Katy said. "A strawberry waffle, coffee and orange juice. Moira?"

"The egg scramble with cheese and ham, coffee and juice, please," Moira said. When the waiter left, Moira leaned toward her mother. "Mum, I...honestly, I needed to be with you." That was surprisingly true. She hadn't wanted to be alone with her confusion regarding last night. And she hadn't wanted to be in the house if Michael and Josh had arrived early with ideas for the day's filming or eager to hear what she wanted to do next. They had lots of tape. Plenty for an hour's show, even if they decided not to do a live segment on Saint Patrick's Day. Which, of course, the Leisure Channel was expecting.

"Are you all right, Moira?" her mother asked.

She squeezed her mother's hand across the table. "A little confused, Mum, that's all."

"Danny?"

"Am I that obvious?"

"No, you're practically rude to him."

"Mum, you like Michael, right?"

"He's trying very hard. And he's handsome indeed. Probably more so than Danny, though I am prejudiced toward the Irish lad. You say he's dependable and he works hard, and he likes the theater and music and a ball game."

"Yes. He's willing to try anything. He's polite and courteous, and in the same business I am." Moira fell silent as their waiter arrived with juice and coffee. When he had gone, Katy leaned toward her.

"You make it sound as if you're dating off a computer matchmaking program."

"But I'm not, Mum. I've enjoyed him. Enjoyed being with him, I mean. I like the theater and all, too. He's a great companion."

"So is a Great Dane."

"No, he's nice, he's fun… I've really enjoyed being with him," she repeated without conviction.

"And…" Katy said, then hesitated, shaking her head. "You're hedging, daughter. All right, this isn't something you want to discuss with your mother, so I'll go first. Your father is a great companion, but I can tell you quite frankly that I…that I also find him quite exciting."

"What?" Moira said, startled.

"Well, I wasn't born yesterday. And I like to think I raised children with morals, but being compatible sexually is not a bad thing."

"Whoa, Mum," Moira said, laughing, then shutting up as their food arrived.

"This isn't a bad place. They're fast and efficient," Katy said.

"I'm so glad you like it, at least."

"Thus far," Katy said, cutting into her waffle. "If we're talking, let's talk. Don't go being all horrified that I like your father. We're not that decrepit yet. Honestly, child, where do you think you and your siblings came from? I do realize that children don't like to think of their parents in such a light—"

"No, I certainly know where we came from, it's just that…"

"I don't want you sharing more than necessary with me, no details, daughter. I'm just trying to really understand your dilemma."

"I'm attracted to them both," Moira said. She leaned forward, speaking more softly. "Does that make me bad, Mum?"

"My dear child, I adore your father, and we've had a good marriage. No, we don't burn with passion the way we did when we were kids, but we're comfortable together, and we do still have our moments. No life is a mass of excitement hour after hour, there's always the mundane. But we do have our moments, and we cherish them still. And that's what's kept us together sometimes when we've disagreed and been at one another's throats. It's human nature, girl. You may be attracted to more than one man. It's when you make a commitment that it must be real. And there's your man."

"What?"

"There's your man. Brolin. He just walked in with what looks like a group of four prizefighters. Don't spin around too obviously."

Despite her mother's words, Moira spun around instantly.

"I said not to be so obvious," Katy protested.

"Sorry." Moira picked up her juice and sipped it, trying to appear casual. "Mum, I should do this, right?"

"You've had a TV show some time now. How have you approached those other celebrities?"

"Until recently, Josh called. Lately it's been Michael's job. And usually we focus on little bits and pieces of Americana, with far more average—though wonderful—people."

"You're not afraid?"

"I'm just not sure how to approach him."

Katy set down her glasses and napkin and rose. "Excuse me, then."

"Mum," Moira began. But her mother was already walking to the table. Moira noticed that, as harmless

as her mother appeared, the men with Brolin immediately rose.

Moira rose instantly to follow her mother, ready to
fiercely protect her should the need arise.

"Excuse me," Katy said very politely. "Jacob, it's
Kathleen Kelly. Do you remember me?"

Brolin rose with a huge smile. He was a big man. Not
just tall, but big. Iron gray hair, deep blue eyes. A face
filled with character. Wrinkled like a bloodhound's,
yet somehow still very pleasant.

"Kathleen!" he said, and, stepping past his bodyguards, he took her mother's hands.

"Then you do remember me?"

"Of course, how could I forget?"

Moira stood stone still a few feet behind her mother.

"I knew you were here, of course. I'd meant to stop
by Kelly's—after Saint Patrick's Day."

"Really?"

"Of course. I'd heard you'd married Eamon Kelly
and moved to the States. Kelly's is known in the homeland, Katy. My, you haven't changed a bit."

"Ah, well, that's kind, but it's been over thirty years."

"I still say you haven't changed a bit."

"Jacob, come now. We both look a great deal more…
tired," Katy said, and laughed. Moira stood dumbfounded. Was her mother flirting? No, not really, but…

"Katy, did you come here to find me?" Brolin asked.

She shook her head. "I was just having breakfast
with my daughter. I'd love you to meet her. In fact,
she's been meaning to call you."

"Oh?" Brolin looked past Katy and saw Moira standing there. He smiled broadly for Moira. "Why, she's just
like you, Katy." He strode past his bodyguards, taking
Moira's hands and giving her a kiss on both cheeks.
"Now, lass, why were you going to call me?"

"I, uh, I'd love to have a few words with you on tape for an American travel show, Mr. Brolin," she said. "We're trying to show the magic of Saint Patrick's Day in America. Actually, a lot of it is focused on the old saying that everyone is Irish on Saint Patrick's Day." She paused, wondering if she was babbling. She had been taken by such surprise. Did her father know Brolin, too? If he did, wouldn't he have mentioned it when Seamus and Liam had been talking about the man with such awe?

Brolin looked to one of the big men at his side. "We can fit something in somewhere, can't we? We will. Call the hotel room tomorrow and we'll set you up. Will you and your mum join us?"

"I'm afraid we can't, we have to get back," Katy said. "But indeed, Jacob, we'd be more than thrilled to have you as our guest when your obligations are finished here."

"How are things at Kelly's Pub?" Brolin asked.

"Busy. You know a pub on Saint Patrick's Day," Katy said.

He nodded. Moira was surprised to realize that he was studying her. "Well, now, that's fine. And yes, I'd love to visit you and Eamon and your family."

"Then we'll be seeing you, Jacob." She smiled at his guards. "Please excuse the interruption."

Jacob Brolin kissed Katy's cheek, and Katy took Moira's arm. "Time to leave, I think," she murmured, starting out of the dining room.

"Don't forget to call, Moira," Brolin called.

Moira stopped to turn back. "Thank you."

"Come along now," her mother said. "In all these years, you've surely learned how to make a proper exit."

"I didn't finish breakfast."

"I'll make you eggs Benedict. This is our exit."

"Mum! Our exit is going to be rather embarrassing if I don't pay the check!"

"Oh. Oh, of course," Katy said, then stood by the table as Moira summoned the waiter and left the money.

Out on the street, Moira looked at her mother. "I—I had no idea you knew him."

"I don't really know him. We met, many years ago."

"Was he...was he...?"

"Was he what?"

"I don't know. Like a great love in your life long ago or something?"

Katy shook her head impatiently. "You're mocking me, daughter."

"No, Mum—"

"The younger generation always thinks they're the first to discover sex and passion, but it's been going on for centuries, Moira." She started down the street toward the subway station.

"Mum, I was about to tell you that I was impressed—"

"Well, don't be."

"Mum, he's a very important man."

"He's a man like any other. He just knows both sides of the problem."

"But how did you meet him? I thought we were from Dublin? And you've never been involved in politics."

Katy looked at her with sheer exasperation. "You're from Boston, you live in New York, and you've traveled all over. And you know something about the American Civil War. Fathers fought sons, brothers were against one another, families were divided."

"Yes, but they were fighting for a cause, for something that had more to do with what they believed than where they were born—"

"Trust me, the fellow fighting for his plantation, his

income, cared where he was born, and believe me on this—every man has a cause. Life is what it is. Catholics have married Protestants. People move. People living in the tiniest town in Limerick might be politically active, while a man living in Belfast might wear blinders and walk to and from work daily, not really caring who's in power, just so long as he can take his vacation in Spain. Moira, do you know why we came to the States?"

"Dad wanted a pub in America. The economy wasn't great at home, and he'd read about America all his life. It was a dream and a new beginning."

"All that's true. But we married, and moved, after a cousin on my father's side was killed. She should have known what she was in for—she was active in a violent group. She inflicted her share of violence and received it in return. That's what your father couldn't bear. A life in which children were taught to hate. She was a kid when she was killed, Moira. Twenty-one. I wanted revenge, but your father had the kind of courage to say no and walk away. And he's lived with that kind of courage every day of his life, teaching you all that a man's color, race or religion doesn't matter, just the mettle of the man. Brolin, too, learned that kind of commitment. He wasn't always lily white, but he learned his lessons the hard way. I've watched his career from afar. He's one of the few people in power to realize that hate can be taught, that it's passed on from generation to generation. He knows that even if you can't erase decades—or centuries—of bloodshed, oppression and, on both sides, cold-blooded murder, you can work hard to create a new world where men and women talk instead of shoot."

Moira stood openmouthed, staring at her mother, stunned.

Katy went up the subway stairs and started down the street. Moira followed her. "Mum, where are you going?"

"Walking. I—I want to go see your brother's boat."

Moira followed her. "Mum?"

"What?" Katy snapped.

"Um, if you really want to see Patrick's boat, we have to cross the street and go that way," Moira said.

Katy spun and stared at her, smiled, then laughed out loud. "Sorry," she murmured.

Moira walked up and hugged her mother. "I always loved you for breakfast every morning, for harping at us to get out of bed for school, for being there with tea and whiskey when we had colds. I loved you for down pillows and fluffy comforters, and for being the world's greatest mum. And I never doubted that you were smart, but I never knew how very wise you were, and just how incredibly wonderful. Forgive me for not seeing all that you were."

Katy pulled away from her, patting her cheek. "There are tough choices in life, daughter, always, for everyone."

"Tell me more about Brolin," Moira said. "How did you meet him?"

Her mother hesitated, then said, "My cousin died. She had been living in Northern Ireland, and I met him at the funeral. It's not a time I like to remember. Come on, let's get going. I want to see that boat. It's March now, we'll be able to get out in it soon enough. Sometimes I wish we'd moved to Florida. I do love the water. And Patrick has been out checking that boat over so many times this year. He's getting restless, I think. He does love the ocean. And I'm glad. It keeps him coming in to Boston."

They had reached the dock leading to Patrick's boat.

One thing she'd always known about her mother: she could outmove a power walker. Moira was almost breathless.

"The gate is locked," Katy said with dismay.

"I doubt it. The people around here are fairly casual." Moira pushed the gate open. "See…it should be locked, but it never is."

They walked down the dock. A sharp wind blew in. March was always an unpredictable month.

"Ah, there she is," Katy murmured.

The boat was called *Siobhan*. She was beautiful and sleek, freshly painted, with sails and a motor. Patrick had only had her pulled out of dry dock a few weeks back, anticipating the coming of good weather.

Moira saw that, beneath the tarp Patrick had over the helm, there were a number of boxes. "I guess he's been out here, stocking her up," Moira murmured.

"Well, of course he's been out here. It's where he said he was going. Why did you say that?"

"Oh, I don't know. I think Siobhan has been worried about him a few times. He's getting involved with that group supporting orphans. At least, that's what he's been saying."

Katy spun on her. "If that's what he's been saying, that's what is. When you love someone, you trust him."

"Of course," Moira murmured.

"You're talking about your brother, Moira."

"Hey, don't worry, I love my brother. I just hate to see any trouble between him and Siobhan."

"They'll weather this. They're lucky. They were young when they met. But they really love each other. Sometimes, it isn't easy to trust someone. But when you make it through, well, then you know your heart has been in the right place."

"Mum, don't worry. I always defend Patrick. I haven't wanted to deck him in almost ten years now."

Her mother smiled but stared at her very seriously. "Let your brother manage his affairs. You've got to worry about your own situation now, don't you? What do you feel, Moira? Thinking isn't a bad thing, but what you feel is usually much more important."

Moira hesitated, staring at her mother. "Mum, I don't know what I feel. Do I spend my life waiting for an exciting, combustible, perhaps even dangerous wild card, or trust in someone who's right here, with all the right virtues? There's a lot to be said for compatibility. If I had any sense, I'd certainly go for dependable, just as…"

"Just as I did?" Katy suggested, then she shook her head, smiling. "You've got it all wrong. Your father was the wild card, the one with the real beliefs, the dreams, the one taking me away from everything I had known and loved. He said that we were going to get to America or be damned. Choices are never easy. And never clear-cut. To this day, I admire other men, but I love your father. He was my gamble, and I played against the odds. I played by instinct, and I played by heart." She turned and started walking along the dock. "Let's get on home now, eh? Your business associates have probably been calling all morning."

Katy started off again at her usual brisk pace. Moira followed.

Strange morning indeed. She'd gotten what she'd set out for.

And a great deal more.

12

Moira was surprised to see how late it had gotten when they returned to the house. Colleen was finishing cleaning in the kitchen, but a squeal from the family room assured them that the house was not empty.

Katy Kelly arched a brow to Colleen.

"Gina is in there with Granny Jon, Siobhan and all the kids," Colleen explained. "Molly and Shannon are fascinated. They think Siobhan should have twins so they can play with babies all the time."

"Oh, dear, all Siobhan needs is twins!" Katy said, heading into the family room.

"Where's everyone else?" Moira asked.

"Dad's already downstairs setting up. He says that Mondays are usually slow, but since it's almost Saint Patrick's Day..." She shrugged.

"Patrick?"

"Who knows? He's off."

"Danny? Josh? I'm assuming Josh was here, if he's left Gina for the day."

"Yes, Josh is downstairs with Dad, helping out. And Michael and Danny are out—together."

"What?" Moira said incredulously. She felt a chill on the inside as a sheen of sweat broke out on the outside. "Danny and Michael left here together?"

Colleen glanced at her sharply. "You took off this morning without leaving any hint of your filming schedule. Josh reminded Michael that you'd been going to do a musical overlay or something, showing the doors of some of Boston's finest pubs. Those not quite as fine as Kelly's, of course, but worthy of note. Danny mentioned that he knew every pub in the city, from the most elite to the down and dirty. Anyway, they went out together—in Dad's car, as a matter of fact—to scout out pub doors. What's the matter? You look as white as a ghost."

Moira shook her head. "Nothing," she said, a bit too quickly. "Nothing at all. I just can't see the two of them getting along."

Colleen narrowed her eyes, setting down the dish towel she'd been using and walking over to Moira. "You never told Michael that once upon a time you had a fling with the old family friend, huh?"

"Colleen…"

"You didn't, did you?"

"It didn't matter. We both know there have been other people in our lives," Moira said. "We never felt it necessary to give names, dates and license numbers."

Colleen laughed softly. "Well, no, not if he dated some girl in L.A. or Ohio. But you brought him home when Danny was staying here."

"I didn't think that it mattered. I really didn't."

"But now they're out together and you never told him and… Oh!" Colleen exclaimed, staring at her very closely.

"Oh, what?"

"That's where you were last night."

"What?"

"You were with Danny."

"Colleen, will you shut up!"

"As long as you don't lie to me."

"How do you know I wasn't in my room?"

"I couldn't sleep, so I went to find out if you wanted to make tea or talk or something. Oh, my God."

"Colleen, stop, please."

"I thought you were really in love with Michael. Then again, I didn't think you'd ever really be out of love with Danny. You can be so stubborn... Of course, Danny does come and go, and Michael really is one wicked hunk, but... You have to make up your own mind, of course. Though if it were me...well, to be honest, sex is so important in a relationship—"

Moira could hear footsteps coming from the family room. She clapped her hand over her sister's mouth. "Please..."

Colleen tugged free of Moira's hold. She looked toward the family room. "Whoever it was turned back. Do guys talk, do you think? Oh, Lord, Moira, do you think they're out together talking about you? What do men say, do you think?" She broke off, wincing. "Lord, what am I saying? Sorry, you must be really miserable. I know you. You'd never just... I mean, there had to be a reason. I love you, and this must be so difficult. Don't worry, they're not going to come to blows. If I know Danny, he won't say a word to Michael. Honestly. It's going to be all right. I'll make tea. According to Granny Jon, that solves everything. Maybe you need some whiskey in yours. That can be arranged."

"No," Moira said. "I'm going down to the pub. Cover for me with Mum and Granny Jon and Gina, please?"

"Sure, sure, I'll say you needed to talk to Josh." Her sister sensed her misery, caught her by the shoulders and gave her a kiss on the cheek. "Honest to God, it will be all right."

"It's not all right. Michael is really good and decent and trusts me—"

"And maybe now, if you decide he's the right man, it will be without hesitation. Moira, you didn't turn into the town slut." Colleen stared at Moira, shaking her head. "Hey, kid, no one's going to do anything worse to you than you're doing to yourself." She sighed. "You met Michael right after the Christmas holidays, right?"

Moira nodded.

"And knowing you, you saw him a zillion times before anything happened."

"No, we went out about twelve times in January, then at the beginning of February—"

"Okay, I'm not really that detail oriented, at least not right this minute," Colleen said. "And when is the last time you really went out in the last…however many years it was since you last hooked up with Danny?"

Moira shook her head.

"No one?" Colleen gasped.

"I went out."

"But you went that long without…without sleeping with anyone? Boy, and I just thought that you were really discreet. Moira, don't go beating yourself up over this. Trust me, by the standards these days, you're practically a nun. Please, don't be so upset."

"I'm not upset, I'm confused. I really do love Michael. And I guess that I've always loved Danny. But I should have…refrained."

"He didn't exactly drag you down into the cellar, huh? Were you drinking?"

"No. But I really need a drink now."

"Yeah, maybe you do. Hey, big sis, I'm here, okay?" Colleen hugged her tightly once again. "Any time, any circumstances. I'm here."

"Thanks. I'm going downstairs for that whiskey."

Moira kissed her sister quickly on the cheek and escaped. As she closed the door to the spiral stairway, she could hear Gina asking for her and Colleen making an excuse.

Her father and Josh were at one end of the bar. Her father was calling out names, while Josh went through open liquor boxes on the floor, trying to supply the right bottles for the empty spaces in the wells.

"Hey, there," Josh called.

"Welcome, daughter."

"Hey, Dad. Josh. Hey, Josh, how long have—have the guys been gone? Are we going to tape the pubs today?"

"They were going to call the crew from the road," Josh said. "They really don't need either of us for this. Of course, it isn't Dan's job at all, but he seemed to want to help. And he does know the pubs of Boston."

"Oh, yes, that he does," Moira muttered, striding behind the bar to the Irish whiskey. She poured herself a shot while both her father and Josh stared at her. She smiled sheepishly at her father. "Bad night. I didn't get any sleep."

"I was afraid you were going to tell me that a couple of hours alone with your mother had made you crazy," Eamon said.

"Dad!"

"You were the one running for the whiskey, girl, not me."

"Mum and I had—" She paused, remembering the way Jacob Brolin had instantly remembered her mother after thirty years. "Mum and I had a lovely time out together."

"Good. Your mother is a wonderful woman, and you should appreciate that."

"I do. I told you, no sleep," she said.

"Gina and the twins okay?" Josh asked.

"Yep. The other kids are entertaining them," she said. She swallowed her whiskey in a single gulp. It burned like a son of a gun. Just what she needed. Almost like a slap in the face. Guilt was now, beyond a doubt, settling down hard on her.

She heard a noise from the rear of the bar and looked back. Maybe they were wrong. Maybe Danny was in his room.

But it wasn't Danny. It was Jeff Dolan. He was setting up the instruments and doing sound checks.

"Hey, Jeff," she said. "Need any help?"

She left the bar area quickly, aware that her father and Josh were studying her way too closely—and they both knew her too well.

"Sure, Moira," Jeff said, "though I'm almost done here. I was going to get something to eat, walk around awhile, before we had to get started tonight. It's going to be a long one, for a Monday. Well, for me. We don't usually play on Mondays, you know. Plug in that amp for me, please?"

"Sure." She did as bidden.

Jeff gave her a long sideways glance, brown eyes curious. "You all right?"

"Of course."

"I saw you talking to that guy the other night."

"That guy?"

"Drinking the blackbird, sitting in the corner." He grinned. "In fact, I heard you. I would have come up and applauded but…is he a cop?"

"He gave that impression."

"Yeah? Well, you told him. I'm surprised the guy didn't come right up to the stage and frisk me."

"I thought your record was as white as snow these days?"

"I'm whiter than snow," Jeff said, reaching down to straighten a few wires. "But there's no way to clean up your record."

"Jeff," she said very softly, "is something going on here?"

"No," he replied, too quickly.

"You're lying."

"No, I'm not. Really. Hey, why aren't you working?"

"The guys are off taping pub doors."

"Ah."

"Jeff—"

"You want to get a sandwich with me?" he asked.

"We can go upstairs and I can dig something up for you. Of course, the kitchen staff should be here by now, too."

"No, do you want to go out and get something with me?" he persisted.

"I— Sure. Of course," she said. He was going to talk to her. But not here. "I'll just go up for my purse."

"Your dad pays us decently. I can buy you a pop and a sandwich."

"Okay, great."

They walked toward the bar. "Dad, Josh, I'll be right back. Jeff wants to get a grinder."

Eamon, looking up from his stock list, frowned. "Jeff, you're always welcome to any food in the place."

"Thanks, Eamon. I had a hankering for one of those grinders at Zeno's, down the street."

"And I'm really in a mood for a gourmet coffee," Moira added. "I promise, we'll be right back."

"Take your time," Eamon said. "Josh here is proving to be an excellent pub keeper."

"Keeping at it, just in case the film thing ever fizzles," Josh told her. But Josh knew her well, and he was watching her suspiciously.

As they started out the door, she heard her father swear as he slammed his head against the bottom of the bar, trying to rise quickly. "Moira!"

"What is it, Dad?"

"You stay with Jeff."

She looked at him, surprised. "Dad, it's broad daylight."

"They just had it on the news. They've found another dead girl."

"He's telling the truth," Josh said, handing her father a bottle of tequila.

"Another prostitute?" she asked.

"An Irish girl," her father said.

"Dad, I'm American, not Irish. And Jeff is going to pimp for me so I can become a prostitute, okay?"

"Moira Kathleen!"

"Dad, I'm sorry. It's horrible, really horrible. But please, you don't have to worry. I won't go off with any strange men. I'll stick to Jeff like glue."

"If I'd known, I'd not have been so fast to let your mother and you off alone this morning," Eamon said.

"Dad, I swear, I'll be careful."

"Did you want a sandwich, Josh?" her father asked. "Maybe you should be going with them."

"Eamon, I ate too much breakfast a very short while ago," Josh said. "And I'm helping you here, right? I worry about your wayward daughter, too, but I have to admit, she usually uses good sense. Well, sometimes."

"Eamon, I'll guard her with my life, I swear it," Jeff said patiently.

Eamon nodded. "Well, on with you, then. But come back quickly."

"Sure thing, Eamon," Jeff said.

They walked outside. "It really is terrible," Moira murmured.

"The dead girls?"

She nodded. "I didn't see the news, though. Did you?"

He nodded. "Your father had it on before you came down. Thank God I don't know anyone in the business now."

"Now?"

He shrugged. "In my wild days, I knew several working girls. Hey, you know I did some pretty bad shit when we were kids. Drugs. Hell, they got me for vandalism, and armed robbery, though I wasn't the one with the gun. I shaped up with your dad's help. I have a beer now and then. No drugs. No guns. Okay, a little nicotine…" He pulled a pack of cigarettes from his jacket and lit one as they headed down the street. "That's why your cop the other night made me nervous."

"You're nervous about more than that, aren't you?"

Jeff waved his cigarette in the air. "Rumors, Moira. Nothing more than rumors."

"And what are the rumors?"

He shrugged and inhaled deeply before answering her. "Jacob Brolin."

"What about him?" She tensed, praying suddenly that this had nothing to do with her mother.

"Well, he's a bigwig. And a moderate. And you have a huge population tired of bloodshed and violence in Northern Ireland. But you've had decades now, too, of a group—an ever-changing group, of course—who still believe that only violence has the power to change anything. And you have to remember, the Republic of Ireland was won through violence."

"Jeff, please, I don't know what you're talking about."

"Moira, don't be a dunce. Assassination."

She stopped dead still on the sidewalk. "Assassination?"

"Moira, there could be a dozen lunatics in the street ready to do something violent, either because they're psychotic assholes or because they don't believe in moderation and negotiation."

"So what does that have to do with us? If it's that obvious, surely Brolin knows it. He walks around with—" She broke off and started over. "Surely he walks around with a bodyguard. And he probably has a police escort, too."

"Of course, of course. And I'm not in on anything, I swear it. There was just some talk about blackbird being some kind of a code word. And Kelly's being a place where people might meet and find one another."

She gasped, staring at him in horror. "That's terrible! And it can't be true. We need to tell the police."

"Apparently, they already know. Hence your guy ordering the blackbird the other night."

She let out a long breath. "Rumor. Where did you hear this rumor, Jeff?"

"Oh, Moira—"

"I need to know."

"There's the sandwich shop."

"Jeff, I need to know."

He sighed deeply. "Seamus. Seamus said he'd heard people whispering one night. It was dark…after hours. He didn't know what was going on, and he was afraid. He talked about it in the pub, thinking he was safer surrounded by friends. I told him to keep his old mouth shut."

"Jeff, you should go to the police with what you know."

"What do I know? That Seamus—who's half-deaf— heard whispers? Blackbird is the name of the band.

And a drink. And the police are aware there could be crackpots in the city. What could I possibly tell them that they don't already know? I'd get myself arrested on some trumped-up conspiracy charge, and that would be that."

"Jeff—"

"Your father's right, Moira," he said, stopping at the door to the sandwich shop. "Don't trust any strangers. And be damned careful, even in the pub. If you want to know more, you're going to have to ask old Seamus. Now, there's a fellow who *could* go to the police—but he won't. Yeah, Seamus is one straight arrow. He came to the States, worked his ass off and became a model citizen. But I sincerely doubt that he'll talk to you, and I can guarantee he won't go to the police."

"Why not?"

"Because it's dangerous to let anyone know that you know too much," he told her.

"But if—"

"Trust me, the radicals, the moderates and even the just-don't-really-cares have excellent intelligence systems. The police are here already. We're usually filled with our regulars, the lunch crowd and the cocktail crowd. The dinner crowd, and those who come in for the music. And most of them look familiar to me after all this time. But I've been watching the people in the bar lately. Lots of strangers."

"There are always strangers in the pub."

"Yes, but trust me. There are more than usual. I bet even Brolin's people are here already. Jesus, Moira, trust me on this. Keep out of it—completely."

"It's my father's pub."

"Nothing is going to happen in your father's pub. And there's nothing that any of us could tell Brolin's people that they don't already know."

"If everyone is so smart, how come so many people have been killed through the years?"

"Because there are too many people who see their side as a just and true cause, and they're willing to die for it. You need to keep your mouth shut, and Seamus needs to keep his mouth shut. Ignorance isn't just bliss, Moira, it's life. Okay, they're beginning to stare at me from inside for keeping this door open so long. We've got to go in. And I'll never say a word about any of this to you in front of anyone else. Now, what kind of sandwich you want?"

When she returned to Kelly's with Jeff, her father was gone. Chrissie had come in and was working the bar. Patrick and Josh were sitting at one of the front tables, drinking coffee and talking to a blond man of about forty-five, nicely dressed, long legs casually stretched out from his seat at the table.

The stranger saw Moira as she entered. He stood, bringing both Patrick and Josh to their feet.

"Moira, I don't think you've met Andrew McGahey as yet. He works with the Irish Children's Charities group. Andrew, my sister Moira. And you have met Jeff Dolan, right?" Patrick asked.

"Moira, how do you do?" McGahey said. His accent wasn't Irish. It was New York City, if anything. He went on to shake Jeff's hand. "Of course I've met Jeff. I've heard the Blackbirds many a time now. Wonderful group."

"Thanks," Jeff said.

"Coffee, you two?" Patrick asked.

Moira lifted her cup. She hadn't forgotten to stop for the gourmet coffee she had told her father she was craving.

"I'm fine," Jeff said.

"Moira, did you have any more plans for the day?" Josh asked.

"What?"

"Plans. For taping. The guys are off with the crew. They called in, and they're doing fine with the pub door segment. Was there anything else you wanted to do today?"

She'd forgotten about her own show. Forgotten that she'd detoured Josh and company from a delightful vacation to come home to film Saint Patrick's Day.

"Uh, no, not today. But," she said hastily, "I think I can get an interview with Brolin. I have to call his people back in a bit for a time and a place, but I think it will work out."

"You got Brolin," Josh said appreciatively.

"I think," she murmured.

"You didn't tell me that," Jeff said.

"Or me," Patrick said.

"Well, it just happened. This morning," Moira murmured uncomfortably. She didn't mention her mother's role, not because she didn't want to give credit where it was due, but because she didn't know if Katy wanted people knowing that she had been, at the least, acquainted with Brolin in Ireland.

"Great," Josh said. "If we're done for the day, though—or if I'm done, at least—I'm going to take Gina sight-seeing."

"Hey, thanks for the help down here," Patrick told him.

"Not at all," Josh said, waving goodbye.

"Where's Dad?" Moira asked.

"I'm not sure," Patrick said, frowning. "He got a call, asked us to man things and took off like a shot." Her brother looked unhappy. "I asked him what was wrong, and I was going to follow along, he was so damned white. But he told me he needed me here."

"That's strange. You're sure he was all right?"

"No, he wasn't all right. But I couldn't knock him down and insist he tell me what was going on. He will, in his own good time. And by the way, Andrew came by today specifically to meet you."

"Oh?" She looked at the blond man.

He smiled. A mature charmer, tall and good-looking, with a single dimple. He had an air of casual sophistication.

"I'm hoping you can help us along with your show, somewhere along the line."

"Ah," she murmured. "How?"

"Airtime."

She nodded. "Of course. Did you mean…now? For this show?"

He shook his head. "Oh, no, we're just putting the whole thing together now. Your brother has been doing our legal work. I'm hoping to get Jeff and his group to do a special CD for me, with the proceeds going to my cause. Once we get it going, we'll be hitting the news stations, papers and all, but with your show…well, it would be nice to touch the heart of America's travelers. They usually have money."

"What exactly is your charity doing?" she inquired.

"Moira, you're sounding like an inquisitor," Patrick murmured.

"I need to know," she told her brother. She didn't know what was goading her on, but she was being rude. "I want to make sure you're trying to teach kids about art and literature, language and mathematics, computer science. I mean, you're not conducting a school for the manufacture and use of weapons, are you?"

"Moira," Patrick said angrily.

"It's all right," Andrew said, smiling. He folded his hands on the table, looking at Moira earnestly. "There was a lot of violence in the seventies and early eighties, even into the nineties. Did you know that half the population of Ireland is under fifty years old? Bad times caused a lot of emigration. And a lot of orphans, or kids growing up in single-parent homes. A lot of poverty. Ireland is coming along financially now, both in the North and in the Republic. But we still have a generation coming into the working world that has grown up with little assistance. Young adults with little education and few skills. We're hoping to change that."

"Well, then, when you get your charity up and rolling, I'll be happy to see what I can do," Moira murmured. Patrick was still staring at her as if he wanted to kick her leg under the table. Even Jeff was watching her with a slightly rueful expression. Was she becoming ridiculously paranoid? Every politician in the world took a chance, trying to change things, even trying to make a better world. There was always someone out there with the capacity for violence.

"Thanks," Andrew said. "Hey, I can show you one really special kid." He took out his wallet. She almost jumped back, wondering for a moment if he was reaching for a gun.

He flipped open his billfold, showing her the picture of a young woman of about eighteen, with long dark hair. "Jill Miller. Both folks killed. She was blinded in the explosion that took their lives. A car bomb. Anyway, she's a wonderful natural musician. She plays the guitar like an angel. She's got the talent, and she wants to come to the States, to go to Julliard."

Moira nodded. "Well, I hope she makes it," she said softly.

"She will," Andrew assured her. "The world is filled

with trouble. Eastern Europe, Africa, and naturally we need to learn to help ourselves right here in the States, too. God knows, AIDS is an epidemic killing us all. But I think that this is a good cause. In my mind, there's never been anything to outdo the value of a good education."

"Yes, of course," Moira murmured.

"And it's not a bad thing for those of us who have done so well in the States to give back," Patrick said.

"You're an American," she reminded her brother.

"I'm American, as well, born and bred in New York, as I'm sure you can tell," Andrew said. "But I'm first generation, just like you. My parents talked so long about doing something like this that I've finally realized they were right. Anyway, thanks for listening. And I'll appreciate your help, whatever you're willing to give."

"Like I said, I'm very willing to see what you're doing."

"And I'll want to show you—really show you. When the time is right." He smiled at Moira, then turned to her brother. "Hey, Patrick, I think it's closing in on cocktail hour. I'd like to try one of those specialties of the house. A blackbird."

Moira thought he was staring straight at her as he said the words.

A blackbird. Sure. They hadn't made any in years, but what the heck, it was becoming popular now.

"One blackbird, coming right up. You sit, Patrick. I'll make him his drink. I think I'm becoming an expert."

As she rose, the pub door opened. Moira turned toward it.

Her father was standing there, his face gray, beyond ashen.

"Dad!" she cried with alarm, rushing to him.

He didn't protest, but he didn't seem to notice that she had his arm.

"Dad? Dad, are you all right?" she asked. "What is it?"

Patrick was standing, as were Andrew and Josh, everyone looking at Eamon.

"I need a chair," he muttered.

Patrick was instantly at his other side. They walked their father to a chair at a table. Andrew moved back instantly, allowing Eamon to sink into the chair.

"Do you need your pills?" Moira asked anxiously. "Is it your heart?"

"My heart is fine, girl."

"I'll get Mum."

"No, not yet." He waved a hand dismissively in the air.

"I'll get a whiskey," Patrick said.

"That I need."

"Dad, please, what is it?" Moira asked anxiously.

Patrick set a shot glass of whiskey on the table before his father. Eamon picked it up, put it to his lips, cast his head back and swallowed the shot whole.

He set the glass down, staring at it.

Then he looked at the foursome surrounding him.

"Seamus is dead," he said softly.

13

Long moments of disbelief followed Eamon's announcement.

"Dead!" Moira exclaimed.

Seamus, dead? No. Seamus, so good a friend, a man who had been in their lives like a family member, dead. She didn't speak words of denial. She knew by her father's face that it was true. Tears stung her eyes at the loss. What had happened to him? Had they not paid enough attention to his health? Had he been ailing? What?

Then a niggling of fear and suspicion swept through her sorrow. She looked at her brother accusingly. "Patrick, I told you to walk him home last night."

"I did walk him home, straight to his door," Patrick said, staring at his father. "He was fine. He was certainly not drunk, and he…he was fine."

"How? What happened?" Jeff asked.

Eamon shook his head, staring at Moira. "Don't go blamin' your brother, now, Moira. I'm sure he did as he said. Seamus died trying to help another, so it appears. It was the strangest thing. His neighbor, the old fellow downstairs, must have been having a heart attack and known it. He was found right outside his door, dead as well. The best the police could piece it all together, Mr.

Kowalski must have called out for help, trying to get Seamus to come down. Seamus… Seamus apparently fell down the stairs in his hurry." Eamon was quiet for a moment. "He broke his neck. They say it must have been instant. He didn't suffer. That's all the good they could tell me. He didn't suffer." He buried his head in his hands for a moment. "They were just lying there, the two of them. If the UPS man hadn't needed a signature for a delivery, they might have lain there…well, until one of us went to find out why he wasn't in the pub tonight."

"A UPS man found them?" Patrick asked, his voice strange.

Eamon nodded. "He saw them through the glass door and called the police. The police arrived and called the medical examiner's office. Apparently they died in the wee hours of the morning. When the police… when they'd investigated and taken the bodies away, they called me. Seamus was an organized man, neat with paperwork. He'd left my name and number right in his wallet and by his phone upstairs. I'm Seamus's executor. He had no family. We were his family. The pub was his real home. Here in America."

"Kowalski had relatives," Patrick said dully.

Eamon looked at his son. "No, not really. Like Seamus, he never married. That's what the police said. There's a grandnephew in Colorado somewhere."

"Strange," Patrick murmured. "Maybe Seamus was more addled than I thought. He told me that Kowalski had kids and that there were people in and out all the time."

"No," Eamon said, frowning slightly. "Not according to the police. I was there awhile with them, answering what questions I could about Seamus."

"You told them that Seamus was here last night, right?" Jeff Dolan asked.

"Well, of course. I hadn't known, though, that you walked him home last night, Patrick. I'm glad to hear it. He had friends with him to the end."

"I left him at his front door—on the street," Patrick said. "I think he was a little put out. He didn't think he really needed an escort, he'd been watching his drinking. I asked him to let me walk him to his door, but he kept insisting he was fine."

Eamon put a hand on his son's shoulder. "And he probably was fine, then. The officers investigating the accident seemed certain they'd pieced it together right. Kowalski had come out to his doorway, right in the midst of his heart attack. Seamus must have been up the steps already when he was called back. You were with him, Patrick, just remember that. He loved you kids, our family." He sighed, looking around. "He loved this place. He spent his last night here. We were his family, and he'll have us through the last respects, as well. His funeral will be what he wanted. I don't know what will be happening with Kowalski. The nephew will be coming for his body. There's to be an autopsy on both men—there always is when there's a situation like this—but we should be able to wake Seamus by Wednesday night and have his funeral on Thursday morning. Saint Patrick's Day. That would have pleased him. He had a great faith in God, and he loved Saint Patrick's Day."

They all sat there in silence, watching Eamon, not knowing what to say. Moira was afraid to look at her brother. She wasn't sure what she would see. Her eyes kept filling. She remembered the times she had given Seamus a hard time. Arguing with him that they were Americans. Insisting that he get over it and quit re-

living the Easter Rebellion. She could see him on the
bar stool, telling her that he could well handle another
Guinness. She remembered when they had all been
younger, when he seldom came to the pub without some
kind of special chocolate in his pockets for the kids.

And still, somehow, no matter what her father said,
something about his death wasn't right. She was hurt
and angry...and suspicious.

She felt ill. Absolutely ill.

"Well," Eamon said, "I'm going to have to go up and
tell your mother and grandmother. Colleen and Siobhan. And the kids." He looked at Moira as if he'd been
reading her mind. "And the kids," he added. "He loved
it when the kids were here. He said he could stuff his
jacket with candy again and see little eyes light up. He
should have had his own family. He would have been a
fine father." He shook his head. Then he looked around
the pub. There was a single man on a bar stool and one
couple at the back having a late lunch or early dinner.
"And things go on," Eamon said. "The place will be
jumping tonight. Without Seamus. Still, it would be the
old Irish way. Death is a passage, and the fullness of a
man's life is to be celebrated at its end."

"Dad," Moira said, "you go up and see Mum and
Granny Jon, and we'll manage down here."

"Ah, now, daughter..."

"She's right, Dad," Patrick said. "Spend the evening
getting some rest. With Mum. You can talk about celebrating a man's life all you want, but I know how you're
feeling. You lost one of your best friends. Tomorrow
you'll be making his funeral arrangements."

"Flannery's," Eamon said, nodding. "Flannery's.
That's where he wanted to be waked. Actually, in the
old days, we might have waked him right in the bar and
lifted a pint or two over the coffin. Now that, Seamus

would have liked. But Flannery's. That was his choice. His coffin was chosen, his plot bought. He didn't leave me much to do for him but be there."

"I'll take you on up, Dad," Patrick said.

"I can make it," Eamon said.

"Dad, let me go up with you," Patrick insisted.

Before any of them could move, the pub door opened again. A wild gust of wind blew in, and Michael and Danny were there, silhouetted in the dying afternoon light. "Evening, folks," Danny said. "I've been teaching Michael here a few good Irish drinking songs. He's got them down pat. Ready, Michael? Here we go…come on, Michael, join in."

Danny began to sing, Michael joining him and doing the Irish accent quite well right along with Danny, who purposely deepened his brogue.

"The dear old lady, God bless her! She jumped into the drawer of her dresser. For the north wind blew and sailed, and the black-heart banshee wailed, oh, that dear old lady, God bless her, a-lying in the drawer of her dresser!"

They finished the ditty together. Michael seemed very proud and pleased.

The group in the pub stared at them both.

Danny frowned, stepping in the doorway, bringing Michael along with him, his arm around the other man's shoulders. "We're not really wasted, you know. We stopped in a few pubs along the way," Danny said, "but honest, Moira, I didn't bring your Michael home drunk."

Michael was frowning, as well, as he stared at Moira. "We did a great job, I think. You and Josh will have to see the tape, of course. And we did stop in a few pubs, but…" He trailed off as he realized she was clearly upset. "Are we late? Did we miss something?"

Danny was suddenly dead sober and serious. "What's wrong? What's happened?" he asked.

"Seamus is dead," Moira said.

"My God," Danny breathed. "What happened?"

"Seamus?" Michael murmured.

"My dad's friend, seventh stool down, you met him," Patrick said briefly.

Danny walked straight over to Eamon, kneeling at his side. "Eamon, I'm so sorry. Are you all right?"

"Aye, son, I'm good, thank you. He'd lived himself a full life, a good life. Could have been longer…but he was, at the least, up in his years. Doesn't seem to matter how old a body is, though. When he's gone, he's missed. There's just an emptiness, you know?"

"Aye, Eamon." Danny was frowning. "Did his body give out? I didn't know his exact age, but he seemed a fine and healthy man."

"I'll explain," Moira said, rising. "Patrick was taking Dad upstairs. My mother and grandmother and the others have to be told."

"Come on, Dad," Patrick said softly.

Eamon stood. Moira felt the tears stinging her eyes again as she watched her father. He suddenly seemed old. The loss hit her again. She gripped the back of her chair. "Dad, you go on up. You and Mum need each other tonight."

Eamon touched her cheek, then allowed Patrick to lead him to the rear. He stopped suddenly, looking back. "Danny?"

"Aye, Eamon?"

"You'll host the place tonight for me, eh? There will be the usual customers coming in, and you know the right way. We'll do his wake and his funeral proud, but there must be words for his friends tonight."

"I'll see to it, Eamon. I swear," Danny promised.

Patrick and Eamon disappeared through the door behind the bar. Danny stared at Moira.

He might have visited a few pubs, but he was stone cold sober now. "What happened?" he demanded.

Moira watched him closely. "According to the police, the man who lived on the first floor—"

"Kowalski?" Danny interjected.

"Yes. Apparently he started having a heart attack. Maybe he had just heard Seamus come in. He called to him. Seamus tripped on the stairs in his hurry to reach him. Kowalski was found dead of a heart attack. Seamus was found by him at the foot of the stairs. His neck was broken."

Danny looked down for a long moment. Moira saw that he had gripped the back of the chair her father had just vacated. His knuckles were as white as her own.

"When did it happen?" he queried.

"Sometime early this morning."

Danny still wasn't looking at her. She couldn't see his eyes, but when he looked up at last, she couldn't even begin to read his expression. Suddenly he pushed the chair away and started striding toward the door.

"Where are you going, Dan?" Jeff asked.

"You just told my father you'd be the host here tonight," Moira called after him.

He paused, his back to her for a minute. Then he turned. "I will be. I'll be back within the hour."

He started out once again, then swung around, returning to the table.

Andrew McGahey had been sitting there, awkward and silent, through it all. Now Danny stopped dead right in front of him. "Who the hell are you?" he demanded.

"Danny!" Moira said, horrified.

"Andrew McGahey, Irish Educational Charities," McGahey said flatly. He didn't offer Danny his hand.

"Oh," Danny said. He stared at the man a moment longer, then exited the pub with long strides.

Moira found herself taking the part of the stranger she had so mistrusted. "I'm really sorry, Mr. McGahey," she said. "This isn't Danny's place. He had no right to be so rude."

"He loved old Seamus," Jeff said quietly.

"It's quite all right, and please, just call me Andrew," McGahey said. "Look, I'm going to get out from underfoot right now. Please extend my deepest sympathies to your father and the rest of your family, and tell Patrick we'll talk at a better time." He reached for Moira's hand. She allowed it to be taken. He shook it briefly, nodded to the others, then departed the pub.

Moira felt Michael's hands on her shoulders. Strong, supportive. Guilt didn't even kick in. She was still feeling too stunned.

She offered him a weak smile but moved away, walking to the pub door. Above the etched Kelly's in the cut glass of the upper part of the door, she could see the street.

Danny hadn't gone that far. He was across the street, looking from the pub door down the street to the corner where a turn would lead to Seamus's house.

As Moira watched, Andrew McGahey walked over to him. Danny watched him come. Then McGahey blocked her view of Danny. She could only assume the two men talked. Then they walked off in opposite directions, McGahey to the right, Danny toward the corner. Moira couldn't see exactly where he went without opening the door, but she didn't need to. She knew he was walking toward Seamus's house.

She felt Michael behind her once again. "Tell me what I can do," he said softly. He turned her around to face him. She started to cry. The tears she'd been blinking back streamed down her face. Michael took her in his arms very gently. "It's all right, it's all right," he said softly. "Sounds as if he departed the world in a very noble way. He led a good life."

"He's gone," she said simply, against his chest. Michael, rock solid, there with her. She felt in her heart then the way she had betrayed him. He was here with her, while Danny was running off somewhere, half-cocked. And Seamus...

Seamus with his strange mutterings. Jeff telling her that people needed to keep their mouths shut. Blackbird. Politicians. Talk of assassination. Seamus, Seamus, Seamus...

Seamus had been afraid. Talking. Unnerved. And now Seamus was dead. He had gone to the aid of a friend. A friend dead from a heart attack. He had tripped, fallen.

Or had he?

Seamus, if...

If what?

Seamus, if something was going on, if the picture we see is a lie, I swear, we won't just let it go, we'll find the truth.

"He's gone, and you should cry," Michael soothed. "You lost an old friend. Oh, honey, I am so sorry. Hey, I'm not worth much in a pub, but it's slow as a snail in here right now. Go into the office, or upstairs with your folks."

Moira pulled back, looking at him. She covered his cheek with her palm, shaking her head. Michael. He didn't deserve... But that would have to wait. Seamus was gone. Tears blurred her eyes again. Michael was right. She needed some time to pull herself together, but she could see behind him now. Chrissie was at the bar, talking to Jeff, her head bowed, her crying audible.

And Moira's tears were drying. Suspicion was setting in far more deeply and, with it, a sense of indignation and a longing for the truth.

Whatever it might be.

"No, Michael," she said. "Thank you for the thought. But I told my dad we'd manage."

"You know, you could just put a Closed Due to Death in the Family sign on the door," Michael suggested.

She shook her head, drawing away from him with a slight smile. "I can't. It wouldn't be my dad's way. It wouldn't be the Irish way. Seamus's friends, bar cronies, will arrive tonight. They'll need their drafts. They'll need to talk about him. I'm all right. Honestly. And thank you. Would you check on that couple in the back for me? I'm going to tell Chrissie to take a few minutes. The band will be coming in, so Jeff won't be able to help. We're not busy this minute, which is good."

Michael nodded as if understanding that her way to cope was to start moving. "I'll be here," he promised.

"You really are incredible," she told him.

"Thanks." He started to walk away, then came back to her. "This isn't the time," he said. "But remind me, I need to talk to you later."

"Sure."

He left. She walked to the bar, hugged Chrissie, cried with her for a minute. Then she sent Chrissie to the office, offering her the night off. Chrissie wouldn't take it. There would be a wake at Flannery's Wednesday night, but this would be the night when everyone learned of Seamus's passing, and Chrissie needed to be a part of it, too.

It seemed that as soon as she sent Chrissie back, people began slipping in. A group from the business offices down the street, the dinner crowd.

Just when she was beginning to think she couldn't

handle the bar and the floor, and that Michael didn't know enough about what he was doing, she saw her brother come down with Colleen. Behind the bar, Colleen took a moment to hug her tightly, no words needed. Then she joined Patrick, working on the floor. When the pub was really filling up, Danny finally returned. He had a green ribbon with him, and he roped off Seamus's stool, then set a rosary on top of the ribbon. Liam arrived just as he finished. Danny put an arm around Liam and began talking to him.

Old Liam began to cry, tears running down his wrinkled cheeks. He took his stool, next to Seamus's empty place. Other regulars were there, as well. Sal, the Englishman Roald and his wife. Danny spoke briefly to Jeff, then went up to the small stage, where the other musicians had gathered. He took the mike from Jeff and asked to make a statement. He addressed those who had just stopped by as well as those who considered Kelly's a home away from home. He told them that Seamus wasn't with them anymore and described his hurry to help a fellow man and his quick death for his pains. He spoke about Seamus as a man and a friend, then said that a round would be served on the house in his honor. He hoped that every man and woman there would offer up a prayer and a toast to Seamus, who had heard the banshee's wail and gone to meet the God in whom he had so deeply believed.

He stepped down from the dais, and the band played "Amazing Grace" while Moira and the others quickly served drafts for the prayer and the toast.

As she stood behind the bar busily pouring ale, Moira noted that Kyle Browne, in a mauve sweater tonight, was at the corner table he'd occupied the first time she'd seen him.

She decided to serve him his draft.

She called to Chrissie that she would be on the floor for a minute. Chrissie nodded in acknowledgment.

Moira walked over to Kyle Browne. "Did you know Seamus?" she asked, setting the draft down.

"No, but I'm very sorry to hear of his death."

"Thank you. So what have you seen?"

"As yet? Well, as I've said, I'm watching."

"I've been told this isn't a good place to talk," she said.

"Oh?"

"I think that Seamus might have kissed the Blarney Stone in his youth. He got carried away talking, sometimes."

"Oh? And what was he saying?" Browne asked her, leaning forward, pretending to accept the draft.

"I was actually thinking of wandering down to the police station," Moira said. "Asking about my friend Seamus myself."

"Good," Browne said. He leaned back in his seat, watching her. "I'll be there."

Moira nodded and walked away from him, wondering if she was losing her mind. Had she just hinted to a police officer that someone in her father's pub was a killer? No, she had done more than hint.

Behind the bar again, she found herself shaking. Patrick had walked Seamus home. That meant that Patrick had been the last one to see him alive. Except—if her suspicions were correct—for the killer, and maybe Kowalski. Though most likely he'd heard the noise of Seamus's fall, come out to see and had his heart attack on finding the body. If she went to the police, would it be tantamount to suggesting that her brother had somehow caused what happened? Managed to give Mr. Kowalski a heart attack and bring Seamus crashing down the stairs? After all, her brother was right here, while the killer might be only a figment of her imagination. Unless Patrick…? No. She wouldn't go there.

Arms slipped around her from behind. Michael. "Are you doing all right?" he asked gently.

"Fine. And you've been great on the floor," she told him.

"I'm not so sure. I think I'm wearing a great deal of corned beef and cabbage. Didn't actually have a meal, but the mashed potatoes and gravy I had to lick off my wrist were really great."

"Glad to hear it," she told him, then noted that a woman at a table was waving a credit card in her hand and looking at Michael.

"I think you're being summoned."

"Yeah, looks likes it. Maybe she's a big tipper."

"Hey, go for it."

He lifted his chin. "I'm an associate producer. I don't keep the tips, I put them in Chrissie's jar."

Moira smiled, taking his hand, brushing a brief kiss on the back of it. There was so much she was going to have to deal with once they got through all this. "I'm sure you're making her a bundle. And I'm sure she appreciates it."

"I'd better go take care of that."

"Right. You don't want another customer walking out on you."

"What?"

"Remember when the folks walked out on you? You don't want it to happen again. The pub can probably stand the loss, but your ego was severely injured, remember?"

"I'm on it."

"Good man."

"You bet."

Michael walked off. Moira saw Liam sitting, staring at his empty glass.

She walked down the bar, took his glass and refilled it. Liam was a slow drinker. He still liked his beer warm.

"You okay?" she asked him.

He nodded. "Who will I argue with now?" he asked her mournfully.

"Dad. He's always good for an argument," Moira assured him. She touched his face. "You be careful with yourself, you hear? We really need you now."

Liam nodded. He lifted his glass. "To Seamus."

"To Seamus," she agreed.

When she turned, Josh was behind the bar waiting for her. He didn't ask her how she was doing. He gave her a hug. "You coherent?" he asked.

"Yup, I'm doing fine."

"This is a note from your mum. And I have a question for you. Who is Sally Adair?"

"Oh!" Moira exclaimed, clapping a hand over her mouth. "She's a friend. A wiccan."

"She practices witchcraft, you mean?"

"Yes, she lives in Salem. We went to Catholic school together."

"And now she's a witch?"

"She's a Universalist and a wiccan. I sent her an e-mail about what I was doing, and she suggested we do some taping in Salem. You know, it's a great city for getting into holidays. I take it she called?"

"Yes, she just wanted to know your schedule."

"I'll have to call her."

"Call her in the morning. I told her that a friend of the family had died, and that you'd call her in the morning."

"She knew Seamus. She'd understand."

"Moira, I don't want to put pressure on you, but what do you want to do? Call off any more taping? We can put together a program with what we've got."

"No, no… I think there's a lot more we can do. I want to help my dad in the morning, though, make sure everything is set. They'll have a wake on Wednesday night…and bury him Thursday morning. That is, if the autopsy is done and the body is released. And I still need to talk to Brolin's people about that interview."

"All right, Moira. You need tomorrow morning for your dad, then we'll worry about the show. Take it easy tonight—wow, that's a dumb statement. Tonight's in full swing, and it doesn't look as if you're taking it easy at all."

She smiled. "You know, it's been the best thing for me. I almost feel guilty about sending my dad upstairs."

"Don't feel badly. He's been with your mom."

"I've forgotten about the kids and everything."

"Everyone's fine. I took Gina back to the hotel a while ago. Patrick and Siobhan's three are in bed a while, all curled up with their mum. The pub is running smoothly. What I was saying is that you can take all the time you need tomorrow with your dad, then figure out what else you want to do about taping. Just let me know."

"This is your show, too, Josh."

"The show is mine, but not this episode. This one is all yours, and it's going to be great. I'm going to take off now. But you know, if you need me, I'm just a call away."

"You know, Josh, you really are the best man in my life. Thank God we never got intimate."

He smiled and kissed her cheek. "Good night."

When Josh left, she realized she was still holding the note her mother had sent down. She opened it quickly.

"Brolin's people called. Instead of calling, you should stop by for a personal chat tomorrow afternoon and set up what you want to do. Love, Mum."

"What's up?"

Jeff Dolan had come to the bar. The band was on break.

Moira wasn't sure why, but she quickly crumpled the note in her hand and despite her father's warnings of clogged plumbing throughout the years, inconspicuously washed it down the drain in the sink next to the taps.

"Nothing. How are you doing?"

"Good. And you?"

"Fine."

"Jeff."

"What?"

"Do you think Seamus talked too much?"

Jeff paled. "He fell down the stairs trying to help a friend. We'll never know. Can I have a draft? It's been a hell of a hard night."

"Of course."

She poured him a beer.

Michael walked over to her, setting down a bar rag. He offered her a rueful smile. "It's all under control now. The place is thinning out. You should go up to bed."

"Soon," she said.

He sighed. "Moira, I wish there was something I could do for you. I'm an outsider here."

"No, Michael, it's not that."

"I *am* an outsider. And I guess you need your family. And friends," he added with a strange note. "I'm going to head back to the hotel. Unless you want me to stay."

"Michael, you've done so much."

"I'm going to do more. I'd like to hold you and comfort you, but it seems you really want to be alone."

"I'm just fine. Really. Working is good."

"I understand. I *will* hold you and comfort you, though, you know."

"A pub is a different kind of place, Michael. I'm good here. Picking up glasses, scrubbing them will be good."

"Josh said he talked to you. You know how to reach me. I'll wait to hear from you."

"Thank you," she said softly.

"Want to walk me to the door?"

"Sure."

She came out from behind the bar and allowed him to slip an arm around her shoulders as they walked to the door. There, he paused and kissed her lightly on the lips. She frowned suddenly. "What did you want to tell me?"

"Tomorrow," he said.

"Now. You can tell me now."

He paused, looking around the pub.

"I'm not sure…"

"I'll get my coat. We'll step outside."

She slipped her coat from the hook by the door and stepped out with him. It was warmer than it had been. The walk was clear of ice. Maybe spring really was on the way.

"What is it?"

"I still don't think I should be telling you this now," he said.

She shook her head. "Why? What is it?"

"Maybe something you already know. But… I ran a check on your friend Danny."

"What?"

"I'm sorry, I couldn't help myself."

"A check?"

"I have some sources. Anyway, I'm ashamed to admit it, but I was jealous and worried. He seems…a little dangerous. And…well, I wasn't sure if you really knew him."

"In what way?" she asked.

"Well, he's from Belfast—"

"I know that."

"But did you know why he grew up with the uncle who brought him here all the time?"

"His parents died."

"They didn't just die. His father was shot and killed by an off-duty member of a British army unit. He had a baby sister who was shot and killed at the same time. His mother died a year later, in the middle of a rock-throwing war between rival factions."

Moira stared at him. No, she hadn't known any of those things about Danny. She hadn't known about her own mother and father, and she sure as hell had never known that Danny's past had been so bitter and violent.

"My God," she breathed.

"Moira, I'm telling you because what happened to him was certainly horrible, but he also…well, my sources say that he has been involved with some really radical groups in Northern Ireland. I just want you to be careful. Keep your distance from him as much as you can."

"You went out with him all day," she murmured.

"Well," he said ruefully, "if I can't be with you, I intend to keep an eye on him."

She moistened her lips and nodded. The entire day had been strange. And sad. Suddenly she wanted a tea with whiskey and a full night's sleep, so she could have a few hours in which to forget everything.

"Moira, I'm sorry to do or say anything to upset you.

I just want you to be careful. The door to the top floor of the house locks, right?"

"Right," she murmured. She didn't tell Michael that Danny had keys to every lock the Kellys had.

"Your friend could be nothing more than a great guy with a spotty past," Michael said. "But lock yourself in at night. Protect yourself. You're very precious, especially to me," he told her.

She nodded again. She tried not to think about the fact that he was doing everything so decently, while she had betrayed him with the very man from whom he wanted to protect her.

"Get back into the pub before I leave," he said.

She nodded and went in. As she walked to the bar, she wondered if he had noticed that she had been too stunned, tired or simply shell-shocked to offer him so much as another hug good-night.

When she walked behind the bar, she was stunned to see Granny Jon sitting on the bar stool to the left side of Seamus's empty seat. "I came for a nightcap, child. I needed one this evening," she said, lifting a brandy snifter to Moira. "A blackbird," she said. "Join me?"

"Of course. Give me a second."

Moira made herself a drink, then went to stand before her grandmother. They clicked glasses. "To Seamus," Granny Jon said. Moira was startled by the volume of her voice. Rich and deep. It reached every ear in the pub. "To Seamus. And to all men of peace. And may all who would kill innocent men, women and children for their cause, no matter what it might be, be damned."

She downed her drink. The pub was silent, watching her.

Then Jeff Dolan cried, "To Seamus and the Irish. To the golden age of learning, and a future of peace."

"Salute!" someone called.

Glasses throughout the pub were raised.

Granny Jon set her snifter on the bar. "Good night," she said softly to Moira, and walked around the bar, heading for the stairs.

Patrick came to stand next to his sister. "What was that all about?" he murmured worriedly. "You don't think that this has…unhinged her a little?"

"She's in pain," Moira replied.

"Yeah," Patrick said. "Do you want to go up? Colleen, Danny and I can close down. You've really been working tonight. It must have been a long day."

She was ready to demur, determined to stick it out strongly to the end, then she changed her mind. "All right. Thanks, Patrick."

She turned and left him, following her grandmother's footsteps up the stairs. When she reached the landing, she hesitated, wanting to lock the door then, with her brother and sister still downstairs. They both had keys. Probably not on them. And then again, whom would she be locking the door against? Her brother—or Danny?

She walked down the hallway, passing her room to listen at her grandmother's door. She could hear water running in the bathroom.

She went to her room, washed her face and brushed her teeth by rote and started to climb into bed. Her mind seemed to be running at a million miles an hour. She was exhausted, but she was never going to sleep.

Lie down, just lie down…

She crawled in. Seamus was dead. Her mother knew Jacob Brolin from way back. Danny's entire family had died tragic deaths. She had slept with him. Jeff had told her that something might be going on in the pub. Seamus was dead. He had talked. Granny Jon had come downstairs and made a strange speech...

She jumped out of bed and walked to her grandmother's door. She tapped on it lightly.

"Yes?"

"It's me, Granny, Moira."

"Come in."

Granny Jon was awake, lying in her bed, watching a television that had no sound coming from it.

Moira walked over and sat on the edge of her bed. Granny Jon arched a brow, then stretched out her fingers, curling them around Moira's.

"That was quite a toast you gave downstairs," Moira said.

Granny shrugged. "I may be old, but I like to let my mind be known now and then."

"Are you worried about something?" Moira asked her. "Something going on?"

"I'm sad. We've lost an old friend. And maybe I am a little worried. There's a lot going on these days."

Moira stared at her, then changed the subject. "You know, I take it, that Mum was once acquainted with Jacob Brolin?"

Granny Jon nodded. "Naturally."

"What do you think is going on?"

Granny Jon shook her head. "Just a feeling in these old bones, my girl. And, I suppose, a history filled with a violence I never want to see repeated. It makes me angry, because Ireland is such a wonderful country. Ah, Moira, you've been there. Is there anything like a summer's day in Connemara? The wind blowing over the grass...all of the island. In the North, the Giant's Causeway, those ancient rocks rising like bizarre steps cast down on the earth from heaven above. You can almost believe the legend of Finn MacCool."

Moira smiled and began musing. "Finn MacCool, warrior, leader of the Fianna, who defended Ireland from foreign invaders. He was strong and had the gift of second sight. He could suck his thumb and gain wisdom by doing so." She smiled. "I remember that Mom and Dad couldn't get Colleen to stop sucking her thumb when she was a little girl. She would argue with them that sucking her thumb was going to make her smart like Finn MacCool."

Granny Jon smiled. "Well, now, very good. But it wasn't just Colleen who used Finn as an excuse to suck her thumb. I believe she got the idea from you. I need a trip home. I want to go to Armagh again and see the great cathedral rising out of the land, and the fields rolling and green and so lovely. It's a magical place. I need to see it again."

"You've been back many times."

"I know, but I get homesick. I love the States, and I'm proud to be a citizen. But I want to drive around and see the beauties of my youth."

"We need to plan a trip, then," Moira said lightly.

"We'll see. Let's get through the next few days, eh?"

Moira nodded. She hugged her grandmother. "I love you very much."

"I know, Moira. And I love you, too. Dearly. We're all very, very proud of you, you know. And of Patrick, and Colleen, too, of course."

"May I ask you something?"

"My girl, in life, we can ask anything we like. Getting an answer is an altogether different thing."

Moira smiled. "Will you tell me the truth about Danny?"

"What truth is that?"

"I never knew before that his father and sister were murdered."

Granny Jon was silent for a minute. "Where did you hear that?"

"I'd rather not say. Is it true?"

"Yes, they were killed before his eyes."

"Why didn't anyone ever tell me?"

"Danny never talks about it. I imagine it's a painful subject for him. Even after all these years."

"But it's important. It's something that could…"

"Could what?"

"Well, it could definitely make someone…"

"Crazy? Is that what you're trying to say?"

"No, no, not crazy. Just…radical."

"Some people, maybe." Granny Jon shrugged. "As it happened, he was raised around the world. He puts his feelings into his writing."

Moira realized that her grandmother was not going to speak ill of Daniel O'Hara. Even so, she had learned what she needed to know. Michael had told the truth.

"Granny Jon…maybe it's not a good time to be making speeches. Even if you're only making a toast to an old friend."

"I'm an old woman, girl, and I can speak my mind when I choose. That's a gift that comes with age."

"You're not all that old."

"Oh, yes, my dear, I am."

"Seamus was old, but there was no reason we should have lost him."

"Ah, Moira, you feel his death deeply, I know. We all do."

"It's more than that," she murmured.

"You're feeling something in your young bones, eh? Well, then, I promise I'll behave and keep my feelings to myself, if you'll be doing the same."

"Discretion is my middle name," Moira promised.

"Give me a kiss, then, and let me get some sleep."

Moira kissed her grandmother, then rose reluctantly. She was tempted to ask her to move over and let her share the bed.

She walked to the door, wondering why she felt such a strange and deep-seated fear. She decided she wasn't going to frighten her grandmother.

But she wasn't going to leave.

She was going to take a seat right outside her door for the time being.

She opened and closed the door silently and nearly screamed aloud when she almost tripped over something in the hallway. A body, a man. Kneeling, sitting, crouching? It didn't matter. Even as a scream formed in her throat, the man moved. He was instantly up. Before the terrified sound could rip from her lungs, a hand was clamped hard over her mouth.

14

"Shh."

She was shaking in his hold but didn't really need the voice, even in so hushed a monosyllable, to know it was Danny. She had felt him. Been close enough to breathe in his scent.

"Moira, it's me. Dan. Shh."

She choked back sound but continued to stand there, shaking. Danny. The man she had known so well and never really known at all.

He released her. She forced herself not to run screaming down the hall. "What are you doing here?" she whispered furiously.

"Watching over your grandmother."

He was watching over someone?

"Why?" she asked.

"I don't know," he said flatly. "Not exactly. What are you doing here?"

"I live here."

"In your grandmother's room?"

"She *is* my grandmother."

"Right. But what are you doing here *now?*" he asked.

She was unnerved but also determined to stand her ground. "Watching over my grandmother."

He was silent. In the shadowy hallway, she couldn't begin to read his expression.

"You can go to bed," he told her. "I intend to stay here awhile."

Moira bit her lip, wondering if this wasn't like the wolf offering to guard the lamb. They were in her home. Her father and brother were both asleep down the hall. The house was full of people.

He couldn't possibly be planning on doing anything.

So what was he worried about? And what was *she* worried about?

"I intend to stay here. You can go to bed," she told him.

She felt Danny's eyes in the shadows. He took her hand suddenly. "Fine. That's my place against the wall, there. That's yours."

He stubbornly sat down. She sat next to him stiffly. They were still close enough to touch. She didn't know whether to be afraid or not.

To just start screaming or not…

"Really, you can go—" she began.

"I'm not moving."

"Neither am I."

"Then we'll just have to sit here together, won't we?" he said.

And so they sat.

Time ticked by. At some point she must have fallen asleep. She woke suddenly, with a sense of alarm, not knowing why, or even where she was or what was going on for a moment. Then she knew. Her neck hurt. She had fallen asleep with her head on his shoulder. And he was suddenly sitting up, alert, tense, listening in the shadows.

Moira straightened without letting out a sound. As tense as he, but she didn't hear a thing.

He leaned very close to her. "Your family is all home for the night?" he mouthed.

She nodded. Then she realized she didn't really know. Patrick, Colleen and Danny had all still been downstairs when she had come up. She had gotten ready for bed and gone straight into her grandmother's room. She really had no clue as to whether they had come up and gone to bed or not.

Danny rose, silent as a wraith. She stood beside him. To her horror, her knee cracked. He paid her no attention but started moving down the hallway to the entry. On bare feet, Moira tiptoed behind him. He came to a sudden halt, turning around, frowning severely and motioning that she should turn back. She glared at him indignantly.

He turned again, tense. Then she saw his body suddenly ease. He turned to her. "It doesn't matter now. They're gone."

"Who's gone?" she inquired.

"I don't know. I wish I did."

"I didn't hear anything."

"You were sleeping."

"Well, what did you hear?"

"Something…at the main door."

"Like what?"

"Like…a key in a lock."

"Oh," she said. He was lying. Her family had keys to the front door, and he had a key. No one else. She looked at her watch. It was just after five.

"Mum could be getting up soon," she said, staring at him flatly.

He looked at her, jaw at a slight angle and locked.

"What is suddenly the matter with you?" he asked.

"Nothing is the matter with me," she said, hoping she didn't sound nervous. "My mother wakes up very early. The household stirs. You can leave now, and I'll be very careful to lock up in your wake."

"You don't want me in your house?" he said. It was more of a statement than a question.

"Danny, this was a hard day. You're right. I don't want you up here."

"All right. It is almost morning. And the threat is gone."

"What threat? Maybe you're the only threat around here."

She realized that she was at the head of the hallway and he was in front of her. She was rather like a dachshund trying to pretend it was a Doberman, with her family safely behind her. But she had begun this. She needed to bluff it out.

"I'm a threat?"

"Yes. I think you are."

She thought he would argue. She was even afraid he would get angry and go after her. This time she was ready to scream before he could come anywhere near her.

But he didn't approach her. He turned and headed for the stairway to the pub, leaving the house without ever looking back.

Moira remained in the hallway, shivering, for long moments.

Had he really heard something? *Was* her grandmother in some kind of danger, just for speaking her mind?

And damn it, was Danny not just a loose cannon but one primed and ready to strike?

She started to walk to her room, then hesitated. She paused at Colleen's door, then quietly twisted the knob.

Her sister was sound asleep.

At the door to the master bedroom, where Patrick

slept with his family, she paused longer. To Colleen, she could easily explain her presence. She couldn't sleep. She wondered if Colleen, too, was awake and in need of company. Patrick was sleeping with his wife. If Siobhan awakened, what explanation could she give? *Sorry, Siobhan, excuse me, I was just checking up on my brother.*

Still, she had to be sure. She tried the knob, hoping that they hadn't locked the door. Of course, if the door *was* locked, that had to mean Patrick was in bed. Siobhan wouldn't lock the door if her husband wasn't in.

Seconds ticked by. Moira twisted the knob as silently as she could, thanking God that her father kept everything in good working order, all hinges oiled.

She looked in. Stared against the darkness. A nightlight burned from the bathroom, but the bed was in shadow. The light was left on for the kids in the adjoining room.

After a moment, however, she could make out the bed. There was only one body in it.

She stood there, feeling icy cold and frozen in place. Then she closed the door quickly, realizing that Siobhan could awaken with her standing there. She walked down the hallway to the kitchen and was about to turn on the light when she heard a key turning in the lock to the door that led to the pub.

She froze against the refrigerator. The pounding of her heart seemed so heavy and hard that she was sure the sound would give her away.

If Danny had returned, she was going to scream. She was going to waken the whole house and tell her father that they had to get Daniel O'Hara out of their home.

But it wasn't Danny. As she watched in silence, her brother entered the house, his shoes off and in his hand. He closed the door very quietly. Locked it. On his stocking feet, he started through the entry to the hallway.

"Took you a while to close up, eh?" Moira said softly from the shadows.

Patrick spun around, pale as a sheet, and stared at her. "Damn it, Moira, what is the matter with you lately? Are you trying to wake the whole house?"

"Where have you been?"

"Are you my newly elected parent?"

"Where have you been?"

"Why don't you talk a little louder so my wife can ask me that question and she and I can have a real fight?"

"Patrick, I asked you—"

Her brother strode to her in the shadows. "Out, Moira, with friends."

"On the night Seamus died?"

"Yeah, on the night Seamus died. It's kind of an Irish thing, you know? I was with some other friends of Seamus's, as a matter of fact. Now, if you have any more questions, why don't you put them down on paper? I'm going to try to sleep for a few hours."

He left her standing in the kitchen and started down the hallway. She was both furious, and afraid. She loved her brother.

But where the hell had he been?

Had he come back to the house before, sensed that there was someone there and waited? No, that didn't make any sense. He could have come in at any time and had a reasonable explanation. He lived there.

She was suddenly really tired. And it was after five.

Maybe a few hours' sleep would make things a little better.

She walked to the main door and studied it. She

wondered if the top bolt still slid. It hadn't been used since they'd gotten out of high school.

She tried it. It groaned and at first wouldn't budge. Then it slid home. She walked through the house to the door that led to the curving stairway. Once upon a time there had been a chain bolt on it. The chain was missing now. It didn't matter, or shouldn't have mattered. There was an alarm system on the pub.

She turned from the door and walked down the hall. She headed for her own room but didn't go in. She went to Granny Jon's room, slipped in, locked the door and carefully settled next to her grandmother. She put her head down, thinking she still wouldn't be able to sleep.

She'd locked the doors. And still, she had to wonder if she was locking out the danger that might threaten her household or locking herself in with it.

Amazingly, she was so tired that she slept.

She woke to the sound of her mother's panicked voice.

"Eamon! Moira's not in the house!"

She'd slept with her head at the foot of the bed. She bolted up, turned to see her grandmother rising and staring at her with surprise. She offered a rueful smile and leaped up. She was so tired she was dizzy. She raced out the door to the hallway where her mother was standing, tears starting to flood her eyes.

"I'm here, Mum. I'm here."

"Oh, Moira, dear," Katy said, taking her into her arms. "I'm so sorry. I was going to awaken you to go with Dad to Flannery's, I didn't mean to pry, and then I saw that you weren't there…and there's just so much going on lately that…"

"I'm here, I was just… I, uh, I just decided to crawl in with Granny Jon."

Katy pulled away and nodded as if she understood.

"I do want to go with Dad, though. I'll hop in the shower, then be right out."

When Moira emerged, her father and sister were dressed and waiting.

"Do you want some breakfast, Moira?" Katy asked.

"No, Mum, I'm fine."

"Have a quick cup of tea."

She would have refused, but her mother was already pouring it. She looked at her father, her eyes offering an apology for keeping him waiting.

"Is Patrick coming with us?" she asked, taking the tea from her mother and sipping it.

"Patrick is going to stay with his wife and children," Eamon said. "Whenever you're ready, Moira."

She gulped the tea, kissed her mother on the cheek and followed her father and sister out the door. Flannery's was only about five blocks away, so they decided to walk.

She and Colleen sat on either side of Eamon as they went through the arrangements. Seamus had already picked out his coffin, they discovered. It was a simple one, but with a carved claddagh on the lid above a large cross. The mortuary attendant told them that it was a stock piece for them, so many of their clientele were Irish. The attendant had spoken with the medical examiner's office, and they expected to be able to pick up the remains that afternoon. The wake could be on Wednesday night, as Eamon wanted, and the funeral could be held Thursday morning. Father Mulligan was already aware of the death and would read the service.

As they walked home, Eamon told them, "There were two things he always said he wanted. He told me he wanted to look down from heaven and see you girls doing 'Amazing Grace' in the church. And he wanted me to do a eulogy with every word polite and full of flattery, whether I choked on the words or not."

"We'll sing, don't worry," Colleen said. Then she hesitated. "But what if…what if we break down, Dad?"

"You won't. But if you did, that would be fine with Seamus."

When they returned, the household was up. Siobhan was putting coats on the kids. "We're going down to pick out some flowers for Seamus. Brian thinks that we should choose a very special wreath for him."

Shannon walked to Moira, who bent down and hugged her. "Molly thinks that we should put a few chocolates in the box with Seamus, so he can look down from his place with Jesus and think of us and remember that we loved him. Do you think it would be okay for us to put a few chocolates in with him?"

"I think it would be lovely," Moira said, squeezing her niece.

"Brian says they'll melt and get yucky," Molly said, coming up.

Moira looked at Brian, who looked very mature and serious in his winter coat. "Brian, I don't think that it will matter too much. I had a friend who buried a few cigars with her dad. Since it's your granddad who has the final say in everything, I'm pretty sure it's going to be okay to bury Seamus with a few chocolates. I think it will make you feel good. That's what matters."

Siobhan gave her a grateful smile, taking the little girls by the hands. "We're off."

"Where's Patrick?" Moira asked.

"Still in the shower. He can catch up with us—if he chooses to," Siobhan said briefly.

"Hey, I'll come with you," Moira said. Siobhan frowned at her but made no protest. When they had gotten down to the street, her sister-in-law stared at her. "Were you just trying to get out of the house without your father swearing that you might need an armed escort?"

"No," Moira protested. But Siobhan was still staring at her. "All right, maybe. But not really on purpose… okay, I guess it was Freudian or something. I'll really come to the flower shop. Then I do have a few errands."

As they walked, Siobhan allowed the kids to move a few feet ahead. "It's got to be hard for you right now. Even before this accident with Seamus, your dad was all worried about the murders. Frankly, I don't see the danger. Not that I'm saying anyone deserves to be murdered, but if there is a new serial killer out there, he's targeting prostitutes."

"I know. And I'm sure Dad knows. Have you tried to leave the house alone at night?"

"Yeah, the night you came in. I was only going to a dinner my folks were giving. Your father drove me. My parents aren't a mile from here. But don't feel bad—it's not just your father. My father drove me back."

"I guess we should be thankful we have them," Moira said.

"Yes, I know. Something like this happening to Seamus makes you realize how delicate life can be."

"It does," Moira murmured.

Siobhan was watching her curiously. "Have you met Andrew McGahey?"

"Yes. Just yesterday."

"And…?"

"And what?"

Siobhan shrugged. "I find him…smarmy."

"Smarmy?"

"I don't trust him."

"Really?"

"Oh, he gave us a tape about the kids in Ireland…

but he's rich himself, grew up in the Hamptons, and I haven't heard about any of his own contributions. He's been in Ireland often enough. But I haven't figured out what he does for a living, except spend his parents' money."

"I really didn't see him long enough to make a judgment," Moira said.

Siobhan shrugged. "Maybe I'm wrong. But I think smarmy fits him perfectly. I don't know, maybe if I actually see him do something I'll change my mind. So far, it seems he's at his most passionate when he talks about fishing. He likes Patrick's boat."

"I agree about one thing—we'll have to see what the man does," Moira murmured. Siobhan's words disturbed her. Siobhan and Patrick were definitely having their differences. She loved her sister-in-law, and she was very sorry to see it.

And she was mistrusting her brother herself.

"Maybe we're just getting older and more like our dads than we want to be—paranoid about everything," Moira murmured.

They reached the flower shop. Siobhan was a great mother, keeping patiently sane and quiet while the children all explained just what they wanted for Seamus. Moira picked out a bouquet for the funeral. Seamus was the kind of fellow who would want donations to a good charity given in his memory rather than too many flowers. But they were his family, as her father had said, and some flowers were necessary.

When they finished, Moira glanced at her watch. Nearly noon.

"Where are you off to?" Siobhan asked.

"I—" She hesitated briefly. *The police station, because I don't trust people living in our own home.*

She couldn't say that. And she sure as hell didn't

mean to implicate her brother in anything. She just
wanted to voice her concerns.

"I have a few things to check on for the show," she
lied.

"Well, I'm glad I got you out of the house without a
lot of grief," Siobhan said. "I won't be back for a while
myself. There's a subway station right up the street. I'm
going to take the kids to see my folks."

"Great. Tell them hello and best wishes for me,"
Moira said.

"Will do."

They parted and went in opposite directions. As
Moira walked, she wondered if she was doing the right
thing. She was going to the police with rumors they'd
already heard about. And what was she going to tell
them? That Seamus might have had a few things to tell
them, but Seamus was dead? She loved her brother, but
he couldn't really be doing anything wrong. She simply
couldn't believe it. Then there was the fact that they
had a guest staying with them who had real cause to
be a gun-toting radical...

She wasn't at all sure. And ridiculously, she found
herself looking over her shoulder as she approached the
station. What did she think? That there were eyes
following her everywhere?

She saw a man outside the station, leaning against
the wall, smoking a cigarette. When he saw her, he
tossed the cigarette away and walked toward her.
He was in a very basic suit and overcoat this time. It
was Kyle Browne. He made his way to her as she approached the door.

"You probably don't want to go in there," he told her.

"Why?"

"I think we should walk, maybe get some coffee,

talk. But you don't want to be seen in the police station."

She hesitated, then stepped around him. "I think I should go in."

"Suit yourself."

She kept walking; he didn't stop her. She got all the way to the door, and he still made no move to stop her. She turned and headed toward him.

"I'm not sure what good this does. As if people don't know you're a cop."

"I'm not exactly a cop."

"What exactly are you, then?"

"Different agency," he said. He let out an impatient sound. "This is an international situation, surely you realize that."

"Are you FBI?" she inquired.

He was already moving ahead of her. "You go into that station," he told her, "and the name badges you'll read will be O'Leary, Shaunnessy, O'Casey, and maybe you'll find a Lorenzo, a Giovanni or an Astrella. Sure, the local cops are on guard duty."

"I had wanted to see somebody about Seamus," she murmured.

"The autopsy report just came in. Broken neck. Kowalski died of a heart attack. Just like the cops read it at the scene."

"So it was…natural?"

"If you want to call a broken neck natural."

"I'm telling you, my father—"

"Your father is probably pure as the driven snow," Kyle said impatiently.

"Then what—"

"There's a coffee shop right up here. Let's slip in."

They did so. The place was narrow, with tables stretching far back. Kyle headed for the farthest corner. They sat and ordered two coffees from a disinterested waitress.

He didn't talk again until their coffee had been served. "So, what do you know?" he demanded.

"I'm sure I know a lot less than you do. I wanted to go in and talk to someone to make sure that what happened to Seamus really was an accident."

"Why? What was Seamus doing?"

"Doing? Nothing. But he was talking."

"Saying?"

"That there were whispers in the pub. Rumors about a conspiracy or something. A plan to attack Brolin when he was in the city. And apparently the code word *was* supposed to be blackbird. You ordered a blackbird."

"I thought I'd see what feathers rustled when the word came up."

"It is a drink and also the name of the house band."

"Yes, of course. And not a bad code name. Innocent enough. All you have to do is use it in conversation and see what response you get. So who's in on it?"

"You're acting as if I know."

"You must know something. Your brother has been involved in a lot of anti-Union politics lately."

"He wants to educate orphans. That's hardly anti anything," she murmured protectively. "And actually, isn't the whole thing absurd? Any nut could pull out a gun at a parade—"

"But any nut would have to get close enough. And I'm assuming the trigger man doesn't want to get the death penalty."

"There is no death penalty in Massachusetts—"

"There can still be a death penalty for a federal crime," Kyle said impatiently. "But I'm assuming our man wants to get away with murder."

"Get away with murder as in make it appear like

an accident? Like someone breaking his neck falling downstairs?"

Kyle shrugged.

"Then why would you need a 'piece'?"

"A piece? Who was talking about a piece?"

"I... I don't know. It was just something I over-heard."

"You've got to think. Who?"

"I don't know. It was outside the pub. People whispering. I never saw their faces. They were in shadow."

"Think. What about the voices?"

"Just whispers."

"Come on, now, you must have recognized something."

"I didn't."

"Did they see you?"

"I... Yes, I guess so. I think one of them brushed past me, pushing me down on the ice."

"And you didn't see anything, think anything, feel anything, hear anything more?"

"Yeah—I felt pain when I landed on the ice."

"Then what?"

"Then a friend was picking me up."

"A friend? What friend?"

"Dan O'Hara."

"And you saw him come out from the pub to help you?"

"No, I..." She'd had no idea where Danny had come from that night.

Browne kept studying her. "You know, your friend has a shady past."

"I know that..."

"You know his father was shot and killed?"

"Are you after my brother or Danny? Or someone else in the pub?"

"Your band man deserves a lot of watching, as well."

"Well, that's what you've been doing, right? Watching."

"Miss Kelly, you don't seem to understand. You may be in personal danger. It's important that you come to me with anything you learn, anything at all."

Kyle was staring at the door. She felt at a disadvantage; she couldn't see what he did. She twisted. Two uniformed officers had come into the coffee shop. As she turned to face Kyle, he lifted a hand as if waving to them.

She lowered her head, feeling her stomach turn. There was too much that she hadn't known about Danny.

And she'd slept with him. Fallen into her pattern of physical and mental familiarity and longing.

"You've got to protect yourself," Kyle said. "Stay near those you know from other walks of life. Your partner, your New York lover."

"What about my family?" she asked dully.

"Your family will be occupied with the death of your friend."

"They are, but...the pub is open. After the wake to-morrow night, it will be crawling with people."

"I'll be there. You'll be safe."

"The way Seamus was safe?"

"Look, this is all you have to do. Keep your mouth shut. Pretend you don't know a damned thing. For God's sake, don't snoop. Keep out of it completely. But if you hear anything, anything at all, come to me. Don't let people see you looking for the police. You'd be waving a red flag, just like a matador teasing a bull."

"What do you suggest I do? Lock myself in my room?"

"Live your life normally. Keep out of it. And tell me everything."

"I've told you what I know."

"No, you haven't."

"I haven't?"

"You didn't mention the fact that it was your brother who last saw Seamus alive."

"He walked him home. Seamus went inside alone."

"So he says."

"How did you know that?"

"It's my job to know. I'm good at my job. Now, go about your normal life. And keep your mouth shut, unless you're talking to me."

"I'm supposed to be filming in the area."

"Don't film in or around the pub right now."

He rose, finished with her. "Want me to walk you back?"

"No, thanks, it's broad daylight, I'm not far, and I've got a few errands to run."

They exited the shop together. Kyle lifted a hand to the cops at the front. They waved in turn.

Kyle watched her as she started down the street. She walked to the first corner, then turned, not sure where she was going. She didn't really have errands; she just wasn't ready to go home. She felt dull and afraid, sick at heart.

Then she knew. No matter how tough Kyle Browne might be, Seamus had died. And though it certainly appeared to be an accident, that didn't make it so.

She ducked into a drugstore and pretended to read cold remedy boxes. She purchased one, looking around all the while. Her next stop was a shoe shop, then a clothing store. She bought a blouse, watching all the while.

Finally, she headed in the direction she had determined to go.

* * *

"Where's Moira?" Dan asked Eamon, who was be-hind the bar checking his inventory again. Dan had thought she was safe enough that morning, at Flan-nery's with her father and sister.

"She went out with Siobhan and the kids."

"Where'd they go?"

"Buying flowers. Of course," Eamon said with a frown, "that was some time ago. Then I think Siobhan was taking the kids to spend some time with her folks."

"You think Moira went with her?"

"Maybe."

"You know, maybe I'll call them and find out," Dan said.

Moira wasn't with her sister-in-law.

"Do you need her?" Eamon asked.

"No, not really. I just wanted to see if I could give her a hand."

Eamon shook his head. "Well, she might be with that fellow of hers."

"True," Dan said, feeling something knot in his stomach. "What do you think of him, Eamon?"

"Good-looking fellow."

"Yeah."

"Very bright."

"Yeah."

"Seems willing to bend over backward for her."

"Yeah."

"And…"

"And?"

"He's an American. Doesn't fly in and fly out every time he gets her heart going."

"Eamon, you know I love her. But I wasn't settled in my heart and mind."

"Ah, well, that's life, eh?"

"You think I've lost her?"

"Well, now, you know, she's a fine daughter, but she's not quite shared her feelings with me. Looks like a good thing for her, though. The fellow is part of her business. Works for her, with her. Dotes on her. Takes her places. Like they say, what's not to like?"

"Yeah, Eamon, I guess you're right," Dan said, turning away. He needed to get out.

"Danny?"

"Yeah?"

"There's still something in her eyes when she looks at you. Something sparks when I see you arguing with one another."

"Thanks, Eamon."

Dan walked out the door.

Moira took a circuitous route to the T station to catch the subway. Once there, she bought her ticket, wondering if she had become completely paranoid. She tried very hard to survey the crowd around her, but it was impossible. She had seldom seen the subway system this busy during the day.

When she emerged from the subway, she was certain that she hadn't been followed. She hurried along with brisk steps.

When she reached the hotel, she slipped into the ladies' room and waited a few minutes, then found a house phone. She was afraid she might have difficulty getting through to Jacob Brolin's room, but the operator connected her right away, and she was answered by a deep, very businesslike male voice with a rich brogue.

"My name is Moira Kelly," she told the man. "Mr. Brolin said that I might stop by today."

The man asked her to wait just a minute, then asked if she was in the hotel and if she could come right up.

Brolin had an appointment with city officials soon, but he would love to see her.

Moira headed for the elevator.

He sat in a chair in the lobby, watching her. She didn't see him, of course, because he kept his newspaper high, blocking his face.

When she was gone, he let the newspaper fall.

It was perfect. Everything was going according to plan.

One of the huge men who had been with Brolin downstairs at the restaurant opened the door to the suite. "Hello, Miss Kelly, welcome. Mr. Brolin will see you in the den. Can I get you some coffee or tea?"

"Oh, no, thank you."

"Nonsense, you must have some tea," Brolin called from the doorway to the room. "A meeting of the Irish, from the old country and the new, we must have tea."

Moira smiled and shrugged. "I guess I'll have tea."

She approached Brolin, smiling and offering a hand. He took her hand, then kissed both her cheeks. "Actually, I'm a coffee man myself, but everyone seems to want the Irish to drink tea. Wherever I go, they serve tea in my honor."

"We can have coffee," Moira said politely.

"Which do you prefer?"

"Either. I've had a bit of coffee already today."

"So have I. We'll stick with the tea."

He ushered her into the den, indicating a comfortable armchair. "So, now, shall we discuss what you'd like me to do on your show?"

"I'd like you to say and do whatever you want," Moira told him. "What I do is a travel show about the wonders of America, sometimes big events—which I think we can consider Saint Patrick's Day in Boston to be—and sometimes small events, like a quilting bee in Nebraska. I love to do shows on what makes us special in America, which includes all our different ethnic backgrounds. Of course, Irish emigration to America has been huge over the years. The Irish have certainly put their stamp on this country." She paused as the large man came in with the tea.

"Thank you, Peter," Brolin said.

"Yes, sir, my pleasure."

Peter left them.

Moira leaned forward. "Actually, Mr. Brolin, I didn't come to see you about the show."

"Oh?" He arched a brow, offering her a deep smile. "I never met your father, but I know many people who have. By all accounts, he's a truly fine man. I never had an affair with your mother, if that's what you've come to discover."

Moira stared at him for a moment. "Oh, no! I didn't come to quiz you about my mother, Mr. Brolin."

"Ah. Well, that wasn't much of a fine moment for a politician, eh? Offering information where none was requested."

"Mr. Brolin—"

"If you'll be good enough to call me Jacob, I'd be delighted to call you Moira."

Moira nodded, taking a breath. "Jacob, I want you to know you're in danger."

A slight smile curled his lips. "I've been in danger, you know, from the day I was born."

He wasn't being patronizing. He was reminding her gently that he knew his business and his life very well. He saw the distress on her face and knew that she was genuinely concerned. "Strange, but peace is a dangerous way to some. But I'm grateful, truly grateful, that you would come here to say this to me."

"Mr. Brolin—Jacob—I'm afraid that something may be going on in my father's pub. There's a rumor going about that it was to be…a meeting place, I guess, for people arranging to assassinate you while you were here in Boston."

He set down his tea and leaned forward, hands together, listening intently. "What have you heard?"

"I can tell you what I've pieced together—which I'm afraid seems totally vague. We have a house band, a very good band, which plays Irish music. Pop, as well, but a lot of Irish music. They're called Blackbird. We also have a drink called a blackbird. My dad invented it years ago, though I hadn't heard an order for that drink in a very long time. Apparently, the word was to be used between people when they came into the bar to connect with other people. If someone made a mistake in looking for a contact, it could be easily solved, since the word also signified the drink and the band. My father had a very good friend who died the night before last. He fell down a flight of steps, trying to help the man who lived beneath him, or so the police assume, since they found both men dead."

"I'm assuming autopsies were done?"

"Yes," Moira said, a little frustrated. "And Mr. Kowalski, the man living downstairs, died of a heart attack. Seamus died of a broken neck."

Brolin was silent.

"But you see, Seamus had been muttering about hearing strange whisperings in the bar, about the name blackbird the night before he died."

"I see."

"I really believe that someone, and I'm afraid it might be someone I know, might be part of a plot to kill you. And it isn't just me. There's a government man who has been coming into the pub, watching people."

"A government man, you say."

She nodded. "I've spoken with him."

"And what has he told you?"

"To be careful, really careful. To stay around friends who aren't Irish."

"Ah, that's difficult, when your father owns the pub."

"Yes."

"So this man told you to be careful, and you came straight to me?"

"I thought you had to be told. Of course, I don't really know anything solid at all, it's just that…that I felt you had to be warned. Maybe you shouldn't ride in the parade."

Brolin's smile deepened. "There may be many people walking around Boston right now who would like to kill me."

"I know."

He leaned back in the sofa, still watching her with a half smile.

"You're a very brave young woman."

"Not at all."

"You're here."

"Yes, but everyone knows that I want to interview you for the show."

"True."

He leaned forward again. "Moira, I agree with what the government man told you. You must be very careful. Stay close to good friends and family, preferably in groups. And keep quiet about your suspicions regarding the death of your father's friend. And…" He hesitated, but only for a moment. "We'd had word about the rumors. Actually, there are several possible danger zones in the city. Comes with the territory. We Irish like to be dramatic. What more noticeable than an Irishman killed on Saint Patrick's Day? I'm afraid that the situation is prime for people who still believe that terrorism is the only way. Naturally we've looked into many rumors regarding trouble here. We're watching your father's pub, as well, and though a man such as myself is always vulnerable, I have some strong support behind me. We have computer technology to trace people and the friendship of the government to help us. This is a free country, and no one can make your dad's place into an inquisition chamber. Again, I thank you sincerely for coming to me. Now, I want you to pretend that you know nothing, and watch out for your personal safety. You must behave as if everything is completely normal. Go about your business, but be wary. Most important, watch out for yourself. For me, will you take care to do that?"

She nodded, not really feeling assured, just colder. Brolin had heard that there might be a conspiracy.

Stemming from Kelly's.

"When is your father's friend's funeral?"

"Thursday morning."

"What time?"

"The church service is at nine. We'll be at the graveyard around ten."

"Ah. The parade starts at eleven," Brolin mused. "Will it work for you if I give you that interview you want right after the parade? I believe that I get off the float at about one in the afternoon."

"I would love the interview whenever you have time to give it."

"You're frowning, Moira. You're afraid that I'm not going to live long enough on Saint Patrick's Day to spend time with you."

"Oh, no! You've got to live."

"I will," he promised her. "I will." He rose. "Come, we're going to give you an escort downstairs and pretend that all we've talked about is the interview. We'll do it at Kelly's. As soon as I'm free from official duty, I'll come to the pub."

"It will be crowded to the gills," she said worriedly.

"And I'll be delighted to be the center of attention in an authentic Irish-American pub," he told her. "Trust me, we will survive it. And we'll drink to Ireland, and to America."

Moira rose to join him. He reached for her hand.

The tall blond man was just outside in the parlor area of the suite, glasses low on his nose as he read from a file folder.

"Peter, we're going to escort Miss Kelly down," Brolin said.

"With pleasure," Peter assured him, setting aside his file and rising.

As he did so, Moira noted that his tailored suit covered a shoulder holster and gun. Brolin was certainly being protected, but she wondered if any amount of strength and firepower could stop someone who was really intent on murder, especially if—as she feared— they were willing to die to achieve it.

Peter opened the door for them, stepping into the hallway first. Brolin spoke casually about the weather. Strange, it had been so cold, so much snow that winter, ice on the walks, and now, suddenly, the days were warming, almost as if the heavens were bringing spring a few days early, just for Saint Patrick's Day.

"We're expecting a high in the sixties tomorrow," Brolin said as they stepped into the elevator and pushed the button.

"That will be nice," Moira replied casually. "It was

a rough winter. Even in Manhattan, we had snow piled on the sidewalks."

They reached the lobby and walked together into the center. Brolin made a point of kissing her cheeks.

"It will be wonderful to chat on camera with such a lovely young lady," he said, his voice carrying to the registration desk and beyond. "I look forward to it. I have a few old tales I can tell on camera for you. And a few new ones, too, of course."

"Thank you so much for your time, and thank you so much for agreeing to the interview," Moira responded.

She thanked Peter and said goodbye, then headed for the large main doors. She knew without looking that they stood in the lobby and watched her until she was headed down the street.

As she went down the steps to catch the T to the pub, she was deep in thought regarding her conversation with Brolin. *So they knew.* There were several possible danger zones, but Kelly's Pub was one of them, and they had known.

There was nothing for her to do. Everyone was warned. The Irish were watching; the American government and the police were watching. She had done all she could. Now all she had to do was watch out for herself.

And pray that her brother wasn't a terrorist.

And Danny…

She had to go about normally. Work, stay with groups of people, act as if she knew nothing, suspected nothing.

The wake was tomorrow night; the pub would be very busy. It would be busy tonight, as well. She had to help her father; that would be normal.

Tonight…tomorrow night.

Saint Patrick's Day.

She remained deep in thought.

And never noticed the man following her down into the bowels of the T station.

15

As she hurried down the steps to her train, Moira wondered again at the number of people. She had been on the South Side, a busy enough place and often filled with tourists, but it still seemed like a lot of commuters. She found a spot just behind the worn line on the pavement in front of the tracks, anxious to make sure she got on the train. As she stood waiting, she noticed movement on the tracks. A few rats running feverishly here and there. She wondered how many of them died, run over or electrocuted. She couldn't help feeling sorry for the creatures, even if their species tended to be disease-ridden and had carried the fleas that spread bubonic plague to Europe.

From the distance, she heard the arrival of the train. The crowd started to surge forward.

Suddenly it didn't seem like the natural surge of a crowd. She was being pushed.

"Whoa, excuse me," a heavyset man behind her apologized, as he was pushed against her.

"Hey!" a woman at her side cried with alarm.

Moira tried to slide between them, realizing she was dangerously close to the edge.

"Who the hell is pushing?" another man cried angrily.

But as he spoke, there came another massive crush as someone at the rear tried to get closer, shoving everyone forward.

"Stop!" the woman screamed.

Another hard push nearly sent Moira flying. Grabbing at the coat of the man to her right, she kept from soaring over the edge of the platform, but the impetus at her back sent her sprawling.

Her lower body was on the platform.

Her upper body hung over it.

She lay breathless and stunned. She noticed the rats again. Scampering around at a maddened speed.

Of course. The train was coming. Trying to rise and looking the tracks, she saw the nose of the vehicle bearing down on her with the speed of lightning.

"Back off!" someone from the rear shouted with furious authority.

She desperately tried to gain her balance.

"Jesus!" breathed the woman at her side.

The fat man was down, reaching to get hold of her legs and help her as she struggled to get on the platform.

"Back off!" she heard again, and then there were more hands, grabbing her, angling for a good grip. She was lifted off the platform.

The train whizzed by her, groaning and screeching as it came to a halt, the nose a hundred feet beyond her. She felt the wind it created on her face, so close that it was like facing a twister. Her hair tangled before her eyes. She swept it back, blinking, balancing, turning into the hands that still held her so strongly.

"Danny!" she gasped with shock.

His hair was as windswept as hers. The look on his face was dark and strained. His teeth were clenched.

"Are you all right?" the heavyset man asked, catching her arm. Despite her brush with death, people were still pushing around them to get on the train.

"Fine, fine."

"You shouldn't be allowed on the streets," Danny muttered.

"Don't get mad at her because other people are so rude," the woman gasped.

Danny didn't seem to notice the people around them, either those brushing by to get on the train or the two who had risen to her aid and now her defense.

"You could have been killed," he said.

"You could have killed her," the big man said.

Danny turned and stared at him. Whatever the man saw, he didn't like. He hurried past them to get on the train.

"You tell him where to go, honey," the woman said, stepping on the train, as well.

Moira was shaking too badly to move, to do anything other than stare at Danny. What the hell was he doing there?

She'd fallen on the ice. And he had been there.

She'd tripped—or been pushed—in the pub, and he'd been there.

And here…now…

How could one man orchestrate such a mob scene? How could he zero in on her? Any one of the people close to the edge of the platform might have been killed.

"Moira, are you all right?" The question didn't seem to be voiced with concern. He was still angry. Maybe she wasn't supposed to be all right.

She pulled away from him. "Yes, thank you. I'm fine. I'd just as soon get off this platform, though."

"Let's go out and get a cab."

They exited the T station. She tried to keep from shaking, from giving away any of her thoughts or feelings. He had taken her arm again. She wanted to scream and wrench away from him. But that wouldn't be acting normally. Since he was holding her, he could surely feel her shaking. That was all right. She might have been decapitated. Or sliced cleanly in half.

It would only be normal to be shaking.

They came to the street. The sun was blazing. Danny still held her arm as he shook his head with disgust. "Jesus, Mary and Joseph," he breathed. "Where were the T attendants? There should have been someone down there, stopping that kind of mob crunch."

She looked at him. "It all happened in a matter of seconds," she said.

"There should have been someone there. In fact, a report should have been filed. And people should have been arrested."

"Which people?" she asked, staring at him. "There's no way to tell who started pushing and no one to arrest."

He didn't answer but took her elbow, hurrying her along the main street. "I guess the best place to get a cab is over by the aquarium," he said.

"Danny?"

"What?"

"How the hell did you happen to be in that T station?"

"I was looking for you."

"Why?"

"I was worried about you."

"Why?"

"That should be obvious."

"Because you think I'm in danger? Not just 'Shut up and don't speak Gaelic' danger but real danger?"

"You seem to be having a lot of strange difficulties these days."

"All explainable, of course. A slide on the ice, tripping over my own purse, which I had somehow lost and not seen by the bar. And now…a crowd in a subway."

"You could have been killed."

"Yes, this time. But you were there to save me. Pretty incredible."

He cast her a sideways glance. "You think I would push you under a train?"

"I didn't say that. I just said it's incredible that you were there. How in God's name would you think to look for me at that T station?"

"Well, let's see. No one knew where you were, but your mother was talking earlier this morning about Brolin wanting to talk about an interview with you. That's his hotel." He pointed.

"How did you know that?" she inquired.

"I read the newspaper. The entire city knows where he's staying. I didn't need to be Sherlock Holmes. Neither did you."

"Your timing was convenient."

"My timing was heaven-sent. That fat man would have had you both in the gulley in his gallant efforts."

"Hey, he was a stranger who was trying to save me."

"Right. A good man. But also an incompetent one."

They were nearing the aquarium, and as Danny had suggested, there were plenty of cabs. He started to hail one, then hesitated. "Do you want to go back? Do you want to get a drink somewhere first?"

"No," she said quickly. "I have to get back. I have work to do."

"Ah, yes, of course. Work must go on."

He lifted his hand, flagged down a cab. Moira slipped into it; Danny followed. "So what's your plan?"

"My plan?"

"You said you had work to do."

"Yes."

"So…what's on your taping schedule for what's left of today?"

She didn't have a schedule, but as she stared at him blankly, she came up with one. "I'm going to be out of the city."

"I thought your show was on how Boston celebrates Saint Patrick's Day?"

"Actually, my plans have changed. But it's great that you're here, Danny. In Boston. I'll be able to leave for the rest of the day and know that you'll be here with Dad. He's going to need a lot of help today. The morning was hard for him, making the arrangements for Seamus."

Danny fell silent. She felt his presence so close to her in the cab. He still looked just like the man she had known for so many years. Tall, straight, striking in his long leather coat, hair smoothed back, face somewhat taut, eyes enigmatic as he trained them out the window on the scenery they passed. She saw his hand where it lay on the seat between them. The long fingers, neatly clipped nails. He had powerful hands. Watching his hand where it lay, she was tempted to reach out and touch it. She bit her lip. She knew him far too well in that regard. His shoulders appeared broad in the coat. He had an exceptional build, lean, wiry, not an ounce of fat on his frame. He possessed a very strong jawline and striking features. Those eyes, hazel, not hazel, amber, gold. In the cab, she could breathe in the scent of his cologne. She knew what lay beneath the clothing; the problem was she hadn't really known the inner man. It chilled her to think what he must still feel in the lonely dark of night. He had watched his father and sister shot down. That would surely create a wealth of bitterness in a man's heart. He had to want revenge. How far was he willing to go to take it?

He turned and stared at her suddenly, as if reading her mind. "I wish you would trust me," he said quietly.

"I do."

"You're a poor liar, Moira. You always were."

"There's something going on, Danny, and we both know it."

"Isn't it a pity we don't know more?"

"I think you *do* know more."

"And I think there's a lot you're not telling me."

"There's nothing I could possibly tell you, Danny."

He turned his gaze to the window again. In another few minutes they were outside the pub. Danny paid the driver, and they exited the cab.

"Thanks," Moira said briefly, heading for the door.

"For the cab ride, or for rescuing you from dismemberment?" he asked dryly.

"Both," she murmured, and escaped through the doorway to the pub.

The dining area was still half-filled with the end of the lunch crowd. Liam was on his stool, with Eamon leaning on the bar from the opposite side. They smiled and waved as she walked in; she still thought that her father looked terribly sad, and older today. He was going to miss Seamus so much.

"Hi, Dad."

"Hi, daughter. Everything all right?"

She nodded, coming to him, hugging him. "And you? How are you holding up?"

"Well. Very well. You know, it's best to talk to people. And talk about people. And keep moving, keep going."

"You're sure you're all right?"

"I'm where I should be. Working. And with friends. My friends, Seamus's friends."

"Moira Kathleen," Liam said, "don't y'know? That's the way of the old Irish wakes. Sitting with the one passed on, right by the coffin, lifting pints as we gathered round, just talking. The waking and the funeral have never really been for the dead but for those left behind."

"Of course, Liam."

"We should have had two nights of waking, Eamon," Liam said.

"Seamus told me what he wanted, and wrote it down, as well. I'm following the man's wishes, Liam, nothing more." Eamon turned his attention back to her. "If you have work to do, Moira, you go ahead and do it."

"Dad, I'll be here with you tonight when it gets busy," Moira said. "But may I borrow the car? I'm thinking of taking a camera up the coast a bit, to Salem. Tomorrow I've got to edit and get the main tape out, then coordinate with Michael and Josh regarding the live feed we're going to do of the parade."

"He's called twice," Eamon said.

"Who?"

"Michael. Best give him a call."

"Can I use your desk?"

"Of course."

Moira went into her father's office and sat behind his desk. She wasn't sure that what she was doing was right—perhaps she should remain at the pub during the afternoon, as well. But she really needed to get away. Danny would be at the pub.

And Patrick...

Well, it didn't seem that anyone ever really knew where Patrick would be.

She put a call through to Sally Adair at the Magik

Maiden, her friend's shop in Salem. Sally answered, delighted to hear from Moira and glad that she was coming up.

"But are you sure? I read in the paper today about your old friend Seamus. This must be a hard time for you."

Harder than you can imagine, Moira thought.

"That's partly why I'd really like to come up today. I need to get away. I'm not bringing a crew, just a hand-held camera. If it's all right with you—and you're willing to sign a waiver, of course—I'll film a bit in the shop, and then you can escort me around to see the town's Saint Patrick's Day decorations."

"I'd love it."

Sally extended her sympathy to Moira's dad and family, and they chatted a minute longer, then Moira hung up and tried Michael in his hotel room. He wasn't there, but she hadn't really expected him to sit around all day waiting. She called his cell phone and found him.

"Hey, beautiful, I've been looking for you."

"You knew I was going with Dad, and then I had a few errands. And I went to see Jacob Brolin. He's going to come to the pub after the parade and let me interview him here."

"Fantastic! I knew you could get him."

"I'm delighted, but we won't have him for the original airing, since we need to get the tape we have in tomorrow if we want to show it with the live feed. They'll have to edit him in for the repeat of the broadcast at night."

"I'm sure that will be fine. So…were you planning on staying around to help your dad today?"

"Actually, no. How soon can you meet me here?"

"Ten minutes, why?"

"I want to take a trip up to Salem."

"Oh?"

"I'd like some tape from Salem to compare to Boston's festivities. Nothing major, just the handheld camera."

"Moira, whatever you want. I've been reviewing what we've got and made arrangements to get the tape out tomorrow once we've finished up. Plus I made the last of the arrangements for the live setup."

"Great. Thanks, Michael."

"Hey, it's my job, remember? Besides, in all honesty, Josh has done a lot of the work."

"It's his job, too," she reminded him. "Is he at the hotel?"

"I believe he is. Editing the pub door thing."

"I'll give him a call."

"I've got the camera. If you can't reach him, we can just take off and leave him a message."

"Great."

She hung up and went to the bar. She looked around, but Danny hadn't followed her in.

"Do you know where Danny is?" she asked her father.

"Haven't seen him," Eamon replied.

"How about Patrick?"

"Your brother went out a while ago, said he was going to meet Siobhan at her folks' place."

"You're sure you haven't seen Danny?"

"He took off a few hours back. Haven't seen him since."

Moira wished that he had come in, that she could see him and know he was here. It was making her uneasy not to know where he was.

"Think he's in his room?"

"No, I don't think he's there, but give a knock on his door if you're worried."

Moira nodded, then walked toward the back of the pub. At Danny's door, she hesitated, listened, then knocked. He didn't answer. She tried the door and found it open. Walking into the room, she found that he kept it impeccably neat, bed made, clothing put away, only a jacket over a chair. A notebook computer was running on the desk, and next to it were several maps of Boston. She hesitated, then curiosity got the best of her. The file that was running was something called *Sara's Night*. She began to read.

"There was only one thing to do when taken in by the Royal Ulster Constabulary under the Special Powers Act. Lie. And Sara lied."

Moira kept reading.

The soldiers were none too gentle when they broke into the house. Naturally, they came in the dead of night, when the fog lay heavy over the streets. She had always thought there would be a warning, but she was wrong. She had barely lifted her head from the bed when they dragged her from it. The nightgown she'd worn was torn off her, just as the sheets were stripped from the bed. They were taking no chances that she might have a weapon hidden somewhere on her body or in her bed.

When they finished with their search, she was shaking and humiliated, and wondering what weapon could be so minute that she might have hidden it in the orifices they violated.

Clothes were thrown at her. She dressed.

They took her to the "Infamous Place," Long Kesh, with barbed wire and towers that sported machine guns. She was taken alone, which frightened her more than anything. This wasn't a general sweep of all suspected terrorists. This was aimed at *her*.

When she arrived, she was escorted to the man in charge. She knew his name. And his reputation.

"Miss O'Malley, is it?" he asked, reading from a folder. She had been seated in a chair before his desk, and he was speaking politely. She had heard about prisoners being tortured, terrorized. This man was being courteous. Courtesy, she had learned, was deadly.

"Yes. Sara O'Malley. And I've done nothing."

"You were recognized, Miss O'Malley, as the woman who pretended to be distressed, who lured Sergeant Hudson from his car while your friends set a bomb beneath it. Hudson and three soldiers were killed when that bomb went off."

She had been willing to give her life, or so she had believed. But she had never imagined what it would be like when a bomb went off, when an explosion ripped through the air, the fire, the screams, the smell of human flesh burning...

"I don't know who thought they saw me. I was nowhere near the scene."

He leaned forward. "Poor silly girl. I don't really want to see you go to prison...or die. You're a young thing, with your whole life ahead of you. You could escape, run to America. What I want from you are the names of the men who are doing the bombing. It's very easy. You give me the names. I help you escape."

"I can't give you names. I wasn't there."

He nodded, as if accepting her word. "Fine, we'll give you some time to think about it. Maybe you will come up with something."

She'd had no idea that a man had been standing behind her until she was blindfolded. A hood fell over her head. Arms reached for her. "Call the lady's escort, please."

Her escort.

She never knew exactly where she was taken. Or how many soldiers "escorted" her.

She had been willing to give her life…

In the end, they left her on the concrete, still blindfolded.

The hours passed in a nightmare. She imagined the smell of the burning bodies once again. She shivered with the cold. Names. She couldn't give names…

They brought her into the office again the next day.

"Miss O'Malley, have you thought of anything to tell me?" he asked her.

She shook her head. "No."

"I'm sure in time you will. Meanwhile, let me have you escorted back to your cell."

She tried not to let him see the way she was shaking. Her lip trembled.

"I'm sorry—did you think of something to say?"

She shook her head, trying to steel herself for what was to come. The "escort" arrived. She tried very hard not to think or feel. One of the soldiers, bending over her, whispered, "Hudson was my cousin." When he finished with her, silent tears fell down her cheeks in such a flood, she nearly choked on them.

"Enjoying the story?"

Moira slammed down the screen of the laptop, stepping back in horror. Danny had come into his room. He was leaning against the doorway, staring at her with narrowed amber eyes.

"Danny…"

He moved toward her. "I asked you if you're enjoying the story."

"What do you care what I think? I'm sure you have plenty of fans."

"Do *you* ever buy my books?" he asked politely.

"Of course. Sometimes. I will now, of course."

"Of course. You want to see how it ends."

"I've got to go."

"Right. You have work to do today."

"Yes."

She tried to brush past him, but he caught her arm. He didn't hurt her, just brought her too close against him.

"What did you want?"

"What?"

His body seemed as hot as a furnace. His hold on her flesh reminded her of the lean power in his arms and chest. The anger in his eyes seemed to shoot through her.

"You're in my room. What did you want?"

"Nothing."

"Just nosy?"

"No... I was...looking for you. To make sure you'd help my father if he needed it until I got back. I'll only be gone four or five hours."

"You're a fool, Moira."

"The computer was there—"

He shook his head with impatience. "Do you think I give a damn if you read what I write?"

"I've got to go," she insisted.

"Moira, damn it, you need to talk to me."

"Why, Danny, when you've never really talked to me?" she asked.

"You're shaking."

"I've got to go."

"Moira?" She heard her father's voice as he called from the bar.

"Let me go. My father is calling me."

His eyes pinned her for another moment, and he pulled her slightly closer. "Moira, I... Damn," he muttered, then released her, almost pushing her away.

He watched as Moira fled past him.

16

"Michael is here," Eamon said as she rushed to the bar. "Let me get the car keys."

"Thanks, Dad. I'll be back for the post-dinner rush."

"Thanks, but you go do your own work. I can manage the pub."

"I'll be back," she said firmly, catching the keys as he tossed them to her.

Michael was standing at the door, waiting, a backpack with camera equipment thrown over his shoulder. He slipped an arm around her shoulders as she joined him at the door.

"You're shaking."

"Am I? Just a little chill. Let's go."

The attendant at the garage brought the car around. When it arrived, Michael set a hand on her shoulder. "I think I should drive."

She was about to protest, but he was right.

They pulled onto the road.

"Are you sure you want to do this today?" he asked her, sliding a hand over hers. "This is a rough time for your family. Even I could see that Seamus was much more than a customer."

"Yes, I'm fine. I'm happy to be getting out of the

city. And I've given so little attention to what I've been doing, I'll be amazed if we have a show left."

"You're not supposed to worry about the technical aspect of the operation, Moira. You're the talent."

"I'm also a producer."

"Josh is on top of everything. You don't need to worry. And," he reminded her lightly, "you do have me."

"I've used and abused you both."

"I love it when you use me, you know."

He was teasing. His fingers tightened around hers, and she smiled again, but she was sure it was a sick smile. He didn't know that she had betrayed him. With a man who might be planning murder. Who might already have tried to murder *her*.

Then again, Danny had been there, picking her up each time. Of course, if he'd failed in his attempts to cause her harm, what better way to disarm her suspicions than by being the man to rescue her?

What about the night she had come downstairs? They had been alone together for a very long time. He could have done something then. What? Slit her throat in a bed in her father's house?

"Moira, what's wrong? I'm here, you know."

She looked at Michael. What was wrong, indeed? Here was a man most women would kill to be with. He had done nothing wrong; she had. But she wasn't ready to come clean with him—not while all this was going on. And she knew she couldn't resume their relationship until she had done so.

"I don't know. I suppose I'm just upset, worried about a lot of things."

"You know, we don't need this segment. We could just take the day off. Find a charming New England inn and…forget about everything."

"Oh, Michael, I'm so sorry, I've been horrible, and—"

"It's all right. We'll go to Salem."

He kept driving, then said, "I'm sorry—I think I upset you more, telling you what I found out about O'Hara."

"It looked like you two were getting along fine on your pub door excursion."

"Yeah, well…" Michael murmured ruefully. "I think I'm sorry about what I told you. I should have kept my mouth shut."

"Why?"

"Because we did have a decent day. You know, it's a little intimidating when the family friend turns out to be a man who looks like real competition."

"He isn't competition," Moira murmured. Lord, she was lying. Or maybe she wasn't. Some things didn't change easily. Maybe Danny would always have a physical power that beckoned to something in her senses. And maybe the sheer logic of everything she knew about him would be enough to convince her that even if he wasn't contemplating murder, he wasn't what she was looking for in life.

"No, I guess not. He told me that if I made you happy, no one could ever wish me greater blessings in life. Sounded a lot like your brother. We had an interesting day." He fell silent for a moment, then said in a serious tone, "You think there's something going on in your dad's bar, don't you?"

"Pub," she corrected automatically, giving him a rueful shrug. "There is a difference. And there could be something going on anywhere," she murmured.

"I think you should stay close to me for the next few days. Will you?"

She turned and looked at him. "I'm with you now, and we're on our way out of town."

"So let's have a good day."

"Michael," she murmured. "I—"

"No more talk about the pub or Seamus. You have your interview with Brolin, and everything is going to be all right."

"How can it be all right? Seamus is dead."

He was quiet for a minute, then said, "Moira, I talked with your dad. I know what happened, and I know you're disturbed. But it was an accident. A man trying to help a friend. Now let's just try to enjoy the day, okay?"

She smiled and agreed, but inside she was still cold and worried.

"Josh, where did she go?"

Dan had barely waited until Moira left his room to call her business partner, hoping he would be in his room at the hotel.

"Hang on," Josh said. "I just got in, but I've got a message here. They went to tape in Salem, with Moira's friend Sally Adair. I never met her. Do you know her?"

"Yes, I met her years ago. She used to live around here, then moved up the coast. Are you going to join them?"

"I wasn't planning to. I'm assuming Moira planned on using just the handheld camera, and since Michael is with her, he can handle it."

Dan hadn't closed the door to his room; he was startled to see Patrick Kelly standing in the doorway.

He lifted a hand in acknowledgment of Patrick's presence.

Patrick smiled and nodded, waiting for him to finish his conversation.

"I think I'll take a drive up," Dan said. "Just in case they need a hand."

Josh was silent for a minute. "Dan, I'm sure they're going to be fine. And...you know, this is none of my business, but...she's been seeing Michael steadily ever since they met."

"I know. Look, if it turns out that he's what she really wants to be happy, I swear, I'll back off so far you'll never know I was around. Moira has been really upset though, lately, with Seamus and all... Why don't you drive up with me?"

"All right. But if we don't move—"

"We'll move now. Right now. We can catch them. They just went out the door."

"All right. I'm on my way."

"Where are you moving to?" Patrick asked from the doorway.

"Salem."

"Dad said Moira had taken off with Michael to see Sally." Patrick studied Dan. "You don't think you should leave the two of them alone?"

"Maybe I should. But I'm not going to, not now, in the midst of everything here...with Seamus's loss and all. Hell, did you need me for something?"

Patrick shrugged and laughed. "Actually, I came to see if you wanted to take a drive up to Salem."

"*You* were planning on following them?"

"Yup."

"Why?"

"I guess I'm a little worried about her. And Michael...well, maybe she's madly in love with him, but he hasn't really known her that long. I'm her brother. I've known her forever, and if she needs support right now, I think I'm better qualified to offer it. And I had a feeling you might be willing to join me."

"Yeah, I'm willing. And Josh is on the way."

"Good. That makes it okay for us to go up and you to get into the middle of her relationship, right?" Patrick asked. "Never mind, don't answer. I'll drive."

"Hey, do me a favor. Make sure your dad is going to be okay, then keep a lookout for Josh. Give me a minute here. I'll be right out."

"Sure."

Patrick left. Dan dialed the phone again. He never called Liz on the house phone. This time, however, he did.

"Liz, tell me you've got something new for me."

"All right. This charity fellow that Patrick Kelly is working with… Andrew McGahey. There's a man walking a really fine line. Want to hear about him?"

"Shoot."

"You're on the house line," she accused him suddenly.

"Just tell me quickly what you've got."

"He was in Belfast several times in the last few years. Each time he went, he had a number of meetings with Jacob Brolin—and members of the Real IRA. You need to keep your eye on him—and Patrick Kelly. Although I will say this, McGahey has been doing all the right things legally for that charity. His papers have all been filed correctly."

"Well, of course. Patrick Kelly is a good attorney," Danny said dryly.

"There's been another man in the pub, as I'm sure you know."

"I'm aware of Browne."

"Good. Watch yourself. He's not working alone."

"I know the main prize, Liz. I've been watching out for Browne. Jesus, there should be something else by now. Have you gotten anything else on Michael McLean?"

"Why? Are you itching to take the fellow down? Don't go getting obsessive."

"Just keep at it," he said. Obsessive? Well, yes, he could be obsessive. And he wasn't even sure why. He'd managed to spend the afternoon with Moira's new beloved and discovered that if there was something behind the facade, it was damned well hidden. The guy had been decent all day, humorous, intelligent. It appeared that he really loved Moira, which should have made Dan feel some guilt, but didn't. Maybe he was wrong, and the guy was simply perfect, and he himself had blown everything over the years.

"I told you," Liz said wearily, "every record we have squeaks. Don't go getting tunnel vision. There's too much at stake."

"I don't have tunnel vision." Maybe he did. Liz was right; there was too much at stake.

"You know that Moira Kelly went to see Brolin today."

"Yes, of course, I know that."

"Good. You've been on that line too long."

"I was on it too long the second I called you," he said impatiently. "Listen, I want to see what you have."

"On what?"

"McGahey, Patrick, the charity. And on McLean."

"Dan…" she said warningly.

"I want to see what you've got. It's my ass on the line here, big-time. Now I'll get off the phone." He hung up, grabbed his coat, patted the inner lining to make sure he had everything and went out. He spoke quickly with Eamon, praying the man would tell him that he was fine and had plenty of help. Eamon said exactly that.

Dan hurried outside to join Patrick. They waited on the street for Josh to arrive.

As they passed the sign telling them that they were entering Salem, Michael asked Moira where she wanted him to park.

"There's nothing much by the shop. I usually park in a space around the common when I come here. It's only a few blocks to her shop, and the town is really charming."

Michael drove past pretty houses to park in the first space he could find around the common. He took the camera from the trunk, and they walked along the street, past the Hawthorne Inn toward the waterfront.

She grinned at him. Getting away from Boston had been good. She felt as if she had cast aside a burden, if only for a short time. She could almost forget that tomorrow would bring a wake, that Seamus was dead.

"One more block to Sally's shop."

The camera was over his shoulder. He took her hand as they walked. She didn't protest.

"Ah, there you are."

Sally was standing outside her shop, as if supernaturally aware of just when they would arrive.

"See, she is a witch, she's expecting us," Moira told Michael seriously. She moved ahead, hugging her friend. Sally had ink-dark hair that went well with the slinky black caftan she was wearing. The V neck of her garment displayed the silver pentagram she wore. Silver orbs dangled from her ears and highlighted her almost powder blue eyes.

"You must be Michael," Sally said, stepping forward and extending a hand.

"I must be. Sally, great to meet you. I admit, you're my first witch."

"Sally. I love the window," Moira said, looking into the display window, where her friend had created an Irish tableau with fairies and leprechauns and a charming statue of Saint Patrick.

"Thanks. You don't think it's overkill? I had such a good time." She grinned at Michael. "The Irish may be very Catholic in general, but they do love their fairies, leprechauns, banshees and the rest."

"Michael comes from an Irish family, too."

Sally laughed. "Probably not quite as Irish as yours. Is anyone—even in Ireland—as Irish as your dad? Hey, come on in," Sally said, slipping her arm through Moira's, leading her into the shop and whispering a mile a minute, as she tended to do. "He's a hunk. Of course, I'd already heard he was good-looking. The others are already in the shop."

"The others?" Moira asked, frowning, pulling back. But they were inside, and she came to a standstill, frozen as if she'd suddenly been sheathed in ice. Patrick, Josh and Danny were all there. Josh had a camera and was already filming, Patrick was studying a display case, while Danny seemed to be perusing the sachets of herbs that offered to heal or bring money, love or peace of mind.

"Hey, what took you so long?" Josh asked cheerfully.

"What the hell are you doing here?" Moira exploded without thinking.

Josh frowned. "Sorry. I thought I was part of this."

Moira quickly gathered her wits. "No, Josh, I'm sorry, I—"

"I don't think she meant you in particular, Josh," Patrick said.

"Or you," Danny murmured, so softly Moira wasn't sure she really heard him.

"You didn't know they were coming? How nice that

they've surprised you," Sally said cheerfully, apparently missing Moira's tone. "Anyway, the window is special for Saint Patrick's Day. I have some books on Ireland over there. Oh! And there's my banshee. Isn't she great?"

The banshee *was* great. She was swathed in black and seemed to float in the air in the archway between the front of the shop and the rear. She had a strangely beautiful porcelain face, with dark eyes and a mournful expression.

"She's very impressive," Moira heard herself murmur.

"She's beautiful," Michael said.

"Well, originally, banshees must have been beautiful," Sally said. "You see—"

"Wait, wait," Josh protested. "Moira, sit down with Sally. You can interview her about the banshee."

A few minutes later she was seated in a chair alongside Sally, the banshee swaying to Sally's right. Moira introduced the piece and filming began.

Sally's discussion of the banshee made a nice complement to Granny Jon's tales. When she was done, Moira smiled and looked at Josh. "I think it's perfect."

"Really? I did well? You're going to use the tape?" Sally asked.

"It was great."

"And I won't end up on the editing room floor?" Sally queried.

"No way," Danny said. Moira looked at him, irritated that he would answer such a question in her stead. "Well, she was definitely more interesting than the pub doors we taped," he said with a shrug. He spoke lightly, but the way he stared at her disturbed her. He was still angry, she thought, that she had been on his computer, reading what he had been writing.

"Well, then, I have to take you to lunch to celebrate," Sally said.

"No, we'll take you to lunch, for your wonderful speech," Moira said.

"I insist," Sally said.

"We're going to make big bucks on you, Sally. Let the production team of Whalen and Kelly take you out," Josh insisted.

"All right," Sally agreed. "Randall and Meg will be here in just a minute. They do palm reading," she explained to the others. "They're wonderful, if anyone is game for a palm reading."

"I'm afraid I'm more game for lunch," Josh said. "It's nearly three. I'm going to embarrass myself with abdominal rumblings soon."

"Why don't you guys go ahead? I'll call my friend Martin McMurphy, so he'll be expecting us all. Just introduce yourselves—he'll have a table."

Michael, near Moira, leaned to her and whispered softly, "Martin McMurphy? Is that name for real?"

A smile twitched her lips. So what if Danny, her brother and Josh were here? She was in a crowd; she was safe. She just needed to steer clear of Danny. She was going to make the day a pleasant one.

"All right, we'll head on out."

"The restaurant is completely decorated. Leprechauns—and the usual stuffed wiccans, ladies in black, none on broomsticks—are decorated with green bows. Marty also owns House of Haunts. It's a year-round spook house, but he's added some extra banshees, evil leprechauns and green-glowing skeletons for Saint Paddy's Day. He says you're welcome to run tape there, as well."

"I'm for it. But lunch first. So how do we get to this place?" Josh asked.

"Straight down the mall. The restaurant is across the street in a quaint little eighteenth-century house. The horror house is right next door."

"Well, since we're all still standing here, I'll do the heading on out," Patrick offered. As he started out the door, the Pelhams—Randall and Meg, Sally's palm readers—came slipping through the door. They were both at least sixty and could have passed for thirty. Randall's head was shaved, and he had a Yul Brenner look. Meg had apparently been born with the kind of platinum blond hair that turned to shimmering silver with age. She had an abundance of it, streaming down her back and over the long black cloak she wore. Sally explained that she was off to lunch and they headed for the door.

"Moira," Meg called just at the last moment.

She stopped, looking back.

"Have a nice lunch. But be careful. There's a darkness around you."

"A darkness?" Moira murmured.

Meg looked worried. "Just avoid darkness. Scoot, go, go. I'm sorry I stopped you."

Moira gave Meg a quick kiss on the cheek and hurried out. The others followed. As they headed down the street, she realized Danny was right behind her. It was that aftershave. She knew it so well.

"Hey," she accused him suddenly and angrily as he came up beside her. "I asked you to help my father."

"Your father is fine. He's with Liam, Chrissie is there, Colleen was on her way down, and Jeff and the band were coming in early, in case they needed to help out."

"Really? You talked to my dad?"

"I did, and so did your brother."

"Why are you here?"

"I'm worried about you."

"Why? I seem safe enough when you're not around."

He caught her shoulders, swinging her around to face him. "You really think I'd push you under a subway?"

She stared at him stubbornly, her chin in the air. The others were ahead of them and kept walking, unaware of the drama playing out behind them.

"Moira, I'm a writer. I put things on paper. Is Stephen King a mass murderer? Is Dean Koontz a psychotic killer?"

"Let's just have a nice lunch, Danny."

"Yeah, right. And when we get back, why don't you search my room, see what else you can find?"

She ignored him, pulling away and hurrying to catch up with the others.

A few minutes later they arrived at Martin McMurphy's restaurant. He greeted them with pleasure. He was tall, sandy-haired, freckled and immensely charming. As they walked to the table, Moira nudged Sally. "There's an adorable guy for you."

"He's a great friend, but I'm afraid his boyfriend likes him, too."

"Oh. Sorry."

"Don't be sorry, they're both two of the best friends I've ever had." Sally laughed. "You'll meet Dirk later. He works in the haunted house."

They sat at a table done up with a green tablecloth, green napkins and leprechaun salt and pepper shakers. The place was usually a theme café, with model monsters, gargoyles, fake spider webs in the corners and little plastic rats to hold the menus. Now the witches and goblins were all decked out in green.

Martin waited on them himself. As they waited for the meal, Michael produced a release form, and then

Josh followed Martin and Moira around the room, filming. When the food arrived, they all took their places at the table again. The food was delicious, and the green beer was crisp and cold. Coffee was served with McMurphy's Finest Shortbread, and no one was able to pick up the check because McMurphy refused to give them one.

"But we're a crowd," Sally protested.

"And this is the best kind of business expense," Martin retorted.

"This has been wonderful, but we've got to be getting back, I'm afraid," Moira said.

"You've got to do the haunted house first," Sally told her. "It only takes a few minutes."

"Dirk will be waiting for you," Martin insisted.

"Do you mind if we tape in the haunted house?" Moira asked him.

"I want you to go in and become delightfully spooked," he said. "No taping—I can't give away my trade secrets. Besides, scary things aren't so scary in the light."

They thanked him for his hospitality and headed for the spook house next door. There they were met by Dirk. He was tall and striking, with dark eyes and hair, fine cheekbones and a quick smile. He kissed Sally's cheek and smiled broadly as everyone was introduced. "All right, then, I guess I should give my usual spiel. Being a little bit scared is fun, being really frightened is not. This doesn't look like a crowd to be really frightened. Or even scared," he said with a sigh. "But if anyone is upset at all, just yell, and we'll get you right out into the open air, okay?

"And now…" He swept his arm dramatically through the air, gave a low bow and opened another door, ushering them in.

The place was well done, with black lights and realistic effects. Moira walked in with Sally, and they paused together in the first room, the den of Bram Stoker, who was writing while horrid visions of vampires danced on the walls. The next room highlighted the contrast between the witch of legend and the true wiccan, who honored the earth as the mother and respected all things within the universe. Next came a room filled with werewolves, vampires, demons, mummies and, special for the upcoming holiday, crazed leprechauns and evil banshees. A vampire was bent over a bed where a beautiful young woman slept in a silk gown. As Moira went to study the tableau, both the victim and the vampire suddenly turned, the woman dripping fake blood, the vampire snarling. Moira let out a startled scream, and her brother, Michael, Josh and Danny were instantly at her side.

"Moira?" Patrick said.

"I was startled." She laughed. The vampire and victim had resumed their deadly pose, as if they had never moved.

"There are live performers throughout," Sally told them. "Those two should get a raise."

Danny was right behind Moira. She rushed ahead, not wanting to be close to him. Michael had asked Sally something, and the two were walking together, deep in conversation, while Josh told Patrick that they really should do a separate show on Salem.

They entered a room with psychedelic lighting and a floor that rotated. Moira moved quickly, wanting to shake Danny. She found herself spinning, then emerged into a pretend graveyard. Mist rolled across tombstones. Banshees swept through the air, letting out mournful cries. A figure dressed as the grim reaper suddenly leaped out from behind one of the tombstones.

Moira jumped, startled again, but she smiled rather than screamed as the figure circled her, not touching her but tapping his scythe on the floor. "You guys are good," she told him softly, moving on. The grim reaper didn't say a word, just walked among the tombstones, ready to startle the next guest. Moira hurried on, hearing the revolving floor rotate, bringing the rest of her party from beyond.

She passed through a doorway hung with fluttering gray silk.

Here was a church scene, with mourners standing by an open grave. Above the dead man floated another of the black-draped banshees.

She walked through another doorway and found herself in a hall. Eerily lit signs pointed in either direction. She moved to the right and found a door warning of the dangers of the countryside. In this scene, there was misted light and a rainbow. A leprechaun sat on a pot of gold at the foot of the rainbow. But as she approached, something triggered the leprechaun. He spun around, offering a face of pure evil. There was something so eerie about his expression that she suddenly found herself uncomfortable. She quickly exited the room and returned to the hallway, only to find herself completely turned around, and going back the way she had come.

She found herself in the graveyard again. Music played, low and macabre. "Sally? Guys?" she called softly. It seemed they had come and gone. "Hello?" she murmured, hoping the black-clad grim reaper would reappear to show her the way out.

Nothing. The banshees floated by, singing in a high-pitched wail that made her flesh crawl.

"Damn it!" she muttered, and started for a doorway. A sixth sense warned her that she was being followed.

She spun. The grim reaper. "There you are. I don't believe it, but I'm lost. Can you show me the way out?"

He walked past her and stopped, blocking the doorway.

Suddenly he drew his black-clad arm from beneath his cloak. The light caught on something in his hand. A knife. A big knife, glittering in the dim light.

"No need for that, I'm already scared," she told him.

She gasped, stunned, as he reached out and grabbed her, twisting her into his arms. She felt the blade of the knife at her throat. A ragged whisper touched her ear as he pulled her close against him.

"Iss binn beal 'na thost!"

Despite the blade at her throat, Moira screamed.

17

The creature shoved her forward. Moira raced through the door and down the hallway, took the wrong turn and burst into the rainbow room again.

The leprechaun turned, grinning evilly.

The right, the right, she had to go to the right to get out. But somehow she found herself in the graveyard again, colliding in the dim light with a man. She screamed.

"Moira, it's me."

Danny. He gripped her shoulders, shaking her slightly. "Why did you walk off like that? We've all been going in circles, looking for you."

Lights suddenly came on. The grim reaper—revealed as a tousle-haired college kid with his hood and mask removed—came rushing into the graveyard scene, followed by Dirk. "Moira, I'm so sorry. Are you all right? You rushed on ahead. What on earth frightened you so badly?"

Glaring lights betrayed the fact that the gravestones were nothing more than foam and the flying banshees black-clad figures on strings as the others came rushing in. Michael and Sally came from the revolving floor behind her, Patrick and Josh from the forward doorway.

She stared at the grim reaper. "He threatened me with a knife!"

"Adam?" Dirk said with bewilderment and anger, staring at the kid.

"I didn't threaten anyone with a knife," the boy protested, and looked at Moira earnestly. "Honestly, I only carry the scythe. And it's rubber—look." He proceeded to show her how the blade of his weapon moved, bending at his slightest touch.

"Someone threatened me," she murmured. "With a real knife. And he—"

Sally came over to her, wrapping her arms around her. "Moira, I'm so sorry. We should have all stayed together. But none of the employees ever carry real weapons. Ever."

Moira realized that they were all staring at her. She was never going to convince them that she hadn't managed to let her imagination get out of control.

Michael came up to her then, putting his arms around her. "Maybe a haunted house wasn't such a great idea right after the death of a friend," he murmured, smoothing her hair.

She allowed him to hold her and turned in his arms, looking at Sally and the three men before her: Danny, her brother and Josh. She was suddenly certain that none of Dirk's employees had threatened her. And someone here knew she wasn't lying.

Whichever one of them had threatened her.

"Iss binn beal 'na thost," she said softly, repeating the Gaelic words the attacker had whispered. "A silent mouth is melodious."

"A silent mouth is melodious?" Michael asked, frowning as he tightened his arms around her securely. His tone, however, suggested that, despite his longing to have faith in her, he was losing it. "Moira, honey, what is that?"

"An Irish proverb," Patrick said, watching his sister and looking puzzled. "My grandmother used it often enough when we were kids."

"When my folks said it, it meant shut the hell up," Sally said lightly.

"Sweetheart, that's not really a threat," Michael said softly. "It's rather pretty. An Irish proverb. I like it."

"Dirk," Sally said, "I guess we should get out of here."

"Yes, of course. Adam, it's all right. Take a few minutes. We won't let any more groups through for a while."

"Thanks," Adam said, but he still hesitated, approaching Moira but maintaining a safe distance from her. "I'm real sorry if I frightened you."

"You didn't," she told him.

He frowned, nodded and passed by. She could just imagine what he would have to say if he was with friends and happened to flick a television to the Leisure Channel and catch her show. "Man, I met that lady once, and let me tell you, she is one pathetic wacko!"

"Come this way," Dirk said. "I'll get you all out of here."

They followed him. With the lights on, Moira saw how small the place really was, and how unbelievably *un*realistic. He led them into a gift shop that led to the front porch of the house.

"Look, I'm really sorry. I should have kept you together and stayed right with you," Dirk said.

Sally put a hand on his arm. "It's all right. Moira doesn't usually overreact like this. She's been under a lot of stress."

"I haven't been under stress," she insisted, knowing it was a lie.

"Moira, going home after being away is always stressful. Especially when you're Irish," Sally murmured. "And then Seamus... Anyway, Dirk, thanks."

"You're welcome, but I am so, so sorry," he said again.

Moira walked up to him. "Please, you and Martin have been wonderful. The restaurant is great, and this place is the best in Salem. Really. I look forward to coming back."

"Thanks."

"But we've got to get home. My dad will need help tonight, I'm certain," Moira said.

"Yes, we've got to get back," Patrick said.

Everyone began saying goodbyes. Moira escaped to the sidewalk with Sally and hugged her friend.

"Honestly, Moira, I'm so—"

"Please, don't you dare tell me you're sorry again. You've been wonderful. Listen, as soon as this Saint Patrick's thing is over, we'll make real plans to get together." Sally nodded, and Moira glanced at her watch. "It really is getting late."

"I'll go find the others."

Moira knew when Danny came up behind her a moment later.

"I thought you didn't speak Gaelic?" he said.

She spun around. "You know, Danny, I can also tell you how to say kiss my ass in Gaelic but that doesn't mean that I speak the language. Yes, I know a few words. I've heard it my whole life. Why? Was that you in there, testing me?"

"What?"

"Did you steal one of the costumes and threaten me, just so you could come out and call me a liar?"

He crossed his arms over his chest. "Moira, now you're being absurd."

"Am I?"

The others were coming out behind him. Moira walked past him, linking arms with Sally again. "Walk with me so I can have a few minutes with you before we take off. You know, it's true, since we've both moved away, we hardly see one another anymore."

"Moira…"

"I'm all right, really. Let's move on ahead."

When they had gotten out of earshot, she asked Sally, "Where were you all when I went ahead? Still together?"

"Um…wow, I'm not really certain. No, we weren't actually all together. I was talking to Dirk in the Bram Stoker room. He was out of there like a bat out of hell when he heard you scream. Most of the walls in there are false. You can travel the whole place in a matter of minutes if you use the pathways behind the walls. I tried to follow him, and I think I came in by the other door. I don't even remember right now. Why?"

"I just wondered," Moira said, frustrated, but trying not to let Sally see it.

"Moira, it couldn't have been a real knife. There aren't any in the place."

"Well, I was definitely fooled."

"And why would someone threaten you with a knife, then come out with an old saying our grandparents used? I know there's no one saner than you in this universe, but maybe you…maybe you have been working too hard."

"Maybe," Moira agreed. She looked back, making sure the others were still a distance away. It was almost five o'clock; the streets were dark. Maybe they were even too far away. She didn't like the darkness anymore. She wasn't sure if she wanted to be with people or if she felt safer alone. She could see Josh and Michael carrying the cameras, with Danny and Patrick behind them. She looked at Sally again. "Please, don't be worried about me. I'm fine. You're sure you weren't with anyone else?"

"Well, yes, I told you, I was with Dirk."

Sally was perplexed. Moira decided that she wasn't going to say any more—her questions weren't getting her anywhere.

As they crossed the street, Michael caught up with them. "We're parked at the common, so I guess we should split up here."

"I guess," Sally said. "Michael, it was so nice to get to meet you. And, Moira, please take it easy, and send your parents my love and sympathy."

As she spoke, Danny reached them.

"Where are you parked?" he asked Michael.

"At the common."

"Wait for us to drive around and we'll follow you home."

"That isn't necessary," Michael told him.

"I'd like to be behind my sister," Patrick said, coming up.

"We're all going back to the same place," Josh said, joining them. He took Sally's hand, thanking her and telling her that it had been great to meet her.

Moira kissed her friend on the cheek one last time. "See you soon," she promised, and started walking. Michael caught up with her, slipping an arm around her shoulders.

"Hey, are you all right?"

"I'm fine," she lied.

He didn't try to talk again as they walked to the car. She was grateful. When she slid into the passenger seat, she leaned back, exhausted. She had been afraid. Terrified. It had happened in split seconds. Or had it happened at all? The ghouls in the horror house weren't supposed to touch the customers, but she had been touched. Or was she losing it? The evil leprechaun had made her uneasy. Maybe...

No. Someone had purposely scared her.

But she hadn't been hurt. She'd been frightened, then released. Naturally. The place was small, filled with people. Someone was bound to come quickly once she screamed. Of course, if the blade had crossed her throat...

And here she was, alone with Michael. What if it had been him? What if, for some bizarre reason, he wanted to kill her? She was alone in a car with him. Night had come. He was driving. He could drive anywhere...

Except that he hadn't started the car.

He was looking in the rearview mirror.

"There they are, behind us," he murmured.

"If you lose them on the road, don't worry about it."

"I won't lose them."

They drove down the street, turned and headed out of town. Moira looked out the window. They passed the restaurant and the haunted house. She noticed a group of kids on the next street, in front of a gingerbread Victorian. One boy was sitting on a parked car, something in his hand. It glinted in the streetlight. A knife.

She sat up straight, staring at the kid as they passed. He was out of makeup, but she still recognized him as the boy who had played the vampire.

"Stop the car!" she told Michael.

"What?"

"Stop the car. Pull to the curb and stop the car."

"Moira, are you sick?" he asked, doing as she asked. She jumped out of the car, ignoring the question.

She might have been insane at that moment; she almost hoped so. She wanted to look insane and scary. She strode across the street, dodging traffic heedlessly, aware that Michael was hurrying behind her and not caring. She was dimly aware that Patrick had pulled over, as well.

She reached the group of kids ahead of everyone else and walked up to the car, eyes narrowed, teeth gritted. The kid looked at her with real alarm in his eyes, trying to jump off the car and get away, but she caught him by the lapels of his jacket before he could do so.

"You!"

She *was* insane. He was still holding the knife, and it was real.

"You little two-bit jerk," she breathed furiously.

He was surrounded by his friends, but his face was white and the other kids were dead silent. "Why did you do that to me? And don't even think about lying, because I know it was you."

"I didn't hurt you. I was just supposed to scare you!"

He was probably sixteen. And though he might have been a big man at his high school, he suddenly looked like just a sixteen-year-old kid.

"Who told you to scare me?"

"A man… I needed the money. He came by maybe an hour before you did. Lady, he gave me a hundred bucks, and I really needed it."

"*What* man?"

By then Michael had reached her. He had her by the shoulders. "Moira—"

"Let me go, Michael." She returned her attention to the boy. "Tell me, *what man?*"

The others had reached them. Danny took the kid by the shoulders, spinning him around. "She asked you a question."

"I'm going to call my mother."

"Good. She can come down to the police station with us."

"Hey, it isn't even a real knife. Okay, it's a knife, but it's a magician's prop. It's steel, but it retracts. Please, man, you can't call the cops on me! Please."

"Then answer the lady's question!" Danny roared. The kid might have been frightened of Moira, but he was terrified of Danny.

"What man?" Moira repeated more calmly.

The kid shook his head. "He didn't give me a name. And it was dark… He talked to me in the haunted house. He was tall, I think. A little taller than me. He…" He looked around at all of them, staring from Josh to Patrick, Danny to Michael. He swallowed hard. "He… he, oh, man, I don't know. He was tall…like all your friends. I think his hair was brown. He was a nice guy. Said he just wanted to pull a prank on a friend. Scare her, whisper a few Irish words. I don't even know what I said. Honest. He made me memorize the words. You gotta understand—he gave me a hundred bucks. I had a fender bender in my dad's car, and my mom covered me, and I've got to pay her back. If my dad found out, he'd have made me quit the football team. You don't know my dad. He'll kill me. Honest, I am so sorry, lady, so sorry. I'll do anything. I'll give you the hundred bucks, just please don't call the police. I swear to God I'll never do anything like it again."

"Let him go," Moira told Danny softly.

"Let him go?" Danny asked indignantly.

"We should call the police," Patrick said firmly.

"I think he's right," Josh murmured.

"No, just let him go."

Danny slowly released his hold on the boy. "Remember," he said softly, "we can come back and get you any time."

"I swear, I'll give you the money—" the kid began, but Moira was already walking across the street to the car. She had all she needed. She hadn't been threatened by anyone who had been with her.

She thought Michael was behind her at first, but knew before she turned that it was Danny. That aftershave again. "I think an apology would be nice."

"I'm sorry," she said stiffly.

"And I'm not so sure that walking away is a good thing."

"Why?"

"You don't know who paid the kid."

She stopped and turned. "And you know damn well that there's no way to find out. If I call the cops, they'll drag the kid down to the station, where he'll cry and try to remember more about the man, but he won't be able to. He talked to him in the dark. The kid is scared out of his wits now, and it will only get worse if we do drag him down there. Let's just go. I think I've proved my point. I'm not crazy."

"I never suggested that you were crazy," he said softly.

Danny sighed. Michael had caught up to them. Patrick and Josh were still dodging cars. "Hey, Moira, you should really call the cops. Who the hell would want to scare you like that?" Michael said now.

She couldn't tell him that as long as it hadn't been one of them, it didn't really matter.

"Who knows, maybe someone who hates travel shows," she said lightly. "Please, guys, let's just go home."

They both stared at her unhappily as the other two caught up.

"Please," she repeated.

Michael sighed, walking around to open the passenger door so Moira could slide into the car. As he went to the driver's side, she saw, in the rearview mirror, that the others were getting into their car, as well.

As they drove, she felt the anger drain from her. Despite the fact that someone had paid that kid a hundred dollars to frighten her, she was relieved.

It hadn't been one of them.

Exhausted, she leaned back.

"My shoulder is here," Michael said softly.

"Thanks. I'll take it."

She was amazed to find herself able to doze against him as he drove. When she awoke, they had reached her father's garage. Michael was prodding her gently, fingers brushing her hair from her face. "We're here."

She climbed out of the car just as Patrick drove up behind them. When they had been joined on the sidewalk by the others, Moira smoothed her hair and said, "Not a word about any of this to Mom and Dad, you understand?"

"You should have called the police," Danny said irritably.

"Would you listen to me for once? My father is dealing with enough right now. Not a word. I mean it."

They all stared at her, jaws locked. She felt a sudden surge of wisdom regarding men. None of them liked being told what to do.

She turned and headed toward the pub, the rest of them following her.

The place was a zoo. Word of Seamus's death had been in the paper, and more old friends had turned up to drink to his memory.

Moira wasn't sure what the men behind her decided to do. The minute she came in, she stowed her purse and coat and hopped behind the bar. Seamus's old friends from his days at the shipyards had heard the news and forsaken their local pubs to come here. They talked about the difficulties of their work, of the times Seamus had done something funny, of the times he had stood up for other men when conditions had been bad.

She was serving a Guinness when she heard a man say, "The obituary was really beautiful. Eamon told us you wrote it up. That was nice, Dan. A real tribute to the man."

She swung around. Danny was behind the bar, filling a tray of wineglasses with Chablis.

"Thanks, Richie."

"You're a talented man with a pen."

"It's not difficult to write about a man like Seamus," Danny said.

"Yeah, the pen is something," the man named Richie said. "Mightier than the sword. A weapon like no other, so they say."

"The written word can cut like a knife," Danny agreed. He picked up the tray. Moira hadn't realized that she was blocking his way out of the bar area until he looked at her and said, "Excuse me."

"I could have gotten those for you. You didn't have to come back here."

He said nothing as he walked past her. A few minutes later, her father was behind her. "You're needed on the floor," he told her softly. She turned and looked at him with surprise.

"For Seamus. The dock fellows have asked for you and Colleen to do 'Amazing Grace.' And 'Danny Boy.'"

She nodded, wondering if she was too unnerved to get through the songs. She walked out, met her sister on the floor. Colleen squeezed her hand. They walked up to the band. Jeff made the announcement that the

next two songs would be in honor of Seamus and anyone was welcome to join in.

From the time they'd been little, they'd been singing "Amazing Grace." Eamon Kelly had always been
proud of his daughters' natural ability to harmonize
together. They fell into it instantly now, the pipes adding a mournful tone. They went straight from "Amazing Grace" into "Danny Boy," Moira nearly cutting her
palms with her nails, her hands clenched so tightly as
she sang the words.

They finished to applause and Liam's teary-eyed
statement that, "Sure, but old Seamus is looking down
now, happy in heaven that he had the love of women
such as yourselves."

Moira smiled stiffly. Colleen had little trails of tears
trickling down her cheeks. Moira hugged her sister
tightly and slipped behind the bar.

Danny was there again, making a drink.

"What's that?" she asked sharply.

"A blackbird. For the fellow in the corner."

She looked. Kyle Browne was back. She should bring
the drink, take the chance to talk to him, tell him what
had happened that day.

"I'll take it to him."

"No, Moira, I'll be taking this."

She watched Danny leave the bar, watched as he delivered the drink. She couldn't hear anything over the
music and the crowd. She could see, though, that they
were talking. Both men were tense.

"Moira, another Guinness this way, darlin', please,"
Liam called to her.

She served the drink to Liam, squeezed his hand
affectionately and started along the length of the bar,
making sure everyone was all right, still trying to keep
an eye on Kyle Browne and Danny.

"Miss...hey! You're Moira Kelly, right? Wow, that's smart, you're... Kelly's Pub."

Moira looked at the young woman who had spoken. She was probably about Moira's age, but she had a slightly haggard appearance, as if she had put in a lot of miles over the years.

"I am Moira Kelly. And welcome to Kelly's. Can I get you anything? Would you like to see a menu?"

"No, this is fine for me. One beer. I have to get home. But I've seen this doorway forever. I grew up in a pub, too. Well, not a pub. A bar. Nothing so nice as this." She flashed Moira a smile that made her look younger. "I've always wanted to come in here. Tonight I did. There's a good feeling here, not like...not like a few of the places I go."

Looking at her, Moira suddenly thought she knew why the other woman had such a sad, hardened appearance. She continued speaking, her words seeming to verify Moira's thoughts. "I've been so nervous lately... two girls dead. Those prostitutes. Strangled. It makes a woman nervous to step into a bar."

"Do they know that the killer has been finding the women in bars?" Moira asked. She felt sorry for her and was glad that she had come in—as long as it wasn't for the purpose of solicitation. This was her father's very reputable place of business.

The woman, with huge dark eyes, circles under them, looked at her as if she had read her mind. "I'm just here for a drink," she said, sounding a little bit desperate.

"Of course," Moira said instantly.

The woman lowered her voice. "I think he must be meeting them in bars. In fact... I was at my dad's place the other night, doing some stocking, down below the bar. And I'm not certain...but I thought I saw the girl who was killed in there. With a man. A nice-looking man, and of course, she was a beautiful girl…once. I've been watching the papers. I saw her face… I think."

"Did you go to the police?"

"Are you kidding?"

"Someone is murdering people," Moira said very softly. "The police won't—"

"You don't understand. You don't go to the cops from my father's place." She hesitated. "More drugs go through his bar than come out of Colombia. Someone would kill me for sure if I went anywhere near the police."

"More people could die—"

"But I'm not certain what I saw. Maybe it wasn't her. And the guy… It was dark. I don't know that I'd recognize him."

"But—"

"I shouldn't have talked to you, but I'm scared. I shouldn't have come in here. I don't belong in a place like this."

"You're welcome in here. Come in any time—for a beer."

"Of course," the girl said, and laughed.

Then, suddenly, the strangest expression came over her face. She was staring at a point beyond Moira.

Moira turned. The young woman was looking into the antique mirror above the bar that advertised Guinness. Moira stared into the mirror. She couldn't see anything but heads moving and people sitting. There was a watery reflection of the band, Danny picking up empty glasses from the table next to Kyle Browne's, her brother and Michael, in the center of the floor, serving plates of food.

Moira turned to look at the young woman.

She was gone.

Moira swore.

"What's up?" Chrissie came up and asked her, worried.

"There was a girl in here, a frightened girl. I think she was a prostitute, and she said something about maybe having seen one of the murdered girls in her father's bar, but she refused to go to the police...and then she disappeared."

Chrissie looked at her. "Moira, every prostitute and 'escort' in the city is probably nervous right now. She probably went home. And if she does know anything, I bet she will wind up speaking to the police sooner or later."

"She's afraid. Her father has a bar where a lot of drug deals go down."

"Well, she's gone. There's nothing you can do now."

"I'm worried about her."

"Moira, I know you always want to help everyone, but there's nothing you can do, so just forget it. We've got our own problems here, these days."

Moira was afraid that Chrissie was going to start crying over Seamus again.

"The girl sounds smart enough to watch what she's doing, Moira," Chrissie said.

"I guess you're right."

"Don't say anything to your father if you ever want to take ten steps on your own again," Chrissie warned.

"You're right about that," Moira murmured. She went behind the bar, got busy and decided that Chrissie was right. There was nothing she could do, and she did have her own problems. Big problems. Kyle Browne was still in the corner. Alone.

Moira decided this was her chance. She quickly put together another blackbird. Before she could take it to the man in the corner, though, she was interrupted.

"Miss Kelly, your song was beautiful."

She stopped, staring at the young man who had spoken to her. He had dark hair, hazel eyes and looked familiar.

"You don't remember me."

"Yes…"

"I'm Tom Gambetti. Your taxi driver. Remember? I dropped you off here the night you arrived."

"Oh, yes, of course. I'm sorry: it's just been really crazy here."

"I see that. I gather that this is a tough time for your family. But you and your sister really did just do a great tribute."

"Thanks. We've done those songs forever. Put us in a karaoke bar, though, and we're just awful, I promise." He was pleasant, but she still needed to escape. "Tom—"

"I know, you're busy. I'm not trying to be a pest. I'm just reminding you that I'm around if you should need transportation." He grinned. "Besides, I *am* half Irish. Your dad's pub is great."

"Thanks. And I have your card. I promise, I will call you if I need a taxi."

She slipped past him and took the drink she had made to Kyle Browne.

"Miss Kelly, how nice to see you."

"You, too."

"Did you need to talk to me?"

"I was nearly pushed onto the subway tracks this morning."

"Oh?"

"And someone paid a kid in a haunted house to frighten me with a trick knife. *Iss binn beal 'na thost.*"

"What?"

"It's Gaelic," she said. "It means, 'A silent mouth is melodious.'"

"Did you call the police?"

"No. What could they have done? The kid couldn't describe the man who had paid him."

He looked at her thoughtfully. "Sounds something like, take care, or you'll be sleeping with the fishes. You should heed the warning. Do like I told you. Stay away from everyone who could possibly be involved."

"Well, it's a little late for that, and I don't know who the hell is involved, anyway."

"Maybe you should be keeping as far away from your 'friend' O'Hara as you can."

She stared at him. "Danny was with me when I questioned the kid, and he didn't identify Danny as the man who had paid him to scare me."

"Maybe the kid took one look at your friend and decided he'd rather face the police. Or maybe I'm wrong. Maybe your brother is up to no good. Or your pal Jeff over there. Hell, maybe your dad is still fighting a war."

"If you say another word about my father—"

"Can you get into O'Hara's room?" he interrupted. "I bet you can. In fact, I believe you've been in there before. You might find something very interesting in there, if you chose to look."

"What are you insinuating?"

"Me? I don't insinuate."

He was right, though. She did have a way into the room.

"Don't stand here any longer," he told her. "And think about what I said."

She turned and left him, retracing her steps to the bar. Danny was onstage with the band. He and Jeff were singing together, an old Irish drinking song that Seamus had loved.

Josh approached her. "Things are winding down here, so I'm going to go. I won't see you in the morning. I'm going to the studio to finish editing and get the tape out. You stay here, get some rest. Take care of your folks."

"I should be helping you."

"I have Michael if I need help. I know you'd like to see the tape yourself, but you know you can trust me. We're partners, remember?"

She kissed his cheek. "Thanks, Josh."

"Stay home, stay with family, you got it?"

"I got it. Give Gina and the twins hugs and kisses for me."

Josh walked to the door, then stood there, waiting. Michael came over to her. "Maybe you should come back to the hotel with us."

She shook her head slowly. Was she being a total idiot? He would forgive an indiscretion. And she would be safe at a hotel. Away.

All right, she was a total idiot. She was going to stay here.

"Thank you, Michael. But tonight my place is here."

"I understand."

No, you don't, she wanted to insist, but she didn't. He cupped her face gently, gave her a soft kiss and reminded her that he and Josh would be at the studio most of the day.

The crowd thinned further. Moira noticed that Kyle Browne was gone. Andrew McGahey had arrived and was at a table in conversation with her father and brother. Colleen came over to the register and rang up a check. "I'm giving last call," she told Moira.

"Good idea."

"You look tired as hell," she said.

"Hey, we're working hard here. It's a good thing it's

your face that's getting so famous—you're getting some major dishpan hands."

"It's worth it. I'm glad we're here. For Dad. For Seamus."

The bar began clearing out in earnest. Moira saw that Andrew McGahey was gone. So was her brother.

Had he left with McGahey or gone upstairs with his wife?

At the tail end of the night, Patrick came back from wherever he had been. Colleen, Moira, Patrick and Danny helped Eamon and Jeff clean up. Then Eamon told Jeff to go on home, he'd been going above and beyond. Colleen and Moira suggested that their father go upstairs; Patrick firmly insisted that he do so. When they were down to the last few glasses, Moira told her sister and brother to go on up.

"Hey, kid, you worked today," Colleen told her. "I can finish."

"And I can help her," Patrick said, staring at Moira sternly. He and the others had kept their word, not saying anything about the scare in Salem. But Patrick was giving her his older-brother stare, trying to be fierce.

"Please," she said, "I've got some extra energy to burn. You two go up."

She knew that Danny was staring at her, more than baffled by her obvious intention to be alone with him. He was all-out suspicious. She didn't look up, just kept cleaning glasses.

"All right. But don't get carried away here. A cleaning crew will be here in the morning."

Moira nodded, and her brother and sister left. She kept washing the glass. What the hell was she doing?

Why did she just want, with her whole heart, to prove that Danny was innocent? Or did she just want that one last chance to sleep with him before…

…before admitting he was a cold-blooded assassin who just might be willing to kill even her?

She swallowed hard.

"That glass must be very, very clean," he said.

She looked up. His amber eyes were on her intently. His features, taut and tired, were compelling and hard. The glass slipped from her fingers to land in the sudsy water without breaking.

"Well, thank God you've got such energy. I'm beat. I'll let you finish up."

To her amazement, he turned and walked to his room, closing the door behind himself.

She set down the glass, turned off the water and dried her hands. She walked to his door, contemplated knocking, but didn't.

She reached for the door, hoping he hadn't locked it. He hadn't. He was stretched out on the bed, leaning against the headboard, arms folded over his chest, watching the door. He'd known she was coming.

"All right, just what the fuck are you up to?" he demanded.

"I didn't want to be alone."

"I see. You accused me of trying to throw you onto the subway tracks. You thought for sure I'd tried to knife you in that haunted house, threatening you. So sure, come spend some time with me."

"All right. Never mind," she murmured, deciding to leave. She was no good at this.

He moved with the speed of lightning, ending up in front of her, his hands on her, drawing her in. He locked the door.

"Hell, I don't care why you're here. I only care that you are."

There was nothing subtle or seductive about him. He put both hands on her waist, pulling her close, then found the hem of her sweater and pulled it over her head. Danny knew how to remove clothing quickly. He didn't fumble at all but found the clasp of her bra, and in seconds it landed on the floor. He lowered his head, his lips closing over her breast. Despite herself, the magic of his mouth, the heat of his laving tongue, sent currents of fire sweeping through her.

She tugged at his hair. "Danny…"

"What?" He mouthed the word against her flesh.

"I need a shower."

He didn't release her. One hand remained on her hip, while the other slid lower, roamed over her jeans between her thighs.

"Danny…"

He groaned and looked at her. "Great. I feel like Vesuvius, and all you want is a shower."

"It's been a long day." She slipped past him, heading for the bathroom. She shed the rest of her clothing along the way, aware that he was watching her. She turned on the shower quickly and stepped beneath the hot spray, lathering with the speed of light. She knew that he would follow her.

He did. A moment later, he was behind her. The steam billowed around them as he took the soap from her. His hands, filled with the suds, moved over her back. Curled over her buttocks, came around to the front. She bit her lip, feeling the steam, feeling what he could do to her. She closed her eyes. He was an extremely talented and imaginative man with soap. Hands curving over her breasts, fingers splayed, erotically moving over her nipples. Down her torso, moving with light pressure over her hips, at an angle over her abdomen, down, between her thighs. The soap fell to the floor. His fingers pressed, entered, explored. Her breath was coming quickly; she leaned against him. Felt the steam of the shower enter her with the rotation of his touch. She let a soft groan escape her as she turned to face him, the lather on her body covering his. He found her mouth, kissed her deeply, wetly. Her fingers fell from his chest, swiftly downward, found the hardened length of him. His arms tightened around her. *She had been in love with him so much of her life. No one could do what he did. No one felt like him, laughed like him, talked like him, touched like him, made love like him.*

She broke off the kiss, gasping uneasily. "This…is too slippery."

"Slippery?"

"Yes, I'm getting out."

"You wanted to get in."

"I know…but… I want to make love, not break a leg."

She stepped from the tub, grabbed a towel, wrapped it around herself and exited the bathroom, closing the door behind her.

She had seconds, just seconds. She dropped to her knees by the bed, looking beneath it. The door from the bathroom opened. Danny hadn't bothered with a towel. Sleek, wet, naked and still hard as timber, he stared at her. She jumped to her feet, looking at him.

"What the hell are you doing?"

"I dropped my ring."

"It's on your finger."

"I know. I just put it back on."

He strode over to her, lifting her chin. "Curiosity killed the cat," he said.

She stared at him. "Are you going to kill me, Danny?"

He ran his fingers through his hair, frowning. "Jesus Christ! It's an expression, Moira. Look, do you want to stay—or go?"

She didn't answer him.

He unwrapped the towel from her body. "Stay, or go?"

Her silence must have been the answer he wanted. He cupped her chin, kissed her lips. His mouth ran gently along the left side of her throat. Down between the valley of her breasts. He dropped to his knees. Hands cupped her buttocks. His tongue moved.

She stood shaking. She couldn't do this.

Warmth, fire, staggering sweetness, filled her.

Oh, yes, she could, quite easily.

She gripped his shoulders, her fingers locked into his hair as she surged against him. Shivered, burned, knees giving, body rigid, going weak. She feared she would collapse. She forgot her self-imposed mission. He rose, supporting her when he felt her give, letting her fall against him. Within seconds they were on the bed, locked together, Danny aggressive, inside her like steel, so hard and forceful he seemed to have become a part of her. She melded against him, forgetting everything then but the sensations that rocked and overwhelmed her, the hunger, the need…the volatile, breathless peak, the eruption of climax.

Later, she lay beside him, staring into the darkness. This was so wrong. But she had to—*had to*—know.

"And to think," he murmured, "my pride nearly forced me to make you stay away."

"I need to go," she whispered, a little desperately.

He rolled her over, staring at her. "Listen to me, and for the love of God, believe me. I am not trying to kill you."

"We're still in my dad's house," she whispered.

"I don't give a damn where we are. I would have wound up sleeping in the hallway tonight if you hadn't come here."

"Why?"

"I think that someone did try to get into the house the other night."

"Why?"

"I'm not sure."

"There was no sign of a break-in. My father would have noticed if there had been. Only the family and you have keys."

"Ah, there we are. Me again. Go to sleep, Moira, I'll wake you in plenty of time to get upstairs before your family wakes up."

She could stay, she thought. And when he fell asleep…

"You'll be fine," he said, as if reading her mind. "I wake up at the drop of a pin."

Tomorrow night, then. She would have to get back here while he was still at the wake. It was her only chance.

"I should go up."

"You should sleep."

"I'm still…restless."

"Too much energy to burn," he murmured. "Hmm… let me help you out with that."

She felt his hands, the subtle caress of the tip of his tongue.

Soon she wasn't restless at all. Just exhausted. She fell into a deep sleep. Dreamless. She might as well have been…

Dead.

She didn't want to waken when she felt his touch on her shoulder.

"It's morning, Moira. Time for you to get upstairs. And by the way, when are you going to quit pretending that you're still with Michael? I think the next time

I see his arm around you, or watch you go up on your toes for a delicate little kiss, I'm going to haul off and deck the guy."

18

Moira spent the day with her family, watching Brian, Shannon and Molly for a while in the morning, then helping her dad make phone calls so everything would be perfect for Seamus's wake and funeral. She made sure that the substitute band was coming in, since Blackbird had been given the night off. The group would probably be in with the rest of the mourners after the wake, and they would probably wind up playing. But they had all known Seamus, and they were all to be given the time.

The wake would end at ten. At that time, everyone would be invited back to Kelly's. There would be food and drink, and no one would be charged.

When Michael called from the studio, she tried to explain it to him. "The wake will run from seven to ten. Colleen, Patrick and I will take turns being here during that time for an hour each."

"Why?" Michael asked her.

"It's…it's just the way we do things."

"So your dad is going to allow anyone in? Why doesn't he just put up a notice that he's having a private party?"

"Because…well, I think it's a way to really honor Seamus. In the old days, Ireland was known for her hospitality. Strangers were never turned away. Seamus was…part of that spirit of Ireland. There were no strangers to him, just people he hadn't met yet. I rather like it. I think it's part of what can be so beautiful about the nature of the Irish."

"Your dad's going to go broke feeding people." He sighed. "I guess I'm not Irish enough to really understand, but hey, I'm here to weasel my way in. Where you go, my love, I will be. And what you do, I will support."

Tremendous guilt swept through her. But it would be good if Michael came back to Kelly's with her when it was her turn to host the bar during the wake.

That would keep Danny from thinking that he had to be with her.

"By the way, the editing is going great, and the live feed will run from twelve till twelve-thirty. And you've got a great place on the dais to watch the parade."

"Thanks, Michael," she said softly.

"It's my job, ma'am. Just my job," he teased.

She hung up after telling him she would see him at Flannery's that night. She was due there with her family at six.

The afternoon went quickly. Patrick and Danny were both in attendance all day as they readied everything for the family's departure. Moira served in the bar for a while, then helped her mother, Granny Jon, Colleen and Siobhan upstairs; Katy Kelly was preparing a lot of food for that evening.

When she was alone with her sister, chopping vegetables, Colleen spoke to Moira softly. "You're looking haggard, kid. You were downstairs again last night."

Moira stared at her sister, startled.

"You've got to make a decision, you know."

"Decision?"

"Regarding Michael. I saw him watching you last night."

"Colleen, I just want to get through tomorrow—"

"I know. I understand. It's just that…well, I think he's starting to suspect something's going on between you and Danny. He doesn't say a word, but the way he was watching last night…well, you know, he is a man, and he has his pride as well as his feelings."

"I just have to get through tonight and tomorrow. Things will be better after tomorrow, although…"

"Although what?" Siobhan asked, coming into the kitchen and joining the conversation.

"I don't know. Everything seems very…strange, lately."

"Why?" Colleen asked. "What else has happened?"

"Happened?" She felt guilty, looking at her sister, wondering if Colleen, too, knew that something was going on in the bar, if she knew that Kyle Browne was a Fed looking for a would-be assassin.

"What's strange?"

She thought of the one thing she could say. "There was a girl in the bar last night. I'm certain she was a prostitute—pretty, well dressed."

"A hooker? In Kelly's?" Colleen said. "Dad would be furious."

"She wasn't soliciting. She was just having a drink because she was afraid to be out alone with a killer on the loose."

"What was so strange?" Colleen persisted.

"Well, she was talking to me, saying maybe she had seen one of the victims, maybe even the killer. But she wouldn't go to the police. I think her father deals drugs."

"Then what?" Siobhan asked.

"She looked into the mirror over my head and turned

white. When I looked into the mirror to find out what she was staring at, she disappeared."

"Obviously she saw something that scared her," Siobhan said.

"Yeah, like the cop who sits in the corner every night ordering blackbirds," Colleen said.

"You know he's a cop? How?" Moira asked.

"Jeff told me he's almost sure of it."

"You know, once we get through all this…if you're still worried," Siobhan said, "I'll take a walk to the police station with you, and you can tell them about the girl and what you heard. Maybe you'll feel better then."

"It probably won't do much good," Colleen said. "First, they'd have to find her, and this is a big city. Then they'd have to get her to talk. And maybe she didn't really see anything at all."

"You're right," Moira told her sister. "But Siobhan is right, too. It might make me feel better."

Later on, when Siobhan was helping her arrange cookies on a plate, her sister-in-law looked at her and said, "There's more bothering you than a conversation you had with a girl at the bar. It's Danny, isn't it? His being here is getting to you."

"No," Moira lied.

Siobhan shrugged. "I think you're lying. You'd like to believe he's come to stay. You don't want to face the truth. Well, take it from me, the truth is always better than doubt. I'd give my eyeteeth to know the truth now."

"Patrick adores you," Moira said, defending her brother.

"I'd like to believe that. I might, if he were with me more. I think he's even forgotten that he has kids. He keeps talking to Michael about taking the boat out and bringing Andrew McGahey along, so they can all talk about Ireland. Guess what? He hasn't mentioned bringing me or his kids on this exciting first trip of the season."

Siobhan walked away.

Finally it was time to get dressed and ready, and then they were on the way to Flannery's. Molly and Shannon had their chocolates to go into the coffin. Siobhan had wondered whether or not to let Molly see Seamus in his coffin, but the undertaker had done such a fine job that her worries had been laid to rest.

"I still don't understand, Auntie Mo," Molly said to Moira when they were standing beside the coffin. "Mommy says it's like he's sleeping. Why does he want to sleep in a box?"

"Well, Molly, Seamus is really in heaven, with God. His body is resting in the box, and we'll bury him, and that way, when we want to say a prayer for him or think about him a lot, we can go to the cemetery, to his grave, maybe bring him a flower."

"Or a pint," Danny suggested wryly from behind her.

"Bring him a little something," Moira continued, "and feel close to him. But Seamus himself, his soul, the real Seamus, is with God." She picked up her niece. "Here, I'll lift you, Molly. You can set your chocolates right in his hand. Next to the rosary Auntie Mo just put in."

Molly put her chocolates in the coffin. Shannon did the same. Even Brian, the doubter, had brought a Snickers bar.

Soon it was time for the doors to open to the public. Eamon Kelly, Katy by his side, still knelt at the coffin. A moment later he rose and took a seat in the first row of pews. The first hour had begun.

Patrick had returned to the pub, to tell any lost mourners the way to Flannery's, and to let them know they would be welcome at the pub later.

Michael, Josh and Gina arrived, without the twins. Gina whispered to Moira that they'd managed to get a baby-sitter. Josh told Moira that he and Gina would head to the pub with her when it was her turn to go; she told him that Michael was coming with her, and that she would appreciate it if they would stay at the funeral home so they could bring Colleen back for the last shift.

From then on, it was wild. Seamus had never married, but he'd acquired his share of lady friends. The room was so crowded that Moira took to the halls. She heard the keening from within as friends from the old country cried over the loss. When she went back inside, she sat with her father, as people kept coming up. Friends from the bar. Friends with whom Seamus had worked. All shook her hand and told her how wonderful a man Seamus had been. Finally Moira rose again, needing some breathing room. As she walked from the viewing room, she was startled to run into Tom Gambetti.

"I just came to pay my respects," he told her, as if he was embarrassed to be there.

"That's very nice of you. Please, go on in."

"If I'm being too pushy…?"

"No, no, you're fine. I'll see you at the pub later— you're more than welcome, if you'd care to come by."

He nodded his thanks.

Moira went into the broad windowed hallway that ran along the front of the building. She could see Danny outside on the porch, lighting a cigarette. Many people approached him. He listened, shook hands and apparently accepted condolences on behalf of the family. She narrowed her eyes when one woman, middle-aged, with silver gray hair, approached him carrying a brown parcel. He leaned low, kissing her cheek, apparently thanking her for coming.

When she walked away, the woman no longer had the parcel.

"You doing okay?" Michael came up to her, slipping an arm around her shoulders. His hand moved to her nape, and he massaged her neck.

"I'm fine."

"It's almost time for us to go back to the pub."

She saw Danny come back into the funeral parlor. To her surprise, he walked into one of the viewing rooms that wasn't in use.

"Moira?"

"Oh, yes, we have to go. In just a few minutes. Excuse me, Michael, I'm going to try to find my father."

She slipped through the crowd, not sure why, but knowing that she didn't want Michael to know her destination. She walked up to Siobhan and asked her if she'd seen Danny.

"No, not in a while."

"I think I saw him slip into a room over there. Can you find him while I speak to Dad? Tell him that we need him to…carry something. Heavy."

Siobhan left. When Danny came out with her, he didn't have the bundle. Moira avoided them and raced into the room. No bundle, but there was a drapery over a coffin stand. She rushed to it. The brown bundle was there. She felt it. Not a gun. She sighed in relief, realized it was a group of folders.

She could hear people talking just outside the room.

"What did she want?" It was Danny.

"I don't know, Danny. Moira just said that you were needed," Siobhan responded.

"Well, where the hell is she?"

"Probably with Eamon, by the coffin."

They moved off.

On an impulse, Moira grabbed a few of the folders

and shoved the bundle back where it had been. She slipped the folders beneath her jacket and hurried out. Michael was in the hallway.

"Moira, everyone is looking for you. You needed something moved?"

"Never mind, the funeral parlor people took care of it. It was a flower arrangement," she babbled quickly. "Hey, let's go."

"Don't you want to tell your dad we're leaving?"

"He'll know. Let's go, Michael. Now."

Patrick had taken his own car; Moira and Michael took her father's. She was silent as they drove. Michael slid a hand over hers. "I love you."

She smiled at him weakly.

"You're so distant."

"This is almost all over."

"Yes."

They reached the pub. Things were quiet. The substitute group was setting up, and Patrick was behind the bar, serving the lone man in a business suit who was sitting there. The tables were empty.

"We're here, Patrick. You can head back. I don't think Siobhan wants to stay much longer with the kids. I was thinking she could come home with Colleen when she leaves. Josh and Gina will be with her, too. Then you can stay with Mum and Dad until I get back."

"Sounds good," Patrick said, rubbing his neck. "Guess I'm on my way back, then." He paused, looking at his sister. "You all right? Michael is here with you, anyway."

"I'll break the bottle over the head of any asshole who comes in here and scares her," Michael said.

Patrick nodded. "Good deal." Then he grabbed his coat and was gone.

"Michael, that guy is just drinking beer. Can you

step behind the bar for a few minutes? I think I'll use Danny's bath to freshen up," Moira said, seeing her chance.

"Sure."

He stepped behind the bar, and she hurried into Danny's room. She tore through the closet, heedless of the mess she made.

Nothing.

He had stopped her when she'd looked under the bed. She crawled beneath it and caught her breath.

There was the gun. She didn't know a damned thing about firearms, but this had to be a sniper's rifle. A really good, high-tech one. There was a scope on it. The gun was taped to the underside of the bed. She crawled out, tears in her eyes. It was time to call the police.

When she stood, she was dizzy, so she sat at the foot of the bed for a minute. She felt the file folders she had stuffed under her black suit jacket poke against her flesh. She pulled them out, tears still stinging her eyes. There were names on the folders. Her brother's name was on the first. She flipped through it. There were pictures, records. Her vision blurred.

The next one bore the name Michael Anthony McLean. She opened it idly, wiping her eyes. Michael's picture leaped out at her. Or was it Michael's picture?

Blurred. It was the tears in her eyes. No…it was Michael. Yes, surely. Dark hair, blue eyes, same face…

"So you know. I was afraid you'd seen the way that whore stared at me the other night in the bar."

The door was open. Why hadn't she heard it open? She stared across the room. Michael was standing there. He entered the room and closed the door.

The band started playing just outside, the closed door doing little to muffle the sound.

So you know…the whore…

The picture of Michael. Close…so close…but not Michael.

Denial, disbelief, made her talk desperately. "Michael," she said, "Danny's planning on assassinating Jacob Brolin—"

"Yes, of course, good try," he said coldly. "That was the plan, of course. To get you going on Danny, discover the rifle…who the hell knew that you would find a picture of the real Michael McLean?"

The sudden clarity of the truth that had been around her all along was staggering. It was too horrible to believe. And yet…

God, there it was, staring her in the face!

She stood, her eyes glued to his. She didn't even think to scream, she was still so stunned, though part of her mind knew it wouldn't have mattered even if she had screamed; the music was way too loud.

"I don't understand, Michael," she murmured, bluffing. "We have to call the police. Danny has a rifle taped under his bed—"

"And you have the dossier right in front of you that proves I'm not who I say I am," he said coldly. Leaning against the door, he stared at her. His eyes were like chips of blue ice. When he spoke, it wasn't with the level voice and even accent she had known. His tone was harsh—and his brogue was heavy. "You know, Moira, I had planned to be with you, right from the beginning. That's one of the reasons I've always been so adept at my chosen vocation. I'm good with women. But, though you really won't believe this, I never lied when I said that I loved you. I've been trying to figure if it might be possible to really become Michael McLean—who is, of course, dead, you must realize. Do this one last job, a triumph for freedom, and then live a normal life. Marry you. But you were supposed to help me set up your old friend for a fall, not sleep with him. You did sleep with him, right?"

"Look, Michael, I don't know what you're talking about."

"Of course you do. Blackbird. You knew something was going on in the pub. An attempt to assassinate Brolin. This was to be the meeting place. And it was. Dan O'Hara was to be the perfect fall guy—arrested for the crime. You were to help with that, though you didn't know it, and you were moving along in just the right direction. But now...you know. You betrayed me, Moira. You pretended to love me, and you fucked him."

The horror, the magnitude of what had being going on struck her full force. From the time he had taken the job with her, he had been planning this. No, from before that time. He had found a man with the right look and the right credentials, and he had killed that man, then applied for and won the job in his stead. He had taken the time to court and seduce her. He had studied her family, the pub. He had been so thorough, so careful. And when he hadn't been with her...

He had been strangling prostitutes.

"I—I love you, Michael," she lied. He was between her and the door.

He shook his head. "No. We were apart too much. And you didn't mind. I minded. And I needed company. Actually, you're a lot like those whores, Moira. You couldn't keep your mind on me, you lie and cheat, and you're nosy as hell. I didn't think I'd have to kill you—I was spending a lot of time on that fantasy where I married you in the family church and was welcomed like a son into the bosom of the family. A pretty fantasy. I should be grateful you cheated. Because Michael McLean is going to have to disappear now. After tomorrow, of course. But...well, I'm going to have to deal with you first. And Danny boy… I'll have to deal with him later."

"Michael, my family is going to be home any minute. And…you're wrong about all this. I love you, we can—"

"Oh, Moira, please! I don't think you're stupid, and you know damn well I'm not. You really have complicated matters, but…let's go."

"Go? I'm not stupid. Where do you think I'm going with you?"

He started walking toward her. She jumped up, but there was no way out of the room except through the door he was blocking. Still, she was desperate to preserve her life at all costs. She screamed, praying someone would hear her over the band. He reached the bed, and she crossed to the other side. It was hopeless. She tried to race past him, but he caught her viciously by the hair. She screamed again, trying to wrestle away.

That was when she saw his hands.

He wore gloves. And carried a cloth with a strange, sickly-sweet odor.

Fighting wildly, she tried to avoid his hand. She kicked, screamed, bit. The hand, and the cloth, came over her mouth.

She tried not to breathe.

Eventually she had to.

He caught her before she could sink to the floor. He lifted her up and met her eyes with his own, the cold, ice-blue eyes of a killer, before the light began to fade.

Fade out…

The world became black and existed no more.

Moira wasn't there. Dan was irritated, cursing the fact that she had been looking for him immediately after he received the files. He'd flipped through them all quickly, then focused on the one about Michael. He'd immediately realized that something wasn't quite right. He had been studying the file when Siobhan called.

He went all over the funeral home looking for Moira. He even waited in front of the ladies' room. When a gray-haired dowager in a pillbox hat came out, he apologized and headed into the room where Seamus's remains lay. He checked with her family. She hadn't told anyone she was leaving, but Eamon told him that she had probably headed to the pub with Michael, as planned.

As soon as Eamon said the words, something clicked in Dan's mind. He excused himself and left, hurrying to the empty viewing room where he had stashed the files. Heedless of who might be watching him, he dug through the stack.

A few were missing. Moira must have them. He didn't know why or how he was so sure of that, only that he was.

Suddenly his mind processed what he had seen.

Dropping the files, which scattered all over the floor, he strode through the outer room, deciding that it would probably be just as quick to walk the distance as to try to flag down a cab. But as he walked out, someone called to him, "Hey, heading for the pub?"

It was a young man, brown-haired, hazel-eyed. Maybe twenty-six or twenty-seven.

"Who the hell are you?" Dan demanded.

"Tom Gambetti."

Dan stared at him blankly, grudging every second that passed.

"I'm a cabdriver. I drove Moira home when she got off her plane."

"You're a cabdriver?"

"Yes."

"Your cab is here?"

"Yeah, right there."

"Great. I *am* headed for the pub, and I need you to get me there as quickly as you can."

When they pulled up in front of the pub, Dan told Tom to wait right there, then strode inside. There was no one at the bar except a man complaining of no service. One of the band members came up at that point, offering to help him. "Hey, buddy, cool it. I'll find you a beer. There's been a death in the family. Bad time, you know."

Dan ignored the customer and addressed the band members. "Where's Moira Kelly?" he asked.

"She came in here just a few minutes ago with some man. Took off to freshen up or lie down or something like that. She must be really broken up about that guy's death. Her friend went to look for her, and when he came out with her, he said she was in really bad shape. Could hardly stand. He was supporting her. Said he was going to take her back to the family, that she was in no condition to hold down the fort."

Dan's insides seemed to congeal. He raced to his room, throwing open the door. The spread was askew, nearly on the floor. The closet door was open, clothing everywhere.

Whatever had happened, it had happened quickly. He closed the door. The musician was still behind the bar.

"How long ago did they leave?" he asked tensely.

"A couple minutes ago. Literally. They walked out just before you walked in."

"Thanks."

Dan burst out to the street. As he stared up and down the sidewalk, the cabdriver stuck his head out the window. "Hey, if you're looking for Moira, they just left. Looked like she was sleeping. I waved, but the guy driving wasn't paying any attention."

Dan was instantly in the cab. "Turn around. Follow them."

"Follow them? I don't know where the hell they were going."

"They're only seconds ahead. You can find them."

"Wait a minute! Who are you and what—"

"Damn it, turn around, follow them. Her life is at stake."

Tom Gambetti apparently believed him. He spun the cab around and began to take the streets of Boston like a madman.

"Careful, we don't want a cop on us—not unless we find them first. Hey, there they are. They're in her father's car. Turn here."

"This is a one-way street—"

"Turn anyway."

Gambetti did. Dan had to admit the guy could drive. They missed a tan Suburban by inches. Moments later they were in traffic, just three cars behind Eamon Kelly's.

"What now?" Gambetti asked.

"Keep on him," Dan said, keeping his eyes steadily on the vehicle ahead. They were at a light, wedged between a Corsica and delivery van, when Eamon's car made a sudden turn.

"Shit, I'm going to lose him," Tom Gambetti swore.

"Never mind, we know what direction he's going. Turn as soon as you can."

Gambetti did as he was told.

"Pull over to the curb," Dan said when they reached the wharf. "Just let me out. And listen." Dan was scratching a number on a scrap of paper as he spoke.

"Call this number. Tell them you're calling for Dan O'Hara. Tell them to get to the wharf, to the *Siobhan,* as quickly as they can. Tell them lives are at stake. Understand?"

"Yeah, of course." He was fumbling in his pocket. "I've got a cell phone right here. Hey, you sure you don't want to call yourself?"

Dan was already gone, sprinting down to the docks.

She wasn't dead. Yet. Her head pounded; her stomach churned. She felt as if she were being tossed around by a cruel hand.

She opened her eyes very slowly. Colors dimmed by pale light floated in her vision. She could hear voices. Men…talking. She fought to clear her vision. She blinked, thinking she was seeing things. She was on a narrow sofa, looking at a compact dining booth in front of her. There were flowers on the table. Suddenly she recognized her surroundings. She was in her brother's boat; he always arranged to have flowers on the table, for Siobhan, for their first sail of the season.

The men…arguing. Who were they? What were they saying? She closed her eyes again, listening, trying to ignore the pain in her head, still her stomach and discern what was going on and how to survive.

"One damned day. We needed one more damned day. This was asinine."

"Don't you get it, man? She had a fucking file. She knew the picture wasn't me."

"Great. So now she's got to disappear tonight. That screws tomorrow."

"We can come up with a different plan. We've got the best weapon in the world, we just need a point to fire from. I'll need another new identity, though."

"This has to be done. It would have been perfect if

you could have been near Moira. So close, and yet you still could have disappeared into the crowd."

"It would have been great, but now we need a new plan."

"It was that O'Hara bastard," Michael—for she didn't know how else to think of him—said.

"We should have fixed him to begin with."

"He was to take the fall."

"Fucker wasn't who he said he was, either. Obviously he's on the inside somehow. How the hell else did he get that kind of dossier on you?"

"Damned if I know. Hurry up—we need to get this boat out of here, drown the girl and sink it."

"Why didn't you just strangle her? Seems like you were getting pretty adept at that."

"Get the boat moving. I'm going to make sure she's still out."

Moira heard footsteps. Despite the pounding in her head, she leaped up. Patrick kept a loaded gun in the safe in the master cabin. She wasn't a great shot, but point-blank, she couldn't miss.

She made it to the master cabin just as the hatch opened. She heard Michael swearing. Terror filled her, but she slammed the door and locked it. Her fingers were frozen and shaking as she jerked open the latticed closet door and started twirling the numbers on the safe.

They clicked home.

"Moira, come out. I'm still trying to make this painless."

The safe opened just as the flimsy door to the cabin burst inward.

She reached into the safe for the gun. It was gone.

She stared into the empty safe, then into the eyes of the man she had known as Michael McLean. He watched her dispassionately from the doorway.

"Your brother is as easy as you are, Moira," he said. "I guess he never mentioned that he and his buddy Andrew McGahey brought me down to the boat on one of those mornings when you were being the family girl. Good old Patrick, expecting no evil. He never knew I spotted the safe. And a safe like that…well, it's no problem to a man such as meself."

There was another weapon in the cabin. Maybe one he didn't know about.

She made a dive across the small room, flinging open the top drawer of the bedside table. Her fingers curled around the knife.

She knelt on the bed, the hilt of the knife in both hands. "Come near me and I'll kill you, I swear it."

He smiled slowly. "Moira Kelly, you're no killer, and you know it. Give me the knife."

She raised it as he came near, then slashed at him when he leaped at her, cutting his arm severely. He didn't seem to notice the pain. He caught the knife with his right hand, her throat with his left. The knife was wrested from her. He pressed her downward on the bed, straddling her, his fingers around her throat in a death grip.

"It's going to be a while before we reach the open sea. You know, I wasn't lying to you, Moira. I really fell in love with you. Enjoyed you wholeheartedly. Why don't you try to make it up to me?"

She was nearly choking.

"Can't answer? Sorry."

He eased his hold.

She still couldn't move, but she looked into his eyes as she spoke. "When I'm gone, they'll search for me. They'll find you."

"Who is ever going to think that I've taken you out on your brother's boat?" he asked, smiling. "Oh, babe,

I'm sorry that it has to end this way. Want to draw it
out a little longer? Entertain me? Live? Hope that some
miracle will occur, and you won't have to die?"

He reached out to touch her face.

A sound like a growl suddenly erupted from the
doorway.

"Touch her, you pile of shit, and I'll shoot you in the
balls so you can bleed to death in agony!"

Michael was startled enough to roll halfway off
Moira.

They both froze for a minute. There was Danny, hair
tousled as always, standing in the doorway. He had a
gun in his hand. Not a big rifle with a scope, but a small
weapon that, in the tiny room, looked just as lethal.

Danny. The man she had condemned...

"Move, Moira," he commanded.

She tried to flee, but Michael still had the knife. She
felt the point in her back when she would have leaped
up. She froze

"Trust me, I learned a trick or two in my youth,"
Danny said softly. "I can shoot you before you can
do more than scratch her. But I think she's been hurt
enough, don't you?"

Danny took aim. Michael eased away with the knife.
"You fucking traitor," he told Danny. "You bastard. You
should have been the one killing Brolin. God knows,
you stupid bastard, you should be at the forefront of
the fight."

"Oh, I believe in the fight. A fight of words and negotiation and persistence. Not a fight of killing children and innocents."

Footsteps. She heard footsteps coming up behind
Danny.

He heard them, too, and turned, but Moira cried out,
"Danny, it's all right. He's a cop."

Danny hesitated at her words.

Kyle's gun exploded. The bullet seemed to burst directly into Danny's chest. Into his heart.

19

Moira screamed. A shriek of horror that went beyond fear for her own life. She raced toward Danny, who had fallen facedown on the floor, but Michael caught her around the waist before she could crouch to see if he was still alive.

"You shouldn't have shot him," Michael told Kyle.

Caught in Michael's arm, Moira was beyond hysterical. She clawed at his arm, kicked, spat, tears blinding her eyes. "You!" she raged at Kyle. "A cop!"

"I never said I was a cop."

"FBI—"

"I never said I was anything, Miss Kelly. I let you believe what you wanted. I did spend an entire day sitting in front of the police station, waiting to catch you. Ah, Miss Kelly, you were so mistrustful of those you knew. You helped us right along."

She kicked out at him, the man who had killed Danny. She caught him right in the belly, and he doubled over, stunned and groaning in agony.

She lashed out again, kicking backward. She managed to catch Michael's shin, but though he might have been in pain, he didn't release his hold on her. Instead he slammed her against the wall, and her head began to spin again.

FREE Merchandise is 'in the Cards' for you!

Dear Reader,

We're giving away FREE MERCHANDISE!

Seriously, we'd like to reward you for reading this novel by giving you **FREE MERCHANDISE** worth over $20 retail. And no purchase is necessary!

You see the Jack of Hearts sticker above? Paste that sticker in the box on the Free Merchandise Voucher inside. Return the Voucher today... and we'll send you Free Merchandise!

Thanks again for reading one of our novels—and enjoy your Free Merchandise with our compliments!

Pam Powers

Pam Powers

P.S. Look inside to see what Free Merchandise is **"in the cards"** for you!

W e'd like to send you two free books like the one you are enjoying now. Your two books have a combined cover price of over $10 retail, but they are yours to keep absolutely FREE! We'll even send you 2 wonderful surprise gifts. You can't lose!

"A COMPELLING STORY...
INTRICATE AND FASCINATING."
—TAMI HOAG
NEW YORK TIMES
BESTSELLING AUTHOR
ON DARK ROAD HOME

KAREN
HARPER
NEW YORK TIMES BESTSELLING AUTHOR
FALLING
DARKNESS
A SOUTH SHORES NOVEL

MARTA
PERRY
ECHO
OF
DANGER

REMEMBER: Your Free Merchandise, consisting of **2 Free Books** and **2 Free Gifts**, is worth over $20 retail! No purchase is necessary, so please send for your Free Merchandise today.

YOUR FREE MERCHANDISE INCLUDES...

2 FREE Books **AND** 2 FREE Mystery Gifts

FREE MERCHANDISE VOUCHER

2 FREE BOOKS and 2 FREE GIFTS

Please send my Free Merchandise, consisting of
2 Free Books and **2 Free Mystery Gifts**.
I understand that I am under no obligation to buy
anything, as explained on the back of this card.

191/391 MDL GLTQ

Please Print

FIRST NAME

LAST NAME

ADDRESS

APT.#   CITY

STATE/PROV.   ZIP/POSTAL CODE

NO PURCHASE NECESSARY!

SUS-517-FM17

"Want to hear a good Irish expression, Miss Kelly?" she heard Kyle Browne grate the words out. "The back of my hand to the front of your face."

The blow was stunning. She melted against the cabin wall like a water balloon thrown against concrete. Stars burst in her vision.

"Jesus, don't leave bruises all over her," Michael swore.

"It needs to look convincing, like he beat her up, and then she shot him. Now let's move. We don't have forever."

She felt Michael dragging her up from the floor. He was strong, but she was deadweight. She saw Danny's body stretched out on the floor. She wanted to cry out in sheer agony once again, yet her lips refused to open.

Danny had fallen on top of his gun.

But the knife had wound up just inches from her hand...

As Michael fumbled with her weight, she shifted and fell again. Intentionally, this time.

On top of the knife.

She managed to curl her fingers around it. She let him lift her then, prodding her before him. The hallway was narrow. As he shoved her along, Kyle Browne followed, but he was caught in the passageway behind Michael. Halfway along, before reaching the area where the hallway broadened into the salon area, Moira decided to make her move. Fury and pain aided and abetted her effort. She twisted and struck, using all her strength to force the blade through Michael's flesh and muscle.

Shock stopped him as much as the injury. He stared at Moira, who looked at him with tears of loathing and defiance. His face had drained of color.

"Move it, Michael," Kyle commanded.

Michael had no breath to reply.

Moira took that moment to run. She raced down the hallway and up the three steps that led topside. She leaped out on deck and slammed down the hatch, locking it.

A bullet tore through the hatch just seconds after she moved away.

The hatch would not stay locked long.

Another bullet ripped through it...

And another.

She ran to the stern, where the dinghy was tied. They'd left the dock, and the tiny boat was her only way back. She dropped to her knees and struggled against the rocking waves to untie the ropes that held the small rowboat in place. Perhaps, she thought, she should just jump in the water.

She wouldn't last long, she knew. This time of year, the ocean was lethally cold. She would have only a few minutes' grace if she threw herself into its inky depths.

Just as she untied the dinghy, she was grasped from behind, dragged to the deck and thrown flat.

She looked up. Michael was standing over her. He didn't have a gun or a knife, but that didn't stop him. He reached for her, his hands winding around her throat.

She fought him, her will to survive strong enough to drive her to struggle even when all hope was lost. She slammed against his wrists, bucked against him, clawed his arms. She couldn't loosen his grasp against her throat. Her breath was going...

Somewhere, distantly, she heard an explosion. She thought at first that it was the sound of dying.

Then, miraculously, Michael was gone and she could breathe.

She gasped, choked, tried to inhale, tried to see past the patches of darkness that had formed before her eyes. At first she heard only the water lapping against the hull of the boat. Then she became dimly aware of the sounds of a struggle. She sat up, then blinked furiously. A man was down, sprawled over the hatch, his legs trailing along the deck. Further to the fore, near the helm, two men were struggling.

She stumbled forward. Kyle Browne was the man lying over the hatch. His eyes were open, but he saw nothing. He was dead.

She carefully tried to sidle around him, but the waves rocked the boat, throwing her against the dead man. She steadied herself and reached the helm just in time to see Danny and Michael go over the side of the boat together. A pool of blood stretched along the deck and over the hull.

Danny had been shot. In the chest. It was amazing that he had even gotten up. He was bleeding to death. And he was in the water...

"Danny." She meant to cry out his name, but she merely croaked.

She rushed to the side and leaned over. A hand rose from the water, and she reached for it, desperate with fear.

A head rose to join the hand. Her heart sank. Michael. His face no longer seemed human, it was knotted into such a snarl of hatred and malice.

He jerked on her hand, and the motion sent her tumbling into the water.

It was cold, so cold it stole the breath she had just regained. She was barely aware at first that her hand had been jerked free by the impetus of her fall. For long moments she seemed to speed downward into the freezing stygian depths. She realized that she would die if she didn't force herself to act. She kicked hard and began to surface. She broke through the waves, but the boat seemed impossibly far away. Her muscles didn't want to work; her arms didn't want to move. Her teeth chattered hard, and it seemed ridiculously difficult to breathe. She forced herself to head for the boat. She reached it, but couldn't reach high enough to grasp the rail and pull herself up.

Suddenly she was propelled upward. Her midriff met the rail, and she crawled over, fell, gasped for breath. Danny! Danny had to be alive. Shaking violently, she crawled over to look into the water again. He was rising, using long strokes against the icy waves to reach the boat. He made it to the hull, and she reached out with both hands to pull him to safety.

"Danny." It was a whisper as she saw the golden glint of his eyes. As she spoke, he was suddenly jerked under again.

"No!" It was a scream, but nearly silent. Michael must still be there, still alive, still attacking Danny. She rushed to the dead man and shoved him aside searching for his gun. She found it and half walked, half crawled to the side where Danny had last surfaced. She desperately searched the dark water, holding the gun in both hands.

A ripple...

A hand...and then a head appeared. Someone was swimming toward her again. Fingers curled over the hull.

"Moira, help me up."

Danny!

She set the gun down and reached for him, using all her strength. Somehow she succeeded in pulling him high enough, and they fell together onto the bloody decking.

They lay there for several seconds, both shivering

violently, gasping for breath. Then Moira jerked into motion, going for the gun again.

He rose, stretching out his arm, gently taking the gun from her.

"He might come after you again."

"No."

"But—"

"He won't be coming back up to the surface again, Moira."

She let him have the gun, but she kept staring at the water, barely aware of how frozen she was until she felt Danny behind her again, covering her shoulders with a blanket. Still she stared at the waves lapping against the boat. So black.

He pulled her against his chest. "Moira, he won't be coming back up," he repeated softly.

She heard a whirring sound; it was a helicopter above them. Danny began to wave wildly, and they heard a male voice over a loudspeaker.

"The Coast Guard is on its way. The Coast Guard is on its way."

The helicopter remained above them as Danny held her. Knowing it was over, Moira began to shake more violently.

"You're alive," she said through chattering teeth. "But he…he shot you in the chest. Point-blank. I saw him…"

"I'd been getting a little wary lately. Bulletproof vest."

She turned to look at him, barely aware anymore that she felt like a Popsicle. "Are you a cop? And you didn't tell me—"

"No, Moira, I'm not a cop."

"Then what are you?"

"An Irishman," he said with a rueful smile. He

opened his mouth to offer a further explanation, then didn't. He took her into his arms suddenly, kissed her lips with a warming fervor, then held her against him. She could hear the motor of the Coast Guard vessel as it came near.

From then on, the rest of the night became a blur.

20

There had been so many surprises that night. As she had guessed, Michael McLean wasn't really Michael McLean. The real Michael McLean, a quiet man long estranged from his family, a solitary man with film as his only love, had been murdered shortly after his arrival in New York City the previous December, shortly after meeting up in a bar with the terrorist Robert McMally, who had been on the lookout for just such a man. Kyle Browne was not a cop, nor was Kyle Browne his name. There was a real Kyle Browne who was an FBI agent, and the name had been chosen with the expectation that someone would verify his identity with the government agency.

Moira gained a greater understanding of the intricacies of what had been going on in her own home through one of the greatest surprises of the evening—the fact that Jacob Brolin was aboard the Coast Guard cutter that came to rescue them from the *Siobhan*. That he hugged her warmly was certainly pleasant and rewarding, but the way he greeted Danny was astonishing. Danny might have been his long-lost son. With a cup of steaming cocoa in her hand and more warm blankets around her, Moira stared at the two men.

"All right, what is going on?" she demanded. "If

you're not a cop," she accused Danny, "you must be something with the… Irish government? Northern Ireland government?"

He shook his head. "I'm a writer and a lecturer, Moira, just as I have always been."

"And a very good friend," Brolin said.

"Actually, we met because of your mother."

"My mother?" Moira asked blankly.

Danny shrugged. "I want to see peace in Northern Ireland more than anything, and my way to work for that is writing about the lives that have been destroyed through the violence. But there was a time when my uncle's way—talking—didn't seem to do anything, and since I'm not a perfect human being, there were years when I was very bitter, something of a hothead and nearly convinced that a promise I had made to myself might be nothing more than the idealistic dream of an idiot. I might have gone a different way. Your mother gave Jacob Brolin's name to my uncle, and I spent a summer with him." He hesitated. "What you know now is true, my father and sister were gunned down. I watched them die. I swore on that day that I would do anything in my power never to let another child like my sister die for the hatreds of her elders."

"I'd made a few of the mistakes Danny was in danger of making," Jacob told her. "I come from a long line of Protestant Orangemen. I fell in love with a Catholic. My family's refusal to accept her sent me to the other side…where I learned harsher lessons. That's another story. Danny is writing it now."

Moira stared at Danny. "Why didn't you tell me what was going on?"

"I couldn't let him tell you anything," Brolin said. "Michael McLean looked like a golden boy on paper. We were afraid the contact man might be Andrew Mc-

Gahey, making contact through your brother. And Jeff Dolan…he's clean now, but with his past, we couldn't take any chances. McLean and your brother had your love and your trust. Who knew what you might say to them. We had our suspicions about Kyle Browne, but we didn't want to move against him, because we still didn't know who he was meeting."

"And they set Danny up. They put that gun under his bed."

"Yes. Remember the night your purse disappeared?" Danny asked.

"Yes," she murmured.

"I believe they stole your purse to get your key copied, and then all they needed was the appropriate moment to get the gun into my room. They not only meant to assassinate Jacob but to see the murder pinned on me."

"But the whole thing is…so complex," Moira breathed. "How—"

"They were both part of a splinter group calling themselves the Irish American Liberation People. They collect money from Americans who think they're giving to children maimed in the violence, but it really goes to arm the IRA. The American government has been trying to close in on them, but there was never enough evidence. They were good, I'll hand them that. They were able to falsify documents, create new identities for themselves and steal the lives of other men."

"Aren't you worried? There must be others who wish you harm," Moira murmured to Jacob.

"There will always be someone who disagrees with the peaceful process," Jacob told her lightly. "But there are so many people who support me, and I like to believe that, having been on both sides and known the tragedy of each, I can make a real difference."

"So, Danny…you work for Jacob?"

"No."

"He's my friend," Jacob said. "And he had an in at Kelly's. When we knew something was brewing at the pub—sorry, no pun intended—I called Danny and set him up with a contact through my office, and he agreed to keep his eyes on the events in the pub."

Moira found herself shivering again, looking at Danny. "From things he said… I think that Michael… Robert McMalley was the one murdering prostitutes."

Danny's eyes met hers. He knew what she was feeling. She had trusted a man, slept with a man, who had come to take human life so lightly that no one mattered if they threatened his goals in any way.

His eyes held hers. "We'll probably never know exactly what happened."

"Almost back to shore," Jacob said lightly, pointing ahead.

There was an emergency vehicle waiting. Moira didn't want to go to the hospital and said that she was fine, but Jacob Brolin insisted. Her neck was a definite shade of blue, he said, and Danny had most likely a few broken ribs.

She stared at Danny, dumbfounded. He shrugged. "Yeah, I think he's right. I would be dead if Jacob hadn't warned me it was time to start being careful. Thing is, the vest saves your life, but being shot that close…"

At the hospital, Moira didn't want to leave Danny's side, but she was gently, politely forced into another room for medical care. She was in a cubicle alone, waiting for word about Danny's X rays, when she heard Brolin, who had been doing the talking with the police thus far, suddenly begin talking to someone else.

She heard her father's voice, deep and concerned. Then her brother and her mother.

"I am perfectly calm," Katy Kelly announced, sounding only a shade shrill. "And I want to see my daughter."

A moment later Katy came bursting into the cubicle. She stopped at the curtain and looked at Moira in her hospital gown, stretched out on the gurney.

"Eamon!" she cried to her husband, who had come in right behind her. "Look what they've done to me baby."

Katy promptly passed out.

Luckily Eamon was there to catch her.

Eamon looked at his daughter. "Ah, lass, she's the strongest woman I've ever known—you just don't threaten her children."

He couldn't drop his wife, so his enveloping hug for his daughter came only after an orderly had appeared, an ammonia vial had been broken, Katy had come to and the hug could be a family affair.

Soon after, Patrick, Colleen and Granny Jon were with her in the small space, as well, and the way she was kissed, hugged and enveloped by her family made her realize that she had to be one of the luckiest people in the world. When Patrick held her in his arms, she was able to whisper, "Patrick, oh, my God, I am so, so sorry. There were times…"

"When you were suspicious of me," he whispered back. "It's okay. I understand. I love you, and I'm so sorry I didn't see what was going on in time."

Then the police insisted on speaking to Moira. They ushered her family out, except for her parents, who refused to go.

Katy Kelly gave the police only so much time, then put her foot down and forced them out. Moira would give them any information they needed once she was declared fit and well and had had some rest, Katy informed them in no uncertain terms.

When they were gone, Moira told her mother, "I don't want to rest. I just want to see Danny."

"We'll see to it," Eamon said firmly, and she was taken to the cubicle where Danny's ribs had just been wrapped. He was sliding into the clean shirt the Kellys had brought from the house. Moira rushed to him, suddenly bursting into tears.

Danny held her. "Ah, Moira, my love. It's all right now. Truly. Oh, hug me, darlin', just not quite so tightly, please."

"He should be staying in the hospital," the stern-looking doctor on duty said.

"For observation," Danny told him. "Believe me, sir, these good people will observe me." He looked into Moira's eyes. "No one can watch me better than she," he added softly.

She didn't leave his side. It would have done little good to attempt to go to bed or sleep that night, anyway. None of the Kelly household slept, except for the children. Siobhan would explain things the best she could to them when they awakened in the morning. As for the rest of the family, they hadn't been able to return to the house until nearly four a.m. Seamus's funeral was still planned for nine.

Eamon gave the eulogy, a fine speech. Moira was to have performed another rendition of "Amazing Grace" with Colleen, but since her voice remained a throaty croak, Colleen was on her own. She, too, did beautifully.

Seamus was duly laid to rest. Jacob Brolin had quietly attended the funeral service at the church; at the graveyard, he gave a short speech, honoring Seamus as both a fine Irishman and a fine American.

Moira had spent a few minutes closeted with Josh. Colleen was going to take over her sister's announcing duties for the live feed, because not only was Moira's voice gone, she had been invited to ride with Jacob Brolin on his float.

Moira did, however, do her own interview with Jacob Brolin at the pub that afternoon, surrounded by a full house, with a real Saint Patrick's Day bash in full swing. Jacob was wonderful, talking reasonably about both sides of the conflict. Many people in the North had legitimate complaints, he said, and he meant to see to them. They needed more Catholics on the police force, more good faith among men, and yes, they had a long way to go, but they had also made immense strides in the direction of peace. "Northern Ireland is beautiful," he said, "and there is one thing that draws all of us together, and that is the desire to let the world know just how beautiful, and to welcome travelers with the hospitality of old. Our future lies in our ability to lay out a level playing field for all men. Oscar Wilde once said, 'If one could only teach the English how to talk, and the Irish how to listen, society would be quite civilized.' We all need to learn how to talk—and how to listen."

The pub had been open to the public throughout, and Brolin's speech was heartily applauded by all. Many of the customers were amazed that Eamon had gone ahead with the opening of the pub that afternoon, after everything his family had faced.

Eamon had said, "Why not? Close the pub? I've never had more reason to celebrate in my life. My child was in danger, but she is here with me, and I am a blessed man, with all my family and my friends. Saint

Pat was looking out for us from up above, and I'll be thanking God for the rest of my days."

There had been no way to keep what had happened from the newspapers and the networks, and Kelly's Pub became famous across America that day.

Josh ably handled the media, arranging for questions from four to five, then the absence of cameras in the pub thereafter.

It was busy, and Moira insisted on remaining behind the bar, washing glasses as she listened when it was time for Danny to be quizzed by the reporters.

Being Danny, he managed to explain the truth, tell a story and speak lightly all the while. At the end of the session, a seasoned reporter asked him, "What's next for you, Mr. O'Hara? Will you be going home to enter Irish politics?"

"Oh, no," Danny replied. "I'm staying in America. I'm getting married, you see."

Moira was so startled she dropped a glass in the water. Still in shock, she met Danny's eyes.

"If she'll have me," he said softly.

Epilogue

The street had changed. There were handsome shops all along it now.

Danny stood on the sidewalk, taking a moment, as he always did in Belfast, to go back in time. Not to dwell on the misery of loss. Just to remember the family that had once been his.

He did love Belfast and all the North. They had been to Armagh just the other day, visited Tara, walked along endless hills of rolling green, felt the expanse, the wildness, the beauty and the magic of ancient times. Then they had returned to Belfast, and joined the hustle and shove of the busy city.

Today it seemed especially important for him to stand here. The last year had been the best of his life.

He would never forget his youth. In a corner of his heart, there would always be the pain of his loss. Yet even though that pain would never go away—*should* never go away—it had changed. The pen really *was* worse than the sword. He had done a great deal to change the world, or, at least, his world. His parents, he thought, would be proud. And Moira… Moira had allowed him to find his own peace, and a man could truly bring it to others only when he had found it in himself.

"Danny!"

He saw her coming down the street. She was in green. Kelly green, at that. A neat little suit that displayed the length of her legs and the indentation of her waist. Her hair, shining in the sunlight, bounced and waved over her shoulders. There was a slight touch of concern in her blue-green eyes as she reached him, taking his hand, placing a light kiss on his lips before studying his eyes again.

"Are you all right?"

He smiled. "Absolutely."

"I was worried. I didn't know where you had gone."

Okay, so he had ducked out on the luncheon. Andrew McGahey was being honored in the grand ballroom of the hotel for his efforts on behalf of the children of Ireland. And Andrew wasn't alone. He and Sally Adair had been introduced at the wedding, and they had been together ever since. Of course, Andrew remained a dedicated Catholic. Sally was still a wiccan. Maybe they would make it anyway. Anything was possible in America.

Danny had listened to most of the speeches, had watched his brother-in-law be merciful to the crowd and accept his plaque with a few words only, thanking his family and the Irish in America. Then a rather longwinded professor had taken the dais, and Danny had given in to the overwhelming urge to take a walk. It was important for him to come here. He always did, wherever he came back to this city of his birth.

"This is where it happened?"

"Yes."

She squeezed his hand. "Danny?"

He arched one brow. It still amazed him that they

were man and wife. He had always loved her, but he had known when they were very young that he hadn't been right for her. That he had a few demons to battle himself. And then…

There had been times when she had lain beside him shivering, and he had known that she was still haunted by her memories. A man who had said he loved her while needing other women…and disposing of them as easily as if they were laboratory rats who had fulfilled their purpose and needed to be destroyed.

All in all, though, they had come through quite well. The wedding had been spectacular. Mass at the family church in Boston, Moira in a shimmering long dress and veil, not quite traditionally white, but a combination of white and silver and mauve that seemed to spread magic with every move she made. Naturally the reception had been at Kelly's.

They'd taken two weeks on a remote private island in the Caribbean. There had been times when they had spent hours just talking. Times when they had just made love, a little desperately on some occasions, gently on others. Either way, it had only mattered that they'd had one another, that they were together, a bastion against the past, a team to forge through the future.

Life was good. He had Moira. It was impossible to love anyone more. Humbling to be so loved in return.

Incredible to have such understanding.

His book, written about the events that had formed Jacob Brolin's life and political perspective, was due out in a month. It was sure to cause some controversy.

That was fine. He still liked a certain amount of controversy. There was nothing like a good, hard-fought argument to be waged—and won. And of course, Moira was opinionated, so they had lots of heated discussions, and lots of wonderful moments of passionate apology. He had become a resident alien in New York City; Moira had already, in the single year of their marriage, taken six trips to Ireland with him. Their first trip, they had come alone, here, to Belfast, then traveled beyond, into the North.

Their second trip, they had taken Granny Jon and the family to Dublin. Everyone had come, including Siobhan and the children. They had made a day out of traveling down to Blarney to show the kids the castle and, of course, kiss the Blarney Stone. Katy Kelly had remarked that it seemed rather unnecessary, since most of the time they were all full of it to begin with.

It had been a great trip. Showing Ireland to children for the first time, showing them the source of so many of the tales they had heard, had been wonderful. Seeing Molly's eyes widen for a ride on a chubby Irish pony through fields of emerald, Brian's fascination with the tales of knights in shining armor, and Shannon's pleasure in the quaint charm of the small towns.

Moira had brought her own brilliance to their travels. She had expanded her show, and they now did segments on American vacationers returning to their roots in foreign countries. Colleen's was still the face on hundreds of magazine covers, but she had also taken to hosting more shows for her sister. That allowed Moira more travel time. For himself, it was easy. Writing was an exercise of the mind. Of course, it helped to see all the places that stirred his imagination and brought back the trials and triumphs of history, near and far.

Life was good. He couldn't imagine that anything could be better.

"Danny," Moira said again.

He looked at his wife. *Wife.* He smiled. "Sorry, love, I was wandering."

She shook her head. "I worry about you when I

know…you've come here. I think about my family. Patrick, Colleen…my folks. When I see Molly, Brian and Shannon, and I think about what happened… I know I couldn't have come through…as you did."

"I only come here because I loved them so much. It's a way of saying hello, telling them they'll always be with me."

She smiled. "You feel that they're here, with you, a little bit?"

"Maybe. But I'm okay, Moira. I have been for years. Never as good, though, as since I've been with you."

Shoppers passed them by. A pretty woman walking a dog smiled and said hello. A man in a tweed cap tipped it to them.

"Hmm…"

"What?"

"I was actually waiting for us to be alone somewhere incredibly beautiful and romantic…"

"Excuse me, but my city *is* incredibly beautiful and romantic."

"Oh, I know, I know. I meant like our bedroom in the hotel, the lights all muted, music playing, roses in a vase…"

"Champagne in a bucket? A tub full of suds? You wearing nothing but bubbles here and there, at strategic spots?"

"Something like that."

"I like it—let's go."

"Wait, Danny, the point was that I want to tell you something. And I've just decided to tell you here."

"Great. Get me all hot and bothered, then make me stand on the sidewalk where I can't do a damn thing about it."

"Danny, we're going to have a baby."

He couldn't have imagined that anything could be better, but he'd just been proven wrong.

"We're…pregnant?"

"No. *I'm* pregnant, but *we're* having a baby."

He folded his wife into his arms. Kissed her. Tenderly. On her lips, both cheeks, her forehead, her lips again. "A little Irishman," he whispered.

"Or an American woman," she reminded him.

He cradled her face in his hands. Studied her eyes, kissed her lips again. "Whichever, I'm thrilled. I'm… God, I'm thrilled." He smiled and looked up. "Hear that, Mum? A grandchild." Suddenly he got a questioning look in his eyes.

"You're certain?"

"Absolutely."

"Maybe we should test again."

"Why?"

"Because then you can tell me again, in the romantic room, with the music, the champagne…"

"Danny, I won't be drinking champagne any time soon," she told him.

"I didn't intend for you to drink it. I think it would be better for you to, oh, wear it," he told her.

"Oh." She smiled. "Shall we go?"

He put his arm around her, and they started down the street.

"My God, I'm shaking," he said. "I'm going to be a dad. To a wee bit of an Irishman."

"Or an American girl."

"Maybe it will be a lass," he agreed. "A little Irish lass."

"Or an American boy."

"Fine. Have it your way—the first time," he teased. Then he stopped again in the street, cradled her face once more, kissed her and drew her to him.

"The best of Ireland, and of America, will be in our son or daughter," he said softly.

"Oh, Danny, that's lovely."

"You think so?"

"Yes."

"Good, then let's move on. I'm definitely in the mood for champagne."

* * * * *

FATAL AFFAIR

Marie Force

1

The smell hit him first.

"Ugh, what the hell is that?" Nick Cappuano dropped his keys into his coat pocket and stepped into the spacious, well-appointed Watergate apartment that his boss, Senator John O'Connor, had inherited from his father.

"Senator!" Nick tried to identify the foul metallic odor.

Making his way through the living room, he noticed parts and pieces of the suit John wore yesterday strewn over sofas and chairs, laying a path to the bedroom. He had called the night before to check in with Nick after a dinner meeting with Virginia's Democratic Party leadership, and said he was on his way home. Nick had reminded his thirty-six-year-old boss to set his alarm.

"Senator?" John hated when Nick called him that when they were alone, but Nick insisted the people in John's life afford him the respect of his title.

The odd stench permeating the apartment caused a tingle of anxiety to register on the back of Nick's neck. "John?"

He stepped into the bedroom and gasped. Drenched in blood, John sat up in bed, his eyes open but vacant. A knife spiked through his neck held him in place against the headboard. His hands rested in a pool of blood in his lap.

Gagging, the last thing Nick noticed before he bolted to the bathroom to vomit was that something was hanging out of John's mouth.

Once the violent retching finally stopped, Nick stood up on shaky legs, wiped his mouth with the back of his hand, and rested against the vanity, waiting to see if there would be more. His cell phone rang. When he didn't take the call, his pager vibrated. Nick couldn't find the wherewithal to answer, to say the words that would change everything. *The senator is dead. John's been murdered.* He wanted to go back to when he was still in his car, fuming and under the assumption that his biggest problem that day would be what to do about the man-child he worked for who had once again slept through his alarm.

Thoughts of John, dating back to their first meeting in a history class at Harvard freshman year, flashed through Nick's mind, hundreds of snippets spanning a nearly twenty-year friendship. As if to convince himself that his eyes had not deceived him, he leaned forward to glance into the bedroom, wincing at the sight of his best friend—the brother of his heart—stabbed through the neck and covered with blood.

Nick's eyes burned with tears, but he refused to give in to them. Not now. Later maybe, but not now. His phone rang again. This time he reached for it and saw it was Christina, his deputy chief of staff, but didn't take the call. Instead, he dialed 911.

Taking a deep breath to calm his racing heart and making a supreme effort to keep the hysteria out of his voice, he said, "I need to report a murder." He gave the address and stumbled into the living room to wait for the police, all the while trying to get his head around the image of his dead friend, a visual he already knew would haunt him forever.

Twenty long minutes later, two officers arrived, took a quick look in the bedroom and radioed for backup. Nick was certain neither of them recognized the victim.

He felt as if he was being sucked into a riptide, pulled further and further from the safety of shore, until drawing a breath became a laborious effort. He told the cops exactly what happened—his boss failed to show up for work, he came looking for him and found him dead.

"Your boss's name?"

"United States Senator John O'Connor." Nick watched the two young officers go pale in the instant before they made a second more urgent call for backup.

"Another scandal at the Watergate," Nick heard one of them mutter.

His cell phone rang yet again. This time he reached for it.

"Yeah," he said softly.

"Nick!" Christina cried. "Where the *hell* are you guys? Trevor's having a heart attack!" She referred to their communications director who had back-to-back interviews scheduled for the senator that morning.

"He's dead, Chris."

"Who's dead? What're you talking about?"

"John."

Her soft cry broke his heart. *"No."* That she was desperately in love with John was no secret to Nick. That she was also a consummate professional who would never act on those feelings was one of the many reasons Nick respected her.

"I'm sorry to just blurt it out like that."

"How?" she asked in a small voice.

"Stabbed in his bed."

Her ravaged moan echoed through the phone. "But who… I mean, *why?*"

"The cops are here, but I don't know anything yet. I need you to request a postponement on the vote."

"I can't," she said, adding in a whisper, "I can't think about that right now."

"You have to, Chris. That bill is his legacy. We can't let all his hard work be for nothing. Can you do it? For him?"

"Yes…okay."

"You have to pull yourself together for the staff, but don't tell them yet. Not until his parents are notified."

"Oh, God, his poor parents. You should go, Nick. It'd be better coming from you than cops they don't know."

"I don't know if I can. How do I tell people I love that their son's been murdered?"

"He'd want it to come from you."

"I suppose you're right. I'll see if the cops will let me."

"What're we going to do without him, Nick?" She posed a question he'd been grappling with himself. "I just can't imagine this world, this *life,* without him."

"I can't either," Nick said, knowing it would be a much different life without John O'Connor at the center of it.

"He's really dead?" she asked as if to convince herself it wasn't a cruel joke. "Someone killed him?"

"Yes."

Outside the chief's office suite, Detective Sergeant Sam Holland smoothed her hands over the toffee-colored hair she corralled into a clip for work, pinched some color into cheeks that hadn't seen the light of day in weeks, and adjusted her gray suit jacket over a red scoop-neck top.

Taking a deep breath to calm her nerves and settle her chronically upset stomach, she pushed open the door and stepped inside. Chief Farnsworth's receptionist greeted her with a smile. "Go right in, Sergeant Holland. He's waiting for you."

Great, Sam thought as she left the receptionist with a weak smile. Before she could give in to the urge to turn tail and run, she erased the grimace from her face and went in.

"Sergeant." The chief, a man she'd once called Uncle Joe, stood up and came around the big desk to greet her with a firm handshake. His gray eyes skirted over her with concern and sympathy, both of which were new since "the incident." She despised being the reason for either. "You look well."

"I feel well."

"Glad to hear it." He gestured for her to have a seat. "Coffee?"

"No, thanks."

Pouring himself a cup, he glanced over his shoulder. "I've been worried about you, Sam."

"I'm sorry for causing you worry and for disgracing the department." This was the first chance she'd had to speak directly to him since she returned from a month of administrative leave, during which she'd practiced the sentence over and over. She thought she'd delivered it with convincing sincerity.

"Sam," he sighed as he sat across from her, cradling his mug between big hands. "You've done nothing to disgrace yourself or the department. Everyone makes mistakes."

"Not everyone makes mistakes that result in a dead child, Chief."

He studied her for a long, intense moment as if he was making some sort of decision. "Senator John

O'Connor was found murdered in his apartment this morning."

"Jesus," she gasped. "How?"

"I don't have all the details, but from what I've been told so far, it appears he was dismembered and stabbed through the neck. Apparently, his chief of staff found him."

"Nick," she said softly.

"Excuse me?"

"Nick Cappuano is O'Connor's chief of staff."

"You know him?"

"Knew him. Years ago," she added, surprised and unsettled to discover the memory of him still had power over her, that just the sound of his name rolling off her lips could make her heart race.

"I'm assigning the case to you."

Surprised at being thrust so forcefully back into the real work she had craved since her return to duty, she couldn't help but ask, "Why me?"

"Because you need this, and so do I. We both need a win."

The press had been relentless in its criticism of him, of her, of the department, but to hear him acknowledge it made her ache. Her father had come up through the ranks with Farnsworth, which was probably the number one reason why she still had a job. "Is this a test? Find out who killed the senator and my previous sins are forgiven?"

He put down his coffee cup and leaned forward, elbows resting on knees. "The only person who needs to forgive you, Sam, is you."

Infuriated by the surge of emotion brought on by his softly spoken words, Sam cleared her throat and stood up. "Where does O'Connor live?"

"The Watergate. Two uniforms are already there.

Crime scene is on its way." He handed her a slip of paper with the address. "I don't have to tell you that this needs to be handled with the utmost discretion."

He also didn't have to tell her that this was the only chance she'd get at redemption.

"Won't the Feds want in on this?"

"They might, but they don't have jurisdiction, and they know it. They'll be breathing down my neck, though, so report directly to me. I want to know everything ten minutes after you do. I'll smooth it with Stahl," he added, referring to the lieutenant she usually answered to.

Heading for the door, she said, "I won't let you down."

"You never have before."

With her hand resting on the door handle, she turned back to him. "Are you saying that as the chief of police or as my Uncle Joe?"

His face lifted into a small but sincere smile. "Both."

2

Sitting on John's sofa under the watchful eyes of the two policemen, Nick's mind raced with the staggering number of things that needed to be done, details to be seen to, people to call. His cell phone rang relentlessly, but he ignored it after deciding he would talk to no one until he had seen John's parents. Almost twenty years ago they took an instant shine to the hard-luck scholarship student their son brought home from Harvard for a weekend visit and made him part of their family. Nick owed them so much, not the least of which was hearing the news of their son's death from him if possible.

He ran his hand through his hair. "How much longer?"

"Detectives are on their way."

Ten minutes later, Nick heard her before he saw her. A flurry of activity and a burst of energy preceded the detectives' entrance into the apartment. He suppressed a groan. *Wasn't it enough that his friend and boss had been murdered? He had to face* her, *too? Weren't there thousands of District cops? Was she really the only one available?*

Sam came into the apartment, oozing authority and competence. In light of her recent troubles, Nick couldn't believe she had any of either left. "Get some tape across that door," she ordered one of the officers. "Start a log with a timeline of who got here when. No one comes in or goes out without my okay, got it?"

"Yes, ma'am. The Patrol sergeant is on his way along with Deputy Chief Conklin and Detective Captain Malone."

"Let me know when they get here." Without so much as a glance in his direction, Nick watched her stalk through the apartment and disappear into the bedroom. Following her, a handsome young detective with bed head nodded to Nick.

He heard the murmur of voices from the bedroom and saw a camera flash. They emerged fifteen minutes later, both noticeably paler. For some reason, Nick was gratified to know the detectives working the case weren't so jaded as to be unaffected by what they'd just seen.

"Start a canvass of the building," Sam ordered her partner. "Where the hell is Crime Scene?"

"Hung up at another homicide," one of the other officers replied.

She finally turned to Nick, nothing in her pale blue eyes indicating that she recognized or remembered him. But the fact that she didn't introduce herself or ask for his name told him she knew exactly who he was. "We'll need your prints."

"They're on file," he mumbled. "Congressional background check."

She wrote something in the small notebook she tugged from the back pocket of gray, form-fitting pants. There were years on her gorgeous face that hadn't been there the last time he'd had the opportunity to look closely, and he couldn't tell if her hair was as long as it used to be since it was twisted into a clip. The curvy body and endless legs hadn't changed at all.

"No forced entry," she noted. "Who has a key?"

"Who *doesn't* have a key?"

"I'll need a list. You have a key, I assume."

Nick nodded. "That's how I got in."

"Was he seeing anyone?"

"No one serious, but he had no trouble attracting female companionship." Nick didn't add that John's casual approach to women and sex had been a source of tension between the two men, with Nick fearful that John's social life would one day lead to political trouble. He hadn't imagined it might also lead to murder.

"When was the last time you saw him?"

"When he left the office for a dinner meeting with the Virginia Democrats last night. Around six-thirty or so."

"Spoke to him?"

"Around ten when he said he was on his way home."

"Alone?"

"He didn't say, and I didn't ask."

"Take me through what happened this morning."

He told her about Christina trying to reach John, beginning at seven, and of coming to the apartment expecting to find the senator once again sleeping through his alarm.

"So this has happened before?"

"No, he's never been murdered before."

Her expression was anything but amused. "Do you think this is funny, Mr. Cappuano?"

"Hardly. My best friend is dead, Sergeant. A United States senator has been murdered. There's nothing funny about that."

"Which is why you need to answer the questions and save the droll humor for a more appropriate time."

Chastened, Nick said, "He slept through his alarm

and ringing telephones at least once, if not twice, a month."

"Did he drink?"

"Socially, but I rarely saw him drunk."

"Prescription drugs? Sleeping pills?"

Nick shook his head. "He was just a very heavy sleeper."

"And it fell to his chief of staff to wake him up? There wasn't anyone else you could send?"

"The senator valued his privacy. There've been occasions when he wasn't alone, and neither of us felt his love life should be the business of his staff."

"But he didn't care if you knew who he was sleeping with?"

"He knew he could count on my discretion." He looked up, unprepared for the punch to the gut that occurred when his eyes met hers. Her unsettled expression made him wonder if she felt it, too. "His parents need to be notified. I'd like to be the one to tell them."

Sam studied him for a long moment. "I'll arrange it. Where are they?"

"At their farm in Leesburg. It needs to be soon. We're postponing a vote we worked for months to get to. It'll be all over the news that something's up."

"What's the vote for?"

He told her about the landmark immigration bill and John's role as the co-sponsor.

With a curt nod, she walked away.

An hour later, Nick was a passenger in an unmarked Metropolitan Police SUV, headed west to Leesburg with Sam at the wheel. She'd left her partner with a staggering list of instructions and insisted on accompanying Nick to tell John's parents.

"Do you need something to eat?"

He shook his head. No way could he even think about eating—not with the horrific task he had ahead of him. Besides, his stomach hadn't recovered from the earlier bout of vomiting.

"You know, we could still call the Loudoun County Police or the Virginia State Police to handle this," she said for the second time.

"No."

After an awkward silence, she said, "I'm sorry this happened to your friend and that you had to see him that way."

"Thank you."

"Are you going to answer that?" she asked of his relentless cell phone.

"No."

"How about you turn it off then? I can't stand listening to a ringing phone."

Reaching for his belt, he grabbed his cell phone, his emotions still raw after watching John be taken from his apartment in a body bag. Before he shut the cell phone off, he called Christina.

"Hey," she said, her voice heavy with relief and emotion. "I've been trying to reach you."

"Sorry." Pulling his tie loose and releasing his top button, he cast a sideways glance at Sam, whose warm, feminine fragrance had overtaken the small space inside the car. "I was dealing with cops."

"Where are you now?"

"On my way to Leesburg."

"God," Christina sighed. "I don't envy you that. Are you okay?"

"Never better."

"I'm sorry. Dumb question."

"It's okay. Who knows what we're supposed to say or do in this situation. Did you postpone the vote?"

"Yes, but Martin and McDougal are having an apoplexy," she said, meaning John's co-sponsor on the bill and the Democratic majority leader. "They're demanding to know what's going on."

"Hold them off. Another hour. Maybe two. Same thing with the staff. I'll give you the green light as soon as I've told his parents."

"I will. Everyone knows something's up because the Capitol Police posted an officer outside John's office and won't let anyone in there."

"It's because the cops are waiting for a search warrant," Nick told her.

"Why do they need a warrant to search the victim's office?"

"Something about chain of custody with evidence and pacifying the Capitol Police."

"Oh, I see. I was thinking we should have Trevor draft a statement so we're ready."

"That's why I called."

"We'll get on it." She sounded relieved to have something to do.

"Are you okay with telling Trevor? Want me to do it?"

"I think I can do it, but thanks for asking."

"How're you holding up?" he asked.

"I'm in total shock…all that promise and potential just gone…" She began to weep again. "It's going to hurt like hell when the shock wears off."

"Yeah," he said softly. "No doubt."

"I'm here if you need anything."

"Me, too, but I'm going to shut the phone off for a while. It's been ringing nonstop."

"I'll email the statement to you when we have it done."

"Thanks, Christina. I'll call you later." Nick ended

the call and took a look at his recent email messages, hardly surprised by the outpouring of dismay and concern over the postponement of the vote. One was from Senator Martin himself—"What the fuck is going on, Cappuano?"

Sighing, he turned off the cell phone and dropped it into his coat pocket.

"Was that your girlfriend?" Sam asked, startling him.

"No, my deputy."

"Oh."

Wondering what she was getting at, he added, "We work closely together. We're good friends."

"Why are you being so defensive?"

"What's your *problem?*" he asked.

"I don't have a problem. You're the one with problems."

"So all that great press you've been getting lately hasn't been a problem for you?"

"Why, Nick, I didn't realize you cared."

"I don't."

"Yes, you made that very clear."

He spun halfway around in the seat to stare at her. "*Are you for real?* You're the one who didn't return any of my calls."

She glanced over at him, her face flat with surprise. "What calls?"

After staring at her in disbelief for a long moment, he settled back in his seat and fixed his eyes on the cars sharing the Interstate with them.

A few minutes passed in uneasy silence.

"What calls, Nick?"

"I called you," he said softly. "For days after that night, I tried to reach you."

"I didn't know," she stammered. "No one told me."

"It doesn't matter now. It was a long time ago." But if his reaction to seeing her again after six years of thinking about her was any indication, it *did* matter. It mattered a lot.

3

The Loudoun County seat of Leesburg, Virginia, in the midst of the Old Dominion's horse capital, is located thirty-five miles west of Washington. Marked by rolling hills and green pastures, Loudoun is defined by its horse culture. Upon his retirement after forty years in the Senate, Graham O'Connor and his wife moved to the family's estate outside Leesburg where they could indulge in their love of all things horses. Their social life revolved around steeplechases, hounds, hunting and the Belmont Country Club.

The closer they got to Leesburg, the tenser Nick became. He kept his head back and his eyes closed as he prepared himself to deliver the gruesome news to John's parents.

"Who were his enemies?" Sam asked after a prolonged period of silence.

Keeping his eyes closed, Nick said, "He didn't have an enemy in the world."

"I'd say today's events prove otherwise. Come on. Everyone in politics has enemies."

He opened his eyes and directed them at her. "John O'Connor didn't."

"A politician without a single enemy? A man who looks like a Greek god with no spurned lovers?"

"A Greek god, huh?" he asked with a small smile. "Is that so?"

"There has to be *someone* who didn't like him. You can't live a life as high profile as his without someone being jealous or envious."

"John didn't inspire those emotions in people." Nick's heart ached as he thought of his friend. "He was inclusive. He found common ground with everyone he met."

"So the privileged son of a multi-millionaire senator could relate to the common man?" she asked, her tone ripe with cynicism.

"Well, yeah," Nick said softly, letting his mind wander back in time. "He related to me. From the moment we met in a history class at Harvard, he treated me like a long-lost brother. I came from nothing. I was there on a scholarship and felt like an imposter until John O'Connor took me under his wing and made me feel like I had as much reason as anyone to be there."

"What about in the Senate? Rivals? Anyone envious of his success? Anyone put out by this bill you were about to pass?"

"John hasn't had enough success in the Senate to inspire envy. His only real success was in consensus building. That was his value to the party. He could get people to listen to him. Even when they disagreed with him, they listened." Nick glanced over at her. "Where are you going with this?"

She mulled it over for a moment. "This was a crime of passion. When someone cuts off a man's dick and stuffs it in his mouth, they're sending a pretty strong message."

Nick's heart staggered in his chest. "Is *that* what was in his mouth?"

Sam winced. "I'm sorry. I figured you'd seen it…"

"Jesus." He opened the window to let the cold air in, hoping it would keep him from puking again.

"Nick? Are you all right?"

His deep sigh answered for him.

"Do you have any idea who would have reason to do such a thing to him?"

"I can't think of anyone who disliked him, let alone hated him that much."

"Clearly, someone did."

Nick directed her to the O'Connors' country home. They drove up a long, winding driveway to the brick-front house at the top of a hill. When he reached for the door handle, she stopped him with a hand on his arm.

He glanced down at the hand and then up to find her eyes trained on him.

"I have to ask you one more thing before we go in."

"What?"

"Where were you between the hours of ten p.m. and seven a.m.?"

Staring at her, incredulous, he said, "*I'm* a suspect?"

"Everyone's a suspect until they aren't."

"I was in my office all night getting ready for the vote until five-thirty this morning when I went to the gym for an hour," he said, his teeth gritted with anger, frustration and grief over what he was about to do to people he loved.

"Can anyone confirm this?"

"Several of my staff were with me."

"And you were seen at the gym?"

"There were a few other people there. I signed in and out."

"Good," she said, seeming relieved to know he had an alibi. "That's good."

Nick took a quick glance at the cars gathered in the driveway and swore softly under his breath. Terry's

Porsche was parked next to a Volvo wagon belonging to John's sister Lizbeth, who was probably visiting for the day with her two young children.

"What?"

"The whole gang's here." He pinched the bridge of his nose, hoping to find some relief from the headache forming behind his right eye. "They'll know the minute they see me that something's wrong, so don't go flashing the badge at them, okay?"

"I had no plans to," she snapped.

Nonplussed by her tone, he said, "Let's get this over with." He went up the stairs and rang the bell.

An older woman wearing a gray sweat suit with Nikes answered the door and greeted him with a warm hug.

"Nick! What a nice surprise! Come in."

"Hi, Carrie," he said, kissing her cheek. "This is Sergeant Sam Holland. Carrie is like a member of the family and keeps everyone in line."

"Which is no easy task." Carrie shook Sam's outstretched hand and sized up the younger woman before turning back to Nick, her approval apparent. "I've been telling Nick for years that he needs to settle down—"

"Don't go there, Carrie." He made an effort to keep his tone light even though his heart was heavy and burdened by what he had to tell her and the others. How he wished he were here to introduce his "family" to his new girlfriend. "Are they home?"

"Down at the stables with the kids. I'll give them a call."

Nick rested his hand on her arm. "Tell them to leave the kids there, okay?"

Her wise old eyes narrowed, this time seeing the sorrow and grief that were no doubt etched into his face. "Nick?"

"Call them, Carrie."

Watching her walk away, Nick sagged under the weight of what he was about to do to her, to all of them, and was surprised to feel Sam's hand on his back. He turned to her and was once again caught off guard by the punch of emotion that ripped through him when he found her pale blue eyes watching him with concern.

They stared at each other for a long, breathless moment until they heard Carrie coming back. Nick tore his eyes off Sam and turned to Carrie.

"They'll be here in a minute," she said, clearly trying to maintain her composure and brace herself for what she was about to hear. "Can I get you anything?"

"No," Nick said. "Thank you."

"Come into the living room," she said, leading the way.

The house was elegant but comfortable, not a show place but a home—a place where Nick had always been made to feel right at home.

"Something's wrong," Carrie whispered.

Nick reached for her hand and held it between both of his. He sat that way, with Carrie on one side of him and Sam on the other, until they heard the others come in through the kitchen.

Hand-in-hand, John's parents, Graham and Laine O'Connor, entered the room with their son Terry and daughter Lizbeth trailing behind them. Graham and Laine, both nearly eighty, were as fit and trim as people half their age. They had snow-white hair and year-round tans from spending most of their time riding horses. When they saw Nick, they lit up with delight.

He released Carrie's hand and got up to greet them both with hugs. Terry shook his hand and Lizbeth went up on tiptoes to kiss his cheek. He introduced them to Sam.

"What're you doing here?" Graham asked. "Isn't the vote today?"

Nick glanced down at the floor, took a second to summon the fortitude to say what needed to be said, and then looked back at them. "Come sit down."

"What's going on, Nick?" Laine asked in her lilting Southern accent, refusing to be led to a seat. "You don't look right. Is something wrong with John?"

Her mother's intuition had beaten him to the punch. "I'm afraid so."

Laine gasped. Her husband reached for her hand, and right before Nick's eyes, the formidable Graham O'Connor wilted.

"He was late for work today."

"That's nothing new," Lizbeth said with a sisterly snicker. "He'll be late for his own funeral."

Nick winced at her choice of words. "We couldn't reach him, so I went over there to wake him up."

"Damned foolish of him to be sleeping late on a day like this," Graham huffed.

"We thought so, too," Nick conceded, his stomach clutching with nausea and despair. "When I got there…"

"What?" Laine whispered, reaching out to grip Nick's arm. *"What?"*

Nick couldn't speak over the huge lump that lodged in his throat.

Sam stood up. "Senator, Mrs. O'Connor, I'm so very sorry to have to tell you that your son's been murdered."

Nick knew if he lived forever, he would never forget the keening wail that came from John's mother as Sam's words registered. He reached for Laine when it seemed like she might faint. Instead, she folded like a house of cards into his arms.

Carrie kept saying, "No, no, no," over and over again.

With Lizbeth crying softly behind him and Terry's eyes glassy with tears and shock, Graham turned to Sam. "How?"

"He was stabbed in his bed."

Nick, who continued to hold the sobbing Laine, was grateful that Sam didn't tell them the rest. He eased Laine down to the sofa.

"Who would want to kill my John? My beautiful, sweet John?"

"We're going to find out," Sam said.

"Sam is the lead detective on the case," Nick told them.

"Excuse me," Graham mumbled as he turned and rushed from the room.

"Go with him, Terry," Laine said. "Please go with him."

Terry followed his father.

Lizbeth sat down on the arm of the sofa next to her mother. "Oh, God," she whispered. "What will I tell the kids?"

Painfully aware of how close John was to his niece and nephew, Nick looked up at her with sympathy.

"That he had an accident," Laine said, wiping her face. "Not that he was killed. You can't tell them that."

"No," Lizbeth agreed. "I can't."

Laine raised her head off Nick's shoulder. "Where is he now?" she asked Sam.

"With the medical examiner."

"I want to see him." Laine wiped furiously at the tears that continued to spill down her unlined cheeks. "I want to see my child."

"I'll arrange it tomorrow," Sam said.

Laine turned to Nick. "There'll be a funeral befitting a United States senator."

"Of course."

"You'll see to it personally."

"Anything you want or need, Laine. You only have to ask."

She clasped his hand and looked at him with shattered eyes. "Who would do this, Nick? Who would do this to our John?"

"I've been asking myself that question for hours and can't think of anyone."

"Whoever it is, Mrs. O'Connor, we'll find them," Sam assured her.

"See that you do." As if she couldn't bear to sit there another second, Laine got up and made for the door with Lizbeth and Carrie following her. At the doorway, Laine turned back to Nick. "You know you're welcome to stay. You're a part of this family, and you belong here. You always will."

Touched, Nick said, "Thank you, but I'm going to head back to the city. I need to spend some time with the staff."

"Please tell them how much we appreciate their hard work for John."

"I will. I'll see you tomorrow."

"Mrs. O'Connor," Sam said, rising to face Laine. "I'm so sorry to have to do this now, but in this kind of investigation, the first twenty-four hours are critical…"

"We'll do whatever we can do to find the person who did this to John," Laine said, her tearstained face sagging with grief.

"I need to know the whereabouts of you and the other members of your family between the hours of ten p.m. last night and nine o'clock this morning."

"You aren't serious," Laine said stiffly.

"If I'm going to rule out any family involvement—"

"Fine," Laine snapped. "The senator and I entertained friends until about eleven." She glanced at Carrie, who nodded in agreement.

"I'll need the name and number of your friends." She handed Laine her card. "You can leave the information on my voicemail. And after eleven?"

"We went to bed."

"You, too, ma'am?" Sam asked Carrie.

"I watched television in my room until about two. I couldn't sleep."

"And you?" Sam asked Lizbeth.

Her expression rife with indignation, Lizbeth said, "I was at home in McLean with my husband and children."

"I'll need a phone number for your husband."

Lizbeth met Sam's even gaze with a steely stare before she stalked from the room and returned a minute later with a business card.

"Thank you," Sam said.

The three women left the room.

"You really had to do that today?" Nick asked Sam when they were alone. "Right now?"

"Yes, I really did," she said, looking pained. "I have to play by the book on something this high profile. Surely you can understand that."

"Of course I do, but they just found out their son and brother was murdered. You could've given them fifteen minutes to absorb that before you went into attack cop mode."

"I have a job to do, Nick. When I make an arrest, I'm sure they'll be relieved that his killer is off the streets."

"What the hell difference will that make to them? Will it bring John back?"

"I need to get back to the city. Are you coming?"

Taking a long last look around the room, remembering so many happy times there with John, Nick followed her out the front door.

4

Feeling as if the world had quite simply come to an end, Graham O'Connor leaned against a white split-rail fence to look out over the acres that made up his estate but saw nothing through a haze of tears and grief. *John is dead. John is dead. John is dead.*

From the moment Carrie called them to say Nick was waiting at the house, Graham had known. With the most important vote of John's career scheduled for that day, there was only one reason Nick would have come. Graham had known, just as he had always known there was something shameful about a father loving one of his children more than the others. But John had been extraordinary. From the very earliest hours of his youngest child's life, Graham had seen in him the special something that inspired so many others to love him, too.

His face wet with tears, Graham wondered how this could have happened.

"Dad?"

The sound of his older son's voice filled Graham with disappointment and despair. God help him for thinking such a thing, but if he'd had to lose one of his sons why couldn't it have been Terry instead of John?

Terry's hand landed on Graham's shoulder, squeezed. "What can I do for you?"

"Nothing." Graham wiped his face.

"Senator?"

Graham turned to find Nick and the pretty detective approaching them.

"We're going back to Washington," she said, "but before we do I need to confirm your whereabouts last night. After ten."

He somehow managed to contain the hot blast of rage that cut through him at the implication that he could have had something to do with the death of the one he loved above all others—except for Laine, of course. "I was right here with my wife. We had friends over, played some bridge and went to bed around eleven or so."

She seemed satisfied with his answer and turned next to Terry. "Mr. O'Connor?"

"I was…ah…with a friend."

Terry's womanizing had gotten completely out of hand since a DUI derailed his political aspirations weeks before he was supposed to declare his candidacy for the Senate. It made Graham sick that Terry was no closer to settling down and having a family at forty-two than he had been at twenty-two.

"I'll need a name and number," the detective said.

Terry's cheeks turned bright red, and Graham knew what was coming next. "I…ah…"

"He doesn't know her name," Graham said, casting a disgusted look at his son.

"I can find out," Terry said quickly.

"That'd be a good idea," the detective said.

"It's not a coincidence, is it, that this happened on the eve of the vote?" Graham said.

"We're not ruling anything out," the detective said.

"Check Minority Leader Stenhouse," Graham said. "He hates my guts and would begrudge my son any kind of success."

"Why does he hate you?" she asked.

"They were bitter rivals for decades," Nick told her. "Stenhouse has done everything he could to block the immigration bill, but it was going to pass anyway."

"Take a good look at him," Graham said, his chest tight with rage and his voice breaking. "He's capable of anything. Taking my son from me would give him great joy."

"Can you think of anyone else?" she asked. "Anyone who might've tangled with your son, either on a personal or professional level?"

Graham shook his head. "Everyone loved John, but I'll think about it and let you know if anyone comes to mind."

Nick stepped forward to embrace him.

Graham wrapped his arms around the young man he loved like a son. "Find out who did this, Nick. Find out."

"I will. I promise."

As Nick and Sam walked away, Graham noted the hunched shoulders of his son's closest friend and trusted aide. To Terry he said, "Get the name of your bimbo, and get it now. Don't show your face around here again until you do."

"Yes, sir."

On the way back to Washington, Nick checked his cell phone and read through the statement his office had drafted.

With tremendous sorrow we announce that our colleague and friend, Senator John Thomas

O'Connor, Democrat of Virginia, was found murdered in his Washington home this morning. After Senator O'Connor failed to arrive for work, his chief of staff, Nicholas Cappuano, went to the senator's home to check on him. Mr. Cappuano found the senator dead. At the request of the Metropolitan Police, we'll have no further statement on the details of the senator's death other than to say we will do everything within our power to assist in the investigation. Subsequent information on the investigation will come from the police.

We will make it our mission to ensure passage of the landmark immigration legislation Senator O'Connor worked so hard to bring to the Senate floor and to continue his work on behalf of children, families and the aged.

Our hearts and prayers are with the senator's parents, Senator and Mrs. Graham O'Connor, his brother Terry, sister Lizbeth, brother-in-law Royce, niece Emma and nephew Adam. Funeral arrangements are incomplete but will be announced in the next few days. We ask that you respect the privacy of the O'Connor family at this difficult time.

Nick nodded with approval and read it again before he turned to Sam. "Can I run this by you?"

"Sure." She listened intently as he read the statement to her. "Sounds like they covered every base."

"The part about the investigation was okay?"

"Yes, it's fine."

Nick placed a call to Christina. "Hey, green light on the statement. Go ahead and get it out."

Christina replied with a deep, pained sigh. "This'll make it official."

"Tell Trevor to just read it and get out of there. No questions."

"Got it."

"You guys did a great job. Thank you."

"It was the hardest thing I've ever had to do," she said, her voice hoarse.

"I'm sure."

"So, um, how'd it go with his parents?"

"Horrible."

"Same thing with the staff. People are taking it really hard."

"I'm on my way back. I'll be in soon."

"We'll be here."

Nick ended the call.

"Are you all right?" Sam asked.

"I'm fine," he said stiffly, still pissed that she had talked alibis with the O'Connors so soon.

"I was just doing my job."

"Your job sucks."

"Yes, a lot of times it does."

"Do you ever get used to telling people their loved ones have been murdered?"

"No, and I hope I never do."

As bone-deep exhaustion began to set in, he put his head back against the seat. "I appreciated you saying the words for me back there. I just couldn't bring myself to do it."

She glanced over at him. "You were very good with them."

Surprised by the unexpected compliment, Nick forced a weak smile. "I was in uncharted waters, that's for sure."

"You're close to them."

"They're family to me."

"What does your own family think of that?"

They hadn't taken the time to compare life stories the first time they met. They'd been too busy tearing each other's clothes off. "I don't have much of a family. I was born to parents who were still in high school and was raised by my grandmother. She passed away a few years ago."

"What about your parents?"

"They breezed in and out of my life when I was a kid."

"And now?"

"Let's see, my mother is married for the third time and was living in Cleveland the last time I heard from her, which was a couple of years ago. My father is married to a woman who's younger than me, and they have three-year-old twins. He lives in Baltimore. I see them once in a while, but he's hardly a father to me. He's only fifteen years older than me."

Her silence made him realize she was waiting for him to say more.

"I remember the first weekend I spent with the O'Connors. I thought families like theirs only existed on TV."

"They always seemed almost too good to be true."

"They're not, though. They're real people with real faults and problems, but they have such a strong belief in giving back and in public service that it's impossible to be around them for any length of time and not be sucked in. They changed my whole career plan."

"What were you going to do?"

"I'd considered accounting or finance, but after a few meals at Graham O'Connor's table, I was bitten by the political bug."

"What's he like? Graham?"

"He's complicated and thoughtful and demanding. He loves his family and his country. He's fiercely patriotic and loyal."

"You love him."

"More than any man I've ever known—except his son."

"Tell me about John."

Nick thought for a moment before he answered. "If his father is complicated, thoughtful and demanding, John was simple, forgetful and lackadaisical. But like his father, he loved his family and his country and was proud to serve the people of Virginia. He took those responsibilities seriously but didn't take himself too seriously."

"Did you like working for him?"

"I liked being around him and helping him to succeed. But from a political staff perspective, he could be a bit of a handful."

"How so?"

Nick paused, considered and decided. "Right now, my chief goal is to protect his legacy and ensure he's afforded the dignity and stature he deserves as a deceased United States senator."

"And *my* goal is to figure out who killed him. If I'm going to do that, I'll need you and the rest of your staff to be forthcoming. I can do it faster and more efficiently with your help than without it. I need to know who he was."

Nick wished he couldn't smell her, wished he wasn't so aware of her. And more than anything, he wished he didn't so vividly remember the night he'd spent lost in her. "I was furious," he said in a soft tone.

"When?" she asked, confused.

"On my way to his place this morning. If he hadn't

been dead when I got there, I might've killed him my-self."

"Nick…" Her tone was full of warning, reminding him not to forget who he was talking to.

"If you want to know who John O'Connor was, the fact that his chief of staff was on his way to haul him out of bed—*again*—should tell you everything you need to know."

"It doesn't tell me everything, but it's a start."

5

Sam's memories of Nick Cappuano should have faded over the years, but they hadn't. He remained a larger-than-life character from a single night that shouldn't have meant as much as it had. But she *had* forgotten the reality of him—his height, easily six-three or -four, broad shoulders, chocolate brown hair that curled at the ends, hazel eyes that missed nothing, olive-toned skin, strong, efficient hands that changed forever what she expected from a lover, crackling intelligence, and the cool aura of reserved control she'd found so fascinating the first time she met him.

Cracking that control had been one of the best memories from her night with him. When he didn't call, she'd wondered if their intense connection had scared him off. But now that she knew he *had* called, that he *had* wanted to see her again…that changed everything.

"Can I ask you something that has nothing to do with the case?" she said as they cut across the District on the way to the Watergate where he'd left his car. Along the way, they noticed a few American flags already lowered to half-mast in John's honor. The word was out, and the official mourning had begun.

"Sure."

Her heart raced as she picked at a scab she'd mistakenly thought healed long ago. "When you called me… after…that night…do you remember who you talked to at my house?"

He shrugged. "Some guy. One of your roommates maybe."

Knowing the answer before she even asked, she said, "You didn't get his name? I lived with three guys."

"Shit, I don't know. Paul maybe."

"Peter?"

"Yes. Peter. That was it. I talked to him a couple of times."

Gripping the steering wheel so tightly her knuckles turned white, Sam wanted to scream.

"Was he your boyfriend?"

"Not then," she said through gritted teeth.

"Later?"

"He's my ex-husband."

"Ah! Well, now it all makes sense," he said but there was a bitter edge to his voice that she understood all too well. She was feeling rather bitter herself at the moment.

"Too bad you didn't give me your cell number instead of your home number."

"I only had a department cell then, and I never used it for personal business." They were quiet until she pulled into the Watergate. "I'd like to interview your staff in the morning," she said as the car idled.

"I'll make sure they're available." He rattled off the Hart Senate Office Building address where she could find them.

"In the meantime, here's my card in case you think of anything that might be relevant. No matter how big or how small, you never know what'll crack a case wide open."

He took the card and reached for the door handle.

"Nick," she said, her hand on his arm to stop him from getting out.

Looking down at her hand and then up to meet her eyes, he raised an eyebrow.

"I would've liked to have gotten those messages," she said, her heart racing. "I would've liked that very much."

He sighed. "I can't process this on top of everything else that's happened today. It's just too much."

"I know." She raised her hand to let him go. "I'm sorry I brought it up."

He surprised her when he reached for her hand and brought it to his lips. "Don't be sorry. I really want to talk about it. Later, though, okay?"

Sam swallowed hard at the intense expression on his handsome face. "Okay."

He released her hand and opened the car door. "I'll see you in the morning."

"Yes," she said softly to herself when he was gone. "See you then."

Frederico Cruz was a junk food addict. However, despite his passion for donuts, his ongoing love affair with the golden arches, and his obsession with soda of all kinds except diet, he managed to maintain a wiry, one-hundred-seventy-pound frame that was usually draped by one of the many trench coats he claimed were necessary to staying in character.

In some sort of cosmic joke, Sam had drawn the dietary disaster area known as Freddie for a partner. In the midst of the HQ detective pit chaos, Sam watched fascinated and envious as he chased a cream-filled donut with a cola. She swore that spending most of every day with him for the last year had put ten unneeded pounds on her. "Where are we?" she asked when he put down the soda can and wiped his mouth.

"Still at square one. The neighbors didn't hear anything or see anyone in the elevator or hallways. I sent a couple of uniforms to pick up the security tape—not an easy task, I might add. You'd think we were planning to send G. Gordon Liddy back in there or something. I had to threaten them with warrants."

"What was the hang-up?" Sam asked, eyeing his second donut with lust in her heart.

"Resident privacy, the usual bull. I had to remind them—twice—that a United States senator had been murdered in his apartment and did they really want any *more* unfavorable publicity than they're already going to get?"

"Good job, Freddie. That's the way to be aggressive." She was forever after him to get in there and get his hands dirty. In turn, he nagged her about getting a life away from the job.

"I learned from the best."

She made a face at him.

"We also seized everything from the senator's home and work offices—computers, files, etc. The lab is going through the computers now. We can hit the files tomorrow."

"Good."

"What's your take on the O'Connors?"

"The parents were devastated. There was nothing fake about it. Same with his sister."

"What about the brother?"

"He seemed shocked, but he says he was with a woman whose name he doesn't remember."

"He'll have to produce her if he's going to rely on her for an alibi."

"He's painfully aware of that," Sam said, smirking

at her recollection of Terry O'Connor's discomfort and Graham's obvious disapproval.

"That's what he gets for sleeping with a stranger. Imagine going up to someone you slept with to ask for her name."

Sam's face heated as memories of her one-night stand with Nick chose that moment to resurface. "Easy, Freddie. Don't get all proper on me."

"It's just another sign of the moral decline of our country."

Groaning at the familiar argument, she said, "Any word from the M.E.?"

"Not yet. Apparently, they had a backlog to get through."

"Who comes before a murdered U.S. senator?"

He shrugged. "Don't kill the messenger."

"My favorite sport."

"Don't I know it? The guy who found him checked out? Cappuano?"

"Yeah." Sam decided right in that moment not to tell Freddie about her history with Nick. Some things were personal, and she didn't want or need Freddie's disapproval. She was still dealing with her own disapproval for bringing up their former personal relationship in the midst of a murder investigation. "He was at work all night with other people from the staff, which I'll confirm tomorrow."

"So what's next?"

"In the morning, we'll interview O'Connor's staff and pay a visit to the senate minority leader," she said, filling him in on Graham O'Connor's long-running feud with Stenhouse.

Freddie rubbed his chiseled cheek. On top of his many other faults, he was *GQ* handsome, too. Life wasn't fair. "Interesting," he said.

"Senator O'Connor questioned the timing—on the eve of the biggest vote of his son's career as a senator."

"Someone didn't want that vote to happen?"

"It's the closest thing to a motive I've seen yet. When we talk to his staff tomorrow, we need to cover both sides—the political and the personal. Who was he dating? Who might've had an axe to grind? You know the drill."

"What's your gut telling you, boss?"

He knew she hated when he called her that. "I'm not loving the political angle."

"The timing works."

"Yeah, but would a political rival cut off his dick and stuff it in his mouth?"

Freddie cringed and covered his own package.

"We're going to keep that detail close to the vest and see where it takes us. But my money's on a woman."

"You know what's bugging me?" Freddie asked.

"What's that?"

"No sign of a struggle. How does someone get a hold of your dick and do the Lorena Bobbitt without you putting up a fight?"

"Maybe he was asleep? Didn't see it coming?"

"Someone grabs my junk, I'm *wide* awake."

"Spare me the visual, will you, please?"

"I'm just saying…"

"That it was someone he knew, someone he wasn't surprised to see."

"Exactly." He picked up the second donut and took a bite. With a dollop of white cream on his lower lip, he added, "He had one of those butcher block knife things in his kitchen. The butcher knife was the one holding him to the headboard."

"So the killer didn't arrive armed."

"It doesn't seem so. No."

Standing up, Sam said, "I want to see those tapes. What the hell is taking them so long?"

Driving from the Watergate to the office, Nick should have been thinking about what he was going to say to his staff. They'd be looking to him for leadership, for answers to questions that had no answers. But rather than prepare himself for what would no doubt be an emotional ordeal, he kept hearing Sam's voice: "I would've liked to have gotten those messages."

Pounding his hand on the steering wheel, he let loose with an uncharacteristic string of swears. Like it wasn't enough that John had been murdered. To also have to face off with the one woman from his past who he'd never worked out of his system was…well, calling it unfair wouldn't do it justice.

He knew she wanted to talk about what happened all those years ago and why they never saw each other again. It made him so mad to think about her malicious ex not giving her the messages. But he couldn't process the implications of this discovery in the midst of the mayhem caused by John's murder. Dealing with Sam Holland solely on a professional level would take all the fortitude he could muster, never mind getting personal.

Years ago, when she failed to return his calls, he'd been angry and hurt—so much so that he hadn't pursued it any further, which he now knew had been stupid. He couldn't help but wonder what might have been different for him—for both of them—if she had gotten his messages and returned his calls. Would they still be together? Or would it have burned out the way all his relationships inevitably did?

He realized, with a clarity he couldn't explain or understand, that they would probably still be together.

He'd never had that kind of connection with anyone else, which was why he'd been so acutely aware of her all day today.

6

After spending an excruciating hour with his grieving staff, Nick sent them home with orders to be back to work at nine in the morning to meet with the detectives and to plan the senator's funeral. He instructed them not to discuss the case or the senator with anyone and to avoid the press in particular.

He lowered himself into his desk chair, every muscle in his body aching with fatigue as the sleepless night and agonizing day caught up to him.

"Have you eaten?" Christina asked from the doorway.

Nick had to think about that. "Not since the bagel I puked up this morning."

"There's pizza left from before. Want me to get you some?"

Not at all sure he'd be able to get it down, he said, "Sure, thanks."

"Coming right up."

She returned a few minutes later with two slices that she had warmed in the microwave.

"Thank you," he said when she handed him the plate and a can of cola. Her blue eyes were rimmed with red, her face puffy from crying. "How're you doing?"

With a shrug, she collapsed into a chair on the other

side of his desk. "I feel like all the air has been sucked out of my lungs, and I can't seem to breathe."

"I know you cared for him a great deal," Nick said haltingly. They'd never discussed Christina's feelings for John.

"For all the good it did me."

"He loved you, Chris. You know he did."

"As a friend and colleague. Big whoop."

"I'm sorry."

"So am I because now I have to live the whole rest of my life wondering what might've happened if I'd had the courage to tell him how I felt."

"I'm kind of glad you didn't."

"I'm sure you are," she said with a laugh.

"Not because of work. I loved him like a brother. You know that. But he wasn't good enough for you. He would've broken your heart."

"Probably," she said. "No, definitely."

"If it makes you feel any better, I was confronted with a blast from my romantic past today. We spent a memorable night together six years ago, and I haven't seen her since—until she walked into John's apartment this morning as the detective in charge of the case."

Christina winced. "Awkward."

"To say the least."

"Do you trust her to handle the case?"

"Sam's a damned good detective."

"I thought you hadn't seen her in six years."

"Doesn't mean I haven't read about her."

"Hmm," she said, studying him.

"What?"

"Oh, nothing." Her eyes widened all of a sudden. "What's her last name?"

"Holland."

"Oh my God! She's the one who ordered the shoot-out at that crack house where the kid was killed!"

"Yes."

"But, Nick, do we really want *her* investigating John's murder? Couldn't we get someone else?"

"I trust her," Nick said. "She has one blemish on an otherwise stellar career. And think of it this way, she's got something to prove right now."

"I guess you're right," she said, still wary. The phone on Nick's desk rang, and Christina reached for it. "Nick Cappuano's office." Once again her eyes widened, and she stammered as she said, "Of course. One moment please."

"Who is it?" Nick asked.

"The president," she whispered.

Nick quickly swallowed a mouthful of pizza and reached for a napkin and the phone at the same time. "Good evening, Mr. President." He had met President Nelson on several occasions—mostly in receiving lines at Democratic Party fund-raisers—but a phone call from him was unprecedented.

"Hello, Nick. Gloria and I just wanted to tell you all how sorry we are."

"Thank you, sir. I'll pass that along to the staff. And thank you for the statement you issued to the press."

"I've known John since he was a little boy. I'm heartbroken."

"We all are."

"I can only imagine. I also wanted to make myself available for anything you might need over the next few days."

"I appreciate that. I know Senator and Mrs. O'Connor would be honored if you could speak at the funeral."

"*I'd* be honored."

"I'll work with your staff on the details."

"Let me give you my direct number in the residence. Feel free to use it."

Nick took down the number with a sense of disbelief. "Thank you."

"I spoke earlier with Chief Farnsworth and made the full resources of the federal government available to the Metropolitan Police. I'm sure you'll be close to the investigation. If there's anything you feel they could be doing that they're not, don't hesitate to contact me."

"I won't, sir."

The president released a deep sigh. "I just can't imagine who would do such a thing to John of all people."

"Neither can I."

"Do you think Graham and Laine would be up for a phone call?"

"I'm sure they'd love to hear from you."

"Well, I won't keep you any longer. God bless you and your staff, Nick. Our thoughts and prayers are with you all."

"Thank you so much for calling, Mr. President." Nick put down the phone and looked over at Christina.

"Unreal," she said.

"Surreal," he added, filling her in on what the president had said.

She began to cry again. "I keep waiting for John to come bounding in here asking why we're all sitting around."

"I know. Me, too."

"I actually had a few people ask me today how this affects their jobs," she said with disgust.

"Well, you can't blame them. They have families to support."

"Couldn't they have waited a day or two to bring that up?"

"Apparently not. I'll talk to them about it tomorrow and tell them we'll do our best to get them placed somewhere in government."

"What'll you do?" she asked.

"Shit, I don't know. I can't think about that until after we get through the funeral. The two of us, maybe a couple of others, will be needed for a while until the governor appoints someone to take John's place. Whoever it is will want to bring in their own people, so we'll help with the transition and then figure out what's next, I guess."

Christina looked so sad, so despondent that Nick felt his heart go out to her. "Why don't you go home, Chris? There's nothing more we can do here tonight."

"What about you?"

"I'll be going soon, too."

"All right," she said as she got up. "I'll see you in the morning."

"Try to get some sleep."

"As if."

He walked her to the door and sent her off with a hug before he wandered into John's office. The desk had been swept clean and the computer removed. If it hadn't been for the photo of John with his niece and nephew on the windowsill, there would've been no sign of him or the five years he'd spent working in this room. Nick wasn't sure what he hoped to find when he sat in John's chair. Swiveling to look out the window, he could see the Washington Monument lit up in the distance.

Resting his head back, he stared at the monument and finally gave himself permission to do what he'd needed to do all day. He wept.

* * *

Sam arrived home exhausted after a sixteen-hour day and smiled when she heard the whir of her father's chair as he came out to greet her.

"Hi, Dad."

"Late tonight."

"I'm on O'Connor."

The side of his face that wasn't paralyzed lifted into a smile. "Are you now? Farnsworth's got you right back on the horse."

She kicked off her boots and bent to kiss his cheek. "So it seems."

Celia, one of the nurses who cared for him, came out from the kitchen to greet Sam. "How about we get ready for bed, Skip?"

Sam hated the indignation that darted across the expressive side of his face. "Go ahead, Dad. I'll be in when you're done. I've got a couple of things I want to run by you."

"I suppose I can make some time for you," he teased, turning the chair with his one working finger and following Celia to his bedroom in what used to be the dining room.

Sam went into the kitchen and served herself a bowl of the beef stew Celia had left on the stove for her. She ate standing up without tasting anything as the events of the day ran through her mind like a movie. Under normal circumstances, she'd be obsessed with the case. She'd be thinking it through from every angle, searching out motives, making a list of suspects. But instead, she thought of Nick and the sadness that had radiated from him all day. More than once she had wanted to throw her arms around him and offer comfort, which was hardly a professional impulse.

Deciding it was pointless to try to eat, she poured

the rest of the soup into the garbage disposal and stood at the sink, her shoulders stooped. She was still there twenty minutes later when Celia came into the kitchen.

"He's ready for you."

"Thanks, Celia."

"He's been kind of…"

"What?" Sam asked, immediately on alert.

"Off. He hasn't been himself the last few days."

"The two-year anniversary is coming up next week."

"That could be it."

"Let's keep an eye on him."

Celia nodded in agreement. "What do you know about Senator O'Connor?"

"Not as much as I'd like to."

"What a tragedy," Celia said, shaking her head. "We've been glued to the news all day. Such an awful waste."

"Seemed like a guy who had it all."

"But there was something sort of sad about him, too."

"Why do you say that?"

"No reason in particular. Just a vibe he put out."

"I never noticed," Sam said, intrigued by the observation. She made a mental note to find some video of O'Connor's speeches from the Senate floor and TV interviews.

"Go on in and see your dad. He so looks forward to his time with you."

"The stew was great. Thank you."

"Glad you liked it."

Sam went into her father's bedroom where he was propped up in bed, a respirator hose snaking from his throat to the machine on the floor that breathed for him at night.

"You look beat," he said, his speech an awkward staccato around the respirator.

"Long-ass day." Sam sat in the chair next to the hospital bed and propped her feet on the frame under the pressurized mattress that minimized bedsores. "But it feels good to be doing more than pushing paper again."

"What've you got?" he asked, reverting to his former role as the department's detective captain.

She ran through the whole thing, from the meeting with Chief Farnsworth to reviewing the tapes the Watergate had finally produced. "We only got traffic in the lobby. Nothing jumped out at us, but I'm going to show them to his chief of staff in the morning to see if he can ID anyone."

"That's a good idea. Why do you get a funny look in those blue eyes of yours when you mention the chief of staff? Nick, right?"

"I went out with him once." She spared her father a deeper explanation of what "going out" had meant in this case. "A long time ago."

"But it was hard to see him?"

"Yeah," she said softly. "I found out he *did* call me after that night. Guess who took the messages and never gave them to me?"

"Oh, let's see, could it be our good friend Peter?"

"One and the same, the prick."

Skip's laugh was strained. "You able to be objective on this one with your Nick from the past part of the mix?"

Surprised by the question, she glanced up at him and found him studying her with sharp, blue eyes that were just like hers. "Of course. It was six years ago. No biggie."

"Uh huh."

She should have known he would see right through her. He always did.

"You need to get some sleep," he said.

"Whenever I close my eyes, I'm back in that crack house with Marquis Johnson screaming. And then I break out in a cold sweat."

"You did everything right, followed every instinct." He gasped for air. "I wouldn't have done it any differently."

"Do you ever think about the night you got shot?" She had never thought to ask that until she'd been haunted by her own demons.

"Not so much. It's all a blur."

Her cell phone rang. Sam reached for it on her belt and checked the caller ID. She didn't recognize the 703 number. "I need to take this."

"Go on."

She kissed her father's forehead and left the room. "Holland."

"Sam, it's Nick. Someone's been in my house."

Her heart fluttered at the sound of his deep voice. This was *not* good. "Has it been ransacked?" she asked, making an effort to sound cool and professional.

"No."

"Then how do you know someone's been there?"

"I *know*. Stuff's been moved."

"Where do you live?"

He rattled off an address in Arlington, Virginia.

Even though it was out of her jurisdiction, she grabbed her coat. "I'm on my way."

7

Thirty minutes later, Sam stormed up the stairs to Nick's brick-front townhouse.

He waited just inside the door and held it open for her. "Thanks for coming."

"Sure." She stole a quick glance around a combined living room/dining room where it appeared nothing was out of place. In fact, the space seemed better suited to a furniture showroom rather than someone's home. "How can you—"

He grabbed her hand. "Come."

Startled, she let him lead her into his office, which was as neat as the other rooms but more lived in than what she had seen so far.

"See that?"

Following the direction of his pointed finger, she studied a small stack of books on the desk. "What about it?"

"It's at an angle."

"So?"

"It's not supposed to be."

"*Seriously?* You called me over here at eleven o'clock at night because your stack of books isn't anally aligned?"

With a furious scowl, he grabbed her hand again and

all but dragged her upstairs to his bedroom. *Now we're talking! Relax, Sam, he's not dragging you off to bed as much as you wish he were.* Reminding herself that she was investigating a break-in at the home of a player in a homicide investigation, she pushed aside her salacious thoughts and tuned in to what he was showing her.

Pointing to the dresser, he said, "I didn't leave it like that."

A tiny scrap of white fabric poked out through the closed drawers. Deciding to humor him, Sam leaned in to inspect the cloth. "It's not possible your tighty whities got caught in the drawer and you didn't notice?"

"No, it's not possible," he said through gritted teeth.

She stood up and studied him like she had never seen him before, as if she hadn't once seen him naked. "Have you always been so anal?"

"Yes."

"Hmm."

"What does that mean? Hmm? Aren't you going to call someone?"

"To do what?"

"To figure out who's been in my house!"

"Nick, come on."

"Forget it. Go home. I'm sorry I bothered you."

His eyes, she noticed, were rimmed with red. She ached at the thought of him alone and heartbroken over his murdered friend. "Fine. If you really think someone's been in here—"

"I do."

"I left my phone in the car. May I use yours?"

He handed her his cell phone.

"This is Detective Sergeant Sam Holland, MPD. I need a Crime Scene unit," she said, giving the address.

When she hung up, she turned to find him watching her intently.

"Thank you."

She nodded, unsettled by the heat coming from his hazel eyes. Had she caused that or was it the fault of the person who had supposedly invaded his private space?

An hour later, Sam sat with Nick on the sofa, out of the way of the Arlington cops who were dusting for prints.

"How do you think they got in?" Desperate to maintain some semblance of distance from him, she spoke in the clipped, professional tone she used to interview witnesses.

"I have no idea."

"Does anyone have a key?"

"John had the only other one."

"Where did he keep it?"

"I'm not sure. I gave it to him in case I ever locked myself out."

"Which probably never happens."

"It hasn't yet."

"You don't use the security system?" she asked.

"It came with the place. I've never had it turned on."

"You might want to think about that."

"Really? Gee, thanks for that advice, Sergeant."

She shot him a warning look.

"I'm sorry," he said, dropping his head to run his fingers through thick dark hair.

Sam licked her lips, wishing she could do that for him.

"I don't mean to snap at you. It's just the idea of someone in my *home*, going through my stuff… It has me kind of skeeved out."

"Any idea what they might be looking for?"

His shoulders sagged with fatigue. "None."

Sam's heart went out to him. He'd had a horrible,

painful day, and she wished she could find an appropriate excuse to hug him. She made an effort to soften her tone. "Is it possible someone is trying to find something here they couldn't find at the senator's place?"

"I can't imagine what. Neither of us ever took anything sensitive out of the office. There're all kinds of rules about that."

"What kind of sensitive stuff was he involved with?"

"After the midterm election, he was appointed to the Senate Homeland Security Committee, but most of his work was in the areas of commerce, finance, children, families and the aged. None of that was overly sensitive."

Watching his tired face with much more than professional interest, she was dying to address the elephant in the room—the six years' worth of unfinished business and the tension that zipped through her every time she connected with those hot hazel eyes of his. "Is it possible he was involved in something you didn't know about?"

Nick scoffed. "Highly doubtful."

"But possible?"

"Sure it is, but John didn't operate that way. He relied on us for everything."

"You alluded earlier to him being high maintenance for the staff. Other than having to wake him up in the morning, how did you mean?"

Nick was quiet for a long moment before he glanced at her. "This is all for background, right? I won't read about it in tomorrow's paper?"

"I think we've missed the deadline for the morning edition."

"I'm serious, Sam. I don't want to say or do anything to cause his parents any more grief than they're already dealing with."

"It's for my information now, but I can't guarantee it'll stay that way. If something you tell me helps to make this case, it's apt to come out in court. As much as we might wish otherwise, murder victims are often put on trial right along with their killers."

"That's so wrong."

"Unfortunately, it's just the way it is."

Nick made an A-frame out of his hands and rested his chin on the point. "John was a reluctant senator. He used to joke that he was Prince Harry to Terry's Prince William. Terry was the anointed one, groomed all his life to follow his father into politics. While Terry always lived in the public eye, John had a relatively normal life. For some reason, the press took an unusual interest in Terry's comings and goings. His name was mentioned on the political and gossip pages almost as often as his father's, and this was long before his father announced his retirement."

"It must've been tough to deal with all that attention."

Nick laughed, which chased the tension from his face. "Terry loved it. He ate it up. He was Washington's most eligible bachelor, and he took full advantage, let me tell you."

"That doesn't sound like a smart political strategy."

"Oh, it wasn't. He and the senator—his father, I mean—had huge, knock-down brawls over his lifestyle. I witnessed a few of them. But somehow Terry managed to stay one step ahead of the scandalmongers—that is until he got arrested for drunk driving three weeks before he was supposed to announce his candidacy for his father's seat. No amount of spin can get you out of that."

"Ouch. I remember this. It's all coming back to me now."

"Graham was devastated. Before today, I've never

seen him so crushed. That this son he'd placed all these hopes and dreams on had so totally let him down…"

"How did Terry take it?"

"Like a wounded puppy, like it was someone else's fault. He was full of excuses. John was totally disgusted by him. At one point, he said, 'Why doesn't he just be a man and admit he made a mistake?'"

"Did he say this to Terry?"

"I doubt it. They were never really close. Terry loved all the attention, and John did his best to stay well below the radar."

"Until Terry forced him into the spotlight," Sam said, starting to get a clearer picture of the O'Connor family.

"Yes, and *forced* is the right word. John wanted nothing to do with running for the Senate. In fact, I remember him grousing about how 'lucky' he was that he'd just turned thirty, which is the minimum age to run for the Senate. He was sitting atop a nice little technology firm that made a chip for one of the DoD's weapons systems. He and his partner were very successful."

"What happened to the company when John ran for Senate?"

"His partner bought him out and later sold the company."

"Would he have any reason to want John dead?"

"Hardly. He made hundreds of millions when he sold the company. The last I knew, he was living large in the Caribbean."

"What about Terry? Is he still harboring resentment that his younger brother got the life he was supposed to have?"

"Maybe, but Terry wouldn't have the stones to kill him. At the end of the day, Terry's a wimp."

Regardless of that, Sam made a note to look more closely at Terry O'Connor.

"Sergeant?" The lieutenant in charge of the Crime Scene unit approached them. "We're just about done here. We didn't find any sign of forced entry at either door or any of the ground-floor windows."

"Prints?"

"Just one set." He glanced at Nick. "We assume they're yours, but we'll have to confirm that."

Nick swore softly under his breath.

"Thanks, Lieutenant." Sam handed the other officer her card. "I'll write up what I have if you'll shoot me your report as a courtesy. There may be a connection to Senator O'Connor's murder."

"Of course."

After a perfunctory cleanup of the dust left over from the fingerprint powder, the other cops left a short time later.

"Do you want some help cleaning up?" she asked Nick when they were alone.

"That's all right. I can do it."

He stood and extended a hand to help her up.

Sam took his hand, but when she tried to let go, he tightened his grip. Startled, she looked up at him.

"I'm sorry I dragged you over here for nothing."

"It wasn't nothing—" Her words got stuck in her throat when he ran a finger over her cheek. His touch was so light she would have missed it if she hadn't been staring at him.

"You're tired."

She shrugged, her heart slamming around in her chest. "I haven't been sleeping too well lately."

"I read all the coverage of what happened. It wasn't your fault, Sam."

"Tell that to Quentin Johnson. It wasn't his fault, either."

"His father should've put his son's safety ahead of saving his crack stash."

"I was counting on the fact that he would. I should've known better. How someone could put their child in that kind of danger… I'll just never understand it."

"I'm sorry it happened to you. It broke my heart to read about it."

Sam found it hard to look away. "I, um… I should go."

"Before you do, there's just one thing I really need to know."

"What?" she whispered.

He released her hand, cupped her face and tilted it to receive his kiss.

As his lips moved softly over hers, Sam summoned every ounce of fortitude she possessed and broke the kiss. "I can't, Nick. Not during the investigation." *But oh how she wanted to keep kissing him!*

"I was dying to know if it would be like I remembered."

Her eyes closed against the onslaught of emotions. "And was it?"

"Even better," he said, going back for more.

"Wait. Nick. *Wait*." She kept her hand on his chest to stop him from getting any closer. "We can't do this. Not now. Not when I'm in the middle of a homicide investigation that involves you."

"I didn't do it." He reached up to release the clip that held her hair and combed his fingers through the length as it tumbled free.

Unnerved by the intimate gesture, she stepped back from him. "I know you didn't, but you're still involved.

I've got enough problems right now without adding an inappropriate fling with a witness to the list."

"Is that what it would be?" His eyes were hot, intense and possibly furious as he stared at her. "An inappropriate fling?"

"No," she said softly. "Which is another reason why it's not a good idea to start something now."

He moved closer to her. "It's already started, Sam. It started six years ago, and we never got to finish it. This time, I intend to finish it. Maybe not right now, but eventually. I was a fool to let you slip through my fingers the first time. I won't make that mistake again."

Startled by his intensity, Sam took another step back. "I appreciate the warning, but it might be one of those things that's better left unfinished. We both have a lot going on—"

"I'll see you tomorrow," he said, handing her the hair clip.

Sam felt his eyes on her back as she went to the door and let herself out. All the way home, her lips burned from the heat of his kiss.

8

Early the next morning, as she stood over the lifeless, waxy remains of Senator John Thomas O'Connor, age thirty-six, it struck Sam that death was the great equalizer. We arrive with nothing, we leave with nothing, and in death what we've accomplished—or not accomplished—doesn't much matter. Senator or bricklayer, millionaire or welfare mother, they all looked more or less the same laid out on the medical examiner's table.

"I'd place time of death at around eleven p.m.," Dr. Lindsey McNamara, the District's chief medical examiner, said as she released her long red hair from the high ponytail she'd worn for the autopsy.

"That's shortly after he got home. The killer might've been waiting for him."

"Dinner consisted of filet mignon, potatoes, mixed greens and what looked like two beers."

"Drugs?"

"I'm waiting on the tox report."

"Cause of death?"

"Stab wound to the neck. The jugular was severed. He bled out very quickly."

"Which came first? The cut to the neck or the privates?"

"The privates."

Sam winced. "Tough way to go."

"For a man, probably the toughest."

"He was alert and aware that someone he knew had dismembered him," Sam said, more to herself than to Lindsey.

"You're sure it was someone he knew?"

"Nothing's definite, but I'm leaning in that direction because there was no struggle and no forced entry."

"There was also no skin under his nails or any defensive injuries to his hands."

"He didn't put up a fight."

"It happened fast." Lindsey gestured to O'Connor's penis floating in some sort of liquid.

Sam fought back an unusual surge of nausea. This stuff didn't usually bother her, but she had never seen a severed penis before.

"A clean, fast cut," Lindsey said.

"Which is why the killer was able to get the knife through his neck while he was still sitting up in bed."

"Right. He would've been reacting to the dismemberment. He might've even blacked out from the pain."

"So he never saw the death blow coming."

"Probably not."

"Thanks, Doc. Send me your report when it's ready?"

"You got it," Lindsey said. "Sam?"

Sam, who had reached for her cell to check for messages, looked over at the other woman.

"I wanted you to know how terrible I felt about what happened with that kid," Lindsey said, her green eyes soft with compassion. "What the press did to you...well, anyone who knows you knows the truth."

"Thank you," Sam said in a hushed tone. "I appreciate that."

By seven o'clock, Sam was in her office wading

through four sets of phone records drawn from the senator's home, office and two cell phones. Her eyes blurry from the lack of sleep that she blamed on Nick's kiss and the memories it had resurrected, she searched for patterns and nursed her second diet cola of the day. Most of the calls were to numbers in the District and Virginia, but she noticed several calls per week to Chicago that usually lasted an hour or more. She made a note to check the number.

A few other numbers popped up with enough regularity to warrant a follow-up. Sam made a list and turned it over to one of the other detectives who had been assigned to assist her.

Grabbing another soda and a stale bagel left over from yesterday, she stopped to brief Chief Farnsworth before heading out to meet Freddie on Capitol Hill. A crush of reporters waited for her outside the public safety building. When she saw how many there were, she briefly considered going back to ask a couple of uniforms to help her get through the crowd. Then she dismissed the idea as cowardly and stepped into the scrum.

"Sergeant, how close are you to naming a suspect?"

"How was the senator killed?"

"Who found him?"

"What do you think of the headlines in today's paper?"

That last one made her stomach roil as she could only imagine what the papers were saying about the detective the department had chosen to lead the city's highest profile murder investigation in years. She held up a hand to stop the barrage of questions.

"All I'll say at this time is the investigation is proceeding, and as soon as we know anything more, we'll hold a press conference. I'll have no further comment until that time. Now, would you mind letting me through? I have work to do."

They didn't move but also didn't stop her from pushing her way through.

Rattled and annoyed, Sam got into her unmarked department car and locked the doors. "Fucking vultures," she muttered.

Outside the Hart Senate Office Building, she dropped two quarters into the *Washington Post* box and tugged out the morning's issue where a banner headline announced the senator's murder. In a smaller story below the fold, a headline read, Disgraced Detective Tapped to Lead Murder Investigation. Sam released a frustrated growl when the words appeared jumbled on the page as they often did during times of stress or exhaustion. *Goddamned dyslexia.* Taking a deep calming breath, she tried again, taking the words one at a time the way she'd trained herself to do.

The story contained a recap of the raid that had led to the death of Quentin Johnson and stopped just short of questioning her competence—and the chief's.

"Great," she muttered. "That's just *great.*" Tossing the paper into the trash, she took the elevator to the second floor where Freddie enjoyed a glazed donut while he waited for her.

"Did you see the paper?" he asked, wiping the sticky frosting from his mouth with the back of his hand.

She nodded brusquely, and before he could get into a further discussion about the article, she brought him up to speed on the possible break-in at Nick's, the autopsy and the phone records. Gesturing to the door to Senator O'Connor's suite of offices, she said, "Let's get to it."

After a thorough look through the remaining items in John's office where they found nothing useful to the case, Sam and Freddie worked their way up from administrative assistants through legislative affairs people to the staff from the senator's Richmond office to the communications director. They asked each of Senator O'Connor's employees the same questions—where were you on the night of the murder, did you have a key to his apartment, what do you know about his personal life, and can you think of anyone who might've had a beef with him?

The answers were the same with few variations—I was here working (or at home in Richmond with my husband/wife/girlfriend), I didn't have a key, he guarded his privacy, and everyone liked him, even political rivals who had good reason not to.

"Who's next?" Sam asked, feeling like they were spinning their wheels.

"Christina Billings, deputy chief of staff," Freddie said.

"Bring her in."

"Ms. Billings," Sam said, gesturing the pretty, petite blonde to a seat across the conference room table. Sam always felt like an Amazon next to tiny women like her. "Let me begin by saying how sorry we are for your loss."

The sympathy brought tears to Christina's blue eyes. "Thank you," she whispered.

"Can you tell us where you were the night of the senator's murder?"

"I was here. With the vote the next day we had so much to do to get ready for the aftermath—press conferences, appearances on talk shows, interviews… We were doing everything we could to ensure the senator got the attention he deserved." Her shoulders sagged, almost as if life had lost its purpose. "He'd worked so hard."

Intrigued by the gamut of emotions emanating from Christina, Sam said, "You were here in the office the entire night?"

"Except for when I left to get food for everyone."

"What time?" Freddie asked.

"I don't know. Maybe around eleven or eleven-thirty?"

Freddie and Sam exchanged glances.

"Where did you get the food?"

She named a Chinese restaurant on Capitol Hill, and Sam made a note to check it out later. "Did you go anywhere else?"

"No. I picked up the food and came right back. Everyone was hungry."

"Do you have a key to the senator's apartment?" Freddie asked.

Nodding, she said, "He gave it to me some time ago so I could pick up his mail and water the plants when he was in Richmond or Leesburg."

"When was the last time you used it?"

Christina thought about that. "Maybe three months ago. He's been in town for most of the session working on gathering the votes needed for the immigration bill."

"What do you know about his personal life?" Freddie asked. "Was he dating anyone?"

Her expression immediately changed from grief-stricken to hostile. "I have no idea. I didn't discuss his love life with him. He was my boss."

Something in the tone, in the flash of the blue eyes, set off Sam's radar. "Ms. Billings, were you romantically involved with the senator?"

Christina pushed back the chair and stood up. "I'm done."

"The hell you are," Sam snapped. "Sit down."

Trembling with rage, her lips tight, Christina turned

and met Sam's steely stare with one of her own. "Or what?"

"Or we'll do this downtown. Your choice."

With great reluctance, Christina returned to her seat, her body rigid, and her hands clasped together.

"Before we continue, I'll advise you of your right to have counsel present during this interview."

Christina gasped. "Am I under arrest?"

"Not at this time, but you may request an attorney at any point. Do you wish to continue without counsel?"

Christina's nod was small and uncertain. Her posture had lost some of its rigidity at the mention of lawyers.

"I'll ask you again," Sam said. "Were you romantically involved with the senator?"

"No," Christina said softly.

"Did you have feelings of a romantic nature for him?"

Christina's eyes flooded. "Yes."

"And these feelings were unrequited?"

"I have no idea. We never discussed it."

"How did you feel about him dating other women?" Freddie asked.

"How do you think I felt?" Christina shot back at him. "I loved him, but he didn't see me that way. To him I was a trusted aide and a friend he could count on to pick up his mail."

"What were your specific duties as his deputy chief of staff?" Sam asked.

"I oversaw his daily schedule, kept his appointment calendar, supervised the administrative assistants, and basically managed his time."

"So you worked closely with him?" Freddie asked.

"Yes."

"More closely than Mr. Cappuano?"

"On many days. Yes."

"And in all this time you spent with him, he had no idea how you felt about him?" Sam asked.

"I went to great lengths to hide it from him and everyone else. He was my boss. I felt like a bad cliché."

"So no one else knew?"

"Nick had figured it out, but I didn't know that until after the senator was…killed," she said, her voice trailing off.

"Why didn't you leave?" Sam asked, working hard to contain her fury at Nick for keeping this from her.

"Because he needed me. He said he'd be lost without me." Christina shrugged. "I know that sounds so pathetic, but it was better than nothing."

"Was it?" Sam asked.

"If you're implying I killed him because he didn't notice me as a woman, you're way off."

"People have killed for less."

"I didn't. I loved him. Receiving that phone call from Nick was the single most devastating moment of my life." After a long moment of silence, Christina started to push back her chair. "May I go?"

"Before you do," Freddie said, "let me ask you this— you say you kept his schedule and managed his life. Did I get that right?"

"Yes."

"So wouldn't you know who he was seeing outside the office?"

Christina's jaw clenched with tension.

"Is that a yes?" Freddie asked.

"There were several," Christina finally said.

"We'll need a list," Sam said. "I'd also like a list of anyone else you know of who had a key to his apartment and his appointment calendar for the last six months—by the end of the day, please."

With a curt nod, Christina got up.

"Stay available," Sam said before the other woman could leave the room.

"What does that mean?"

"Exactly what you think it means."

The moment the door slammed shut behind Christina, Sam turned to Freddie.

"I know what you're going to say." He counted off on his fingers. "A break in the alibi at the same time as the murder, a key to the apartment, unrequited love…"

"It's almost enough to arrest her," Sam said.

"Except?"

Sam sighed. "I believed her when she said his death was the most devastating thing that's ever happened to her."

"Doesn't mean she wasn't responsible for it."

"No, it doesn't."

"I'll do some digging around in Ms. Billings's background."

"Freddie, you read my mind. We also need to look into who would stand to gain financially from the senator's death."

"Would the chief of staff know that?"

"He might. He's next. Do you want to go grab some lunch before we get to him?"

"I thought you'd never ask." Freddie stretched, rubbing his belly with glee. "Something for you?"

"A salad." She slapped a ten-dollar bill into his hand. "Low-fat dressing."

He made a disgusted face. "Coming right up."

The moment he was gone, Sam marched into Nick's office and slammed the door.

"Well, good afternoon to you, too, Sergeant," he said with a small, private smile that let her know he'd been thinking of her since they'd kissed the night before.

"Save the charm for someone who's interested."

He raised a swarthy eyebrow in amusement. "Oh, you're interested. But if you want to play hard to get, don't let me stop you."

"What happened last night can't happen again."

"It can, and it will."

"Not until this case is closed, Nick. I mean that." Deciding it was time to move past their personal debate, she planted her hands on her hips. "Were you planning to mention that your deputy was in love with the senator?"

Nick looked stricken. "She *told* you that?"

"I got it out of her. One of my special talents."

"I'll bet," he said dryly.

"Why didn't you think it was important enough to share with me?"

"It was personal, and I didn't see how it was relevant."

"*Everything* is relevant, Nick! This is a *homicide* investigation!"

"I'm sorry. It never occurred to me that it would matter."

"She left here to get food at the exact time the M.E. has placed the time of death. She had a key to his place. She was in love with him."

Nick's handsome face went pale. "You can't possibly be suggesting—"

"I can, and I am."

"There's no way, Sam. She adored him. She was devoted to him. She could never have harmed him."

"How well do you know her?"

"I've worked with her for five years. She's a great colleague and friend."

"What do you know about her background?"

"She grew up in Oregon, came here for college, and has been working for the legislative branch since she graduated. She's worked her way up from the admin level."

"You trust her?"

"Implicitly."

"What level clearance does she have?"

"Secret."

Sam tugged the notebook from her back pocket and made a note to get a hold of the background check Christina Billings would've been required to undergo for a government security clearance. "What about you?"

"Top secret."

"As of when?"

"As of the senator's appointment to the Committee on Homeland Security and Governmental Affairs. Before that it was secret."

"Who else has top secret?"

"Only the senator."

"Who're his heirs?"

Nick considered that. "Well, I suppose it would be his niece and nephew, Emma and Adam."

"But you don't know for sure?"

He shook his head.

"Who would?"

"Probably his father and their attorney, Lucien Haverfield."

Sam wrote down Haverfield's name.

Freddie came into the room carrying two bags of takeout. "Start without me, boss?"

"We're talking heirs," Sam told him. "Mr. Cappuano believes it's most likely the senator's niece and nephew."

"Makes sense," Freddie said. "Are we doing this here or in the conference room?"

Nick gestured to a small table. "Here is fine with me."

"Let me grab the recorder," Freddie said.

"Do you mind if we eat in here?" Sam asked Nick. "Detective Cruz gets cranky if he doesn't get his midday influx of grease on time."

Nick smiled but Sam noticed his eyes were tired and sad. "No problem. I eat at that table more often than I do at home."

"Speaking of home, did you notice anything else out of place or missing?"

He shook his head.

"Let me know if you do."

"So you believe me? That someone broke in."

She replied with a small nod and had trouble meeting his intense gaze, startled to realize she was afraid of what she might find in those incredible hazel eyes.

"Am I interrupting something?" Freddie said when he returned with the recorder.

Sam cleared her throat. "No. Let's get this done. We've got a lot of ground to cover today."

9

After a quick stop at the Chinese restaurant on Capitol Hill where they confirmed that Christina Billings had in fact picked up takeout around eleven the night before last, Sam drove Freddie back to the office.

"So," he said. "Do you want to tell me what that was all about before?"

"What?"

"You and Cappuano. I felt like a third wheel on a hot date."

Sam shot him a glance. "What the hell are you talking about?"

"Well, gee, let's see." Counting on his fingers, he said, "Pregnant pauses, simmering gazes, and of course the entertaining innuendo. Need I continue?"

Unnerved that Freddie had noticed the sparks flying between her and Nick, she realized she should have known her savvy partner would have tuned in to what she had tried so hard not to encourage during their hour-long interview with Nick. The effort to keep things professional and focused had left her drained. "You're imagining things."

"No, I'm not. What gives, Sam?"

"Nothing. I barely know the man." That much was

true—sort of. "Whatever you *think* you saw was the result of your overactive and undersexed imagination."

"Wow," Freddie said on a long exhale. "Who said anything about sex?"

Simmering with retorts she didn't dare pursue, Sam pulled into the parking lot at the public safety complex.

Before she could get out, Freddie stopped her. "What happened on that trip to Loudoun County yesterday?"

"Nothing." Now, *that* was true.

"I'm your partner, Sam." He gripped her jacket to keep her from escaping. "Talk to me."

She tugged her arm free of him. "There's nothing to say! We've got a million things to do, and you've got time to grill me about something you're *imagining*?"

"I'm a trained observer—trained in large part by you. I don't care what you say, there was enough heat in that room to burn down the capitol."

Sam fumed in silence. This was *exactly* why she told Nick that what happened the night before couldn't happen again. She didn't need any more aggravation right now.

In a softer tone Freddie said, "Whatever's going on, I hope you're being careful. You've got a lot at stake right now."

"Thanks, Freddie. I'm glad you reminded me of that. Otherwise I might've forgotten about the child who died on my watch."

"Sam—"

"We have work to do."

"I'm on your side. I hope you know that. If you want to talk—"

"Thank you. Can we get to work now?"

With a deep sigh, he reached for the door handle.

Sam stalked inside, again pushing her way through

the gaggle of reporters gathered in the foyer. Leaving them wanting and frustrated gave her tremendous joy.

She felt bad about being so testy to Freddie who'd been a pillar of support in the wake of the Johnson case, but she didn't want to hear what he'd have to say about her past relationship with a witness—a relationship she hadn't disclosed, knowing that if she did, she'd be taken off the case. That couldn't happen. She desperately needed a big win on a high-profile case like this one to get her career back on track.

That was why she planned to work around the clock, if that's what it took, to break this case as fast as she could—long before anyone found out that she had once spent a night with the man who'd found the senator dead. If she was unsuccessful and her superiors discovered that she'd had yet another lapse in judgment, she could kiss her hard-won career goodbye. And then what would she do? What was she without this job? *Who* was she? No one.

Shaking off that unpleasant thought, Sam told Freddie she'd be back after the press conference and headed for Chief Farnsworth's office. On the way, she stopped in the restroom to splash cold water on her face. Looking up at her reflection, she was startled by the bruised-looking circles under her eyes, the pale, almost translucent skin made more so by weeks of sleepless nights, and eyes that couldn't hide the torment.

She had told them she was ready to come back, had assured the department psychologist she could handle anything the job threw her way. But could she handle seeing Nick Cappuano again? Could she handle how it had felt—even six years later—to be engulfed once again by those strong arms, to be kissed by those soft lips, to be on the receiving end of those heated eyes? *God!* Those eyes of his were flat-out amazing.

"Stop, Sam," she whispered to the face in the mirror, a face she barely recognized. "Please stop. Do your job and stop thinking about him. Think about the senator."

Reaching for a paper towel, she blotted the excess water from her face and took a deep breath. "The senator," she said once more as she prepared to stand next to the chief at the press conference.

The questions were brutal.

"How can you trust someone with Sergeant Holland's poor judgment to oversee such an important investigation?"

Chief Farnsworth, bless his heart, made it clear that she was the detective best suited to lead the investigation, and she had his full confidence and trust.

As Sam imagined what he'd have to say about her relationship with a material witness, she swallowed hard. *Enough of that,* she thought. *You've made your decision where he's concerned. It was one night, so stop thinking about it. Yeah, right. Okay.*

Once the reporters were done attacking her, they moved on to more specific questions about the investigation.

"Do you have any suspects?"

The chief nodded at Sam to take the question. "We're considering a number of possible suspects but haven't narrowed it down to one yet."

"What's taking so long?"

"The senator led a complex, complicated life. It's going to take some time to put all the pieces together, but I'm confident that we'll bring the investigation to a satisfactory conclusion."

"Any word on funeral plans?"

"You'll have to ask his office about that."

"Can you tell us how the senator was murdered?"

"No."

"Was his apartment broken into?"

"No comment."

"Was there a struggle?"

"No comment."

The chief stepped in. "That's it for now, folks. As soon as we have more to tell you, we'll let you know." He ushered Sam off the stage and into his office. "You did a good job out there. I know that wasn't easy." Studying her for a long moment, he said, "You're not sleeping well."

She shrugged. "Got a lot on my mind."

"Maybe you should talk to Dr. Trulo about a prescription—"

Sam held up a hand to stop him. "I haven't reached that point yet."

"I need you at the top of your game right now."

"Don't worry. I am."

"I like this Christina Billings for a person of interest."

"I don't know," Sam said, shaking her head. "The people in the office said the food was hot when she returned with it, so it seems like she went straight back. The records at the parking garage show she returned twenty-eight minutes after she left."

"Could she have gone to his place before the restaurant?"

"She'd have had to drive across the District to the Watergate, kill him and get back with Chinese in half an hour. Not enough time. Plus, the knife severed his jugular. The blow would've sprayed blood all over her. Cappuano, the chief of staff, said she had on the same suit the next morning that she'd worn the day before because they pulled an all-nighter at the office to get ready for the vote the next day. Based on that, I'm on the verge of ruling her out."

The chief rubbed at his chin as he thought it over. "Do some digging into her. She had motive, opportunity and a key. Don't rule her out too quickly."

"Yes, sir."

"Same thing with his brother. Again, we have motive, opportunity and no alibi if he can't produce the woman he says he was with."

"Right. We're going to talk to him more formally. Another thought that's been running around in my head is the sister and brother-in-law, Lizbeth and Royce Hamilton."

"Why?"

"Their kids are most likely the senator's heirs. The O'Connor parents will be here at six to view the body. I'll ask Graham O'Connor about his son's will, and I've got Cruz digging into their finances. Then there's Stenhouse, the O'Connors' bitter political rival. He went home to Missouri for a long-planned fund-raiser today, but we've got an appointment with him in the morning."

"What do you think of that angle?"

"Not much, which is why I didn't stop him from going to Missouri. There's no way he had a key to the place, and I'm convinced that whoever did this was someone John O'Connor was close to."

"Girlfriends?"

"Billings is getting us a list of women he's seen socially in the last six months and anyone who had a key. I'm also going to ask the senior Senator O'Connor if there might be keys still floating around from when he lived there."

"The surveillance videos were no help?"

"We couldn't I.D. anyone and neither could Cappuano. The video captures activity in the lobby and elevator areas but not at individual doors, so that didn't help much. It was a cold night, and everyone was bundled up pretty tight with hats and scarves. We had trouble making out faces."

Startled, the chief looked up at her.

"What?"

"People were bundled up…"

"What about it?"

"Is it possible Christina Billings had a coat she ditched after the killing?"

Intrigued, Sam puzzled that over. "That would explain why the suit wasn't ruined."

"Exactly. Might be time to get a warrant to search her car."

"Jesus," Sam said. "Why didn't I think of this?"

"You would have. I think you've got a timing problem where she's concerned, but it seems to me like you've got every base covered, Sergeant."

"I'm trying."

They were interrupted by a knock on the door.

"Come in," the chief called.

The door opened and Freddie stepped into the room, looking nervous and uncertain.

"Detective Cruz."

"Hello, sir," Freddie stammered. "I'm sorry to interrupt, but the officers going through the documents taken from the senator's apartment have uncovered a life insurance policy that I think you need to see, Sergeant Holland." He handed it to her.

Sam scanned the document, her eyes widening at the two-million-dollar amount. An involuntary gasp escaped when she saw the beneficiary's name: Nicholas Cappuano.

* * *

Twenty minutes later, Sam stormed past Nick's startled staff straight into his office and slammed the door behind her.

He never looked up from what he was doing when he said, "Back so soon, Sergeant?"

"You son of a bitch!"

He finally glanced at her, but there was steel in his normally amiable eyes. "Care to explain yourself?"

"How about *you* explain *yourself.*" She slapped the insurance policy down in front of him.

Without breaking the intense gaze, he reached for the document. "What's this?"

"You tell me."

He finally looked away from her. "It's an insurance policy."

"To me it looks like a *two-million-dollar* insurance policy," Sam clarified. "Flip to the last page."

He did as she asked. *"I'm* the beneficiary?" he asked with what appeared to be genuine shock.

"As if you didn't know."

"I didn't! I had no idea he'd done this!" An odd expression settled on his face. "So…that's what he meant." His voice faded to a whisper.

She wanted to demand he say more but waited for him to collect his thoughts.

"I once told John, back when I first met him and figured out who his father was, that I couldn't imagine in my wildest dreams ever being a millionaire. He said, 'You never know.'" Nick ran his hand reverently over the pages of the policy. "Then about a month ago, the subject came up again because I made a joke about how rich I'm getting running his office. He said I still had plenty of time to be a millionaire and that what I was doing—what we're all doing—was more important than money." Nick looked over at Sam. "That was the first time it seemed to me that he really embraced the significance of the office he held. Then he said I could be a millionaire sooner than I thought and walked away."

"You didn't ask him what he meant by that?"

He shook his head. "It seemed like a throwaway line at the time, but now it takes on more significance."

"Do you think he knew he was going to die soon?"

"No, but he had a sense that he was going to die young. He'd get into these maudlin discussions when we'd been drinking. We called them his philosophical moods."

"Did he have these moods often?"

Nick considered that. "More often lately, now that you mention it. Christina asked me last week if I thought he might be depressed."

"Did you?"

"*Distracted* might be a better word than *depressed.* He definitely had something on his mind."

"And you have no idea what?"

"I tried to talk to him about it a couple of times, but he brushed it off. Said he was focused on the bill and getting it passed. I chalked it up to stress."

"You really didn't know about the insurance?"

"I swear to God. Give me a polygraph."

Sam studied him for a long moment. "That won't be necessary. Congratulations, looks like you're finally going to be a millionaire."

"Hell of a way to get there," he said softly.

The last of the steam she'd come in with dissipated. "Nick…" She resisted the powerful urge to walk around the desk and embrace him. Clearing the emotion from her throat, she said, "His parents are coming in at six. They want to see him. Do you think maybe you could come, too? It might help them to have a familiar face there."

"Of course."

"I could take you and bring you back later so you don't have to deal with the parking situation over there."

"Sure." He stood up and reached for the suit coat that was draped over the back of his chair.

Sam's mouth went dry as she watched the play of his muscles under the pale blue dress shirt he had worn without a tie. His hands were graceful as he adjusted his collar. She remembered the way those hands had felt moving over her fevered skin so many years ago. The memory shouldn't have been so vivid, but there it was, as bright and as real as if it had happened only yesterday.

He caught her watching him. "What?"

Her face heated. "Nothing."

Without looking away from her, he came around the desk and stopped right in front of her. He reached out and ran a finger over her cheek. "I think about it, too. I never stopped thinking about it."

"Don't." She wondered how it was possible that he had read her mind so easily. "Please."

"Even in the midst of everything else that's going on, even as I plan my best friend's funeral, even as I deal with a traumatized staff and John's parents, I want you. I think about you, and I want you."

"I *can't*, Nick. My job is on the line. My whole career is riding on this investigation. I can't let you do this to me right now."

"What about later? After it's over?"

"Maybe. We'll have to see."

"Then that'll have to do." He gestured for her to lead the way out of his office. "For now."

10

"What's the plan for the funeral?" Sam asked Nick as they sat in heavy traffic on Constitution Avenue.

"He'll lie in state at the capitol in Richmond for forty-eight hours, beginning on Friday. The funeral will be held at the National Cathedral on Monday with burial at Arlington a week or two later. It takes a while to get that arranged."

"I didn't realize he was a veteran."

"Four years in the Navy after college."

"If possible, I'd like to attend the funeral with you in case I need you to identify anyone for me."

"Sure. I'll do what I can."

"Thank you." She wanted to say more but found her tongue to be uncharacteristically tied in knots. After a long, awkward pause, she glanced over at him. "I, um, I appreciate the help you're giving me with background and insight into the senator's relationships."

"Have you spoken to Natalie yet?"

Sam's brain raced through the various lists of friends, family, coworkers, and acquaintances. "I haven't heard of a Natalie. Who is she?"

"Natalie Jordan. She was John's girlfriend for a couple of years."

"When?"

Nick thought about that. "I'd say for about two years before he ran for the Senate and maybe a year after he was sworn in."

"Did it end badly?"

"It ended. I was never sure why. He wouldn't talk about it."

"Yet you saw fit to toss her name into a homicide investigation."

He shrugged. "You were mad I didn't tell you Chris was in love with him. Natalie was important to him for a long time. In fact, she was the only woman I ever knew of who was truly important to him. I just thought you should know about her."

"Where is she now?"

"Married to the number-two guy at Justice. I think they live in Alexandria."

"Did he ever see her?"

"Sometimes they'd run into each other at Democratic Party events in Virginia."

"Would she still have a key to his apartment?"

"Possibly. They lived together there for the last year or so that they were together."

"Did you like her?"

Nick rested his head against the back of the seat. "She wasn't my type, but he seemed happy with her."

"But did you *like* her?"

"Not really."

"Why not?"

"She always struck me as a social climber. We rubbed each other the wrong way—probably because I couldn't do anything to advance her agenda so she didn't have much use for me."

"Knowing he dated someone like that seems contrary to the picture you and others have painted of him. To me, he wouldn't have had the patience for it."

"He was dazzled by her. She's quite…well, if you talk to her, you'll see what I mean."

"What do you think of his sister and brother-in-law?"

Nick appeared startled by the question. "Salt of the earth. Both of them."

"What's his story? Royce Hamilton?"

"He's a horse trainer. One of the best there is from what I've heard. Lizbeth has been crazy about horses all her life. John always said she and Royce were a match made in heaven."

"Any financial problems?"

"None that I ever heard of—not that I heard much about them. I saw them at holidays, occasional dinners in Leesburg, fund-raisers here and there, but we don't travel in the same circles."

"What circle do they travel in?"

"The Loudoun County horse circle. John adored their kids. He talked about them all the time, had pictures of them everywhere."

"What did Senator O'Connor think of his only daughter marrying a horse trainer?"

"Royce is an intelligent guy. And more important, he's a gentleman. The senator could appreciate those qualities in a potential son-in-law, even if he wasn't a doctor or a lawyer or a politician. Besides, Lizbeth was wild about him. Her father was smart enough to know there'd be no point in getting in the way of that."

"What about her? Could she have had some sort of dispute with John?"

Nick shook his head. "She was completely and utterly devoted to him. She was one of our best campaigners and fund-raisers." He chuckled. "John called her The Force. No one could say no to her when she went out on the stump for her 'baby brother.' There's no way she had anything to do with this." More emphatically, he added, "No way."

"Did she have a key to the Watergate apartment?"

"Most likely. Everyone in the family used the place when they were in town."

"That place has more keys out than a no-tell motel."

"It was just like John to give keys to everyone he knew and think nothing of it."

"Yet he was the only other person in the world who had a key to your place. Can you see the irony in that?"

"He led a bigger life than I do."

"Tell me about your life," she said on an impulse.

He raised that swarthy eyebrow. "Who's asking? The woman or the detective?"

Sam took a moment to appreciate his quick intelligence, remembering how attractive she had found that the first time she met him. "Both," she confessed.

He glanced at her, and even though her eyes were on the road, she felt the heat of his gaze. "I work. A lot."

"And when you're not working?"

"I sleep."

"No one—not even me—is that boring."

He flashed her a funny, crooked grin that she caught out of the corner of her eye. "I try to get to the gym a couple of times a week."

Judging from the ripped physique she had been pressed against the night before, he put those gym visits to good use. "And? No wives, girlfriends, social life?"

"No wife, no girlfriend. I play basketball with some guys on Sundays whenever I can. Sometimes we go out for beers afterward. Last summer, I played in the congressional softball league, but I missed more games than I made. Oh, and every other month or so, I have dinner with my father's family in Baltimore. That's about it."

"Why haven't you ever gotten married?"

"I don't know. Just never happened."

"Surely there had to have been *someone* you might've married."

"There was this one girl…"

"What happened?"

"She never returned my calls."

Shocked and speechless, Sam stared at him.

"You asked."

Tearing her eyes off him, she accelerated through the last intersection before the turn for the public safety parking lot. "Don't say that to me," she snapped. "You don't mean that."

"Yes, I do."

She pulled into a space and slammed the car into park.

He grabbed her arm to stop her from getting out. "Calm down, Sam."

"Don't tell me what to do." She tugged her arm free of his grasp. "And save your cheesy lines for someone who's buying. I don't believe you anyway."

"If you didn't, you wouldn't be so pissed right now."

"Do you want to know what happened to your friend?"

With one blink, his hazel eyes shifted from amused to furious. "Of course I do."

"Then you have to stop doing this to me, Nick. You're winding me up in knots and pulling my eye off the ball. I need to be focused, one hundred percent *focused* on this case, and *not* on you!"

"What about when you're off duty?" The teasing smile was back, but it didn't steal the sadness from his eyes. "Can I wind you up in knots then?"

"Nick…"

Fixated on the drab-looking public safety building,

he sighed. "We're about to go in there and take John's parents to see him laid out on a cold slab, and yet, all I can think about right now is how badly I want to kiss you. What kind of a friend does that make me? To him or to you?"

His tone was so full of sadness and grief that Sam softened a bit. "You were a great friend to him, and in the last twenty-four hours, except for the whole kissing thing, you've been helpful to me, too. Can we keep it that way? Please?"

"I'm trying, Sam. Really I am, but I can't help that I feel this incredible pull to you. I know you feel it, too. You felt it six years ago—as strongly as I did—and you still do, even if you don't want to. If we had met again under different circumstances, can you tell me the same thing wouldn't be happening between us?"

"I have to go in now." Her firm tone hid her see-sawing emotions. "His parents are probably waiting for me, and I don't want to drag this out for them. Are you coming?"

"Yeah." He opened the door. "I'm coming."

Freddie met them inside. "We've got the O'Connors in there." He pointed to a closed conference room door. "And the Dems from Virginia the senator had dinner with the night he was killed are in there."

Sam glanced back and forth between the two closed doors. "Will you take Mr. Cappuano and the O'Connors to see the senator, please?" she asked Freddie.

"No problem."

She rested a hand on Freddie's arm and looked up at him. "Utmost sensitivity," she whispered.

"Absolutely, boss. Don't worry."

To Nick, she said, "I'll catch up to you."

He nodded and followed Freddie into the room where

Graham and Laine O'Connor waited with their daughter and another man who Sam assumed was Royce Hamilton. With a brief glance, Sam noticed that both O'Connors had aged significantly overnight.

"Senator and Mrs. O'Connor, my partner, Detective Cruz, will take you to see your son. I'll join you in a few minutes."

"Thank you," Graham said.

With a deep breath to change gears and force her mind off the intense conversation she'd just had with Nick, Sam entered the room where two portly men sat waiting for her. She judged them both to be in their late sixties or early seventies.

Upon her entrance, they leapt to their feet.

"Gentlemen," she said, reaching out to shake their hands. "Detective Sergeant Sam Holland. I appreciate you coming in."

"We're just *devastated*," drawled Judson Knott, who had introduced himself as the chairman of the Virginia Democratic Party. "Senator O'Connor was a dear friend of ours and the people of the Commonwealth."

"I'm not looking for a sound bite, Mr. Knott, just an idea of how the senator spent his last few hours."

"We met him for dinner at the Old Ebbitt Grill," said Richard Manning, the vice chairman.

"How often did you all have dinner together?"

The two men exchanged glances. "Every other month or so. We offered to reschedule that night because he had the vote the next day, but he said his staff had everything under control, and he had time for dinner."

"How did he seem to you?"

"Tired," Manning said without hesitation.

Knott nodded in agreement. "He said he'd been

working twelve- and fourteen-hour days for the last two weeks."

"What did you talk about over dinner?"

"The plans for the campaign," Knott said. "He was up for re-election next year, and although he was a shoo-in, we take nothing for granted. We've been gearing up for the campaign for months, but now…" His blue eyes clouded as his voice trailed off. "It's just such a tragedy."

"What time did you part company after dinner?"

"I'd say around ten or so," Knott said.

"And where was he headed from there?"

"He said he was going straight home to bed," Knott said.

"Who will take his place in the Senate?"

"That's up to the governor," Manning said.

"No front-runners?"

Knott shook his head. "We haven't even talked about it, to be honest. We're all just in a total state of shock right now. Senator O'Connor was a lovely person. We can't imagine how anyone would want to harm him."

"No one in the party was jealous of his success or bucking for his job?"

"Only his brother," Manning said with disdain. "What a disappointment *he* turned out to be."

"Was he jealous enough to kill the senator?"

"Terry?" Knott said with a nervous glance toward the door, as if he was afraid the O'Connors might hear him. "I doubt it. It would require he get his head out of his ass for more than five minutes."

"The O'Connors had their problems, like any family," Manning added. "But they were tight. Terry might've been jealous of John, but he wouldn't have done this to his mother." Shaking his head with dismay, he said, "Poor Laine."

"We saw them outside," Knott said. "Our hearts are broken for them."

"Thank you for coming in." Sam handed each of them her card. "If you think of anything else, even the smallest thing, let me know."

"We will," Manning said. "We'll do anything we can to help find the monster who did this."

"Thank you." Sam saw them out and headed for the morgue.

11

Following the O'Connors into the cold, antiseptic-smelling room, Nick thought he had properly prepared himself. After what he had seen yesterday, he should have been able to handle anything.

However, nothing could have prepared him for the sight of John lifeless, waxy, and so utterly *gone*. Nor could he have prepared for Laine's reaction.

With one look at her son's face, John's mother fainted into a boneless pile. It happened so fast that no one was able to reach her in time to keep her head from smacking the cement floor.

"Jesus, God!" Graham cried as he dropped to his knees. "Laine! Honey, are you all right?"

"Mom," Lizbeth said as tears rolled down her face. "Mom, open your eyes."

Several tense minutes passed before Laine's eyes fluttered open. "What happened?"

"You fainted," Lizbeth said. "Do you think you could sit up?"

"I need to get out of here. Take me out of here, Lizzie."

Lizbeth and Royce helped her mother up. Without another glance at the body on the table, they escorted her from the room.

"Are you all right, Senator?" Nick asked when they were alone.

His complexion gray, his hands trembling, Graham O'Connor fixated on the white bandage covering the neck wound that ended his son's life. "It's all so wrong, you know?" the older man said in a hoarse whisper.

"Sir?"

"Standing over the body of your child. It's wrong."

Nick's throat tightened with emotion. "I'm sorry. I wish there was something I could say…" He kept his voice down so Detective Cruz, who was minding the door, wouldn't hear them.

Graham reached out haltingly to caress John's thick blond hair. "Who could've done this? How's it possible someone hated my John this much?"

"I just don't know." Nick looked down at John, wishing he had the answers they so desperately needed.

"Do you think it could be Terry?"

Shocked, Nick whispered, "Senator…"

"He never got over what happened. He resented John—maybe even hated him—for taking his place in a job he felt was his."

"He wouldn't have killed him over it."

"I wish I could be so certain." Graham looked up at Nick with shattered eyes. "If it *was* Terry… If he did this, it'll kill Laine."

Nick could only imagine what it would do to Graham.

"Um, excuse me," Sam said from behind them. "I'm sorry to interrupt."

Nick wondered if she had heard them speculating about Terry.

"Can I get you anything, Senator? Would you like to sit for a minute? I could get you a stool—"

Graham's expression hardened as he turned to Sam.

"You can tell me you've found the person who did this to my son."

"I wish I could," she said. "I *can* tell you we're working very hard on the case. If you want to come with me to the conference room, I can update you and your wife on what we have so far."

The senator turned back to his son and stroked John's hair. Tears pooled in Graham's already-bloodshot eyes. "I love you, Johnny," he whispered, leaning over to press a kiss to John's forehead. Graham's shoulders shook as he clutched the sheet covering John's chest.

Nick had never seen such a raw display of grief. After a moment, he rested a hand on Graham's shoulder. The older man remained hunched over his son until Nick gently guided him up.

"Oh God, Nick," he sobbed, pressing his face to Nick's chest. "What're we going to do without him? *What'll we do?*"

Nick wrapped his arms around Graham. "I don't know, but we're going to figure it out. We're going to get through this." He glanced up to find Sam watching them with an expression of exquisite discomfort. Embarrassed by his own tears, he returned his attention to the senator. "Why don't we let Sergeant Holland fill us in on the investigation?"

Graham nodded and stepped out of Nick's embrace. With a long last heartbroken look at John, Graham headed for the door.

Swiping at his face, Nick followed him.

Sam directed them to the conference room where Lizbeth and Royce sat on either side of a pale and drawn Laine. Someone had gotten her a glass of water and an ice pack for her head.

Graham went to his wife, reached for her hands and drew her up into his arms.

Nick couldn't look. He simply couldn't bear to witness their overwhelming agony. Turning from where he stood in the doorway, he stepped out of the room.

"I'll…ah…give you a moment," he heard Sam say as she followed him.

In the hallway, she joined Nick in resting her head against the cinderblock wall. "Are you all right?"

"I was," he said with a sigh. "I was doing a really good job of convincing myself, despite what I saw yesterday, that he was in Richmond or at the farm. But after that, after seeing him like that…"

"Denial's not an option anymore."

"No."

Soft words and sounds of weeping drifted from the conference room.

"I've never before felt like I didn't belong with them. Not once in all the years I've known them, have I ever felt I didn't belong…until in there…just now…" His voice caught, and he was surprised when her hand landed on his arm.

"They love you, Nick. Anyone can see that."

"John was my link to them. That's gone now." His head ached, his eyes burned. Hating the uncharacteristic bout of self-pity but needing her more than he'd needed anyone in a long time, he sighed. "He's gone… my job…everything."

Sam squeezed his arm and then removed her hand abruptly when Freddie came around the corner.

Seeming to sense he was interrupting something, Freddie paused and looked to her for guidance.

"They needed a minute after seeing him," she said. "Could you do me a favor and find Mr. Cappuano some water?"

"That's not necessary," Nick protested.

A nod from Sam sent Freddie off.

"You didn't have to—"

"It's water, Nick."

"Thank you." He glanced over at her. "How're you holding up?"

"I'm tired."

"And?"

"And what?"

"Something else."

She cast her eyes down at the floor and kicked at the tile with the pointed toe of her fashionable black boot. "I'm pissed. Seeing those people." She nodded toward the conference room. "Others like them. Something like this happens to them and their lives are permanently altered. That bothers me. A lot."

"You care. That's what makes you such a good cop."

"I don't know too many who'd call me a good cop lately."

Taking her hand, he saw that he'd startled her with his public display of affection. "There's no one else I'd rather have on John's case. No one." He surprised her further when he kissed the back of her hand and released it.

Before Sam could chew him out for the risky PDA, Freddie returned with a cold bottle of water for Nick.

"Thank you."

"May I have a word, Sergeant?" Freddie said.

"Of course," Sam said. To Nick, she added, "Tell them we'll be right in."

Sam followed Freddie into the conference room across the hall and closed the door. "I know what you're going to say, and it's not what you think."

"Guilty conscience, Sergeant?"

Since his question was accompanied by a teasing

smile she didn't remind him that she outranked him by a mile and an insubordination complaint wouldn't look good on his record. "Not at all."

"The financials came back on all the principal players."

"And?"

"Royce Hamilton is up to his eyeballs in debt."

Sam's heart reacted to the burst of adrenaline by skipping in her chest. "Is he now?"

"There's a lien on their house, which is mortgaged to the hilt."

"And his kids were O'Connor's likely heirs. Very interesting, indeed."

"We also found a regular monthly payment of three thousand dollars from the senator's personal account to a woman named Patricia Donaldson. I ran the name and came up with hundreds of hits, which I've got some people checking into."

"We can ask his parents who she is."

"Third thing, the tox screen on the senator was clean, except for the small amount of alcohol we already knew about. No drugs, prescription or otherwise."

"Okay, that's good," she said, starting for the door. "One less thing to figure out."

"Wait," he said. "I wasn't done."

She waved an impatient hand to encourage him to proceed.

"They found porn on his home computer. A lot of it."

"Kids?"

"None so far, but what's there is hard-core."

She smoothed her hands over her hair. "Christ, can you believe a United States senator would take such chances?"

Freddie frowned at her use of the Lord's name. "What do you suppose it means for the case?"

"I don't know. Let me think about it. Any word on the warrant to search Christina Billings's car and apartment?"

"I just checked when I went back to get the water and nothing yet."

"What the hell is taking so long?" she fumed. "If we don't have it by the time we finish with the parents, I'll get the chief involved."

"What about Hamilton?"

"After we get the wife and in-laws out of there, we'll go at him."

Freddie's eyes lit up with anticipation. "Good cop, bad cop?"

"If necessary."

"Can I be bad cop this time? *Please?*"

She shot him a withering look that said "as if."

"I *never* get to be bad cop," he said with a pout. "It's so not fair."

"Grow up, Freddie," she shot over her shoulder as she crossed the hall to where the O'Connors waited. Before she opened the door, she took a moment to collect herself, to take her emotions out of the equation. She appreciated that Freddie knew her moods well enough by then not to question what she was doing or why. "Ready?"

He nodded.

Sam opened the door. "I'm sorry to keep you waiting." She did her best to avoid looking directly at the four faces ravaged by grief as she took them through what the police knew so far, leaving out anything that would compromise the integrity of the investigation.

"So you're telling me that after two days, you've got absolutely nothing?" Graham said.

"We have several persons of interest we're taking a hard look at," Sam said as the chief slipped into the room. She nodded at him and returned her attention to the O'Connors. "I wish I could tell you more, but we're working as hard and as fast as we can."

Graham turned to the chief. "I've known you a lot of years, Joe. I need the very best you've got."

Chief Farnsworth glanced at Sam. "You're getting it. I have full faith in Sergeant Holland and Detective Cruz as well as the team backing them up."

"So do I," Nick said quietly from where he stood against the back wall.

Senator and Mrs. O'Connor turned to him.

With his eyes trained on Sam, Nick said, "I've known Sergeant Holland for six years. There's no one more dedicated or thorough."

As Sam fought to keep her mouth from dropping open in shock at the unexpected endorsement, Senator O'Connor held Nick's intent gaze for a long moment before he stood and held out his hand to his wife. "In that case, we should let you get back to work. We'll count on you to keep us informed."

"You have my word, Senator," Chief Farnsworth said. "I'll show you out."

"Before you go," Sam said, "can you tell us who Patricia Donaldson was to your son?"

Graham and Laine exchanged glances but their expressions remained neutral.

"She was a friend of John's," he said.

"From high school," Laine added.

"A friend he paid three thousand dollars a month to?"

"John was an adult, Sergeant," Graham said, appearing nonplussed to hear about the payments. "What he did with his money was his business. He didn't have to explain it to us."

"Where does she live?" Sam asked.

"Chicago, I believe," Graham said.

Interesting, Sam thought, that the senator knew, without a moment's hesitation, the exact whereabouts of his son's friend from eighteen years earlier. She debated pushing him harder and might have had the chief not been in the room. In the end, she decided to pursue it from other angles.

"If there's nothing else, I'd like to take my wife home," Graham said with a pointed look at Sam.

"We realize this is an extremely difficult time for you, but we may have other questions," she said.

"Our door's always open," Graham said, helping his wife from her chair.

Lizbeth and Royce got up to go with them.

"Mr. Hamilton," Sam said. "A minute of your time, please?"

Royce's eyes darted to his wife.

"Go ahead, Daddy." Lizbeth kissed her parents. "Take Mom home. We'll be by after a while."

After Graham and Laine left the room with Chief Farnsworth and Nick following them, Sam turned to Lizbeth. "We'd like to speak to your husband alone, Mrs. Hamilton."

Tall, blond, blue-eyed and handsome in a rugged, hard-working way, Royce slipped an arm around Lizbeth's shoulders. "Anything you have to say to me can be said in front of my wife."

Sam glanced at Freddie, who handed her the printout detailing the Hamiltons' financial situation. "Very well. In that case, perhaps you can explain how you've come to be almost a million dollars in debt." Only because she was watching so closely did she see Royce tighten the grip he had on his wife's shoulder.

"A series of bad investments," Hamilton said through gritted teeth.

"What kind of investments?"

"Two horses that didn't live up to their potential, and a land deal that's tied up in litigation."

"We're handling it," Lizbeth said.

"By mortgaging your house?"

"Among other things," Lizbeth said, her tone icy.

"What other things?"

"We're considering a number of options," Royce said, adding reluctantly, "including bankruptcy."

"You expect us to believe the daughter of a multi-millionaire is on the verge of bankruptcy?"

"This has nothing to do with my father, Sergeant," Lizbeth snarled. "It's our problem, and we're handling it."

"Are your children the heirs to your brother's estate?"

Lizbeth gasped. "You think…" Her face flushed, and her eyes filled. "You're insinuating that we had something to do with what happened to John?"

"What I'm asking," Sam said, "is if your children are his heirs."

"I have no idea," Lizbeth said. "We weren't privy to the terms of his will."

"But he was close to your children?"

"He adored them, and they him. They're heartbroken by his death. And you think we would've done that to them—to *him*—over *money*?"

Sam shrugged. "He had it, you needed it."

Shaking with rage, Lizbeth moved out of her husband's embrace and stepped toward Sam. Speaking in a low, fury-driven tone, she said, "I had only to ask, and he'd have given me anything. *Anything.* There would've been no need for me—or Royce—to kill him for it."

"So why didn't you? Why didn't you ask him for help?"

"Because it was *our* problem, our business. Other than my husband and children, there was no one in this world I loved more than John. If you think my husband or I killed him, I encourage you to prove it. Now, if there isn't anything else, I need to take care of my parents."

"Stay available," she said to their retreating backs.

After they were gone, Sam turned to Freddie. "Impressions?"

"Pride goeth before the fall."

"My thoughts exactly. They'd rather declare bankruptcy than let her family know they're in trouble."

The door opened, and the chief stepped into the room. "What was that about with the son-in-law?"

"Nothing," Sam said, deciding it was just that. "Tying up a loose end."

"You know Nick Cappuano?" the chief asked.

Sam cleared her throat. "Technically, yes. I met him once, six years ago. I hadn't seen him since until yesterday. He's been a tremendous asset to the investigation."

"That was quite a show of support from someone you hardly know."

She shrugged. "It seemed to be what the senator needed to hear."

"Indeed." The chief's shrewd eyes narrowed as he studied her. "Is there anything else you want to tell me, Sergeant?"

He was handing her the opportunity to come clean. But if she told him she'd slept with Nick, had feelings for him—then and now—she'd be off the case and maybe off the force. It was too much to risk. "No, sir," she said without blinking an eye.

"Anything I can do to help?"

"We're waiting on a warrant to search Billings's car

and apartment. If you could exert some muscle to speed that up, we'd appreciate it."

"Consider it done." He started to leave, but turned back. "Get me an arrest, Sergeant. Soon."

"I'm doing my best, sir."

12

Sam spent two hours with Freddie and the other detectives assigned to the case going over everything they had so far. While she was with the O'Connors, the lab came back with the report from John's apartment—nothing was found in the sheets, the drain, or elsewhere in the apartment that didn't belong to the victim.

Beginning to feel frustrated, Sam doled out assignments, told Freddie to meet her at Senator Stenhouse's office at nine the next morning, and sent him home. Fifteen hours after she'd started her day, she returned to her office to find Nick in her chair with his feet on the desk.

"Comfortable?" she asked, leaning against the door-frame.

He dropped his cell phone into his suit coat pocket. "You were my ride."

"Oh shit. Sorry. You waited all this time? You could've grabbed a cab."

"I was hoping to talk you into dinner."

"I can't. I've still got a million things I need to do." She paused, looked closer. "Did you *clean* my desk?"

"I just straightened it up a bit. How can you work in such a messy space?"

"I have a system. Now I won't be able to find anything!"

"You need to eat, and you need to sleep. What good will you be to anyone if you make yourself sick?"

"So in addition to bringing your anal retentiveness to my workplace, you've put yourself in charge of making sure I eat and sleep?"

His face lifted into a cocky, sexy grin. "Happy to oblige on both fronts."

"Food, yes. Sleep? No way in hell."

He shrugged, apparently pleased with the half victory. "Who's this?" he asked, picking up a photo from her desk.

"My dad." In the picture, Sam stood to the side of her father's chair, her arm around his shoulders. "He was injured on the job almost two years ago."

"I'm sorry. What happened?"

Stepping into the cramped office, she bumped his feet off the desk and sat. "He was on his way home in his department vehicle and saw a car weaving through traffic. He followed it for a mile or two before he pulled it over."

"He was a traffic cop?"

She shook her head. "He was deputy chief and three months shy of retirement. Anyway, he approached the vehicle, knocked on the window, and the driver responded with gunfire. He doesn't remember anything after stopping the car. The bullet lodged between the C3 and C4 vertebrae. He's a quadriplegic, but through some miracle, he can breathe on his own when sitting up. We've learned to be grateful for the small things."

"I remember reading about it, but I didn't realize he was your father. Happened on G Street?"

"Yes."

"Did they ever get the guy?"

"Nope. It's an open investigation. I work on it whenever I can, and so does every other detective in this place. It's personal to me, to all of us."

"I can imagine. I'm sorry."

She shrugged. "Life's a bitch."

He stood up, stepped around her, pushed the door closed, reached for her and held her tight against him.

Appalled by the lump that settled in her throat, she wrestled free of him. "What was that for?"

He kept his arms around her. "You seemed to need it."

"I don't." She placed her hands on his chest to put some distance between them and to calm her racing heart. "I can't be alone in here with you. People will talk, and I don't need that."

He reached for the door and opened it. "Sorry."

Sam was relieved to find no prying eyes on the other side of the door and annoyed to realize she *had* needed the comfort Nick offered, that it somehow helped. The discovery left her unsettled.

"What?" he asked, studying her with those intense hazel eyes that made her melt from the inside out. "You're staring."

"I was just thinking…"

He tipped his head inquisitively. "About?"

"You've aged well. Really well."

"Gee, thanks. I think."

"That was a *compliment*," she said, rolling her eyes.

"Thanks for clarifying. Of course, I could say the same to you. You're even sexier than I remembered— and I remembered *everything*." He took a step to close the distance between them.

Her heart tripping into overdrive, she held up a hand to stop him. "Stay out of my personal space."

"You're the one who started handing out the *com-*

pliments," he said with a grin that she much preferred to the grief she'd witnessed earlier.

"Temporary lapse in judgment brought on by fatigue and hunger."

"Then how about that dinner?"

"Pizza and you're buying."

"That could be arranged."

"Speaking of arranged, the M.E. is set to release the senator's body to the funeral home in the morning."

Nick immediately sobered, and Sam was sorry she'd dropped it on him that way. "Okay. Once the funeral home is done, the Virginia State Police will accompany him to the state capitol in Richmond," he said. "I was going to ask you if I could get into his place to get some clothes. The funeral director needs them."

"After dinner. I'd like to go back there anyway. Poke around some more."

"It's a date."

She turned off her computer and the lamp on her desk. "It's not a date."

"Semantics," he said as he followed her from the office.

"It's *not* a date."

Over thick-crust veggie pizza and beer at a place where everyone seemed to know Nick, Sam asked him about Patricia Donaldson.

"Who?"

"According to his parents, she was a high school friend of John's who lives in Chicago."

His eyebrows knit with confusion. "I've never heard of her."

"He sent her three thousand dollars a month, has for years, called her several times a week and talked for as much as an hour."

Nick shook his head. "I don't know anything about her." He seemed puzzled, distressed even. "How's that possible?"

"Did you know he was into porn? Big-time into it?"

Pausing mid-bite, he returned the pizza to his plate and wiped his mouth. "No. How do you know?"

"It was on his home computer."

His expression shifted from startled to disgusted. His breathing slowed as he fixated on a spot behind her. He was quiet for a long time. "I wish I could say I'm totally surprised, but I'm not. He took such chances with his reputation and his career."

"What else besides this?"

"Women. Lots of them. It was like he was looking for something he just couldn't seem to find. He'd be all hot over someone and a week later she'd be history."

"Did they have anything in common?"

"They were all blonde and well endowed. Every one of them. One Barbie doll after another. It got so I didn't even bother to make the effort to remember their names."

Sam swallowed the last of her beer in one long sip and had to admit she felt recharged after the meal. "Christina Billings sent over a list of the women he'd dated during the last six months. We're working through it now. I bet we'll find his killer among the Barbies."

"I doubt it."

"Why do you say that?"

"You said it was a crime of passion, right?"

She nodded.

"None of them were around long enough to feel the kind of passion you'd have to feel to do what was done to him—except Natalie, but that was over and done with years ago. If she were going to kill him, she probably would've done it a long time ago."

"We're going to talk to her tomorrow."

"How do you do it?" he asked.

"Do what?"

"Keep up this pace. It's relentless."

"You spent a night in your office this week. You do what it takes to get your job done. That's all I'm doing. Usually it's worse than this. I often have multiple cases going, but thanks to the forced vacation my load has been light lately."

"But dealing with murderers and victims and medical examiners… It's got to be so draining."

"It can be. Other times it's exhilarating. There's nothing quite like putting all the pieces together and coming out with a picture that leads to conviction."

"Did you always want to be a cop?" He hadn't asked that question the first time they met, when she had just made detective.

"That subject is kind of complicated."

"How so?"

She fiddled with the handle on her mug. "I'm the youngest of three girls. I think I was about twelve when it dawned on me that the only reason I'd been born was because my father wanted a son so desperately."

"You can't know that for sure."

"Oh, yes I can. My mother all but told me."

"Sam…"

She hated the sympathy that radiated from him. "So, knowing I'd disappointed him just by being born, I set out to win his approval every way I could think of. Name a high school sport—I played it. I went with him to Redskins games, Orioles games. He even branded me with a boyish nickname."

"You'll be Samantha to me," Nick declared. "From this moment on."

She sneered at him. "I don't let *anyone* call me that."

"You're going to have to make an exception because to me there's nothing boyish about you. You're *all* woman. Every beautiful, sexy inch of you."

Her face heated under the intensity of his gaze. "I'll allow an occasional Samantha, but don't overdo it. And not in front of anyone else."

"I'll save it for only the most important, *private* moments," he said with a grin that melted her bones. "So, you became a cop to please him, too."

"Huh?" she asked, captivated by his hazel eyes.

"Your father."

"Oh. Right. At first that's what it was about. I won't deny that. But I discovered I have a knack for it—or I thought I did until recently."

"You do. You can't let one incident shake your confidence or your faith in yourself."

"You sound like the department shrink," she said with a chuckle. "And while I know you're both right, there's something about a dead kid that shakes you to the core even when you know you did everything right." Sam fixated on a spot on the wall as the horror of it all came back to haunt her once again. She'd never forget the sound of Marquis Johnson's agonized shrieks after his son was hit by gunfire.

"What happened that night?"

The sick weight of it settled over her and turned a stomach so recently satisfied by food. She'd had a hard time choking down anything for weeks after the incident. "I'm not supposed to talk about it. I have to testify at the probable cause hearing next week."

Under the table, he took her hand, linked his fingers through hers and resisted her efforts to break free. "Stop," he said softly. "Just stop, will you?"

"Someone might see," she hissed.

"No one's looking at us, and the tablecloth hides a world of sin. There's nothing quite like a good table-cloth."

Sam gently extricated her hand and folded her arms while pretending not to notice the wounded look that crossed his face. "I'll bet you've done your share of public sinning."

"I'll never tell," he said, his lips quirking with amusement. "Is it so difficult for you?"

"What?"

"Sharing the burden."

"It's impossible," she confessed. "My inadequacy in that regard has caused me some major problems in my life."

"What kind of problems?"

"The marriage kind for one." She wished for something else to drink since her mouth was suddenly as dry as the desert. Glancing at Nick, she found him watching her with the patience of a man who had nothing but time. She reached for his half-empty glass of beer and took a long drink.

"Why'd you get divorced?"

Sam mulled it over, wondering if she should have this conversation with a man she was wildly attracted to but who was off limits to her. After a long pause, she decided what the hell? Why not? "My ex-husband claimed I didn't need him."

"And did you?"

"No," she snorted. "He turned out to be a total loser."

"Since he failed to deliver a couple of critically im-portant messages, I'd have to agree with you there."

"I made such a big mistake with him," she sighed.

"I didn't see him for what he really was until it was too late. I didn't listen to people who tried to warn me."

Nick straightened out of the slouch he'd slipped into. "Was he... I mean... He didn't *hit* you, did he?"

"No, but it almost would've been easier if he had. At least I could've fought back against that. His thing was passive aggression. He wanted total control over me. I let it go on for far longer than I should have because I didn't want to admit I'd been so incredibly wrong. Damned foolish Irish pride."

Despite her resistance, Nick moved closer. "I want to wrap my arms around you right now," he said gruffly against her ear, his warm breath sending goose bumps darting through her. "I hate the idea of someone making you feel inadequate."

"I let him," Sam said, the pillars of her resistance toppling like dominoes. She wanted Nick's arms around her, wanted to lean her head on that strong, capable shoulder. For the first time in longer than she could remember, she wanted the comfort he offered. No, she *needed* it. What should have been terrifying was actually rather exhilarating. "Can we go?"

"Sure." He put some bills on the table, got up and offered her his hand.

"We've left the safety of the tablecloth," she reminded him as she stepped around his outstretched arm on her way to the door.

Grinning, he followed her out.

Heads bent against the blustery cold, they walked a block to where they'd parked her department vehicle. An odd chill that had nothing to do with the cold ran up her spine as she unlocked the door on the dark street. Glancing around, she expected to find someone watching her, but saw no one. Just her overactive imagination, she thought, as she reached over to unlock the passenger door for Nick.

He slid in next to her. "Before we go to John's place, I need to get my car."

"Okay." Sam started the car to get the heat going, but sat with her hands propped on the wheel.

"What's wrong?"

She gripped the wheel. "I'm sorry I can't give you more right now, Nick." Glancing over, she found him watching her intently. "It's not because I don't want to."

He reached over to caress her face. "I know that."

His touch sent a burst of longing sizzling through her, but she tamped it down. "Can you be patient with me?"

"I spent years wishing for another chance with you, Sam. I'm not about to bail just because it isn't going to be easy."

She released a deep sigh of relief. "Good."

"But after this case is closed…"

"I'll be right there with you."

"What we had six years ago is still there," he said, gazing into her eyes.

"So it seems."

"Whatever it is, I've never had it with anyone else."

"I haven't either. I was so sad when you didn't call. I couldn't believe I'd been so wrong about you."

"*Ugh.* That makes me furious. When I think about what we might've had, all these years…"

"Let me close this case," she said, her voice hoarse and tense. "The minute I close this case…"

Nick seemed to be resisting the urge to haul her into his arms. "Samantha?"

Surprisingly, the dreaded name didn't sound so bad coming from him. "Hmm?"

"We steamed up the windows."

"And we didn't even do anything!"

"Yet," he said, his voice full of promise.

Finding him harder to resist with every passing second, she shifted the car into drive and forced herself to focus on the road.

13

Sam left Nick at the congressional parking lot, and timed her drive across the city to the Watergate. At that hour of the night, traffic was light but an accident on Independence Avenue screwed up her timing. She'd have to try again tomorrow night to determine whether Christina Billings would've had enough time to drive across the city, commit murder, and drive back with a stop to pick up Chinese food in twenty-eight minutes.

Reaching for her cell phone, she called to check on the search of Billings's car.

"I was just going to call you," Detective Tommy "Gonzo" Gonzales said. "We got a hit for blood on the front seat."

"I knew it!" Sam cried. "I'll bet she wrapped up her coat and left it on the seat. The blood soaked through!"

"Wait," Gonzo said. "Before you get too excited, she said she cut her hand scraping ice off her car two weeks ago and had to get three stitches. She has a raw-looking pink scar on her right hand and produced the form from the E.R. with wound care instructions. We're checking the blood anyway, but I'll bet a month's pay it's going to be hers. She willingly gave us a sample."

"*Son of a bitch*. We can't catch a single break in this one."

"We've narrowed down Billings's list of the senator's recent girlfriends from six to two. The other four could prove they weren't in the city that night."

Sam added visits to the two remaining Barbies to her ever-growing to-do list for the morning. "Do me a favor and set up some plainclothes coverage for the senator's wake. Make sure you coordinate with Virginia State Police and Richmond."

"Sure thing. Do you want observation and video or just observation?"

"Let's tape it. Make sure the officers you send have the photos of the senator's family and girlfriends, so they'll know who to watch for."

"I'm on it."

"Thanks for the good work, Gonzo."

"You got it. Try to get some sleep tonight, Sam."

"Yeah, sure."

As she sat in the tangle of cars held up by the wreck, Sam banged her fist on the wheel in frustration that came from multiple sources. She couldn't stop thinking about Nick and how understanding he'd been when she put their fledgling relationship on hold. How often did she allow herself to lean on someone? Never. However, she couldn't lean on someone who was a material witness in the homicide case she was investigating. As much as she wanted to, she just couldn't.

She edged the car forward and finally cleared the accident. When she arrived at the Watergate, Nick was waiting for her in his black BMW.

"What took so long?" he asked as he stepped out of the car.

"Accident on Independence."

"You should've taken Constitution."

"Well, I know that *now*. Nice ride," she said, admiring the gleaming Beamer. "The taxpayers take good care of you."

"I have few vices," he said with a grin as he slid an arm around her. "Cars are one of them."

She scooted out from under his arm before they entered the lobby. "No PDA," she growled. Flashing her shield to the officer at the security desk, she gestured to the bank of elevators. "We're taking another look at the senator's apartment."

The officer nodded and waved them through.

They rode to the sixth floor where the door to John's apartment was blocked by yellow crime scene tape. Sam plugged in the code to the police lock and pushed open the door. Lifting the yellow tape, she encouraged Nick to go in ahead of her.

She heard his deep inhale and watched his broad shoulders stoop as the memories came flooding back to him. Placing her hand on his arm, she stopped him. "You don't have to be here. I can get the clothes for you."

"No," he said softly. "I can do it."

"Take a minute. I'm going to wander."

Sam walked through the luxurious apartment where a light sheen of fingerprint dust remained. Picking up knickknacks, opening drawers and checking behind the television, she looked for anything that might have been missed the first time through. She had no doubt the place had been put together by a decorator—probably when the senior Senator O'Connor lived there. It was odd, really, how little of John O'Connor could be found in the apartment.

In the senator's bedroom, the bed linens had been stripped and sent off for DNA analysis. A single hair could have blown the case wide open, but all the fingerprints, fibers and DNA were John's. Since the apartment had not yet been cleaned, blood stained the wall behind the bed as well as the beige carpeting, and co-agulated on the bedside table. The blow to the jugular would've been messy. Blood would have burst like a geyser from the wound, soaking the killer.

Sam stood at the foot of the bed and let her mind wander. Had he fallen asleep sitting up? Or had he sat up in surprise when the killer appeared? Obviously, he'd been naked in bed. Had he thought he was going to have sex with the woman who appeared in his bedroom? Was that how she gained easy access to his privates? Sam was absolutely convinced it was someone he knew well, which was why he hadn't had much of a reaction to finding her in his apartment.

"What's going on in that head of yours, Sergeant?" Nick asked from behind her.

"He was asleep," Sam said, her eyes fixed on the headboard where the gaping hole in the beige silk upholstery was a glaring reminder of what had happened there almost forty-eight hours ago. "Dozing. The TV was probably on."

"It wasn't on when I got here."

"She could've shut it off. Whoever it was, she was someone he wasn't surprised to see."

"She?"

"They were lovers." Sam spoke in a monotone as the scene played itself out in her imagination.

"Did he let her in?"

Sam shook her head. "She was waiting for him and took him by surprise. She had the knife behind her back. Maybe she was naked, too, which is why there's no one on the security tapes leaving with blood on their clothes. He thought he was going to get lucky, and that's how she managed to get a hold of his penis. By the time he became aware of the knife, she had already severed it. The pain would've been monstrous. He probably lost consciousness. If he came to before she killed him, he would have asked why. Maybe she told him, maybe she let him wonder."

"Would she have been strong enough to get a knife through his neck with one shot?"

"Good question. And you're right—it would've taken a tremendous blow to go all the way through his neck and lodge in the headboard. She would've been enraged by something he did or failed to do. Rage and adrenaline breeds strength. It could've been a promise he made and didn't deliver on or maybe she caught him with another woman. People have killed over less. When she was done, she took a shower to get rid of the blood that would've been all over her. Then she cleaned the bathroom and scrubbed it so well there wasn't so much as a hair on the floor. The water in the tub had dried by the time he was found, so we can only speculate that she showered. But none of the towels had been used. If she used one, she took it with her. Before she left, she might've taken a long last look at him. She was filled with regret that he couldn't be what she needed him to be, but at the same time she was angry with him for making her do this."

"You're good, Sam," Nick said, his tone reverent.

As if she had been in a trance, Sam looked up at him. "What?"

"The way you describe it… If I were a juror, I'd convict."

"All I have to do now is prove it and figure out who did it."

"You will." He moved to the closet, opened the doors and contemplated the row of dark suits, dress shirts in white, various shades of blue and some with pinstripes. There were easily a hundred ties to choose from.

Peeking into dresser drawers, Sam asked, "Did he ever wear anything besides suits? Where're the jeans? The sweats?"

"He didn't keep a lot of that stuff here."

"Where else would it be?"

"At his place in Leesburg."

"He has a second home?"

Nick nodded. "A cabin near his parents' property. We both use it as a retreat from the insanity of Washington."

"Why didn't you say anything about it the other day?"

"To be honest, it never occurred to me. I'm sorry. I wasn't thinking clearly then. I'm still not. Between what happened to John and seeing you again…"

"Take me there."

"Now?"

She nodded.

"It's almost midnight. You've been at it for eighteen hours. I can take you tomorrow."

Shaking her head, she said, "I won't have time tomorrow. If you drive, I'll nap in the car—if you can stay awake that is."

"I'm fine. I do my best work from midnight to three a.m."

His comment was rife with double meaning that Sam refused to acknowledge. Her face, however, heated with embarrassment as she helped him decide on a dark navy suit, pale blue silk dress shirt and a tie decorated with small American flags. They unearthed a garment bag, and Sam zipped it over the suit.

"Underwear?" she asked.

"He didn't wear it in life."

"How in the hell do you know that?"

Nick laughed. "We were at a luncheon with the

Daughters of the American Revolution a year or so ago, and everyone was starting to leave when one of the blue hairs came to tell me the senator needed me at the head table. I went into the room, and he was sitting all by himself."

"How come?"

"Apparently, he'd managed to split his pants and was in need of an exit strategy."

Sam laughed at the picture he painted. "Let me guess—he was in commando mode?"

"You got it. So I found him an overcoat—not an easy feat in July, I might add—and got him out of there with his pride intact."

"Where did that fall in your job description?"

"Under 'other duties as assigned,'" he said with a sad smile that tugged at her heart.

"All right then. No underwear. Shoes?"

"Would you want to spend eternity with your feet encased in wingtips? The tie will be bad enough. I'm sure I'll hear plenty about that when we meet up again in the afterlife." He reached for her hand and linked their fingers. "Thank you for helping me with this."

Flustered, she extracted her hand and jammed it in her pocket. "It's no problem."

"Is choosing clothes for the deceased part of *your* job description?"

"This is definitely a first."

On their way out of John's bedroom, Nick looked at her in a way that reminded Sam of what he wanted from her. A burst of yearning took her by surprise. Sam wasn't a woman who yearned, especially for a man. She was focused, efficient, dedicated to her work and her family, hard nosed when she needed to be, and independent—fiercely and completely independent. So it should have been unsettling to want a man as much as she wanted Nick.

Truth be told, she had fantasized about him for years after the night they spent together. She had followed Senator O'Connor's career and watched hours of congressional coverage in the hopes of catching a glimpse of the senator's trusted aide. But only rarely had she seen Nick. He apparently kept a much lower profile than his illustrious boss.

In the parking lot, he held the passenger door of his car for her.

She slid into the buttery soft leather seat and sighed with contentment. When he turned the car on, she quickly discovered the seats were heated and felt like she'd gone straight to heaven. "This car suits you."

"You think so?"

"Uh huh. It's classy but not showy."

"Is that a compliment, Samantha?"

She shrugged.

He reached for her hand as they headed out of the city. When she tried to resist, he held on tighter. "No one but us, babe."

"There's no tablecloth to hide under."

He flashed that irresistible grin and laced his fingers through hers. "Give me just this much, will you?"

Since he'd asked so nicely and it really wasn't much, she didn't argue with him even if the simple feel of his hand wrapped around hers set her heart to galloping and put her hormones on full alert. Guilt was mixed in there, too. She had no business spending this much time with him or wanting him so fiercely. But since it was dark and she was tired and no one was looking, rather than push him away, she tightened her grip on his hand.

14

Sam hadn't expected to sleep. But the combined lull of the moving car, the heated seats, Nick's hand wrapped companionably around hers…

"Wake up, Sleeping Beauty. We're here."

Coming to, Sam looked out at the vast darkness and was able to make out the shape of a cabin in front of the car. "Let's get to it."

The rush of frigid air slapped at Sam's face. She followed Nick up the gravel path to the door and stood back while he used his key in the lock.

Inside, he flipped on lights.

Sam blinked a comfortable living area into focus. Big, welcoming sofas, a flat-screen TV mounted on the wall, overflowing bookshelves on either side of the stone fireplace, framed family photos and a couple of trophies. Here, at last, was Senator John Thomas O'Connor.

She shrugged off her coat, pushed up the sleeves of her sweater, tugged the clip from her hair and got to work. Two hours later, she had discovered that John loved Hemingway, Shakespeare, Patterson and Grisham. His musical taste ran the gamut from Mellencamp to Springsteen, Vivaldi to Bach. She had sifted through photo albums, yearbooks and a file cabinet that seemed to have no rhyme or reason to anyone other than its owner.

She perused a series of essays John wrote for his senior project at Harvard, detailing the roles of government and the governed. The essays were bound into a small navy blue volume with smart gold embossing.

"He was proud of that," Nick said from the doorway to the office.

Startled, she glanced up at him. She had *almost* forgotten he was there.

"His father had the book made and gave it to everyone who was anyone." Nick stepped into the room and handed her a steaming mug.

"*Oh*, is that hot chocolate?" she asked, soaking in the mouthwatering aroma.

"I figured it was too late for coffee." He had removed his suit coat and released the top buttons on his dress shirt. Her eyes fixated on a dark tuft of chest hair.

"You figured right. Fat free, calorie free, I hope." Swirling her tongue over the dollop of whipped cream on top, she took a moment to appreciate the taste. Looking up at him again, she found his hazel eyes locked on her. "What?" she asked, her voice shakier than she intended it to be.

"It's just…you…and whipped cream. It's giving me ideas."

She swallowed, hard.

"I like your hair down like that," he added.

Choosing to ignore the comments and the flush of heat that went rippling through her body, she returned her attention to the book John had dedicated to his father. A photo slid out from between the pages and fell to the floor. Sam put her mug on the desk and leaned over to retrieve the picture of a strapping blond boy of about sixteen in a football uniform.

"What've you got there?" Nick asked.

"Looks like a photo of John when he was in high school." She turned it over to find the initials "TJO" and a date from four years earlier. "Oh. It's not him. Who's TJO?"

Nick took the photo from her, studied the likeness, and then turned it over. "I have no idea, but he could *be* John when I first met him."

"Did he have a son, Nick?" She thought of Patricia Donaldson and the three-thousand-dollar-a-month payments.

"Of course not."

"You're sure of that?"

"I'm positive," he said hotly. "I've known him since he was eighteen. If he had a son, I'd know it."

"Well, if that's not his son, whoever he is, he bears a striking resemblance to John." Sam tucked the photo into her bag with plans to ask the senator's parents about it in the morning. "He had quite a thing for Spider-Man, huh?" She gestured to the shelves in the corner that housed John's extensive stash of Spider-Man collectibles.

Nick smiled. "He was obsessed."

She picked up a carved placard from the desk that bore Spider-Man's signature saying, With Great Power Comes Great Responsibility. Studying it for a long moment, she glanced at Nick. "Did he believe this?"

"Very much so. Despite his sometimes lackadaisical approach to his job, he took his responsibilities as seriously as he was able to."

"But not as seriously as you would have."

"Let's just say if our roles had been reversed, I would've done a lot of things differently."

"Have you ever wanted to be the one in the corner office?"

"God no," he said with a guffaw. "I work much better as the guy behind the guy." He seemed to sober when he remembered he had lost his guy when John died.

"With his parents' okay, I'd like to have a team go through here more methodically tomorrow." She stretched and got up. "I'm running out of gas after twenty hours."

"I'm guessing you'll want to talk to his parents about that photo," Nick said, "so why don't we crash here and go see them in the morning?"

Her eyes darted up to meet his. "I'm not sleeping with you."

"I'm not asking you to," he said with a sexy smile. "There's a guestroom I use when I'm here. I'll take John's room."

Sam ran it around in her mind as she finished her hot chocolate. Technically, the cabin wasn't a crime scene, so she didn't have an issue there. She was exhausted, he didn't look much better, and she *could* knock a few things off her to-do list in the morning if she stayed in Leesburg, including another discussion with Terry O'Connor if he was available.

"All right," she said, even though she would've preferred separate hotel rooms, but hotels were in short supply in that corner of the county. She got up to follow Nick down the hallway to the bedrooms.

"Bathroom's in there," he pointed. In the guestroom, he rooted through an antique chest of drawers and pulled out a large T-shirt. "One of mine if you want something to sleep in. There're extra toothbrushes and anything else you might need in the bathroom closet."

"Thanks," she said, embarrassed and shy all of a sudden—two emotions she rarely experienced.

He slid a hand around her neck to draw her in close to him. For a long, breathless moment he just looked at her before he kissed her forehead. "I'll see you in the morning. Holler if you need anything."

Devastated by the simple kiss, she watched him cross the hall, her heart pounding and her hands damp. She hated being off balance and out of kilter, which of course was why he had done it. Feeling defiant, she used the bathroom and then left the shirt he had given her on the bed as she stripped out of her clothes and slid naked between the cool sheets.

Less than a minute later, she was out cold.

"Sam. Honey, wake up. You're dreaming."

Sam could hear him but couldn't seem to force her eyes open.

"Babe."

Her eyes fluttered open to find Nick sitting on the bed.

When he brushed the hair back from her face, she realized she was sweating and her heart was racing.

"Are you okay?" he asked.

"Mmm, sorry." It occurred to her that she must've been loud if she had woken him. She glanced at him, noticing he wore only a pair of sweats, and let her eyes take a slow journey over his muscular chest.

"It was a doozy, huh? The dream?"

"I don't know. I never remember the details, just the fear." She rubbed a weary hand over her cheek and wished for a glass of water. "Did I…um…say anything?"

He replaced the hand she had on her face with his own. "You kept saying, 'Cease fire, hold your fire.'"

"Shit," she said with a deep sigh.

He stretched out next to her on top of the comforter and settled her head on his shoulder. "It was a traumatic thing, Sam, but it wasn't your fault."

Steeped in the masculine scent of citrus and spice, she closed her eyes against the rush of emotion and absorbed the comfort he offered. Just for a minute. His chest hair brushed against her face, making her want him so fiercely. "If only I could forgive myself as easily as you've forgiven me."

He brought her closer to him.

"Um, Nick?"

"Hmm?"

"I'm kind of naked under here."

"Yeah, I noticed."

As all the reasons this was a bad idea came crashing down on her, she attempted to struggle out of his embrace. "I can't," she whispered. "I can't have this. I can't have you."

"Yes, you can."

Her face still pressed to his chest, Sam gave herself another second to wallow in the scent that she'd never forgotten. "Not here. Not now."

He released a deep, ragged breath. "I missed you, Sam. I thought about you, about that night, so often."

"I did, too," she said, her eyes closed tight against the onslaught of emotions she'd only felt this acutely once before.

"I've never wanted anyone the way I want you. If you're in the room, I want you."

"I seem to have the same problem."

"We've got a few hours until daybreak. Would it be okay if I just held you until then?"

"I'd love nothing more, but it's too tempting. *You're* too tempting."

Sighing again, he released her and sat up. He leaned

down to press a soft kiss to her lips. "See you in the morning."

Sam watched him go, knowing she'd never get back to sleep with every cell in her body on fire for him.

15

Sam corralled her hair into a ponytail, strapped on her shoulder holster, clipped the badge to her belt, and adjusted her suit jacket over the same scoop-necked top she'd worn yesterday. When she was ready, she took a long look around to make sure she wasn't leaving behind any sign that she had spent the night for the team she planned to send in there later that day. Satisfied by the quick sweep of the room, she emerged to find Nick waiting for her in the living room. Somehow he managed to appear pressed and polished in yesterday's clothes. His face was smooth and his hair still damp from the shower.

"Ready?" he asked.

She nodded.

Wrapping her coat and his arms around her, he hugged her from behind and pressed kisses to her neck and cheek before he finally let go.

The spontaneous demonstration of affection caught her off guard. Unless it was leading to sex, Peter had never bothered with the random acts of affection that Nick doled out so effortlessly. Nick seemed to *need* to touch her if she was near him. That she liked it so much was just another reason to keep her distance.

The O'Connors' home was located two miles up

the main road from John's cabin. Once again, Carrie met them at the door and was surprised to see them out so early.

"Are they up?" Nick asked.

"They're having breakfast. Come on in." She led them into the cozy country kitchen where Graham and Laine sat at the table lost in their own thoughts. Neither of them seemed to be eating much of anything.

Both had dark circles under their eyes. Weariness and grief clung to them.

"Nick?" Graham said. "You're out early. Sergeant."

Carrie handed mugs of coffee to Sam and Nick.

"Thank you," Nick said.

"I'm sorry to barge in on you so early." Sam stirred cream into her coffee and wished it was a diet cola. "But I have something I need to ask you."

"Of course," Laine said. "Whatever we can do to help."

Sam retrieved the photo from her bag. "Who is this?" She placed the photo on the table between them.

They looked at the photo and then at each other.

"Where'd you get this?" Graham asked.

"At the cabin," Nick said. "The photo was tucked into the essay book you had made for him."

"It's John's cousin, Thomas," Laine said, glancing up at Sam with cool patrician eyes. "His father is Graham's brother Robert."

"I don't remember John mentioning a cousin that young," Nick said.

Laine shrugged. "There were almost twenty years between them. They were hardly close."

"He looks an awful lot like your son," Sam said, testing for reactions.

"Yes, he does," Graham said, his expression neutral. "Is there anything else?"

"Do you know where I can find Terry?" Sam said.

The question seemed to startle both O'Connors.

"I believe he's working in the city this morning," Graham said.

"The address?"

He rattled off the name and K Street address of a prominent lobbying firm, which Sam wrote down in the small notebook she pulled from her back pocket. "If you have no objection, I'd like to send a team into the cabin today to make sure we're not missing something that could help with the case."

"Strange people in John's home?" Laine asked, visibly disturbed by the notion.

"Police," Sam clarified. "They'll be as respectful as possible."

"That's fine," Graham said with a pointed look at his wife. "If it'll help the investigation, do it."

"Can you tell me, Senator, who might still have keys to the apartment at the Watergate from when you lived there?"

Graham pondered that for a moment. "Only my family."

"No staffers or aides?"

"My chief of staff had one, but I distinctly recall him giving it back to me when we left office."

"Any chance he might've had others made, given them to other people?"

"No. He was a guard dog about my privacy. He didn't even like having the key himself."

"Are you aware, either of you, that John spoke with Patricia Donaldson in Chicago several times a week for an hour or more each time?"

Again the O'Connors exchanged glances.

"No, but I'm not surprised," Graham said. "They were close friends as children."

"Just friends?"

"Yes," Laine said pointedly, so pointedly in fact that it raised Sam's hackles and her radar. There was more to this story. Of that she had no doubt. She'd be speaking to Patricia Donaldson as soon as she could arrange a trip to Chicago.

"John is still due to be moved today to Richmond?" Laine asked Nick.

He nodded. "The motorcade is leaving Washington at noon."

"We'll be going down to Richmond this afternoon," Graham said. "The state police are escorting us and clearing the way for us to get in and out before they open it to the public."

"The staff will have a private viewing in the morning," Nick said.

"You got the clothes they needed?" Laine asked.

"Yes. I'm heading to the funeral home from here. Um, about the funeral… Have you decided who you want to have speak on behalf of the family?"

"You do it," Laine said with a weary sigh.

"Are you sure? You wouldn't rather have a family member?"

"You *are* family to us, Nick," Graham said. "You'll do him proud. We know that."

"I'll do my best," he said softly. "We should let you get back to your breakfast."

"We'll see you Monday, if not before," Laine said.

Nick leaned over to kiss her cheek. "I'll be in touch."

She squeezed the hand he rested on her shoulder. "Thank you for all you're doing. I know it can't be easy for you."

"It's an honor and a privilege."

Patting his hand once more, she released him.

Nick hugged Graham and kissed Carrie on his way

out of the kitchen. With his hand on the small of her back, he steered Sam to the front door. Once they were outside, he took a deep, rattling breath of cold air.

Since there was little else she could do to comfort him, she held his hand between both of hers all the way back to Washington.

After fighting their way through rush-hour traffic, Nick pulled up to the Watergate with fifteen minutes to spare before Sam's appointment with Senator Stenhouse.

"So much for going home to change first," she grumbled. "Freddie will have a field day with this."

"Tell him you worked all night. Won't be a total lie."

"It'll be a good excuse to remind him that I outrank him and can order him to shut up. He likes that."

Nick smiled and reached for the inside pocket of his suit jacket. He withdrew a small leather case and handed her his business card. "Call me? My cell number is on there."

She took the card, stuffed it in her pocket and reached for the door.

He stopped her before she could get out. "Talk to me before Monday so we can arrange to go to the funeral together if you still want me to help you ID people."

"I do. I'll be in touch."

"Remember to eat and sleep, will you?"

"Yeah, right," she said on her way out the door.

Nick waited, probably to make sure her car started because he was polite that way, and then pulled into traffic just ahead of her.

On the way to Capitol Hill, Sam called Gonzo and asked him to oversee the sift through John O'Connor's cabin.

"It's not a crime scene, so I'm not interested in fingerprints or DNA. I'm just looking for anything we don't already know about him."

"Gotcha. So we got confirmation that the blood in Christina Billings's car was her own."

"Well, I guess that closes that loop," Sam said. "There's no way she made it across town, killed him, showered, cleaned up the bathroom and got back with Chinese food in twenty-eight minutes. Not in this town with this traffic, even at midnight."

"No way is right," Gonzo agreed. "I'll get a team together and get out to Leesburg this morning."

"You'd better notify Loudoun County, too, so we don't have jurisdictional trouble." She paused before she added, "Full disclosure—I crashed in the guest-room there last night. I needed to see his parents in the morning, and it saved me some time. Cappuano slept in the senator's room."

"Okay."

"If you could keep that tidbit to yourself, I'd owe you one."

He laughed. "I like having you indebted to me. Just let me know if there's anything else I can do."

"There is one thing," she said, playing the hunch. "Do a run on Graham O'Connor's brother, Robert. I need the deal on his family, offspring in particular. If you can get photos, even better."

"Will do," Gonzo said. "I'll call you with what I find out. So, um, you saw the papers this morning I assume…"

Sam's stomach took a queasy dip that reminded her she hadn't eaten or had either of the two diet colas she usually relied upon to jumpstart her day. "No, why?"

"Destiny Johnson is calling you a baby killer."

"Is that so?" Sam growled, the dip in her stomach descending into the ache that dogged her in times of stress. Two doctors had been unable to determine the cause. One had suggested she give up soda, which simply wasn't an option, so she lived with her stomach's annoying ability to predict her stress level.

"Don't take it to heart, Sam. Everyone knows that if she'd been any kind of mother, her kid wouldn't have been hanging out in a crack house in the first place."

"But she has the nerve to call *me* the baby killer." Of all the things she could've said, that hurt more than anything.

"I know. She made some pretty serious threats about what she'd do if you testify against her deadbeat husband next week. I'm sure you'll be hearing from the brass about it."

"That's great." She rubbed her belly in an effort to find some relief. "Just what I need right now."

"Sorry. You know we're all standing behind you. It was a clean shoot."

"Thanks, Gonzo." Her throat tightened with emotion she couldn't afford to let in just then. Clearing it away, she said, "Call me if you find anything useful at the cabin. I did a surface run last night, but I was operating on fumes. I could've missed something."

"Leave it to me. I'll let you know when we finish."

She gave him the O'Connors' phone number so he could get a key to the cabin from them and signed off. Weaving her way through traffic, she made it to Capitol Hill with minutes to spare and took off running for the Hart Senate Office Building.

Freddie was pacing in the hallway outside Senator Stenhouse's office suite. "There you are! I was just about to call you." His astute eyes took in her day-old suit and landed on her face.

"I worked all night, I haven't been home to change yet, and yes, I've heard about Destiny Johnson," she snapped. "So whatever you're going to say, don't bother."

"As usual, a night without sleep has done wonders for your disposition."

"Buzz off, Freddie. I'm truly not in the mood to go ten rounds with you."

"What were you doing working all night? And why didn't you call me? I would've come back in."

"I went through O'Connor's place again and then his home in Leesburg."

Freddie raised an eyebrow. "By yourself?"

"Nick Cappuano was with me. He told me about the place in Leesburg and took me there. Otherwise I never would've found it. Do you have a problem with that?"

"Me?" Freddie raised his hands defensively. "I've got no problems, boss."

"Good. Can we get to work then?"

"I'm following you."

"Nice digs," she muttered under her breath as Stenhouse's assistant showed them into a massive corner office that was triple the size of that assigned to the junior senator from Virginia.

Stenhouse, tall and lean with silver hair and sharp, frosty blue eyes, stood up when they came in. He dismissed the assistant with orders to close the door behind her. "I'm on a tight schedule, Detectives. What can I do for you?"

Wants to play it that way? Sam thought. *Well, so can I.* "Detective Cruz, please record this interview with Senate Minority Leader William Stenhouse." She rattled off the time, date, place and players present.

"You need my permission to record this," Stenhouse snapped.

"Here or downtown. Your choice."

He glowered at her for a long moment before he gestured for her to proceed.

"Where were you on Tuesday evening between ten p.m. and seven a.m.?"

"You can't be serious."

Turning to Freddie, she said, "Am I serious, Detective Cruz?"

"Yes, ma'am. I believe you're dead serious."

"Answer the question, Senator."

Teeth gritted, Stenhouse glared at her. "I was here until ten, ten thirty, and then I went home."

"Which is where?"

"Old Town Alexandria."

"Did you see or speak to anyone after you left here?"

"My wife is at home in Missouri preparing for the holidays."

"So that's a 'no'?"

"That's a 'no,'" he growled.

"How did you feel about the immigration bill Senator O'Connor sponsored?"

"Useless piece of drivel," Stenhouse muttered. "The bill has no bones to it, and everyone knows that."

"Funny, that's not what we've been told, is it, Detective Cruz?"

"No, ma'am." Freddie flipped open his notebook and rattled off the statement the president had issued days earlier, calling the immigration reform bill the most important piece of legislation proposed during his first term.

Stenhouse's glare could've bored a hole through a lesser cop, but Sam barely felt the heat. "Were you irritated to see Graham O'Connor's son succeeding in the Senate?"

"Hardly," he said. "He was nothing to me."

"And his father? Was he nothing to you as well?"

"He was a prick who overstayed his welcome."

"How did you feel when you heard his son had been murdered?"

"It's a tragedy," he said in a pathetic attempt at sincerity. "He was a United States senator."

"And the son of your longtime rival."

Awareness dawned all at once. "Did he tell you I did this? That bastard!" He stalked to the window and stared out for a moment before he turned to them. "I hate his fucking guts. But do I hate him enough to kill his son? No, I don't. I haven't given Graham O'Connor a thought in the five years since we saw the last of his sorry ass around here."

"I'm sure you've had cause to give his son more than a passing thought in the same five years."

"His son was in the Senate for one reason and one reason only—his pedigree. The O'Connors have the people of Virginia snowed. John O'Connor was even more useless than his father, and that's not just my opinion. Ask around."

"I'll do that," Sam said. "In the meantime, stay available."

"What does that mean? Congress will be in holiday recess after tomorrow. I'm heading home to Missouri the day after."

"No, you're not. You're staying right here until we close this case."

"But it's Christmas! You can't keep me here against my will."

"Detective Cruz, can I keep the senator here against his will?"

"I believe you can, ma'am."

"And do we have a jail cell with his name on it if we hear he leaves the capital region?"

"Yes, ma'am. We absolutely do."

Stenhouse breathed fire as the detectives had their exchange.

Sam took three steps to close the distance between them. Looking up at the senator, she kept her expression passive and calm. "Neither your rank nor your standing mean a thing to me. This is a homicide investigation, and I won't hesitate to toss you in a cage if you fail to cooperate. Stay available."

With that, she turned, nodded at Freddie to follow her, and left the room.

She was gratified to hear Stenhouse yell to his assistant, "Get Joe Farnsworth on the line. Right now!"

Terry O'Connor spent the days he was sober in a closet-sized office on Independence Avenue. Judging from the lack of anything much on his desk, Sam deduced the job was bogus and most likely a favor to his illustrious father.

Terry's already pasty complexion paled when the detectives appeared at his door.

"Good morning, Mr. O'Connor," Sam said. "We're sorry to interrupt your work, but we have a few follow-up questions for you."

"Um, sure," he said, gesturing to a chair.

Sam took the chair while Freddie hovered in the doorway.

"I have to leave soon," Terry said. "We're going to Richmond."

"Yes, I know. We won't keep you long. Have you made any headway in producing the woman you were with on the night of the murder?"

Terry seemed to shrink further into his chair. "No."

"Did you kill your brother, Terry?"

Misery turned to shock in an instant. "No!"

"You had good reason to want him dead. I mean,

after all, he was living the life that should've been yours and was about to know real success as a senator when the immigration bill passed. Maybe that was just too much for you."

"I loved my brother, Sergeant. Was I jealous of him? You bet I was. I wanted that job. I *wanted* it. Down here, you know?" He gestured to his gut. "I'd prepared for it my whole life, so yeah, it bothered me that he had it when he didn't even want it. But killing him wouldn't change anything for me. You don't see the Virginia Democrats lined up outside my office wanting me to take his place, do you?"

"No."

"So what was my motive in killing him?"

"Pleasure? Revenge?"

"Do I look like I've got the energy to care that much about anything?" he asked, his tone heavy with utter defeat.

Sam stood up. "I'd still like the name of the woman you say you were with that night."

Terry sighed. "So would I, Sergeant. Believe me. So would I."

Outside, Sam turned to Freddie. "What do you think?"

"I don't want it to be him. I mean, think of those poor parents if it *was* him…"

Freddie's endless compassion could be alternatively comforting and aggravating. "He's a lot more than jealous of his brother. Check out that hole-in-the-wall office. You think it didn't bug the shit out of him that baby brother was snuggled into that suite in the Hart Building?"

"Enough to kill him?"

"I don't know. I still see a woman for this, but I'm

not ruling out the brother angle. Not yet. I'm giving him until the funeral is over to produce his alibi and then he and I are going to have a more formal chat." She paused before she added, "I need to go home and get changed. Do you mind if we make a quick stop?"

"Nope. You know I like seeing the deputy chief."

"He likes you, too, for some unknown reason."

"My wit and charm are hard to resist."

"Funny, I seem to have no problem resisting."

"You are a rare and unique woman, Sergeant."

"And you'd do well to remember that."

Freddie laughed and followed her to the car.

16

Sam wasn't surprised to receive a call from Chief Farnsworth as she drove home.

"Good morning, Chief. I assume you've heard from Senator Stenhouse."

"You assume correctly. Is it really necessary to retain him, Sergeant?"

"I believe it is, sir. He had a number of political reasons to want to see John O'Connor dead, not the least of which was his hatred for the senator's father."

"*Hate* is a strong word."

"It's his word." Glancing at Freddie she said, "Correct me if I'm wrong, Detective Cruz, but I believe the senator's exact words in reference to Graham O'Connor were, 'I hate his fucking guts.'"

Freddie nodded his approval.

"Detective Cruz has confirmed my account, sir."

"Tread carefully on this front, Sergeant. Stenhouse can make my life difficult, and if my life is difficult, so is yours."

"Yes, sir."

"The media is burning a hole in the back of my neck clamoring for information. How close are we to closing this one?"

"Not as close as I'd like to be. I don't have a clear-cut suspect at the moment—a few who had motive and opportunity—but no one's popping for me just yet."

"I'd like to see you when you get back to HQ."

"About what was in the paper this morning?"

"Yes."

"I can handle that, sir. There's no need—"

"My office, four o'clock," the chief said and ended the call.

"Shit," she muttered as she returned the cell phone to her coat pocket.

"They have to take those kinds of threats against an officer seriously, Sam," Freddie said. "They have no choice."

"She's a grieving mother who's looking for someone to blame. I'm convenient."

"Too bad she can't see that her crackhead husband is the one to blame, not you."

Sam parked on Ninth Street, rested her hands on the wheel, and looked over at Freddie. "Listen, in the event that she's not blowing smoke, there could be some trouble in the form of stray bullets flying at me. I'd understand if you wanted to partner up with someone else until this blows over."

"Nice try, Sergeant, but you're stuck with me."

"I could have you reassigned."

"You could," he conceded. "But let me ask you this—if someone was taking pot shots at me, would you bail?"

"No."

"Then why do you think I would?"

Under his junk food–loving, cover-boy exterior, Freddie Cruz was made of stuff Sam respected. "All right then," Sam said, attempting to return things to normal. "When you get your pretty head blown off, don't come crying to me."

He stuck out his jaw. "You really think my head is pretty? You've never told me that before."

"Shut *up*," she groaned, reaching for the door handle. "Jesus."

"I've asked you to refrain from using the Lord's name in vain."

"And I've asked *you* to refrain from preaching your Holy Roller crap to me." There. Back to normal.

The ramp that led to Skip Holland's front door was a stark reminder of the changes wrought by an assailant's bullet. Inside, Sam called for him and smiled when she heard the whir of his chair.

"There's my daughter who blows her curfew and stays out all night."

"I left a message that I know you got." She bent down to kiss his forehead. "So don't give me any grief."

"Morning, Detective Cruz. Have you eaten?"

"Earlier." Freddie squeezed Skip's right hand in greeting. "But you know me, there's always room for more."

"Celia made eggs. I think there's some left."

"Don't mind if I do." Freddie flashed Sam a grin as he headed for the kitchen.

She rolled her eyes. "Why do you have to encourage him?" she asked her father.

"He's a growing boy. Needs his protein."

"I hope I'm around when his metabolism slows to a crawl the way mine has." She reached for the mail stacked on a table. "You look tired."

"I could say the same for you, Sergeant. What kept you out all night?"

"Working the case. You know." She glanced at him, caught a hint of something in his wise eyes. "What?"

"I can still read."

"Oh." She released her hair from the ponytail and

combed her fingers through it in an attempt to bring some order to it. "You saw the thing in the paper. She's looking for someone to blame."

"What's being done?"

She knew he meant by the department and wanting to quell his fears she told him of the meeting Farnsworth had called.

"He'll take you off the streets. Off O'Connor until you've testified."

"He'll take me off kicking and screaming. I can't let a useless excuse for a mother like Destiny Johnson get in the way of the job."

"She has a lot of friends—angry friends with guns. Farnsworth won't have any choice but to put you under protection after the threats she's made."

"If I go under, the case goes with me. I'll be surprised if they haven't already picked her up for threatening the life of a police officer."

"No doubt, but just because she's locked up doesn't mean the threat's been neutralized."

Sam leaned over to press another kiss to his forehead. "Don't worry."

A look of fury crossed the expressive side of his face. "You can say that to me? When I'm sitting in this chair incapable of doing a goddamned *thing* when the life of my daughter, *my child*, has been threatened by someone who has not only the will but the means to follow through? Worry is all I've got. Don't take that away from me, Sam, and don't patronize me. I expect better from you."

"I'm sorry. You're right." She expelled a long deep breath as her stomachache returned with a vengeance. Navigating his new reality was a slippery slope, even almost two years later. "Of course you're right."

"You're to take this seriously and do whatever you're

told by your superior officers. I'm trusting Joe to do his part, so I need your word that you'll do yours."

She reached for his hand and squeezed the one finger that could still feel it. "You have it."

"Go get changed and then come down to have some breakfast."

Because he was her dad and needed to feel like he still had control over something, she did what she was told without reminding him that she was thirty-four and didn't have to.

Over eggs and toast, she and Freddie hashed out the case with Skip while Celia helped him with a cup of coffee.

"I agree with you about the female angle, the act of passion," Skip said.

"We haven't encountered a woman yet with the emotional baggage toward O'Connor that this would've required," Freddie said.

"We're talking to some ex-girlfriends when we leave here, so we're hoping to get lucky," Sam said.

"You're looking for a cool customer," Skip said, slipping into the zone. "Someone who keeps tremendous anger bottled up under a refined exterior. You'll find she's been abused or had complicated relationships with the significant men in her life—father, ex-husband, ex-lover. Men have disappointed her in some way and whatever the senator did was the final straw. The breaking point."

"Damn," Freddie said reverently. "You two are something else. She sees these things as clearly as you do."

Celia smiled at him. "It's in their genes. I wonder sometimes if I should be afraid, spending as much time as I do with people who can slide inside a criminal's mind as easily as these two can."

"Enough about our genes." Sam stood as she downed

a last swallow of soda. "Thanks, Celia, for the chow, and you for the consult." She kissed her father's cheek. "See you tonight."

"I won't hold my breath," he said with a dry chuckle. To Freddie he added, "She uses me for a place to keep her considerable wardrobe."

"Seems to me she uses you for a lot more than that. Always a pleasure, Chief."

"All mine, Detective. The Skins are playing at home Sunday night if you want to stop by to watch the game. Celia tells me there'll be snacks. Maybe even a beer or two if I'm good."

"Snacks, beer *and* football?" Freddie reached out to squeeze Skip's hand. "Hard to resist an offer like that. I'll do my best to come by. Thanks for breakfast, Celia. It was fabulous as usual."

"Anytime, Detective," Celia said, blushing a little as even the strongest of women tended to do when on the receiving end of Freddie's formidable charm.

Outside, Sam paused before she got into the car. "I, ah, I just wanted to say thanks for that in there."

Freddie's eyebrows knitted with confusion as he studied her over the top of the car. "For what? Eating your food like I just got rescued from a deserted island?"

"No." She struggled to find the words. "For treating him like he's still a normal guy, a normal person."

"He is." Freddie maintained the puzzled air of innocent befuddlement. "Why would I treat him any other way?"

"You'd be surprised the way people treat him sometimes." They got into the car. "I'm only going to say this once, and if I hear you repeated it I'll deny it with everything I've got. Understand?"

"Gee, I can't wait to hear this. You leave me breath-less with anticipation."

"Your sarcasm and significant dietary failings aside, you're a special guy, Freddie Cruz. A one-in-a-million good guy." She glanced over to find him staring at her with his mouth hanging open. "Now that we've got that bullshit out of the way, what do you say we get back to figuring out who killed the senator?" When Freddie failed to reply, she said, "For Christ's sake, will you quit looking at me like I just hit you with the Taser?"

"Might as well have," he muttered. "Might as well have."

That he didn't mention her disrespectful use of the Lord's name told her she'd truly shocked him with the compliment, which made for a satisfying start to what promised to be a shitty day.

They found Natalie Jordan at home alone in Belle Haven, an upscale development of stately colonial homes in Alexandria. Red brick, white columns and black wrought iron fronted hers. The home reeked of old money and Virginia aristocracy.

"Nice crib," Freddie said, gazing around at the well-kept grounds.

"Looks like Natalie landed herself a sugar daddy after all," Sam said as she rang the doorbell. Chimes pealed inside.

Natalie answered the door dressed in a salmon-colored silk blouse, winter white wool pants and two-inch heels. A gold chain bearing a diamond the size of Sam's thumb encircled her slender neck, and her blond hair was cut into a sleek bob that perfectly offset her thin, angular face. Sharp blue eyes were rimmed with red and dark circles marred her otherwise flawless complexion. Sam could see what Nick had meant when he'd described Natalie as "quite something."

No slouch in the fashion department herself, Sam was immediately intimidated. Her stomach twisted. Willing the pain away with a quick deep breath, Sam flashed her badge. "Detective Sergeant Holland and Detective Cruz, Metro Police."

"Come in," Natalie said in a honeyed Southern accent. "I've been expecting you."

"Is that so?" Sam said as they followed her to a living room ripped from the pages of the *Town & Country* holiday issue.

"Senator O'Connor and I were involved for a number of years. I assumed you'd want to speak to me at some point. May I offer you something? Coffee or a cold drink?"

Before Freddie could accept, Sam said, "No, thank you. Do you mind if we record this conversation?"

Natalie shook her head, and Sam gestured for Freddie to turn on the recorder.

Sam began by noting the people present and the location of their interview. "Can you tell me where you were on Tuesday between the hours of ten p.m. and seven a.m.?"

While Natalie might have been expecting them, she clearly hadn't been expecting that. "I'm a *suspect*?"

"Until we determine otherwise, everyone is. Your whereabouts?"

"I was here," she stammered. "With my husband."

"His name?"

"Noel Jordan."

"And where might we find him to confirm this?"

"He's the special assistant attorney general at Justice." She rattled off an address in the city. "He's at work right now."

With the wave of her hand to encompass the room, Sam said, "Swanky digs for a guy on a government salary."

"His family has...they're wealthy."

"Can you tell me the nature of your relationship with Senator O'Connor?"

Hands twisting in her lap, Natalie said, "We were involved, romantically, for just over three years."

"And it ended when?"

"About four years ago," she sighed. "A year or so after he was elected."

"Were you in love with him?"

"Very much so," she said with a wistful expression that had Sam speculating that Natalie's feelings for the senator remained intact.

"Why did the relationship end?"

"I wanted to get married. He didn't." She shrugged. "We argued about it. Several times. After one particularly nasty disagreement, he said our relationship had run its course and we should think about seeing other people."

"And how did you feel about that?"

"Devastated and shocked. I loved him. I wanted to spend my life with him. I had no idea he was that unhappy."

"Did he love you?"

"He said he did, but there was always something... off, I guess you could say. I was never entirely convinced he loved me the same way I loved him."

"Must've pissed you off to get dumped by the guy you'd planned to marry."

Raw blue eyes flashed with emotion. "I was too crushed to be pissed, Sergeant. And if you're wondering if I killed him, I can assure you I didn't. In fact, I was quite certain I was over him until I heard he was dead."

Tears suddenly spilled down her porcelain cheeks. She wiped at them with a practiced gesture that indicated she'd done a lot of crying in the last few days. "Since then, I can't seem to turn off the waterworks." Pausing for a moment, she added, "I have a nice life now with a man I adore, a man who's good to me. I'd have nothing to gain by harming John."

"Do you still have a key to the senator's apartment at the Watergate?"

"I, um, I don't know." She appeared genuinely perplexed. "I might."

"So you had one when you were dating?"

"I lived with him there for the last year or so of our relationship." Red blotches formed on her cheeks. "I don't recall giving the key back to him when I moved out."

"I need to ask you something of a personal nature, and I apologize in advance if it offends you."

"Everything about this offends me, Sergeant. A good man, a man I loved, has been murdered. It offends me on a very deep level."

"I understand. However, my job is to find out who killed him, and to do that I have to ask you about his sexual preferences."

Taken aback, Natalie said, "What do you mean?"

"Was he into anything kinky?"

Her cheeks went from blotchy to flaming. "We enjoyed a satisfying sex life if that's what you're asking."

"Did he tie you up?" Sam asked, playing a hunch based on the type of porn they'd found on his computer. "Did he get rough? Want more than the usual deal?"

"I don't have to answer that," Natalie stuttered. "It's my personal business, *his* personal business."

"Yes, it is, but aspects of his murder were intensely

personal, so if you'd answer the questions, I'd appreciate it."

Natalie took a long deep breath and exhaled it as she spun a huge diamond engagement ring around on her finger. "He was a creative lover."

Sam used her trademark steely stare to let Natalie know she'd have to do better than that.

"*Yes*," she cried. "He tied me up, he could be rough, he asked for more than the usual deal." Descending into sobs, she added, "Are you satisfied?"

"Were *you?* Did you go along with it because you wanted to or because you felt you had to?"

"I loved him," she said in a defeated whisper that set Sam's already frazzled nerves further on edge. "I loved him."

"Did he ever bring other people into the relationship? Male or female?"

"Of course not," Natalie sputtered. "No!"

"Mrs. Jordan, I'm going to need you to stay available until we close this case."

"My husband and I are due to leave for Arizona in a few days to visit his parents for Christmas."

"You're going to have to change those plans."

Wiping her face, she said, "Do I need an attorney, Sergeant?"

"Not at this time. We'll be in touch."

17

"Go ahead and say it," she muttered to Freddie when they were back in the car.

"Say what?"

"I was too hard on her. I'm a mean, insensitive bitch. Whatever's on your mind."

"I feel sorry for her."

She hadn't expected that. "Other than the obvious, why?"

"Did you notice the one thing she *didn't* say?"

"How about we skip the Q&A, and you tell me what you observed, Detective."

"She said she 'adored' her husband. She never said she loved him. How many times did she say she loved O'Connor? Four? Five?"

Startled, Sam could only stare at him.

"What?" he asked, squirming.

"We might just be making a detective out of you yet."

Freddie flashed that *GQ* smile, and damn it if her heart didn't skip a beat. He was so goddamned cute.

She started the car. "You know, you can feel free to jump in when we're interviewing people."

"And interrupt your groove? I wouldn't dream of it. Quite a pleasure to watch you work, Sergeant Holland. Shame on me if I spend a day with you and don't learn something."

"Are you sucking up?" She shot him a suspicious glance as she drove through Belle Haven. "What do you want?"

"Other than lunch, I couldn't ask for anything more than I already have. Where are we heading now?"

"We've got two more ex-girlfriends to knock off the list, and then I'd like to have a word with Noel Jordan."

"Are we going to ask the exes about their sex lives?"

"Damn straight."

He sighed. "I was afraid of that."

Tara Davenport, age twenty-four, worked the lunch shift at a high-end restaurant that catered to the Capitol Hill crowd. Sam presented her badge to the maître d'. "We need a few minutes with Tara Davenport."

"She's working. Can you come back at end of shift? Around five?"

"This isn't a social call. I can speak with her in a private space you'll provide or I can haul her out of here in cuffs and take you with us for interfering with a police investigation. What's it going to be?"

Looking down his snooty nose at her, the stiff said, "Wait here and keep your voice down, will you?"

"Mean and scary," Freddie murmured, drawing a laugh from Sam.

"Thank you."

"You would see that as a compliment."

"How else should I see it?"

They watched the stiff tap a slender but well-endowed young blonde on the shoulder and point to Sam and Freddie. He signaled to them, and they followed Tara to the back of the busy restaurant. On the way, more than a few patrons took notice of them. For some reason, that pleased Sam, so much so she hitched her hands into her pockets and put her weapon and badge on full display.

"Class act, Sergeant," the maître d' seethed.

"The next time myself or any of my colleagues appear at your door, perhaps you'll consider cooperating."

"You have fifteen minutes. After that you'll need a warrant to set foot in here again."

"Will I need a warrant if I wish to return for a follow-up visit, Detective Cruz?"

"No, ma'am, in most cases an informal interview of a potential suspect in a homicide investigation doesn't require a warrant."

The stiff paled. "Homicide?"

"Step aside and let me do my job," Sam said in a low growl. "So much as knock on that door and I'll haul your skinny ass downtown and put you in a cage with some guys who'd love nothing more than to make you their bitch."

He swallowed hard and moved to let them by.

"Mean *and* scary," Freddie said again.

Choking back a laugh, Sam opened the door to the break room where Tara Davenport waited, pale and trembling. As she introduced herself and Freddie to Tara, Sam questioned whether the woman had the physical strength to put a butcher knife through John O'Connor's neck.

"Is this about John?" she asked softly after agreeing to allow them to record the conversation.

"It is. Can you provide your whereabouts on the night of the murder? Tuesday, from ten p.m. to seven a.m.?"

Rattled but firm, Tara said, "I was out with some friends, early in the evening, but home by ten."

"I'll need you to give Detective Cruz a list of the people you were with. Do you live alone?"

She nodded.

"So no one can verify your whereabouts after ten?"

"No."

"No one saw you arriving home? Neighbors?"

"Not that I can recall."

"How and when did you meet Senator O'Connor?"

"I met him about six months ago. He was a regular here. He and his chief of staff, Nick, came in for lunch a couple of times a week when the Senate was in session."

Sam's belly twisted at the mention of Nick, whom she'd studiously tried to block from her mind all day. Remembering his muscular chest and the tender way he'd cared for her after the dream infused her with heat. She shrugged off her coat and slung it over a chair.

"John always asked to be seated in my section. He liked to tease and flirt. After a few months of that, he asked me out to dinner."

"Did that surprise you?"

"It did. I mean, he's a United States senator. What does he want with a waitress?"

"What *did* he want?"

"At first, I thought he was lonely," she said, her green eyes filling. "The first few times we went out, we talked for hours. He took me to nice places."

"You must've felt like Cinderella," Freddie said.

"In some ways, I did. He was a perfect gentleman, and so very handsome."

"Did you fall for him?" Sam asked.

"Yes," she whispered. "If you knew John at all, you'd know it would be hard not to."

"So what happened?"

Playing with her fingers, Tara said, "We had dated

for a few weeks when he asked me to spend the night with him."

"And did you?"

Looking down at her lap, she nodded. "It was lovely. *He* was lovely." She swiped at tears. "We couldn't get enough of each other."

"Did you have a key to his place?"

"He gave me his once when I was meeting him there, but I gave it back to him that same night."

"Why did it end?" Freddie asked.

"He, ah…he was looking for more than I was willing to give."

"In the relationship?" Sam knew the answer before she asked.

Tara shook her head, her cheeks blazing with color. "In bed."

"What happened to lovely?"

"I wish I knew. After a few times, it changed. He became rough, almost aggressive. And he wanted… things…that I'm not into."

"What kind of things?"

"Is this really necessary?"

"I'm sorry, but it is."

"He…"

"I know this is terribly difficult for you, Ms. Davenport, but we're looking for a killer. Anything you can tell us that will aid in our investigation is relevant."

Tara took another moment to collect herself. "He wanted bondage and…anal."

"Did you have anal sex with the senator, Ms. Davenport?"

"No! I said no! I don't do that. I'm not into that."

"And how did he take it when you refused him?"

"He was mad, but he didn't try to force me."

"Honorable," Freddie muttered. "Did you see him again after you refused?"

She shook her head. "I never heard from him again."

"How did you feel about that?" Sam asked.

"I was sad, devastated. I thought we had something special, and then it was just…over. Like you said. For a few weeks, I felt like Cinderella. It was right out of a fairy tale."

"But he wasn't your Prince Charming," Freddie said.

"No."

"Did he ever ask you about bringing other people into your sexual relationship?" Sam asked.

Tara's face lit up, her cheeks flaming. Bingo.

"Ms. Davenport?"

"Once," she said softly. "He said it would be amazing for me to have two guys at the same time." A shudder rippled through Tara's petite frame.

"Did it seem to you that he'd done that before?"

"Yes."

"And you said what to this request?"

"I told him that I was perfectly satisfied with just him. He seemed annoyed that I said no."

"That must've been disappointing," Sam said.

"It was."

"Were you disappointed enough to kill him, Ms. Davenport?"

She blanched. "*Kill him?* You think I *killed* him?"

Her shock was so genuine that it all but knocked her off the list of suspects. "If you could just answer the question."

"No, I wasn't disappointed enough to kill him. I didn't kill him."

"Have you told anyone else about why your relationship with the senator ended?"

"No. It's not something I'd ever talk about with even my closest friends. It's mortifying, to be honest."

"How did you feel when you heard he was dead?"

"Sad. I was overwhelmed with sadness. But to be honest, I wasn't entirely surprised that someone killed him. If you treat people the way he treated me, it's going to catch up to you eventually."

"I need you to stay available and in town for the time being."

"I'm working through the holidays," she said, her voice flat, devoid of hope or animation. "I'll be here."

"I have trouble understanding his type," Freddie said when they left the restaurant.

"You would. Do you think he was gay?"

"And in the closet? Working it out on women?"

"He certainly went for a type. The porcelain blonde. No way Tara is strong enough to get a knife through him on one stroke."

"I was thinking that very same thing." He paused and seemed to be pondering something. "So you know how we always joke that we spend more time together than we do with our own families?"

"*You're* the joker. I'm the serious law enforcement professional."

"Yeah, whatever."

"Your point?"

"I've known you a long time. Partnered with you over a year."

"Do you have a point? 'Cause if you could get to it in this decade, I'd like to get back to work."

"I have a point," he huffed. "It's just when she mentioned Cappuano in there, your face got all red and you had to take your coat off."

"I was hot! So what?"

"You were *flustered*. And you're *never* flustered."

Her stomach picked that moment to make its presence known. *Never flustered? Ha!* She spent half her life flustered but apparently did a good job of hiding it.

Freddie stopped on the sidewalk and turned to her. "Tell me the truth, Sam. Are you into him?"

She chose her words carefully. "The job, it takes almost everything I have. I work, I take care of my father, I help my sisters with their kids whenever I can. That's my life."

"Do you think I'd begrudge you wanting more?" His warm brown eyes flashed with emotion. "You think that?"

"He's off limits. There's no point talking about something I can't have."

"Why can't you have him?"

"He's a witness! He found O'Connor. He'll be wrapped up in this until sentencing."

"He didn't kill anyone. He's on our side."

She shook her head. "It's a murky ethical pit, and you know it."

"You're right. It's not clean. Few things in life ever are. But he wants this closed as much as we do, if not more. He *flusters* you, Sam. That's an amazing thing, if you ask me."

"I'd say *unsettling* is a better word." Glancing up at him, she added, "You won't say anything about this at HQ, will you?"

"Give me some credit, and while you're at it, ask your friend Cappuano if there's any chance the senator was gay."

"He'll say no."

"Humor me, and before you drag me into another interview that includes questions about peculiar sexual appetites, you're going to have to do something about mine."

She turned up her nose. "Your sexual appetite?"

"Nope." He chuckled and rubbed his belly. "The other one."

Sam pulled rank, insisted they have lunch at a vegetarian sandwich shop and was treated to Freddie's vociferous complaints about the lack of grease.

"Can't even get a stinking French fry in this place," he muttered as Sam downed her small veggie sub and wondered if it really had fewer than six grams of fat. No doubt every gram would find its way to her ass.

"If you're done sulking, we need to hit Total Fitness on Sixteenth."

He raised an eyebrow. "Are you taking up working out to go with this diet you're on?"

"Just because I choose to eat healthily doesn't mean I'm on a diet. Another of the senator's ladies works at the gym as a personal trainer." She consulted her notebook. "Elin Svendsen."

Freddie perked right up. "Swedish?"

"Sounds like it."

"Blonde, buff *and* Swedish? This day is suddenly on the upswing."

"Why, Freddie, I thought you were above such base human emotions as lust."

"Just because I'm choosy doesn't mean I don't enjoy a little eye candy as much as the next guy."

"This insight into the male psyche is fascinating. Truly."

"I'm here to serve."

Elin Svendsen was not only buff, she looked like she'd be capable of kicking some serious ass when provoked. Easily five-ten or -eleven, with white blonde hair, icy blue eyes and a figure that could stop a train dead on its tracks, Sam decided she wouldn't want to meet up with Elin in a dark alley.

They caught her between clients and followed her into the club's juice bar, which wasn't due to open for another hour. They declined her offer of fruit smoothies.

"Do you mind if I make one for myself? My energy is starting to flag. Been a long morning."

"Not at all," Sam said. "Do *you* mind if we record this?"

"Nope."

Noticing Freddie had his eyes glued to Elin's every movement, Sam nudged him to get his head back in the game.

He replied with a chagrined smile.

Elin joined them at the table with a strawberry smoothie. "If you're here to ask if I killed John O'Connor, I didn't."

"Where were you the night of the murder, between ten p.m. and seven a.m.?"

"I had a date and was home by two or so."

"Alone?"

She nodded.

"Your date's name?"

"Jimmy Chen. He's a member here. We go out once in a while. No biggie."

"You never left your house after you got home?"

"Not until I left for work the next morning."

"Where did you meet the senator?"

"Here. He hired me to train him, we hit it off, one thing led to another…"

"And how long ago was this?"

"Three or four months ago." Sam did some quick

math and realized he was seeing Elin and Tara at the same time.

"Do you have a key to his apartment?"

"I set him up with some home workout equipment, and he gave me a key so I could get in when he was at work to put it together."

"Did you give the key back to him?"

She thought about that for a moment. "You know, I don't think I ever did. Hmmm."

With a glance, Sam handed the ball to Freddie.

"Oh, um, what was the nature of your relationship with the senator, Ms. Svendsen?" he asked.

Sam had never seen him so tongue-tied around a woman and planned to poke at him about it the moment they left.

"Mostly we had sex."

Freddie's face flushed with embarrassment.

Sam sat back to enjoy the show. Folding her arms, she sent the message that she had no plans to bail him out.

"Could you, or I mean, would you mind if I asked you to be more specific about the, ah, sex you had with the senator?" Using Sam's words, he added, "Was it, um, the usual deal or more?"

Seeming to cue in to Freddie's exquisite discomfort, Elin smiled as she leaned toward him. "It was more, Detective. Much more. We were very well matched sexually."

Freddie cleared his throat.

"Were you still tearing up the sheets with the senator when he was killed?" Sam asked, realizing they were going to be there all day if she waited for Freddie to get on with it.

"No, we called it off a month or so ago."

"Whose doing?"

"Mine." She shrugged. "I was getting bored. It was time to move on."

"How did he take it when you ended it?"

"He was fine with it. This wasn't a love match, Sergeant. It was purely physical."

"Did he ever try to bring other people into the relationship."

"He did more than try." Elin seemed to be enjoying the effect she was having on Freddie. "We had a couple of memorable threesomes."

Sam glanced at Freddie to find his mouth hanging halfway open. She wanted to smack it shut.

"Male or female?" Sam asked.

"One of each on two separate occasions."

"Who sought out the extra parties?" Sam asked.

"I did. I know a lot of people from working here, and it was easier for me in light of who he was."

"What was his interaction with the other guy?"

"Hardly any. He was for me, not John."

"So John didn't have any kind of sex with him?"

Elin thought about that for a minute. "I think the guy sucked John's dick, but John didn't do anything to him."

"Did these 'extras' know who he was?"

"Nope. We just introduced him as 'John.' We didn't get into our life stories."

Sam left her with the standard line about staying available.

"Detectives?" Elin said as they headed for the door. They turned back to her.

"He wasn't 'the one' for me, but he was a good guy. He didn't deserve to be murdered."

Sam nodded and pushed open the door, thinking the definition of "good guy" was all a matter of perspective.

"Did you enjoy that?" Freddie snapped the moment they were back in the cold air.

"Enjoy what?"

"Making me ask her those questions."

Sam stopped and turned to face him. "If you can't ask the questions, *any* question, *any* time, you shouldn't be carrying a gold shield, Detective."

"You're right." He sagged a bit as the anger seemed to leave him all at once. "I know you are, but it's just so freaking embarrassing asking a woman I've never met about what kind of sex she had with a dead senator."

"You think I like it any more than you do? It's part of the job. The best way to figure out who killed him is to figure out who and what he was."

"You're right, and I apologize for going queasy on you. It won't happen again."

"Yes, it will," she said with a sigh. "The day it doesn't bother you to ask those kind of questions is the day you're no longer Freddie Cruz. It's supposed to bother you. Just don't let it stop you from doing what needs to be done."

"I won't," he vowed. "See what I mean about learning from you? That's what I meant. Right there."

"Kiss my ass, Cruz."

"While that's a lovely offer and one I take very seriously, I don't think it would be appropriate in light of our professional relationship. You know, with you being my superior officer and all."

She used her best withering look to shut him up. "If you're quite through, can we go see what Noel Jordan has to say about his wife's ex?"

"One thing we can say for Svendsen is that she certainly would've had the strength to get that knife through him in one shot."

"No doubt. And she had a key."

"The part about her breaking up with him threw me, though. I can see her being pissed if he dumped her, like he did with Davenport, but if she's the one who pulled the plug, what's her motive in offing him?"

"That's only her side of the story. Who knows how it really went down? She can tell us she dumped him because he's not here to refute it."

"Here again, I find myself learning from you."

"Keep that up and you're going to piss me off. I like her for the murder. So far, more than anyone else, I like her."

"I liked her, too," he joked.

"I could tell by the tongue hanging out of your face, but she's too scary and experienced for an innocent boy like you. She'd chew you up and spit you out."

"And that would be bad how exactly?"

"Pardon me while I get busy poking out my mind's eye."

18

Gonzo called as they made their way toward the Justice Department on Pennsylvania Avenue.

"What've you got?" Sam asked.

"Nothing so far at the cabin, but I did that run you asked for on Robert O'Connor. Sixty-five years old, lives in Mechanicsville with his wife Sally, age sixty-three. They have three grown children—Sarah, forty, Thomas, thirty-six and Michael, thirty-four. Five grandchildren."

"Son of a bitch," Sam muttered. "They lied to me."

"Do you want me to do some more digging?"

"No, that's okay. Were you able to get pictures of the kids?"

"Yeah, I shot them to your email."

"Thanks, Gonzo. Let me know if you turn up anything at the cabin."

"It's slow going. I'll call you when we're done."

"Who lied to you?" Freddie asked when she had ended the call.

"O'Connor's parents." She explained about the photo she had found at the cabin. "I think John had a son they swept under the rug. I'm going to Chicago tomorrow to find out."

"Want me to tag along?"

"No, I can take this one alone. I need you to confirm the info we got from Davenport and Svendsen about the people they were with the night of the murder. I'd also like you to check security at both their buildings. See if you can catch them coming home that night—or more importantly, going back out."

"Got it," he said, making notes. "I would've done that run you had Gonzo do."

"Don't pout, Freddie. An investigation of this magnitude requires we make use of all available resources."

After navigating building security and handing over their weapons—something that always left Sam feeling twitchy—she and Freddie were escorted to Jordan's office. As special assistant attorney general, he sat right next door to the attorney general himself. Jordan was tall with an athletic build, short blond hair that looked like it would be wildly curly if left to grow and sharp blue eyes. He wore a dark pinstriped suit that had clearly been cut just for him. *Nothing off-the-rack for this guy*, Sam thought, as she noted his almost startling resemblance to John O'Connor. Apparently, the late senator wasn't the only one who went for a "type."

"Detectives," he said, standing to shake their hands. He gestured for them to make use of the chairs in front of his desk. "What can I do for you?"

"You're aware that your wife had a long-term relationship with Senator O'Connor?"

"I am."

"Did she ever talk to you about him?"

"Occasionally, but nothing more than an off-hand comment or two. She respects me too much to throw him in my face. My wife and I are happily married, and none of our former relationships factor into our marriage."

"Did you ever meet the senator?"

"A few times. I'm active in the Virginia Democratic Party, and obviously he was as well."

"Did you like him?"

"I didn't dislike him, but neither would I say we were anything more than casual acquaintances. So he dated my wife? Big deal. She's a beautiful woman who had several relationships before me. I don't expect that her life—or mine—began the day we met. Although," he said, softening, "in many ways, mine did begin with her."

"Can you confirm your whereabouts on the night of the murder? Tuesday between ten p.m. and seven a.m.?"

He consulted a brown leather book. "On Tuesday evening we attended the annual Christmas fund-raiser/silent auction for the Capital Region Big Brothers and Big Sisters here in the city. We were home by ten, in bed by ten-thirty. We made love and went to sleep. Is that enough information?"

"Has your wife ever mentioned anything about her relationship with the senator that made her uncomfortable?"

For the first time, Jordan's cool composure wavered. "Uncomfortable in what way?"

"Any way."

"No, but like I said, we've never felt the need to share the intimate details of our past relationships."

When Sam stood up, Freddie followed her lead. "I know you had plans to be out of town for the holidays," she said, "but you'll need to remain in the area."

"I'm due to leave for Europe on the third of January. Work-related travel."

"Hopefully by then we'll have cleared this up. Until we do, you and your wife are required to stay local."

"Thoughts?" she asked Freddie after they had reclaimed their weapons. Relieved to have her gun back, Sam slid hers into her hip harness.

"First, he knew we were coming. Had that appointment book nice and handy."

"No doubt the wife tipped him. But guess what? He lied about one thing."

"What's that?"

"The Big Brothers/Big Sisters thing?"

Freddie nodded.

"That was *last* Tuesday. I know because I was there."

Freddie released a low whistle.

"It doesn't mean one of them killed the senator, though. It only means there's something he doesn't want us to know or his date book is messed up. We still can't place either of them at the Watergate."

"So we file this tidbit away and continue to work the case?"

"Exactly. The thing between the senator and Natalie was over years ago. Where's the motive?"

"True," Freddie said.

"My take is that he's crazy in love with her, still wonders how he ever managed to snag her and he's glad O'Connor's dead. He didn't kill him, but he sees it as a favor that someone else did."

"So you think he was threatened by the senator?"

"Big time," Freddie said. "He knows he wasn't the love of Natalie's life."

"Good. That's good. Crazy how much he looks like O'Connor, huh?"

"I'd say *creepy* would be a better word."

"Agreed. I want you to look into those 'other relationships' of hers that he referred to. Find out if any of the other men in her life met with an untimely demise, and while you're at it, do a search for unsolved cases involving dismemberment. The senator might not have been the first."

"Local or national?"

"Start local and see what pops. I'll be authorizing overtime for both of us, so while you're at it, get me everything you can find on the three women we met today. No detail is too big or too small. If they have a tattoo, I want to know what it is and where."

"Tramp stamps," he wrote as she snickered at the term. "Got it. You're really sure it was a woman, aren't you?"

"Every fiber of my being tells me this was a love affair gone very wrong."

"Or someone wants us to *think* that."

"We can't rule that out," she conceded.

"In light of what we've learned today, we also can't rule out that it might've been a love affair with a *man* that went very wrong."

"Right again," she said. "Nothing is ever as cut and dried as we'd like it to be, is it?"

"Nope."

"You've had a few girlfriends."

"So?" he said warily.

"Don't you compare notes on past relationships?"

His face flooded with color. "Depends on how serious it is with the new one and whether or not she asks."

"Is it weird that Natalie Jordan never told her husband that things got kinky with the senator?"

"I don't know, Sam. That falls into a serious gray area. What guy would want to know that his woman did it *all* with the ex?"

"Hmm. It just seems strange to me that she's never even alluded to it. I mean, they're *married*. And you saw his face. He had no idea what I was talking about."

"Did you share that kind of stuff with Peter?"

"Bad example. We weren't your typical married couple."

"Sorry to dredge up the past, but I think you'd be in a better position to answer your own questions than I would be, having never been married myself."

"Yeah, I guess, but I hardly had the kind of marriage where major sharing factored in."

"So what's next?" he asked, seeming anxious to change the subject.

"I need to go back to HQ, write up what we have so far, and deal with the brass on this thing with the Johnson case."

"What'll you do if they put you under?"

"*If* they do, it'll only be for a couple of days at most—one of those days I'll be in Chicago, another one we're taking off because we'll need to recharge, and then Monday is the senator's funeral. With all the local police and Secret Service who'll be there, I can't imagine they'll stop me from going. I can pull the strings from the sidelines, but I'm not letting it go."

"Even if they order you to?"

"Especially then."

"Righteous."

Back at her desk, Sam downed a soda, opened the email Gonzo had sent, and discovered the real Thomas O'Connor was a thirty-six-year-old man with dark hair and eyes. She made a note to ask Nick whether John had ever mentioned having a cousin of the same age. Regardless, the man on her screen was not the boy in the picture, and she now had positive confirmation that Graham and Laine O'Connor had lied to her about the boy. But why? Why would they deny their own grandchild? Sam had no idea, but she intended to find out.

Her stomach clenched with pain as she read—and

then re-read—an email from the chief's admin, confirming her four o'clock appointment. Checking her watch, she realized she had just a few minutes to get there on time. She stood up, but the pain had other ideas. Collapsing back into her chair, she put her head down and tried to breathe her way through it. A bead of sweat slid down her back.

This was a bad one, but it had been getting progressively worse over the last few months despite her best efforts to ignore it. Sooner or later, she was going to have to do something about this "nervous stomach" situation, possibly even give up diet cola as she'd been told to do. But not now. No time for that now. When the worst of the pain had passed, she tested her shaky legs, took another long deep breath and set out for the chief's office.

She was waved right in but stopped short just inside the door. When Farnsworth called in the brass, he called in the brass. Seated in a wide half-circle in front of Farnsworth's desk were Deputy Chief Conklin, Detective Captain Malone, Lieutenant Stahl and Assistant U.S. Attorney Miller. Sam glanced at Miller's shoes, saw the stiletto heel, and confirmed it was Charity, one of the identical triplets who worked for the U.S. Attorney. Neither Faith nor Hope would be caught dead in stilettos.

"Well," Sam said, as the pain resurfaced with an ugly vengeance. Determined to stay cool, she took shallow breaths and slipped into the remaining chair. "You didn't tell me we were having a party, Chief. I would've brought snacks."

"Sergeant," Farnsworth said, his handsome face tight with stress that only added to Sam's. "Before we get into the Johnson matter, go ahead and brief us on the status of the O'Connor investigation."

Folding her hands tightly in her lap, she brought them up to speed, holding back the details about the senator's peculiar sexual appetites. She had decided to do her best to keep that out of the official record in deference to his parents and family.

"So almost seventy-two hours out, we don't have so much as a suspect?" Stahl said.

Sam made an effort not to show him what a jackass she thought him to be. "We have several individuals of interest we're actively pursuing. In addition, I believe the senator had a son who was kept hidden from the public. I request permission to travel tomorrow to Chicago to further investigate this thread."

"How's it relevant?" Stahl snapped.

Repulsed by the roll of fat around his belly and the huge double chin that wiggled when he talked, Sam said, "If it's true, the senator's relationship with the mother could be very relevant."

"I'll authorize the travel," Malone said, pulling rank on Stahl who fumed in silence.

"Thank you, Captain," Sam said.

"The Feds are sniffing around," Farnsworth said. "I've managed to hold them off thus far, but with every passing day, it's getting harder."

"Understood. We're moving as fast as we can."

"All available resources are at your disposal, Sergeant," Farnsworth added. "Use whatever you need."

"Yes, sir. Thank you."

"Now, on the other matter, we've got Mrs. Johnson on a seventy-two-hour hold."

"You aren't planning to charge her, are you, sir?" Sam asked.

"AUSA Miller is considering charges."

"If I may, sir," Sam said. "While no one would mistake Destiny Johnson for mother of the year, I have no doubt her heartbreak is genuine."

"That doesn't give her the right to threaten the life of a police officer," Farnsworth said.

"She has good reason to be pissed with Sergeant Holland and the department," Stahl said.

"Lieutenant, I find your attitude counterproductive," Farnsworth said. "You can get back to work."

"But—"

Captain Malone flipped his thumb toward the door.

With an infuriated glance at Sam, Stahl hauled himself out of the chair and waddled to the door. After it closed behind him, Farnsworth returned his attention to Sam. "We have to take her threats seriously, Sergeant. You're extremely vulnerable in the field, so until you've testified on Tuesday, we're putting you under. Limited duty, permission to work from home, no field work."

"Since I'm going to Chicago tomorrow, taking Sunday off, and attending the senator's funeral on Monday, that shouldn't be a problem."

"About the funeral…" Deputy Chief Conklin said.

"I believe the local and federal security required to bring in the president will be sufficient to protect a lowly District sergeant," Sam said with what she hoped was a confident smile.

"The Secret Service will have to be made aware of the threat and your planned presence at the service," Conklin said. "I'll take care of that."

"Appreciate it," Farnsworth said. He leaned forward to address Sam. "I want you to take this very seriously. Johnson has a lot of friends, and all of them—fairly or unfairly—blame you for what happened in that house. They don't care that you didn't fire the shot. They care that you gave the order."

"Yes, sir." Since she blamed herself, too, she could understand where they were coming from.

"AUSA Miller, has Sergeant Holland been adequately prepared for Tuesday's court appearance?"

"She has, Chief. We've been through it several times, and she's never wavered from her initial statement."

"I'll let you get back to work then," Farnsworth said. "Thanks for being here."

"No problem." With an encouraging smile for Sam, Charity got up and left the room.

"If there's nothing else, I've got a few more threads to tie up before my tour ends," Sam said.

"There's just one more thing," Farnsworth said, reaching for a file on his desk.

Sam refused to acknowledge the twinge of pain that hovered in her gut. "Sir?"

"I had lunch with your father earlier this week."

"Yes, sir, he mentioned that. I know he appreciates your visits." To the others, she added, "All of you."

"And I know you go out of your way to downplay your family's history with this department."

"I don't want nor do I expect special treatment because of the rank my father attained prior to being injured in the line."

Farnsworth replied with a hint of a smile. "Regardless, he was curious as to whether I'd gotten the results of the lieutenant's exam."

Just those words were enough to override any success she'd had in keeping the pain at bay. It roared through her, leaving her breathless in its wake. When she was able to speak again, she said, "I'm aware it's a source of embarrassment to my father and to you as my superior officers that I've been unable to pass the exam on two previous attempts."

"What I'd like to know is why the fact that you're

dyslexic isn't mentioned anywhere in your personnel file."

Stunned, Sam opened her mouth and then closed it when the words simply wouldn't come.

"I've done some basic research on dyslexia and discovered that standardized tests are one of the dyslexic's greatest foes."

"Yes, but—"

"Allow me to finish, Sergeant. I have to admit this information was a relief to me." He gestured to the deputy chief and captain. "To all of us. We've been hard pressed to understand how the best detective on this force has been unable to attain a rank that should've been hers some time ago."

"I...um..."

"You passed this time," Farnsworth said. "Just barely—but you did pass."

Sam stared at him, wondering if she had heard him correctly.

He rifled through some other papers until he found what he was looking for. "With the distinct exception of Lt. Stahl, you've received outstanding superior officer recommendations, high marks on your interviews and evaluations. We also factored in the graduate degree in criminal justice you earned from George Washington. All in all, you make for an ideal candidate for promotion." He looked up at her. "Under my discretion as chief of police, I'm pleased to inform you that your name will be included in the next group of lieutenants."

"But, sir," Sam stammered, "people will talk. They'll scream favoritism."

"You met the criteria. The test score is only one element, and no one but the people in this room will know it was low."

"I'll know," she said softly.

"Sergeant, do you believe you've earned the rank of lieutenant?"

"If I didn't, I wouldn't have sat for the exam in the first place, but—"

"Then you should have no further objection to a promotion you have earned and deserve. You'll be taking command of the detective squad at HQ."

Staggered, Sam stared at him. "But that's Lieutenant Stahl's command."

"He's being transferred to internal affairs."

The rat squad, Sam thought, her stomach grinding under the fist she had balled tight against it. "You're setting me up to have a powerful enemy."

"Lieutenant Stahl is skating on very thin ice these days," Captain Malone said. "I don't believe he'll give you any trouble, and if he does, he'll deal with us. Let me add my congratulations, Sergeant, on a well-earned and highly deserved promotion. I look forward to working with you in your new role."

"Thank you, sir," Sam said, still shocked as she shook his outstretched hand and then Conklin's.

"Ditto," Conklin said, following Malone from the room. "You've earned it."

"Thank you, sir."

When they were alone, Sam turned to the chief.

"You'll piss me off if you ask if this is because I'm your chief or your Uncle Joe," he said, his tone full of friendly warning.

"I was just going to say thank you," Sam said with a smile that quickly faded. "Will the, ah, dyslexia be added to my jacket?"

"It'll remain your personal business, provided it continues to have no bearing on your ability to do the job."

"It won't."

Farnsworth sat back in his big chair and studied her.

"I have to ask how you managed to get two degrees while battling dyslexia."

"I got lucky with professors who worked with me, but everything took me twice as long as it took everyone else. And I've always choked on standardized tests. I just can't get them done in the time allotted."

"I can only imagine how much harder you've had to work to compensate. Knowing that only adds to my respect for you and your work." He stood up, came around the big desk, and offered his hand. "Congratulations."

Sam's throat closed as her hand was enfolded between both of his. "Thank you, sir. I'll do my very best to be worthy."

"I have no doubt. Let me know what you uncover in Chicago."

"I will, sir. Thank you again. For everything." She closed the door behind her, managed a nod to the chief's admin, and made for the nearest ladies' room. The relief, the sheer overwhelming relief, left her staggered. She gave herself ten minutes to fall apart before she pulled it together, wiped her face and blew her nose.

Studying her reflection in the mirror, she whispered, "Lieutenant," as if to try it on for size. For once her stomach had no comment. Taking that as a positive sign, she splashed cold water on her face and decided to leave on time for a change. The report could be written and transmitted from home. Besides, she needed to go tell the only other person in the world who would care as much as she did that she would soon become Lieutenant Holland.

19

Before Sam could call for him, she heard the chair.

"What's this? Home on time?"

She went to him, rested her hands on his shoulders and was startled to encounter sharp bones where thick muscle used to be. Jarred by the discovery, she bent to kiss his forehead. Eye to eye, she said, "I should be furious with you."

"For?"

"Don't play coy with me."

"It should've been in your jacket. From day one. I've always said that."

"It wasn't for a reason. I don't want people feeling sorry for me or treating me differently. You know how I feel about it."

"That fierce pride of yours is only going to get you so far."

"And my daddy is going to get me the rest of the way?"

"I simply gave him a piece of information he didn't have. What he did or didn't do with it was up to him."

"No, Dad, it was up to *me*. I don't want you interfering in my career. How many times do I have to say it before you get the message?"

"I've been duly chastised. Now, are you going to tell me what he did with it?"

"Not until you've suffered a little first. What's for dinner?"

He followed her to the kitchen. "That's mean, Sam."

"Are you being mean to your father again?" Celia asked.

"Believe me, he deserves it. Oh, jeez, is that *roast beef?*"

"Sure is. Are you hungry?"

"Starving. I didn't even realize it until right this very minute." She peeked into a pot and groaned. "Mashed potatoes? God, my ass is growing just smelling it."

"Now you stop that," Celia said as she served the meal. "You have a lovely figure that I'd kill for. How was your day?"

"The usual chaos."

"Nothing special?" Skip asked. "Nothing different?"

Sam pretended to give that some significant thought. "Not really. Freddie and I are working the case, pulling the threads. Got a couple of good angles to pursue."

"What are they doing about Johnson?" Skip asked.

Hanging on their every word, Celia fed him and herself with a practiced hand.

"I was ordered to 'lay low' until I testify on Tuesday."

"To which you said…?"

She shrugged. "I'm fine with it. I have to go to Chicago tomorrow, I'm taking most of Sunday off, and have the funeral on Monday. I should be fine."

"Should be isn't good enough." He swallowed, cleared his throat and turned his steely blue eyes on his daughter. "Anything else happen at your meeting with Farnsworth?"

Deciding she had tortured him long enough, she said, "Oh, you mean about the promotion?"

He growled.

"I got it." She took another bite of mashed potatoes and tried not to think about the calories. "You can soon call me Lieutenant, Chief."

"Yes," he whispered. "Yes, indeed."

"Oh that's wonderful, Sam!" Celia jumped up to hug and kiss her. "That's just wonderful, isn't it, Skip?"

He never took his eyes off his daughter. "It sure is. Come give your old man a hug."

Pained that he'd had to ask and embarrassed by Celia's effusiveness, Sam got up and did her best to work around the chair. With her lips close to his ear, she whispered, "Thank you."

"For?"

Sam pulled back to smile at him. "Love you."

"When you're not being mean to me, I love you, too."

Two hours later, Sam was laboring her way through the report of the day's activities on her laptop when Celia knocked on the door.

"Sorry to interrupt your work, but I thought you might enjoy some warm apple pie. It's so darned cold out."

Sam moaned. "Tell me it's fat free, calorie free and can't find an ass with a roadmap."

Chuckling, Celia handed her the plate. "All of the above. I swear."

"If the nursing gig doesn't pan out, you might consider a life of crime. You're a convincing liar."

"You've made your father very proud tonight, Sam. He's always proud of you, but he wanted this promotion for you. More, I think, than you wanted it for yourself."

"I don't doubt it." Sam used a finger to swirl a dollop

of whipped cream off the pie and pop it into her mouth. "Sometimes I feel so selfish where he's concerned."

Celia lowered herself to the edge of Sam's bed. "How do mean? You're here for him every day, despite a demanding, time-consuming job."

"It would've been better…for him anyway…if the shot had been fatal. I can't imagine how he stands living the way he does, confined to four small rooms and wherever he can go in the van the union bought him. But I wasn't ready to lose him, Celia. Not then and not now. I thank God every day that bullet didn't kill him. As much as I hate the way he has to live now, I'm so grateful he's still here."

"In his own way, he's accepted it and come to terms."

"I wish you could've known him." Sam sighed. "Before."

"I did," Celia said with a smile, her pretty face blazing with color and her green eyes dancing with mirth.

"You've never told me that! Neither of you ever did!"

"I met him at the Giant, about two years before he was wounded. I helped him pick some tomatoes in the produce aisle, he asked me out for coffee and that was the start of a lovely friendship."

Sam slipped into detective mode as she narrowed her eyes. "Just friends?"

Laughing, Celia said, "I'll never tell."

"You dirty dogs! How did you slide this by me? By everyone?"

"You weren't looking," Celia said, her expression smug. "Why do you think I asked to be assigned to his case?"

"You love him," Sam said, incredulous.

"Very much. In fact, we've been talking about maybe…getting married."

Sam's mouth fell open. "Seriously? You said he's been down lately, worried about something. Is this it?"

"It's one of several things. He's been terribly upset about what happened to you in the Johnson case and fretting over your safety as well as the promotion he thinks you've been due for some time now."

"I wish he wouldn't spend so much time worrying about me."

"Sam," she said with a smile. "You're his life. His heart. He loves your sisters and their children very much, but you…"

"I know. I've always known that."

"And you've always struggled to live up to it."

Startled, Sam stared at her. "Been doing a lot more than nursing around here, haven't you?"

"I hope I haven't overstepped."

"Of course you haven't. You're already family, Celia. I don't know what we would've done without you the last two years."

"So you wouldn't mind too much if I married him?"

Sam put down the plate and reached for the older woman's hand. "If you make him happy and can bring some joy to whatever time he has left, the only thing I can do is thank you for that."

"Thank *you*," Celia said, her eyes bright with emotion. "It matters to him, to both of us, that you'd approve."

"I guess I need to get busy looking for another place to keep my clothes."

"Why?"

"You crazy kids won't want me underfoot."

"He wants you to stay. We both do. There's no reason for you to move out. I'll take one of the other bedrooms up here. We'll work it out. I'm here most of the time anyway. I don't expect much will change."

"This'll change everything for him, Celia. It'll give him a reason to keep fighting."

"Perhaps. I'll consider myself blessed for whatever time we get."

"Did he bully you into telling me?"

"He was afraid it would upset you, so I offered."

"You can tell him that not only am I fine with it, I'm thrilled for him. For both of you."

"That means a lot, Sam. I'm tired of hiding it. He's the most remarkable man I've ever known and the best friend I've ever had."

"Ditto," Sam said with a smile as Celia got up to leave. "Thanks for the pie."

"My pleasure. Don't work too hard."

When she was alone, Sam had to resist the urge to call her sisters to share the huge scoop that had just fallen into her lap. "Not my news to tell," she muttered, deciding that maturity wasn't much fun at all.

While Celia's news had surprised her, Sam realized it shouldn't have. With hindsight, she could see there was something special between her father and his devoted nurse. Their banter, the carefree caresses Celia showered him with even though he couldn't feel them, the genuine affection.

Comforted by Celia's disclosures, Sam finished the pie and turned back to her report. She ran through it twice more before she sent it off to Freddie, who always checked them for her before she passed them up the food chain. If he wondered about the random mistakes, odd phrasings or twisted wording, he never said. Rather, he corrected the errors and returned the reports to her without comment.

Might be time to bring him into the loop, she thought. Dyslexia had cast its long net over every corner of her life, and until its diagnosis in sixth grade, she had believed herself to be as stupid as she was made to feel by teachers who had no idea what to do with her and parents who had been frustrated by her less-than-stellar performance in school.

Giving it a name had helped somewhat, but the daily struggles that went along with it were exhausting at times.

With the report finished, she finally allowed her thoughts to drift to Nick. As if floodgates had opened, she was overwhelmed by emotions and yearnings she had managed to resist all day. She had a list of questions she wanted to run by him, so she had every reason to take out the card he had given her. The call was about the case, right? There was nothing wrong with reaching out to him in a strictly official capacity. If she was also dying to tell him about her promotion and her father's pending marriage, what did that matter?

She flipped the card back and forth between her fingers for several minutes until her stomach twisted with the start of the dreaded pain. Thinking of the case and *only* the case, she dialed his cell number.

He sounded groggy when he answered.

"Oh God, did I wake you?"

"No, no." A huge yawn made a liar out of him. "I was hoping you'd call."

Deciding to keep it strictly business, she said, "I have some questions. About the case."

"Oh."

She winced at the disappointment reverberating from that single syllable. "You sound… I don't know… kind of lousy."

"It's been a lousy day, except for the very beginning when I was with you."

Without saying much of anything he had managed to

say it all. And she knew she couldn't tell him what she needed to tell him over the phone. "You're at home?"

"Uh huh."

"Do you mind if I come by? Just for a minute?"

"Are *you* at home?"

"At the moment."

"You're just going to 'drop by' all the way over here in Arlington? And only for a minute?"

"I need to talk to you, Nick. I need… Oh hell, I don't even know what I need."

"Come. I'll be waiting. And, babe? You don't ever, *ever* have to ask first. Got me?"

She melted into a sloppy, messy puddle of need and want and desire. "Yeah," she managed to say. "I'll be there. Soon." Her heart doing back flips, Sam reached for her weapon, badge and cuffs. She released her hair to brush out the kinks and primped for a few more minutes before she headed downstairs to tell her dad she was going into work for a while. Celia told her he was already asleep.

"He was especially tired tonight." She held Sam's coat for her. "You'll be careful, won't you?"

"Always." Impulsively, she turned to kiss Celia's cheek on her way to the front door. "See you."

He'd turned on the outside light for her. A simple thing, but it evoked such a powerful sense of homecoming that Sam sat there for several minutes reminding herself of why she was there—and why she wasn't. "It can't be about you," she whispered. "Not now. This is about finding justice for John O'Connor. Nothing more."

But when Nick came to the door looking so…well… *lost* was the best word she could think of, nothing else mattered but him.

"Nick." Closing the door behind her, she let her coat drop to the floor and reached for him.

They stood there, arms wrapped around each other, comfort seeping through to warm the chill she had brought in with her.

Raising her hands to his face, she looked up at him. "What is it?"

Shrugging, he said, "Everything." He leaned his forehead against hers. "I've gone from having every minute of every day programmed to not knowing what the hell to do with myself, which gives me way too much time to think."

Even after what she had learned that day about John O'Connor, she was still able to feel Nick's pain over the loss of his friend and boss. Used to his unflappable, polished demeanor, seeing him disheveled in a ratty Harvard T-shirt and old sweats was jarring. Sometime in the course of that long day, the shock apparently wore off and gritty grief set in.

"I'm glad you're here." He shifted to press her against the closed door. "I've been worried about you. That stuff in the paper…"

"We're handling it."

"I don't like the idea of you being unsafe." The light caress of his hand on her cheek caused her heart to lurch. He leaned in, bringing with him the scent of spice and soap.

"Nick, wait—"

His lips came down hard and insistent on hers, sucking the breath from her lungs and the starch from her spine. If he hadn't been holding her up with the weight of his body, she might have slid to the floor. Somehow he maneuvered them so her legs were hooked over his hips, his hands were full of her breasts and his tongue was tangled up with hers—all in the scope of thirty seconds.

Having forgotten everything she'd vowed in the car the moment she saw his grief-stricken face, Sam wove her fingers through his damp, silky hair and pressed hard against his straining erection. Then they were moving, falling. She yelped against his lips and clung to him as he lowered them to the sofa.

Tearing at clothes, desperate for skin, for contact, for relief, they wrestled through layers until there was nothing left between them but raging desire.

"You're just like I remembered." His tongue darted in circles around her nipple, and his hands seemed to be everywhere at once. "Tall and curvy and strong... soft in all the right places." Nick gazed with reverence at breasts that had always seemed too big to her, but he appeared to like what he saw.

Need zipped through her, leaving her desperate and panting. "Nick..." She tugged at him to align them for what she wanted more than the next breath. "Now."

"Condom," he said through gritted teeth. "Wait a sec."

She stopped him from getting up. "I'm on the pill. We get tested—"

"So do we." He slid one arm under her shoulders while his other hand cupped her bottom and tilted her into position to receive him.

Overwhelmed by desire, Sam let her legs fall open to take him in.

He held her gaze as he entered her with one swift stroke.

She cried out as an orgasm ripped through her with more force and fury than anything she'd ever experienced.

He froze. "Oh, God, did I hurt you?"

"No, *no!* Don't stop. *Please.*"

Watching him, feeling him, there were no recriminations. There wasn't room for thoughts of anything but him as he began to move, slowly at first and then faster as his closely held control seemed to desert him. She remembered that from the last time, how he'd let go with her, in a way she suspected he didn't often allow himself.

With his arms wrapped tight around her, he pounded into her, the smack of flesh meeting flesh the only thing she could hear over the roar of her own heartbeat.

Sam met each thrust with equal ardor, and when he sucked hard on her nipple, she cried out with another climax that took him tumbling over with her.

"Jesus," he whispered when he'd recovered the ability. "Jesus Christ. I didn't even offer you something to drink."

She laughed and tightened the hold she had on him, letting one hand slide languidly through soft hair still damp from an earlier shower. "What kind of host does that make you?"

"A crappy one, I guess," he said, turning them over in a smooth move.

Stretched out on top of him, still joined with him, Sam breathed in his warm, masculine scent and reveled in the comfort of strong arms wrapped tight around her. It was almost disturbing to accept that she had never experienced anything even remotely close to this, except during the one night she spent with him so many years ago. How foolish she had been then to assume that what she'd shared with him would show up again with someone else. She was wise enough now, old enough, jaded enough, to know better.

But even as the woman continued to vibrate with aftershocks and tingle with the desire for more, the cop resurfaced with disgust and dismay. "This was a very bad idea," she muttered into his chest.

He curled a lock of her hair around his finger. "Depends on your perspective. From my point of view, it was the best idea I've had in six years."

Sam studied him. "It must be the politician in you."

Eyebrows knitting with confusion, he said, "What must?"

"The way you always seem to have the right words."

He framed her face with his big hands. "I'm not feeding you lines, Sam."

His sweet sincerity made her heart ache with something she refused to acknowledge. "I know." The emotions were so overwhelming and new to her, she did the first thing that came to mind. She tried to escape.

His arms clamped around her like a vise. "Not yet." He brushed his lips over hers in a gesture so tender it all but stopped her heart. Her eyes flooded with tears that she desperately tried to blink back.

"What?"

She shook her head.

"Sam."

Letting her eyes drift up to meet his, she said, "I like this. I know I shouldn't because of everything… but I like it."

"Sex on the sofa?"

"This." She had to look away. It was just too much. "You. Me. Us."

"So do I." He kissed her softly. "So does this mean we're together now?"

A stab of fear went through her. She just wasn't ready for the magnitude of what this had the potential to be. "Why does it need a label? Why can't it just be what it is?"

Once again, the flash of pain she saw on his face

bothered her more than it should have. "And what is it exactly, Sam? I want far more from you than just a sex buddy."

"That might be all I can give you right now."

He sighed. "I suppose I'll take whatever I can get." When his lips coasted up her neck, he made her shiver. "We could move this somewhere more comfortable. There's a big soft bed in the other room."

Her stomach ached as reality stepped in to remind her of why she'd needed to see him. "There're things we need to talk about. Stuff about the case."

"We'll get to it. Can I just have a few more minutes of this first?"

Because he seemed to need it so much, she said, "Okay."

20

The bed, as advertised, was big and soft. How he managed to coax her into it was something she planned to think about later when she reclaimed her sanity. It would be so easy, so very easy indeed, to curl into him and sleep the sleep of the dead. But the grinding sensation in her gut was an ever-present reminder of the conversation she needed to have with him.

"What's wrong?" he asked as his talented hand worked to ease the tension in her neck.

"Nothing, why?"

"I had you on the way to relaxed, and now you're all tight again."

"We need to talk."

"So you've said. I'm listening."

"I can't do cop work naked."

Laughing, he said, "Is that in the manual?"

"If it isn't, it should be."

Sitting up, he reached for the pile of their clothes he had deposited on the foot of the bed, found the T-shirt he'd been wearing when she arrived, and helped her into it. "Better?"

Engulfed in the shirt that carried his sexy, male scent, she was riveted by his muscular chest. "Um, except you're still naked."

"I'm not the cop." He reached for her hand, brought it to his lips. "Talk to me, Sam."

The dull ache sharpened in a matter of seconds.

"Something's wrong," he said, alarmed. "You just went totally pale."

"It's nothing." She tried and failed to take a deep breath. "Just this deal with my stomach."

"What deal?"

"It gives me some grief from time to time. It's nothing."

"Have you had it checked?"

"A couple of times," she squeaked out.

"Babe, God, you're in serious pain! What can I do?"

"Gotta breathe," she said as the pain clawed its way through her, making her feel sick and clammy. "Sorry."

"Don't be." He fitted himself around her, held her close and whispered soft words of comfort that eased her mind.

She closed her eyes, focused on the sound of his voice and drifted. The pain retreated, but the episode— worse than most—left her drained and embarrassed. "Sorry about that."

"I told you not to apologize. You have to do something about that. You might have an ulcer or something. I can get you in with my friend. He's awesome."

"It seems to crop up whenever I'm nervous about something, which I'm finding is fairly often."

"You're nervous about what you have to say to me?"

She tilted her head and found his pretty hazel eyes studying her intently. "I guess I am."

He sat up, propped the pillows behind him and snuggled her into his chest. "Then let's get it over with."

"Cops don't snuggle."

"Make an exception."

"I think I've already made quite a few," she said dryly.

"Make another one."

Before the pain could come back to remind her she was powerless against it, she took the plunge. "I have to ask you something. It's probably going to upset you, and I hate that, but I have to ask."

"Okay."

"Is there any chance John was gay? Or maybe bi?" She felt the tension creep into his body, and then just as quickly it was gone.

He laughed. He actually *laughed*. "No. Not only no, but *no fucking way*."

"How can you know that for sure? Some men hide it from their friends, their families…"

"I would've known, Sam. Believe me. I would've known."

"You didn't know he had a son."

And just that quickly he was tense again. "You don't know that, either."

"I'm all but certain of it. The picture?"

"What about it?"

"His parents lied. His cousin Thomas, the son of Robert O'Connor? He's thirty-six, dark hair, dark eyes." She sat up straighter and shifted so she could see his face. "Surely you must have heard him talk about a cousin who was the same age as him?"

Nick mulled that over. "I can't say I ever did. Maybe they weren't close. I don't think Graham and his brother are."

"Either way, the kid in the picture isn't his cousin. His mother lied to me today, and his father didn't refute it. The monthly payments—stretching twenty years— the weekly phone calls, catching his parents in a big, fat lie, the startling resemblance to the senator... It doesn't take a detective to add it all up, Nick."

"But why...wait." He went perfectly still. "One weekend a month."

Baffled, she said, "Excuse me?"

"He required one weekend a month with no commitments. Usually the third weekend. Never would say what he did with the time. In fact, he was always kind of weird about it, now that I think about it."

"And you just thought to mention this now? What the hell, Nick?"

"I'm sorry. It was just so much a part of our routine that I didn't think anything of it until right now."

"I bet if I do some digging, I'll find him booked on a regular flight to Chicago."

All the air seemed to leave Nick in one long exhale. "Why didn't he tell me? Why would he keep something like this hidden from me? From everyone?"

"I don't know, but I'm going out there tomorrow to find out."

"You are?"

"I'm on an eleven o'clock flight."

"Does she know you're coming?"

Sam shook her head. "Element of surprise. I don't want to give her time to put away the pictures or send the kid out of town."

"And you think this has something to do with his murder?"

"I can't say for sure until I've spoken to the mother, but for some reason they've kept him hidden away for twenty years. I want to know why."

"Politics, no doubt."

"How do you mean?"

"A teenaged son with a baby would've been a political liability to the senator. I should know. As the offspring of teenaged parents, I can attest to the embarrassment factor in a family with zero public presence."

Sam ached from the pain she heard in his voice.

"Graham O'Connor would've wanted this put away in a closet," he concluded.

"His own grandchild?"

"I don't think it would've mattered. The O'Connor name wasn't always the powerhouse it is now. He had a few contentious campaigns around the mid-point of his career. If the timing coincided, this could've ruined him. He would've acted accordingly."

"At the expense of his own family?"

"Power does strange things to people, Sam. It can be addicting. Once you get a taste of it, it's hard to give it up. I've always found Graham to be a kind and loving—albeit exacting—father, but he's as human as the next guy. He would've been susceptible to the seduction of power." Nick paused, as if he was pondering something else.

"What are you thinking?"

"I'm wondering how, considering you're certain he had a son, you also think he might've been gay."

"Just a vibe we've picked up on the investigation. Nothing concrete. I've told you my gut says it was a woman he'd wronged, but then Freddie goes and ruins that by pointing out that it could've just as easily been a love affair gone wrong with a guy."

Nick shook his head. "I can't imagine it. There was never anything, *anything* in almost twenty years of close friendship that would make me doubt his orientation. Nothing, Sam. He was a skirt-chasing hound."

"So I've discovered. But he wouldn't be the first guy to use that as a front to hide his real life."

"I suppose."

"You're upset. I'm sorry."

He shrugged. "It's just...you think you know someone, really know them, only to find out they had all these secrets. He had a son. A *child*. And in twenty years, he never mentions that to his closest friend? It's disappointing at the very least."

It was also a betrayal, she imagined. That the family he'd considered his own—his only—had kept something of this magnitude from him.

As if he could read her thoughts, he said, "Did they think I'd tell anyone?"

"You shouldn't take this personally, Nick. It won't do you any good."

"How else should I take it?"

Looping an arm around him, she bent to press her lips to his chest and felt the strong, steady beat of his heart. "I'm sorry this is hurting you. I hate that."

He enfolded her in his arms. "It goes down easier coming from you." Tilting her chin, he fused his mouth to hers.

"I should go," she said when they resurfaced.

"Stay with me. Sleep with me. I need you, Samantha." He dropped soft, wet kisses on her face and neck. "I need you."

"You're playing dirty."

"I'm not playing."

Something other than pain settled in her gut, something warm and sweet. This was a whole new kind of powerlessness, and it felt good. Really good. She let her hand slide over the defined chest, the ripped abdomen and below. Finding him hard and ready, her lips followed the path her hand had taken. His gasps of pleasure, his total surrender, told her she had succeeded in taking his mind off the pain and grief, which made everything that was wrong about this feel right.

* * *

They began the next day the same way they finished the one before.

As her body hummed with rippling aftershocks, she pressed her lips to his shoulder. "This is getting out of hand."

"We've got six years of lost time to make up for."

His lips moving against her neck made her tremble. "I need to go soon," she said. "I have to shower and change and get to the airport."

"I'm taking the staff to Richmond today to see John," he said with a deep sigh. "I'd rather be going with you."

"I wish you could." She reached up to caress his face and found the stubble on his jaw to be crazy sexy. Replacing her hand with her lips, she said, "I forgot to tell you my news."

"What news?"

"I made lieutenant."

His face lit up with pleasure. "That's awesome, Sam! Congratulations."

"It won't be official for a week or so." For a moment, she thought about telling him how it happened but decided against it. "And my dad is marrying one of his nurses."

"Wow. Do you like her?"

"Yeah. A lot."

"Where's your mother?"

"She lives in Florida with some guy she hooked up with when I was in high school. They ran off together the day after I graduated. Nearly killed my dad. He had no idea."

"Ouch. That sucks. I'm sorry."

"Yeah, I guess I should be grateful that she stuck

around long enough to get me through school, but it wasn't like she was *there* for me or anything."

"I saw my mother three times when I was in high school."

Sam cursed herself for being insensitive. "I'm sorry. I didn't mean to complain."

He shrugged. "It was what it was."

"At least you had your grandmother."

"And she was a real treat," he said with a bitter chuckle.

Intrigued, she shifted so she could see him. "She wasn't good to you?"

"She did what she could, but she always made it clear that I was a burden to her, that I was keeping her from traveling and enjoying her retirement." He paused, focused on her fingers. "When I was about ten, I heard her talking to my dad—her son. She said she'd done enough, and it was time for him to step up and take over, that he was an adult now and there was no reason he couldn't take care of his own child. He said he would, and I got all excited, thinking I was going to get to go with him."

Her stomach twisted with anxiety for the ten-year-old boy. "What happened?"

"I didn't see him again for a year."

"Nick… I'm sorry."

"He sent money—enough for me to play hockey, which I loved. I poured all my energy into that and school. Ended up with an academic scholarship to Harvard and played hockey there, too. That was my escape."

Listening to him, she wanted to give him everything he'd been denied as a child and wished she had it to give.

"Anyway," he said, running a hand through his hair,

"someday hopefully I'll have my own family and it won't matter anymore."

And that, she thought, *is my cue to go.* She sat up and reached for her clothes at the foot of the bed.

"It's only seven. You've got time yet." His hand slid from her shoulder to land on her hip. "I could make you some breakfast."

"Thanks, but I've got to go home, take a shower, get changed, check in at HQ," she said as she jammed her arms into her shirt and dragged it over her head. *Air and space*, she thought, *and we're not talking about the museum. That's what I need. Some air, some space, some perspective. Distance.*

Twirling her bra on his index finger, his full, sexy mouth twisted into a grin. "Forget something?"

She snatched it away from him and jammed it into her pants pocket.

Laughing, he reclined on the big pile of pillows.

She felt the heat of his eyes on her as she ducked into the bathroom. Re-emerging a few minutes later, she found him out of bed and wearing just the sweats he'd had on the night before. The pants rode low on narrow hips, and that chest of his... It should've been gracing the covers of erotic romance novels rather than spending its days hidden behind starched dress shirts and silk ties. Tragic. Truly a waste of good—no, *great*—man chest.

"You're staring."

"And you're hot. Seriously. Hot."

"Well, um, thanks. I guess."

His befuddlement amused and delighted her until she remembered that she'd been plotting her escape. Suddenly, morning-after awkwardness set in, leaving her tongue-tied and uncertain as she tugged on her sweater. "Good luck with your staff. Today. In Richmond."

"Thank you." He reached for her hand, brought it to his lips. "Will you tell me what happens in Chicago?"

"If I can, I will. That's the best I can do."

"That's all I can ask." Releasing her hand, he caressed her cheek. "When will I see you?"

Before she knew it the words were tumbling from her face as if her mouth was on autopilot. "There's this thing tomorrow. Family dinner at my dad's. If you want to come." All but stuttering now, she added, "I'd understand if you didn't want to because there're so many of us—"

He stopped her with a finger to her lips. "What time?"

"Dinner's at three." Her cheeks grew warm with embarrassment. "But if you want to come earlier, we could take a walk. Check out the market. If you want."

"I want." He slid his arms around her waist and brought her in snug against him. "I really want."

She should've been prepared by then for the way her legs turned to jelly when he kissed her in that particular proprietary way, but the sweep of his tongue, the pressure of his hands on her ass holding her tight against his instant arousal...no way in hell she could prepare for that.

"So," he asked, peppering her face and lips with kisses, "does *this* mean we're together? I mean, *you're* asking *me* to do stuff." His teasing grin did nothing to offset the serious look in his eyes.

With her hands on his chest, she managed to extricate herself. At the bedroom door, she paused and turned back to him. "I've crossed every line there is to cross here, Nick."

"I know that," he said, his expression pained.

"If the job requires it, I won't hesitate to cross back."

"I wouldn't expect anything less."

Satisfied that he understood, she left him with a nod and a small smile.

He followed her downstairs. "Sam?"

She swung open the inside door. "Hmm?"

Framing her face with his hands, he said, "Fly safely."

She winced.

"What?"

"I hate to fly. Hate it with a passion. I've been trying not to think about it."

Grinning, he leaned his forehead against hers. "Just close your eyes and try not to think about it."

"Yeah, right," she said, rolling her eyes. "Okay, I'm going now."

"Okay, I'm letting you." Except he didn't. He hung on for a moment longer. "Be safe. This thing with that Johnson woman… Be careful." He kissed her. "Please."

"I always am."

"Guess what?"

"What?"

His lips landed on hers for another mind-altering kiss. "You're pretty damned hot yourself."

Sam gave herself one last minute to sink into the kiss.

With what appeared to be great reluctance, he finally released her.

21

Nick stayed at the door to watch her walk to her car. *Damn*, if the woman didn't make his mouth water with that curvy body and long-legged gait. The whole package was a huge turn-on. He acknowledged they were walking a fine line that was causing her great ethical conflict, but Nick could only be grateful for the second chance they'd been given. And despite her reluctance to acknowledge that this was an actual relationship, he had no intention of messing it up this time.

Long after she should have driven away, she sat at the curb. He wondered if she was on the phone. Tipping his head so he could better see her face, he noticed it was tight with frustration. He cracked the door, heard the unmistakable click of a dead car battery and waved at her to come back in.

Furious, she got out, slammed the car door and started back up the stone pathway to his door. She was halfway there when the car exploded.

The blast was so strong it shattered the storm door and propelled him backward onto the floor. His head smacked hard on the tile, but he fought through the fog to remain conscious so he could get to her.

Barefooted, shirtless and panic-stricken, he crawled through the glass calling for her. The quiet neighborhood had descended into bedlam. He heard people screaming and could smell the acrid smoke coming from the burning car. "Sam! *Sam!*"

Blood flowed from a cut on his forehead. He swiped at it and started down the stairs, ignoring the pain of jagged glass under his feet. *"Samantha!"* Frantically, he scanned the small front yard, the street, the neighbors' yards.

A moan from the bushes behind him caught his attention. "Sam!" He rushed to the huddled form in his garden and had the presence of mind to realize that the miniature evergreens he had planted the summer before had most likely saved her life. "Sam! Sam, look at me." With the scream of sirens in the distance, he gently turned her head. Other than a knot on her forehead and a shocked glow to her eyes, he didn't see any obvious injuries.

"Bleeding," she whispered. "You're bleeding."

"I'm fine." He picked branches from her hair, brushed dirt from her cheek. "Do you hurt? Anywhere?" Releasing a long deep breath, he swayed with lightheadedness. "Babe. Jesus." Sitting with her in the garden, he did battle with the blood pouring from his forehead. He held her tight against him and whispered soothing words as she trembled in his arms.

"Need to call. HQ. Report it."

"I'm sure someone called 911. Just stay still until we get you checked out."

"My ears are ringing."

"Mine, too. You didn't hurt anything else?"

"Chest hurts." She trembled. "God, Nick. Oh my God." Clutching her stomach, she rocked in his arms.

He tightened his hold on her. "Shh, babe." The blood coming from the cut on his forehead seemed to finally be slowing. "Breathe. Deep breaths."

An Arlington police officer approached them. "Are you folks all right?"

"I'm on the job." She showed him the badge she pulled from her tattered coat pocket. "Detective Sergeant Holland. Metro."

"Are you hurt, Sergeant?"

"I don't think so, but it was my car that went up. I need to get word to my brass."

"I'll call it in for you." Until the cop handed Nick a blanket, he'd forgotten he was wearing only the now-torn sweats. "And I'll send the paramedics right over."

"Thank you, Officer…"

"Severson."

"Thank you," Sam said again. When they were alone, she glanced at Nick. "I'm sorry."

"What the hell for?"

"For bringing this to your home." She sniffed and wiped her nose. "I never thought they'd really try to kill me. I never imagined they had the balls."

"Don't you dare apologize to me, Samantha. You're a victim here."

"Your windows are broken. Your neighbors', too."

"Screw that. It's glass. It can be replaced. But you…" His voice hitched with emotion. Brushing his lips over the lump on her forehead, he took a deep shuddering breath. "There's no replacing you. I ought to know. I tried for six years."

"Nick," she said, haltingly, "I'm supposed to hold it together and do my job, but this…" She fixed her eyes on the firefighters hosing down what was left of her car.

"Nothing's going to happen to you. I won't let it."

Smiling now but still shaky, she turned to him and wiped the drying blood from his brow. "And how do you intend to do that?"

"By not letting you out of my sight."

"Nick—"

"Sergeant Holland?" Officer Severson said. "The paramedics are ready for you."

"We're not finished," she told Nick as she gestured the paramedics over. "We'll talk about this later."

"You bet your fine ass we will."

Remarkably, Nick's injuries were more serious than Sam's. He required five stitches to close the cut over his left eyebrow and stitches in his right foot after doctors removed several slivers of glass. In addition, he had a slight concussion and a minor case of hypothermia from the hour he spent half-dressed in the cold.

Sam, on the other hand, had only a bump on the head and an ugly bruise on her breastbone where she'd connected with the bushes. When she allowed her mind to wander to what could've happened, she was beset by the shakes. She decided it was better if she didn't think about it until she had to. Standing at Nick's bedside, watching the plastic surgeon stitch his forehead, Sam's knees went weak as the needle passed through his flesh. Nothing freaked her out more than needles—not even airplanes.

The TV was tuned to John's public wake in Richmond, with special coverage of the O'Connor family's poignant visit the day before. Nick was riveted to the coverage, but Sam was riveted to the needle.

"You'll have a scar," she whispered.

"No way," the doctor protested. "He'll be good as new."

"Damn," Nick said with a grin. "I was hoping for a gnarly scar."

"It's not funny," Sam snapped.

"Hey." He squeezed her hand. "Why don't you wait outside? You're pale as a ghost."

"I'd rather stay in here where there're needles than face what's waiting for me out there."

"And that would be?"

"I heard the lieutenant and the captain are here, no doubt media, too. It'll be all over the news that I spent the night with you."

"We'll deal with it, babe."

"*I* will deal with it. *You* will say nothing, you got me?"

"I'm not going to let you get reamed for something we both had a hand in."

"You're a *civilian*. You won't help me if you try to fight my battles for me, Nick. You have to promise me you'll resist the urge to speak."

"Or?"

"I'll have Freddie toss you in the can until the dust settles."

"You wouldn't dare."

"Oh no?" She leaned in close to his battered face, but not too close to the needle. "Try me."

The doctor smiled. "I think I'd listen to the lady if I were you—unless you want to be back for more stitches."

"The *lady*," Nick said, never taking his eyes off Sam, "is sadly deluded if she thinks she can order me around like one of her collars."

"*Ohhh,*" Sam said. "Listen to him spewing cop talk." Reaching behind her, she grabbed her cuffs and snapped them on him and the bed rail so fast he never saw it coming.

"*What the fuck?*" He tugged on the cuffs, clanked them against the metal rail. "*Goddamn it, Sam!*"

"Ah, you need to stay still unless you want a needle straight through to your brain," the doctor said.

"I'll be back to get him after I've dealt with my

bosses," Sam said to the doctor. "Keep him quiet until then."

"Yes, ma'am," the doctor said, seeming awestruck by her brassiness.

"You're going to pay for this, Samantha," Nick growled.

She brushed a kiss over the uninjured side of his forehead. "Be back soon." Over her shoulder, she added, "Behave." As she walked away, the furious clatter of cuffs made her smile. "That'll teach him to screw with me." Her smile faded when she encountered Lieutenant Stahl's angry scowl in the waiting room. Realizing she was still braless, she pulled her tattered coat closed and crossed her arms.

Stahl gestured her to a deserted corner. Captain Malone followed them.

"Sergeant," Stahl said. "I'd like an explanation for what you were doing at the home of a material witness—overnight."

"Yes, sir, Lieutenant, I'm fine. Thanks for asking."

"How about we add a rap for insubordination to your growing list of problems?" Stahl retorted.

"Lieutenant," Captain Malone said, the warning clear in his tone. To Sam, he said, "Your injuries were minor?"

"Yes, sir. Bump on the head, bruised sternum."

"And your companion?"

Sam gave him a rundown of Nick's injuries. "Was anyone else hurt?"

"No. The street was deserted. Luckily, it was a weekend."

Yes, luckily, Sam thought, feeling a tremble ripple through her as she realized how truly lucky she—and Nick—had been. "Has Explosives gotten anything on the car?"

"They're there now. Our people are bumping heads with Arlington. The chief was on the phone with their chief asking for some latitude when I left."

"I'm sorry to have caused all this trouble, sir."

"You start down that path, you're gonna piss me off."

"What were you doing with Cappuano?" Stahl asked.

This time, Malone didn't bail her out. Rather, he watched her with wise gray eyes that she knew from experience didn't miss a thing.

"We're friends," she said haltingly. "We met at a party six years ago. I hadn't seen him again until the, ah, until the senator was murdered. Cappuano has been cleared of any involvement and has been a tremendous asset to the investigation in a civilian capacity. Sir."

"I'm taking you off the O'Connor case, effective immediately," Stahl said, puffed up with his own importance.

"But—"

"Not so fast, Lieutenant," Captain Malone said.

"This is my call, Captain," Stahl huffed. "She's *my* detective."

"And I'm *your* captain." Malone dismissed Stahl by turning his back to him.

The foul look Stahl directed at Sam would have reduced a lesser woman to tears. Fortunately, Sam wasn't a lesser woman. She directed all her attention and focus on the much more rational captain.

"Sergeant, I'm disappointed in the judgment you've exhibited by getting involved with a witness," Malone said.

"Exactly—" Stahl sputtered.

"Lieutenant!" the captain roared. "Get back to your squad." When Stahl didn't budge, Malone added a fierce, *"Now."*

With one last hateful glance at Sam, Stahl stalked out of the emergency room.

"As I was saying," Malone continued, "you've shown poor judgment with this involvement, but in the more than twelve years you've been under my command, I've never once had reason to question your judgment. I know you, Holland. I know how you think, how you operate and have had many an occasion over the years to appreciate your high ethical standards. So, the way I see it, the only way you hook up with a witness in the midst of the most important case of your career is if it's serious."

Sam might've swallowed her tongue—if she could've opened her mouth. "Sir?" she squeaked.

"Are you in love with this guy? Cappuano?"

"I...ah... I..."

"It's a simple yes or no question, Sergeant."

"Don't be ridiculous. Of course I'm not in love with him," Sam sputtered, but the words rang hollow, even to her. Apparently, they did to him, too.

Looking satisfied, he studied her again, long and hard. "I'm going to give you the benefit of the doubt. I'm going to assume you've done nothing to compromise this investigation, that when you say Cappuano has been invaluable to you, you're being completely aboveboard with me."

"I am, sir."

"In that case, for now you're to have no comment to the press about your relationship with him. We'll let the media folks spin it. I'll take care of that." He sat and gestured for her to take the chair next to him. "As for the bombing—"

"If you take me off O'Connor, you're going to have to take my badge, too."

"Sergeant, there's no need for ultimatums. You've been through a traumatic thing."

"Yes, I have, and by tomorrow morning, everyone in the city will know who I'm sleeping with. They'll know Destiny Johnson meant it when she said she'd get even with me for what happened to her kid. They'll know I'm no closer to a suspect in the O'Connor case today than I was the day it happened. They'll know all that, and then they'll hear that my own command didn't have enough confidence in me to let me close this case. Where will that leave me?"

"You're a decorated officer. Soon to be a lieutenant. This is a setback. That's all it is."

"On top of another setback. You want me to take command of the detective squad. I won't have an ounce of authority left if you take this case away from me."

"Your safety has to be a consideration. They've come at you once. They'll come at you again."

"Next time, I'll be ready. I screwed up this time because I didn't take her seriously. I know better now."

"I've got to talk to the chief about this. He's having a fucking cow. Gonzo and Arnold have Destiny Johnson in interview right now. Because we've had her in lock-up since yesterday, she's playing dumb on the bombing."

Freddie came rushing into the Emergency Room, looking pale and panicked. "Oh, thank God," he said when he saw Sam talking with Malone. "Thank you, Jesus."

"If you hug me, I'll have you busted down to Patrol," Sam snarled at him.

Freddie stopped just short of the embrace, bent at the waist and propped his hands on his knees. "I heard it on the radio," he panted. "Scared the freaking shit out of me."

"He's swearing," Sam commented to Malone. "He only does that in extreme circumstances. I'm honored."

Freddie tipped his face, met Sam's eyes. "You almost got blown up. I'm sorry if I don't find that funny."

"I'm fine, Cruz," she said, touched by his concern. "You can relax."

"What are we doing?" he asked Malone, his eyes hot with anger and passion. "What can I do?"

"Gonzo's got Destiny in interview," Sam told him.

"I was thinking on the way over here," he said, still breathing heavily. "What if it's not Johnson?"

"How do you mean?" Malone asked.

Freddie stood up straight. "Destiny spews in the paper yesterday, right?"

Sam and the captain nodded.

"So say someone wants to hose up the O'Connor investigation? What's the fastest way?" Before they could answer, he said, "Take out Sergeant Holland and have the full wrath of the department focused on Johnson. Presto. O'Connor is back burner. Senator or not, no one takes precedence over a dead cop."

"That's an interesting theory, Detective," Malone said, clearly impressed.

Sam was filled with pride. Young Freddie was coming along very well. Very well, indeed.

"You think it's possible?" Freddie asked, full of youthful exuberance.

"It's solid, Cruz," Sam said. "Good thinking." She paused, thought for a moment and decided. "I want you to go to Chicago and talk to Patricia Donaldson. I want to know if her kid is John O'Connor's son. I want the whole story. Tell her she can either spill it to you, or we'll get a warrant for DNA. Don't come back until you know every detail of her relationship with O'Connor. He went out there the third weekend of every month.

I want to know if he was banging her. I want to know how. You got me?"

"Without you?" His normally robust complexion paled again.

"A bomb just blew off your training wheels, Detective." Sam winced at the pain in her chest as she rose. "Get your ass to Chicago." She grabbed the lapels of his ever-present trench coat and pulled him down so his face was an inch from hers. "You get yourself hurt in *any* way, and I'll kill you. You got me?"

"Ma'am." He swallowed hard. "Yes, ma'am."

She retrieved the paper with her ticket information from her purse. "Be on that eleven o'clock flight and get back here as fast as you can. Report in tonight."

"Watch your back, Cruz," Malone added. "If they've got eyes on Sergeant Holland, they're on you, too."

"Yes, sir." Freddie stood there for a second longer, beaming at the two of them.

"What the hell are you standing there grinning like a goon for?" Sam asked.

"I'm going. I won't let you down. I'll call you as soon as I've got anything."

"Go!" After he scrambled through the ER doors, she glanced at Malone. "Sheesh, was I ever that green?"

"Nope," he said without hesitation. "You came in with the sensibilities of a captain. Why do you think I've been watching my back all these years?"

Staggered by the compliment, Sam stared at him. "I'm sorry if I've let you down."

"I'll bet your friend is wondering where you are. Why don't you go on back and check on him? I'll give you both a lift when he's sprung."

She rested a hand on his arm. "Don't let them take me off O'Connor, Captain. Don't let them."

"I'll do what I can."

22

Sam made her way back down the long hallway, pausing just before Nick's room to lean against the wall and collect herself. She couldn't stop thinking about what Malone had said. Was she in love with Nick? Was that why she'd allowed things with him to progress even though she knew it was wrong and could get her into a shit load of trouble? Had she maybe always loved him? Way back to the first time they met?

With a soft groan, she tipped back her aching head. She hadn't loved Peter but discovered that far too late. When Nick failed to call her after their night together—or so she thought—she'd been seriously depressed. Peter came to the rescue, offering a shoulder to cry on and a friend to lean on. It had been easy, too easy she later realized, to get swept up by him.

Now, on top of everything else she'd learned about him, she knew he intercepted Nick's calls while pretending to offer comfort, proving he was an even bigger asshole than she had given him credit for being. He had robbed her of a lot more than four years of her life. He had taken her self-esteem, caused her to question her judgment, stolen her self-respect and left her confidence in tatters.

A smart woman would be leery of making another

mistake after the whopper she'd made with Peter. A smart woman would go slow with Nick, would take her time, would make sure she was doing the right thing. As the clank of metal against metal reminded her she had a very angry man to deal with, she decided she clearly wasn't as smart as she'd always thought.

Pasting a big smile on her face, she stepped into the room, her stomach aching from the tension. "Great! You're all done."

All but smoking with rage, Nick said, "Get these things off me, Sam. Right now."

"I'd be happy to." She dug the key out of her pocket and dangled it in front of him. "But before I do, let's get one thing straight. I need you to stay out of my work stuff. Agree to that, and I'll let you go."

"How do you know I don't plan to let *you* go once you unlock me?"

The question sent a surprising jolt of fear through her. "Well, I guess that'll be up to you, won't it?" she said with more bravado than she felt.

"Unlock me. Now."

"Not until you agree."

"I'm not agreeing to anything while I'm locked to a bed. If you want to unlock me and talk this through like rational adults, then that's fine."

She studied his furious, handsome face for a long moment. "You're awfully sexy when you're pissed." Leaning down, she kissed the bandage over his left eye.

The kiss seemed to defuse him, but only somewhat.

"I'm sorry I locked you up." When his face twisted with skepticism, she said, "I *am* sorry. But you have no idea how difficult it is to be a woman in this profession or the daughter of a fallen hero. The last thing I need is some guy on a white horse riding to my rescue as if I can't handle things myself. As it is, I spend most of every day waiting for it all to blow up in my face."

"Like it did today?"

"A joke?" she asked, incredulous. "You're joking about a bomb?"

"Sorry," he said with chagrin, "it was too good to pass up. Doesn't mean I think it's funny. Quite the contrary." With his free hand, he captured one of hers and brought it to his lips. "Unlock me. I promise not to kill you."

Knowing that was the best she was going to get and encouraged by the tender gesture, she released the cuffs.

He made a big dramatic show of rubbing his sore wrist for a minute before he got up to reach for his jeans and sweater.

Still uncertain about just how angry he really was, Sam stayed on the far side of the bed while he got dressed. She winced at the flash of pain that crossed his face as he slid his injured foot into an old running shoe the cops had brought from his house.

"Um, Captain Malone is going to take us…well… I guess to my house if you don't mind."

"I don't mind," he said in a testy tone.

Swallowing the lump in her throat, she added, "I'd appreciate it if you don't discuss what happened earlier with him."

"What? That my girlfriend or sex buddy or whatever you are was nearly blown to bits in my front yard? I shouldn't mention that?"

She rubbed at eyes gone gritty with exhaustion. After an almost-sleepless night with him, she'd planned to catch a couple of hours on the plane if her nerves allowed it. "I'm asking you to do this for me. He was a lot cooler about me getting caught with you than I expected him to be. It would just be better if you stayed out of it."

He came around the bed and backed her up to the wall. "You want me to stay out of it?"

"Um, yeah, that would help." Only her hands on his chest kept him from completely invading her space.

"Let's get one thing straight, Samantha. I've been the guy behind the guy my whole career, and that's fine with me. But if you think, for one second, I'm going to ride shotgun in my personal life, you've got the wrong lapdog on your leash."

While she should have been pissed at a comment like that, she was ridiculously turned on. She looped a hand around his neck and brought him down for a kiss intended to make him forget all about being mad with her.

With his hands on her hips, he jerked her tight against him.

"I don't want a lapdog," she said when she finally came up for air. "That's not what I'm asking you to be."

"What *are* you asking me to be?"

"Do we have to decide that right now? It's bad enough the whole town's going to know we're sleeping together."

"Damage done," he said with a bitter laugh that jangled her already frazzled nerves.

"That's easy for you to say. Your job isn't on the line."

"No, it's not. I lost my job when my boss got himself murdered. Remember?"

"I don't want to do this. I don't want to be sniping with you when we've got so many bigger things to deal with."

"See what you just said there? *We* have so many bigger things to deal with? You just made my point."

She studied the floor for a moment before she found

the courage to bring her eyes back up to meet his. "I'm not used to *we*."

He laughed, but at least the anger seemed to be gone. "And you think I am? This is all new ground for me, too, babe."

"I'm sorry we're being forced to go public before we're ready."

"Something tells me that nothing about you and me is going to be simple or easy. We may as well get used to it. At least you're calling us 'we' now. That's progress."

Ignoring that, she said, "So you'll be cool with the captain?"

"I'll be cool."

With her eyes fixed on his, she kissed him softly. "You really are super sexy when you're all steamed up."

"Is that so?"

She loved how embarrassed he got when she said stuff like that. "Uh huh." After patting his face, she headed for the door.

"Samantha?"

She turned back.

"You owe me twenty-six minutes in handcuffs, and I fully intend to collect."

Damn him! When all her attention and focus was needed to deal with the captain and whatever was waiting for her at home, all Sam could think about was being cuffed and at Nick's mercy for twenty-six minutes. Her whole body tingled with anticipation.

Turning to glare at him, she was rewarded with a shit-eating grin that told her he knew he had rattled her.

"You really are super sexy when you're all steamed up," he whispered, earning another furious glare. When he tried to hold hands with her, she tugged hers free and jammed it into her coat pocket where she encountered the cuffs and her bra. Her head pounded, and she began to believe it was possible for a head to actually blow off a neck. As they approached the waiting area, her stomach took a nasty dip that caused her to gasp with pain.

"What?" Nick asked, taking her arm to stop her.

"Stomach."

"Why don't we get someone to look at that while we're here?"

She tugged her arm free. "It's been checked."

"It needs to be checked again," he said, rubbing his hands up and down her arms.

"It's better." She stepped out of his embrace. "No PDA in front of the captain or anyone else."

"You're not giving me orders, remember?"

"Nick—"

"Sam."

With a growl of frustration, she marched into the waiting room several strides ahead of him.

Captain Malone put down the *Time* magazine he'd been flipping through and stood up. "Ready?"

"Yes, sir. Ah, this is Nick. Nick Cappuano." Gesturing to Nick without looking at him, she added, "Captain Malone."

While Sam's stomach grinded, the two men sized each other up as they shook hands and mumbled, "Nice to meet you."

"On behalf of the department," Malone said, "I apologize for your injuries and the damage to your home."

"Not your fault," Nick said. "However, I'd like to know what's being done to find the person who tried to kill Sam."

Sam stared at him, her mouth hanging open. Was *that* how he planned to stay out of it?

"Let's get you two out of here, and we'll talk about

it on the way." He waved his hand and two uniformed officers appeared. "We've got press up the wazoo outside the E.R., so Officers Butler and O'Brien are going to get you out through the main door upstairs. I'll get my car and meet you there."

"Thank you, sir," Sam said. The moment the captain was out of earshot she pounced on Nick. "*That's* you staying out of it and being cool?"

"What? He knows we're sleeping together. Wouldn't I look like a jerk if I didn't even ask? Do you want him to think I'm a jerk? Wouldn't it be better for you if he likes me? If he can see why you'd risk so much to be with me right now?"

"*Ugh!*" She stalked after the uniforms, pretending not to hear him laughing behind her.

By the time they had parked in front of her father's Capitol Hill home, Nick was the captain's new best friend. They'd bonded over their shared concern for Sam's safety as well as their passion for the Redskins, politics and imported beer. If Sam hadn't already been on the verge of puking, she would be now for sure.

She suspected they were using the small talk to mask the underlying tension that surrounded them all as they contemplated what could have happened that morning and the staggering array of implications they were left to contend with. For that reason, and that reason only, she decided not to kill Nick for defying her.

Her stomach clutched when she saw the chief's car parked on Ninth Street. No doubt he and her father were in there concocting a plan to lock her up somewhere until she testified.

As they approached the house, Sam glanced at Captain Malone. "Um, sir, could you give us just a second?"

"Sure. I'll see you in there."

After he had gone inside, Nick turned to her. "I know what you're going to say, but I was just trying to make conversation—"

She went up on tiptoes to plant a kiss on him.

Startled, he said, "What was that for?"

"Just wanted to."

"Are you intentionally trying to keep me off balance?"

"It's not intentional, but if it's working…"

"I figured I was in for another tongue-lashing—and not the good kind."

She smiled. "I just wanted to tell you that my dad has some feeling in his right hand, so when I introduce you…" She shrugged. "If you wanted to squeeze his hand, it'd mean something to him. And to me."

Nick put his arms around her, drew her in close and kissed the top of her head. "Thank you for telling me."

"He's going to be all wound up about the bomb and stuff, so he might not even notice you. Don't be offended by that."

"I won't."

"I hope you didn't use up all your charm on the captain," she said, rubbing her belly, "because my dad's the one who counts. You know that, right?"

"Of course I do. It's going to be fine, babe. Don't worry or your stomach will start up."

She eyed him with amusement. "Starting to see the pattern?"

"Yep. Let's get this over with before you work yourself into a full-blown episode."

"Might be too late," she muttered. Taking one last deep breath, she led him up the ramp to the front door and stepped into a room full of cops.

Celia pounced on her. *"Oh my God, Sam!"* Her tears dampened Sam's cheek. Stepping back to run her hands over Sam as if to take inventory, Celia said, "Are you all right?"

"I'm fine." She did a little spin. "See? Everything still attached and working."

Celia raised an eyebrow. "You lied to me last night when you said you were going to work."

Sam squirmed under her future stepmother's stern glare. "Um, yeah, I do that every now and then. Lie, that is. Is that going to be a problem for you?"

Celia cast an appreciative glance at Nick over Sam's shoulder and smiled. "If he's the reason, I guess I can forgive you. This one time."

Sam introduced her to Nick, and when she couldn't avoid it for a second longer, she met her father's steely stare from across the room. She went over to him and bent to kiss his cheek. "I'm sorry you were worried."

"I went past worried about three hours ago, but we'll get to that. Who've you got with you?"

Knowing her father was already fully aware of who Nick was, Sam nodded to Nick anyway. "Dad, this is Nick Cappuano."

As instructed, Nick squeezed Skip's right hand. "Pleased to meet you, Deputy Chief Holland."

"Excellent sucking up. I'd say someone prepared you well to meet her old man."

"I wouldn't know what you mean, sir."

Skip's eyes danced with mirth. "That from this morning?" he asked, referring to the bandage over Nick's eye.

"Yeah, but I'll live."

Sam re-introduced Nick to Chief Farnsworth.

"Detective Higgins, ma'am," the other cop said to Sam. "Explosives."

"I've seen you around," Sam said, although she couldn't believe he was a detective. With his sandy hair cut into a flat top over a baby face, he barely looked old enough to be out of the academy. "What'd you find?"

"Two EDs on your car." For the benefit of Nick and Celia, he added, "Explosive devices—one on the ignition and a backup. Only one detonated. Both of them go, we're not having this conversation."

Sam swallowed hard and didn't object when Nick's hand landed on the small of her back.

"That's not all," Higgins said. "When we did a sweep of the other cars in the area, we found two more attached to a black BMW."

Nick and Sam gasped.

"Registered to you, Mr. Cappuano."

As if all her bones had turned to mush, Sam sank to the sofa. "Why?" she whispered. "Why would they target him?"

"We were just discussing that when you came in," Chief Farnsworth said. "If it's Johnson or their pals, the best theory I've heard yet is 'you take mine, I'll take yours.' Revenge, pure and simple. Johnson wanted you either dead or decimated. How would they've known his car?"

"I've been in it," Sam confessed. "Recently. And I've had the feeling someone was watching me a few times."

"Detective Cruz suggested a link to O'Connor rather than Johnson," Malone said. "Worth looking into, especially since they targeted Nick, too."

Farnsworth turned to Nick. "Do you know of anything Senator O'Connor was involved in that had ties to terrorists or terrorism?"

"He was on the Homeland Security Committee, working mostly on the immigration issue, but he was briefed on counterterrorism initiatives. We both were."

"I want to take apart that bill he was sponsoring, line by line," Sam said. "Maybe I've totally missed the boat on this. I've been thinking jilted lover, but they don't tend to plant bombs."

"No," Malone agreed. "They tend to dismember."

"Which is why I've focused most of my attention on his love life." Sam got up to pace. "We've uncovered a slew of recent ex-lovers, a few with complaints about some of his, um, fetishes." She sent a sympathetic glance to Nick since he was hearing this for the first time. "But maybe Cruz is right. Maybe the Lorena Bobbitt was intended to throw us off."

"He was *dismembered?*" Higgins squeaked, his baby face gone pale.

"A detail we've managed to keep out of the press," Farnsworth said with a pointed look at his detective.

"Yes, sir." Higgins got up to leave. "I need to get back to the lab where it's safe."

Sam rolled her eyes. "Run back to your cave, Higgins, and leave the dirty work to those of us in the field."

"You can have it. I'll send you details on the EDs when I have more, but I can tell you they were crude and you got lucky, Sergeant. Damned lucky."

"Yeah," Sam said. "I know." She saw him out and turned to find every man in the room focused on her.

No doubt sensing a battle royal in the making, Celia stepped into the kitchen.

"Before you all get going," Sam said, "I have something I want to say, and I want you to listen to me without interrupting."

When they agreed with their silence, she pushed her fist into her aching gut and took a second to look each of them in the eye—Dad, her hero and her rock; Chief Farnsworth, beloved friend and respected leader; Captain Malone, boss and mentor; and Nick, quickly becoming more important than anyone. All of them cared about her. She had no doubt about that, just as she had no doubt they'd go to any lengths to keep her safe.

"I'm sure you two have cooked up a plan to toss me into a safe house for the weekend," she said to her father and the chief, "but that's not going to happen." Before they could protest, she held up a hand to stop them. "I'm going to continue to work this case until I close it, and I'm not going to let punks or terrorists or whoever strapped an ED to my car and Nick's take me off the streets. The minute they think they have that kind of power over me, I'm done on this job and you know it."

Pausing, she made eye contact with each of them again. "I know you're worried, and I know you care. But if you care about me at all, don't ask me to be a coward. I won't deny that bomb scared the shit out of me." She let her gaze fall on Nick. "When I saw your face covered with blood, my heart almost stopped. So I'm going to get them. If for no other reason than they hurt you, and that's simply unacceptable to me."

Nick's hard expression softened into a smile that engaged his eyes and filled her heart with emotions she had never experienced quite so strongly before.

To Farnsworth, she said, "Let me do my job. I'll take every precaution I can. I'll run things from here, stay as close to home as I can, but I won't hide out. I dare any of you to tell me you wouldn't rather go down in the line than run scared from scum who think they can take us out like yesterday's garbage."

A full minute of silence ensued, during which she noticed Farnsworth and Malone watching her dad and understood they were going to take their cues from him.

"I'd like to see that immigration bill," Skip finally said. He glanced at Nick. "I'm a political junky in my spare time. I might catch something in there we can use."

"I'll get it for you." Nick checked his watch as he stood up. "My staff should be back from Richmond by now, so let me make a call. What format do you prefer?"

"A fax would work. We can pop it right into my reading device. I can see two pages at once that way." Skip rattled off the number and followed Nick into the kitchen.

"I'm going to go lean on the lab to speed things up with the boomer," Malone said as he pulled on his coat.

Sam was left alone with the chief. "I know what you're going to say."

"Do you?"

She squirmed under the heat of his stare. In a rush of words, she said, "I'm sorry I lied to you about Nick. But I was so afraid you'd take me off the case, and after Johnson I *needed* it. You know I did. I tried to fight what was happening between us, but he was just *there* for me, every step of the way and I, um... Why are you smiling?"

"In some ways, you're exactly the same as you were at twelve, you know that?" He took a step closer to her, the smile fading. "But if you ever, *ever* lie to me again, Sergeant, I'll have your badge. Are we clear?"

"Crystal," she said, swallowing hard. "Sir."

"Get O'Connor cleaned up—and fast. I don't want any more bad publicity for you or the department."

"Yes, sir."

He called out his good-byes to Skip and Celia before donning his coat.

"Chief? Thank you for understanding why I have to do this."

"I would've done the same thing myself. In fact, your dad predicted your little speech almost down to the last vowel. We were ready for you."

"Well, sheesh," she huffed. "Here I was thinking I'd handled you, and *I'm* the one being handled?"

"You gotta get up a lot earlier in the morning to get one past a couple of crusty old vets like us. Truth is, we would've been disappointed if you'd done it any other way. You're a chip off the old block, Holland."

"Thank you, sir. You couldn't pay me a higher compliment."

"I know." He glanced toward the kitchen. "You think about what it would do to him if something happens to you. It'd be the end of him. You think about that."

"Yes, sir," she whispered as she watched him go down the ramp.

23

With Nick outside on the phone, Sam went into the kitchen where her dad was reading the bill.

She bent to kiss his cheek. "Thanks for the help. I hate feeling like I've totally missed the point on this one."

"Don't know for sure yet that you have. Just because it's taken a few twists and turns doesn't mean you aren't on the right path."

"That's true."

"Seems like a nice kid."

"Who? Higgins?"

"No," he said grinning. "Nick."

"Oh, right." She wasn't ready to go down *that* path with him just yet. "So, hey, I hear you've been keeping secrets."

"You're one to talk, and which secrets are you referring to?"

Sam raised an eyebrow as she slipped into a kitchen chair.

"Oh. Celia."

"Uh huh," Sam said, delighted by the faint blush that appeared on his ruddy cheeks.

"Well, I was going to tell you."

"Except you were too chicken so you got her to tell me."

"Something like that."

Sam laughed. "I'm happy for you."

"Really? You are?" His relief was almost as comical as his embarrassment.

"Of course I am. She's terrific. What would we have done without her the last couple of years?"

"No kidding. Thing I can't understand is why she'd want to shackle herself to this?" With his eyes, he took in his useless body, the chair, the whole situation.

"She loves you. I think it's that simple."

"She's not in it for the house or the pension, in case you wondered."

"I didn't."

"Sure you did, because I've trained you to be as cynical as I am."

"Well, maybe it crossed my mind for an instant, but listening to her talk about you…she's genuine."

"I think she is," he said, seeming incredulous. "In fact, she wants to sign something that says she gets nothing, you know, after…"

"Which says to me she should get it."

"See? That's what I think, too. It wouldn't bother you or your sisters if she got a cut?"

Sam stood up to rest her hands on his shoulders and brought her face down to his. "All I want is you, here with us, for as long as we can have you, for as long as you want to be here."

"You haven't forgotten, have you? About our deal?"

Sam thought of the prescription bottle she had stashed in a safe-deposit box. "No."

"And you're still willing? If the time comes…"

Fighting back the sting of pain in her belly and her heart, she kept her voice steady when she said, "If the time comes."

He released a long deep breath. "Good. Okay. Let

me get back to this. I'll report in if anything jumps out, Sergeant—or should I say Lieutenant?"

"Not quite yet." She kissed his forehead. "Thanks for the help."

"My pleasure."

And she could see that it was. He seemed more vital, more alive in that moment than he had in a long time. She should've been bringing him into her cases on a more formal basis all along and vowed to do so going forward. His mind was as sharp as ever, and if using it gave him a reason to stay in the fight, then she'd use it and no doubt benefit from it.

Nick ended the call with Christina and stashed the cell phone he'd borrowed from Sam in his pocket. He rested against the porch rail and let his eyes wander up and down the quiet street. Some of the townhouses were painted in a variety of bright colors while others were fronted by brick or stone. The red brick sidewalks sloped and curved over tree roots. Black wrought iron gates added a touch of class to the Capitol Hill neighborhood.

Was someone out there right now watching him? Hoping to get another shot at Sam? Or at him? The thought sent a chill chasing through him as he contemplated the sudden changes in his life. Last Saturday, he spent the morning in the office and then played in a pickup basketball game at the gym. He went out for a few beers with the guys he'd played with and went home alone.

Now, a week later, John was dead, he was in love with Samantha Holland and someone had tried to kill them both. Any doubt that he was in love with her had evaporated during the interminable trip through shattered glass to get to her after the bombing. He'd had just enough time to imagine a return to the empty existence his life had been without her to be certain he loved her.

Three doors down on Ninth Street, a metal "For Sale" sign caught his attention as it banged against a brick-front townhouse. The creepy sound reminded Nick of ghost towns and spaghetti Westerns. Another trickle of fear crept along his spine as he took a long look up and down the deserted street.

"What're you doing out here in the cold?" Sam asked as she joined him on the porch.

"Nothing much." He extended a hand to her. "Where's your coat?"

"I'll share yours." She slipped her arms around his waist and burrowed into his coat. "Mmm. Warm."

As Nick held her close, he wondered how he had survived, how he had lived without her for all the years since he first met her. He closed his eyes and rested his cheek on the top of her head.

"What are you thinking about?"

He couldn't tell her he loved her. Not now. Not in the midst of murder and chaos and not when she wasn't ready to hear it. Later, he decided. There'd be time. He would make sure of it. "That you showed a lot of spine before, letting them know you planned to stay on the case."

"Yeah, well, apparently they predicted that's what I'd say and had planned for it." She looked up at him. "I just cashed in every good judgment and sterling moral code chip I've earned in twelve years on the force to bring you into my life." With a coy smile, she added, "I hope you're going to be worth it."

Realizing the huge step she was taking, he framed her face with his hands and kissed her. "I will be. I promise."

"I was kidding."

"I wasn't."

She brought him down to her and sucked the breath out of his lungs with a passionate kiss.

"Sam," he gasped, burying his face in the elegant curve of her neck. "God."

"What? What is it?"

"When I think about what might've happened." He raised his head, met her sparkling blue eyes and was grateful. So very grateful. "I know this is all so new, but the thought of losing you…again… I don't want to lose you."

"You won't. Nothing's going to happen to me."

"They could take a shot at you right now. We're totally exposed standing out here."

She reached up to caress his face. "You can't do this. If you're going to be with me—"

"If?"

She smiled. "I get hurt every now and then. I have close calls—not like I did today—but stuff *happens*. You can't let fear rule you. That's no life for you—or me." She hesitated, as if there was something else she wanted to say.

"What?" He sensed her tension before he felt it. "Babe. What?"

"When I was married," she said haltingly, "Peter obsessed about my safety, my whereabouts, my cases. It wasn't healthy, and while it wasn't the only problem we had, it made a bad situation much worse. It was totally suffocating."

"I hear what you're saying, and I understand. I really do. I'll do my best to give you room to breathe, but you've got to give me some time to adjust, okay? I'm not used to the woman I care about being nearly blown up in my front yard. It's going to take me a while to get used to the dangers that go with your job."

"Fair enough."

He brushed his thumbs over the deep, dark circles under her eyes and pressed a gentle kiss to the lump on her forehead. "You're whipped. Do you think you could sleep for a bit?"

"I guess I could try, but my mind is racing. I want to get everyone here later when Freddie gets back to start all over again. We're missing something. I know we are."

"You won't be any good to anyone if you run yourself into the ground. How about a nap to recharge?"

She flashed that coy smile he'd come to love. "Only if you join me."

"*Here?* With your dad in the house?"

"He can't shoot you."

"That's not funny. He can have me killed. Easily."

"I was married, Nick. He knows I've had sex."

"Not with me."

"I'll bet he doesn't think we were baking cookies last night."

"That's what we were doing. If he asks, that's *exactly* what we were doing. Baking cookies—all night long."

Laughing, she took his hand to lead him inside. "We're going to crash for a bit," she said to Celia. "Freddie is due back later tonight. If we conk out big time, will you wake us up when he gets here?"

"I sure will, honey. Can I get you two something to eat?"

"I don't think I could eat yet," Sam said, running her hand over her belly.

"Me either," Nick said. "But thanks anyway." He glanced at the kitchen where Skip was still engrossed in the immigration bill. "If you could fail to mention to Chief Holland that I'm upstairs, too, that'd be cool. In fact, I'd pay you."

Celia chuckled and waved them up. "I'll see what I can do."

Feeling like a teenager sneaking into his girlfriend's room—a goal he'd never managed to achieve back then—Nick followed Sam up the stairs.

She closed the bedroom door and pulled off her sweater.

He winced at the ugly purple bruise on her chest. If he hadn't stopped breathing, he might've enjoyed watching her strip. "I agreed to a nap. I didn't agree to nudity."

"You want me to sleep, right?"

"Uh huh."

She wiggled out of her jeans and panties and came at him with intent in her eyes. "I sleep best in the nude."

He took a step back and encountered wall. "He's going to know. If a babe like you is my daughter, I've got her room bugged to make sure guys like me don't get in." Without allowing his eyes to leave her face, he said, "So he's going to know I'm up here with his daughter—his beautiful, sexy, *naked* daughter—and he'll call some of his cop buddies. They'll drag me into a dark alley to rip the limbs from my body one by one, and then toss what's left of me in the Potomac."

Laughing, Sam slipped her hands under his sweater and eased it up and over his head, catching him off guard when she nuzzled his nipple. That's all it took to make him rock hard.

"With an imagination like that, you should consider a career in fiction."

He kept his hands limp at his sides. Maybe if he didn't leave prints on her he'd walk away with his life.

"You really think you can resist me?" she asked, trailing kisses from his jaw to his collarbone as her breasts rubbed against his chest.

"My life depends on it."

Her lips glided over his chest to his belly. "All that tough talk from before…" She unbuttoned his jeans, pushed them down and sank to her knees in front of him. "I think I'm about to make you my lapdog."

Sensing where this was going, he tried to escape.

In a move that both startled and stirred him, she pinned him to the wall.

He groaned, his fingers rolling into fists as her hot mouth closed around him. "Sam…*please.* I thought you liked me."

"I do," she said, dragging her tongue in circles that made his head spin. "I really do."

A bead of sweat rolled between his shoulder blades, straight down his spine. "He'll *know,* and he'll kill me."

She managed to laugh as she sucked. Hard.

"Jesus." His breathing became labored, the heat of her mouth unbearable. "Sam, honey, come here."

"So you're willing to play now?"

"Yeah." He helped her up, lifted her and sank into her in one easy movement. "Hell, you only live once, right?"

She gasped from the impact.

"Okay?" he asked.

Her arms encircled him, and he bit back a moan when she made contact with the bump on the back of his head. "Yes," she sighed. "*So* okay."

If he had to suffocate, he decided, he wanted to do it between Samantha Holland's spectacular breasts, engulfed in her jasmine and vanilla scent. Dropping a gentle kiss on the bruise, he walked them—carefully, since his jeans were still twisted around his ankles— to the bed and lowered her.

"Nick."

"What, babe?"

"Fast." She clung to him. "I want it fast."

His heart staggered, and he had to bite his lip to keep from losing it right then and there. Knowing she could be noisy, he captured her mouth as he gave her what she wanted. Had *anything* ever been this good? No. Nothing. Ever. She was tough and courageous on the job, yet here with him she was all girl—warm, soft, fragrant girl. Her moan echoed through her and into him the instant before she lifted off.

He muffled her cries, or at least he hoped to God he did, before he pushed hard into her one last time and let himself go.

24

Freddie sat in front of Patricia Donaldson's two-story home for a long time. He couldn't imagine asking her the questions he needed to ask but knew it was long past time he got over the queasiness that struck him whenever he had to ask people personal questions—especially about their sex lives.

Perhaps if he got a sex life of his own, then he wouldn't be so put off by asking about what other people did in their bedrooms. He'd been raised a Christian, had taken his religion seriously and had saved himself for marriage. That's how he ended up a twenty-nine-year-old virgin, a fact he had shared with no one, lest he be ridiculed by his colleagues.

He'd had plenty of girlfriends and had done his share of fooling around, but he'd yet to have the full experience. Lately, he'd been thinking too much about what he was missing. And with no marital prospects on the horizon, he wondered how much longer he could hold out.

Since they'd interviewed that personal trainer the other day, Elin Svendsen, he had fantasized about her obsessively. The way she hinted at the nasty stuff she had done with Senator O'Connor... What Freddie wouldn't give for one night with her. Maybe once they cleared the case, he'd be in the market for some personal training of a different sort.

In the meantime, he needed to go into that house and ask Patricia Donaldson if her son was John O'Connor's son, if she'd continued a sexual relationship with the senator and if so, what kind of sex she'd had with him. The thought of asking those questions of a woman he'd never met made him sick.

Even if he sat there all night, he'd never be fully prepared. And since Sam was waiting for him to get this information and get it back to her, Freddie emerged from the rental car and headed up the flagstone walkway. With one last deep breath to settle his nerves, he rang the bell. Chimes echoed through the house. He waited a full minute before a fragile-looking blonde opened the door. Her blue eyes were rimmed with red, her pretty face ravaged with exhaustion. If this woman hadn't recently lost someone she loved, Freddie would turn in his badge.

"Patricia Donaldson?"

"Yes?"

"I'm sorry to disturb you, ma'am. I'm Detective Freddie Cruz, Metro Police, Washington, D.C." He showed her his badge.

She took the badge from him, examined it and handed it back to him. "This is about John."

"Yes, ma'am. I wondered if I might have a few minutes of your time?"

With a weary gesture, she stepped aside to let him in.

Freddie followed her to a comfortable family room, noting the photos of the handsome blond boy scattered throughout the house. The place appeared to have been professionally decorated, but had retained a warm, cozy atmosphere.

When he was seated across from her, Freddie said, "You were acquainted with Senator John O'Connor?"

"We've been friends for many years," she said softly.

"I'm sorry for your loss."

Her raw eyes filled with tears. "Thank you." She brushed at the dampness on her cheeks.

"You were just friends?"

"Yes," she said without hesitation.

Freddie reached for a framed photo on an end table. "Your son?"

"Yes."

"Handsome boy."

"Thank you."

"I can't help but notice his striking resemblance to the senator."

She shrugged. "Maybe a little."

Freddie returned the photo to the table. "Is your son at home?"

"He went to do an errand at school. He's a junior at Loyola."

Relieved to know the boy wasn't in the house, Freddie pressed on. "In the course of our investigation, we've uncovered a series of regular monthly payments Senator O'Connor made to you for the last twenty years." Even though he knew the facts by heart, Freddie consulted his notebook. "Three thousand dollars, paid by check, on the first of every month."

Her hand trembled ever so slightly as she reached for the gold locket she wore on a chain around her neck. "So?"

"Can you tell me why he gave you the money?"

"It was a gift."

"That's a mighty big gift—thirty-six thousand dollars a year, totaling more than seven hundred thousand over twenty years."

"He was a generous man."

"Ms. Donaldson, I realize this is a very difficult time for you, but if you were his friend—"

"I was his best friend," she cried, her hand curling into a fist over her heart. "He was mine."

"If that's the case, I'm sure you want us to find the person who killed him."

"Of course I do. I just don't see what you need from me."

"I need you to confirm that your son Thomas is John O'Connor's son."

"Do you, Detective?" she asked softly. "Do you really need me to confirm it?"

Her easy capitulation flustered Freddie. He'd expected to have to work for it. "I'd appreciate if you could tell me about your relationship with the senator, from the day you met him through to his death."

She paused for a long moment, as if she were making a decision, and then began to talk so softly that Freddie had to strain to hear. "My family moved to Leesburg the summer before eighth grade. I met him on the first day of school. He was nice to me when no one else gave me the time of day, but that was John. It was just like him to make the new girl feel welcome." Lost in her memories, she seemed to have forgotten Freddie was there.

He took notes, knowing Sam would expect every detail.

"We became friends—unlikely friends."

"Why unlikely?"

"His father was a United States senator, a multimillionaire businessman. Mine worked at the post office. We weren't exactly from the same universe, but John was the least status-conscious person I ever knew.

He couldn't have cared less about his father's position, which of course drove his father crazy.

"Over time, our friendship grew and blossomed into love. His parents never liked me, never welcomed me into their home or their family. That made John sad, but it didn't keep us apart. He was the love of my life, Detective, and I was the love of his. We knew it at fifteen. Can you imagine?"

"No, ma'am." He couldn't imagine it at twenty-nine. "I can't."

"We were overwhelmed by what we felt for each other and determined to be together forever, no matter what it took." She glanced down at her lap, her fingers twisting nervously. "I was sixteen when I got pregnant. My parents were devastated, but his were outraged. His father was in the midst of an ugly re-election campaign, and all they cared about was the potential scandal. They offered me a hundred thousand dollars to have an abortion."

Freddie kept his expression neutral.

"I refused to even consider it. I was under the illusion that John and I would find a way to be together, to raise our child together. I had no idea then how far people with power could and would go to get what they wanted. Within a week, my father was transferred to a post office in Illinois."

"What did John say about this?"

"What could he say? He was going into his senior year of high school. His parents still had him under their thumb."

"Did he see the baby?"

She nodded. "He and his parents came out for a day when Thomas was born. The senator pitched a holy fit when I named him Thomas John O'Connor, but they had taken John away from me—away from us—they weren't going to deny my son his father's name. I had my limits, too."

"What was your relationship with John like after the baby was born?"

"We talked on the phone as often as we could. We made plans to be together." Her hands trembled in her lap. "After he graduated from high school, his father got him an internship in Congress for the summer and then they shipped him off to Harvard. It was more than a year before we saw each other again."

"He was an adult by then. Why didn't he stand up to his parents?"

"They controlled the money, Detective, the money he was using to support his son while he was in college. He did what he was told."

"And after college?"

"His father threatened to disown him if he married me, because if he did, people would find out about 'the kid' as Graham called him, and there'd be a scandal." Her voice had gone flat and lifeless. "As much as John loved me and Thomas, he wouldn't have been able to live with being disowned by his father." She leaned forward. "Don't get me wrong, Detective. I hate Graham O'Connor for what he denied me, what he denied Thomas and mostly what he denied John. But John loved his father, and more, he respected him despite everything he had done to us. John was a good man, the best man I've ever known, but he didn't have it in him to turn his back on his father. He just didn't. I accepted that a long time ago and learned to be satisfied with what I had."

"Which was what exactly?"

"We had one weekend a month to be a family, and we made the most of it. John was a wonderful father to Thomas. Between visits, he was completely available to him, and they talked most days. My son is devastated by his father's death."

"And no one ever questioned his resemblance to the senator in light of the fact that he had his name?"

"No," she said. "Amazingly, we got away with it. The O'Connors managed to thoroughly bury us here in the Midwest. During John's campaign and the first few months he was in office, we played it cool and didn't see much of each other. Once the attention faded, we were able to pick things up again. The media never caught so much as a whiff of us."

"I'm curious as to why he sent you monthly payments, rather than giving you a lump sum. His parents had money, and he became a wealthy man himself when he sold his company."

"He took good care of us, but he liked sending the monthly payments. He said it made him feel connected to Thomas and to me."

"I apologize in advance for what I'm about to ask you… But I need to know where the senator slept when he was here."

Her eyes flashed with anger and embarrassment. "Where do you think he slept?"

"Was he involved with other women?" Freddie hated the pain his question obviously caused her.

"Yes," she said through gritted teeth. "But my son doesn't know that, and I'd prefer to keep it that way."

"It didn't bother you? That he was with other women?"

"Of course it bothered me, but I didn't expect him to be celibate the other twenty-seven days a month."

"Did you discuss the other women in his life?"

"We did not."

"Not even when he was with Natalie for three years?"

"He had his life, and I had mine," she snapped. "One weekend a month, we belonged to each other."

"Have you ever been married?"

She laughed. "Where do you think I would've stashed my husband on the third weekend of every month when my longtime lover came to visit?"

"So that's a no?"

"I've never been married."

"When he was here," Freddie said, trying not to stumble over the words, "you had sexual relations with him?"

"I don't see how that's relevant to the case."

"It's relevant, and I need you to answer the question."

"Yes, I had sex with him! As much and as often as I could! Are you satisfied?"

"Was there anything, um, unusual about the kind of sex you had with him?"

She stood up. "We're finished here. I won't allow you to come into my home and debase the most important relationship in my life."

Freddie stayed seated to give her the perceived advantage as he dropped the final bomb. "Did he ever try to get you to have rough sex or anal sex with him?"

She stared at him, astounded. "I want you to leave. Right now."

"I'm sorry, ma'am, but you can answer the question here or I can take you back to Washington so you can answer it there. It's your call."

Her hands on her hips, her eyes shot daggers at him. "John O'Connor was never anything but a perfect gentleman with me. Every woman should have a lover as gentle and sweet. Now if there's nothing further, I want you to leave my home."

"Will you be attending the funeral in Washington?"

"Since there's no longer an O'Connor in office, I

can't see any reason for my son and me to hide out anymore. We're planning to go. John's attorney called me today to tell me we need to be at the reading of the will the day after the funeral. I'm sure Graham and Laine are thrilled about that."

"Have they ever had any contact with Thomas?"

"Not since the day after he was born."

"The media will be all over you."

He admired the courageous lift of her chin. "John suffered over the fact that he couldn't acknowledge his son. The least I can do for him is rectify that now that he's gone."

"I'm sorry again for your loss, Ms. Donaldson, and I'm sorry to have upset you with my questions."

She shrugged off his apology. "If it helps the investigation, then I guess it will have been worth it."

"You've been a big help."

At the door, she said, "Detective? Get the person who did this to my John." Her eyes filled with new tears. "Please."

"We're doing everything we can."

25

The Watergate lobby was mobbed, but when Nick walked in the mob went silent, parting to allow him passage to the elevator. He recognized some of the faces—his grandmother, his father, Mr. Pacheco from seventh grade science, Lucy Jenkins who'd lived next door and Graham O'Connor. Why was he here? With the vote this afternoon, John wouldn't have time for one of their regular lunches.

Nick tried to tell him John was busy, but Graham wouldn't listen. He just smiled, like he knew something Nick didn't know. Behind him, was that… Sam? Sam Holland? She hadn't returned his calls, but that was a long time ago. He'd always wanted to see her again. Reaching out, he tried to get to her.

She smiled and slipped away.

"No! Not again. Come back. Sam!"

John's sister Lizbeth cried and clawed at him, her face red and swollen. "John's hurt! Help him, Nick. Help him!"

Nick ran for the elevator, pushed the up button frantically, but the doors wouldn't open. Banging on the metal doors until his hands were bruised, he finally bolted for the stairs and ran up six flights. Gasping for air, he emerged into the hallway. A woman dashed from John's apartment carrying a bloody knife, her face covered by a knitted scarf.

"John!" Nick sprinted into the apartment.

"Hey, Cappy," John said, emerging from the bedroom, blood coursing from the open wound in his neck. "What's up?"

"John…" Nick pressed his hands against John's neck, trying to make it stop. How could he lose this much blood and stay conscious? "Help! Somebody help us!"

"It's okay, Cappy." John's hand landed on Nick's shoulder. "I'll be all right."

Nick looked up to find John's face morphing into a smiling skeleton. He screamed.

"Nick," Sam said. "Wake up. Babe, wake up."

His head ached, his mouth was dry, his eyes gritty. "What?"

Sam brushed the hair off his forehead and kissed his cheek. "You were dreaming."

Nick rested a hand over his racing heart. "John was there. He was still alive. There was so much blood. I tried to make it stop." His throat tightening, he closed his eyes. "I couldn't stop it."

She held him close, running her fingers through his hair. "You couldn't have stopped it," she whispered.

"The stuff I've found out about him…since it happened… None of it matters. He was my friend."

"Yes." She pressed her lips to his forehead. "That'll never change."

"He was the closest thing to a brother I've ever had. We had this…language. It was all ours. The staff used to shake their heads when we'd get going. They had no idea what we were talking about. But we did. We always did."

Sam tightened her hold on him.

"I miss him," he whispered. "I really miss him. I just can't believe I'm never going to see him again."

"I'm sorry. I wish there was something I could say."

"You're helping." He raised his head, met her eyes.

She leaned in to kiss him. "I want to get the person who did this for his parents and his family. But mostly I want it for you."

"I'm apt to be a bit of a mess for a while."

"That's all right."

He rested his hand over the hideous bruise on her chest. "This is a hell of a time for us to be starting something. You know that, don't you?"

"Worst possible time."

"So it stands to reason we'll be able to deal with just about anything if we can get through this."

"I guess we'll find out." She smiled and caressed his face. "I need to get back to work."

"I know. Did you sleep?"

"Big time. I didn't think I would."

"You needed it. We both did." He leaned in to kiss her once more. "Are you or your dad going to mind that I plan to stay here with you until this is over?"

"No. I like having you here, and he doesn't really care, despite the grief he might give you."

"I need to go home at some point to get some clothes and make sure the condo association took care of getting the windows fixed."

"We can arrange that." She sat up and stretched. "I'm going to grab a shower. Care to join me?"

"I'd love to, but I'm not going to push my luck. I'll go after you."

"Wimp."

"Yep."

She laughed as she slipped into a robe, and the sound warmed him. He was surprised to realize she had made him feel better, even as the sickening images from the dream lingered. After Sam went into the bathroom, he sat up, gripping his pounding head. The concussion they'd called minor was making a major statement, and whatever they'd used to numb the cut over his eye had worn off, leaving a dull, throbbing ache.

He felt kind of foolish about unloading on Sam, but she hadn't seemed to mind. Having someone to share the ups and downs with was something he could get used to—as long as that someone was her.

He stood up and groaned when his injured foot protested. Reaching for his jeans, he pulled them on and took a good look around the messy room. Sam had a way of exploding into a space, which was in direct conflict with his need for order. Beginning with the clothes piled on the floor, he went to work on the clutter. By the time she emerged from the bathroom fifteen minutes later, the place was almost livable.

Her eyes all but popped out of her skull. "It's like you can't help yourself!"

"Just straightening up. No biggie."

"I won't be able to find anything!"

"You couldn't find anything before."

"I knew *exactly* where everything was."

"No way," he scoffed. "You're a slob, Samantha." He bunched the towel she had wrapped around her into his fist and tugged her close enough to kiss. "A sexy, gorgeous slob, but a slob nonetheless."

Pouting, she tried to break free of him. "Just because I'm not an anal retentive freakazoid, doesn't mean I'm a slob."

"Freakazoid? I'm hurt." With another hard kiss he released her so she could get dressed. "This is going to be a problem when we live together."

"*Live* together?" she sputtered, choking on the words. "Where the hell did *that* come from?"

"You don't have to act like the idea is totally repulsive."

She shoved her long legs into jeans. "We haven't even been together a week, Nick. I mean…come on."

Not wanting her to see that she'd hurt him by being so dismissive, he turned away from her to look out the window. He churned with things he'd like to say to her, arguments and persuasions she was clearly not ready to hear. As he stared out into the darkness, a shadow across the street caught his eye. Zeroing in for a closer look, he realized someone was watching the house. He ignored the screaming pain in his foot and the pounding in his head when he bolted for the door and flew down the stairs.

Sam called out to him.

Blasting through the front door and down the ramp, he was almost hit by a car as he ran into the street. The blare of the car's horn startled him, taking his attention off the shadow for just an instant, but that was all it took.

"Watch out, asshole!" the driver yelled out the car window.

By the time Nick recovered his bearings the shadow was long gone.

"*Shit!* Son of a bitch!"

"What're you doing?" Sam screamed from the porch.

"Someone was there," he said, his breath coming out in white puffs in the cold air. "I saw him. Watching the house."

"So you just run out half-cocked, not to mention half-dressed?"

"What else was I supposed to do?"

She had her hands on her hips in a gesture he recognized by now as her seriously pissed stance. "Um, I don't know. Maybe tell the *cop* who was in the room with you?"

He limped back to the ramp and started up to where she waited for him. "I didn't think of it. All I thought about was getting him."

"And what were you going to do with him once you got him?"

Squirming under the heat of her blue-eyed glare, he shrugged. "I would've figured something out."

"That's *exactly* how civilians get themselves killed by the hundreds every year, thinking they can take the law into their own hands."

"I don't need you to lecture me or to keep using the word *civilian* like it's some kind of vermin."

"Vermin's got to be smarter than you just were."

"I almost had him."

"You almost got flattened by a car!"

Fuming, they stood there spitting nails at each other.

"Um, 'scuse me, but ah, I'm back," Freddie said from the sidewalk. "You said I should come here and, um…"

"Come up," Sam said, never taking her eyes off Nick. "Go in. I'll be right there."

"Gotcha, boss," Freddie said with a sympathetic smile for Nick as he went by them. "Good to see you again, Mr. Cappuano."

"Likewise," Nick said, still focused on Sam. "And you can call me Nick."

"You should've told me what you saw," Sam said after the door closed behind Freddie. "If you had, I could've called it in, and maybe we would've nabbed him. Instead, you go off on a Rambo mission that yielded squat."

Nick contemplated that. "You might have a point."

"I *might?* Really? Wow, thanks."

"I'm sorry, all right?" He ran a hand through his hair in frustration. "I just reacted. So shoot me for wanting to get whoever is stalking you."

"How do you know they're not stalking *you?*"

"Because I'm a whole lot more boring than you are."

"You're not boring. Stupid occasionally, but never boring."

"Thank you. I think."

"Did you get a good look at him?"

He shook his head. "Nothing but a shadow, but that shadow was definitely watching this house."

"If you see him again, *tell me.*" She pinched his chest hair and tugged just hard enough to raise him to his tiptoes and bring tears to his eyes. "Don't you *dare* risk yourself like that again. You got me?"

"I got it," he said through gritted teeth. After she released him, he rubbed a hand over his chest. "I only let you get away with that shit because I was taught it's bad manners to flatten a woman, even if she deserves it."

"Whatever," she retorted on her way back into the house where Skip, Celia and Freddie waited for them.

Skip's sharp eyes skirted over Nick's bare chest and feet.

"Um, I'm going to go find a shirt," Nick said, starting up the stairs.

"Might not be a bad idea," Skip said.

"Leave him alone, Dad," Sam said. "He's already convinced you're going to have him killed."

"Also not a bad idea. Why didn't I think of it?"

"Dad..."

"Relax and let me have some fun with the boy, will you? I so rarely get to have any fun these days."

Freddie smirked.

"What're you smiling at, Cruz?"

The smile faded. "Not a thing, ma'am. Not one thing."

"I assume you're not just here to bum another meal. What've you got for me?"

"Some of the others are heading over from HQ to help out," he said. "Want me to wait and brief everyone at the same time?"

"Give me the highlights."

By the time he had run through it, she had paced a path in the living room rug.

"I was thinking on the plane ride home," Freddie said, "that the other women he dated were like substitutes for the one he couldn't have. All of them resemble her in basic features, and I'm no shrink, but maybe he turned on the kink with them because he was frustrated he couldn't be with the one he wanted."

"That's probably why he freaked when Natalie pressured him about getting married. In his own twisted way, he felt like he was already married, even if he was unfaithful to her. I mean, how does he marry someone else when she's off raising his kid in Siberia?"

Nick came down the stairs, his hair wet from the shower.

"You heard all that?" Sam asked, alarmed by his pale face and flat eyes.

"Enough to get the gist."

"I'm sorry," she said, surprised when he shook off her sympathy.

"Don't protect me. Do your job. Find out who did it."

"Okay," she said, understanding that he was absorbing the blow the best way he knew how. Turning back to Freddie, she was interrupted when the front door swung open. In flooded most of the HQ detectives, carrying platters of food, six packs of beer and soda, and armloads of chips. Each of them paused to squeeze Skip's hand on their way into the kitchen to deposit the food.

"What the hell is this?" she asked Gonzo.

"They take a stab at you, they take one at all of us," he said, his chocolate brown eyes fierce. "Everyone's on their own time. Give us something to do."

Touched and on the verge of choking up, she said, "Thank you."

"They posted the LT list today. Congratulations."

"You'll be there soon enough," she said with a twinge of guilt over how she'd gotten there. Gonzo made detective a couple of years after her, so at least she hadn't snagged a spot from him. "For sure."

He shrugged. "We'll see."

"There was someone out there." She gestured to the door. "Nick saw him watching the house. He went vigilante on me and scared the guy off."

"I'll call it in and get someone posted outside."

"If it was just me, I wouldn't want it. But my dad's here and Celia…"

"Say no more. We're on it." He glanced over at Nick. "So. You and the witness, huh?"

She winced. "Don't."

Gonzo's handsome face lit up with amusement. "I won't, but others will. You have to know that."

"Hopefully, the gossip mill will run its course and the story will die a natural death when someone else fucks up."

"Not before you take some serious abuse."

"I can handle it."

"Sam?" Nick said. "Why don't you come have something to eat?"

"He likes to feed me," she whispered to Gonzo.

"Nothing wrong with that."

Thirty minutes later, after everyone had eaten, Sam

called them into the living room. "Let's get back to work."

"Before we do that," Freddie raised his Coke bottle in salute to Sam, "a toast to my partner, soon-to-be *Lieutenant* Holland."

As Sam glared at him and plotted his slow, painful death, the room erupted into applause and whistles. She glanced at her father and found him watching her, his eyes bright with emotion.

He nodded with approval and pleasure—more pleasure than she'd seen on his face in two years.

"All right," she said, putting a stop to the merriment before they forgot they were there to work on a homicide. "Thanks for the food, the toast and the help. I appreciate it. Before we go any further, I need to ask if you all mind that Nick is here. He's been very helpful to us on the investigation—"

"He's been critical," Freddie said.

Sam sent him a grateful smile. "Still, if anyone's uncomfortable…"

"No problem for me," Gonzo said.

The others mumbled their agreement.

Sam released a breath she hadn't realized she'd been holding and turned to Freddie. "In that case, Cruz, let's hear what you found out in Chicago."

"You got it, boss."

26

"I also dug into the girlfriends like you asked me to," Freddie said, consulting his notebook. "Tara Davenport has no tattoos or unusual piercings. The people she says she was with on the night of the murder confirm her story, and security tapes show her arriving home at 10:18 and leaving again at 9:33 the next morning. Elin Svendsen's date, Jimmy Chen, a major muscle head, confirmed they had dinner and went to a dance club for a couple of hours. He dropped her off at her apartment just after two in the morning. The building has minimal security and no video, so I couldn't confirm that she stayed in for the rest of the night. She has a tattoo on her left breast—a heart with a Cupid's arrow—and both nipples are pierced."

"I don't even want to *know* how you found that out," Sam said, drawing chuckles from the other detectives.

"Not the way I would've preferred, that's for sure."

"Go, Cruz!" Detective Arnold said with a bark of laughter.

"Aw, our little boy's growing up," Gonzo said, dabbing at a pretend tear.

"Up yours, Gonzo."

In deference to her partner, Sam stifled the urge to laugh. "Is that it?"

"You didn't tell me to," Freddie continued, "but I dug a little deeper on Natalie Jordan. St. Clair was her maiden name, and I got a hit on that. Apparently our girl Natalie lost her college boyfriend in a suspicious fire in Maui about fifteen years ago."

"You don't say." Blood zipped through Sam's veins as pieces began to fall into place. Whether they were the right pieces, she'd soon find out.

"She and the senator had been broken up for years when he was killed," Skip said. "Hardly the same thing."

"True," Sam said. "Give us the details on the fire, Cruz."

"Brad Foster, age twenty-one, killed in a suspicious house fire while on a two-week vacation in Maui with Natalie St. Clair."

"Two weeks in Maui for a couple of college kids?" Gonzo asked with a low whistle.

"Apparently, Foster's family was loaded. His parents owned the beach house. Anyway, from the reports I found in the newspaper, Natalie went out for a morning walk and while she was gone the house went up. Police suspected arson but couldn't prove it. Her alibi for the time of the fire was flimsy. They looked really closely at her but never charged her with anything."

"Good work, Cruz," Sam said. "We'll have another chat with Mrs. Jordan tomorrow."

"I should also add that I found no unsolved dismemberment cases in the District, Virginia or Maryland," Freddie said. "I can widen the search if you think it's worth it."

"Hold off on that for now. Gonzo, what do you have from the search of O'Connor's cabin?"

"Nothing other than some additional references to

the kid, Thomas—cards, letters, artwork from when he was younger—but you've already got that."

"What about the immigration bill, Dad?"

Skip took them through the finer points of the proposed law. "There's a lot of passion on both sides of this issue. There are those who feel that keeping our borders open to people in need is what this country is all about—'give me your tired, your poor, your huddled masses…'" When he was greeted with blank stares, he added, "Emma Lazarus? The poem engraved on the Statue of Liberty? Did you people go to school?" Rolling his eyes, he continued. "The other side argues that immigrants are a drain on the system, that charity should begin at home and we can't take care of the people who are already here."

"Would killing the senator kill the bill, too?" Sam asked Nick.

"That's exactly what it did. We had it sewn up by one vote. The Senate's in recess until January. Depending on who they get to take John's seat and whether he or she supports the bill, we might get lucky and get it back to the floor for a vote sometime next year. But either way, the supporters will have to start all over to make sure they have the votes. Even a month is a long time in politics—plenty of time for people to change their minds."

"So if someone was out to stop it altogether, killing him would accomplish that," Sam said.

"It'll certainly delay it indefinitely. Getting a bill through committee and on to the floor for a vote is no simple process. It took more than a year of writing, rewriting, compromising, meetings with various lobbies and interest groups, more compromise. Not simple."

Listening to him, Sam had a whole new appreciation for how John's death had affected Nick's professional life. The failure to pass the immigration bill had to be a bitter defeat on top of the personal tragedy. "In that case, his murder seems too well timed to be coincidental."

"Someone couldn't bear to see him get this win, you mean," Freddie said.

"Which takes us right back to his brother Terry," Sam said.

Nick shook his head.

"Speak," Sam said.

"I've said this before—Terry doesn't have the balls to kill his brother. He's an overgrown boy trying to live in a man's world. This would take planning and foresight. Terry's idea of making a plan is deciding which bar to hit on a given night."

"Still," Sam said, "he had motive, opportunity, a key and can't produce his alibi. I want to bring him in tomorrow morning for a formal interview."

"Can't that wait until after the funeral?" Nick asked, beseeching her with those hazel eyes of his.

"No. I'm sorry. I wish I could spare the O'Connors any more grief, but the minute they lied to me about Thomas, they lost the right to that courtesy. In fact, I could charge them with obstruction of justice."

"But you won't," Nick said stiffly.

"I haven't decided yet."

"I noticed Terry never completed the court-ordered safe driving school after his DUI," Freddie said.

Sam smiled as she turned to Gonzo and Arnold. "Will you pick up Terry O'Connor in the morning? While he's our guest, we'll have another chat with him about his alibi. Coordinate with Loudoun County."

"Can do," Arnold said.

"You're barking up the wrong tree," Nick said, frustration all but rippling from him.

"So noted." To the others, she said, "What've we got on the bombing?"

Higgins gave them an in-depth analysis of the four crude, homemade bombs they'd found attached to Sam's car and Nick's. "We got a partial print off one of the EDs on Mr. Cappuano's car, and we're running it through AFIS now," he said, referring to the Automated Fingerprint Identification System.

"We've worked our way through the Johnson family and the majority of their known associates," Detective Jeannie McBride said. "For the most part, they were hardly sympathetic to hear you'd nearly gotten blown up but were adamant that they had nothing to do with it." With a chagrined expression, she added, "A few said they wished they'd thought of it."

"Nice," Nick muttered.

"We didn't pick up any vibe that an actual order had come from either of the Johnsons," McBride said.

"And it would have," Sam said. "After six months undercover with them, I can tell you nothing happens without one of them ordering it."

"Agreed," McBride said.

Sam ran her fingers through her hair, which she had left down the way Nick liked it. "I've got a bunch of shit running around in my head, so I want to go through it from the top if no one minds."

When the others nodded in agreement, she began with Nick finding the senator's body in his apartment. "He's murdered on the eve of a vote that would elevate his standing in the Senate by passing legislation on a hot-button issue. The murder itself, at least on the surface, is personal, with all the trimmings of a love affair gone wrong. However, as Detective Cruz correctly pointed out, the dismemberment could've been intended to throw us off, to send us down the personal road. Keep in mind there was no forced entry and no sign of a struggle, leading us to believe the killer was someone he knew, someone he was comfortable with and not surprised to see."

"And someone who had one of the many keys he'd given out," Freddie interjected.

"Yes. We've interviewed three of his past lovers, discovered he had a few fetishes, and uncovered a son his family kept hidden from the public for twenty years. The mother of that child appears, for all intents and purposes, to have been the love of his life and, for some reason, the only one who didn't experience his wilder side. It would stand to reason that his often-cavalier treatment of other women and his fixation with Internet porn stem directly from the stymieing of the most important sexual relationship in his life. That it wasn't allowed to flourish or take its natural course, set him up for all kinds of psychological issues that he worked hard to keep hidden from even the people closest to him." She glanced at Nick and found him staring at the wall, his face impassive.

"The senator's relationship with his parents, his father in particular, was complicated by the teenage pregnancy and the resulting child. When John reached adulthood, his father threatened to disown him if he married Patricia Donaldson or acknowledged his son. If Ms. Donaldson is to be believed, protecting his political career and reputation was more important to Graham O'Connor than his own grandchild." She looked to Freddie for confirmation. With his nod, she continued. "On the same night he discovered the senator's body, Mr. Cappuano reported an intruder in his house, which the Arlington police investigated. Toss in Destiny Johnson's threats in yesterday's paper and the bombing today. Is that everything?" She looked to Freddie. "Am I forgetting anything?"

"Stenhouse."

"Right—the O'Connors' bitter political rival. His motive would be derailing the bill and deflecting the accompanying glory that would have fallen on John, the son of a man he told us he hated."

"But he would've had no way into O'Connor's apartment," Freddie said. "Or at least he wouldn't have had a key."

"Which keeps him at the bottom of the list, but still a person of interest," Sam said. "A man in his position could probably get a key if he wanted one badly enough. So how's it all related? How's our dead senator related to a break-in at his chief of staff's house? If we've ruled out Johnson, how's it related to a bombing at the same location?"

"Maybe it isn't," Skip said.

All eyes turned to him.

Sam's brows knitted with confusion. "What do you mean, Dad?"

"Goes back to timing. What else has happened this week?" Before Sam could reply, he said, "In the course of the investigation, you've rekindled an old flame." He glanced at Nick. "Who might be put out by that?"

"We're both single, so other than my superiors, I can't think of anyone," she said, wondering where he was going with this.

"Are you sure?"

And then, all at once, she knew exactly what he was talking about—or rather *whom*. "Peter," she gasped. "Oh my God." Curling her fist into her stomach, she had to sit when her legs would have buckled under her.

The room fell silent. Her rancorous divorce, complete with restraining orders and accusations of mental cruelty and emotional abuse, was hardly a secret to any of them.

Nick sat next to her, and Sam didn't object when his arm slid around her shoulders.

"He was outside the house," she whispered. "That was him before. He was watching us that night after we had pizza. I felt *something*, but I blew it off, chalked it up to nerves. I'll bet he was in your house, too."

"What would he want there?"

"First rule of combat," she said softly. "Know your enemy."

Nick turned to Skip. "What do we do?"

Skip shifted his furious eyes to Gonzo. "Call Malone. Report in, and then pick up Gibson."

"Yes, sir." Gonzo signaled to Arnold, his partner, and they left.

"I'm going with you," Freddie said, following them.

Sam got up and grabbed her coat off a hook by the door. "I just need some, ah, air." She rushed through the front door.

Nick was right behind her.

She struggled against his efforts to embrace her. "Just leave me alone, will you?"

"The hell I will." He pulled her in close and tightened his arms around her. "Don't push me away, Samantha."

"*He was watching us!* He was in your house! Because of *me!*"

"It's not your fault. Don't take it on."

"*How can I not?* He's obsessed." Another thought occurred to her all of a sudden.

"What?"

"The EDs," she whispered, the ramifications so huge, so monstrous it was almost too much to process.

"You don't think…"

She looked up at him. "That he'd rather kill me than see me with you? Yeah, I do, and if he couldn't take me out, getting rid of you would be the next best thing."

"Jesus."

"I told him everything about you after that night we spent together. When you didn't call, I told him about the connection we'd had, how I'd never had that before with anyone else. I thought he was my friend." She took a deep, rattling breath to stave off the pain circling in her gut. "He'd remember that. He'd know you were important, a real threat. The first real threat since he and I broke up."

"He'd be jealous enough to want to kill us both?"

"Destiny Johnson handed him the perfect opportunity with her tirade in the paper yesterday," Sam said as the whole thing clicked into focus with such startling clarity she wondered how she could've missed it. "If it had worked, the cops would naturally blame her or her friends. No one would've thought to look at him. It was so easy. He wouldn't have been able to resist." The pain gnawed at her insides, making her sick and weak.

"Would he know *how* to build a bomb?"

"You can get how-to instructions for just about anything on the Internet these days." She winced at the claws stabbing her gut. "Higgins said the EDs were crude. I guess we were lucky Peter screwed it up."

"You're in pain."

"Just need to breathe," she panted.

He loosened his hold on her. "What can I do? You're scaring me, Sam."

Clutching her midsection, she looked up at him. "I've dragged you into a nightmare."

"I'm exactly where I want to be—where I've wanted to be since the night I met you. And if I get my hands on that ex-husband of yours before you do, I'll be sure to let him know that he might've sent us on a long detour but we found our way back to each other." He kissed her, gently at first and then with more passion when she responded in kind. "Despite him, we found our way back, and nothing's going to get in our way this time. Nothing and no one."

"Especially not a couple of bombs," she said with a weak smile.

"That's right." He returned her smile. "How's the belly?"

"Better," she said, surprised to realize it was true.

"We're going to do something about that. As soon as this case is closed, you're going to see my doctor friend Harry."

"You and what army will be taking me?"

"You'll find out if you don't go on your own."

Her heart hammered in her chest as she studied him. "There're things…about me…that I need to tell you, stuff you should know before you decide anything."

Cradling her face in his hands, he looked down at her with his heart in his eyes. "There's nothing you could tell me that would make me not want to be with you. Nothing."

"You don't know that—"

His mouth came down hard on hers, stealing the words, the thoughts, the air and every ounce of reason. When he had kissed her into submission, he said, "I do know that."

"But—"

"I love you, Samantha. I've loved you from the first instant I ever saw you across a crowded deck at that party and for all the years since. Having you back in my life is the single best thing that's ever happened to me. So there's nothing, nothing at all, you could tell me that would change my mind about you or what I want from you."

Sam rarely found herself speechless, but as she looked up at his beautiful, earnest face—the face she had dreamed about during her miserable marriage— she simply couldn't find the words.

Without breaking the intense eye contact between them, he brushed his lips over hers in a kiss so sweet and undemanding that her knees went weak.

"Later," he said. "We'll have all the time in the world. I promise."

27

They borrowed Celia's car to go to Arlington. After an upsetting day, the neighborhood had returned to tranquility, and the media had thankfully moved on to the next story. At Nick's house, the windows had been repaired, but broken glass crunched under their feet in the foyer and upstairs in his bedroom. "I'll still be cleaning up glass a year from now," he joked, attempting to make light of it since he could feel the distress radiating from her.

"I'm sorry."

"Don't go there, Samantha." He threw jeans, sweaters, underwear, T-shirts and socks into a large duffel bag. With the funeral scheduled for Monday, he packed a dark suit, dress shirt and tie into a garment bag and tossed a pair of wingtips into the duffel. In the bathroom, he grabbed what he needed as fast he could, not wanting her to be there any longer than necessary after what happened earlier.

He'd told her he loved her. Just blurted it out because he thought she needed to hear it right then. He told himself it didn't matter that she hadn't said it back. She would. Eventually. But what if she didn't? What if she'd been swept up by the craziness of the investigation, and he'd read her all wrong? No. That wasn't possible. Couldn't be possible.

"Nick?"

"What, babe?"

"You just went all still. What're you thinking about?"

He cleared the emotion and fear from his throat. "I'm wondering if they found Peter."

"They'll call me. They know he's mine once they bring him in."

"You're going to confront him?"

"I'm going to nail him."

"Why don't you let someone else do it? Why does it have to be you?"

"Because it does."

"That's it?"

She shrugged. "Yeah."

"What if I ask you not to?"

"Don't."

"Would it matter? If I did ask?"

"It would matter. And I'd take that in with me, and it'd throw me off. I want to be at one hundred percent when I confront that miserable excuse for a human being. So don't send me in there dragging baggage. Don't do that to me."

"Is that what I am? Baggage?"

"What the hell happened between my house and here?"

He zipped the duffel. "Nothing. Not a goddamned thing."

She grabbed his arm and spun him around to face her. "Are you mad that I didn't say it back?"

"What're you talking about?" he asked, his heart aching.

"You know." Her tone softened as she raised her

hands to his face. "Everything is so insane—the investigation, my psychopathic ex-husband, your loss and your job situation, my stomach...even the freaking holidays are bearing down on me. After what I went through with Peter, I'm different than I used to be. I'm more cautious. I haven't been cautious with you, though, and that scares me." She laughed. "It terrifies me, actually."

"You have nothing to fear from me."

"I know that, but I've screwed up so badly in the past. I need time, when I don't have fifty other things on my mind, to think and to process everything that's happened this week. I can't do that right now. But if it helps at all, I can tell you I'm moving in the same direction you are."

"It does help to know that." He reached for her hands and brought them to his lips. "Will you promise me one thing?"

"If I can."

"Will you spend Christmas Eve with me here? No matter what happens in the next few days, will you save that one night for me?"

"We usually go to my sister's..."

"We can do whatever you want on Christmas Day."

"All right."

"Promise?"

"I promise." She went up on tiptoes to kiss him. "I can't believe Christmas is Wednesday, and I haven't bought a thing for anyone. What about you?"

"Not too many people on my list. I usually get something for Christina, the O'Connors, my dad's twins, John..."

"I'm sorry. I wasn't thinking. About your family situation."

"Don't sweat it." He shut off the light in the bedroom and led her downstairs.

She stood in the living room with her hands jammed into her coat pockets. "What you said earlier, about us living together?"

"Too much, too soon. I get it."

"What I was going to say is if, you know, we get to that, I couldn't live here. It's too far from the city and my dad."

"Okay."

"That simple?"

"It's just a house."

She studied him. "When are you going to turn into a jerk?"

"Any minute now. I've been meaning to get to that."

Her cell phone rang, and she pulled it from her pocket. "It's Freddie." She put it on speaker so Nick could hear. "What've you got?"

"No sign of him at his place, but we found wires, plastic and fertilizer sitting right out on the table. Gonzo requested a warrant for a full search, and we're just waiting on that now."

She sat down. "I was hoping it wasn't him. I was really hoping…"

"I'm sorry. We've issued an APB. Every cop in the city is looking for him. We'll get him, Sam."

"Thanks. Go on home. Get some sleep. Meet me at HQ at eight. We'll put in a half day."

"I'll be there. Are you okay?"

"Overall, I've had better days, but I'm okay. See you in the morning."

Nick dropped the duffel and suit bag by the front door and joined her on the sofa.

"I was so hoping he was just stalking me and we

wouldn't be able to pin the EDs on him. I didn't want it to be him."

Nick put his arm around her and brought her in to rest against him. "I know, babe."

"The papers tomorrow will be all about me—the bomb, my relationship with you, my psycho ex-husband. They'll rehash Johnson, run through my dad's unsolved case." She scrubbed at her face. "I hate when the story is about me. It's been about me too often lately."

"You're so tired," he said, kissing her brow. "Do you want to sleep here tonight?"

"I'd rather stay close to home until we get Peter. He knows my dad is an Achilles heel of mine."

Standing, Nick held out a hand to help her up.

She surprised him when she wrapped her arms around him. "Can we just do this for a minute?"

He kissed the bruised bump on her forehead. "For as long as you want."

They were interrupted several minutes later by a knock on the door.

"Wonder who's here at this hour." Nick swung the door open and was startled to find Natalie Jordan on his doorstep. "Natalie? What're you doing here?" He wouldn't have thought she even knew where he lived.

Her eyes rimmed with red, she said, "May I come in for a minute?"

Nick glanced back at Sam, who nodded. He showed Natalie into the living room.

"I was hoping you'd be here," Natalie said to Sam. Her face was splotchy, as if she'd been crying for hours.

"What can I do for you?" Sam asked.

To Nick, Natalie said, "Would it be possible to get a glass of water?"

Nick made eye contact with Sam. "Sure." When he

returned with the water, Natalie had taken a seat on the sofa and was focused on her hands in her lap.

Sam looked at him and shrugged.

"Here you go," Nick said, handing Natalie the glass of water.

"Thank you."

"It's really late, Natalie," Nick said. "Why don't you tell us why you're here?"

"It's so unreal," she said softly. "I still can't believe it…"

"Mrs. Jordan, we can't help you if we don't know what you're talking about," Sam said.

Looking up at them with shattered eyes, Natalie said, "Noel. I think he…"

"What did Noel do?" Nick asked, his heart beating harder all of a sudden. He wanted to take Natalie by the shoulders and shake it out of her. "What did he do?"

"He might've killed John."

"Why do you say that?" Sam asked.

Nick noticed that she'd slipped into her cop mode, all signs of her earlier dismay over Peter gone.

"He's been acting funny, leaving at odd hours, long silences. He seems very angry, but he won't tell me why."

"When I talked to you earlier in the investigation, you didn't mention any of this."

"I hadn't put two and two together yet."

"Tell me what you think you've put together."

"That night," Natalie said haltingly, "the night John was killed, we went to bed together, but I woke up in the middle of the night and he was gone."

"You never mentioned that before."

"He's my husband, Detective." Natalie's eyes flooded with new tears. "I couldn't believe it was even possible. I didn't want to believe it's possible."

"So what changed?" Nick asked. "Why did you come here?"

"You were John's friend," Natalie said to Nick. "I thought you'd want to help find the person who did this to him."

"Of course I do! But I want the truth!"

"So do I! I loved him! You know I did. Noel was jealous of him. I couldn't even mention John's name without setting him off."

"What do you think set him off enough to want to kill him?" Sam asked.

"We saw John a couple of weeks before he died. It was at a cocktail party the Virginia Democrats had at Richard Manning's house." Natalie wiped new tears from her cheeks. "John came over to me, gave me a friendly hug and kiss. We talked for a long time, just catching up on each other's lives. It was nothing. But I looked over at one point and saw Noel watching us. He looked like he could kill us both on the spot."

"Why didn't you mention any of this to us the other day?" Sam asked.

"I didn't want to believe it."

"You still haven't said what changed your mind."

"I asked him." She ran a trembling hand through her disheveled hair. "Straight out. 'Did you kill John?' He denied it of course, but I don't believe him." To Nick, she said, "I didn't know what to do, so I came over here, hoping you'd put me in touch with Detective Holland."

"Do you have somewhere you can go where you'll be safe?" Sam asked.

Natalie nodded. "My parents' home in Springfield."

"Give me some time to look into this," Sam said.

"He's powerful," Natalie said. "You'll never be able to pin this on him."

"If he did it, I'll pin it on him," Sam assured her.

Natalie stood up to leave. "I'm sorry to barge in on you. I heard about what happened earlier. I'm glad you weren't seriously hurt."

They walked her to the door. "Tomorrow, I'll want to get all of this on the record." Sam pulled her ever-present notebook from her back pocket. "Write down your parents' address and a phone number where I can reach you."

Natalie did as she asked. "Thank you for listening." To Nick, she added, "I know I was never your favorite person—"

"That's neither here nor there."

"Anyway, thank you."

They watched her walk to her car.

"She's full of shit," Nick said, his eyes intensely focused on Natalie's car as it drove away. "I don't believe her for one minute."

"What don't you believe? That her jealous husband could've killed the man his wife never stopped loving? That's as good a motive as I've heard yet."

"I know Noel Jordan. He's not made of that kind of stuff. If you ask me, she is, though. I could very easily see her losing her shit with John and killing him for not loving her enough. After what we heard earlier about her ex-boyfriend dying in a suspicious fire, you believe it's possible, too."

"Why would she come here, seeking out the lead detective on the case, if she was the one who did it? Think about that, Nick."

"Why didn't you ask her about what happened to her boyfriend in Hawaii?"

"I didn't want to tip my hand on that just yet. As long as she thinks we don't know about it, she might be more forthcoming."

"I don't like her. I've never liked her, and I don't care

what you say, she's lying. She'll do anything it takes to advance her agenda, even if it means tossing her husband under the bus."

Sam checked her watch. "I wonder what time Noel goes to bed."

"You're actually going to do something with that pile of bullshit she just fed you?"

"Of course I am. This could be the break we've been waiting for."

He ushered her out of the house and locked the door behind them. "You're wasting your time."

"It's my time to waste."

"It's almost midnight."

"I know what time it is. If you'd rather stay here, I can go by myself."

"You're not going anywhere by yourself as long as your ex-husband is out there waiting for another chance to kill you."

"I don't need you to protect me, Nick. I'm more than capable of taking care of myself."

Silently, he ushered her into the car and a few minutes later took the exit for the George Washington Parkway, heading toward Alexandria. "You really think I could go home and go to bed and actually *sleep*, knowing you're out here by yourself confronting a potential killer while your ex waits for his next opportunity?"

"I've been in tighter spots."

"That was before."

"Before what?"

"Before me."

"I'm not one of those women who finds this whole alpha-male act sexy. In fact, it's a major turn-off."

"Whatever."

They rode to Belle Haven in stony silence. Sam didn't speak until she had to direct him to the dark house. She retrieved her gun and badge from her purse and tucked them into her coat pockets. "Wait here."

As if she hadn't spoken, Nick emerged from the car and followed her up the walk.

"I told you to wait!"

"You're not going in there alone, Sam. It's either me, or I call 911." He held up his cell phone defiantly. "What's it going to be?"

They engaged in a silent battle of wills until Sam finally said, "Don't say a word. Do you hear me? Not one freaking word." She spun around and marched up the front stairs to ring the bell. It echoed in the big house. They waited a couple of minutes before a light went on upstairs. Through the beveled windows next to the door, Sam watched Noel come down the stairs.

He peeked through the window before he opened the door. "Sergeant Holland?" Blinking, he glanced at Nick.

"Yes," Sam said. "I'm sorry to call on you so late." Begrudgingly, she added, "I believe you know Nick Cappuano."

"Of course. Come in." Noel's blond hair stood on end. He wore a T-shirt from a road race with flannel pajama pants and hardly resembled the second-ranking attorney at the U.S. Department of Justice she had met the other day.

Nick and Noel shook hands as he ushered them into the house.

"What can I do for you?"

"Is Natalie here?" Sam asked, feeling him out.

Noel's genial expression faded. "She flew out of here in a rage after we had a fight earlier. She must be at her parents' house."

"Is that something that happens often?" Sam asked. "The rages?"

"It's not the first time, but I think it's going to be the last. I can't believe what she accused me of! She thinks I could actually *kill* John O'Connor. Can you even imagine?"

"People have killed over jealousy before."

"I see that she's voiced her suspicions to you." Noel ran his hands through his hair. "What do you want, Detective?"

"Why did you tell me that you attended the Big Brother/Big Sister event the night John was killed?"

"Because I had it in my date book."

"Your date book was off by a week."

Noel seemed startled to hear that. "My secretary keeps it up for me." He thought for a moment. "You know, you're right. It was two weeks ago. I'm really sorry about that. Things have been insane at work lately, and at home…"

"What's been going on at home?" Nick asked.

Sam glowered at him. "I'll ask the questions." Turning back to Noel, she said, "Things have been tense between you and Natalie?"

"More so than usual since we saw John at a fundraiser a couple of weeks ago. She knows how I feel about her talking and flirting with him in public, so what does she do? Flaunts her 'friendship' with him right in front of my face—and everyone in the room is talking about the two of them. How do you think that makes me feel?"

"Disrespected?" Nick said.

"I said to be quiet!" Sam hissed.

Noel directed an ironic chuckle at Nick that infuriated Sam.

"I guess you can relate, huh?" Noel said to Nick.

They followed Noel into the living room where he poured himself a drink from a crystal decanter.

Sam shook her head when he offered them one.

"Don't mind if I do," Nick said, earning another glare from Sam.

"Were you jealous of John?" Sam asked, anxious to wrestle the interview back from the old boys' club.

Noel handed Nick a drink and took a seat on the sofa. "I was sick of him. I was sick of hearing about him, sick of running into him. Mostly, I was sick of being her consolation prize."

"Why didn't you tell me any of this the other day?" Sam asked.

Swirling the amber liquor around his glass, Noel glanced at her. "Because I love her." He smiled, but it didn't reach his eyes. "Pathetic, huh? She has almost no regard for me or my feelings, yet I love her anyway."

"Were you sick enough of John O'Connor to kill him, Mr. Jordan?"

"No! Of course not. I didn't kill him."

"I'd like to give you a polygraph in the morning," Sam said.

"Fine. I have nothing to hide."

"Natalie said she woke up in the middle of the night John was killed and you were gone?"

"I was out running. I do that when I can't sleep."

"Do you think Natalie continued to see John after you were married?"

"We ran into him quite frequently. I've told you that."

"I don't mean in public."

Sam watched as her meaning dawned on him.

"You're not suggesting…"

"I'm not suggesting anything. I'm just asking."

"If she'd been seeing him, it's certainly without my knowledge." He took a long sip of whiskey, and Sam noticed a slight tremble in his hand.

"Do you think there's any way she killed him?"

"I'd like to say no way, but I honestly don't know anymore what she's capable of. I used to think I knew her. All I can say is she's been genuinely distraught since we heard he was dead. No doubt she's more upset than she would've been if it had been me who'd been murdered. And I'm the one who actually married her."

"Do you know about her ex-boyfriend who died in Hawaii?"

He nodded. "Brad. She's had more than her share of heartbreak, that's for sure."

Sam stood up. "I'm sorry to have disturbed you, but I appreciate your candor. I'll have someone contact you in the morning about the polygraph."

At the door, Noel said, "I didn't kill him, Sergeant. But it doesn't break my heart that someone else did."

"I know you're dying to tell me what you think," Sam said as they crossed the 14th Street Bridge on the way back to Capitol Hill.

"I was told to be quiet."

"I don't want to fight with you, Nick. That's the last thing I need right now."

"I don't want that, either. But you're asking a lot expecting me not to worry about you. He tried to *blow you up*."

"We're both kind of raw today," she said, reaching for his hand. "I really do want your impression of Noel."

"So you value my opinion?"

"Yes!"

Laughing, he curled his fingers around hers.

Right away, Sam felt better.

"He didn't do it," Nick said, "but he's not a hundred percent certain that she didn't."

"My thoughts exactly."

"I still say she's the one. She wanted John, he rejected her and she's never gotten over that."

"So why now? What sent her over the edge?"

"Maybe she didn't want to see him get the big win with the immigration bill."

"Why would she care about that? I keep coming back to that, to the timing of it all on the eve of that vote. *Why then?*"

"I can't see how the bill would have any impact whatsoever on Natalie," Nick said.

"Maybe the bill has nothing at all to do with his murder."

"I find that hard to believe."

"Yeah," Sam said, staring out the window. "Me, too."

28

Sam tossed and turned. She dreamed about Peter, Quentin Johnson and Natalie Jordan, and for once she actually remembered the dreams when she awoke with a start, her heart racing. Glancing at the bedside clock, she saw it was just after three and realized Nick wasn't in bed with her. Her eyes darted around the dark room and found him standing at the window, the glow of a street light illuminating his tall frame.

Taking a moment to appreciate his muscular back, she remembered him telling her he loved her and was filled with a warm feeling of contentment and safety that was all new to her. Then she remembered arguing with him over Noel and Natalie, and her stomach took a sickening dip. The soaring highs and crushing lows were just one reason why she'd stayed away from men since she broke up with Peter, who never would've been as civil as Nick had been during a fight. Even though they'd disagreed, Sam didn't doubt for a minute that he loved her. That made him as different from Peter as a man could get.

She got up and went to Nick. Slipping her arms around him from behind, she pressed her lips to his back. "What're you doing up?"

He rested his hands over hers. "Couldn't sleep."

"He's not stupid enough to come back here. By now he knows we're looking for him."

"I think I could kill him if I got my hands on him. I really think I could. Not just because of the bombs, but all those years ago, too. All the years we could've had."

"He's not worth losing sleep over, Nick." She turned him so he faced her and shivered with desire when he ran his hands over her while looking down at her with hot, needy eyes. Looping her arms around his neck, she gasped when he lifted her and carried her back to bed. "I thought you were mad with me."

"I am," he said in an unconvincing tone as he snuggled her against him and pulled the comforter up around them. "Try to get some sleep."

She dragged a lazy finger from his chest to his belly and smiled when he trembled under her touch.

"*Sleep*, Samantha."

"What if I don't *want to,* Nick?" she asked, curling her hand around his erection.

"I'm sleeping," he said with an exaggerated yawn. "And I'm mad with you."

Laughing, she clamped her teeth down on his nipple.

"*Ow!* That hurt!"

"But you're not asleep anymore," she said with a victorious smile as she raised herself up to plant wet kisses on his belly while continuing to stroke him.

His fingers combed through her hair. "You're going to be tired again tomorrow."

"Then I'd better make it count." She straddled him and teased him by sliding her wet heat over his hard length, her nails lightly scoring his chest.

He arched his back, seeking her.

"Maybe you're right," she said, stopping. "We should get some sleep."

Growling, he surged up and entered her with a hard thrust that took her breath away.

"Mmm," she sighed, closing her eyes and letting her head fall back in bliss. "All right, if you insist."

"I insist. Sleep is highly overrated." He brought her down to him and fused his lips to hers, his tongue flirting and enticing.

When she needed to breathe, Sam broke the kiss and moved with painstaking slowness, rising up until they were barely connected, and then taking him deep again. If his sharp intake of air was any indication, he liked it. A lot. So she stopped. "Are you still mad at me?"

"Yes." With his hands on her hips, he tried to control the pace, but she wouldn't be controlled. "Sam…" He moaned, his eyes closed, his jaw tight with tension. "Babe…" Overpowering her, he held her in place and pumped into her. "Come for me. Now."

She rolled her hips, but the orgasm hovered just out of reach. "I *can't*," she whimpered.

Without losing their connection, he turned them over and gave it to her hard and fast, the way she'd told him she liked it, as he sucked her nipple into his mouth and flicked his tongue back and forth.

She cried out when she reached the climax that had eluded her.

Calling out her name, he went with her.

Her fingers danced through the dampness on his back. "You didn't have to do that."

He raised his head and found her eyes in the milky darkness. "Do what?"

"Wait for me." Her cheeks burned with embarrassment, and she was grateful for the dark.

He kissed her. "I'll always wait for you."

"It doesn't always happen."

"It has with me unless you've been faking."

She smacked his shoulder. "I haven't!"

"I know," he said, laughing as he rolled to his side and brought her with him.

"It's been an issue…in the past."

"It's not an issue now."

Reaching up to caress his face, she pressed her lips to his neck and breathed in the warm spicy scent she was quickly coming to crave. "I guess the right partner makes all the difference, even when he's mad with you."

"Especially then." His fingers danced over her hip, sending a new shiver of desire racing through her. "Want to try for a two-fer?"

"That *never* happens."

He eased her onto her back and kissed his way down the front of her. "Baby, I *love* a challenge."

Sam skipped through her morning routine with far more energy than she should have had. Multiple orgasms had multiple benefits. Who knew? With one last glance at Nick sleeping on his belly, she went downstairs in desperate need of a soda. As the first blessed mouthful cruised through her system, she realized she had no way to get to HQ.

Laughing softly, she called Freddie and asked him to pick her up. Since her dad wasn't up yet, she decided to wait for Freddie on the front porch. She surveyed the quiet street, wondering if Peter was out there somewhere watching her and waiting for his next opportunity. They would've called her if they'd found him, so she knew it was possible he was watching her.

"Come and get me, you bastard. You won't catch me off guard a second time."

As she took another long drink of soda, Freddie's battered Mustang came around the corner with a loud backfire.

"Gonna wake up the whole freaking neighborhood," she grumbled.

He pulled up to the house and leaned over to unlock the passenger door.

"Do I need a tetanus shot before I ride in this thing?"

"What's that they say about beggars and choosers?"

She battled with the seatbelt. "I've got to requisition a new ride."

"I'll take care of that for you, boss." He offered her one of the powdered donuts from the package on his lap.

With a scowl, she took one and turned so she could see him. "You've done some good work on this case, Cruz. Damn good."

His face lit up with pleasure. "Thanks. So after I got home last night, I was kinda wired and couldn't sleep, ya know?"

"Uh huh." Her face flushed when she thought of how she'd worked off her own tension.

"I got to thinking that maybe there's some sort of connection besides the sexual kind between O'Connor and one of our people of interest."

"What kind of connection?"

"A domestic—cook, caterer, cleaning lady, gardener."

"Possible. Where you going with it?"

"I know this is way out there, but what if one of the domestics found out about the kid, Thomas, and told someone who'd be infuriated by it?"

"Worth looking into."

"You think?"

"When are you going to start having some faith in yourself and your instincts?"

"I don't know. Soon. I hope."

"So do I, because you're starting to piss me off."

"You know what pisses me off?" He took his eyes off the road long enough to glance at her. "Your scumbag ex-husband. He pisses me off."

"Yeah," she sighed. "Me, too."

"It's all over the papers."

"I knew it would be."

"I have it there. In the backseat if you wanted to…"

Her stomach twisted in protest. "That's all right. Thanks."

"He had pictures of you all over his place. It was totally creepy. There were shots of you from a distance working crime scenes, and he even had a police scanner."

Sam's stomach took a dive at that news. "I should've known he wouldn't just give up and go away. I should've known that."

"This isn't your fault," he said fiercely.

"So Natalie Jordan paid us a visit last night," Sam said, anxious to change the subject. She relayed what Natalie told them and went over their visit with Noel. "I don't think he did it, but I want to get him on a polygraph today. Will you set that up?"

"Sure thing. I don't see Noel for it, either. Nothing about him screamed 'murderer' to me. Natalie, on the other hand, she's a cool customer."

"Nick said she's lying about Noel, but he's never liked her."

"He's got good instincts, though," Freddie said.

"Do me a favor when we get in, ask Gonzo and Arnold to check out this address." She gave him the slip of paper with Natalie's parents' address. "And have them go by Noel Jordan's house in Belle Haven. Get me a couple of hours of surveillance on him before you bring him in."

"Got it. Will do." As they pulled up to the last intersection before the public safety building, he said, "Shit." He pointed at the street leading to HQ, lined with TV trucks bearing satellite dishes.

"Goddamn it."

He scowled at her choice of words. "Let's go in through the morgue."

"Good plan."

They parked on the far side of the building, entered through the basement door and took a circuitous route to the detectives' pit where Gonzo and Arnold waited for them.

"We've got Terry O'Connor in lockup. He's lawyering up."

"Figured."

"They filmed us bringing him in," Arnold said. "It'll be the lead story this morning."

Captain Malone burst through the door. "The chief just got off the phone with a very angry Senator O'Connor. He's threatening to call the president."

"He can call anyone he wants," Sam said. "His son had motive, a key and can't produce his supposed alibi. If he was anyone else, we would've had him in here days ago, and you know it. I need to rule him out."

They stared each other down for a long moment before Malone blinked. "Get him into interview and either charge him or let him go. And do it quickly."

"Yes, sir." To Gonzo, she added, "Bring him up."

29

When Sam and Freddie entered the small interrogation room, Terry O'Connor leaped to his feet. "I didn't kill my brother! How many times do I have to tell you that?"

She pretended to gaze intently into the file she had carried into the room with her. "The reason you're here is you failed to attend the safe driving course the judge ordered after your DUI."

"You aren't serious."

Sam glanced at Freddie.

"She's serious," Freddie said.

"I meant to," Terry stammered.

"Why don't we talk about why we're really here?" the attorney said.

"Give me a lie detector."

Grabbing Terry's shirt, the attorney yanked him into a chair. "Shut up, Terry."

"Mr. O'Connor, have you been advised of your rights?" Sam asked.

"The cops you sent to haul me out of my parents' house before dawn went through all that," he spat back at her.

"Do we have your permission to record this interview?"

"At the advice of counsel," the attorney drawled in a honeyed Southern accent, "Mr. O'Connor will cooperate with this farce—within reason."

"Isn't that good of him?" Sam asked Freddie.

"Real good," Freddie agreed as he turned on the recorder and noted for the record who was in the room and why.

"It's now been ninety-six hours since your brother's body was discovered in his apartment," Sam said. "You say you spent the night of the murder with a woman you met in a Loudoun County bar. Can you give me her name?"

"No," Terry said, dejected.

"Have you found anyone who can confirm you left the establishment with this imaginary woman?"

"She wasn't imaginary!" he cried, slapping his hand on the table.

"Witnesses?"

He slumped back into his chair. "No."

"That kind of puts you in a bit of a pickle, doesn't it?" she asked as Nick's words echoed through her mind—*you're barking up the wrong tree with Terry.* She had to admit that the buzz she got from knowing she had a suspect's nuts on the block and all she had to do was lower the boom was missing here.

"Is there a relevant question coming any time soon?" the attorney drawled.

Sam hammered Terry hard for ninety minutes, reduced him to a whimpering, sniveling baby, but he never deviated from his original statement. Finally, needing to regroup, she asked for a word with Freddie in the hallway.

Malone waited for them outside the observation room door. "Spring him."

Frustration pooled in her aching belly. She nodded

to Freddie. "Tell him to stay local and to get that safe driving class done within thirty days."

"Got it."

When they were alone, she looked up at Malone. "I had to rule him out."

"And you all but have." He lowered his voice. "They brought Peter in thirty minutes ago."

"He's mine."

"No one's saying otherwise. But you know we can take care of him if you aren't up to it—"

"I'm up to it—after he chills in the cooler for a little while longer."

"As a courtesy, I let Skip know we had him."

"Thanks."

"The partial print off the ED on Cappuano's car had similarities to Peter's, but they couldn't make a definitive ID."

"I'll get him to confirm the print is his," she said, more to herself than to Malone.

"With what we found in his apartment, we've more or less already got him." He handed her a rundown of what the warrant had yielded and a folder full of photos that made her sick.

"But he doesn't know that," she said.

"Nope."

She looked up at the captain. "I think I'm going to enjoy this. Does that make me a bad cop?"

"No, it makes you human. Arlington will want him when we're done with him."

With a nod, she left him to go buy another soda and took it back to her office. Closing the door, she dropped into her chair suddenly exhausted and drained. She hadn't seen Peter, except for in court, in almost two years. Their last explosive argument over the time she was spending with her newly paralyzed father had put the finishing touches on what had been a horrible four years for her. The next day, she'd moved her essentials into her father's house and put the rest of her belongings in storage where they remained.

In the ensuing months, Peter had popped up with such annoying regularity that she'd been forced to get a restraining order to keep him from coming around while they hurled accusations back and forth. Since then she'd often had the sensation of being watched or followed, little pinpricks of awareness on the back of her neck that had never materialized into an actual confrontation. In fact, it hadn't occurred to her that he'd still be so invested in her. She should've known better. What made her truly sick was that she had endangered Nick just by spending time with him.

Imagining Peter locked up in a cell in the basement, she smiled. "Let him sit there for a while longer wondering how much we know." The idea infused her with joy as she drank her soda and returned her attention to the O'Connor case.

Nick woke up alone in Sam's bed and shifted onto her pillow to breathe in the scent she'd left behind. He contemplated whether he should stay there until she got home or get up to face her father. Staying in bed all day was definitely the more appealing of the two options. But since he didn't want her to think he was a total coward, he got up to take a shower.

He took his time getting dressed in jeans and a long-sleeved polo shirt. How ridiculous was it that he was afraid to go downstairs to face a man in a wheelchair?

"You're being an ass," he said to his bomb-battered reflection in the mirror. Still, he took another ten minutes to make the bed and straighten up the room while marveling that one woman could own so many shoes.

When there was nothing left to do, he finally started down the stairs and almost groaned when he found Skip by himself in the kitchen. Couldn't even Celia have been there to provide a buffer?

"Morning," Nick said.

"Morning," Skip muttered. "There's coffee."

"Thanks." As Nick filled a mug that had been left by the pot, he felt the heat of the other man's eyes on his back. "Sam got an early start."

"I heard her leave about seven-thirty. Celia's downstairs doing laundry, but she made bacon and eggs. Plates are up there in the cabinet."

"That sounds good." Wondering if he'd be able to eat under the watchful eyes of Sam's dad, Nick brought the plate and coffee to the table. They sat in awkward silence for several minutes before Nick put down his fork and worked up the courage to look over at the older man. "I love her."

"If I thought otherwise you wouldn't have slept in her bed last night. I don't care how old she is."

Taken aback, Nick stared at him. "I wanted to go with her today."

"She wouldn't have let you."

"Still, until this thing with Peter is cleared up..."

"They snagged him this morning at Union Station, buying a one-way ticket to New York."

"Is that so?"

"Yep."

"Well, that's a relief."

"She's gonna have a go at him. I don't know about you, but I'd kind of like to see that."

"How about I drive you?"

Sam took a series of deep breaths to calm her churning stomach before she picked up the folder of material gathered from Peter's apartment, opened her office door, signaled to Freddie, and headed for the interrogation room where she'd asked the uniforms to put Peter. The quiet in the normally buzzing detectives' cubicles told her she'd have a good-size audience watching in observation.

"He's apt to come at me," Sam said to Freddie before they went in. "Don't stop him."

"Are you out of your freaking mind?"

"Let me handle this my way, Cruz."

"Fine, but if it appears he's about to kill you, you'll have to excuse me if I get in the way of that."

"Deal." With a small smile for Freddie, she stepped into the room. Peter had aged since she last saw him. His sandy hair was now shot through with silver, and the face she'd once found handsome was hard and lined with bitterness.

Nodding to release the officer guarding him, Sam stepped up to the table.

"I want someone else," he said without looking at her.

"Tough."

"This is a conflict of interest."

"We're not married anymore, so no it isn't. Detective Cruz, please record this interview with Peter Gibson."

Freddie clicked on the recorder and returned to his post by the door, sending the signal that this one belonged to Sam.

"You've been advised of your rights, including your right to an attorney?"

"Don't need one. You've got nothing on me." Peter raised his cuffed hands. "Is this really necessary?"

"Detective Cruz, please un-cuff Mr. Gibson." When Freddie didn't immediately comply, she said, "Detective."

Freddie stalked past her and released the cuffs. Scowling at her, he returned to the door.

Peter rubbed his wrists. "Kind of a lot of drama over nothing, Sam," he said in the patronizing tone he'd often used on her when they were together.

"Nothing?" She laid out each of the photos of her that had been found in his apartment, hearing the loud nuts-on-the-block buzz that had been missing with Terry O'Connor. "What do you call this?"

"Amateur photography. Is that a crime these days?"

"No, but stalking is."

He shrugged. "A misdemeanor. So charge me."

"Thanks, I will. Hanging around outside my house? Kind of pathetic, even for you."

His genial blue eyes hardened. "I wasn't outside your house."

"Yes, you were. It's sad that you'd rather stalk the woman who divorced you than find someone new to control. Pathetic, isn't it, Cruz?"

"At the very least," Freddie said. "I'd say it's kind of sick *and* pathetic to be fixated on your ex, especially when she's made it crystal clear to the world that she wants nothing to do with you."

If looks could kill, Freddie would've been a goner.

Sam moved around the table so she was behind Peter. "Pissed you off that I didn't want you anymore, didn't it?"

"I didn't want you, either. You were a shitty wife and lousy in bed." He looked up at the dark glass that masked the observation room. "You hear that?" he yelled. "She sucks in the sack!"

"Nick doesn't think so."

Peter tried to surge to his feet, but she shoved him back down.

"I guess you've figured out that we compared notes

and discovered you didn't give me his messages six years ago when you were pretending to be my friend."

"That's not a crime."

"No, but it *is* pathetic. Must've pissed you off this week to see me with him."

"Like I care."

"Oh, I think you do." She leaned in to speak close to his ear. "I think you care a whole lot."

In a jerky motion, he shrugged her off. "Giving yourself a lot of credit, aren't you?"

Returning to the other side of the table, she laid a photo of the bomb-making materials in front of him.

"What's that?" he asked.

"Why don't you tell me?"

A bead of sweat appeared on his upper lip. "I have no idea."

"I think you do." Sam rested her hands on the table and leaned toward him. "You disappoint me, Peter. Four years of living with a cop and you didn't learn a god-damned thing. If you're going to try to kill your ex-wife and her boyfriend, you should know better than to leave fingerprints on the bombs."

"I didn't leave any prints!"

She smiled. Bingo.

His face went purple with rage. "You fucking cunt. Spreading your legs for that asshole ten minutes after you see him again."

Sam leaned closer to him, her stomach burning. "That's right. And guess what?" She lowered her voice so only Peter—and maybe Freddie—could hear her. "When I fuck him, I come every time—sometimes more than once. So it turns out that despite what you always tried to make me believe, *you* were the one who sucked in the sack."

He lunged at her, grabbed her throat and squeezed so hard she saw stars in a matter of seconds.

She heard Freddie moving toward them as she rammed the heel of her hand into Peter's nose, sending him flying backward, blood bursting from his face.

"You *fucking bitch*! You motherfucking frigid whore! You broke my fucking nose!"

"Book him, Cruz." Sam's hand shook as she brought it up to her throat. "Two counts attempted murder, assaulting a police officer, stalking a police officer, possessing bomb-making materials, breaking and entering, violating a restraining order, and anything else you can think of."

Freddie hauled Peter up off the floor and snapped cuffs on his wrists. "With pleasure."

"Does he know you're only half a woman?" Peter screamed. "Did you tell him you're barren?"

Sam's heart kicked into overdrive as pain shot through her gut. "Get him out of here."

Long after Freddie dragged the shrieking Peter from the room, Sam stood there trying to get her shaking hands under control. Finally, she turned to leave the room and found a crowd of coworkers waiting for her.

Captain Malone stepped forward. "Well done, Sergeant."

"Thank you," Sam said, her voice shaky. She heard the whir of the wheelchair before she saw it. *Oh God*, she groaned inwardly at what her father must've heard. The crowd parted to let him through, and her heart almost stopped when she saw Nick with him. "So you heard all that, huh?" Sam said to her dad after the others left them alone.

"Uh huh."

"I'm sorry," she said, her cheeks burning. "It must've been embarrassing for you—"

"That was the most entertaining fifteen minutes of my life—right up until he grabbed you. You should put some ice on your neck. Those bruises are gonna hurt."

"I will." She bent down to kiss his cheek.

"Proud of you, baby girl," he whispered.

She rested her head on his shoulder. How she wished he could wrap his strong arms around her the way he used to. "I think it's finally over."

"I think you're right. Since I'm here, I'm going to go do some visiting. I'll be back in a bit, Nick."

"I'll be right here," Nick said.

"That's what I figured." Skip turned his chair and started down the long corridor, no doubt heading for Chief Farnsworth's office.

Nick held out a hand to her. That he did just that and nothing more finally did it for her. Curling her hand around his, she fell the rest of the way into love with him.

30

"I'm sorry," Sam said when they were in her office.

"What the hell for?" Nick asked.

"For using you and our relationship to stick it to him. I didn't know you were there. I hate that you heard it."

"You think that bothers me?" His hazel eyes were bright with emotion. "You nailed him. That's all that matters. So what did you say that made him go ballistic?"

"It doesn't matter."

"It matters to me."

Reluctantly, Sam told him what she'd said. "I don't want you to think…"

As if he could no longer resist, he put his arms around her. "What?"

Again her cheeks burned with embarrassment and discomfort, but this had to be said. "That I think of what we do…together…as fucking."

"Baby, come on. I know that."

"Because it's so much more than that," she said, looking up at him.

"Yes." He brushed his lips over hers. "It is."

"I love you, too."

He went perfectly still. "Yeah?"

Pleased to have caught him off guard, she nodded.

"Since that night at the party for me, too. I shouldn't have married Peter for many reasons, but mostly because I always loved you. Always."

"Samantha," he whispered, leaning in for a deep, passionate kiss.

"No PDA on duty, or any other time," she mumbled when she came to her senses and remembered where they were.

"Very special occasion." His hands slid down to cup her ass and pull her tight against his erection. "Does that door have a lock?"

With her hands on his chest, she tried to push him back. "Don't even think about it."

"I'm way past thinking."

She went up on tiptoes to roll his bottom lip between her teeth. "I'll make it up to you. I promise."

Groaning, he released her. "I'll hold you to that."

"Um, what he said about me…at the end… We should probably talk about that."

Nick rested a finger on her lips. "Later."

Grateful for the reprieve, she took a deep breath. "So what's with you and my dad?" she asked, grabbing a half-empty bottle of soda from her desk.

"We've reached an understanding of sorts."

Raising a suspicious eyebrow, she studied him. "What sort?"

"That's between me and him."

"I don't like the sound of that."

He tweaked her nose. "You don't have to."

A knock on the door startled them.

"Enter," she called.

Gonzo opened the door. "Um, sorry to interrupt—"

"You're not interrupting anything," she said with a meaningful glance at Nick. "What's up?"

"There's a woman here to see you. Wouldn't give

her name, insists on seeing you and only you. Looks shook up."

"All right. Bring her in." To Nick, she said, "Do you mind taking my dad home? I'll be along soon."

"Sure." He leaned in for one last kiss.

"Don't talk about me with him."

"Dream on," he said, laughing as he left the room. "Put some ice on that neck."

Sam took in the view of his fine denim-clad ass and sighed with delight. That he was hers, all hers, was something she still couldn't believe. She wished she had time to indulge in the happy dance that was just bursting to get out.

Gonzo accompanied a distraught woman to the door and showed her in. "This is Sergeant Holland."

"Have a seat." Sam gestured to the chair and dismissed Gonzo with a grateful nod. "What's your name?"

The woman's manicured fingers fiddled with her designer purse as she looked at Sam with dark, ravaged eyes. "Andrea Daly."

"What can I do for you, Ms. Daly?"

"It's *Mrs*. Daly." She looked down at the floor, sobs shaking her petite frame. "I've done an awful thing."

Sam came around her desk and leaned back against it. "If you tell me about this awful thing, maybe I can help you."

Andrea wiped the tears from her face. "The night the senator was killed…"

The back of Sam's neck tingled. "Did you know him? Senator O'Connor?"

Andrea shook her head. "I've never done anything like this. My family means everything to me. I have children."

"Mrs. Daly, I can't help you if you don't tell me what it is you think you've done."

"I was with Terry O'Connor," she whispered. "I spent that whole night with him at the Day's Inn in Leesburg." She wiped her runny nose. "When I saw him on the news being brought in this morning… I couldn't let that happen. He didn't do it."

"I know."

Incredulous, Andrea stared up at Sam. "I risked my marriage and my family and you *already knew?*"

Sam reached out to her. "You did a brave thing coming here. It was the right thing."

"A lot of good that'll do me when my husband reads about it in the paper."

"It won't be in the paper. If your husband finds out, it'll be because you tell him."

"Do you mean that?"

"Terry O'Connor doesn't remember you. He was so drunk he couldn't even offer a description of the woman he said he'd been with. I'm sorry if that hurts you, but it's the truth. So the only two people who know he was with you are in this room. I know what I'm going to do with the info. What you do with it is up to you."

Overcome, Andrea bent her head. "I've never been unfaithful to my husband before. In nineteen years, I've never so much as looked at another man. But he travels a lot, and we've drifted apart in the last couple of years. I was lonely."

"I understand that feeling—better than you can imagine." Sam raised her fingers to cover bruises on her throat that were starting to hurt. "But if you love your husband and want to make your marriage work, stay out of the bars, go home and fix it. You're lucky this was the worst thing that happened."

"Believe me, I know." She stood and offered her hand. "Thank you."

Sam held Andrea's hand between both of hers. "Thank *you* for coming in. You did the right thing. I had him ninety-nine percent eliminated. You just gave me the one percent I still needed."

"In that case, I guess it was worth it."

"Good luck to you, Mrs. Daly."

"And to you, Sergeant. Senator O'Connor was a good man. I hope you find the person who did this to him."

"Oh, I will. You can count on that." Sam stood at her doorway and watched Andrea leave.

"What was that all about?" Freddie asked.

"Terry O'Connor's alibi."

Freddie's eyes lit up. "No shit?"

"Nope."

"Did you get an official statement?"

"Nope."

"Why not?"

"Because I had nothing to gain, and she had everything to lose. She gave me what I needed. That was enough."

"I continue to be awed not just by your instincts but by your humanity."

"Fuck off, Cruz," she said, rolling her eyes. "Did you get Peter put on ice?"

"Yep. Sent the EMTs down to take a look at his busted schnoz. He's screaming police brutality."

"Self-defense." The fact she had taunted Peter into attacking her wouldn't matter to the U.S. Attorney in light of the evidence they had implicating him in the bombings.

"Damn straight it was."

"What're you hearing from Gonzo and Arnold?"

"Natalie's mother told them she's in seclusion and couldn't come to the door. They didn't push it because all you wanted was confirmation that she was there, and they saw her looking out an upstairs window. Noel spent the day working in his yard and washing his car. No sign of her at the house. Gonzo just took him in for the polygraph."

"Let's set one up for her for tomorrow, after the funeral."

"Got it."

"So where does that leave us?" Sam unclipped her hair and ran her fingers through it. "Our two prime suspects, both with motive and opportunity pointing the finger at each other, but nothing about them is jumping out at us."

"Except her dead boyfriend. That's a red flag."

"If she had anything to do with that, would her husband know about it? Would she have told him all about the boyfriend who'd tragically died in a fire?"

"Hard to say. Murderers can be an arrogant lot. They often want people to know what they've done so they get the credit."

"I didn't get that vibe from Noel. It was more of a 'she was heartbroken' vibe." Sam checked her watch and saw it was after one. "I wanted another go with her, but I think I'll wait until after we polygraph her to see if I need to show my cards on the dead boyfriend. Have Gonzo get her suspicions about her husband on the record at some point today. I'm not liking him for a suspect, but I want it in the file."

"Sounds like a good plan. Do you think it's possible that neither of them had anything to do with it, and she's just trying to get rid of a husband she never should've married?"

"At this point, I'd say anything is possible, but I'm

still left without a primary suspect three days into the investigation. That'll really please the chief."

"How about I write up the reports from this morning?"

"I'd appreciate that." She thought for a moment and realized this was as good a moment as there was likely to be. "Can you come in for a minute?"

"Sure." He shut the office door behind him. "What's up?"

"You know I appreciate your help with the reports, right?"

"It's no problem."

"Well, for me it kind of is." She rubbed a hand over her belly. In a rush of words, she said, "I'm dyslexic. I've struggled with it all my life, and it's mostly under control, but I know you must wonder about the weird mistakes and stuff."

"Why didn't you tell me before? I could've been doing all the reports."

"I don't want that. It's enough that you help me as much as you do."

"You still should've told me. We're partners."

"Do I know everything there is to know about you?"

He squirmed under the heat of her glare. "Most everything."

"We've all got our secrets, Cruz, and the last thing I want is special treatment. I don't expect anything to change now that you know."

"Asking for help doesn't make you weak, Sam. It makes you human."

"That's the second time today someone told me what it means to be human. Don't tell anyone about the dyslexia, all right?"

"Who would I tell?" he huffed. "If you don't know by now that you can trust me—"

"If I didn't trust you, I wouldn't have told you." She paused before she said, "I'm sorry you had to hear that stuff I said to Peter. I know it was embarrassing for you."

"You got him to implicate himself, which is the goal of any interrogation."

"Still…"

"I'm a big boy, Sergeant. I can handle it."

She looked at him with new appreciation. "Copy me on those reports, and you can run your domestic angle in the morning while I'm at the funeral."

"Got it."

"Go home after you finish the paperwork."

He held up a set of keys. "Your new ride, madam."

"Ohhh, what'd you get me? One of the new Tauruses?"

"Yep. Navy blue." He rattled off the parking space number.

"Nice. Thanks."

"I might come by to watch the game later. I mean, if that's all right with you."

"My dad invited you, didn't he?"

"Well, yeah, but…"

"But what?"

He smiled. "Nothing."

She pulled on her coat. "I'll see you later, then. Oh, and thanks for having my back with the scumbag."

"No problem." He followed her out of the office and closed the door behind him. "Sergeant Holland?"

She turned to him, perplexed by his formality.

"It's a great pleasure to work with you."

"Back atcha, Detective. Right back atcha."

On her way out of the detectives' pit, she stopped to peek into the office that would soon be hers. Since the day she made detective, she'd had her eye on the lieutenant's spacious corner office. However, because of her struggles with dyslexia, she hadn't really allowed herself to hope.

She turned to leave and ran smack into Lieutenant Stahl.

"Would you jump in my grave that fast, Sergeant?"

Taken aback by his sudden appearance, Sam stepped aside to let him in and noticed he carried a box.

"You must be feeling quite satisfied." He flipped on the lights and dropped the box on the desk. "Shagged a witness, made lieutenant, stole my command and got away with it—all in the same week."

Sam leaned against the doorframe and let him spew, fascinated by the way his fat chin jiggled in time with his venomous words.

"I mean do you *honestly* think you'd have gotten away with screwing a witness if your daddy wasn't the chief's buddy?" He tossed pictures and mementos into the box. "You can bet internal affairs will be interested in taking a closer look at that. In fact, you might just be my very first order of business."

Sam pretended to hang on his every word while she planned where to put her own things in the space.

"This isn't over, Sergeant. I refuse to turn a blind eye to blatant disregard for basic rules by someone who's gotten where she is because of *who* she is."

Her hand rolled into a fist that she'd love to plant smack in the middle of his fat face, but she wouldn't give him the satisfaction. Instead, she pulled her notebook from her back pocket and reached for a pen.

His eyes narrowed. "What are you writing?"

"Just a note to maintenance. They need to do something about the smell in here." As little red blotches popped up on his fat face, she returned the pad to her pocket. "Good luck in the rat squad, Lieutenant. I'm sure you'll fit right in." Turning, she took her leave.

"Watch your back, Sergeant," he called. "Daddy won't always be there to clean up your messes."

She turned around. "If you so much as look at my father with crossed eyes, I'll personally break your fat-assed neck. Got me?"

He raised an eyebrow. "A threat, Sergeant?"

"No, Lieutenant. A promise."

31

Following the confrontation with Stahl, Sam's stomach burned as she headed for the morgue exit, anxious to avoid the press and get home to Nick. The prospect of a boisterous Sunday dinner with her sisters and their families was looking better all the time. She was on her way to a clean escape when Chief Farnsworth stopped her in the lobby.

"I'm glad I caught you, Sergeant. You need to give the media ten minutes."

She groaned.

"In the aftermath of the bombing, you have to show the public you're alive and actively engaged in the O'Connor case—and you've got to let them know you've cleared Terry O'Connor before the president himself starts calling for my ass in a sling."

"Yes, sir."

"They'll ask about Nick."

Rubbing her hand over her gut, she looked out at the media circus that had taken over the plaza. "I can handle it."

"I'll be right there with you."

"Thank you," she said, knowing his presence would send the signal that the department was firmly behind her.

"You're pale. Do you need a minute?"

"No." She breathed through the pain and buttoned up her coat. "Let's get it over with." The chief followed her into the maelstrom.

The reporters went wild, screaming questions at her.

Chief Farnsworth held up a hand to quiet them. "Sergeant Holland will answer your questions if you give her the chance."

As Sam stepped up to the microphone, the crowd fell silent. "Today, we ruled out Terry O'Connor as a suspect in his brother's murder. We have a number of other persons of interest we're looking at closely." She really wished that was true, but she couldn't exactly tell the media that the investigation had hit a dead end.

"Can you tell us who they are?"

"Not without compromising the investigation. As soon as we're able to give you more, we will."

"Is there anything else you can tell us about the O'Connor investigation?"

"Not at this time."

"How close are you to making an arrest?"

"Not as close as I'd like to be, but it's far more important that we build a case that'll hold up in court rather than rush to judgment."

"Why did Detective Cruz go to Chicago?"

"No comment." No way was she handing them Thomas O'Connor. They would have to figure that one out for themselves.

"Did the Johnson family play a role in yesterday's bombing?"

"No. We've made an arrest that's unrelated to the Johnsons." She looked down and summoned the strength to get through this. "My ex-husband, Peter Gibson, has been charged with two counts of at-

tempted murder—among numerous other charges—
in the bombing."

"Why'd he do it?" one of the reporters shouted.

"We believe he was enraged by my relationship with
Mr. Cappuano."

"Did you know Mr. Cappuano before this week?"

Gritting her teeth, she forced herself to stay calm
and to not make their day by getting emotional. "We
met years ago and had a brief relationship."

"Did you tell your superior officers that you'd had a
past relationship with a material witness?" asked Dar-
ren Tabor from the *Washington Star*. He'd been particularly harsh toward her in his reporting after the
Johnson disaster.

Sam's fingers tightened around the edges of the po-
dium. "I did not."

"Why?"

"I was determined to close the O'Connor case and
believed Mr. Cappuano's assistance would be invaluable, which it has been. Thanks to his help, I'm much
further along than I would've been without it."

"Still, aren't you walking a fine ethical line especially in light of the publicity you received after the
Johnson case?" Tabor asked with a smirk.

"If you examine my more than twelve-year record,
you'll find my behavior to be above reproach."

"Until recently."

"Your judgment," Sam said, working to keep her
cool while making a mental note to check on his un-
paid parking tickets. Issuing a warrant for his arrest
would give her tremendous joy.

"Is it true Mr. Cappuano is the beneficiary of a siz-
able life insurance policy taken out by the senator?"
Tabor asked.

Sam clenched her teeth. How the hell had *that* leaked? "Yes."

"Doesn't that give you a motive?"

"Maybe if he had known about it."

"You believe he didn't?"

"He was as surprised by it as we were. Mr. Cappuano has been cleared of any involvement in the senator's murder."

"Is it serious between you and Cappuano?" Sam wanted to groan when she recognized the bottle-blonde reporter from one of the gossip rags.

"It's been a week," Sam said, laughing off the question.

"But is it *serious?*"

What is this? Sam wanted to shoot back at her. *High school?* "Would I have gotten involved if it wasn't? Next question." She looked away from the reporter's satisfied grin, sending the signal that she was finished with the discourse into her personal life.

"Are you concerned by Destiny Johnson's threats?" another reporter asked.

Relieved to be moving on, Sam made eye contact with the new reporter, a woman she recognized from one of the network affiliates. "Mrs. Johnson is a grieving mother. My heart goes out to her."

"How about Marquis Johnson?"

"As I'm due to testify in his probable cause hearing on Tuesday, I have no comment."

"Sergeant, the second anniversary of your father's shooting is coming up next week. Are there any new leads in his case?"

"Unfortunately, no, but it remains an open investigation. Anyone with information is urged to come forward."

"And how's he doing?"

"Very well. Thank you for asking."

Chief Farnsworth stepped forward to rescue her.

Sam held up her hand to stop him. "I just want to say…" She cleared the emotion from her throat. "That it's an honor to serve the people of this city, and while you've taken your digs at me lately, there's nothing I wouldn't do, no risk I wouldn't take, to protect our citizens. If that's not enough for you, well then you can continue to make me the story rather than focusing on real news. That's it."

As they hollered more questions at her, she pushed through them to the staff parking lot where her gleaming new car waited for her. Only when she was safely inside could she begin to breathe her way through the pain.

Sam called Nick from the car.

"Hey, babe," he said.

She took a moment to enjoy the easy familiarity they had slid into, as if they'd been together for years rather than days.

"Sam?"

"I'm here."

"Everything all right?"

"It is now that I'm talking to you. What're you doing?"

"I'm sitting on your bed trying to write what I have to say at the funeral tomorrow. It's just dawned on me that I have to speak in front of the president and most of Congress."

Sam released a low whistle. "I don't think I could do it."

"Sure you could. You just took on the Washington press corps."

"You saw that, huh?"

"Yep. I heard it's serious between us. Did you know that?"

Laughing, she said, "I've heard that rumor."

"Say it again, Sam," he said, his voice gruff and sexy.

Her heart contracted. "Say what?" she asked, even though she knew exactly what he was after.

"Don't play coy with me. Say it."

"When I see you."

"And when will that be?"

"I'm almost home. Want to meet me outside and go for a walk? I promised I'd take you to the market."

"So you did. Was that *only* yesterday?"

"Sure was. Meet me on the corner in five? If I come in, I'll get trapped, and I need some air."

"I'll be right there."

He was waiting for her when she parked in front of the house and set out toward the corner.

Her heart skipped a beat at the sight of him in jeans and a black leather jacket, and she couldn't help but break into a jog to get to him faster. She hurled herself into his outstretched arms and squealed when he lifted her right off her feet.

His mouth descended on hers for a hot, breathtaking kiss.

"Mmm," she said against his lips. "I missed you."

"You just saw me a couple of hours ago."

"Long time." She burrowed into his neck to nibble on warm skin.

He trembled and tightened his hold on her. "What happened to your ban on PDA?"

"Momentary lapse."

"I like it." He returned her to terra firma and tipped

her chin up. "There was something you were going to tell me?"

She thought about playing coy again, but as she looked up at his handsome face, she found she couldn't do it. "I love you. Big."

His hazel eyes danced with delight. "Big, huh?"

"Scary big."

"Not scary." He hugged her. "Because I love you bigger."

"Not possible."

"Bet?" Laughing at the face she made at him, he slipped his arm around her shoulders for the walk to the market.

A melting pot of crafts, colors, nationalities, smells and textures, Eastern Market was mobbed with last-minute Christmas shoppers braving the damp chill to bargain with bundled-up vendors.

"You aren't going to believe this, but I've never been here," he confessed as they passed a row of fragrant Christmas trees.

She stared up at him. "Are you serious? You've worked a few blocks from here for how long?"

"Well, I worked for a congressman before John, so I guess almost fourteen years."

"That's sad, Nick. Truly pathetic. The flea market is open every weekend, year round."

"So I've heard," he said with a sheepish grin. "I figured, you know, flea market—junk. I never expected all this hand-crafted stuff."

"You can get anything here, and it's usually better than what you can buy in a store."

"I can see that."

"Hey, Sam," one of the vendors called.

"How's business, Rico?"

"Booming, thank God. Heard about you on the news last night. You okay?"

"Just fine. No worries."

"Glad to hear it. Bring your dad down one of these weekends."

"I will."

After several similar exchanges, Nick said, "Do you know *all* these people or does it just seem that way?"

She shrugged as she sorted through a table of fluffy knitted scarves. "This is my hood. I'm a regular." Twisting a hot pink scarf around her neck, she pirouetted in front of him. "What do you think?"

He turned up his nose. "Not your color, babe."

"My niece Brooke firmly believes that no one over the age of four should wear pink."

"That's funny. How old is she?"

"Fifteen going on thirty. You'll meet her later." Returning the scarf to the table, she glanced over at the next kiosk and spotted a beautifully framed painting of the Capitol that she had to have for him. Dying to get a closer look at it, she rubbed her hands together and blew into them. "Do you feel like some hot chocolate?"

"Sure."

"They're selling it right over there."

Eyeing her suspiciously, he looked over to where she pointed. "All right."

Flashing a brilliant smile, she went up on tiptoes to kiss him. "Thank you, honey."

"What're you up to?"

"Nothing." She gave him a little push. "Go."

The moment he crossed the street, she spun around and pounced on the unsuspecting artist in the neighboring booth. "That one. Right there. How much?"

"Three-fifty."

"Sold. Will you take a check?"

"With a license."

"Be quick."

They completed the transaction in record time, and Sam accepted the package wrapped in brown paper moments before Nick returned with two steaming cups of hot chocolate.

"What did you buy?"

"Something for my dad."

"You're a terrible liar, Samantha. Does this mean I have to buy something for you, too?"

"Only if you plan to get lucky in the New Year," she said with a saucy smile.

"In that case, what looks good to you? Sky's the limit."

Laughing and teasing, they were navigating the crowd on their way to the indoor food market when a flash of metal caught Sam's eye. Everything shifted into slow motion as she realized it was a gun. In the span of a second, she shoved Nick out of the way, dropped the painting and her hot chocolate, drew her own weapon and lunged at the shooter.

"Baby killer!" the woman shrieked as she fired an erratic shot.

People screamed and dove for cover as Sam wrestled the heavy-set woman to the ground and struggled to disarm her. Out of the corner of her eye, she saw Nick's black shoe.

"Get back!" she cried as the woman's elbow connected with her cheekbone.

Nick stomped on the woman's hand, and the gun clanked to the cobblestone street.

"Don't touch it!" Sam said to him as she cuffed the crying woman.

"You killed Quentin! *You killed our baby!*"

Something about the voice was familiar. "Marquis

killed Quentin," Sam growled into the woman's ear as she tightened the cuffs. Flipping her over, she wasn't surprised to find Destiny Johnson's sister Dawn under her. "Was anyone hit?" Sam asked Nick.

"I don't think so." He looked down at her with a pale face and big, shocked eyes. "I heard someone call 911."

"Thanks for the assist."

"No problem."

As the market slowly returned to normal around them, Sam sat on a curb with Dawn until a couple of uniforms arrived to take statements and cart her off. Sam promised to write up her portion of the report and get it to them later.

"Nice job, Sam," one of the vendors called to her.

"Thanks," she said as Nick helped her up.

The moment she was upright, the pain she had managed to stave off during the confrontation with Dawn roared through her, leaving her breathless and weak in its wake.

"Jesus Christ, Sam," Nick muttered.

"S'okay," she said, bent in half as she took deep breaths. "Just give me a second." It took several minutes, but she was finally able to straighten only to find his hazel eyes hot with dismay and anger. "I'm fine."

"You're not fine." He took hold of her arm to steer her toward home. "And don't you ever push me out of the way again so you can dive at a gun, do you hear me? Don't ever do that again."

Startled by his tone, she stopped and turned to face him. "It's instinct and training. You can't fault me for that."

"How do you think it makes me feel, as a *man*, when the woman I love pushes me out of harm's way so she can throw herself in front of it? Huh?"

"I have no idea," she said sincerely.

"Well, let me tell you, it makes me feel like a use-less, dickless moron."

"I'm not the kind of woman who needs a big strong man to protect her, Nick. If that's what you want or need, you've got the wrong girl."

"And you think I'm the kind of man who needs his *woman* to protect him? Is that what *you* want?"

"Why are we fighting?" she asked, perplexed. "I saw a shooter. I took her down. What the hell did I do wrong?"

"You pushed me out of the way!"

"Excuse me for not wanting your dumb ass to get killed. Next time I'll let her blow your head off. Would that be better?"

"Now you're just being a jerk."

Stunned and dismayed, she stared at him and said a silent thanks a lot to Dawn for turning their romantic afternoon to shit. "*I'm* the jerk? Whatever." Without a care as to whether he followed her or not, she stomped off toward home. When she got there, she heard voices in the kitchen and figured her sister Tracy's family had arrived. But rather than go see them, Sam went straight upstairs, needing a few minutes to get herself together first.

What's his problem anyway? She fumed as she shrugged off her coat, tossed it over her desk chair and flopped down on the bed. *What did I do besides try to protect his sorry ass?* The ache in her stomach was no match for the pain in her heart. This was exactly why she had stayed away from relationships since she split with Peter. If she never felt this shitty again, it would be just fine with her.

Nick came in a few minutes later, carrying the pack-age she had abandoned in the chaos. "I believe this is yours," he said as he put it on her desk and took off his coat.

She couldn't believe she had forgotten all about the painting. "Thanks."

He sat down on the edge of the bed and brushed his fingers over her sore cheek.

Sam winced when he grazed the spot where Dawn's elbow had connected.

"You should put some ice on that." He laced his fingers through hers. "Between the bump on your head, the bruises on your chest and neck, and now this, you're quite a colorful mess."

"It's not usually like this. I swear to God, it's never this crazy."

"That's good to know, because I don't think I could handle this much drama on a daily basis." He brought their joined hands to his lips and kissed each of her fingers. "I'm sorry I overreacted."

Sam's mouth fell open. "Did you just *apologize*?"

"Yeah," he huffed. "So?"

"I didn't think guys did that. This is a first for me. You'll have to excuse me while I take a moment to enjoy it."

His eyes narrowed. "I'm about to take it back."

She laughed. "Please don't." Reaching up to touch the soft hair that curled over his ear, she studied the face she had come to love so much in such a short time. "I'm trying to understand why you got so upset."

"You did what you were trained to do, and just because I didn't like it doesn't mean you were wrong."

"Wow. This is truly quite a moment for me."

"Samantha..."

"I'll always push you out of the way, Nick. If you can't deal with that, we're going to have problems."

"We're going to have problems anyway. So how

about we handle it this way? When I'm wrong, I'll say so. And when you're wrong, you'll say so."

"I will?"

"Uh huh. That's how it works. That's the *only* way it works."

"Is this you being anal again and cleaning things up?"

"If that's how you want to see it."

"Fine," she conceded. "On the sure-to-be rare instances when I'm actually wrong about something, I'll do my best to admit it. Are you happy?"

"For some strange reason," he said, bending to kiss her, "I really am."

She slid her fingers into his hair to keep him there. "So am I."

32

After dinner, Sam joined her sisters on the porch to share a cigarette. She leaned in to block the air as Tracy lit up while Angela flanked her other side. Each of them took a long drag before passing it on.

"Oh, I needed that," Tracy, who at forty was the oldest, said as she exhaled a steady stream of smoke. She shared Sam's height but had held on to ten extra pounds after each of her three children.

Angela, at thirty-six, had bounced right back to her svelte shape after giving birth to her son Jack five years earlier.

The door swung open, and Angela stashed the cigarette behind her back.

"Mom, Jack is walking back and forth in front of the TV and won't stop," whined fifteen-year-old Brooke, brimming with indignation. Her long dark hair, bright blue eyes and porcelain skin gave her a delicate beauty that was a source of great consternation to her parents as the boys began to take an avid interest in her.

"Sorry," Angela said. "I'll get him."

Tracy stopped her sister and said to her daughter, "Turn off the TV and spend some time with your cousin. All he wants is your attention."

In a huff, Brooke stomped back inside.

"Sorry about that," Angela said. "He loves being with the kids."

"Don't worry about it," Tracy said. "They watch enough TV at home. They don't need to do it here, too."

The door opened again, and this time Sam stashed the cigarette behind her back when she saw it was Nick.

"I was wondering where you all had disappeared to, and your father suggested I check the front porch where I'd find the three of you sharing a cigarette that you think no one knows about. I said, 'What do you mean, Skip? Samantha doesn't smoke.'"

Behind her back, Sam transferred the cigarette to Angela in a move they had perfected over the years. She smiled at Nick. "Of course I don't smoke. Did you need me?"

"I was going to ask if you'd mind if we go to my place tonight."

"I don't mind. I'll be in shortly, and we can take off."

"Okay."

The moment the door closed behind him, Angela took a drag off the dwindling cigarette. "Mmm. Hubba hubba."

Her sisters stared at her.

"Did you seriously just say 'hubba hubba'?" Tracy asked.

"Well, come on. He's yummy. And did he call you *Samantha?*"

Sam shrugged as her cheeks heated with embarrassment. "He likes to call me that."

"You must really dig him to put up with that," Ang said. "How's the sex?"

"Angela!" Tracy said.

"What? Don't tell me you don't want to know, too."

They waited expectantly for Sam.

"It's...you know...amazing."

"I remember amazing sex," Tracy said with a sigh. "At least I think I do."

"Stop," Angela said, bumping Tracy with her hip. "Mike's still hot for you."

"Yeah, I guess. So, Sam, I didn't want to ask in front of the kids, but this insanity with Peter... Are you okay?"

"It's kind of overwhelming to know he hates me enough to want to kill me."

"I think it's more that in his own sick, twisted way he *loves* you that much," Tracy said.

Angela nodded in agreement.

Sam told them about meeting Nick years ago and what Peter had done to keep them apart.

"Motherfucker," Angela muttered.

Sam laughed as she extinguished the cigarette. The sick feeling in her stomach and the lingering foul taste reminded her of why she'd quit smoking years ago. "Tell me how you really feel, Ang."

"I hate that bastard."

"So do I," Tracy said. "Divorcing him was the best thing you ever did. I couldn't stand the way he always had to know where you were and what you were doing. He never would've gone back inside the way Nick did just now. He would've wanted to know what we were talking about."

"I know," Sam said. "When I think about him not giving me those messages... I really wanted to hear from Nick after that night."

"You might've missed the whole Peter saga altogether," Tracy said.

"Maybe everything that happened with Peter, with the babies and stuff, would've happened with Nick and it would've screwed us up just as bad."

Her sisters each slid an arm around her.

"There's no point in going there, Sam," Tracy said. "I haven't had a chance to tell Nick the whole story."

"It won't matter to him," Ang assured her. "He's mad about you. He never takes his eyes off you, but not in the creepy way Peter used to. More of an adoring way."

"He didn't have a family growing up, and I know he wants one."

"There're other ways, hon," Tracy said. "You know that. Don't worry about it right now. Enjoy this time with him. You deserve to be happy after everything you've been through."

"Thank you," Sam said, hugging them. "I'm so glad you guys like him."

"Hubba hubba," Ang said again, and they all laughed.

"Now how about Dad and Celia?" Sam said.

Just as Sam and Nick were getting ready to leave Skip's house, Freddie called. "We've got another body, Sergeant."

A burst of adrenaline zipped through Sam. "Who?"

"Tara Davenport."

"Oh, shit," Sam sighed, remembering the timid Capitol Hill waitress they'd interviewed. "Where?"

"Her apartment." Freddie rattled off the address. "It's bad, Sam. Whoever did this made sure she suffered."

"I'm on my way."

Nick insisted on driving her to the scene. On the way, Sam pumped him for information about Tara.

"She was so sweet," he said. "We always requested her section when we went in for lunch. I can't believe anyone would want to harm her."

"No way this is a coincidence. This has got to be tied to O'Connor. Did he tell you he was dating her?"

"He never came right out and discussed it with me, but I knew. He was so much older than her. I'm sure he thought I wouldn't approve."

"Did you?"

"Not really, but they were both consenting adults, so I kept my opinions to myself."

Since emergency vehicles had surrounded Tara's apartment building, Sam told him to double-park.

Freddie met them at the door to Tara's apartment, his expression grim. "Beaten, bound, raped and strangled."

Steeling herself, Sam followed him into the bedroom. "God almighty," she whispered at the sight of a bloodbath.

Behind her, Nick gasped.

Sam spun around. "You need to step back." Realizing he was on the verge of passing out, she rushed him into a chair and pushed his head between his knees. "Breathe."

"I'm okay," he muttered, looking up at her. His eyes glazed with shock, he shook his head. "Who could do that? Who?"

"I don't know, but I'm going to find out."

"Go ahead. Sorry to wimp out."

Sam left him in the living room and returned to the bedroom as Freddie took photos of the scene. Tara had been bound, gagged and, judging by the bloody pool between her legs, repeatedly raped.

"Who found her?" Sam asked Freddie.

"One of her coworkers got the super to let her in when she didn't show up for work for the second day in a row."

Dr. Lindsey McNamara, the medical examiner, stepped into the room. "Damn. Just when you think you've seen it all…"

"No kidding," Sam said.

One of the Crime Scene officers lifted a baseball bat from the floor. Blood stained the thick end of the barrel. "Looks like this was used for the beating, among other things…"

The women in the room winced.

Sam studied the young waitress who'd been so distraught over her breakup with John O'Connor. "How long has she been dead?"

Lindsey pulled on latex gloves and reached out to close Tara's eyes. "Looks like twenty to thirty hours, but I won't know for sure until I get her into the lab."

"I need a time of death ASAP so I can get a timeline going."

Lindsey nodded. "Who did this to you, sweetie?" the kind-hearted doctor whispered. "Don't you worry. We'll get them." Lindsey shifted her green eyes to Sam. "Won't we?"

"You bet your ass we will."

"Go pick up Elin Svendsen," Sam said to Freddie, working a hunch.

"Really?" The spark of excitement in his voice wasn't lost on Sam. "Will I get hardship duty pay for that?"

"Take her to a hotel and arrange for round-the-clock coverage."

"Got it—take goddess to hotel and watch over her. I think I can handle that."

Sam was relieved to hear him joking again after the hideous two hours they'd just put in at Tara's. "I'm going to send Gonzo out to Belle Haven to pick up the Jordans, too. I want her under protection."

"Noel passed the polygraph."

"Yeah, I got that word an hour ago."

"What're you thinking, boss?"

"Did Patricia Donaldson tell you where she'd be staying in the city when she came for O'Connor's funeral?"

His brows furrowing with skepticism, he said, "No, but I can try to find out."

"Do that. I could be wrong, but I'm going to pull her credit card records to see if she recently bought a plane ticket to Washington."

"Come on, Sam, you're not thinking it's her... That woman was madly in love with him."

"And he was fucking his way through the city while she raised his son in Siberia." Here was the buzz that came when all the pieces started to fall into place. "I'll pull the records, you find Elin."

Sobering, Freddie said, "You can count on me to take very good care of her."

Sam rolled her eyes. "Go easy. You might sprain something."

Emerging from Tara's apartment building, Sam found Nick leaning against her car. "Aren't you freezing?"

"The cold feels good." His face was pale, his eyes watering from the cold or maybe the emotion.

"You shouldn't have followed me in there. I told you to stay here."

"I don't know how you do it," he said softly. "How you can stand seeing stuff like that day after day? I'll never forget what I saw in there."

"I wish I could say it's the first time I've seen something like that."

He reached for her, but Sam shook him off. "No PDA when the place is swarming with cops," she growled.

Jamming his hands into his pockets, he seemed to be making an effort to bite his tongue.

Sam unclipped her hair and ran her fingers through it. "I need some computer time. Do you mind dropping me at HQ?"

"Does it have to be there? You could get online at my house."

She consulted her watch. Ten-forty. "I suppose that would work."

Nick offered to drive her car to Arlington, and Sam was tired enough after the long, draining day to let him.

"This is the time to be on the road." She gestured to the deserted stretch of I-395 as they passed the Jefferson Memorial on their way to the 14th Street Bridge.

"If only it was like this in the morning."

She turned her head so she could see his profile in the orange glow of the streetlights. Anxious to get both their minds off the horror they'd witnessed at Tara's, Sam said, "So tell me, did my family overwhelm you?"

"What? No, of course not. Everyone was really nice."

"They liked you."

"What's the story with your brother-in-law Spencer?"

Sam smiled. "He's a bit much, huh?"

"Ah, yeah. Got a big opinion of himself."

"We only put up with him because he worships the ground Angela walks on. There's nothing he wouldn't do for her."

"Mike's a lot more normal."

"I adore him."

Nick shot her a meaningful glance.

"Not like that," Sam said, laughing. "I just give him so much credit. He's raising Brooke like she's his own—"

"She's *not?*"

Sam shook her head. "Her father was a guy Tracy dated briefly. When they found out she was pregnant he hit the road, and she never heard from him again. She met Mike a couple of years later. After they got married, he adopted Brooke."

"You'd never know she wasn't his."

"That's why I love him so much. We all do. He doesn't treat her any differently than he does Abby or Ethan."

"No, he certainly doesn't," Nick agreed. "I like him even more knowing that about him."

"He's the big brother I never had."

"Which is why he thoroughly grilled me about where I came from, where I'm going and what my intentions are toward you."

"He did *not*," Sam said, astounded.

"Yes, he did. And he made sure your father was able to hear the interrogation. In fact, I'll bet Skip put him up to it."

"I wouldn't doubt it." Turning in her seat, she leaned over to plant a wet kiss on his neck. "Thank you for putting up with that." Because he deserved it after dealing with her family, she tossed in some tongue action, too.

The car swerved. "Hello? I'm going seventy over here!"

She ran her hand up his thigh. "Want to go for eighty?"

He caught her hand the instant before it reached the promised land. "Behave."

"So what did you tell Mike?" she asked, resting her head on his shoulder.

Bringing their joined hands to his lips, he pressed a kiss to the back of hers. "That I've always loved you, and I always will."

Sam sighed with contentment. "I like hearing that."

"Do you know why I wanted to go home tonight?"

"Nope."

"I found out today that you love me, too. I wanted to be alone with you tonight."

A tremble of anticipation rippled through her. "You knew before today."

"I suspected and I hoped, but I didn't know for sure. I worried that maybe we were both caught up in the craziness of the last week."

She raised her head from his shoulder. "Did you really think that was possible?"

He shrugged. "I was afraid I wanted you too much and that somehow I'd screw it up. I almost did a few times."

"I hate knowing you felt that way." Returning her head to his shoulder, she was struck by how alone he was and how badly she wanted to surround him with the love he'd missed out on while growing up without a family. A lump formed in her throat when she thought of one thing he wanted that she couldn't give him.

They rode the rest of the way in silence, both wrapped up in their own thoughts.

Entering his house through the front door, he took her coat and hung it in the hall closet.

"What happened to all the glass?" she asked.

"I paid my cleaning lady double to come in today and deal with it, but we probably shouldn't walk around barefoot for a while."

"How's your foot?"

"Sore."

She winced. "And I had you out walking on it earlier. I never even thought about it. I'm sorry."

He leaned in to kiss her. "No worries, babe. Computer's in the office. I'll take our stuff upstairs."

"Thanks. I'll be quick."

"Take your time. I've got to finish my eulogy."

She went up on tiptoes to kiss him while wishing

there was something she could say to ease his pain. But knowing only time could do that, she let him go and headed for his office. Kicking off her shoes, she sat down to boot up his computer. Before she got to the research she planned to do, she wrote the report on the incident at Eastern Market and saved it to Nick's desktop.

While she waited on the police department system to log her in, she took note of the fastidious order on the dark cherry wood desktop. Feeling mischievous, she nudged the pile of books out of alignment, shifted the container of paperclips so it was off center, turned all the black pens in the pen cup upside down and drew a heart with an arrow through the Sam loves Nick she had written on the blotter.

Pleased with her handiwork, she turned her attention to Patricia Davidson's credit card records. Scanning through the pages, her eyes began to blur with fatigue until she stopped short on an airline charge from two days before John's death. "Well, look at you, Miss Patricia," Sam whispered, the kick of adrenaline making her heart beat faster. "Gotcha!"

She took a moment to look the woman up online to get a visual on her before she called Freddie. "Have you got Elin?"

"We're on our way." He named one of the city's best hotels.

"Jeez, spare no expense, why dontcha," she muttered, imagining the grief she'd get when that expense report landed on Malone's desk.

"Just following orders, Sergeant."

"Patricia Donaldson bought a seat on a flight from Chicago to Washington the day before O'Connor's murder."

Freddie released a long deep breath. "Wow. I totally missed this one. I'm sorry."

"We all missed it."

"But I interviewed her. I should've caught the vibe—"

"Knock it off, Cruz."

"I don't see her having the strength to get that knife through O'Connor's neck. She was almost fragile."

"Rage can make people a lot stronger than normal."

"Yeah, I guess. Would she have a key to his apartment?"

"Maybe she came for conjugals once in a while. It wouldn't surprise me that she had a key—I mean who *didn't* have a key to that place?"

"Right. And don't forget, he could've let the killer in after he got home."

"I still say he was taken by surprise since he was murdered in bed. Anyway, don't let Elin out of your sight, do you hear me?"

"It's a tough job, but someone's got to do it."

33

Sam ended the call and sat back in the big leather chair. Closing her eyes, she let her mind wander through the parts and pieces, hoping something would start to add up. The frustration was starting to get to her as day after day went by without the big break she needed to wrap this up. *I'm missing something. Something big. But what?*

"Everything all right, babe?" Nick asked from the doorway.

Holding out her arms, she invited Nick to join her. "We might be starting to get somewhere. Patricia Donaldson bought a ticket on a flight to D.C. the day before John's murder. We've got people trying to figure out where she's staying in the city. Nothing on the credit report shows her hotel."

"You'll figure it out." He kneeled down in front of her and leaned into her embrace. "What brought on this spontaneous show of affection?"

"I just needed it," she said, resting her cheek on his shoulder. "I'm frustrated, aggravated, pissed that it's taken me so long to hone in on her, that someone else had to die…"

"Well, I'm happy to provide comfort any time you need it." He suddenly stiffened.

"What's wrong?" she asked, pulling back to look at him.

"What did you do to my desk?"

"Nothing," she said, all innocence.

"You did, too. You moved things, and you probably did it on purpose to screw with me."

Sam dissolved into laughter. "You're *such* a freak show." When he would've gotten up to fix it, she stopped him. "Leave it. See if you can do it." She gripped his hands. "Come on. Be strong."

"Why does it bother you so much that I require order?"

"What you require is so far beyond order the sphincter police haven't invented the word for it yet."

"Fine. If you want to make a mess and walk away, that's your problem. It doesn't bother me."

"Yes, it does," she said, laughing to herself at his definition of a mess. He hadn't the slightest idea of what she was capable of in that regard. "I bet you'll sneak down here when I'm sleeping tonight and fix it."

"No, I won't," he said, his eyes flashing with the start of anger.

"It's okay if you do," she cooed. "I'll still love you and all your anal retentive freakazoidisms."

At her words of love, he softened, but only a little.

She ran her fingers through his hair and leaned in to kiss him. "Will you do me a favor?"

"What?" he asked in a terse tone.

"Will you read my report about the shooting at Eastern Market for me? See if I made any mistakes?"

He looked at her oddly as he got up to take her place at the desk.

Sam stood behind him, hanging over his shoulder as he went through the events of earlier, making tweaks here and there. She was relieved that he found no blatant errors.

When he was done, he turned to her. "Want to tell me what that was all about?"

She pursed her lips, wanting to tell him, but feeling shy all of a sudden. "Well, you were there. I was just making sure I didn't miss anything."

He reached for her hand and brought her down to sit on his lap. "You don't need me for that. What is it, babe?"

"I'm dyslexic," she said for the second time that day. "Freddie usually checks me, but since he wasn't involved in this, I didn't feel right asking him. Plus he's baby-sitting one of John's girlfriends at the moment."

"I'm glad you asked me. I'll do it for you any time."

She attached the file to an email to the arresting officer. Then she returned her attention to Nick. "Thank you," she said, pressing her lips to his for what she intended to be a quick kiss.

"You're welcome," he whispered as he ran his tongue over her bottom lip before tipping his head to delve deeper. As he kissed her, he arranged her so she straddled him and took her by surprise when he pulled back to whip the sweater up over her head.

Sam shivered as cool air hit her fevered skin. "Nick—I'm working—I can't right now." As she said the words, she reached for the hem of his shirt, but he stopped her. Moaning with frustration, she found his mouth for another frantic kiss and gasped when he released her bra. "Got to work…"

"Shh," he said, feasting on one breast and then the other.

Surrendering to the sensory assault, Sam gripped his shoulders and tried to convince herself that taking ten minutes for herself didn't make her a crappy cop.

"You have the most beautiful breasts," he whispered, trailing his tongue in circles around her nipple.

"They're too big."

"No," he said, laughing. "They're not. They're utter perfection. In fact, I could sit here all night and do nothing but what I'm doing right now until the sun comes up."

She tilted her pelvis tight against his throbbing erection. "Really? Nothing but this? All night?"

He groaned. "Maybe we could mix it up a bit." Helping her to her feet, he unbuttoned her jeans, hooked his fingers into her panties and divested her of both garments in one swift move before bringing her back to his lap.

"You're kind of overdressed," she said, tugging at his shirt.

"Patience, babe." Raining hot, open-mouthed kisses on her neck, he ran his hands up and down her back, sending shivers of desire dancing through her.

"I don't have any patience. Don't you know that by now?"

He propped her thighs on his legs and then moved his feet apart, opening her.

"What're you doing?" she asked, her words infected with a stammer.

"Touching you."

"I want to touch you, too."

"You'll get your turn." He cupped her breasts and ran his thumbs over nipples still sensitive from his earlier ministrations. "It was infuriating today to hear that bastard call you frigid." His hands coasted down over her ribs. One arm encircled her while his other hand slid through the dampness between her legs. "Feel that?" he whispered. "That's as far from frigid as you can get."

"I hardly ever came when I had sex with him," Sam managed to say. "It made him mad."

"We know you weren't the problem, right?" he asked as he drove two fingers into her.

Sam cried out.

"Did you mess up my desk on purpose?" he asked, his fingers coming to a halt deep inside her.

Laughing, she said, "Maybe!" She wiggled her hips, begging him to continue.

"Fess up or you won't get what you want."

"Yes! I did it!"

"That was easy," he chuckled. "Now you must be punished."

She moaned as he found the spot that throbbed for his touch.

He shifted the arm he had around her so his hand gripped her ass, holding her still for his gliding fingers. When he captured her nipple between his teeth, the combination lifted her into a powerful orgasm that stole the breath from her lungs and brought tears to her eyes.

"So hot," he whispered against her lips. "So, *so* hot."

His fingers continue to tease, and Sam was astounded to feel another climax building. Somehow she marshaled the energy to tear at his shirt, lifting it up and over his head. She ran her hand down his chest to his belly and below, dragging her finger over his steely length.

He inhaled sharply.

"Nick, *please*. I want you."

"You have me, Samantha. I'm all yours. Forever and always." He kissed her as if it was the first time all over again, exploring her mouth with deep, penetrating sweeps of his tongue.

When she couldn't stand the burning need another minute, she worked her way off his lap, pulled him up and stripped him in record time. Dropping to her knees, she took him into her mouth.

"Sam…" He buried his fingers in her hair. "Babe, wait. This was about you. Come up here."

"You said I'd get my turn," she pouted, dragging her tongue over him as she looked up to find his eyes bearing down on her.

"And you will." He helped her up, returned to the chair and brought her down to straddle him once again. "I love you."

She tilted her hips and took him in. Leaning forward she touched her lips to his. "I love you, too."

"I'm never going to get tired of hearing that."

"I'm never going to get tired of saying it."

"Promise?"

She nodded and rolled her hips to take him deeper.

As he released a long deep breath, his eyes fluttered closed.

Sam kissed the bandage above his eye and rode him slowly, each movement taking them both closer…so close.

Suddenly, he wrapped his arms tight around her, stood up and carried her to the sofa without losing their connection.

Hooking his arms under her knees he held her open for his fierce possession. Caught up in the thrill, Sam came with a sharp cry of release that dragged him right down with her.

"Damn," he whispered a minute of heavy breathing later. "Just when I think it can't get any more perfect…"

She brushed the damp hair off his forehead. "It does."

"We're going to kill ourselves if it gets any more perfect."

Sam laughed. "Hell of a way to go."

With his eyes fixed on hers, he kissed her softly.

"I have something I need to tell you," she said, her stomach twisting as she said the words.

"Now?"

Filled with a kind of fear she hadn't often experienced, she bit her bottom lip and nodded.

"So are you going to clue me in on what I'm doing here?" Elin Svendsen said as she paced the fancy hotel room.

"I told you," Freddie said, keeping a tight rein on his libido as he watched her move back and forth. "It's for your safety."

"Are you *sure?*" Her teasing smile shot lust straight through him. He was glad he'd kept his trench coat on. "I'm starting to wonder if you made this whole thing up to get me alone in a hotel room." She sashayed up to him so that her breasts were right at his eye level.

Desperate, he said, "One of John O'Connor's ex-girlfriends was murdered."

Elin gasped. "For real?"

"Would I lie about murder?"

"I don't know. Would you?"

"I never lie about murder."

"I don't get it. He wasn't married or anything."

"Well, he sort of was."

Elin spun around. "What do you mean?"

Freddie told her about the woman and child who'd been banished to the Midwest twenty years ago.

"So you think it's her?"

"We suspect it could be, and we want to keep you safe until we find her."

Elin crossed her arms in a protective gesture that tugged at his heart. "I can't believe he had this whole other secret life."

"Apparently, no one knew. Not even his closest friend."

"I don't sleep with married guys. I know you probably think I'm easy, but I do have morals."

"I never suspected otherwise."

She tilted her head to study him. "You're pretty cute, you know that?"

Freddie's cheeks heated with embarrassment. "Thanks. I think."

Smiling, she added, "We could make this little 'protection mission' of yours a whole lot more fun if you're game."

He swallowed hard. "What do you mean?"

She bent over, her top sliding forward to reveal a tantalizing view of her spectacular breasts. A hint of the Cupid tattoo was visible over the top of her low-cut bra. "Sex, Detective," she whispered. "Dirty, raunchy sex."

Feeling as if he was being tested, Freddie shifted to relieve the growing pressure in his lap. "I'm on duty."

"Who would know?"

"I would." *Sam would know. Somehow, she'd find out, and I'd be screwed in a whole other way.*

Shooting him an "are you for real?" look, Elin shrugged and reached for her bag. "I'm going to get changed."

As soon as he heard the bathroom door close behind her, Freddie closed his eyes and counted to ten. God help him, but he wanted to grab her, toss her down on the bed and have his way with her. Reminding himself that he was *working*, he willed his throbbing erection into submission.

Elin emerged from the bathroom wearing a purple silk nightgown that just barely covered her shapely ass.

Freddie suppressed a groan as she passed by him, leaving a fragrant cloud in her wake.

"Are you *sure* you don't want to have some fun?" she asked as she got settled in the other bed.

"Positive," he said through gritted teeth.

She flipped off the light. "Your loss."

Freddie fell back on the second bed and released a tortured deep breath. He was definitely being tested.

Nick grabbed a blanket from the back of the sofa and spread it over them, arranging them so they lay facing each other. He traced a finger over Sam's frown. "I don't know what's causing you such concern, but whatever it is, we'll get through it together, Sam."

She rested her hand on his chest.

Nick's heart galloped under her touch as he waited for her to gather her thoughts.

"When I was with Peter," she said tentatively, "we tried for a long time to have a baby. We were about to go for infertility treatment when I got pregnant."

Imagining what she was going to say, Nick ached for her.

"I was so excited, even though Peter and I were already having a lot of problems. I know it was foolish to think a baby could fix it, but I still had hope then."

His heart breaking, Nick wiped away a tear that spilled down her cheek.

"I miscarried at twelve weeks."

"Sam… I'm so sorry."

"It was a bad miscarriage. I lost a lot of blood, and it took me a really long time to bounce back. Peter was so devastated. He kind of retreated into himself."

"So you went through it alone."

She shrugged and sat up, moving out of his embrace. "I had my sisters, my family. Angela had Jack a short time later, and he saved me in so many ways. He's my baby as much as he's hers. She even says so."

"He's adorable."

"He's my little man." She wiped her face with an impatient swipe, as if the tears were pissing her off. "A couple of months later, the doctor told me we could try again. Things with Peter had seriously disintegrated, but we both still wanted a baby so we made an effort to fix what was wrong even though I already knew it couldn't really be fixed. For a while, though, things were better. A year after the miscarriage, I got pregnant again, but I didn't know. It was an ectopic pregnancy. Do you know what that is?"

Nick sat up, reached for her hand and tried not to be hurt when she brushed him off. "I've heard of it."

"It's when the embryo implants outside the uterus. In my case, it was in one of the fallopian tubes. I was home alone when the tube erupted. I had almost bled to death when Angela found me."

"Jesus, Sam."

"I was in the hospital for more than a week that time. It was the most painful thing I've ever been through— physically and emotionally. I lost the tube and one of my ovaries. Because of some other problems I'd had with endometriosis, my doctor told me it was unlikely that I'd ever conceive again."

All at once Nick understood what had her so worried. "It doesn't matter, Sam. Not to me. If that's what you're worried about, don't."

"But you want a family. You *deserve* a family after growing up without one."

"We'll have one. We can adopt. There're millions of kids out there in need of homes. It doesn't matter to me how we get them."

"But—"

He leaned over and kissed her. Hard. "No buts. You're the key to everything. I knew that years ago when I first met you, and I know it even more now after living without you for so long. You're what I need most. We'll figure out the rest." Caressing her cheek, he added, "You've already given me so much that I've never had before. I don't want you to spend another second worrying about the one thing you can't give me."

"I told you I'm on the pill, but I'm not. I don't need to be, but I couldn't very well blurt this whole thing out when we were about to make love the other day. I'm sorry I lied to you."

"That doesn't even count as a lie, babe. When the time is right, and we're ready to have a family, we'll work something out."

"You should think about it. You should take some time to make sure—"

He stopped her with a finger to her lips. "I don't need to think about it."

The tension seemed to leave her body in one long exhale, and when he reached for her, she came willingly back into his arms.

"Do you feel better?"

She nodded. "I felt like I was deceiving you by getting so involved with you and not telling you this."

"You weren't deceiving me. It's part of you, Sam. It's part of what's made you who you are, and I love everything about you."

She ran her finger over the stubble on his jaw. "I used to dream about you when I was married. I wondered where you were, what you were doing, if you were happy. We only had that one night together, but I thought about you all the time."

The reminder of what they'd been denied made him ache with regret. "I thought about you, too. I read the paper obsessively, looking for the slightest mention of you."

"I did, too! I knew you were working for O'Connor. I even watched hours of congressional coverage, hoping for a glimpse of you, but you kept a low profile. I hardly ever saw you."

"My profile is probably going to get even lower."

"What do you mean?"

"I checked my voicemail at the office today. Got a few job offers."

"Like what?"

"Legislative affairs for the junior senator from Hawaii, communications for the senior senator from Florida. Oh, and director of the Columbus office for the senior senator from Ohio." With a teasing smile, he added, "What do you think about living in Columbus?"

She curled up her nose. "Is there anything that wouldn't be a major step down?"

"Nope. But that's how it works in politics. Your fortunes as a staffer are tied up in who you work for. If they go up, you go up. If they flame out, so do you."

"Or if they die…"

"Exactly."

"So what're you going to do?"

"I've got some money put away, and there's that money coming from John, too, so I'm not going to make any hasty decisions. In fact, it might be time for a change."

"What kind of change?"

"I used to toy with the idea of going to law school. It's probably too late now, but I still think about it."

"If it's what you want, you should do it."

Nick chuckled as he tweaked her nose. "So you'd be willing to put up with a professional student for a couple of years?"

"Whatever makes you happy makes me happy."

He shifted so he was on top of her. "*You* make me happy."

Sam's arms curled around his neck to bring him in for a kiss full of love and promise. She wrapped her long legs around his hips and arched her back, seeking him.

As Nick slid into her, he was so overwhelmed by love for her it took his breath away. Trying to get a hold of his emotions, he stayed still for a long moment until she began to wiggle under him, asking for more. What had earlier been frenetic was now slow and dreamy. He leaned in to kiss her, managing to hang on to his control until she gripped his ass to keep him inside her when she climaxed.

"Sam," he gasped as he pushed into her one last time, unable to believe they had managed to top perfection.

34

Sam was trying to shake off the sex-induced stupor and open her eyes to go back to work when her phone rang. Checking the caller ID, she saw it was Gonzo. "What've you got?"

"A bloodbath," he said. "They're both dead."

Giving herself a second to absorb the news, she said, "How?"

"Noel was shot twice in the head at close range. Just like the other one, she was tied to the bed and tortured."

"I'm on my way." Sam sat up and started pulling on clothes.

"What's wrong?" Nick mumbled, half asleep.

"Noel and Natalie Jordan were murdered in their house."

He gasped. "Oh my God."

"I've got to get over there."

Reaching for his jeans, he said, "I'll come with you."

"No! There's no need. Peter's locked up, and I have to work."

"I promise I'll stay out of the way."

"You *never* stay out of the way."

"I knew these people, Sam. Don't make me stay home."

He looked so uncharacteristically vulnerable that

her heart went out to him. She understood all at once that more than anything he didn't want to be alone just then. "Okay, but you *will* stay out of the way."

"I promise."

On the way to Belle Haven, Sam arranged for surveillance on Elin Svendsen's apartment building in case Patricia showed up there looking to make Elin her next victim. To Nick, she said, "Can you call Christina? I need the full list of every woman John dated during the years she worked for him."

"All of them?"

"Every one. I want names, addresses and phone numbers. Patricia has been gathering the same info we have. She's had someone digging into his past. I want to know what else she found—or rather *who* else."

"Christina might not have all that."

Sam shot him a withering look. "She was in love with him. You think she doesn't have the full lowdown on all the women he dated? Give me a break. She's probably got every detail down to their bra size in a spreadsheet. Tell her to email the list to me."

While Nick made the call, Sam ordered first shift to be called in early. Rounding up all of John's Barbies was going to take some serious manpower. Her cell phone rang, and Sam took the call from Detective Jeannie McBride.

"We've checked every hotel in the city," Jeannie said. "No hits for a Patricia Donaldson. Do you want me to start checking the burbs?"

Sam thought about that for a moment. "Try Patricia O'Connor, and get some extra people on it. I need that info ASAP."

"You got it, Sergeant."

Sam ended the call, but clutched the phone as they

sped toward the Jordans's house. "I can't believe I didn't get to her sooner."

"She was the love of his life. Why would you think it was her?"

"He was the love of *her* life. Not the other way around. If a guy loves a woman the way she told us he loved her, he's not banging everything he can get his hands on when he's not with her. I think maybe she was still caught up in their teenage Romeo and Juliet romance, but he'd moved on. I'd sure love to talk to their kid. Thomas."

"He must be somewhere local with the funeral the day after tomorrow."

"If he is, we'll find him—and his mother. I just hope we get to her before she gets to another of John's girl-friends."

By the time they arrived, the Jordans' Belle Haven neighborhood was overrun with emergency vehicles.

Gonzo met them, his usually calm demeanor rattled. "I got here as soon as I could after Cruz called to tell me you wanted her picked up. The door was open. I saw him lying in the foyer and immediately called it in. We're getting some shit from Alexandria, so you'll have to talk your way in."

Calling on every ounce of patience she could muster, Sam explained to the Alexandria Police that the Jordan murders were possibly tied to Senator O'Connor's killing. After some territorial squabbling and just as she was about to get ugly with them, they agreed to let her view the crime scene. They made Nick wait outside.

Noel had been taken quickly in the foyer. Sam deduced that he'd opened the door and was shot before he had time to even say hello to the caller.

"He's the number two guy at Justice," she said with a smug smile for the cocky Alexandria detective who'd tried the hardest to keep her out. "You might want to let the attorney general know that his deputy's been murdered."

Flustered, the young detective said, "Yes, of course."

Pleased to have defused some of his arrogance, she went upstairs to see what had been done to Natalie. She'd been bound in almost the exact same fashion as Tara. And like Tara, the blood between her open legs told the story of sadistic sexual torture. "Is that a *hair-brush?*" Sam asked, staring at the object that had been left in Natalie's vagina.

"I think so," the medical examiner said.

Sam grimaced. Judging from the ligature marks on Natalie's neck, she too had been strangled after suffering through a prolonged attack.

Patricia was exacting revenge, one woman at a time.

The Alexandria Medical Examiner estimated time of death at about three hours prior. Sam's gut clenched at the realization that Noel must've just gotten home from the polygraph when they were attacked. If she'd only pieced this together a little sooner, she might've been able to save them.

Since it wasn't her crime scene, she stepped outside after asking the detectives for a courtesy copy of their report.

Nick was once again leaning against the car, waiting for her.

"Same thing as Tara."

"Christ," he whispered. "I didn't like Natalie, but the thought of what she must've gone through..."

Sam ran her fingers through her long hair, fighting off exhaustion that clung to her like a heavy blanket. "I know."

"I've been thinking..."

She glanced up at him to find his face tight with tension and distress. "About?"

"Graham and Laine."

The statement hung in the air between them, the implications almost too big to process.

Sam tossed the keys to him. "You drive while I work."

As they flew across Northern Virginia, Nick's big frame vibrated with tension. "You don't really think…"

"That she'd go after the people she blames for ruining her life? Yeah, I really think."

"God, Sam. If she hurts them…" His voice broke.

She reached for his hand. "We may be way off." But just in case they weren't, she gave the Loudon County Police a heads-up about potential trouble at the senior Senator O'Connor's home. She also forwarded the list of ex-girlfriends that Christina had grudgingly sent to HQ with orders to place officers at each woman's home. The officers were provided with photos of Patricia Donaldson and Thomas O'Connor—just in case she wasn't acting alone. Issuing a second all-points bulletin for both of them, Sam could only pray that the cops got to the other women before anyone else was harmed.

"Should've seen this," she muttered, hating that it had taken her so long to put it together. "So freaking obvious."

"Don't beat yourself up, babe."

"Hard not to when the bodies are piling up."

"I'll bet I know why he was killed on the eve of the vote," Nick said.

Sam glanced at him. "Why?"

"He decided the week before he was killed that he was definitely going to run for re-election. He probably told Patricia that. Maybe he'd promised her one term to satisfy his father and then it would be their time. If

I'm right about that, she wouldn't have wanted him to have the chance to bask in the glow of his big victory on the bill. Not when he was screwing her over—in more ways than one."

"That makes sense," Sam said, buzzing with adrenaline as all the pieces fell into place. Certain now that she was on her way to cracking the case, she called Captain Malone and Chief Farnsworth at home to update them on the latest developments.

"Get me an arrest, Sergeant," the chief said, groggy with sleep.

"I'm moving as fast as I can, sir."

After she ended the call, Nick reached for her hand. "Why don't you close your eyes for a few minutes?"

She shook her head. "I'd rather wait until I have a couple of hours. How about you? Are you okay to be driving?"

"I'm fine. Don't worry about me."

"Too late." She rested her head on his shoulder and went through the case piece by piece from the beginning. All along she'd suspected it would be a woman, one he was close to, who had a key to his place, who he wouldn't have been surprised to find waiting for him in his apartment.

Her cell phone rang. "What've you got, Jeannie?"

"Unfortunately, nothing. We can't find them anywhere in the city."

"Damn it. They must've checked in under other names."

"That's the hunch around here. We're expanding into Northern Virginia and Maryland. I'll keep you posted."

"Thanks."

A Loudon County Police cruiser was positioned at the foot of the O'Connors' driveway when Sam and Nick arrived. He rolled down the window.

"Everything looks fine," the young officer said. "The house is dark and buttoned down for the night. I walked all the way around but didn't see anything to worry about."

"Thanks," Nick said. "We're just going to take a quick look and then be on our way."

"No problem. Have a nice evening."

As Nick drove slowly up the long driveway, Sam studied him with new appreciation. He'd handled the young cop with aplomb—thanking him for checking but letting him know they were going to take their own look—without insulting the officer. "Smooth," she said.

"What?"

"You. Just now."

"You sound surprised that I can actually be diplomatic when the situation calls for it."

She snorted with laughter.

"What's so funny?"

"You are when you get all indignant."

"I'm not indignant."

"Whatever you say."

They pulled up to the dark house, and Nick cut the engine. "I want to take my own walk around."

Sam retrieved a flashlight from the glove box and reached for the door handle.

"Why don't you stay here?" he said. "I'll be right back."

"The way you stay put when I tell you to?" She flipped on the flashlight in time to catch the dirty look he sent her way. "Let's go."

They walked the perimeter of the house, finding nothing out of the ordinary. In the backyard, Sam scanned the property. "Seems like everything is fine."

"I want to see them to make sure."

"Nick, it's two-thirty in the morning, and their son's funeral is tomorrow."

He scowled at her. "Do you *honestly* think they're sleeping?"

Realizing he was determined, she followed him to the front door and cringed at the sound of the doorbell chiming through the silent house.

A minute or so later, Graham appeared at the door wearing a red plaid bathrobe. His face haggard with grief, Sam deduced that he hadn't slept in days.

"What's wrong?" he asked.

"Nothing," Nick said, his voice infected with a nervous stammer. "I'm sorry to disturb you, but there's been some trouble tonight. I wanted to check on you and Laine."

Graham stepped aside to invite them in. "What kind of trouble?"

Nick told him about Tara and the Jordans.

"Oh God," Graham whispered. "Not Natalie, too. And Noel…"

"We think it's Patricia," Sam said, gauging his reaction.

Graham's tired eyes shot up to meet hers. "No… She couldn't have. She loved John. She'd loved him all his life."

"And she'd waited for him—fruitlessly—for her entire adult life," Sam said.

"We think he told her he was running for re-election," Nick said.

"So she assumed he was choosing his career over her and Thomas," Graham said.

"That's the theory," Sam said. "And we think she recently learned there were other women in his life."

"Why are you worried about us?" Graham asked Nick. "We haven't seen her since Thomas was born."

"Because if she's settling old scores, she certainly has a bone to pick with you," Nick said.

Graham ran a trembling hand through his white hair. "Yes, I suppose she does."

"I'd like to arrange for security for you and your wife until we wrap this up," Sam said.

"If you think it's necessary."

Knowing what had been done to Tara, Natalie and Noel, Sam said, "I really do."

Nick hugged Graham. "Why don't you try to get some rest?"

"Every time I doze off, I wake up suddenly and have to remember that John is gone… I keep reliving it, over and over. It's easier just to stay awake."

Nick embraced the older man again, and when he finally released him, Sam saw tears in Nick's eyes. "I know what you mean."

"Yes, I suppose you do."

"I'll see you in the morning. Don't hesitate to call me if you need anything."

Graham patted Nick's face. "I love you like one of my own. I hope you know that."

His cheek pulsing with emotion, Nick nodded.

"There's something I need to talk to you about after the funeral," Graham said. "Save me a few minutes?"

"Of course."

"Drive carefully," Graham said as he showed them out.

Sam slipped her arm through Nick's and led him from the house, taking the keys from his coat pocket on the way to the car. "Are you okay?" she finally asked once they were in the car.

After a long moment of silence, Nick looked over at her. "He's never said that to me before. I've always sort of known it, but he's never come right out and said the words."

"You're an easy guy to love—most of the time."

His face lifted into the grin she adored. "Gee, thanks."

"We've got to do something about your inability to follow orders, however."

"Best of luck with that." He linked his fingers with hers as she drove them down the long driveway. "Thanks."

"For what?"

"For understanding why I needed to see with my own eyes that they're okay."

"They're your people."

"They're all I've got."

She squeezed his hand. "Not anymore."

35

On the way back to Nick's house, Sam arranged for security at the O'Connor home and participated in a conference call with other HQ detectives to map out a plan for coverage of the funeral in the morning. If Patricia or Thomas showed up at the cathedral, they were prepared to snag them going in. Sam planned to wear a wire so she could communicate from the inside if need be. Because she knew Nick needed her support, she hoped she could get through the service without her job interfering, but she knew he'd understand if she had to leave. He wanted John's killer caught as much as she did.

As she followed Nick into his house, she glanced at the front shrubs, recalling once again the sensation of being hurled through the air by the force of the bomb. She shuddered.

"What's wrong, babe?"

"Nothing," she said, trying to shake off feelings that were magnified by a serious lack of sleep.

"It's going to take a while before we can walk in here and not think of it."

"I'm fine," she assured him, amazed once again by how tuned into her he was. "I just need a little more computer time."

He hung their coats in the front hall closet and then stepped behind her to massage her shoulders. "What you need is sleep."

"But—"

"No buts." He steered her up the stairs to his bedroom.

Sam wished she had the energy to fight him as he undressed her and tucked her into bed.

"What about you?" she asked, smothering a yawn.

"I'm going to grab a shower. I'll be there in a minute."

"'Kay," she said, her eyes burning shut.

While she waited for him, Sam's mind wandered through everything that had happened during that long night, replaying each crime scene as she tried to hold off on sleep until Nick joined her. All at once, she snapped out of the languor to discover that nearly half an hour had passed since he'd left her to take a shower.

She got up and went into a bathroom awash in steam. Opening the shower door, she found him leaning against the wall, lost in thought. Quietly, she slipped in behind him and wrapped her arms around his waist.

He startled and then relaxed into her embrace. "You're supposed to be sleeping."

"Can't sleep without you. You've ruined me." She pressed a series of kisses to the warm skin on his back. "Come on."

He shut off the water.

Sam grabbed his towel and dried them both. Taking his hand, she led him to bed. Wrapped in his arms, she was finally able to sleep.

Walking into the National Cathedral for the first time in her life the next morning, Sam gazed up at the soaring spires like an awestruck tourist from Peoria.

She wondered if staring at the president of the United States and his lovely wife like a star-struck lunatic made her any less of a bad-assed cop. In all her years on the job and living in the city, she had caught occasional glimpses of various presidents, but never had she been close enough to reach out and touch one—not that she would because that would be weird of course. Not to mention the Secret Service might take issue with it.

But as President Nelson and his wife Gloria approached Nick to offer their condolences, Sam could only stand by his side and remind herself to breathe as he shook hands with them.

"We're so very sorry for your loss," Gloria said.

"Thank you, Mrs. Nelson. John would be overwhelmed by this turnout." He gestured to the rows of former presidents, congressional members past and present, Supreme Court justices, the chairman of the Joint Chiefs of Staff, the secretaries of state, defense, homeland security and labor, among others. "This is Detective Sergeant Sam Holland, Metro Police."

Sam was struck dumb until it dawned on her that she was supposed to extend her hand. To the president. Of the United States. And the first lady. *Jesus.* "An honor to meet you both," Sam said.

"We've seen you in the news," the president said.

Sam wanted to groan, but she forced a smile. "It's been a unique month."

Gloria chuckled. "I'd say so."

Since both men were speakers, they were shown to seats in the front, adjacent to the O'Connor family. While Nick went over to say hello to them Sam scanned the crowd but saw no sign of Patricia or Thomas. Seated behind the O'Connors were most of John's staff and close family friends whom Nick identified for her when he returned to sit next to her.

She glanced over to find him pale, his eyes fixed on the mahogany casket at the foot of the huge altar. He hadn't eaten that morning and had even refused coffee. Looking back at the throngs of dignitaries, she couldn't imagine how difficult it would be for him to stand before them to speak about his murdered best friend. Disregarding her PDA rule, she reached for his hand and cradled it between both of hers.

He sent her a small smile, but his eyes expressed his gratitude for her support.

The mass began a short time later, and Sam was surprised to discover Nick had obviously spent a lot of time in church. Since she'd been raised without formal religion, the discovery was somewhat startling.

John's sister Lizbeth and brother Terry read Bible passages, and his niece and nephew lit candles. When both of them ran a loving hand over their uncle's casket on their way back to their seats, Sam's eyes burned, and judging by the rustle of tissues all around her, she wasn't alone.

President Nelson spoke of his long friendship with the O'Connor family, of watching John grow up and his pride in seeing such a fine young man sworn in as a United States senator. As the president left the pulpit, he stopped to hug John's tearful parents.

An usher tapped Nick on the shoulder. With a squeeze for Sam's hand, he got up to follow the usher's directions to the pulpit.

Unable to tear her eyes off Nick as he made his way to the microphone, Sam was swamped with love and sympathy and a jumble of other emotions. She sent him every ounce of strength she could muster.

"On behalf of the O'Connor family, I want to thank you for being here today and for your overwhelming outpouring of support during this last difficult week.

Senator and Mrs. O'Connor also wish to express their love and gratitude to the people of the Commonwealth who came by the thousands to stand in the cold for hours to pay their respects to John. He took tremendous pride in the Old Dominion, and the five years he represented the citizens of Virginia in the Senate were the most rewarding, challenging and satisfying years of his life."

Nick spoke eloquently of his humble beginnings in a one-bedroom apartment in Lowell, Massachusetts, of meeting a senator's son at Harvard, of his first weekend in Washington with the O'Connors and how his exposure to the family changed his life.

Sam noticed the O'Connors wiping at tears. Behind them, Christina Billings, Nick's deputy and the woman who'd suffered through unrequited love for John, rested her head on the communication director's shoulder.

Nick's voice finally broke, and he looked down for a moment to collect himself. "I was honored," he continued in a softer tone, "to serve as John's chief of staff and even more so to call him my best friend. It'll be my honor, as well, to ensure that his legacy of inclusiveness and concern for others lives on long after today."

Like the president before him, Nick stopped to embrace Graham and Laine on his way back to his seat.

Sam slipped her arm around him and brought his head to rest on her shoulder. At that moment, she couldn't have cared less who might be watching or who might gossip about them later. Right now, all she cared about was Nick.

The mass ended with a soprano's soaring rendition of "Amazing Grace," and the family followed the pallbearers down the aisle and out of the church.

Dignitaries milled about, speaking in hushed tones as the church emptied. Watching them, Sam realized this was as much an official Washington political event as it was a funeral.

With Nick's hand on her elbow to guide her, they worked their way through the crowd. He stopped all of a sudden, and Sam turned to see who had caught his eye.

"You came," Nick said, clearly startled to see the youthful man with brown hair and eyes and an olive complexion that reminded Sam of Nick's.

"Of course I did." After a long pause, he added, "You looked real good up there, Nicky. Real good."

An awkward moment passed before Nick seemed to recover his manners. "This is Sam Holland. Sam, my father, Leo Cappuano."

"Oh." Sam glanced up to take a read of Nick's impassive face before accepting Leo's outstretched hand. He seemed far too young to be Nick's father, but then she remembered he was only fifteen years older than his son. "Pleased to meet you."

"You, too," Leo said. "I've read about the two of you in the paper."

Nick winced. "I meant to call you, but it's been kind of crazy…"

"Don't worry about it."

"I appreciate you coming. I really do."

"I'm very sorry this happened to your friend, Nicky. He was a good guy."

"Yes, he was."

Neither of them seemed to know what to say next, and Sam ached for them.

"Well," Nick said, "the family's having a thing at the Willard. Can you join us?"

"I need to get back to work," Leo said. "I just took the morning off."

Nick shook his hand. "Give my best to Stacy and the kids."

"You got it." With a smile for Sam, Leo added, "Bring your pretty lady up to Baltimore for dinner one day soon."

"I will. I have Christmas presents for the boys."

"They'd love to see you. Any time. Take care, Nicky." With a smile, Leo left them.

"Dad?"

He turned back.

"Thanks again for being here."

Leo nodded and headed for the main door.

Nick exhaled a long deep breath. "That was a surprise."

"A good surprise?"

"Yeah, sure."

But she could tell it had rattled him. What would it be like to expect so little of your father that you'd be shocked to see him at your best friend's funeral? Sam couldn't imagine.

On the way out of church, numerous people stopped Nick to compliment him on his heartfelt eulogy. He accepted each remark with a gracious smile, but Sam could feel his tension in the tight grip he kept on her hand. When they finally made it outside, he took a deep breath.

Gonzo met them. "No sign of either of them."

Removing the ear piece she'd worn during the funeral, Sam took a measuring look around at the crowd. "I really thought they'd be here, if nothing more than to pour salt in the O'Connors' wounds. She told Cruz they were planning to attend."

"We'll keep looking," Gonzo assured her.

"Any word on autopsies on Tara or Natalie?"

"Nothing yet."

"Get with Lindsey and put a rush on Tara's. We'll have to bug Alexandria for Natalie's." Sam glanced up at Nick, whose attention was focused elsewhere. Lowering her voice, she said to Gonzo, "I need to hang with him for a while longer. Call me if anything breaks."

"You got it."

"Thanks." Taking Nick's arm, she directed him to the row of taxis lined up at the curb.

"It was a good idea you had to take the Metro in this morning," he said once they were in a cab.

"I knew security would make it tough to park anywhere near the cathedral." She snuggled into him and wrapped her arm around his waist. "Are you okay?"

"I've been better."

"You were really great up there, Nick. I was so proud of you, my heart felt like it might burst."

He hugged her tight against him and touched his lips to her forehead. "Thanks for coming. I know you had other things to do—"

She tilted her face to kiss him. "I was exactly where I needed to be. Where I *wanted* to be." Glancing up at him, she found him staring out the window. "Can I ask you something?" she said tentatively, not sure if this was the best time. But she needed to know. For some reason, she *had* to know more.

"Sure you can."

"What you said about growing up in Lowell with your grandmother..."

"What about it?"

"If you lived in a one-bedroom apartment, where did you sleep?"

"The sofa pulled out to a bed."

She bit her bottom lip in an attempt to deal with the sudden need to weep. Her every emotion seemed to be hovering just below the surface, and it wouldn't take much for the floodgates to swing open. "Where did you keep your stuff?"

"I didn't have a lot of stuff, but what I had I kept in the hall closet."

Her heart cracked right in half. "That's why you're so particular about the things you have now, isn't it? And I've made fun of you for that. I'm so sorry, Nick."

"Don't be sorry, babe. You're right to razz me. You lighten me up, and I need that."

"I had no idea…"

"How could you? But it doesn't bother me at all when you tease me about being anal. I swear it doesn't, so please don't stop." He tipped up her chin and flashed the cajoling smile she couldn't resist. "Please?"

She returned his smile with a pout. "If it doesn't bother you, that takes some of the fun out of it."

He laughed. "I love you, Samantha Holland, and all your crazy twisted logic."

Wanting to give him absolutely everything he'd ever been denied, but satisfied for now to hear him laugh, Sam closed her eyes and pressed her lips to his neck. "I love you, too."

36

The cab came to a stop in front of the Willard Intercontinental Hotel, two blocks from the White House on Pennsylvania Avenue.

"The O'Connors reserved the ballroom, and the food here is amazing," Nick said, hoping to convince her to stay for a while.

"I really need to get to work."

"I know. I'm just being selfish wanting you with me."

Sam studied him. "Let me check in with HQ. Maybe I can stay for a few minutes."

Nick watched her while she talked on the phone and wished he could take her home to decorate the Christmas tree he planned to buy. He'd never bothered with a tree before, but this year he wanted the bother. This year, everything was different.

"I'll be there shortly," Sam said as she ended the call. "I'm only a couple of blocks away at the Willard."

"So you can come in?" Nick asked when she had returned her phone to her coat pocket.

She hesitated, but only for a second. "Sure. There's not much else I can do until we get a sighting of one of them."

Before they entered the hotel, Sam rested her hand

on his arm to stop him. "You know it's going to be like this, right?"

"Like what?"

"I'll want to be with you, especially on a day like this, but I'll need to be somewhere else a lot of the time."

Nick smiled, touched by the hint of vulnerability he detected. "I know what I'm signing on for, babe."

"Do you? Do you really?"

Something in her tone and the expression on her face told him this too had been a problem in her marriage. He leaned in to kiss her. "I really do. I'm sorry you can't spend the day with me, but I understand you have a job to do, and in this case, I have a vested interest in you getting it done."

"Okay," she said with a sigh of relief.

"I'm never going to hassle you over your work, Sam," he said as he guided her inside with an arm around her shoulders.

"Never say never. It has a way of screwing up plans, vacations, meals, sleep…"

"I'll do my best to understand, but I'll always be sorry to see you go."

She looked up at him, a small smile illuminating her beautiful face. "I want to be with you today."

"I know, and that counts for a lot."

They checked their coats and wandered into the elegant ballroom where Graham and Laine greeted each guest as they entered the room.

Nick embraced them both.

"You did a beautiful job, Nick," Laine said, grasping his hands.

"Thank you." Nick had such admiration for the aura of dignity the older woman projected even in the darkest hours of her life.

"No, thank *you*, for everything this week. I don't know what we would've done without you."

"It was no problem."

Laine shook Sam's hand. "Thank you for coming today."

"The service was lovely," Sam said.

"Yes," Laine agreed. "I thought so, too."

"Any developments?" Graham asked.

"A few," Sam said. "I'm heading into work shortly, and I hope to know more by the end of the day. I'll keep you informed."

"We'd appreciate that," Graham said. "Nick, look me up in half an hour or so, would you?"

"Sure." With his arm around Sam, Nick steered them through the crowd toward one of the bars in the corner. "I know you have issues with them, so thank you for that…just now."

"This isn't the time or the place."

"Do you plan to do anything about them lying to you?"

"What would be the point? If they had told me the truth, it would've saved me some time. I don't have anything to gain by going after them." She glanced over at the O'Connors who were greeting the senior senator from Virginia and his wife. "In fact, I kind of pity them."

"Because of John?"

"That, too, but also for what they've missed out on with Thomas. And for what?"

"I wonder if they regret what they did," Nick said as he accepted coffee for himself and a soda for her.

"They will if we can prove Thomas's mother murdered John."

Nick shook his head. "What a tangled web."

"It amazes me that people think they're going to get

away with trying to hide a baby. A secret like that is a time bomb looking for a place to detonate."

"True. I see it all the time in politics. The stuff people try to keep hidden usually blows up in their faces during a campaign."

Sam took a measuring look around the room. "I wonder where the cops who are supposed to be protecting the O'Connors are. I don't see anyone."

"Could be undercover."

"If there was a cop in this room, I'd know it."

Lucien Haverfield, the O'Connor family's attorney, approached them. "There you are, Nick. I've been looking for you."

"Lucien." Nick shook hands with the distinguished older man and introduced him to Sam. "Nice to see you."

"Fine job you did today at the funeral."

"Thank you."

"The will is being read tomorrow at two at the O'Connor home. I need you to be there."

"Why's that?" Nick asked, surprised.

"You're a beneficiary."

"But he left me money," Nick stammered. "Insurance money, and a lot of it."

"Can you be there at two?" Lucien asked, clearly not willing to shed any light in advance of the reading.

"Yes, of course."

"Great." Lucien patted Nick's shoulder. "I'll see you then."

"Wonder what that's all about," Nick said to Sam.

"I guess you'll find out tomorrow."

"Yeah." He noticed Graham signaling to him and led Sam over to a table where Graham sat with the Virginia Democrats.

"We'd like to have a word with you upstairs, if you

can spare us a few minutes, Nick," said Judson Knott, chairman of the party.

"Sure," Nick said with a perplexed glance at Sam.

"I'll, um, just wait for you here," she said.

"You're welcome to join us," Graham said. "This involves you, too."

Sam looked at Nick, who shrugged. "Okay," she said.

They followed the other men to the elevator and then to the Abraham Lincoln Suite. Nick took a moment to check out the incredible blue and gold suite, thinking he'd like to bring Sam there sometime when they could be alone. He accepted a short glass of bourbon from Judson. Sam declined a drink. Richard Manning, the party's vice chairman, had also joined them. "What's this all about, gentlemen?"

They gestured for Nick and Sam to have a seat at the dining room table.

"We have a proposition for you, Nick," Judson said.

Nick glanced at Graham and then at Sam. "What's that?"

"We'd like you to finish out John's term," Graham said.

Nick almost choked on the bourbon. "What? *Me?*"

Under the table, Sam grasped his arm.

"Yes, you," Judson said.

"But you have any number of people better suited. What about Cooper?"

"His wife was recently diagnosed with stage three breast cancer. He'll be announcing his resignation from the legislature the day after tomorrow."

"I'm sorry to hear that," Nick said sincerely. "How about Main?"

"He's been carrying on with his son's first grade

teacher for years, and his wife filed for divorce yesterday. It'll be hitting the papers any day now."

"The party's having some troubles, Nick," Manning
drawled. "We need someone of your caliber to step in
and get us through to next year's election. We're hoping Cooper's wife will have recovered enough by then
to free him up to run."

Nick couldn't believe they were serious. He wasn't
the guy. He was the guy *behind* the guy. He named ten
other Virginia Democrats he considered better suited
to the job and was treated to a variety of disqualifying
details about their personal lives that he could've lived
without knowing. She's expecting twins, he's gay and
in the closet—wants to stay there, he's got financial
problems, she's caregiver to a mother with Alzheim-
er's. It went on and on.

"Listen, you guys," Nick said when he had run out
of names to float. "I appreciate you thinking of me…"

"You struck a chord this morning," Judson said.
"With your talk of humble beginnings. The data is
highly favorable—"

"You've *polled* on me?" Nick asked, incredulous.
"Already?"

"Of course we have." Richard seemed insulted that
Nick even had to ask. "Most of Virginia and the rest
of official Washington watched the funeral. You made
quite an impression." Richard directed a charming
smile at Sam. "Between that and your very public relationship with the Sergeant—"

"Don't bring her into this," Nick snapped. "She's
off limits."

Graham rested his forearms on the table and leaned
in to address Nick. "You know how this works. Nothing's off limits, *especially* your personal life. But the
party is prepared to throw its support behind you if you

want it. By this time tomorrow you can be a United States senator. All you have to do is tell us you want it, and we'll make it happen."

"Your name recognition is off the charts right now," Richard added. "Factor in youthful vitality, obvious political savvy, a well-known connection to the O'Connors and you're a very attractive candidate, Nick. Governor Zorn thinks it's a brilliant idea."

A United States senator. It boggled his mind. "I don't know what to say…"

"Say yes," Judson urged.

"It's not that simple," Nick said, thinking of Sam and their fledgling relationship. Could it handle the pressure that would come with a job like this on top of a job like hers? "I need to think about it."

"For how long?" Judson asked. "The governor is anxious to act."

"I need a couple of days."

"Two," Judson said. "I can give you through Christmas, and then we'll need to know."

"Why don't you want it?" Nick asked, beginning to worry about Sam's total silence and the sudden pallor gracing her cheeks.

"Hell," Judson said, "I'm too damned old to keep that kind of schedule. Richard is, too. We want to spend our spare time golfing and hanging out with the grandbabies. We need someone like you to get us through this transition. We're asking for one year, Nick. Give us that, and for the rest of your life you'll be known as Senator Cappuano."

The title sounded so preposterous, it was all Nick could do not to laugh.

Judson and Richard got up to leave. Both shook hands with Graham.

"Sorry again for your loss, Senator," Judson said.

To Nick, he added, "Let me know what you decide by the twenty-sixth."

Nick nodded and shook hands with them. When he heard the door click shut behind them, he turned to Graham and Sam.

"What do you think, Nick?" Graham asked.

"I'd like to know what Sam thinks."

"I, ah, I have no idea what to say."

He could tell by the wild look in her blue eyes that she was having a silent freak-out and decided to wait until they were alone to address it further with her.

"You seriously think I can do this?" he said to Graham.

"If I had any doubt, we wouldn't be here."

Nick studied the other man for a long moment. "This was all your doing, wasn't it?"

Graham shrugged. "I might've suggested that the best man for the job was the one who knew John the best."

"I didn't know John as well as I thought I did."

"You knew him as well as anyone."

Nick looked over at Sam, wishing he knew what she was thinking. No doubt the offer had shocked her just as much as it had shocked him. Standing, he offered his hand to Graham. "Thank you for the opportunity."

Graham held Nick's hand between both of his. "I have nothing but the utmost faith in you, Nick Cappuano from Lowell, Massachusetts. I was so proud of you up there today. You've grown into one hell of a man."

"Thank you. That means a lot coming from you."

A knock on the door ended the moment between the two men.

37

"I'll get it," Nick said. He strolled to the door, opened it and gasped at the face that greeted him. John's face. Rendered speechless, Nick could only stare at the young man. He had a wild, unfocused look to him that put Nick on alert.

"I'm Thomas O'Connor. I understand that my, um, grandfather is here?"

Recovering, Nick said, "Yes. Please. Come in."

As he ushered the young man into the room, Nick experienced the same prickle of fear on the back of his neck that he'd felt once before—the day he walked into John's apartment and found him dead. Sam, he noticed, had stood up and was watching Thomas's every move as he approached Graham.

"Who are you?" Thomas asked Nick.

Surprised that Thomas didn't seem to recognize him or Sam, he said, "I'm Nick Cappuano, your father's chief of staff, and this is my girlfriend, Sam." Nick met Sam's steady gaze with one of his own, using his eyes to implore her to go along with him. Until they knew what Thomas wanted with Graham, he didn't need to know she was a cop.

"You've taken me by surprise," Graham finally said

as he sized up the grandson he hadn't seen since the day he was born twenty years earlier.

"I imagine I have."

"I thought we might see you and your mother at your father's funeral," Graham said.

"She got tied up in Chicago and couldn't make it," Thomas said.

Sam and Nick exchanged glances, and he knew she was picking up the same uneasy vibe.

Thomas turned to them. "You two can take off. I came to see my grandfather."

"That's all right," Nick said, the tingle on his neck intensifying by the minute. "We've got nowhere to be."

Thomas pulled a gun from the inside pocket of his winter coat. Pointing it at Sam and Nick, he said, "Then take a seat and shut up." He gestured to the sofa.

"Thomas," Nick said, taking a step toward him, "you don't want to do this. What difference will it make now?"

The younger man stared at him, his eyes even more wild and unfocused than they were when he first arrived. "Are you serious? What *difference* will it make? My *grandfather* ruined my mother's life. He shipped her off like unwanted garbage to protect his political image."

Sam rested her hand on Nick's arm to pull him back. Nodding her head, she signaled for him to take a seat with her on the sofa.

Once they were seated, Thomas turned back to Graham. "All you cared about was yourself."

"That's not true. I cared about your father, and you, too. I sent money. For years. I made sure you had everything you needed."

"Everything except my father and my family! You took everything from us. We got him for one lousy weekend a month, and you know what he was doing the rest of the time? Fucking his way through Washington with one stupid bitch after another."

Watching Thomas gesture erratically with the gun, Nick's heart slowed to a crawl.

Sam poked his leg to get his attention.

He watched as she raised her pant leg and removed the small clutch piece she had strapped to her calf.

She pressed it into his hand and drew her primary weapon from the shoulder harness she had worn for the funeral, keeping the gun hidden in her suit coat in case Thomas turned to them. Mouthing the word "wait" she used her finger to indicate that he should go right while she went left.

Nick nodded to let her know he understood.

"You know what he told me a couple of weeks ago when I introduced him to my girlfriend? He advised me later that I shouldn't get 'tied down' to one woman. That a man needs to 'mix it up,' that 'variety is the spice of life.' It was a real touching father-son moment, and it was the first time it ever occurred to me that he'd been unfaithful to my mother. She'd waited her *whole life* for him. Ever since you banished her, she's done nothing but wait for him and settle for whatever scraps he tossed our way. And then he comes and tells us he's running for re-election! He actually expected us to be *happy* about his big news. He'd promised us one term. One term for you, his beloved father. Then it would be our turn. He lied about *everything*. Everything!"

"He loved you."

"No, he loved *you!* You were the only one he cared about."

"You killed him," Graham said in a whisper. "You killed my son."

"He had it coming! He was a fucking *whore!* I've

got the investigator's report to prove it. You should see what he got done in just two weeks' time. It was truly revolting."

"That doesn't mean he deserved to die," Graham said. "Natalie didn't deserve what you did to her, either."

Thomas moved so quickly, Sam and Nick couldn't react in time to stop him from pistol-whipping his grandfather.

Graham went down hard, blood spurting from a wound on his forehead.

"Get up!" Thomas shrieked. "Get up and take what's coming to you like a man!"

"You talk about being a man!" Graham screamed back at him. "But what kind of man rapes and murders women?"

Sam held Nick back, giving him the one-minute sign.

"I made them pay for what they did to my mother. They got exactly what they deserved."

"You're a monster," Graham whispered, the blood loss weakening him.

Thomas aimed the gun at his grandfather's chest.

Sam gave Nick the thumbs-up.

They rushed Thomas from behind, each of them pushing a gun into the young man's temples.

"Freeze," they said in unison.

Sam glowered at Nick. "I'll take it from here." She had Thomas disarmed, cuffed and immobilized less than a second later. With her free hand, she tugged her radio off her hip and called for backup.

"What the fuck?" Thomas screamed, fighting the restraints. "You're a fucking *cop?*"

"Surprise," Nick said, unable to resist a smile as adrenaline zipped though his system. Watching her work never failed to fire him up. "Meet my 'girlfriend,' Detective Sergeant Sam Holland, Metro Police Department. You really ought to read a newspaper once in a while."

"Son of a fucking bitch."

"You said it, buddy." Sam tightened her hold on Thomas. "You're under the arrest for the murders of John O'Connor, Tara Davenport, Natalie Jordan and Noel Jordan. You have the right to remain silent."

Nick stayed with Graham while Sam dragged Thomas out of the suite to turn him over to Gonzo for transport to HQ. Nick pressed a handkerchief to the wound on Graham's head.

Tears spilled down the older man's cheeks. "This is all my fault. I caused this. I forced John to lead a double life."

"You did what you thought was right at the time. That's all any of us can ever do."

"Will you find Laine for me? I need to see her."

"As soon as the paramedics get here, I'll get her to the hospital."

"Call Lucien," Graham said. "Have him send someone over to represent Thomas."

Nick stared at the older man. "You can't be serious."

"He's my grandson. What I did to him and his mother drove him to this." Graham closed his eyes and took a deep, rattling breath. "Make the call."

Even though he didn't agree, Nick said, "I'll take care of it." He rested his hand on top of Graham's. "Try not to worry about anything."

"You're going to make an outstanding senator."

"I haven't said yes yet."

"You will." The older man held Nick's hand until the EMTs arrived and whisked him away.

The moment they left with Graham, Sam returned to the suite.

"Whew," Nick said. "That was something."

A cocky grin lit up her gorgeous face. "Just another day at the office."

"For you, maybe."

"You did good—for a rookie."

"Gee, thanks." He wiped the sweat from his forehead, his legs still rubbery. "You called Chicago to check on Patricia?"

"They're on their way to her house as we speak. Thomas had her credit cards in his wallet."

"I feel sorry for her," Nick said. "She's lost them both."

"The whole situation is too sad, but his lawyer will probably mount an insanity defense."

"He was going to kill us all, wasn't he? That's why he said all the stuff he did in front of us."

"I suspect that became his plan when we insisted on staying. I just can't believe I didn't figure this out sooner. I was so sure it was a love affair gone wrong."

"Well, it sort of was when you think about it."

"Yeah, I guess you're right."

"I'm just glad we were here when Thomas confronted Graham." He shuddered. "I don't even want to think about what could've happened."

"It's probably better if you don't think about it."

Nick slipped an arm around her shoulders. "We need to talk about what happened before Thomas showed up."

"Later." She hip-checked him. "No PDA in front of the colleagues."

He slapped her on the ass. "Screw that."

Sam attempted a dirty look but failed to pull it off.

"We make a good team, you know that?" he said.

"As long as you remember who's in charge."

Nick took great pleasure in hooking an arm around her and escorting her down the hallway full of hooting cops. Not even the elbow she jammed in his ribs could detract from his euphoria at having her by his side and John's killer on his way to jail.

In the elevator, she looked up at him, her clear blue eyes full of love. "Thanks for having my back in there."

Hugging her closer to him, he kissed her cheek and then her lips. "Samantha, I'll *always* have your back."

Epilogue

Nick got home from the reading of John's will just after five on Christmas Eve and went straight to the kitchen to dig out the bottle of whiskey he'd kept on hand for John. He poured himself half a glass and downed it in one long swallow that burned all the way through him. Pouring a second shot, he took it with him to sit in the living room where a seven-foot Christmas tree waited to be decorated. Under the tree were six festively wrapped gifts for Sam.

He hadn't heard from her all day, and after her refusal to discuss the Virginia Democrats' offer when they finally got home late last night, he had good reason to wonder if she would keep her promise to spend this evening with him. She hadn't even called to tell him that Marquis Johnson had been remanded over to trial—without incident. Nick had to hear about it on the news.

Still hopeful that Sam would keep her promise to spend tonight with him, Nick went into the kitchen to make the dinner he'd shopped for earlier. By nine o'clock the pasta was rubbery, and he had given up on her. Could she really be *that* freaked out by his job offer? Didn't she know that if she wasn't in favor of it, he wouldn't do it? Disappointment mixed with disbelief. That she would let him down like this, that she would let *herself* down like this…

He stretched out on the sofa with another shot of whiskey. The empty tree was a stark reminder of how his plans for this evening had failed to materialize. Without Sam, what did it matter? What did anything matter?

He must have dozed off because the ringing doorbell startled him awake an hour later. His heart surged with hope as he got up to answer it. He swung open the door, and there she was.

"Hey," he said.

"Hey."

"I thought you weren't coming."

"I almost didn't."

Nick stepped back to let her in and took her coat.

"What do I smell?" she asked, surprised. "Did you cook?"

He shrugged. "Nothing special."

"Did you leave any for me?"

"All of it."

"You didn't eat?"

"I was waiting for you."

Snuggling into his embrace, she said, "I'm sorry. I totally freaked, and I handled this all wrong."

Nick hugged her close, overcome with relief at having her back in his arms after a day filled with uncertainty. He brushed his lips over hers. "Tell me what you're thinking, Samantha. Tell me the truth."

She looked up at him with those blue eyes he loved so much. "I'd be a liability to you. I'm messy and loud and I swear and sometimes I even tell white lies— I don't mean to, but they sneak out before I can stop them. I'm dyslexic, infertile and my stomach runs my life. And then there're the lovely people I come in contact with on a daily basis: drug dealers, prostitutes, murderers, rapists. There's the whole fiasco with the Johnsons—and my ex-husband is headed for prison..."

Even though he was amused by her speech, Nick knew she was dead serious and fought back a smile. "That's not your fault. He tried to kill us both."

"Which will lead people to wonder what kind of woman marries a man like him. They'll question my judgment and yours for getting involved with me. They'll rehash Johnson and every other ugly case I've ever had—and there're a lot of them. It'll reflect poorly on you."

"I'm not running for office, Sam. It's being handed to me for one year, and then it's done."

Rolling her bottom lip between her teeth, she mulled it over. "We'd attract a lot of media attention after everything that happened this week."

"I can handle it if you can."

"I'd hate to be responsible for causing you trouble. I'd hate that."

"I can deal with that, too."

She rested her hands on his shoulders. "You want this, don't you?"

"My life was just fine before. If I say no, it'll be fine after."

"That doesn't answer my question."

"It's something I never dreamed of, something I never even considered before yesterday."

"My dad and Freddie think it's so cool," she said with a shy smile. "They say it would work out fine for us. My dad even thinks it could be a 'grand adventure.'"

Her skeptical scowl amused Nick. "They're very wise men. You should listen to them."

Looking up at him, she said, "Can we eat? I haven't eaten all day, and I'm starving."

He decided not to push his luck since she seemed to be coming around to a decision in her own peculiar way. "Sure."

"Oh!" she said on the way to the kitchen. "You got a tree!"

"I told you I was going to."

"When did you have time?"

"I did it this morning, along with a few other things."

"What other things?"

"A little Christmas shopping," he said with a mysterious smile as he poured her a glass of wine. "And some real estate shopping."

Her eyebrows knitted with confusion.

He served her the reheated shrimp fettuccine Alfredo and carried a tossed salad to the table. "You said you couldn't live way out here in Virginia, right?"

"Uh huh." She dove into the meal as if she was, in fact, starving. "You never told me you could cook like this! It's amazing!"

"You never asked, and I'm glad you like it." After lighting the candles on the table, he sat down across from her. "Anyway, since you can't live here, I bought a place in the city."

"What place did you buy?" she asked, astounded.

"The one that was for sale up the street from your dad's. I looked at it on Sunday when you were at work, I offered this morning and they accepted. I'm meeting with a Realtor after Christmas to list this place."

She sat back in her chair to stare at him. "Just like that?"

"I knew you'd want to be close to your dad and to work."

"Won't you need to maintain a residence in Virginia?"

Implied but not stated was if he became a senator.

"John took care of that. He left me the cabin. That's why they wanted me to come today."

Her eyes went soft with emotion. "Nick… That's wonderful. You love it there."

"I was so surprised and delighted." He reached for her hand and brought it to his lips.

"How's Graham doing?"

"Better. They let him go home today when his blood pressure returned to normal."

"That's good."

"I feel sorry for them. They've got a long road ahead of them coming to terms with all of this. And the media is clamoring for info about John's illegitimate son."

"They should just come clean at this point."

"I think that's the plan. Laine wanted me to tell you how very sorry she is for lying to you about Thomas. She said she panicked when she saw you had his photo."

"It's in the past now. I'm over it."

When they finished eating, Nick picked up their wine glasses and led her to the sofa. "John had so many secrets. Hell, I had no idea until today when the lawyer was doling out his millions how insanely wealthy the sale of his business made him. There were a lot of secrets, but he loved his father. So much. Despite everything. He loved him."

"I can understand that. There's not much my father could do to change how I feel about him."

"You're lucky to have him."

"And I know it."

He studied the face that had become so essential to him. "What're we going to do, Sam?"

"Well, tonight we're going to decorate that tree." She glanced at the tree and then down at the gifts under it. "What's all that?"

"One for every year we missed."

Smiling, she shifted to straddle him. "That's so incredibly sweet."

He pulled her in close.

"Tomorrow," she said, touching her lips to his, "we're going to Tracy's for dinner. The next day, you're going to tell the Virginia Democrats that you're their new senator."

He cradled her face in his hands. "Am I?"

"It's just a year, right?"

"One year."

"It'll be a total mess. You know that, don't you?"

"I *love* a good mess," he said with a teasing grin. "In fact, I *live* for messes."

She smiled. "We're really going to do this."

"We really are."

"I love you, Senator Cappuano."

"I love you, Lieutenant Holland. Merry Christmas."

"Same to you." She leaned her forehead against his and looked him in the eye. "It's gonna be one hell of a New Year."

"I can't wait."

* * * * *

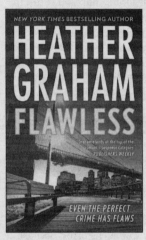

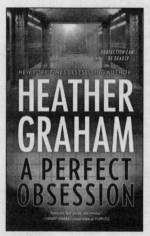

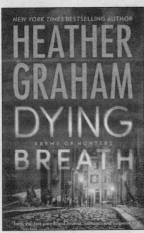

Reading Has Its Rewards

Earn **FREE BOOKS!**

Register at **Harlequin My Rewards** and submit your Harlequin purchases from wherever you shop to earn points for free books and other exclusive rewards.

Plus submit your purchases from now till May 30th for a chance to win a $500 Visa Card*.

Visit **HarlequinMyRewards.com** today

Earn **FREE** REWARDS
HarlequinMyRewards.com
Join Today!

MYR16R1

Get 2 Free Books,
Plus 2 Free Gifts -

just for trying the Reader Service!